Willup Hall

J.M. Ashton

Book Publishing.com

Editing, design, typesetting and publishing by UK Book Publishing

www.ukbookpublishing.com

ISBN: 978-1-916572-88-1

Willup Hall

DEDICATION

To my long ago gone, but not forgotten, parents
Stan and *Freda Ashton* who floated through life
on a cloud of innocence, honesty and love.

ACKNOWLEDGEMENTS

A heartfelt thank you to my patient husband John for all his support, help and encouragement and for feeding me and all the animals when I was busy writing. Love you for enabling me to write undisturbed.

Thank you to my good friend Anne Smith for believing in me and the story, and giving me the confidence to keep going, for giving up her valuable time and knowledge of computers to help sort out my first edit.

To Nick Pal, many thanks for stepping in and helping me recover my lost work and showing me where to find it in the future.

Thank you to Steve Cochrane for his incredible knowledge of the railway lines running during WWII, which stations were open and the then train times of those war years.

Thank you to Joan Jenkinson, my sister, for her help with the French language.

Thank you to UK Book Publishing and staff, especially for Ruth Lunn who has edited the book and been a constant source of advice, support and constructive observations, and to Jay Thompson for his wonderful cover design.

Chapter 1

Willup Hall

I swung my legs out of bed and slowly drank my steaming hot chocolate. I gazed through the window at the sleeping vineyard and at the neat rows of vines. Aurielle had kindly woken me up with a drink and opened the curtains before sunrise. So, this was the day I left for home, Norfolk, Britain. I didn't want to leave, but I had to; no more hoping I didn't have to go, no more wasting time, the war seemed inevitable, it was coming our way and I must flee. I allowed myself time to remember the time I arrived here, and what I had achieved since that day. I cast my mind back to a few weeks ago sitting in the silence of the forest, painting and enjoying the complete peace.

*****

Very slowly and quietly I had leant back against the rough bark of the old tree and breathed out slowly. I had studied my sketch and water wash of the scene before me. I had breathed in the sweet soft smell of the forest peat, pine needles and a musky cool damp. A silent stillness then seeped into my brain, banishing any bad thoughts and troubles of the world.

The early morning sun had risen, sending shafts of light streaking through the branches of the trees. The beams of sunlight had illuminated the head, small antlers, and warm red coat of the grazing young stag in the glade before me. I had worked quietly to capture the early morning stirrings and first light in the forest – the buck wandering into the clearing was an unexpected bonus. Then I revelled in the stillness and beauty of the woods. I felt great peace with the moment in this corner of France. I had sat very still admiring the view in front of me and drinking in the rustling light sounds and sights of a new day in this remote forest on my Tantetta's estate. I was missing my dog Odin, but glad he was back in the Chateau as he would have disturbed every animal or bird now in front of me and for that reason, I had deliberately left him behind in the kitchen. He was part Cocker Spaniel, part Labrador, so had a keen nose that delighted in sniffing out new scents as he snuffled his way through the undergrowth in the woods.

That morning I was convinced nothing could shatter my happiness. It was April 1940: how wrong I was, as the weeks ahead would prove.

I had been up before daybreak to capture the special early morning light before the heat of the day. I had crept quietly from my bedroom and walked past the lake and deep into the forest on a little-known path to the secret glade in the woods to paint and capture the essence of early morning. The young buck appearing was mesmerising, and I had worked quickly with my paints to capture the moment. I remember feeling tired from my intense concentration and a peace crept over me as I surveyed the scene before me.

The news we had every day was not good and it seemed that war was creeping towards France and would destroy our idyllic life, my idyllic life. Hitler had allowed a night of murder and imprisonment of Jewish people on November 9th, 1938, now called Kristallnacht, the night of the broken glass; he had taken control of the Rhineland and marched into Sudetenland to, as he explained 'protect German speaking citizens who lived there'. In March of 1939 he had broken the Treaty of St Germain and occupied Czechoslovakia. There was great economic depression here in France and in Germany after the disastrous Great War which was now causing unrest here and in Germany. Hitler had promised the German people economic success and payback to Europe for Germany losing the Great War. I knew Britain had allowed Hitler to advance on these territories unchecked in the hope of avoiding another war. Appeasement was the name given to Britain's policy. I knew this as I had sat at the kitchen table listening to Joseph and Marcell arguing politics and talking about the current dangerous situation in Europe because of Hitler. I still did not for one minute think it could impact upon my happy life here.

I had been startled by a pheasant squawking and feeling hungry. I'd decided it was time for me to go back home for breakfast. I'd eased my buttocks off the slightly damp ground and realized how stiff I was. The young buck suddenly was on guard, head up, ready to flee. I remembered standing up slowly clutching my sketch pad and paints, not looking at the deer, knowing that if he thought I had not seen him he might just freeze and warily watch me as I left. Not exactly bounding, I had stiffly packed away my paints and made my way through the woods back to the Chateau. I didn't look back, leaving the buck to his area of privacy, to his area of the woods, as I made my way up the forest path to the Chateau where I lived, looking forward to a mug of hot chocolate and a fresh warm croissant.

Forty-five minutes later as I crossed the large lawn behind the Chateau, I could smell coffee and fresh toasted brioche drifting from the open kitchen door and the sounds of voices inside. I entered the cavernous kitchen where Aurielle, the housekeeper, was preparing the breakfast tray with coffee and croissants for Tantetta. My spaniel Odin was behind the door wriggling his body in ecstasy because I was back, and I always fussed and patted him. I loved Aurielle and had given her a hug and wished her good morning. She smiled at me and looked at my sketch, murmuring her approval. Aurielle had my hot chocolate ready, and as usual she had put it onto the large wooden tray painted with beautiful flowers and I would follow her, plus Odin of course, into the hall, up the grand sweeping staircase to my Tantetta's amazing bedroom. The bedroom was vast and decorated with walls covered in hand painted Eau de Nil coloured silk materiel painted with flowers and peacocks. Eau de Nil is an ethereal blue-green colour which was first named after the shimmering waters of the river Nile and has always been a favourite colour of mine. The bedroom furniture was carved, ornate, and typically old French in style. Sitting up in the huge high bed was Tantetta, with her hair plaited to one side and wearing a pure silk negligee in duck egg blue and, as always, she looked elegant even this early in the morning. Her dog Thor, brother to Odin, stretched, yawned, got up and lazily had come to greet us from his wooden dog bed at the side of her bed.

She had greeted us both with a smile, removed her reading glasses and pushed aside the business papers she had been reading. Aurielle set the tray down on a butlers stand by the bed. I, as usual, sat on the side of the bed and kissed Tantetta on both cheeks as

I showed her my morning's work. Meanwhile, Aurielle opened the shutters, letting the early morning sun flood the room with light onto the pale green Aubusson rug covering the honey gold floorboards. On the wall opposite the bed were painted scenes of the Chateau's grounds, grapevines twisted around pictures of wild boar, red deer and dogs on the huge estate which belonging to Tantetta. These had been painted by my uncle who had been an exceptional artist and it had been his way of coping with his World War One injuries and the mental anguish he suffered from the horrors of that awful war. He loved to paint peaceful pictures. It was as if he needed to surround himself with greenery, nature, and everything of beauty in the forests, vineyards, fields, and hills surrounding the Chateau.

I recalled Tantetta picking that day's newspaper from the tray left by Aurielle and reading the headlines. She had sighed and dropped the newspaper onto the embroidered counterpane covering the bed. Looking at me she smiled, a tired sad smile.

"Let me see your sketch again?" she had asked. "Wonderful, you have captured the moment and I love the shaft of sunlight streaking through the tree canopy. Will you paint it again this morning?"

"Yes," I had replied, "watercolour I think."

"Then I will look forward to seeing it when it's finished."

We ate our breakfast in silence, my Tantetta reading the newspaper and me daydreaming about horses as I sipped my hot chocolate. She had leant back on her pillows and said, "I do not like the news of this awful man Hitler; I fear he will bring more destruction and devastation to Europe and France."

I had only half listened as I was thinking that I might ride my mare after breakfast and take Odin and Thor with me around the estate vineyards.

Tantetta had asked sharply, "Cressida, are you listening to me? You must think about returning to England if there is to be a war, you should go home."

"Home, England," I shrieked in horror. "This is my home. No, I love being here with you, I won't leave you."

Tantetta had smiled and replied, "And I love you too, your being here has made me very happy, and this Chateau is your home. However, if war comes here to France, and I fear it will, then I am afraid you must return to England and your family."

Now she had my full attention. I couldn't bear to think of leaving sunny, happy France and Tantetta. The grape harvest, called the vendange, was always a lively fun time to be here, full of hard work and laughter. We grew vines here on ten hectares of land, so life was full of spraying, cutting, and weeding and the vendange, and harvest time, a time of long hours with help from the villagers and friends. We helped each other with the grape harvest, the first crucial step in the winemaking process. I had studied this, the ripening of the grapes, sugar, acid, and tannin levels all part of becoming a viticulturist like Marcell.

My art room was full of my work, how could I consider leaving my lovely sunny studio room I had wondered? "Oh, Tantetta, there is the Maginot line and there are British troops here already, the Germans will never get into France past the wonderful French troops this time, you'll see." I had drunk the last of my hot chocolate, now cold, and blowing her a cheery kiss I had left the room. "You'll see," I gaily said again, my head in the clouds as usual. I had skipped down the huge, curved staircase into the large hall where the walls were covered in paintings, and briskly walked past the round pedestal table and breathed in the fragrant smell of the fresh spring flowers from the garden, went into my art room and put my morning's painting down on my work desk.

I picked up the water jug to take into the kitchen to refill with fresh water for my watercolour paints and stopped to study an oil canvas on an easel, to see where I needed to go next with the work. I always had at least two paintings on the go at the same time so I could leave one for a later review and work on the other. I left my morning work on my desk and made a mental promise to tidy it before I did any more work, as I had promised Tantetta that I would always keep my art room tidy, which I found very hard to do. Before I did anything else it was time to walk Odin and Thor and the best way was to ride my mare Hermes around the lake, so with that thought I left everything and headed outside into the sunshine calling the two dogs to follow me. So, life here was bliss, all sunshine and happiness and I never wanted it to change.

*****

No going back now, I was leaving for England with my new travelling companions, a full horsebox and a war on the way. I dressed and went downstairs to start my journey to an uncertain future. Hermes was loaded into the box; Odin was in the cab, and my new travel companions climbed in beside me. I looked at the dashboard then down the long driveway. And sighing, I reached for the ignition key and turned it. The engine sprang into life.

Chapter 2

How I came to live in France

Poor Tantetta was scared because The Great War had been so cruel, horrible, and difficult for the World, Europe and particularly France. So many men had perished, and my uncle had never recovered from his painful leg injury and the mental scars of seeing young men cut down and dying in such horrible and barbaric ways. My uncle had always been a keen horseman and he hated seeing magnificent horses and mules hurt and destroyed in their thousands during the war. Donkeys, mules, horses, and dogs, even pigeons were used by both armies, and many poor animals died because of the needless conflict. Worst of all though was my uncle and aunt's beloved son and heir who was killed during the conflict. Their daughter had died of scarlet fever when she was only eight years old and then to lose their only son to the madness of a futile war was more than they could ever comprehend. Perhaps that's why my grandmother had suggested to my parents that I live with her sister and her husband knowing I was lonely staying at the Hall on my own and hating boarding school. My Tantetta was an art expert and she bought and sold valuable painting to art galleries and private collectors all over the world. Her name was Henrietta and as children we had amalgamated the French Tante for aunt with Etta, hence Tantetta. I had failed miserably with being away at boarding school, but was able to paint very well and Tantetta had been able to instruct me on how to improve my painting and how to appreciate all art. She took me to visit art galleries in Paris, which had improved my knowledge of the great artists past and present. My French had improved with the French tutor hired to instruct me and my love of winemaking had been instilled in me by simply observing, listening and being hands-on during the vendange, the grape harvest, plus learning from Marcell how to care for the vines. Oh, and the drinking of the wine! There was so much to remember about the pruning and spraying against parasites, and tying up of the vines, the terroir, the natural environment for the grapes which included the topography, soil and climate all contributing to the flavour, aroma, and taste of the wine.

My uncle had owned 2,000 acres most of which was deep impenetrable forest, but it also included a small village. He had found some peace after the war touring the estate on his horse with his paints and sketch book in his saddle bags. Sadly, he had died two and half years ago, not long after my parents had allowed me to move to France, and consequently, I had stayed to keep Tantetta company, only to be still here three and a half years later. Tantetta, with the help of her loyal staff, took on the mantel of responsibility for running the estate she had inherited.

My parents were always travelling abroad because my father worked in the diplomatic service. After the The Great War he had returned home to the family estate in Norfolk, but as a very young Major in the Grenadier Guards had been recalled by the King to join the diplomatic corps. At first my mother always stayed at home with my brother Lysander, sister Portia and me, Cressida. As you can see, my mother loved Shakespeare!

On the plus side, as I have said, Tantetta was a brilliant art expert. I just happened to love painting, was eager to leave boarding school and so, travelling to France and staying in the Chateau really appealed to me. Fortunately, my work and technique had vastly improved under the tutelage of my Tantetta and as she loved to promote young aspiring artists, I was, in her company, privileged to meet an eclectic mix of fascinating people and artists. Tantetta was a renowned art historian, a worldwide respected art dealer, and advised people which artists were worth investing in for the future. She had a Pied-à-terre – well, a grand apartment in the 16th arrondissement near the Place du Trocadero in the heart of Paris – and regularly travelled there to view exhibitions and attend art auctions. She bought art for clients or to keep here in the Chateau whilst waiting for a price rise, or to sell in the gallery she shared with Jean-Phillipe Delacroix, her trusted business partner. Recently Tantetta was leaving the buying at auction to Jean-Phillipe after she had perused the art auction catalogues at home. Jean-Phillipe would then collect and deliver as instructed by Tantetta. The Chateau was filled with amazing paintings for sale, and buyers from across the world would visit us to see them, listening attentively to my Tantetta's advice on art works which she thought most likely to gradually increase in value. Many were on the walls for ever, though, and all my uncle's paintings were kept and rarely sold. He had sold a few when he was alive, and they were gaining in popularity and value. Her advice and help to me was amazing. Recently, she had invested with Jean-Phillipe in a gallery in New York and frequently he had travelled across the Atlantic to take care of the new gallery and choose paintings to exhibit there.

I went through the vast hall into the cavernous kitchen where Aurielle was preparing breakfast for her husband Marcell and his helper Joseph. "A tout a l'heure!" I called as I grabbed an apple from the bowl on the table and headed out towards the farm buildings. Rounding a corner from one of the farm buildings I found Joseph, a sheep between his legs held firmly in place for worming. Joseph looked up startled and the sheep, seizing a chance of freedom, lunged forward, knocking Joseph off his feet. Giggling, I ran to the field, followed by Odin and Thor. I slowed down to approach Hermes my beautiful mare and she whinnied as she trotted over to me. I gave her the apple, threw a lead rope around her neck and led her over to the stables. I took her leather head collar off the hook by her stable and, putting it on, tied her up to the wall, and there I began to groom her. The stables were peaceful and quiet now, but once upon a time they had been full of beautiful hunters, carriage, and farm horses. Hermes had a beautiful rich chestnut coat which gleamed in the sun and a long flaxen blonde mane and tail. I cleaned out her feet to check for stones, wiped her eyes and nose with a cloth, decided not to bother with the saddle but ride bareback. I would lead her to the mounting block, hop on her broad warm back and ride around the lake. We would set off down the shady track leading to a waterfall from which the Chateau got its name where the lake narrowed to a small shallow river. The dogs came too, sniffing and running ahead, using their keen noses to hunt for pheasants to put up. I was so lucky, and even though I knew I was lucky, I didn't truly appreciate just how lucky I was. My life was wonderful, carefree every day. I had no idea how it would all change and so soon.

I loved Hermes and rode her every day unless Marcell needed her for work on the farm, trained as she was to work in harness

as well as under saddle. A Normandy cob, she would be driven in
the trap to take our milk, eggs and vegetable produce to market
in the town. During the vendange she would patiently wait for
the cart to be filled with grapes and then take them to the winery
for the grapes to be tipped into the press. All day long she did
this, patiently walking up and down the rows of vines and then
back to the press.

It was April 1940, and we were preparing the vines, pruning
them, spraying them and hoping for another decent harvest
like last year's. The wine in the winery so far had a good aroma
and looked and tasted as if 1939 had been a reasonable year. I
had learnt so much about the work of Marcell as a vigneron and
wine grower. I had learnt the importance of the terroir which was
about the environment. Climate, soil, topography, the pruning,
and irrigation of the soil and when to harvest the grapes was
so important to know. When they were picked, plus the time
they were in contact with the lees and the temperature during
fermentation was critical, as all these factors went to impart the
flavour and quality that is specific to the site from where the wine
came. This is what makes certain wines unique. Even the oak
barrels made a difference to the flavours of the wine because a
compound living in oak is vanillin which tastes like vanilla. All
this and more I had learnt during my few years living here, and I
hoped to carry on learning more about the winemaking process
which fascinated me.

As I rode down the track the dappled shade was wonderfully
cool in contrast to the rising heat of the morning. It was still early
morning, but already the sun was shedding its heat. The leaves
were bright green and in places they were just beginning to flower
and turn the air into the sweet, mingled perfume of spring. Crisp
greens, and soft lime-coloured leaves glittered and fluttered in

the April sunshine. Hermes' hooves sounded muffled by the forest floor of pine needles as we took the track to the first waterfall. Here I breathed in the pine scented forest and patted Hermes on her warm chestnut neck. Life was bliss and I never wanted it to change. I had holidayed here since I was a child with my parents, my brother and sister, coming every summer for the grape harvest. The first weeks of the summer holidays had always been spent on my parents' estate in Scotland and then we would travel to France for the last weeks of our summer holidays to help with the wine harvest or vendange as it is called. In between these wonderful times with my family, boarding school had been my nightmare. Although my brother and sister were always happy to return to boarding school after our holidays, to their sports and friends, I had hated it, losing weight, and suffering constant headaches whilst at school. When we were young, we had a Governess to educate us at home and enjoyed nature walks around our estate as part of our curriculum. I don't think my freckles and thick wavy auburn hair helped at boarding school, or my inability to master maths, reading and writing. I was a dunce; I was always bottom of the class. I pined for my mother and home, for my dogs, pony, and pets. I did have a good friend at school called Merioneth, but unfortunately her mother became very ill and as her father was a rector with a large moorland Parish on Dartmoor, she was recalled home to help her mother and look after her brothers. After she went home everything at school became even more unbearable.

I was often sent home from school, ill, and my wonderful dotty grandmother, who was expected to be there to look after me, was often away travelling to strange and wonderful places in the world less frequented by tourists. It was my grandmother, called Grandora by her grandchildren (her name was Isadora), who suggested that school was a disaster for me, and it would be a good idea to send me to France to study art.

Tantetta had a brilliant eye for a talented artist with many contacts and was able to locate paintings coming onto the market for the first time in years, often from impoverished families not wanting to publicise their need to sell their family heirlooms. She loved my paintings and told me that I had a gift and her constant supervision helped me to improve. I was originally very nervous about my move to France, but it had been a wonderful decision. Tantetta and I had an instant connection. The best of friends, we shared a love of art, good conversation, good food and wine and a shared sense of humour. My understanding of art and the varied and many mediums and methods used, improved immensely, and my French had become fluent without the need to use books. Best of all, I could ride every day because my wonderful Uncle Edmund had given me, just after my arrival in France, Hermes, an incredibly kind, sweet tempered Normandy cob. I will never forget being called to the stable yard by Uncle Edmund to see the beautiful horse coming down the ramp of a trailer and being told she was mine.

We skirted the lake and cantered up the avenue of lime trees towards the farmyard, with the dogs now trailing behind. Hermes was not sweating when we arrived back, so I slid from her back, brushed her over, took off her bridle and put on her leather head collar. The dogs were panting and flopped down in the shade of the stables. I took Hermes back to the paddock and turning her round at the gate to face me I slipped the head collar off, gave her an apple, a hug, a pat and a kiss. She stayed with me as I checked the water trough and turned on the standpipe to fill a bucket of water to put into the trough.

Joseph came over and filled another bucket to tip into the trough. "Did you enjoy your ride?" he asked.

"Yes," I said, "thank you. What are you doing today?"

"Marcell is sending me to start pruning the Merlot vines on the far side of the middle field. He says they're already putting out new shoots. I am just going to fetch Flavie to put his panniers on as he is taking him to work in the vineyard this morning." Joseph kicked a pebble and looked at the ground. "What do you think about these Nazis? Will they invade France and if they do, will you go home, back to England?' he asked.

"Whatever makes you ask?" I said, astonished he should even think about the possibility.

"They were talking about it at breakfast." He nodded his head towards the Chateau.

"Don't be silly," clever me sniffed. "They will never invade France; our army is too good, and our politicians will negotiate with them and finish all this nonsense about war. We have the Maginot Line, and the British army are here to help us if necessary. There will not be a war."

Joseph looked shocked. "What? Don't you read the papers or listen to the wireless? Germany has annexed Austria now, as you must know, and Hitler has taken control of the Sudetenland, the border of Czechoslovakia last September. They are rounding up and killing Jews in Czechoslovakia and Austria. He has already invaded Poland and you know France and Britain have declared war with Germany. When will you wake up?" he demanded, adding, 'I am thinking I should enlist and fight for our freedom. We are officially at war with Germany, so are Britain and Australia. You can't ignore the Nazis' threat to our country now."

Not believing him about the Jews being murdered I chose to ignore what he said. "No, Joseph, you can't join up! You can't leave your poor mama on her own, she would be devastated," I cried.

"I have to join my French brothers to keep our country safe," he said vehemently. Suddenly he looked passionate, his eyes blazed with anger.

"Marcell will never manage without you," I said, shocked. I realized that he really meant it and he knew I would hate him to leave the estate and face danger. We were short of help on the estate as it was. Many local young men had already left the area to join the army. Joseph had asthma which was why he worked outside in the fresh air and had already failed an army medical in the past. "Joseph, you are needed here," I insisted. "Some people must remain to provide food for the country, and you are a fire fighter for the local community. You are an important member of the village and the estate," I pleaded.

"My country needs me more," he said fearlessly.

I sighed and said, "Oh don't worry, they won't get here, you're as bad as Tantetta who is worried and going on about what we must do to be prepared in case we are invaded."

He shook his head crossly and strode into the paddock to catch Flavie without another word. Seeing Joseph heading his way swinging a halter, Flavie walked off even faster down to the far side of the paddock. It was a casual, but quick walk pretending he was deaf and didn't know that he was about to be caught for work. Joseph shouted in vain for him to stand still as he began eating the grass again with his back to Joseph. Flavie was our mule, a descendant of the horses and mules my uncle had bought after the Great War to save them from the slaughter. This was a sad fate which had happened to many of the English and Australian horses, mules and donkeys left behind after the war. Giggling at Flavie's antics and without another thought of silly war, I headed for the Chateau and my painting room.

When I had arrived to stay here three and a half years ago, my aunt had decided that I should have a designated art room, which was brilliant. I loved my private work room where I could design, plan a painting, or even just dream. I walked into my paradise which smelt of turps and oil paints. Tantetta had chosen a little used day room at the side and front of the Chateau in a round turret with windows on two sides which flooded the room with light. I looked down to the gardens towards the lake on the south-east side through two windows and towards the vineyard and drive, then through two more long windows on the south-west side. I had collected an apple from the apple store and a coffee from the kitchen on my way there. I stared at the blank piece of thick watercolour paper before me and studied my morning sketch, trying to decide if it was the right sized paper. I had already decided to use my watercolours. Swiftly, I taped the paper onto a board, gave it a flat wet wash and then munched an apple as it dried.

Over the last few weeks, I spent there, I would think about Joseph and his thoughts about the situation in Europe. How could it bother us I thought? Japan had invaded China on July 7th, 1937. Nothing to do with us. On April 7th -15th,1939, Italy had invaded and annexed Albania and yes, I knew that last March Germany had incorporated Austria in the Anschluss. They had already signed the Munich agreement in September 1938 with Italy, Great Britain and France forcing the Czechoslovak Republic to cede to Sudetenland. I also knew that last September 87,300 people had been evacuated from the Red Zone, the space between the Maginot Line and the border, and the Siegfried Line in Germany. Many areas of France had to help and cope with these displaced people. In Perigueaux they had 11,375 people arrive with nowhere to stay. They had few clothes, no food or furniture and many had travelled on trains with no food or toilets for days. Sometimes they were referred to as ya-yas because of the German/French accents. To be honest, I wasn't very interested in politics, but I was wondering if I should be. It was the main topic of conversation in the kitchen every lunchtime. Fancy Joseph knowing so much and being interested in what was happening. Well, it was all happening a long way from my haven in France, although the evacuation of so many people should have brought home to me the increasing possibility of war. It did seem to be a bit of a mess and very hard to follow. Since I had arrived in France all I had heard about was the recession in France which now seemed to be taking a back seat in everyday conversation. I drank my coffee, now going cold, and watched Marcell working in the vineyard and Joseph leading Flavie, now carrying panniers, as he headed towards the rows of vines.

I cast my mind back to the day I set to work on my watercolour and time flew by as I concentrated on my work and getting the light streaming through the branches of the trees to look right. I worked with Van Dyke brown and Raw Sienna then Sap green, Aurora yellow and Chromium Oxide green. I lost all sense of time with concentration, and I thought about the words of Paul Cezanne the post-Impressionist: "We live in a rainbow of chaos. A work of art which did not begin with emotion is not art." I was pleased with my drawing of the young buck with his first small antlers, oblivious to me as he browsed in the undergrowth. The light dappled his rich tawny, brown coat and I was sure that I had captured the moment with a light touch of my paints. Twelve-thirty arrived and I put down my brush to stand back and study my work. I would leave it now, go for lunch and see it with fresh eyes later and decide then if it was working and if I liked it. Before I left the room, I had a quick critical look at my painting of Tantetta. She had an interesting face filled with wisdom and I believed that I had captured the essence of her inner beauty. I had already painted her from a photograph, not long after I had arrived, which showed her as a young, beautiful debutante. Now I was painting her yet again, as a surprise for her birthday and I was pleased with its progress. Her long blonde hair was now a soft silver, still shot with strands of blonde and twisted up into an elegant chignon. Her skin was clear and that of an English rose, just as it had been in her youth. She had few wrinkles and classic high cheekbones which even now gave an elegant and beautiful shape to her face with its strong jawline. She had a faintly Roman nose and an aristocrat tilt to her head, but the most remarkable features to her face were her incredible, clear, vivid blue eyes with an outline of almost black around each iris. I had painted her staring straight out of the canvas, looking directly ahead. Those eyes had mesmerised many people in her youth and their piercing clarity still captivated admirers and listeners to what she had to say. I re-covered the painting which I was going to show Jean-Phillipe when he came. He had a good eye and would tell me honestly if it was finished or needed more work.

I was now hungry and so took off my painting smock and went to the kitchen for lunch.

Chapter 3

A Wonderful Life in France

L unch in the kitchen was an important part of our day. Always a relaxed friendly affair, usually just with Joseph, Marcell, Aurielle, Marie Christine and her daughter Elise and me. Tantetta preferred to lunch alone in the day room with her art catalogues and the telephone, because she worked throughout the day. Her lunch was simple. Usually salad or omelette, local cheese or homemade soup – especially soup a l'oignon with croutons and melted cheese on top, also my favourite – served with homemade bread prepared by Aurielle, then taken to her room on a pretty flower-painted tray. On this day in the kitchen the discussion, which often in the past centred around the day-to-day affairs regarding the running of the estate, was again about the events taking place far away. Usually, we would discuss the jobs that needed doing such as the turning of the wine bottles in the cellar, or the produce ready for market that week. The list was always endless. What produce we sent to market was talked about, but included seasonal food grown on the estate and much anticipated by the local housewives.

Recently, though, we had taken to discussing the latest political events and what the Nazis were threatening. Alarmingly, it also included the fear of a German invasion. Mr Hitler was unsettling everyone, he sounded like a thoroughly nasty man. Yet again today, the conversation quickly became all about fascist Italy invading and annexing Albania. Joseph started saying again that he should join the French army, but Marcell and Aurielle joined me in telling him he was needed here, with farming and food production just as important as rushing off to fight with the army. As a part-time village firefighter, he was much relied upon, but it was his mother who needed him more. His father had returned from the Great War and like so many men he had been gassed and his injuries were severe. He was in constant pain. Louisa, his wife, already had a daughter Cecile born before the Great War and after his return they were blessed with the birth of a son, Joseph, in 1920. His father had succumbed to the severity of his injuries and died in 1930 when Joseph was only ten years old. Louisa, now alone, struggled to bring up Joseph and Cecile. Cecile, now married and living in the Lyon area with her new family, rarely visited Louisa and Joseph.

After lunch Marie- Christine and Elise would carry on cleaning the Chateau and twice a week Joseph's mama, Louisa, visited to do the laundry, including the ironing. On those occasions she would naturally join us for lunch in the kitchen. We were increasingly gloomy about the Hitler situation, and I was the only one stupidly optimistic that our French army with the British army, would be able to stop any potential invasion by the Germans. I was convinced that they were worrying for no good reason. How dare Mr Hitler spoil my wonderful, happy life here with my beloved Tantetta, all my companions and animals in this gorgeous Chateau?

As Germany had now invaded Poland without any warning or declaration of war, Joseph, Marcell and Aurielle voiced their worries about this happening here in France as we were now, officially, at war with Germany. We had heard in 1939 that the Nazis had invaded the Polish towns of Katowice, Krakow, Tczew, and Warsaw in surprise attacks. The German wireless had reported that Polish soldiers had attacked the German border town of Gliwice, so it was in retaliation that Germany had attacked Poland. They reported that the Polish soldiers responsible for the attack on Gliwice in Germany had all been shot dead. Most people thought it was just a fabricated story, giving the Germans an excuse to attack and invade Poland, as it was a known fact the town had been attacked by Nazi criminals dressed as Polish soldiers. I thought, well, Poland is a long way away and surely things would settle down. Now they had invaded Poland they wouldn't want to occupy any more countries, surely it would be greedy. That was me, always with my head in the clouds and selfish.

I like a simple fresh herb omelette for lunch and would go back into my art room to paint; all thoughts of any impending invasion banished from my mind. That day I remember looking at a previous painting I had done of Tantetta when she was a debutante. I had used a photograph of her just before her marriage to my uncle Edmund, the Count du Gaillarde, about the time when Henrietta, and her sisters Augusta and Isadora, had all been presented, at court as 18-year-olds, to King Edward VII. Augusta, Henrietta, and my Grandmother Isadora were the daughters of Lord and Lady Rimmington. My Grandmother Isadora met her future husband, Lord Ellesdale, during her year as a debutante. They had settled in Norfolk after their marriage, on the family estate, Willup Hall.

Willup Hall, a moderately small hall, is built of Carstone and Norfolk flint and situated down a long drive lined with beautiful horse chestnut trees and stunningly so in May when they were covered in amazing cream coloured candle-like flowers. The hall, surrounded by parkland, was my home; we had our own stables, coach house and farm buildings. We could see the cattle grazing in the park and we had a herd of zika deer, secretive creatures, so it was always a joy to catch a glimpse of them grazing peacefully. At the back of the Hall, which technically was the front, the lawns swept down to a stream fed by a tributary of the local shallow river where we would paddle or swim when we were children. My father had two sisters Rose-Mary and Lydia-Anne and being the son, he inherited the estate on the death of his father, my grandfather George William the previous Lord Ellesdale.

My father George Albert only lived at Willup Hall when not staying in our family home in Chelsea, London, close to his barracks and his military duties. My mother flitted between London with my father and Willup Hall to be at home with me, my brother and sister. Willup Hall is small as Halls go and the park is small, but we didn't know that during our happy days growing up and running wild in the grounds. We had the most perfect, idyllic, carefree childhood and we loved our home life there. My father was rarely at home, only came to see us when on weekend leave when he would entertain and meet up with their friends. My mother would stay at home with us and my grandparents, her in-laws, who were always there and were very much a part of our lives through those early years. We had pet rabbits, cats, hens, lambs, dogs, and ponies, so life was never dull. There were family parties, paddling or swimming in the shallow clear river; we could ride through the park and go fishing, too. In winters we would go out when it snowed enjoyed sledging and snowball fights. Christmas was always a glorious, happy time. That's how I remember it. Happy sunny days in summer, and snow and fun in winter.

My grandfather, George William, was a kind man and we respected and adored him. He was a great countryman who hunted and kept his own pack of bloodhounds for drag hunting. He had his own well-respected shoot and was an enthusiastic fly fisherman going to his country house in the Scottish borders every year to fish on the river Tweed. He had fished all the great Scottish rivers during his lifetime and was a well renowned fly fisherman as well as a good farmer and keen breeder of cattle and sheep. Any new farming method or machinery was always tried on the estate farms. He promoted the support of rural crafts and good forestry, and the welfare of his estate workers was paramount to his forward-thinking ways. I loved riding around the estate with him on my small pony, Twinkle, and later a bigger pony called Spangles, while he rode one of his many, beautiful big hunters. We would visit the hunt kennels to see the hounds, a mix of Dumfriesshire and Black and Tans, and go on morning exercise with the huntsman Alford Harrington, who, I remember, was always kind to us children. I also visited the gamekeeper Hugh Brownlow and loved playing with the new puppies when they were born. We bred gun dogs, black Labradors and working Cocker Spaniels. Just before I came to France there was a bit of a mix up with the gun dogs when a black Labrador called Venture Scout mated a working Cocker Spaniel called Woodland Wanderer and the resulting litter of six healthy puppies were not considered the 'right sort' of gun dogs for the shoot, so good country homes were found for them all! It just so happened that my Great-Aunt Henrietta wanted a puppy sending to France and so our gamekeeper travelled over to France in person to deliver this precious puppy which she named Thor. I was also allowed to have one as I had been wanting my very own dog for ages, and one puppy was given to Lysander. The other three were found lovely homes on the estate, two with farmers and one little girl puppy went to our vicar Bramwell Stevens and his family. I called mine Odin and Lysander called his Puck. I was now in love with my new puppy, training commenced and going back to school became even more hated by me.

My brother Lysander went away to boarding school when he was twelve years old. Portia and I called him Sandy. He'd been taught by our Governess until then, as we all had. My sister and I missed him terribly as he was the leader in all our games and escapades and such fun. My hero, Lysander, and my sister Portia were always ready to help me climb a tree or get back on a pony if I had fallen off. He was older than me by five and a half years, but not once did he call me a baby or tease me about my curly red hair and freckles. My sister Portia was only three years older than me, very pretty with blonde hair and bright blue eyes just like my brother, and both were very kind to me. I adored them both. I had hazel eyes just like my mother, but why my hair was so ginger and springy with waves and curls, nobody knew. When my brother left for boarding school, we were both very sad, but there was aways so much to occupy our time at home. There were plenty of games to play, our animals to look after, plus lambs to help bottle feed in spring, and, most importantly, my grandparents were always there for us. We had friends to stay with us and life was always very active, busy, and fun.

Then, sadly, our lovely grandfather died, and I remember many people coming to his funeral. He had been a very popular man, a good farmer, huntsman, fisherman, landlord and all-round sporting countryman. He had spoken in the House of

Lords about the rights of farm workers to be housed in decent
cottages and spoke for improved working hours and pay, as well
as on the rights of their children to free education. He was always
keen to improve his livestock and to grow food more efficiently.
He kept a fine well-bred herd of Lincolnshire red cattle and was
an expert on their breeding lines. He also preserved and kept
a small herd of old-fashioned Long Horn cattle and a flock of
Norfolk Horn sheep which he was trying to keep as a pure breed.
Many had been bred to Southdown rams to start a breed called
Suffolk sheep.

He would ride one of his hunters around the estate most days
when he was at home to see what needed doing, to see how the
crops were growing and to talk to his workers and tenant farmers.
He always had all his dogs trailing around after him as he toured
the estate. He was kind, fair and honest to everyone, a loyal friend,
and a great family man. We loved spending time with him, and
I missed him dreadfully after his unexpected, sudden death. My
grandmother was grief stricken and after the funeral she became
quiet and withdrawn, but knew she must take up the reins of the
estate and run it until her son, my father, came home to take
on his responsibilities. My father, however, was now part of the
Diplomatic branch for the British Government in India and it
was not possible for him to assume his duties at home for the
foreseeable future. I don't think he wanted to, anyway. As I saw
it, he was enjoying travelling, and seeing the world, forcing my
grandmother, therefore, to turn to the estate manager, Humphrey
Clayton, to run things after Grandfather's death.

My mother and father seemed to be away more and more
and busier than ever in London. With my father's change of
duty, it became expected my mother would go to India with
him. They were to leave for India after my grandfather's funeral

and this came as a great shock to me. I was so miserable at the thought of my mother going away I found myself riding around the estate alone, unless I accompanied Granger, our groom, or Alford Harrington on early morning hound exercise. I loved sketching and would take all the dogs and ride my pony Spangles, sometimes stopping to sketch. Grandora and I would then meet up for meals – but she was not the same without my grandfather. We used to be a large happy, noisy family at most mealtimes – now we were just two quiet people and strangely, sadly, with very little to say to each other.

Worse was to come. My parents decided I should become a pupil at my sister's boarding school and nothing I said to them would persuade them otherwise. I pleaded with them to let me stay at home – but nothing would change their minds. I hated leaving home and all my animals, but especially my free way of life. My grandmother didn't help, she had become so withdrawn from life I found I couldn't talk to her as once I did. So, off to boarding school I went when I was just thirteen years. Nothing, however, could help me settle into school life.

I had always struggled to read letters on a page; they just seemed so jumbled to me and I forgot what I was reading by the time I had struggled to the bottom of the page. Sadly, I was classed as a dunce, but worst of all was the teasing. This was because I was gawky and even more horrible because I had frizzy, ginger hair and freckles. One girl, who was also teased in my year, became a good friend. Merioneth, from Dartmoor, who was a Rector's daughter. Poor Merioneth was a little bit podgy, was teased because of her weight and it didn't help that she had straight mouse-coloured hair and was very quiet. We were nicknamed Dim and Slim, though I don't know why as Merioneth was not that dim or slim; and I was both. She was brilliant at cookery and sewing classes and her maths was far better than mine. I just happened to be very bad at maths too. In fact, there wasn't really anything I was good at, apart from painting. Anyway, we were happy in each other's company. She helped me with any homework I couldn't do and in turn I helped with her art. She came home to stay with me at Willup Hall one Easter holidays and we had a brilliant time as she got on so well with Lysander and Portia and loved all my animals. I think she loved staying with us because for her it was a real holiday to be away from home and having to help with six brothers. I taught her how to ride on my mother's patient grey mare Polly, and if we just walked the ponies, she enjoyed going out riding.

Then during Spring term at school, she suddenly had to go home to help look after her mother who was ill. Her father was a very busy country Rector, and he was struggling to look after his parish and all the children as well as his poorly wife. Eventually she returned to school looking tired, obviously worn out, and then the awful news came that her mother, having taken a turn for the worse, had died, so she had to go straight home again. She was fourteen and a half years old, and she didn't come back to school – my best friend had gone. I felt more alone than ever. My grandmother had decided to visit India to see some friends living there and travelled on to visit my father and mother. It was then that everything went downhill for me. School was awful and when I was at home it was so quiet. I just missed everyone so much. On top of that I always seemed to be ill with awful headaches.

It was then, thank goodness, that the decision was made that I should came to live in France with Tantetta with no more written schoolwork, plenty of painting, and riding with sunshine every day.

Seriously, how could I not like that?

Now living in France, I had learnt all about the vines and the wonderful art of making good wine. My French had become fluent, and my artwork was improving all the time. My cooking remained 'iffy' despite Aurielle's best efforts to teach me. Coming to France had been the best thing that could have happened to me since my beloved grandfather had died. I was so content and happy and couldn't imagine a different life. I didn't have to try to read or write much anymore. I learnt everything by listening, watching, and doing.

Now I had no idea how much my life was about to change along with the lives of so many innocent people all over the world.

Chapter 4

Reasons for Leaving Britain

I will expand a bit and try to explain why I had lived the good life in France for so long.

In 1936 I had detested boarding school more than ever and I didn't have any best subjects other than art. Then, without Merioneth, the days were even worse. With my Governess, my inability to read had been mostly glossed over. I don't think she wanted my parents to know what a poor student I was and blame her for my failings. Now I was in a class with other pupils it stood out like a sore thumb. I was teased for my poor spelling and my bad schoolwork, but mostly I was teased for my long, curly, wiry red hair, my face covered in freckles, and my name.

As a child my mother had lived in a remote country house in Scotland; she had often been lonely, and reading had been her salvation and passion, her favourite being Shakespeare, hence my name Cressida and my nickname Sid. I became ill at boarding school again with blinding headaches and lost weight, pining for home. I made myself so ill that the school Matron recommended that I was sent home to, hopefully, recover. I found that Grandora had just left for India to visit friends and to see my parents in Kerala. She couldn't stand life at the Hall without my grandfather and decided a trip away would be a good idea. The house was now extremely quiet and although I was pleased to be home, I couldn't be happy with all my family away. I spent more time riding Spangles, walking my father's dogs Trig and Spruce, my new puppy Odin, and of course painting. Finally, I had to return to boarding school, but became ill again with more violent headaches, so severe I would have to lie down in a dark room with a vinegar-soaked flannel on my head and covering my eyes. The headmistress wrote to my parents to tell them that she thought it would be for the best if I left boarding school and advised them to take me home. Meanwhile, they had just been informed that my father's new posting with the diplomatic service was to be in Singapore. My sister tried to reason with me, but she was in a different house at boarding school, was busy preparing for university entrance, and, as we rarely saw each other, I was miserable and lonely. So, at fourteen I left boarding school, and didn't miss it one bit.

Before going out to Singapore, my parents were to return home from India on leave, and it was decided that I should go to Singapore with them. I wanted my mother to stay at home with me, but as she had to accompany my father it was decided I needed to go with them.

On arriving home from boarding school, I was picked up from the station by Clarissa, the estate manager's wife, and taken home to wait for my parents' return. I was a bit in disgrace not able to cope with boarding school, but that didn't bother me one bit. I spent a happy week learning how to cook and bake with Clarissa in her kitchen, riding round the estate visiting tenants with her husband Humphrey, walking all the dogs and spending time with Hugh the gamekeeper, training Odin. My headaches miraculously disappeared.

My parents arrived home at the end of the week, and we discussed my future over dinner. I was always happy to see my mother, but my father was a distant and remote figure in my life. He'd rarely been at home in my early years, and I was a little afraid of him. He'd been in the army as long as I could remember, and he never seemed to play with me even when he was home on leave. Obviously during his time at home, he always had estate affairs to which he had to attend, and this consumed his time. This, I thought, was probably why he preferred relaxing in London when on leave. Our summer holidays were often spent with Mother, but Father was not always with us except on our annual holiday at the end of summer. This was for the harvest of the grapes on my great uncle and aunt's estate in France, where even my father became brown from the sun, and we were all happy and relaxed together. It was rare to see our father relaxed, so we loved these holidays as we were a real family during those happy weeks.

On the first evening of my parents' return home, we ate our evening meal together in silence, each of us deep in our own thoughts with just my mother trying to make conversation. Finally, we finished our meal and what little conversation there was ground to an awkward halt as I held my breath, waiting to hear my father's anger about me leaving school. He then shrugged his shoulders, looked at me and said, "What's done is done, Cressida. I know school is not for everyone, I wasn't too keen when I was sent away, but I loved sport which helped me get through my time there. So how do you fancy coming to Singapore with us?" Shocked I hadn't been shouted at, I was too speechless to answer him. Fortunately, my mother brightly started to tell me all about Singapore – there was horse riding and a good international day school for me to attend and I would no doubt make lots of new friends. I thought quickly, and it was then I remembered an article in a magazine which Merry had read to me about my grandmother's sister Henrietta, my great aunt in France, on how she was considered a world authority in the art world. When we holidayed with her and her husband the Count de Gaillarde at their beautiful Chateau, I had always wanted to learn more about the harvesting of the vines. Could that possibly happen now instead of me going to Singapore? Dare I mention it to my parents? I loved the Chateau, and I could paint and learn so much about the art world from Tantetta, plus my French would improve without having to read books.

I told my mother about the magazine article and how widely respected Tantetta was in the international art world. Good art works generally go up in value or at the very least hold their value so are a good investment. My parents were impressed that I had taken such interest in my Tantetta's career and for some time we chatted about the times we had spent on holiday at the Chateau and the fun we had had there over the years.

My great-aunt and uncle had two children during their long marriage, Henri and Clementine who had been their great pride and joy. But Clementine had died of scarlet fever when she was eight years old and Henri at twenty had been killed in action during the Great War. He had joined the same regiment as my uncle and was serving in the French army when France was brought into the war by a German declaration on August 3rd, 1914. Sadly, he was killed during the First Battle of the Marne. The French casualties were estimated at 250,000 of whom 80,000 were killed. Commandant Edmund Henri Emmanuel de la Bonroille, at twenty years old, was the pride of his parents. Struck down and fatally injured by a bullet, his death devastated his father who never fully recovered. The deaths of his daughter to scarlet fever and then his son on the battlefield, were too much for my Great-Uncle Edmund. He was left in a trough of despair. My Great-Aunt Henrietta kept the Chateau, vineyard and estate going with help from Marcell. His wife Aurielle looked after my great-aunt and uncle and the housekeeping of the Chateau. During the war, despite his despair over Henri's death, my Great-Uncle Edmund had to carry on fighting the German army, serving in the cavalry until during one charge his horse was shot from under him and landed on my uncle, breaking his femur, and smashing his knee cap. The poor horse was put out of his misery. The injury was not repaired properly, so he lived in great pain for the rest of his life. His love of horses, however, was steadfast and at the end of the Great War he managed to buy some of the poor faithful horses and mules which were destined for the slaughterhouse to feed the German prisoners of war. This horrible end to their lives was after all the suffering the animals had endured during the battles – the mud and lack of food, along with all the soldiers who were their best mates.

The horses he bought were taken to the Chateau to rest and recuperate from the trauma of the fighting. Some never worked again, some he sold to friends as good riding, hunting or carriage horses, and some mares bred foals Others were able to work on the estate pulling drays or carriages and were used by my great-uncle to take him around the estate on his good days, to oversee all the work needing to be done or when he carried his sketch book or paints with him.

My parents and I talked until late in the evening around the dining room table. It made a pleasant change to sit and spend time with them as we so rarely saw each other. I heard all about their new move to Singapore and my father's important job working as a diplomat for the foreign office. Finally, I went to bed still not at all sure that I wanted to go to Singapore. The next morning during breakfast our maid Maisie called my mother to the telephone, and I waited for her to return to the breakfast table. She came back into the room beaming and looking very pleased with herself.

My father put down his newspaper and said, "So it looks like it's good news, Rom?"

"Yes, Bertie," said Mother. "It's brilliant. Cressida, my dear, would you like to stay in France at the Chateau with Tantetta and Uncle Edmund?"

I was so shocked and stuttered, "What, I mean when, I mean, for how long?"

"Well, school makes you ill, and you love painting, so my aunt has agreed to tutor you in the history of art and painting, plus you will learn French, and learn about estate management; all about the vines and winemaking. You will spend some time in their apartment in Paris, visit art galleries and the art auction houses, learning how to recognise and choose paintings to buy and sell. A private tutor will be hired to teach you French and history. Your great-aunt and uncle are happy for you to stay with them and continue your education until we return from Singapore. It was your grandmother's idea, and she has already been in touch with her sister, Aunt Henrietta, and it's all been arranged by the two of them."

I threw my arms around my mother and then, a little cautiously, around my somewhat reserved father. "Thank you, thank you so much," I cried. "It's brilliant. Thank you so much, I will love it." My hand flew to my mouth. "But what about my pony, Spangles, and Odin? I can't leave them here alone. What will happen to them, can they come too?"

"You can take Odin with you, but Spangles must stay here – the Marlowe family would like to loan him for their two daughters Birdie and Blythe who already have one pony but need another, as Blythe is outgrowing Star, their pony. They asked me some time ago and you are outgrowing him and can ride any of the hunters or my mare Polly when you want to ride."

"Oh well, that's good I suppose," I said reluctantly. "Can I meet them?"

"Of course you can. Their mother is the Hunt secretary and rides herself. They live near Snettisham, and I know Spangles will be well looked after. Trust me, it's a good home and comes highly recommended by Granger."

Granger was our groom and chauffeur, and I trusted his judgement.

"My Uncle Edmund always has some good horses about the place in France, so you will have something to ride whilst you are there."

"When do I go?" I asked in excitement.

"Well, we leave next weekend, and I would like to think you were safely there before we left for Singapore. You must pack and get some new clothes; I will check out the train times today and we can go shopping tomorrow. Now off you go to sort your clothes with Maisie and decide what you want to take with you."

My father was smiling when he suggested that my mother and I went to London two days earlier, stayed in our London townhouse in Chelsea, and did some shopping before catching my train to Dover. I think he was relieved to have found a solution for his troublesome younger daughter.

"What about Lysander and Portia?" I cried. "When will I see them?"

"I'm sure they will visit you in France, in the holidays, and you will still be able to come home to see them. Now, I shall start making the necessary arrangements for your journey, so go and sort your things out before you go riding Spangles. I can always pop into King's Lynn today for some toiletries and anything else you might need," said Mother.

I was so excited about the journey and my stay in France that at that moment it didn't occur to me that my family life as I had known it was going to be over forever.

Chapter 5

New Life in France

The next three days flew by, and I even managed to meet Birdie and Blythe. I found I liked them so was confident that Spangles would be well looked after whilst on loan to them. The last night in my bedroom soon came and that was the night I had some nerves about my new adventure, as well as sadness at leaving the security of my childhood home. My bedroom walls were adorned in pale pink rose covered wallpaper, and my curtains were plain pink with a border of roses, with an eiderdown of pale green embroidered with a circle of pink roses. I loved my big bedroom and spent hours drawing, painting, or reading here, and now I was leaving this haven for a new adventure. I slept well and left my old teddy on the bed to guard my bedroom, was soon washed, dressed and ready for breakfast. My father took us with Odin to King's Lynn in the station wagon and after saying our goodbyes we were soon on the train, travelling to London. My father was kind and warm, which was unusual. Maybe he was glad to see the back of me.

We stayed in our London town house and went to Fortnum and Mason's for a hamper of luxury food for Great-Aunt Henrietta. I bought new jodhpurs, leather riding boots, some twill slacks, new shorts, and some 'Liberty' print short sleeved shirts for the summer as they were all I ever lived in anyway. My mother insisted I bought two evening dresses and two dresses for daytime, a two-piece costume made of Harris tweed and cardigans for my trips to Paris and any social life in France. I then bought new paints, brushes and 'smocks' to wear when I was painting. Finally, the day came for Odin and I alone to board the train to Plymouth. I hugged my lovely mother tightly and suddenly did not want to let go. I had enjoyed our special time in the house together, the shopping and lunching, the dining out and talking late into the night. It was as if we were just discovering each other as friends, not just mother and daughter – now we had discovered we liked the same things, same jokes and we laughed together. We hoped to see each other each year that I was in France, even though Singapore was such a long way away, but when we met in the future there would be other people there with us most of the time. We just did not know how precious those few days would become to us in the following years when our lives were destined to be so very different and difficult.

I was sad, scared, and excited by my impending trip and was glad to have Odin travelling with me. I travelled from Paddington station to Plymouth and waited for my ferry boat to St Malo. My luggage was taken care of by porters, so all I had to carry was an overnight bag and keep Odin safely secure on his lead.

After staying on the ferry overnight in my own cabin with Odin, we arrived the next morning with the coast of France in view. We soon docked and I was able to take Odin for a walk before we boarded the train for the journey which would take us another six hours. Finally, five days since leaving King's Lynn, I was picked up at the station by Marcell, driving my Great-Uncle Edmund's Rolls-Royce, and after a lengthy journey we finally arrived at the Chateau de la Cascade. I had met Marcell many times when on holiday in France and knew him and his wife Aurielle quite well, so I was pleased to see him pick me up. We arrived at the Chateau, and it looked just as beautiful as usual in the pink glow of the early evening sun. We drove up the long avenue of lime trees and pulled up in front of the stone steps leading to the great lead-studded front door. The Chateau was a pale pink colour with blue shutters at all the windows to keep out the heat in summer or potential invaders of years past. At each of the two corners at the front of the house, were towers with turrets of grey slate like the rest of the roof. It was beautiful and just like a fairy-tale castle. I was very tired but thrilled to be in France where I had always enjoyed summer holidays with my family.

My French was limited – just the basic hello, goodbye and how are you – but I had been studying my new French dictionary and phrase book on my journey down and was keen to practise my new French vocabulary. A maid met me at the door and took care of all my luggage with Marcell's help. Then I was taken to the salon where my Tantetta was reading an art sale catalogue. Tantetta rose and came to greet me warmly with kisses on both cheeks. She held my hands and studied me, smiling. "At last you have arrived, I am so pleased to see you, Cressida; you have grown so much since last time I saw you. How old are you now?"

I hugged my aunt who was just as tall and elegant as I remembered her. "I am nearly fifteen, Tantetta, and I am so happy to be here. Thank you so much for saying that I could stay with you. I promise I won't be any trouble." The words tumbled from me I was so nervous and excited.

"Sit down, let me really look at you." She peered at me intently. "You have a look of your grandmother and your mother. I can see them both in you. So now, is this Odin, Thor's little brother?"

Odin wagged his tail enthusiastically and held out a paw to Tantetta.

"Where is Uncle Edmund?" I asked, curious to know why he was not in the salon with her.

"He is resting, he continues to work too hard and exhausts himself. You will see him later, ma cherie. I can see that you are very tired, you must go to your room, rest, wash and change, before we dine this evening, then perhaps an early night for you, after your long journey I think."

She rang the bell to summon the maid and the young girl who had met me at the door, about the same age as me, appeared and took me upstairs to my bedroom. The smell of the Chateau's interior reminded me of my happy holidays here with Lysander, Portia, and my parents. It smelt of beeswax polished furniture, and delicious smells of French cooking drifting in from the kitchen.

The pedestal table in the vast central hall had a vase with garden flowers carrying a soft perfume of summer and I felt at home, really at home; a great peace washed over me. I was taken up the wide staircase to the first-floor bedrooms, into a large airy bedroom flooded with light and I fell in love with it immediately. In the past when staying here I had shared a room with my siblings. This room had a huge carved French bed painted white and it was covered with an exquisite, embroidered bed cover in pale pink under which was a sort of huge feather pillow thing. I later discovered it was from Switzerland and called a duvet. The tall windows on two walls had white painted interior wood shutters which were open, showing me the view beyond of the long lawn sweeping down to the lake and the dark green woods beyond. It was breathtakingly beautiful, and I felt that I had come home to where I belonged. The walls were covered in a pale grey-blue hand-painted silk wallpaper which was covered in flowers and pink flamingos. I later learnt the colour was called French blue. There was a knock at the door and the maid opened it to allow Marcell and a young man (I later discovered called Joseph) to carry my large trunk into the room. I thanked them in my schoolgirl French, and they left the room. The girl spoke to me in French, pointed at a door near the large ornate wardrobe and, as I didn't have a clue what she was saying, I smiled and said, "Ah oui l'armoire," thanked her, and went to open the wardrobe door so that I could look politely inside. She repeated what she had said, and I realized she was saying bathroom: "Ah salle de Bains?" I said, pointing to the door. She opened the door laughing and I nearly fainted. There was my own bathroom, just for me, and it was huge and beautiful. Black and white and everything in it was huge: the sink, the bath and even the lavatory seemed big with a very high cistern and long pull chain. At home we had a new bathroom on each floor, and they were large and cold with linoleum on the floor and no heating, not places to spend too much time. In winter you had to hop from one foot to the other to keep warm whilst you cleaned your teeth. This one had blue flowers on the sink and toilet, and the huge bath stood on claw feet. There was a big, cosy blue rug on the floor: it was heavenly. I thought it was wonderful. No more trips down a long corridor to a freezing cold bathroom.

I was so tired after my long journey I flopped onto the vast bed and would easily have drifted off to sleep, but the maid started to run a bath for me and whilst it was running, she opened my trunk and started to unpack, putting my clothes away in the huge wardrobe. Meanwhile, Odin went around the room, sniffing everywhere to check out this new place. The maid switched off the tap and I went into the bathroom to have a long soak in the bath whilst my clothes were folded and put away for me, what luxury.

"Attendez, comment vous appelez-vous, s'il vous plait?" I asked, adding, "Je m'appelle Cressida."

The girl giggled as she left. "Je m'appelle Elise."

When I got out of the bath and dried myself on the big soft bath towel, I went into my bedroom and found that one of my new skirts and a twin set had been put out for me to wear that evening for dinner, plus Odin had disappeared, no doubt to play with Thor and have some doggy dinner. A little later there was a knock on my door and Elise had come to tell me my great-aunt and uncle were waiting for me in the salon when I was changed and ready. This was all in French and I only just understood bits of what she had said. I was going to have to improve my French quickly. I cleaned my teeth, brushed my hair, and tied it back with a pale green scarf, but as usual it had a springy life of its own and the curls and waves in my red hair fought against control. I was very excited to meet my Uncle Edmund again as it seemed ages since I had last seen him. When on holiday here last year, I had ridden with him, and we had taken our paints and sketch books. I had enjoyed his company so much, he was so knowledgeable and, fortunately, he spoke excellent English. Thank goodness.

I had dressed in a cotton skirt of pale green poplin and a new pale lilac twinset, tripped down the amazing, curved staircase past the round table with the fragrant summer flowers and to the door of the salon. I gently knocked and opening the large door entered the elegant salon filled with exquisite French furniture and the most wondrous collection of beautiful paintings. My eyes fell on two by Vincent Van Gogh and a Matisse, and then to my great-aunt and uncle who were sitting in comfortable winged chairs, each covered in beige damask either side of the open French windows. I moved swiftly to greet my uncle – I liked him very much. I kissed him on each cheek before he tried to struggle to his feet and then I kissed my aunt again. There was a chair placed next to theirs, waiting for me, and this was placed by the side of a little Louis XV table which held a silver tray on which were three wine glasses and a cut glass decanter filled with white wine. Aurielle, the housekeeper, whom I already knew, came in and poured three glasses of wine for us and brought a plate of green and black olives with little cocktail sticks and a side plate for each of us. I greeted Aurielle in French and thankfully she understood me, which I thought was a good start. I was nervous and thrilled to be offered wine, although of course I had drunk wine before, but only with water in it as well, and only then on very rare occasions. The glasses were only half-filled, and I slowly sipped my wine; it was delicious. Aurielle opened the salon door to let Odin and Thor into the room with their wriggling bodies and wagging tails; they greeted us before settling down. Thor next to Tantetta and Odin snuggling up to me. They obviously had been playing outside and were now shattered. They had not forgotten they were siblings. My uncle patted Odin and said what a lovely dog he had turned out to be, like his brother Thor in size, but not in colour. Thor was a darker blue merle coloured Spaniel taking after his black Labrador father, whereas Odin was tan and white like his Cocker Spaniel mother.

"Does he work like his parents?" Uncle Edmund asked.

"Yes, he is wonderful, he has a very good nose and can pick up a scent quickly. He has been out in the field working with our gamekeeper, but I prefer him with me. I have been learning how to handle him in the field and with the whistle," I replied enthusiastically, and looked proudly at my gorgeous best friend,

Odin. I stroked his long silky ears and he put his head on my lap and sighed contentedly. Even after our long journey, if he was with me, he was happy, and I loved him dearly.

We chatted about my parents and my long journey, and I noticed that my great-uncle had a healthy tan and looked well, but that he had lost weight and he seemed frailer than I remembered. His war wound caused him great pain. We were dining simply so there was a round pedestal table set for us to at the far end of the salon, and Aurielle came in to tell us our meal would be ready in four minutes and invited us to take our seats at the table. We moved over to sit at the table, set with a white damask cloth and white napkins, crystal glasses and Sevres porcelain. My aunt carried the bottle of wine over and poured out some more into each of our glasses. I was little worried I might get tipsy, but the water glasses were filled too and my Tantetta reminded me to drink my water, not just the wine with my meal. We had clear French onion soup, followed by grilled chicken with fresh green beans from the kitchen garden, cheese made locally, and a light lemon soufflé to finish. Everything, cooked and served by Aurielle, was simply delicious, and so French with just the right amount of herbs. I soon learnt that the table in the salon was easier for Aurielle to serve our evening meal – the dining room was far too big with a huge table which could seat up to twenty people.

On this, my first night, I began to think that I would fall asleep at the table, but Tantetta could see I was falling asleep and suggested that I skipped coffee and went to bed. I was so grateful and saying goodnight, thanked them again. The bed was heavenly soft, warm, and comfortable, and with Odin next to me on the floor in his new bed supplied by Tantetta, we were both soon asleep.

So, my new French adventure had begun.

Chapter 6

Chateau de la Cascade

So, my life at the Chateau began and I instantly knew this was my destiny. I painted every day, and I studied French learning about French history, the history of art, about paint colours, light and shadows, perspective, paint mediums and most importantly, how to mix paints. I also learnt about winemaking, how to care for the vines and how the estate was run here in France. I loved everything I had to do, my French improved as did my painting and understanding of the great past and present masters of art. I learnt how to choose a picture for a prospective client and how to buy and sell at auction. Aurielle gave me French cooking lessons so, if I stayed in Paris to attend lectures at the Sorbonne, I could feed myself whilst staying in my great-uncle and aunt's Paris apartment. Although, it must be said, my attempts at cooking were frequently a disaster and I found the faces Joseph pulled when he tasted my culinary mistakes, very funny.

Some weeks after I arrived at the Chateau a horsebox turned up, and Uncle Edmund called me into the stable yard to see what had arrived. Down the ramp came the most beautiful chestnut mare with a flaxen mane and tail – I loved her immediately. My kind uncle told me she was mine, a gift from him for me to keep and ride whilst I was living there. I was ecstatic to be given such a beautiful mare. She was a six-year-old Normandy cob, was broken to ride and drive, and I was speechless as I went to stroke her lovely, sweet, kind face. She put her nose into my hand, gently sniffed me as she looked about with interest at her new home. Her beautiful head, kind eye, broad back, deep chest, sloping shoulders and strong quarters displayed a patient, kind temperament. I called her Hermes and rode her everyday with Odin and Thor running alongside us around the estate.

I had to do schoolwork as well of course, and a local gentleman, a retired professor, Monsieur Dalier, came every afternoon to tutor me in the French language, plus a little Spanish and German. I also studied French history and the history of Britain. Britain and France had through the centuries always been intertwined through royal marriage, war or friendship. We seem to have had plenty of wars between our countries in the past, but somehow become friends again, and our royal families of many years ago had cemented our relations through marriage, well, before the French Revolution.

Every morning after my ride I painted in my studio and then again, after lunch, I had my studies. Later Tantetta would tutor me about the history of art, discussing the merits of artists past and present and their techniques. This helped me to know my own mind and develop informed opinions. I spent many happy hours with Marcell learning about the vines and their care during the year and about the whole process of producing the great wines made here on this estate. I learnt about the importance of the terroir and the best kind of grapes to use here, and when they

needed pruning or spraying. The whole process of winemaking
fascinated me and the different flavours produced by the types
of wood the barrels were made from, what they had previously
contained, the length of time in the barrels and the ageing
process of the wine. The days and weeks passed quickly and every
day I was happy. Even my schoolwork was spent in discussion with
my tutor, and although the need for me to read and write all my
lessons down was not necessary, I still learnt all my work well. He
understood I struggled with the written word but was capable of
absorbing and remembering the verbal discussions we had.

One day shortly after I had arrived at the Chateau, I saw a
man wearing a black beret called Jean-Phillipe Delacroix arrive
and go straight into Tantetta's office. It was later that afternoon,
as I was busy painting a picture of Hermes, with the Chateau and
vineyards in the background, that Aurielle came to my studio and
told me my aunt wanted me in her office. I put down my brush,
took off my paint-smeared smock, washed my hands, and went to
see her, curious to know what it was all about. It was then I was
introduced to Jean-Phillipe. I politely shook hands with a typical
French man, black hair and a small moustache, and I soon learnt
he had a great knowledge of artists and paintings from around
the world and he had an art degree from the Sorbonne. This
was my Tantetta's business manager who lived in Paris, but who
had recently opened an art gallery in partnership with Tantetta
in New York and did much of the buying at auction on my great-
aunt's behalf, spotting up-and-coming new artists in Europe. I
came to respect his knowledge of art as much as I did Tantetta,
soon realizing he could teach me plenty about works of art. I also
came to respect his opinion on my paintings.

Later that year after my arrival, in the summer, Lysander
and Portia came to stay and help with the grape harvest known

as the vendange. They had travelled by train together and were able to tell me more about my parents' work in Singapore and that they were both planning to visit them for Christmas. This surprised me as I had been planning to go home to Norfolk for Christmas, even though I knew my parents wouldn't be there, but I had thought Lysander and Portia would be. I was happy for them to be travelling to Singapore but very disappointed I would not be seeing any of my family for Christmas. This, for the first time in my life.

Lysander and Portia were experienced grape pickers and we all worked hard in the hot sun as we cut the plump grapes and Lysander carried a hotte on his back, which is a large, elongated bucket with leather straps to hold it onto the back of the vendangeur. Joseph also carried a hotte and when full of grapes they were transferred to the basket panniers on the back of Flavie or into the cart pulled by Hermes to take back to the hopper where the fermenting process would begin. Flavie and Hermes have immeasurable patience during the harvest, and I am very proud of them plodding steadily up and down the rows of grape vines, stopping for each vendangeur to tip up their full hotte. That summer we had a canicule, which is French for heatwave, and the Aouta, the harvest mites, plagued us as they climbed into warm places on our bodies to lay their eggs on our skin. Ugh! We knew to keep our wellingtons, shoes, long socks, or long trousers on despite the heat and to wear hats, long sleeve shirts and blouses, but they were still horrible little insects and when the eggs hatched, they caused horrible pain and itching. Over the next three years I became far more experienced during the vendange and managed to avoid these horrible insects, using a host of different lotions which repelled them.

Sandy, the nickname Portia and I called our brother, was now
a student at St Andrew's University in Scotland and had grown
to be a tall, blond, handsome young man of whom I was very
proud. He was hoping to be a naturalist and photographer after
he got his degree. It seemed that he was in love with Scotland,
or someone in Scotland, and didn't seem interested in returning
to Norfolk to run the family estate. He insisted it was my father
who should be retiring from the diplomatic service and running
the estate and farms. It was certainly not for him. Portia was
also at the University of Edinburgh to study law. It amazed me
that she could be so pretty and clever at the same time and also
a thoroughly nice person. How I had managed to be so ginger
haired, freckled and a dunce in my schoolwork defeated me.
However, I knew more than both about the making of good
wine, my painting had improved enormously, and I was getting
better every day with my French vocabulary. I would never be
the brilliant rider like Sandy was out hunting, or a capable show
jumper like Portia always had been at our local pony club, but I
rode every day, and enjoyed the companionship of my beautiful,
gentle horse.

We had great fun that summer. I loved seeing my brother
and sister and was sad when they returned home, but I now had
a new friend in France called Rebekkah whose father was the
local doctor. With my life being very busy, having Rebekkah
to visit, I soon got over any homesickness I felt at their leaving.
Rebekkah was a great friend, the only child of Dr Abe and Esther
Bleumanthall. Born in Paris, she had moved with her parents
to the countryside when her mother had been diagnosed with
asthma. She was a brilliant pianist and cellist who was home-
schooled by Professor Dalier. Being naturally witty and clever,
she was also very funny. Rebbekah didn't ride horses, but she

wasn't frightened of them, and so I would drive into the village with Hermes harnessed up and put to the trap and off we would go for a trip out round the beautiful local tracks and enjoy a picnic. Or we would just go for long bike rides, swim in the nearby river, discussing as we went the merits of Professor Dalier's latest romantic exploits as he was always trying to be an 'amant' to most of the widows in the neighbourhood. We rarely discussed the political situation or the troubles coming out of Germany, we were both disinterested in any thought of war or too naive to imagine anything that could change our happy, peaceful lives. Dr Bleumanthall was a good chess player and he had taught Rebekkah how to play and now she would always beat him at chess. Every time I played against her, I too was hopelessly outmanoeuvred, but I kept trying.

I returned home to Norfolk the first Easter that my parents were away when I lived in France to meet up with my brother and sister and it was fun to see them again, but it was so quiet and sad without my parents and Grandora. The following Easter I took Rebekkah home with me and she loved going out in the trap with my little old pony Twinkle, swimming in the river and cycling off to the local pub for lunch. This was freedom she had not experienced in France before she met me. We were safe around my local area and most people knew me, were very friendly and pleased to see me home. We went to the beach at Holkham or Holme-Next-The Sea with the dogs and walked along the sand dunes. Lysander took us out on his sailing dinghy from Wells and then we would have a barbecue on the beach afterwards. Lysander was very impressed with her ability to beat him consistently at chess and he tried hard every night to beat her, but never succeeded. Rebekkah played our piano beautifully and she played duets with Portia who was a decent pianist, and

it wasn't all classical music either – Rebekkah was a whizz at jazz
and blues. We all loved Louis Armstrong otherwise known as
Satchmo and his group the Hot Fives and Sevens and his 'new'
jazz music. Rebekkah could certainly play his compositions such
as the Dippermouth Blues which would get us up and jiving. The
following Easter Portia was finishing university and wanted to
stay in Scotland because she had a new boyfriend who was very
special, and she was invited to spend Easter with his family and
so, with my parents' blessing, she stayed with them. Lysander put
his doctorate on hold and joined the army and couldn't get any
leave for Easter. Grandora was still travelling abroad in Mongolia,
I think, and never seemed to be home in Britain. So, for the
third year of my time in France, I didn't go home to Norfolk for
Easter and neither my brother nor sister came in the summer for
the vendange.

I did travel home with Tantetta for my sister's wedding that
Christmas and my mother and father flew from Singapore. A long
tedious journey taking them ten days. I couldn't believe she was
marrying so young but was obviously extremely happy and in
love. The wedding was difficult to plan as we were all away in
different parts of the world, but we did, and it was a wonderful
day, the family came together and worked hard to make it a great
success with Alastair, her new husband, and his Scottish relations.
Portia was married in our little village church, decorated with
holly and ivy, white chrysanthemums, and white candles: it was
beautiful. The Hall looked magnificent too and the dining room
glowed softly golden with masses of white candles and decorated
with holly, ivy, and more white chrysanthemums. Portia was so
elegant and slender in a white velvet fitted long gown with long
sleeves and a short white velvet cape trimmed with white fur, and
a lace veil fixed to a diamond coronet belonging to my mother.

Alastair wore a kilt in his family's clan red tartan and looked handsome and dashing with his best man in his kilt of the same tartan. There was no great ball that evening as we all had to leave soon afterwards, but a wonderful reception and it was a joy to see our enormous dining room full of people and so beautifully decorated. It was a very happy occasion but sad too, as we all went our separate ways two days later, leaving our lovely home empty, apart from a few staff. It was heart-breaking leaving my father's dogs even though they were well looked after by Hugh our gamekeeper and Granger our groom-cum-coachman-cum-chauffeur.

A year after I had arrived in France, my Uncle Edmund died. I missed him just like I missed my grandfather, they were both special men who had been brought up to a life of privilege and yet they knew where their duty lay, always looking after their estate workers and never shying from their duty as soldiers during the Great War. They both earned the respect of all who came to know them and were good husbands, family men and horse men. Uncle Edmund had a sense of humour which I loved, and he showed kindness to everyone including all animals, especially dogs and horses. My poor Tantetta was devastated, and I did my best to respect her sorrow, keep her occupied and tried to be there for her during such a sad time. I didn't want her disappearing abroad like my grandmother. His death had been expected, as he became increasingly frail, he just slipped peacefully away, finally free from his pain and the horrors of that awful war. I asked Tantetta if she would like me to go home to Norfolk, but she was shocked and adamant that I stayed as she was glad of my company.

Before a pre-planned road trip, we had Uncle Edmund's funeral, and Tantetta's two sisters had come to stay with us. Augusta, known by us as Auntygusta had travelled from

Switzerland where she lived and Grandora had arrived from Tunisia. It was rare to have the three sisters reunited and so although it was a sad time there were happy moments with the sisters getting together again. I had loved listening to memories of their debutante days and to hear about the current society gossip that was going on.

Several weeks after the funeral we went to Paris to a big international art auction and then we drove to Monte Carlo via Mougins to see Picasso who was spending the summer there with Dora Maar as Tantetta was interested in exhibiting some of his work in New York. We then drove to see a private art collection of various artists, near Arles where Vincent van Gogh had spent some time painting. Works by several artists were coming up for sale including some works by Vincent Van Gogh. It was a fascinating road trip for me. We stopped at Chateau Limon to buy, discuss, and sample their wine and called at other small wineries to sample and buy their wines. It was so leisurely driving down in the in the Rolls-Royce Phantom II Continental drop-head Coupe with the top down and travelling with Tantetta who was the Countess du Gaillarde and it was fascinating to see the enormous respect she generated everywhere she went. Was it the fabulous car or simply her elegance and intelligence? She still had a certain 'je ne sais quoi', a superb style, a confidence, easy authority, and a kindness wherever she went and with those she met. Her steely determination to achieve what she wanted was noticeable, but she did it in the most charming way. Monte Carlo was a revelation in culture and couture for me and I lazed on Tantetta's friend's yacht and swam in the warm Mediterranean Sea. I adored the shifting shades of deep green, aquamarine blues and turquoise fringed with the white froth of the waves gently sliding along the sand and pebble beaches. It was absolute bliss and I loved it. I could have stayed there for ever.

I never saw my parents during my time in France. Sometimes I think that my father forgot about Lysander, Portia, and me. He should have been running the estate in Norfolk, but he didn't seem interested in any responsibilities at home. Being a diplomat for King George V in Singapore kept him very busy and of course there was a wonderful society life that went with it. The scandal of Edward VIII abdicating so he could marry the American lady Wallis Simpson and the Coronation of his brother His Highness Prince Albert of York, later the Duke of York, kept everyone gossiping for months. My parents went home for the Coronation on May 12th, 1937, but did not stay more than one week in Britain before returning to Singapore. They did not visit France to see me. I can imagine my father saying it was quite unnecessary, she's fine where she is, referring to me of course. So, life in rural France for now remained idyllic with the weather, my friends, my horse, my dog, my Tantetta, and me painting every day.

Then the day came that Jean-Phillipe arrived in a distressed state, followed by two strange, Greek Albanian teenagers in a Rolls-Royce along with swarthy, tough-looking armed guards and everything changed for ever.

Chapter 7

Arrivals At The Chateau

Jean-Phillipe arrived and from my art room I saw his van pull up in a cloud of dust as he skidded to a halt on the gravel drive. The year was 1940 and it had been a hot sultry day. I had been engrossed in my painting and was now hungry and admit I was finding it hard to concentrate since the arrival of Jean-Phillipe. I decided to pack up my paints for the day. Next there was a gentle knock on my art studio and Aurielle came in, dropping a mock curtsy and said, "Your Tantetta wants you in her office, Mademoiselle," and with a cheerful grin she departed. I put down the paint brush, cleaned it and took off my paint smeared smock then went to the cloakroom to wash my hands. Crossing the hall to the office, I knocked on her door and went straight in. I didn't usually knock, but then I wasn't usually summoned to go and see her, we just kind of always saw each other throughout the day.

I went into the office and sat down to listen to what Tantetta wanted to tell me. Jean-Phillipe looked on nervously as she told me about her decision for my future. As far as I was concerned, my future was here with my beloved Tantetta, my horse and friends at the Chateau. The year was only just beginning, but the threat of invasion by Hitler and the German army was forever in our minds so even I was getting a little concerned. My mind was full of painting, winemaking and tasting, riding Hermes, walking Odin. I planned the places Rebekkah and I would visit this summer. Basically, the events in Europe had passed me by in 1939 and into the early months of 1940. I had heard British people called it the 'phoney war'. Since war had been declared with Germany there had been no fighting and no bombs had fallen in Britain. I could not conceive anything would interrupt my wonderful idyllic life here in the beautiful French countryside.

Tantetta suggested I sit down – it was rather more formal than usual, so I quickly sat down nervously and waited to hear the news good or bad.

"It's about your future," she said, "As you know there is a threat of invasion by the Nazis here in France."

For once I kept very quiet and held my breath, not ridiculing the suggestion of invasion; there was something about Jean-Phillipe which made me begin to believe that the rumours spreading around the country like a blight, could be true. They were beginning to worry me a little, but I still couldn't believe that it would change my life here.

"I have decided that you must go back to Britain as my sister Isadora has returned home and needs some help running the estate," began Tantetta.

I opened my mouth to protest, but she held up her hand.

"It is not a decision which is up for negotiation. I have made up my mind you are not safe here if the invasion goes ahead and I have discussed it with your parents, and they agree with me. I have managed to buy you a plane ticket to England, and you leave in a few days."

I jumped up in dismay. "No," I protested. "Not so soon. What about Lysander and Portia – why don't they go home instead of me?" I was in tears and nearly shouting.

"Cressida, you have a duty to return home. We must all pull together during these difficult times. England will need more food being produced and you are needed in Norfolk at home where you will be safer," said Tantetta sternly.

"What about you?" I cried. "I won't leave you here alone, you need me here, I'll work even harder." Rebekkah and I had plans for the weekend of the Le Quatorze Juillet. "I can't leave Hermes or Odin here without me, or leave my paintings and my friends," I added selfishly. We always held a party here for Bastille Day and Rebekkah and I were excited about planning the night-time events.

"Now Cressida, calm down, the animals will be well cared for, your paints and paintings will be safe, I am going to join my sister in Switzerland for a few months and Jean-Phillipe is going to the gallery in New York to stay there."

"What about Marcell, Aurielle and Joseph, Marie-Christine or Elise?" I asked.

"They will stay here to run the estate and care for the vineyard until we return," Tantetta replied.

I was so miserable, and I now know how ungrateful I was. How could I refuse to help my grandmother and care for my parents' home? And Tantetta was only thinking about me being safer in England. My brother Lysander had joined the army, was busy training new recruits and couldn't get leave, and if he did, he always stayed on our parents' place in the Scottish Borders to be near his fiancée. Portia had Hamish, her little baby, to look after whilst running their large sheep farm in Scotland, her husband, Alastair, being on duty in the Royal Air Force and flying Spitfires or Hurricanes or something – at that moment I didn't care what. Oh yes, and my parents were still in Singapore! It was impossible for any of them to just pop down to Norfolk to run the estate and how could I refuse to help my grandmother? It was a daunting prospect being expected to run the estate, but I was strangely confident that I could manage. I just didn't want to leave my lovely home in France.

The very next day a strange thing happened as I was working in my studio clearing away my paintings and trying to decide what I had room to take with me – obviously very little as I was flying home. I had never flown in my life, and I wasn't sure if I was excited or a bit scared.

I heard a car flying up the gravel drive and crunch to a stop by the balustraded stone steps at the front of the Chateau. It was a very dirty, mud-splattered car and it was a Rolls-Royce. I was immediately intrigued to see who it was and peered out of the side window from my turret. A man climbed out, opened the boot and took out some luggage. I was transfixed and filled with fear: the man was swarthy, big, and unshaven, but what horrified me, he wore a bandolier across his chest. Another man climbed out from the driving seat, looked all around and then opened the rear door. Out of the car emerged a teenage boy and girl. They all looked very dirty and tired from what seemed, at a glance, to be a long journey. More curious, my Tantetta opened the big front door and greeted the two young people, then waved the two men to take the car round the back to the stables. I took off my painting smock and went into the hall to greet them and find out who they were, just in time to see Tantetta ushering the two young people into the salon. Meanwhile the car was indeed being driven round the back towards the farm buildings and the farmhouse.

I hesitated as I felt that I would be intruding on a private matter if I went into the salon, so I stood in the big hall feeling strangely scared and curious. Aurielle came into the hall from the kitchen carrying a tray of sandwiches and glasses of milk for the visitors, which must have been prepared beforehand. So, I thought, these visitors clearly had been expected. Her normally happy, smiling face looked worried as I opened the salon door for her. I then went through to the kitchen and opened the back door to see where the men had gone. They were unloading more luggage from the boot of the car and Marcell was taking something into the barn. I didn't feel welcome there either, then I noticed the guns propped up onto the car bumper. As I had seen many shooting parties at home, I knew these where not the sort of guns used for pheasant shoots, but these were army rifles, Lee-Enfield's magazine-fed repeating rifle and I knew something very serious was happening. Not knowing what to do next, I decided to take Hermes out for a ride to clear my head and get out of the way. A strange thing to do I suppose, but I felt strange and unsettled and at the time it seemed the right thing to do, thinking that when I got back from my ride everything would be back to normal. With Odin at my side, I ran to the stables and grabbed Hermes' bridle, went into the paddock to catch her and climbed the fence to straddle her broad back. I took her the short way around the lake and galloped up the field back to the Chateau with Odin panting to keep up, but very happy to be out.

Feeling sad, I put Hermes out in her paddock. I gave her a hug and an apple as I was to be leaving her soon, before walking back towards the kitchen door with Odin. The two men were now outside by the car; one was cleaning his gun, the other leant on the car bonnet and studied me as I walked towards them. I ran my eyes over the Rolls-Royce Phantom touring saloon – I did know my Rolls. They both looked sinister to me and as I passed by one of them looked up and our eyes met. I had not met many young men and was shocked to feel a jolt, well feel something all over me of heat, embarrassment I think, I blushed, and he asked me in French if I'd had a good ride. So, he had watched me ride around the lake. I felt sheepish and elated. I told him a bit primly I had, and I asked where they had travelled from. His friend then spoke to him hurriedly in English with a Scottish accent and the man who had spoken to me replied to him speaking English with an Irish accent. Now I was really intrigued.

"Why did you tell him not to tell me anything?" I asked in English.

Both men now looked up at me surprised that I had understood them with new interest and wariness in their eyes.

"So, who are you?" asked the one cleaning his riffle. He was very tense suddenly and his hands seemed poised over his weapon.

I felt rattled by their intrusion into my life at the Chateau and his rudeness so, for the first time in my life, I replied haughtily, "I am The Honourable Cressida Welsby and I live here, and I don't see what that's got to do with either of you." I never used my title or even thought about it, but these two men made me feel uncomfortable here in my home and I wanted to assert some authority or at least hit back at them.

They both stood up and the one with the gun saluted me in a sort of mocking way and the one with the lovely warm hazel eyes held his hand out and said, "I'm Tiff", and we shook hands and both of us seemed in that minute to get a sudden electric shock through our contact. The other man, with the Scots accent, then shook hands with me and Tiff told me his name was Scotty – of course, why wouldn't it be! I now realized how tall they both were, enormous in build, and I realized that they both looked rough, unshaven and dirty because it looked like they had been travelling for days, although neither one told me where they had come from or for that matter who they were.

Aurielle called from the kitchen that a meal was ready, and we all followed her back into the kitchen with Marcell and Joseph coming in behind us. "Sid, madam wants you in the salon."

Brown eyes, who I now knew as Tiff, smiled and said, "So Sid it is then," in a strong Irish brogue.

Flustered, I left the kitchen and went to the salon where I knocked gently again as I entered, something I hadn't done since the day I had arrived until just now, although why I was feeling nervous again, I don't know.

"Come in, Cressida, come and meet our two guests, Malissa and Nico, who will be joining us for dinner this evening and staying with us tonight."

I went over to shake hands and met a very serious dark haired young girl of about my age who looked shattered and worn out. The young man was her brother, and he was about fourteen years old with dark hair, tall for his age and slim. He looked very serious and exhausted but bowed slightly when we shook hands. Aurielle came in with a simple meal and put it onto the round pedestal table in front of the side window. She took out the tray she had brought in with the sandwiches when they had arrived nearly two hours ago. Aurielle had brought us a clear chicken consommé and crusty bread with freshly churned butter and some soft herb cheese. We all sat down and quietly sipped our soup and broke the bread, well I broke the bread to eat, the two young people whom I now knew as Malissa and Nico ate their bread slowly but devoured their soup. Aurielle returned with poached pears and after we had finished our simple meal Tantetta suggested Aurielle should show them upstairs to their rooms where they could rest, and we could talk some more tomorrow before they continued their journey.

When they had left the room with Aurielle, I asked Tantetta where they had come from and who they were and where were they travelling to. Tantetta sipped her coffee and suddenly looked very weary. "They have travelled from Ukraine through Poland and got caught up in the occupation of that country by the Nazis – it was unfortunate they were there at all. Malissa had been visiting a university in Belarus for a chess tournament which should never have gone ahead, and Nico had been studying in Ukraine for six months when Nazi Germany invaded Poland. They are from Albania and needed to travel home, but the unrest there is making the journey they had planned too dangerous, so your father organised an escort for them to bring them here and they are to go on to England."

"Oh, so why is my father, who is in Singapore, involved with two young Albanians travelling to England?" I asked, surprised.

Tantetta didn't answer all my questions but said that my father knew their father through diplomatic channels. She then suggested we all go to bed to be up early in the morning. It was, most probably, going to be a busy day.

It all seemed an unlikely and far-fetched story to me, although I could never doubt the honesty of Tantetta. There was little more to say just now, and I went through to the kitchen to take Odin and Thor out for a walk and again something drew me to the man called Tiff. He was sitting at the kitchen table with Scotty in deep conversation with Marcell and Joseph, Aurielle was wiping pots and listening, but the conversation halted when I went in, and they put away the map they were studying. Marcell got up and said he would show them to their bedrooms over the stables next to the farmhouse where he and Aurielle lived. The two men seemed to fill the vast kitchen with their size and presence, they thanked Aurielle for their meal and got up to follow Marcell. The one called Tiff stopped and asked me if I minded if he walked with me as he realized I was going out with the two dogs.

"Suit yourself," I said and stormed off into the garden which was softly lit round the back with the lights from the Chateau.

"So, I hope you don't mind me joining you on such a beautiful evening. I always take my dog out before I go to bed; it's so relaxing," he volunteered, by way of explaining why he had joined me.

Intrigued, I asked, "What kind of dog do you have?"

"I have a black Labrador called Jessca – unfortunately I have had to leave her behind, but she is with my parents in Ireland, and she is settled and safe there. I hear you have lived here for over three years and that you know every inch of the estate and the countryside around here," he said in a very laid-back way.

"Well yes I do," I replied.

"Even secret places?" He teased.

"Yes, there are some marvellous, secret places that very few people know about, even the villagers don't know where they are," I enthused.

"Your French is excellent, and you can understand the local 'patois', I believe?"

Flattered, I told him that I could. I had chatted with Joseph enough times to pick it up. Intrigued by their arrival I asked about the car and wondered how come they were running around in a Rolls Royce Phantom II Barker touring saloon.

"Oh, it's not mine," he said. "I wish it was, it's a great car, but it belongs to the two young people we brought here today."

"Really," was all I could say in astonishment, adding, "Well it's a fabulous car to maintain high speeds for travelling, if the roads allow."

He then went on, "So you are setting off soon for the docks and on to England with a full lorry, I believe, so I will say 'bonne nuit' and let you sleep and rest before your epic journey. I am pleased to have met you and I hope to see you soon. Take care and keep your wits about you at all times," he added kindly.

"No, you're wrong, I am flying home," I replied.

He smiled and said, "Oh I don't think so..." and then he turned and left me in the garden, puzzled, wondering what he meant 'with a full lorry'; must be a misunderstanding. And then I felt very sad to see him go. With my head in the clouds and wondering about his remarks, I headed for bed. Even then I didn't know that leaving the Chateau would turn out to be the last time for several years before I would return.

Unable to sleep well, I was up before dawn and went to my art room and quickly sketched from memory the two men lounging against the Rolls Royce. I used charcoal for speed. I could roll it up later to take with me. Then I took my box camera outside to take a snap of the car with the Chateau behind it. After this I grabbed my bike and, taking my camera, I pedalled furiously to see Rebekkah before I left for England. It was a beautiful morning with the sun just beginning to warm the earth and my cycle ride through the lush, green French countryside was full of gorgeous country smells of spring and sounds of birdsong. I was there before 6 am, but they were already up and about. The doctor was watering his garden and Rebekkah was sitting in the garden drinking hot lemon tea. Rebekkah and I had become best friends simply because we were both lonely and had been introduced by Tantetta who rightly assumed that we would get on, which we did, instantly. We shared a love of the outdoors and had a similar sense of humour. Rebekkah was the only daughter of Dr Abe and Mrs Esther Bleumanthall, and they had moved from Paris for Esther's health as she suffered from asthma. Dr Bleumanthall was Tantetta's physician, the only doctor for miles around, and he was very popular in the area. In Paris he had been an expert in his field of medicine, ear, nose and throat surgery, but had given it all up and become a General Practitioner for the sake of his wife's health. Rebekkah was home-schooled by the same retired Professor Dalier that I had to teach me and as a result she had few friends in the village or local area. She was a seriously brilliant musician and a first-class chess player. Music was her chosen career path and she had recently been offered a music scholarship in New York which her father had said was ridiculous since it was out of the question for her to travel all the way to America to study on her own. He was adamant he could not leave his patients here to go with her. A keen gardener, he adored his beautiful garden but didn't mention that as a reason for not going with her. Rebekkah had a wicked sense of humour and we giggled and laughed about anything and everything when we were together. I did beat her at tennis as I was taller and had a longer reach. I had grown up trying to beat Lysander and Portia, who were both strong players, but never could. On one trip to Paris, Rebekkah had been allowed to accompany me as she had relatives in Paris and her aunt had acted as chaperone. She had taken us to the Eiffel Tower, Notre Dame Cathedral, and to Montmartre and then one evening during a soiree at her aunt's house Rebekkah had played the piano for us and this recital, heard by an eminent orchestral conductor, had brought about her invitation to the New York Music college with a scholarship.

They knew I had to leave for England soon and that I had come to say goodbye. I had painted a picture of their lovely house on the outskirts of the village, and I gave it to Rebekkah's parents, who were delighted with it. I gave Rebekkah a portrait of herself sitting in their lovely garden under the rose bower. The paintings were small enough for them to keep with them wherever they went in the future and perhaps frame them later.

Rebekkah hugged me with tears in her eyes and I was crying too. She seemed preoccupied and gloomy, so I asked her what was wrong.

"I can't go to New York because my father won't hear of me travelling all that way alone and he says war is coming and he must stay here to help the people who will need a doctor more than ever – and he can't leave them without a doctor."

He had a point and a very good one and he was popular and trusted in the area.

"Well, I am leaving, as you know, but I'm not sure that I'm flying after all. I might be driving the horsebox home, now, instead." Then I began to recount the events of the day before and about the two young Greek Albanians from Northern Epirotes who had arrived yesterday. "They have travelled from Poland and were going to England and then to college there, until their parents can arrange a safe journey home for them." I told her how quiet they both were as they seemed to have had a great trauma and witnessed something dreadful, but I didn't know what. I had realized during our evening meal they were both very intelligent and well educated. Nico was surprisingly old-fashioned for someone so young. Apparently, he spoke several languages and exhibited a sound knowledge of the political history of Europe. His sister was even quieter and according to Tantetta was a genius at battle strategy, a mathematical genius, and a world class chess player. "Another one to beat me at chess," I groaned,

Rebekkah smiled. "I am sure you will be able to play her at some stage before your trip home and you can show her how good you are."

"Very funny," I said. " You know I'm not very good at chess."

"Well, you keep playing me. I know I always win, but you give me a good game and you make me concentrate, so I think you are pretty good really," said Rebekkah kindly.

"Well thank you," I said pleased as Rebekkah had never told me that before.

We chatted briefly about very little of importance, then I dropped my bombshell about the two strange army men and how I felt a connection to the one called Tiff. Wow that soon had her asking me thousands of questions I could not answer, but we giggled over my news. Soon I knew I must leave, and Mrs Bleumantall came out to hug me and wish me bon voyage. The doctor came to thank me for the painting, and we all agreed to meet up here as soon as this nasty period in our lives was over. I hugged Rebekkah and cycled home in tears just in time for breakfast.

Before breakfast I went straight to my studio to check my sketch of the two men and was surprised to see Tantetta already studying it. She was staring long and hard at my charcoal sketch.

"Cressida, this is amazing. You have become an outstanding and brilliant artist. I am so proud of you, to be related to you and to have been a part of your journey to excellence."

I was stunned. "But it's just a quick impression of what I saw," I said.

"Don't touch it again, it's so simple, so well executed and tells everything of the moment you met and of the impending war. Remember, less is often more."

I was so moved to hear this accolade from one of the world's greatest art critics I had tears in my eyes as I hugged her and whispered, "Thank you, Tantetta, I love you so much – that means everything to me."

I followed her out of the room and asked if the two men had anything to do with the boy and girl and would they be taking them to England.

"No, they were sent to find them, rescue them, and deliver them here, and now they have to leave for their next assignment."

"When are they going?" I said, alarmed for no reason that I could understand.

"Now," she said.

I ran through the hall to the front door, yanked it open and ran onto the top stone step just in time to see the still dirty Rolls-Royce rounding the corner of the Chateau from the farmhouse. It slowed down and Scotty was driving, a big grin plastered on his face. Tiff stuck his head out of the window waved to me and blew me a kiss. I waved back and felt overwhelmingly disappointed that they had gone, and I know I was blushing. Back in the hall my aunt looked at me – a surprised look on her face – which in an instant she masked and, putting her arm through mine, marched me to the morning room for breakfast.

We were joined by the two visitors for breakfast, and I found the girl just as quiet as she had been the night before; well, they both were. The young man Nico was dark eyed, and olive skinned, very Mediterranean looking and he politely answered Tantetta's questions about his hobbies and life at home. Malissa was also olive skinned and had thick black hair like her brother. They were both very good looking with a slightly haughty demeanour, which I am sure was not intended, it was just how they were. We were all quiet during breakfast and then Tantetta dropped the 'bombshell', telling me I would not be flying home after all. Thinking I was to be staying at the Chateau, I was about to tell her how relieved I was when she continued that I would be taking the horsebox home with Hermes, Odin, and our two new acquaintances Malissa and Nico. Clearly, I must have looked stunned and Tantetta continued that the change of plan was because it was their parents' wish that they go to England. We needed to leave immediately as the news from the front seemed to change daily and it would be for the best if we were all in England before the Nazis arrived in France.

Later that day Jean-Phillipe arrived seeming even more worried than before and for some reason we had our evening meal earlier than usual. Shortly after, Dr Bleumanthall arrived, looking very grave and went into Tantetta's office with Jean-Phillipe and the two new visitors. Stranger and stranger – I wandered into the kitchen and sat at the kitchen table idly watching Aurielle prepare to leave for home having completed her day's work, her own farmhouse beckoned. She was pensive, and seemed to be a million miles away, in thought, just like me. There was a comfortable silence in the kitchen as we had known each long enough to be able to be happy together and be silent.

Finally, she turned to look at me as she stood by the door ready to go, saying, "You know, Sid, we have had some fun together, what with your weird baking, your jokes and laughter; you have brought us happiness and joy and made us all feel glad to be alive. Pray for better times to come when we will all be together again. God bless you on your journey, and in the future."

I ran to her, and she enveloped me in a great hug and we both had tears running down our faces as we parted. With that she stepped outside into the dark to walk up the path to the farmhouse. I didn't know whether to wait to find out what had been discussed or just go straight to bed, but curiosity compelled me to wait, so I took the dogs into the garden to sit on the swing as they snuffled round in the dark. I sat by the weeping Tamarisk tree which was just starting to flower and colour the garden with its long fronds of pink flowers. Once again, I drank in the smells of the night air and listened to the thick silence broken only by the crickets and croaking frogs, but I was too restless to stay out for long, there was a chill in the air, and it had been a long day.

Back in the kitchen I poured myself a glass of milk and headed for the stairs in time to see Dr Bleumanthall leaving the office and head for the main door. He saw me and stopped. His eyes were full of sadness as he nodded to me, put on his hat and left.

Chapter 8

Alex Bouchet Sets Off

Meanwhile, many kilometres away, Alex was starting on a journey, heading for Spain with his brother, sister, horse, and dog. He had started out full of hope, optimism, and determination, but sometimes on his long journey he had doubts about its success. As usual he had been busy in the bakery one morning, when an interruption from his Aunt Hildegarde changed everything. He loved baking and the magic of the risen dough, the pleasure it gave to people eating his creations, but his dream for the future was to be a winemaker. He had just finished school and wanted to work on a vineyard. It was early April 1940, and the weather was crisp in the mornings, but sunny, and Alex thought of working on just such mornings in the fields, tending the vines instead of being in a bakery. His Uncle Albert wanted him to go into the funeral business with him. He had a steady clientele from the small town and surrounding countryside. Uncle Albert loved carpentry most, but was fed up with making coffins and wanted to carve wood into articles people loved and used, not coffins that some people saw for such a short time and then buried in the ground. The funeral business had belonged to two brothers, but Alex's grandfather had joined the French army in 1911 and was killed in the Great War. Alex didn't want to be a funeral director and coffin maker, he wanted to work in the fields and feel the sunshine, smell the ripening grapes, create complex wine, and learn the skills of the growing and producing of good wine. Now he felt stuck in the bakery. To make matters worse, his father, Bernard, had gone to join the French army in 1939 as a baker to defend France against a possible German invasion. Now Alex had to stay at home and look after his half-brother Claude and half-sister Simone as their Polish mother had rushed home last autumn to nurse her sick mother and had not been heard from since Poland had been invaded by the Nazis.

Alex had lost his own mother when he six years old and had lived alone with his Papa until he had remarried a lady called Yvette. He was close to his Uncle Albert, whom he loved very much, and he had spent lots of time with him learning about woodwork and how to make bow and arrows. His British mother had defied her father to train in nursing during the Great War and when she heard her brother was in hospital in France after being injured badly in the trenches she wanted to go and help him. Her father refused to allow her to go, but when they heard about the Spanish flu pandemic her father wavered and she went to France immediately to fetch her brother home. Whilst in France she fell in love with a French baker called Bernard Bouchet whilst he was delivering bread to the hospital, and she met him daily. Putting aside any thoughts of love, she organised the transportation of her brother back to England and travelled home with him. On finally getting back to England she nursed him at her family home. Because of her prompt attention he escaped the Spanish flu. Finally, after finding him a good home nurse, she decided to return to France and marry the baker with whom she had fallen in love. Her father was furious and never spoke to her again. She had a very happy marriage but had died of tuberculosis when Alex was only six. His father Bernard had tried to contact her family in England, but never received any replies to his letters. Years later, on a trip to Paris, he met and married a Polish girl who was living and teaching there, and they now had two children Claude and Simone and they settled down to married life with Bernard running the bakery alongside his brother Pierre.

Pierre married a German girl, Hildegarde, which met with disproval from his Uncle Albert and their customers in the bakery, so he went to live in Paris to work in a patisserie taking his wife and son Gaston with him. Unfortunately, it was not a happy marriage as Hildegarde was bossy and demanding, always wanting more.

While Alex was still at school, he helped his father in the bakery and had a natural talent for the job. As the threat of war increased, Pierre joined the army as a baker to feed the soldiers and he was glad to get away from Hildegarde and their spoilt son Gaston. Bernard also decided to join up to fight for the freedom of France from the threat of the Nazis. He knew his wife Yvette could run the bakery with help from Alex and he would soon return when the powers in the Parliament Francais, the Senate and the National Assembly sorted out the silly notion of war, but shortly after he had signed up Yvette rushed off to Poland. She hoped to bring her mother back to France with her as there was so much trouble going on with that man Hitler. So, Alex left school and ran the bakery, baking every day, starting at 4 am in the mornings, at the same time looking after his brother and sister. They had a horse to pull the baker's van to take out deliveries which was the best time of the day for Alex as he loved the countryside, the peace, the quiet and the freedom. Most of all he adored the mare Trudi and any spare time he had he loved to groom her and give Claude and Simone rides on her.

Alex was cleaning inside the shop after a busy morning serving customers when he had the visit from Hildegarde and her young son Gaston. He was not expecting her, and he was shocked. She bustled in and started to take an inventory of everything in the shop. He kept quiet and followed her as she wrote on her list what was outside and then she went upstairs to the living area and then downstairs to where the ovens were in the basement, writing all the time. Finally, she informed him she was coming to live there, and he could move into the attic rooms with his brother and sister as she intended to make changes. Firstly, they were to buy a new counter for the bread to separate it from the pies and sausages, and a new floor and new sign outside with her name and Pierre's on it. Then she added the bombshell. The old horse must go, as she was going to get a van for deliveries and learn how to drive. What Alex didn't know was that she was fed up living in Paris on her own with Gaston who was being tormented at school for being part German and overweight. She was very annoyed with Pierre going off and joining the French army, and if the Germans came to Paris, in her mind, everything would be run much better by them. She was fed up with the recession France had been faced with since the end of the Great War. Hitler was a man with a vision, and she liked his ideas. Paris was full of dirty refugees and paying her bills and finding food was increasingly difficult. She was convinced she would be better off running the bakery and, after all, it was mostly hers and Pierre's as he was the older brother. She told Alex she would be back in one week. Alex was horrified – she was bossy, overbearing, and unpopular.

Later that day he harnessed up the mare, a patient, willing, fifteen-year-old Normandy Cob, took his deliveries to his customers and then picked up Simone and Claude from school. He took the mare round the back of the bakery, unharnessed her, washed her down, and left her drying in a stable with some hay. Then he took the children to see Uncle Albert and take him some fresh bread and a pastry tart. As the children played in Albert's big garden by the big store where wood was seasoning for making coffins, Alex told Uncle Albert about the visit from Hildegarde.

"I can't work with her, Uncle, I can't stay there, and I can't bear to lose the mare, and her son is insufferable. I am nearly sixteen years old now; I need to go. I can't bear to watch her cook stodgy food or be ordered around by her."

"Where would you go?" his uncle asked. "I suppose you want to go and work in a vineyard. Why don't you come and work with me here?"

"No, I must get right away from here. I will take the mare and Claude and Simone. I wish my father had thought through the consequences of his joining the army and leaving us here alone."

Silence fell and the mantel clock ticked, and both were lost deep in thought. "I have listened to the news every day and it is getting worse. I don't want you to be forced to join the army, you are too young. The politicians here are bickering, and the English were hoping for peace which has not happened. I fear this awful little Austrian man, Hitler, is intent on the domination of Europe with his frightening Nazi philosophy. Another war so soon after the last one fills me with dread and foreboding. I saw enough suffering caused by the last war. Where would you plan to go?" he asked Alex.

"Spain," said Alex.

Albert shook his head. "It's a very long way and they have just been through a vicious civil war and ended up with the Dictator Franco and his band of fascist followers. He has murdered thousands of political prisoners and created secret police to spy on the citizens. I am not at all sure it is the best place for you to go right now," Uncle Albert said gravely.

"I will not stay here with her," cried Alex. "I am leaving for the south as far away from any war that I can get with or without your help."

"Very well, I will help you. You are quite sure you intend to take the mare and the children?" asked Uncle Albert.

"Of course, I could not leave them here with her," said Alex. "Leave the cart here after you have taken out your orders tomorrow and I will work on it and modify it for you and make a better living space for you all. I have an old map I will bring to your place tonight. Go home now and when the children are in bed, I will come and bring the maps for you to study." Uncle Albert told him.

So later that night they had secret talks about when he should leave, which way he should go and to where he should head. He also had some money for Alex to take with him. He again asked him to reconsider the long journey he planned to undertake. But Alex was certain it was the right thing to do and said 'no', again. Alex was excited to be going now he had made the decision. His birthday was in three weeks' time, and he was convinced it was a good plan for his future. The next few days flew by as Alex had to keep working and baking, planning, and packing. He picked up the baker's cart and at first it didn't look much different until he took a closer look. His uncle had extended the roof slightly to accommodate them all sleeping inside. He had attached a rolled-up tarpaulin which could be rolled right over to keep out any rain.

He had built storage cupboards under the floorboards with one designed like a crate to hold the three hens he knew Alex had. There would only be just enough room to take family, food, horse food, clothes and the so many items he kept realizing he might need. He went to talk to Uncle Albert every night to plan the route down to the smallest detail. Uncle Albert was worried and kept thinking he should go with him, but he had four funerals over the next few days, and it would be for the best if Alex left as soon as possible. The news was bad, but like so many people he thought the British army and the French army would stand firm and stop any invasion. After all, they did have the Maginot Line, the defensive barrier in northeast France constructed in the 1930s and named after the French war minister Andre Maginot, considered to be impenetrable. Alex was a kind, considerate boy with a good sensible head on his shoulders, so Albert had every confidence in him succeeding in his ambition to run a vineyard in the future. Maybe he should go and live with him then and follow his dream of creating beautiful furniture.

Albert used to have ambitions to be a furniture maker, but his father wanted him to follow in his footsteps, the funeral business. So, he had put ambition aside and had made coffins and buried people instead. It was decided Alex would bake extra bread very early on the morning he was leaving, harness Trudi, and, taking the children, leave by four in the morning. Just in case Hildegarde called the police and said he had stolen the horse and baker's cart he would take little, use tracks, and keep away from people and roads. Uncle Albert hugged him that last evening and told him he would drive over in the van when he knew where he was staying and spend some time with him. He told Alex to keep in touch and he would send him any money he needed. Albert had plenty of money earned from long days of hard work Alex was like a son to him – he would eventually inherit all his money and possessions; he would do anything to help him. He gave him a new hunting knife, a bow, and a quill full of arrows, and finally a rifle and bullets. He had built a hidden compartment under the cart to carry these items. He had trained Alex how to use a bow and arrow, taught him how to shoot game and they often went out together on Sundays hunting. He knew Alex could look after himself, but he was still worried; the news did niggle him, but he put it aside. He hoped the threat of war only twenty years after the last horrible, cruel war was only a threat and nothing more.

All their plans came to fruition on a Sunday morning. Alex was up early stoking the oven and preparing a big bake, enough for the shop, his deliveries and enough to take with them on their journey and feed them for a few days. He had loaded up the cart the night before with Albert helping him. They said their goodbyes for the next few weeks and Uncle Albert gave him plenty of money for his journey, more than Alex thought he needed, but Uncle Albert insisted. He assured him, if he needed any more money, to get in touch with his bank as he had instructed them to release funds to him if asked. It was a very sad farewell and with a heavy heart Uncle Albert hugged Alex, wished them all a good journey and gave them his love. Alex was small in stature, slightly built and he looked so young and vulnerable to be embarking on such a long journey. However, Uncle Albert knew he could do it. He trusted him to make the right judgements and he knew he was clever, strong-willed, and capable. In the morning, first Alex loaded the hens into their new wooden crate on the side of the cart and then went to fetch the sleeping children who had been told they were going on holiday and needed to set off on their camping adventure early. He lifted them into their new beds under the canopy of the cart, harnessed up the mare and put her to the cart, made sure his dog Tanner was ready and at his side, and they were off.

Quietly, very quietly, they left the sleepy little town and headed out on their new adventure.

Chapter 9

War Gets Closer

Tantetta saw me in the hall as I was on my way to bed, and she beckoned me over.

"Nico and Malissa have gone to bed but before you go, I want a word with you please. We have more news now about the situation in Europe – when Malissa and Nico were trapped in a hotel in Warsaw, they saw atrocities carried out by the Nazi soldiers against the Polish people, particularly the Jews. They saw them summarily hung, shot, and murdered in the streets, they were beating men, women, and children who they then herded up with rifle buts and marched away to concentration camps. We know this has been going on in Germany since Hitler came to power. He has beaten, imprisoned, and murdered anyone who stood against him. The Jewish people especially have been picked on and they are now banned from many jobs, cannot go into shops or facilities used by other German people; their properties are confiscated, and they are not allowed into universities or schools anymore. Synagogues are being burnt to the ground and the

Jews must wear a yellow star on their clothes, so everyone knows
who they are. Your father arranged for Scotty and Tiff to rescue
Nico and Malissa when their chauffeur went missing in Warsaw
leaving them stranded. Scotty and Tiff were in the area and able
to reach them quickly, find their missing Rolls-Royce and drive
them out of Poland across country just keeping one step ahead
of the Nazis all the way to France."

Apparently, my father had 'pulled strings' being ex-army and
a diplomat to organise the extraction of these two young people
from Poland. It was beginning to dawn on me that obviously they
were special young people, although I was not sure why, but they
had their own chauffeur and their own Rolls-Royce for goodness'
sake. It was also my father who had suggested that they came here
to the Chateau de La Cascade and the Countess de Gaillarde for
safe passage to England and it was then Tantetta proposed that
I should chaperone them home to Britain. So that was that and I
simply could not refuse to go.

In the morning I chatted to Nico who was very reticent to
talk at all about what he knew of France and his travels around
Europe. Over breakfast I talked about the kind of wine we
made here which did seem to interest him a little. His sister had
remained quiet and pensive throughout breakfast, so I decided
to take Hermes out for a ride, with Odin and Thor to accompany
me. The rest of the day went quickly with packing and planning
for the journey. It had been a lovely sunny, warm day and I had
many regrets about leaving this magical place, but there was no
question about it any longer: I must leave and very soon.

Much later that day Jean-Phillipe arrived back from meeting
Armonde, his helper, on the road to Paris to transfer more
paintings brought from the gallery by van and we had an earlier
than usual evening meal, again with very little talk. Jean-Phillipe

told us about some shops shutting in Paris and that many people were leaving their homes and going to the country, that is those people who had homes in the country to go to, or relatives and friends. He said many people were becoming tense over the atmosphere of fear gripping the country and others were carrying on as normal in the cafes, restaurants, and theatres. He told us that Paris was full to bursting with refugees from Holland, Belgium, Poland, and other countries – all were fleeing from the might of the German army. Many German Jews had escaped from Germany to live in Paris and many refugees were trying to get to Spain, Britain, Portugal, America, or Ireland – anywhere away from the war. Sadly, for so many Jewish people, unless they had a visa to travel to these countries, they were often denied entry. It seems many roads were packed with fleeing people and the situation was becoming chaotic. It was so much to take in and absorb, so much horror and so much 'scary' news. After our meal I took Odin and Thor down to the paddock and took Hermes and Flavie an apple each. I then went into the garden where the big garden swing was and sat under the Tamarisk tree. I rocked on the swing and threw balls for the dogs to catch. Restless, I stared up at the darkening evening sky and watched the stars come out, thinking they would still twinkle here when I was back home in England. Unsettled, I went back into the kitchen and poured myself a glass of water, Tantetta came to look for me and at her request I went with her back to her office.

"I have suggested to Dr Bleumanthall that he leaves with Esther and Rebekkah for New York immediately and Jean-Phillipe has offered them the use of his apartment over the art gallery. I have told him it's a perfect opportunity for Rebekkah to take up the place offered to her at the academy for the music scholarship. He has listened to the news brought by Nico and Marisa and reluctantly, for the sake of his family, has agreed to go. He was worried about leaving the community without a doctor, but I know of a French doctor seeking a place in the country who I'm sure will agree to come and live in Dr Bleumanthall's house and care for his patients. Jean-Phillipe will be leaving for America shortly, but, as his flight is from Switzerland, he will be taking more paintings to Switzerland first. I am staying with Augusta, as you know, whilst I sort out and store the paintings in vaults there."

"Surely I should stay here and help Marcell and Aurielle, I could have learnt so much," I began.

My aunt gave me a steely stare with her piercing blue eyes, and I went quiet. "You are more than capable, but you are English and cannot and will not stay here. Should the Nazis invade we now have first-hand knowledge of their incredible cruelty, and you will be safer at home and Isadora needs you more than ever now she has returned to the Hall. George's sudden death hit her hard and she thought that travelling the world would help her to get over the pain of losing him. Well now she is back and it's important her family is with her, and you are her granddaughter. Lysander, Portia and your parents are unable to be in Norfolk at this time, so it's down to you. I also need you to take some important packages for me as they need to be removed from harm's way. The Nazis are plundering art galleries, museums and private homes of priceless art and treasures as they invade, and they will no doubt do the same here. For these reasons I have decided that you will leave for England in the horsebox with Nico and Malissa. You must be prepared to leave the day after tomorrow. You must gather everything you wish to take with you, so we have much to do in the next twenty-four hours."

"Why are Nico and Malissa going with me?" I asked unable to understand the new plans.

"They need to get to Britain to continue their education and they cannot return to Albania now Italy has annexed their country. They were in Ukraine when the Nazis invaded Poland and they witnessed horrific and cruel acts of war. If they had been captured, they would have been sent to the labour camps or their intelligence used to further the Reich's advancement. They have spoken about the murder and imprisonment of Jewish people and about the rounding up and deporting of gypsies as well as the extermination of children with disabilities. Dr Bleumanthall has listened to them and decided it will be wise to go to America immediately. I need you to take these young people to England for their safety."

"How do you know them?" I asked.

"Your father knows their father and he has asked me to help get them to England. As you know your father has already organised their rescue from Poland by two British special forces men. The ones you met. The British Government agreed to help them as their father has a fleet of cargo ships being used to supply goods to Britain. I gather the young man called Tiff made a bit of an impression on you?"

I ignored that innuendo, just smiled and said, "Oh my father knows their father." I was wondering, stupidly, who their father must be, as I fell quiet, trying to digest the enormity of the situation and of my journey ahead. I had learnt to drive the horsebox after my great-uncle died and I had been on long distance rides with Hermes when we travelled to some horse shows and driving events, but driving all the way to the north coast of France and then through part of England seemed daunting. "Where will we sleep?" I asked. "It will take several days to drive to Calais then on to Norfolk."

"You are not sailing from Port of Calais you are heading for St Malo."

"That's too long a sea journey for Hermes," I said worriedly.

"It is the safest option right now and you need to be on your way as soon as possible," Tantetta replied.

"When is Rebekkah leaving?" I asked.

"There is a flight to Gibraltar the day after tomorrow to start their long journey to America and you will be on your way hopefully the same day. Then I leave for Switzerland with Jean-Phillipe travelling with me. There is no time to lose now, we cannot procrastinate; the time has come for us all to leave. The Nazis are on their way, and I doubt our soldiers can hold them back even with the British troops fighting with them. Now I suggest we go to bed; we all need an early start. Jean-Phillipe must go back to Paris tonight and as soon as he returns, I must be ready to leave for Switzerland. He is collecting some more valuable paintings, his personal papers, as well as his passport, and will then fly on to New York from Switzerland. So come now, let's get some sleep. Good night, my dear."

"I won't let you down, Tantetta, I promise," I said and, putting my arms around her shoulders, hugged her.

I went to bed knowing there was no going back to the life I knew and loved so much. My future was uncertain but lay in driving back to England and facing whatever life had in store for me there. I couldn't sleep thinking about the journey and going over and over in my head what I needed to take. Had I packed everything I needed? I must remember Hermes' saddle, her harness, her feed, her bridle, her grooming brushes, her hay – it just went round and round in my head. Finally, I drifted off to sleep and morning came quickly with Aurielle knocking on my door and bringing me a hot chocolate. Five-thirty in the morning and everybody else was up, rushing around preparing for our departure. There was so much to do, and I was still struggling to understand the sense of urgency being shown by everyone else. Unbeknown to me, Marcell had been busy working on the horsebox for the last week. I had been told that it needed some repairs doing to it. So first he had been busy in the cellars doing mysterious building repairs, and now on the horsebox. Why it had all to be done now, I couldn't understand. The weirdest change was that nearly all the paintings hanging on the walls had gone and been replaced with my copies of the paintings I had been asked to do for practice shortly after I had arrived. Only now they all had signatures by famous people. Now it appeared I was a 'forger'. Shortly after I had arrived my aunt had suggested that I copy some of Uncle Edmund's paintings as practice and I had moved on to copy Monet, Gauguin, Matisse, and many others. After my initial copies I had moved on to translate their paintings by putting my own ideas into my paintings as Vincent Van Gogh had done. I had forgotten about this until now. I hadn't signed any and now here they were in original frames and signed by people who were now dead and very good signatures they were too.

I tracked Tantetta down to find out what was going on. She was with Aurielle organising what should be stored away at the Chateau and what could be taken with her as well as what could stay and be hidden locally. I asked why my paintings were hanging with forged signatures. She paused and sat on the chaise lounge. "Your uncle's paintings are not only very dear to me, and I treasure them, but they are becoming popular I am very proud to say. Not only that, but they are also increasing in value, meaning they are something the Nazis could be interested in stealing. These soldiers and their leaders have no honour or scruples, and we must try to be ahead of their devious plans."

"Do you really think they will invade France?" I very naively asked.

"My dear, rumour has it that they are nearly here or that they are on their way and could break through the Maginot Line – that is why there is no time to lose. You will leave at first light in the morning as soon as the horsebox is loaded."

I was shocked by what I heard and remembered my paintings of Tantetta, so I ran downstairs and into my nearly empty art studio, ran to the cupboard and pulled out the paintings; neither were framed. Realizing I was in a panic, Tantetta had followed me downstairs and I heard her gasp as she saw the paintings.

"I had always planned a special occasion to give you these and I honestly thought they would be safe here, now I realize that's not the case at all so you must have them now; I hope you have room for them."

She crossed the room to inspect them more closely then she turned and hugged me. "They are magnificent, Cressida. You are a wonderful and talented artist, and I am so proud of you. I wish Edmund could have seen your work now. They are just incredible; your technique has developed in leaps and bounds." She moved even closer to inspect each one.

"Jean-Phillipe liked them," I said anxiously.

"Well, well, he never once told me about them, I love them and of course they will go to Switzerland with me. Jean-Phillipe should be on his way back now. Poor man, he will be exhausted and there will be room in my car or in our van for these wonderful paintings. I remember my debutante days so clearly when I look at this and when I met your Uncle Edmund. Such happy memories brought alive for me. Thank you, my darling.

"As for your paintings I don't want Marcell and Aurielle punished in any way if the Germans don't find any paintings here as they will expect to. My reputation as an art dealer precedes me so I have mixed some reasonably good new and old artists' work amongst the forgeries. I hope you don't mind too much?" she added as an afterthought with a twinkle in her eye.

I hugged her. "Not in the least. They look pretty good, don't they?" I laughed.

Tantetta added, "I will miss you, my treasure, keep safe and look after my sister Isadora – she needs your help more than ever now. We will try to keep in touch, and we will both be back together here one day all good and God willing. I wish your parents were home in Norfolk, but we must pray that they stay safely out of the way in Singapore."

"Oh, Tantetta, I love you and can't bear to be away from here and from you. Why is this happening to us all?" I sobbed.

"Stay strong, you can be, and you will find strength within you to carry on. Trust me, we will get through this and survive. Look after the two youngsters going with you and your precious cargo."

I thought she meant Hermes. At that moment little did I know to what she was really referring.

"I trust you will do your best and what is always right as you always have. Come into the dining room, I have a map of your route laid out on the table and it shows where we have planned you will stay each night. I have written ahead and organised your overnight stops. The timing is not easy for you, but I think it should go smoothly – it is so important – you must be there on time."

On the table was a large map of France and the route was drawn in black snaking through France on the quieter rough roads and avoiding any large towns. "Nico is a superb map reader and understands the geographical layout of the territory so if you need to change any part of the route slightly, he will be able to show you the way. He has been through the route with me, and he will oversee your progress and map read for you. It is, however, a good idea if you familiarize yourself with it as well."

"How old is he?" I asked incredulously.

"He is nearly fifteen and is very intelligent, as is Malissa. You can rely on both; they are experts in their fields and are in demand for their knowledge back in England."

"Really, that good?" I asked.

"Yes, really that good. You might find them a little strange at times, but they have had a very different upbringing from most people and tragedy has often been part of their very young lives, but they are capable and bright and can handle themselves in most situations. They both understand and can use firearms."

"Why is Malissa so quiet all the time?" I asked. As I was travelling with her for a long time in the confines of the horsebox, I thought it might be a good idea if I understood her better.

"She is a deep thinker and a strategist; her hobbies are war games, and she is a chess grandmaster. She can beat men much older than her. She knows about the history of wars and why they were lost or won. Her talents are needed by important people during the months ahead. She is also an outstanding mathematician and can understand mathematical calculations which confound university students and some professors. Respect her judgement for she is wise beyond her years."

Tantetta surprised me with this news, and I asked no more about my travelling companions. I studied the map and made some brief notes on paper which I hoped I would be able to follow easily. Even if no one else could understand my scribbles. I was getting mixed feelings about my departure. I was frightened, but also excited about the challenge, the adventure of the journey ahead but, oh, so sad to be leaving.

My trunk had been carried downstairs and was ready to be put in the back of the horsebox with my small brown leather suitcase with my overnight travelling stuff in it. I had to fit this behind my driving seat. Some paintings were going home with me and had been rolled up ready for the journey. Marcell and Joseph had been working very hard getting the horsebox ready for our departure, Tantetta's car was ready for travelling, washed, and serviced. The wood on the outside of the horsebox had been re-varnished and it looked very smart. My friends had been amazing, and I was very worried about them staying behind and their safety.

My new travelling companions were very quiet, which I was getting used to and apart from meals they kept themselves away from us; not in a rude way – they helped if necessary but then just disappeared. Tantetta explained that our first night would be on a farm owned by a cousin of Uncle Edmund who had married a farmer and former Captain in the Foreign Legion. She had defied her family to marry the man she loved and had been cut off by the family. Her mother had inherited a good farm and she had passed this on to her daughter when she had died. Her brother inherited the Chateau and lands that went with it, and he still refused to acknowledge his sister even though they were only two miles apart. Fortunately, she had an independent income as well as the farm, so they were comfortable with regard to money. Sadly, though, they did not have children. They were expecting all of us to stay for the first night and had space for us and the animals. They were good people and Tantetta was sending them a case of wine and a large ham as a gift. These items were also loaded in the horsebox which was beginning to look packed out. Just as well it was a big lorry. After that, my next night stop was a day's journey away and we would be staying with an English man who was married to a half-French lady and two of their sons. They were acquaintances of my parents, and they had their own vineyard. His wife ran an antiques business and was in England where she had been selling some of her stock and at this moment was buying a home in Newmarket for them to live in whilst working in England. Their two eldest boys were presently taking their exams at boarding school so it would be handy for their parents to stay near to them when in Britain. The two younger boys would eventually go to boarding school in England so would have a base near their schools.

Organised at last – then all I had to do was get to each destination on time. After these two overnight stops we were to stay in a Hotel de Chambre recommended for us which had its own small paddock for Hermes for the night. Our biggest problem apparently was going to be fuel, and Tantetta was very concerned about that because rationing of food, clothes and fuel was hitting all the people in France very hard. Marcell had filled jerry cans with fuel and put them on the roof of the horsebox, hidden by the hay we were carrying for Hermes. This was to protect them and to keep them hidden from prying eyes. The next was food, as rationing had been in place in France since September 1939; however, we were lucky as we had the farm and lived in a rural community, so it hadn't bothered us too much and with Aurielle such a good cook we simply hadn't noticed any lack of food. It would be a different problem when travelling through France. Aurielle came to the rescue – she had baked and pickled, made jams and honey, plus we had traded some wine for a half side of pig. There was just as much food for Tantetta's and Jean-Phillipe's journey as well. After all this travelling and eating, hopefully we would reach the port in time to catch our boat home to England.

My aunt had instructed Marcell to kill some of our animals now to sell and to give some of the meat to the villagers to avoid them being stolen by the Nazis. We might as well eat them as have them stolen and fed to German soldiers or taken to Germany, she had said. We were lucky we had a chiller room to salt and hang some meat, as we kept some cheeses in a cool place for months before they went to market.

It was now the beginning of the first week in May 1940 and the whole country seemed gripped with worry and doom and fear. It was beginning to worry me as well, and I was anxious to be off now and on my way home. Thor was going with Tantetta to Switzerland and Jean-Phillipe had returned to Paris with some more crates of wine to sell there then he was due back later today with yet more paintings from their gallery to take to Switzerland. They were taking two vehicles: Tantetta's open-topped car and the van used for delivering or collecting paintings. At home she ran around in a little French Citroen 2CV which she was leaving for Marcell and Aurielle to get to market if they didn't use Flavie and his trap, but she had a Rolls-Royce too which had been Uncle Edmund's pride and joy and this journey was deemed special enough to get it out of the garage and ready to travel. This had been another job Marcell had been working on and it was now serviced and fuelled up ready to go. Again, the biggest problem would be fuel and Marcell and Tantetta had been preparing for this and had collected enough petrol in jerry cans to get the car over the Swiss border and the van and its precious load. It had been decided that the regular delivery man who worked for Tantetta would drive the van to Switzerland for them, so Jean-Phillipe would be with Tantetta and navigate. I would very much like to see and hear the two of them on their journey deciding who was right or wrong and who knew the way.

The day flew by with all of us packing, loading, and clearing away our possessions from the Chateau. Aurielle, my lovely, happy friend, worked all day long, but she was very quiet, not her usual joking, light-hearted self. I walked into the garden after our evening meal which we all had together in the kitchen, and I stared up at the peaceful, starry sky and breathed in the scents of the night. When would I be back, I wondered, would it be the same. I stared at the moon and wanted to cry, but no tears came. I was very tired and couldn't settle in the garden as I usually could. Odin caught the scent of something, most likely a mouse, and chased around with his nose in the long grass at the edge of the garden. Our tabby cat called Cesar jumped up beside me on the swing and brushed against me, purring. I stroked him, glad that Aurielle loved the cat and would look after him. Finally, I went upstairs to bed; the Chateau was quiet, but I didn't sleep straight away. I thought about a man called Tiff with friendly, hazel-brown eyes and wondered where he was, and I hoped he stayed safe.

In the morning Aurielle, bless her, came to wake me at 5 am with a mug of hot chocolate made just the way I loved it. Little did I know it would be the last hot chocolate made by Aurielle for me, for a few years. She sat on the chair near my bed. "Sid," she began, "I will miss you so much, you have been such fun living here and brought life, laughter, and love to us all here. Marcell and I will do everything to look after this place until you return, and I just know that you will return one day." With that, she jumped up and hugged me, then went to the door, opened it, turned, blew me a kiss and laughing said, "Oh la la, what a delight they have in store for them at your home in England with your amazing French culinary skills." She ducked as she left the room and, I, laughing, hurled a pillow at her. Aurielle had endeavoured to teach me how to cook, but I just didn't have the talent for cooking, and we had more giggling sessions than lessons at my frequent culinary disasters. Still, there were a few dishes I had become quite good at, and I had taught her how to make Yorkshire puddings and trifle even though, at first, I had to write to Mrs Revill our cook at home to ask for the recipes. We made Chelsea buns and fruit cake, but I couldn't compete with Aurielle's light touch with pastry and her amazing croissants and patisserie.

I showered, washed my hair, dressed in comfy jodhpurs, put on a lemon short-sleeved cotton shirt and a dark blue cashmere jumper to ward off any early morning chills. Finally, I rammed a cloche hat on my head to keep my red curls under control as it was drying, and tied a bright blue and lemon scarf round my neck. I stopped on the stairs and looked carefully around, trying to make sure that I remembered every detail of the day I had arrived and of my wonderful life here. Jodhpurs boots on, and a croissant in the kitchen, then I was silent – I couldn't speak for emotion. Nico came in after me dressed in dark blue long cotton trousers, an open-necked shirt and a dark blue jumper; very neat and tidy; and helped himself to some breakfast. Malissa walked in dressed in a skirt and jumper and started to have her coffee and fruit.

"Malissa, do you have any trousers with you?" I asked.

"No, I have never worn any," she replied.

"Well, we are about the same size so you can have some of mine and if they are too long you can just roll them up. Trust me, they will be more comfortable on our journey," I said.

"Really, I would like that, can I have them to try on now?"

I went out to find my luggage and pull out a pair of trousers for her and gave them to her. She went off and soon came back smiling and showing us her 'new' trousers. Gosh it was nice to see a more human side to her, instead of such a quiet person always reading with nothing much to say. Tantetta walked in and drank some coffee, dressed in slacks ready for her long drive, but somehow even though she was in her sixties she looked so stylish with her long emerald-green silk scarf casually draped around her neck and a beautiful pale blue cashmere bat winged jumper which had fitted sleeves from the elbow to wrist with tiny pearl buttons all the way up. She could still cut a dash in her Rolls. Jean-Phillipe walked in looking rather tired after his epic journey and helped himself to coffee which was in a pot on the giant kitchen stove. He told us that the van driver Armonde had begged for his wife and two children to be allowed to travel with them, and it had been a crowded, noisy journey back to the Chateau. Thank goodness he himself was travelling with Henrietta to Switzerland and that Armonde and his family would be in the van travelling behind them. Tantetta then told him it would be a bit of a squash in the 'Rolls' because of the extra luggage in the car as now they had to take more paintings because of the two children in the van. He added with a sigh that "they couldn't mind under the 'circumstances'". Thor was looking very worried about whether he should come with us and Odin, or stay with Tantetta. She called him to her with reassuring crooning. I loved him so much, just as much as Odin, and I hated saying goodbye to him, but he would be spoilt rotten by Auntygusta in Switzerland so I knew he would be safe and happy there. We all trooped outside to see Marcell loading up Hermes and I went over to talk to her and helped close the ramp. We were well loaded up in the lorry, but there was still plenty of room for Hermes and space to spare. But in the cab, it seemed cramped, with Odin, Nico, and Malissa plus some of our food for the journey. I wasn't sure just how much had been packed for us by Aurielle, though I was to find out later that there was plenty of food, all of which we would be glad of on the journey.

I hugged them all again and without another word because it had all been said, I climbed up into the cab, turned the ignition key, the engine coughed, and the lorry sparked into life.

Chapter 10

Alex Bouchet meets Sid

Alex and his little family travelled well that first morning after leaving their home, and keeping to quiet little-used tracks they didn't see a soul. After five hours he was worried the mare was getting tired or her harness would be rubbing, so he stopped for food and to rest her. Two hours later he travelled on again for four hours, and finding a small wood where they were sheltered and hidden from view, he made camp for the night. The children were so excited to be on holiday and staying out camping all night. Alex made a campfire, cooked some sausages for tea and heated some milk to drink and water to wash in. They all slept in the baker's cart where his uncle had extended the overhead canopy – there was room for them to be very comfortable on a mattress, pillows, and warm rugs. Underneath, Albert had put sheepskins on the cart boards for insulation, so it was very cosy. Tanner stretched out next to them all. The mare was loose, just grazing, and he left the fire lit and hoped it would stay in. They all slept very well. Alex was awake just before four in the morning, stoking the fire and he put the kettle on to make some coffee. The mare had not gone far; he knew she wouldn't. He fed her some hard feed to help her on the journey, prepared some breakfast and woke the children. After Claude and Simone had eaten, they crawled back into their warm nest under the canopy, Alex put the harness on the mare and set off, leaving the children to sleep in the cart.

Three days of much the same, only not panicking as much about the police looking for him or at the very least not worrying about them finding him on the quiet tracks, suggested to him by Uncle Albert, he began to enjoy travelling each day. He just had to keep his fingers crossed that the wooden wheels held up and didn't break on the rough tracks. The weather was good to them, and he had enough food to last them for a week. Early one morning he took his bow and arrow and waited until a big rabbit was busily grazing near where they were camped. He shot it, killing it instantly. He had it skinned, chopped up and boiling in a pan of water before the children woke up. He had found some wild mushrooms and still had plenty of onions stored on the cart. When he knew it was cooked, he put into the frying pan an onion, the wild mushrooms and a knob of butter. When it was browned, he tipped it all back into the big pan ready to eat later. He had flour with him and each morning for breakfast he added two eggs laid by the hens and using water he made crepes cooked on the flat pan and then smeared them with jam or honey. They ate them rolled up like pancakes.

One hot afternoon he came across a beautiful, clear lake half hidden in the woods surrounded by a fringe of gently swaying trees. By the lake was a tiny cottage. He camped by the lake, and they all had a swim to wash and clean themselves. Cautiously, he went over to the cottage and knocked on the door to find out if they could stay there. A middle-aged man with shoulder length black hair shot with silver streaks and a black beard going grey, opened the door. Conker brown from living in the countryside, he looked fit and strong. His French was not brilliant, and it turned out he was Spanish, escaping from the fighting and killing in his country during the Civil War. He knew it was over now, but he had grown to like living in the woods away from people who could be so cruel to each other. He was happy to see Simone and Claude and he shared his food with them all. Alex shared his cooked rabbit. They stayed there for three nights listening to Matias playing Spanish melodies on his guitar as the stars littered the dark blue velvet, dark sky and with only the sounds of the creatures of the night accompanying him.

Alex showed Matias how to use a bow and arrow and how to choose the right wood to make one. Preferably yew, ash, or most hardwoods like oak or maple and they all went out hunting for a suitable tree, a sapling or even the right branch. Claude and Simone loved running along the forest paths. He explained how to get the tillering right and how he could use a soft wood, but not to expect it to last as long as a more durable hard wood. He explained how you could boil the wood to be able to bend it into the shape needed. For the arrows they looked for pine wood, birch, hazel or oak, and he explained about the spine or stiffness of how much an arrow shaft bends. Alex told him that an arrow tip could be made from stone, wood, bone or metal and he explained just as Uncle Albert had taught him about the arrows having the shaft the long spine of the arrow, the fletching made up of feathers creating wind drag and stability and accuracy in flight. The feathers would be different colours and called the cock or the hen feathers. They made an arrowhead: the point of the arrow and lastly the nock, a slotted tip located at the rear of the arrow which slots into the string. This could be made from linen or hemp, sinew, or rawhide. Matias listened and realised how calm and confident this young man was. He also realized learning about bows and arrows was interesting and more complicated than he had imagined. Still, he did learn a lot in four days.

He asked Alex where he was going and when he told him he was heading for Spain he told him, "You don't want to go to Spain, the people in charge are Fascists and they will have no time for you or your brother and sister. The country is still in a mess with many political prisoners still in prison. People have been starving there during the war and I think they will fancy your horse for food. Go further south here in France – try the Bordeaux area or Languedoc or Provence, if it's vineyards you want to work in. You can wander anywhere with your horse down there."

"No, there looks like a war is coming and I need to be somewhere safe not travelling on the road. I do have an address for a former soldier my uncle fought with in the first war maybe I should head there." They looked at the map Alex had brought with him and planned a new route towards Sarlat. Alex asked Matias to go with them. But Matias said he liked the peace and quiet of the woods and preferred to stay where he was. Hopefully the war would not find him here. Matias liked Alex and thought if his two sons had survived the Civil War that they would have been like Alex; he hoped so. He felt an immediate connection to the young man, and he thought he was brave to make the journey with his young brother and sister. He showed Alex how he could throw a knife and aim wherever he liked accurately. Alex practised and was impressed with the skill Matias had with his knife which he used to catch food.

Alex made bread in the cottage for all of them each morning. When the time came that Alex thought he should move on, he didn't want to leave his new friend. The night before he was leaving, whilst the children were asleep, he asked Matias why he had left Spain and ended up living the life of a recluse in France. Matias sighed and stared into the depths of the dark lake. Finally, he told Alex, "When I knew that Francisco Franco had won and beaten Spain's democratically elected Republic, I knew I had to leave or die. I was tired of the fighting and killing. Three years is a long time to see your country fighting brother against brother, father against son, cousin against cousin. The killing was endless, and thousands of prisoners were executed rather than imprisoned. It was bloodshed I was part of, and I had no stomach for it anymore. I fought for the Republic, and we were hunted, assassinated, and murdered. I walked away when I knew my two sons had been killed in the fighting and my wife had died from starvation like so many families. The Nationalists caused such terror and food shortages. I was a schoolteacher and I left to find my eldest son Juan, but all I did was fight and all I saw was bloodshed and betrayal. I became sick of all the killing and hatred. I have found peace here and I don't want to return to my country, but I don't want to be part of another war here. I have killed many times; I am not proud of the part I played in the war. I hope you stay safe with your family, and I wish you all the best in the future."

The next morning Alex left Matias with much sadness, but he knew he needed to find a new life for himself and the children; he couldn't live by the lake forever. He didn't feel so sure of himself anymore and wondered if his journey was a mistake. His actions became more mechanical over the next few days. Rather than the joy it had been to be on the open road in the beginning, it now seemed to be a bad idea and a chore. As he travelled, he used main roads instead of little-known tracks, so he saw more people and realized there was a gloom about the inevitability of war. He stopped to buy food in the little villages through which he passed, but was frequently finding many of these closed or short of food. Nothing seemed to be normal anywhere.

An accumulation of cumulonimbus clouds was beginning to threaten rain so he decided to try and find a quiet track for shelter; on reaching a crossroads he saw a wood to the left and decided it might make a good place to stop, avoid the threatening storm and rest Trudi. He had been walking with her all morning and needed a rest and the children wanted a drink and some food. He was short of food as the last village didn't have a shop open and his provisions were running low. As he walked down the narrow track between the trees towards a clearing in the woods, he was very surprised to see a smart varnished wooden horsebox parked, and a chestnut horse tied up at the side of the box pulling on a hay net. He was nervous of what kind of people owned the horsebox, but was relieved to see there were three young people there. The first thing he did was to say hello and next he took the mare out of the shafts because she needed to graze and drink. He introduced himself to a tallish, slim girl with masses of freckles and bouncy ginger hair pulled back from her face and held down by a hat. He asked her if they had any water to spare for his horse. She told him her name was Sid and her companions were Nico and Malissa. Tanner was busy making his own introductions to a tan and white spaniel, and Alex hoped the dogs made friends and didn't fight. The two dark haired teenagers regarded him with some hostility or maybe it was suspicion, but they said hello and the boy went over to him and shook his hand. They asked where he was going with the horse and cart, and he told them Sarlat. He explained to them about his original plan to go to Spain as he wanted to work on a vineyard and to learn about the winemaking process. He introduced them to his very shy brother,

Claude, and sister, Simone, who were travelling with him. The boy called Nico told him it would take him many weeks to reach the Spanish border the other side of Biarritz and the Germans were very likely to have invaded France by then. He said he didn't think they would be very kind to a boy living like a gypsy with his young brother and sister. He added that Spain had not recovered from the Civil War, and he didn't recommend him travelling there. Alex asked where they were travelling to and he was very surprised when they told him they were going to Britain and that they were going to get the ferry from St Malo. Alex told them his horse was old and they had been travelling for many days and he was worried about her, and he admitted he thought he was travelling too far.

He explained about his aunt taking over the boulangerie and that she had decided to sell the old horse and replace her with a van. He told them everything about his running away to save Trudi from slaughter and how he disliked his bossy aunt and that he could not work with her in the boulangerie which belonged to his father and his uncle. They had both joined the army to fight against the threat of a Nazi invasion. He even told them about his half-brother and sister's mother going to Poland to look after her sick mother and leaving him to run the shop and bake the bread. It was the law in France for a boulanger to make bread every day of the week. The Revolution in1789 had been caused by the shortage of bread to feed the people due to a poor harvest. He didn't want to be baking bread every morning for the rest of his life. Then he mentioned that his mother had been a British nurse who fell in love with his father at the end of the Great War and that she had died when he was six years old.

The girl called Sid listened to his story and then she suggested that he travelled to her aunt's Chateau de la Cascade near

Chateaumelliant. A long journey, but not as far as going to Spain. She agreed to write an introduction for him to her friends Marcell and Aurielle and an introduction to a farm where they could stay tonight. Marcell and Aurielle cared for a vineyard for her great-aunt and would more than likely be pleased for his help there. He should make haste tonight to the Farm belonging to the Albertines where she was sure they would let him stay and help him with his journey. She then offered him and the children food, ham, cheese, tomatoes, fresh bread, apples, and elderflower cordial. He watered Trudi, and Nico gave him some oats for her and food for Tanner. He studied their map, and he showed Nico his old map given to him by his Uncle Albert which interested Nico. They planned the best route for him for that night to reach Moulin a Vent, the Albertines' farm, which was on the way to where he would be heading the next day to reach Chateau de la Cascade. They were very hungry, and he was so grateful for the food and the directions. Sid told him they needed to be on their way to reach their next destination before it was dark, and that Alex should be leaving too. Sid gave him some more ham for his journey and helped him load up ready to leave. Alex felt better to have met some good people on his journey and to have rested Trudi. Now all he had to do was hope it didn't rain and hurry up to get to his next destination without making the mare too tired.

He followed the track suggested to him by Nico using his uncle's map. It was a rough stony track and on more than one occasion he thought the stones would break a wheel on the cart. He finally reached a narrow sort of rough dirt road, lined with trees, and climbing onto the cart he urged Trudi into a trot. It was now drizzling and overcast, and he was anxious to reach the Albertines' farm before dark. He rounded a bend in the road and was depressed to see more long monotonous road stretching out in front with no shelter on either side. Again, he asked Trudi to trot on. As he thought they were reaching the end of the road he could see some trees ahead, so he let Trudi walk; she was blowing, and the drizzle was turning to rain. The sky darkened and he was becoming scared of losing his way and not finding shelter for the night. He walked past the trees onto another long open road and the rain was getting worse. Suddenly he thought he could make out someone walking on the road in the gloom. Hoping they might tell him if he was going the right way to Moulin A Vent, he pulled alongside a small, hunched figure. It was a drenched young girl clutching something to her chest and carrying a large wet carpet bag. She looked lost and exhausted but backed away from him as he spoke to her. Of course, he was wearing an oilskin overcoat and a big hat and looked strange and menacing. He offered her a lift, and she still didn't answer him, so he showed her Claude and Simone sheltering underneath the tarpaulin and only then did she try to climb in. He took her bag and was surprised how heavy it was then he heard a whimper coming from whatever she was clutching to her chest. He literally lifted her onto the cart and under the cover and hurried to climb up to the seat at the front and again ask poor Trudi to trot on. Now he was really frightened he would injure or kill the big-hearted mare who always did as she was asked. Climbing a steady incline, he could again hear the mare blowing and he was thinking they could all die of exposure in the pouring rain when finally, he thought he saw through the rain and evening gloom a bit of a stone wall and a gate post without a gate. He turned down the rough track leading the mare, again hoping, and praying, they had reached a farm. Now the rain was torrential and with his head down he coaxed the tired mare through the downpour along the track. Any farm or barn would do, they just had to stop and rest the mare. In front of him he could just make out there was a building with a steep roof nearly reaching the ground and he was sure he could make out a light inside.

He hammered on the door under a porch, and it was opened by a man who shouted what did he want. "Please forgive me for disturbing you, we are desperately needing shelter and help. Etes- vous Monsieur Albertine, s'il vous plait? J'ai une lettre pour vous » He quickly delved under his oilskin coat and produced the letter from Sid. The man disappeared inside and closed the door, leaving Alex unsure of what to do next. He thought he might cry of cold, fatigue and worry for all of them. The door opened and the man told him to go in quickly. Alex pulled back the tarpaulin and called to Claude and Simone to jump down and then he helped the young stranger with her bag. Tanner followed them; Alex tried to stop him, but the man said, "ca va, venez", and pulling on an overcoat he closed the door behind him and beckoned to Alex to follow him with the mare and cart. He led him to a barn and opened the big doors to let him in. Alex was relieved to find there was room for the mare and cart to go inside and it was warm and dry. One side was full of goats in pens with plenty of straw bedding. Alex quickly unharnessed Trudi and the man hung the harness up on hooks on the barn wall. Alex started to rub Trudi with straw to warm and dry her and reached into the cart to pull out an old jute rug for her. He put hay underneath the rug and rubbed her tired legs with straw. He was directed to put her in a stable which was already bedded down with straw and given a bucket of water for her. The man left him but came back with warm water to take the chill off the mare's water and to make a warm mash for her with some bran. Alex showed him the poor cold hens and he led Alex to another pen to put them in on their own where they gently rubbed them dry. When Alex

was sure that the mare was comfortable, he walked quickly back
to the house and was grateful to walk into the warm room where
a fire burned brightly in the hearth, heating the oven in the wall.
The room smelt of cassoulet and Alex saw the others were already
eating, seated at a big table with their coats hung up near to the
fire to dry. Now for the first time he saw Madame Albertine and
noticed an upright, elegant grey-haired lady perhaps just turned
sixty. She took his heavy oilskin coat, and her husband took it
through the kitchen to a scullery. She filled a bowl with food
from the big pot in the oven and told him to sit down and to eat.
A baby started crying and Madame Albertine picked it up from
an armchair and took it to the slim dark-haired girl to feed it. So
that's what she had been clutching to her chest, a baby. The girl
looked embarrassed and shook her head and went to her bag and
took out an empty bottle. She was nearly crying, and she opened
the bag to show Madame Albertine that she didn't have any milk.
Madame Albertine immediately went into the scullery and came
back with a jug of milk, which she put into a pan to warm, at the
same time adding a little water. She washed the bottle, filled it and
sat down to feed the crying baby. It stopped crying and guzzled
the milk. Alex savoured the delicious meal slowly, allowing the
warmth of the room to enter his bones. Tanner having checked
out the old farm dog stretched out by the fire, he now enjoyed the
crackle of the logs and the warmth. Madame Albertine finished
feeding the child and gave it to the young girl, then went to the
oven and fetched a pudding; a type of cake drizzled with syrup
which was delicious. No words had been spoken during this time.
Alex was grateful as he was too tired to talk. Madame Albertine
beckoned to the children to follow her to a bedroom, carrying
hot water bottles. They first went to Alex and hugged him, kissed
him, and said goodnight. The girl changed the baby's nappy and

when Madame Albertine came back into the room, she washed the baby's bottle, filled it with more milk and put it into a pan of water ready to heat in the night. She told the girl to follow her with the baby and carrying an oil lamp they went upstairs. Alex was shown a bedroom just off the kitchen and he collapsed on the bed into a fluffy warm eiderdown and immediately fell into a deep sleep.

At four in the morning Alex was up, unable to sleep anymore and got up went into the kitchen and made bread using his 'mother yeast' and while it was rising, he ran to the barn to check on Trudi. It was dark and still raining outside. He hoped the Albertines didn't mind him using their kitchen, but he wanted to thank them by baking some bread and he needed some fresh bread to take on their journey. Trudi was sleeping, but she nickered to him as he went through the door. He checked she was warm and resting then he went straight back to the kitchen and carried on baking. When he had finished, he cleaned up the table and after stoking up the fire, made himself a drink. He stared into the fire and dozed again, then right on time he took the bread out of the oven. He went back to the barn to muck out his mare and feed her. The goats bleated to him, so he made sure they all had some sweet hay to chew on and when he got to the top pen, he realized something was wrong with a nanny goat as she lay on the floor groaning and straining. She was trying to give birth, but something was wrong. He went straight to her side and soothing the nanny and crooning to her, he checked the progress of the little baby kid inside her. He could see its legs. He put his hand into the nanny, carefully manoeuvred the kid and helped ease the new baby into the world. When he had finished, he turned around to see Monsieur Albertine watching him.

"Well done, you did a good job there; you've done that before."

"Yes, I have, for my uncle; he's always kept a few goats for some milk."

"Are you close to him?" asked Monsieur Albertine.

"Yes very, my mother died when I was six years old, she was British, my father re-married a Polish girl, she's nice; I like her a lot. She's in Poland now caring for her mother who is ill. Claude and Simone are my half-brother and sister. My father has joined up and I think he is baking for the French army somewhere. Perhaps on the Maginot Line. I have loved watching my father baking and I have learnt how to bake as a result."

Monsieur Albertine leant on the pen gate and let Alex talk. It was obvious he needed to.

"Now my half-German aunt has decided to leave Paris and take over the running of our bakery until my uncle comes home and I just can't stand her, so I have left. My great-uncle Albert is the one person who has always been there for me, no matter what has happened. He is an undertaker and a talented cabinet maker. He agreed with me; if I want to try to be a wine grower then I should have a go. He has always wanted me to work with him yet now he wants to retire and make whatever he wants with wood." Alex smiled wryly.

"Now a war is coming to interfere with all our lives and dreams," said Monsieur Albertine.

"Do you think it really is?" asked Alex innocently.

"We listen to the wireless and the news is very depressing – things are not going well for the French or the British army fighting here," Monsieur Albertine replied.

They both went back to the kitchen for breakfast and found the girl bottle feeding the baby and Madame Albertine giving Claude and Simone their breakfast. Monsieur Albertine told his wife about the new-born kid, and she left immediately to check on it. Alex sat at the table and decided it was time to find out to where the girl was walking and what she was called. She hesitated and didn't seem to understand what he said so he asked again slowly.

"Nadine, my name is Nadine, and my baby is called Jacques," she told him.

"Where are you walking to?" he asked.

"I don't understand you." she replied and turned away from him to attend to the baby.

When Madame Albertine came back Alex said he would get ready to leave. The girl looked startled.

Monsieur Albertine said, "No, don't leave yet, it's still raining heavily; wait and see if it clears up. Don't take the baby and children on the road in this awful weather. Rest for a day or two. We have a friend who we think can take your cart on his lorry and I can take you and the horse in my farm truck. We are making sure we can get hold of enough fuel."

Alex was pleased to be told he could stay there longer. He was tired and Trudi needed the rest.

Later in the morning Madame Albertine was alone in the kitchen when she heard a moan coming from the girl in the scullery. The baby was asleep in a drawer on the table, so she went to find out what was wrong. The girl was trying to reach some clothes drying on a rack and was obviously in agony.

"Let me do that, whatever's the matter? Oh, you are covered in bruises. You need to rest. I have some cream to help those heal. Whatever has happened to you?" asked Madame Albertine.

"It's nothing, I fell, I am fine, but some cream would be good," said the girl.

"Are you English?" asked Madame Albertine.

"NO, definitely not, I am Irish," replied the girl. She walked back to the baby and sat down stiffly. "Thank you for letting me stay here, please don't say anything about my bruises."

Her French was not good, and Madame Albertine wondered who she was, but said no more. Later that day the sun came out and a young boy called Florent cycled over to the farm to see his aunt and uncle and help feed the goats. He played with Claude and Simone and showed them the baby kids. He was the son of the estranged brother of Madame Albertine.

Alex, his siblings, and Nadine stayed with the Albertines, and Alex thought he was in heaven. This was the life he longed for; to be in the countryside and work outside all day. He helped Monsieur Albertine mend a fence and repair a shed roof down in the valley, some way off and hidden from the farm. The next day they moved some of the goats to the field with the barn. For security they needed to be as far away from the farm as possible. In all they spent three nights with the Albertines, and Alex and his family loved every minute they spent with them. Nadine watched them and carried the baby with her everywhere, but didn't join in. She was very quiet and distant.

The day arrived for them to leave and at four-thirty in the morning a lorry drove into the farmyard. They loaded up the cart and off it went. After an early breakfast they all hugged Madame Albertine, very sadly said their goodbyes, and climbed into the farm truck belonging to Gregoire Albertine. They left, waving and shouting to her nephew as he pedalled up the drive after them. After a brief stop for lunch, Gregoire pulled off the road onto a side track and behind some trees they saw their baker's cart waiting for them. It had been dropped off at an agreed location away from prying eyes. When Trudi was unloaded, the nanny goat and her new-born kid were unloaded at the same time. Alex was surprised as he had no idea the goat was on board. "For the baby," explained Gregoire. Again, after repeatedly saying thank you and many sad goodbyes, Gregoire wished them, 'Bonne chance' and left. They had heard the news that the German army was now on French soil, having broken through the Ardennes. They journeyed on with Trudi until nearly dusk and, finding the safe place which they had 'earmarked' on the map, they made their overnight stop.

Next day they set off at five in the morning and travelled steadily for four hours and then stopped for food. At six o'clock in the evening, they were not far from the Chateau and Alex felt glad to be reaching the end of their journey and nervous that he might hate the Chateau or that the people there might not welcome them. They turned onto a narrow, quiet track and through the trees they glimpsed a pale pink Chateau looking like something from a fairy-tale, with two turrets nestled in a parkland setting with rows of vines, and in the distance a line of trees. It looked beautiful and Alex knew it was the right place for him. It just felt peaceful and magical, just as it had for Sid and years before for Henrietta when she had first seen it as a new bride. They turned onto the long drive lined with lime trees which were in flower and perfumed the air. As they approached the Chateau, they saw people coming out to greet them. Alex jumped down and went to Trudi's head to pat her; he then shook hands with first Marcell, then Aurielle and Joseph. He helped Nadine down with the baby and introduced her and lastly introduced Simone and Claude. Tanner was soon running around and checking out his new surroundings with his nose to the ground.

"Ah, you have a Brittany Spaniel – is he a good hunting dog?" asked Joseph.

"Yes, he is, he can find wild boar, rabbits, deer, pheasants. I can show you later." Alex called Tanner to his side and the dog obediently came straight back.

"What do you hunt with?" Joseph asked.

"My gun is a 12 bore, but I also have a bow and arrow. I have hunted with my Uncle Albert who has taught me," Alex replied.

"That's interesting, I hope you can show me," said Joseph. "Come on, I'll show you where to put your horse and goat – oh what a cute little kid. Flavie will be pleased with the company," and he strode ahead with the baby kid in his arms and Claude running after him, followed by Alex leading a tired Trudi now out of the shafts, but still in her harness. The nanny goat ran after them, bleating for her baby. Alex liked Joseph straight away and knew he would get on with him.

"Come on," said Aurielle, "let's get you all fed and then show you your beds; you have the cottage next door to us." She took the baby from Nadine and led her and Simone into the farmhouse. Later, as they all sat around the table, having eaten good food with a glass of wine and sweet fresh water from the well, Alex felt a great contentment wash over him along with serious bone aching tiredness.

He had told them Nadine was his sister – he didn't know why – and Aurielle had seemed a bit surprised, but had not questioned it. No more explanations were offered that night. Sid had written a letter asking them to look after Alex and his brother and sister. No mention of two sisters; not to worry, the help would be useful on the estate. Alex didn't look very strong, but who knows, he had made the journey here and that showed he had a strong character and determination, and he had an open honest face; somehow Aurielle knew, even then, it would work out alright. As Sid had written asking that they be looked after, of course they would. They would do anything for Sid. She loved having a baby to look after and the two children were gorgeous. She just wished and hoped the war didn't spoil their lives too much, but she feared it would.

Chapter 11

Matias Otero

After Alex and his family had left, Matias walked back to the cottage and started his usual morning jobs. He knew it was no good, though as the day wore on, he couldn't understand why he hadn't gone with the family to help them on their journey. He felt restless and for the first time since he had lived by the lake, he felt lonely. That evening he stared at the beautiful lake and saw the golden red sun set behind the darkening trees. The sun looked like it was tangled in the branches and the lake changed colours from blue to gold then black. It was quiet and still, and he was disturbed by his thoughts of his boys growing up, had they lived. He reflected as well on their laughter and the sunny smile of his young wife. He rarely thought about them, it was so painful, but now he did. He had gone to fight for the Republicans after his eldest son Juan had gone to join them. He went to find him and bring him home, but ended up fighting with him. At first, they had no idea how ferocious it would become or how many would die. His son Juan was killed, and he returned home to tell his grief-stricken wife, only to find that his youngest son had gone to fight for the Nationalists. He stayed with his wife and then they both decided he should go and find Jose, their younger son, and bring him home; he was far too young at just 16 years to be fighting. A risky plan as Matias, a Republican, would be tortured, imprisoned, or shot if found by the Nationalists at any time. The country was in chaos with a mass of refugees, orphaned children, deserted old people, all short of money and food, and in the grip of evil barbarism. Everyone feared being summarily executed as many people were being taken away and shot in secret locations or imprisoned without trial and forgotten. With base corruption on both sides, people just disappeared and were never seen again.

Finding Jose proved to be an impossible task and Matias somehow ended up fighting for the Republicans again. He managed to return home to discover that that their son, Jose, had died in the fighting. His wife had subsequently died of malnutrition, illness, and a broken heart.

As the war ended with a frenzy of murders and the killing of innocent people who were unfortunately and often accidentally mixed up in the war, Matias left Spain. There was nothing left for him in his country. The Nationalists were winning and cruelly destroying people, their homes and towns. He walked and walked into Basque country in Northern Spain and on into south-western France. He walked north away from the depravity and sheer madness of war in his homeland, staying briefly in different places on the Camino way, the pilgrims' route. For many days he just kept walking without any aim, looking to find some peace and escape the madness of the vicious war. The war which had turned brother against father, son against mother and divided families with hatred.

He found that peace in the little deserted cottage by a lake which was miles from anywhere. He lived the life of a hermit and fed himself, looked after himself and shunned the outside world.

Now, however, everything changed after he had heard the laughter of the children running through the woods, playing catch and swimming in the lake. He realized what he had been missing: friendship, love, a shared meal, a chat, teaching, and learning new skills.

The next morning Matias was up before the new day had dawned because he had decided he would follow the little family. If a war was on the way they were too young and vulnerable to stand up to the savagery, brutality and inhumanity which would result. War seeped everywhere into the fabric and heart of humanity wherever it was. He had witnessed too much pain and it had destroyed his family; now he would try to protect Alex and his family, and if that meant killing again so be it. Alex had discussed his new plans with him and the direction he planned to travel so he was confident he would find him. Taking the few belongings he still possessed, he loaded up his backpack, carefully concealing his three knives and the rudiments of his small bow and arrows. He was a strong bear of a man in his sixties and confident he could fight anyone and still be able to kill with his bare hands, as he had many times before.

His long stride soon took him into a village to buy some bread. He found he was viewed with suspicion, but he bought bread and milk and managed to learn that the German army was fighting its way to Paris. He decided there was no time to lose and walked until nightfall then made sure he was on his way before dawn every day. He was fit and strong and now had a mission to find the little family. He walked for nearly six days and as light was fading, he chanced visiting a farm on his route. He didn't go down the drive but approached from the fields at the back. Cautiously, he went towards the back door and finding no one around, he knocked, and when no one answered he looked inside through a window and saw a woman weeping. He pushed the door and spoke: "Pardon, Madame, puis-je vous aider?" He filled the doorway with his big frame and stood with his beret in his hands.

The woman turned round and if she was startled, she hid it well. "Who are you?" she asked.

"I am Matias Otero, I have no wish to harm you, I only am here to ask for some water and directions. Then I heard you crying so...." He shrugged his shoulders.

"My husband has died from his injuries from the French police. The thugs have stolen some of our goats and my husband reacted to their insolence. They attacked him and, although strong, not strong enough for four big bullies. They kicked and thumped him, he fell and hit his head, then he died in my arms. I want him to be buried in the graveyard where |I was born and where my family is buried, but my brother will not allow it. He will be buried in the Churchyard. Now I must run the farm alone without my husband." She began to cry again, silently. "My wonderful husband Gregoire had fought in the Foreign Legion against worse men than these fascist thugs. He has been awarded many medals, but their cowardice meant four of them attacked him, three from behind - he didn't stand a chance. I think my brother is behind the attack; he has always hated Gregoire. His wife has enough sense to leave him now and bring the children here and leave him to his gambling, his mistress and his politics and his friends on the far-right. He was never at home looking after the Chateau, which had been my family home for many generations." She fell silent and studied Matias for the first time. "My father had not agreed with me marrying Gregoire, and my brother has carried out his wishes, to the letter, banishing me from ever setting foot on the estate. My mother left me this farm and the rich land with it, which galls my brother as we have looked after the land much better than him. Now he is dangerous and full of self-importance, and he supports the German ideology. Yes, he is very dangerous," she added. Claribel was very upset, she didn't care who this man was. She was just grateful for human company and support.

Matias was moved and left her; returning a while later he knocked on the door again. "I have chopped some logs for you," was all he said.

"Please come in and sit down," Claribel said, putting in front of him a plate of fresh green salad from the vegetable garden and goat's cheese with herbs, with bread she had made earlier. Matias was in very hungry, although he felt guilty eating under the roof of a dead man he'd never known. They drank a little wine, a gift from Cressida, then drank water from the well with a little Vin de Noix made the year before from their own walnut trees. He then told her a little about himself, how he had walked from Spain as the war ended and the Nationalists were winning and how he was sickened with all the killing. How the battle of Ebro had changed his perception of war and he realized the futility of fighting. He had continued to fight for the Republic until January 1939 and realized he needed to leave. He told her how he had been living the life of a hermit for almost a year and had found some peace. That is, he told her, until a young man arrived recently with his horse and cart with two young children, and he had felt the pull of family life. "Just like now, sitting here talking to you," he added.

To his amazement, Claribel then said, "I know who you are talking about. The young man is called Alex, he was here very recently with his two sisters, his brother and a dog called Tanner." She told him about his meeting with Cressida who was travelling to Britain with two companions and her horse and dog. She told him as well about the pouring rain and how wet they all were, and Alex had helped her husband on the farm for the next few days. Because of his help she had some goats hidden away from prying eyes thank goodness. "He had two sisters and a brother Claude who I think was ten years old."

"Two sisters?" said Matias puzzled over what she had told him. So, Claribel told him about the young girl who didn't speak brilliant French and her baby boy. They both wondered how Alex had managed to find her on his journey to Claribel's farm.

They chatted comfortably until a young boy appeared with his mother, Clemence, and his twin sisters. Claribel introduced them to Matias. She began: "Meet Matias Otero, he has been helping me."

Matias solemnly shook hands with Clemence, the young boy and his six-year-old twin sisters. "Pleased to meet you," he said. Matias then went to the door and told Claribel he would leave before it was too late. He thanked her for her kindness and was sorry not to have had the opportunity to meet her husband. He wished her well. "No, please stay at least until after the funeral, I can pay you and I need the help – unless of course you wish to find Alex? I know he is now at my cousin's place, the Chateau de la Cascade, with Aurielle and Marcell and they're all safe there, for now, anyway. As safe as any of us," she added.

Matias needed no more persuasion as he liked her very much, the farm and the food, and she clearly needed help. With that, as if he had been there for ever, he went outside to chop some more wood for the fire.

Chapter 12

Journey Through France

As the engine roared into life, I slowly let out the clutch and the horsebox stalled. Marcell came to my window and shouted to me: "Sid, you must start in first gear, you have a lot of weight on, don't go straight to second as we usually do; she needs driving through every gear now."

I started again and working through the gears we slowly moved off down the wonderful avenue of sweet-smelling lime trees. By the time I had reached the narrow road at the end of the drive to begin our journey, I could hardly see where I was going as the tears streamed down my face. We drove in silence, and I cried in silence until I had to find my handkerchief to blow my nose. After that we remained silent apart from Nico telling me where to turn and driving me mad with his instructions from the end of the drive where he even told me we turned right which of course I already knew. The lorry was very sluggish, and I remember thinking it was going to be a long journey at this slow speed. Nico continued to give me instructions at the junctions and became very irritating, even telling me if we were approaching a hill or bend, but eventually I grew to value his input and concentrate on my driving. Every hill and bend I was told about by Nico, prepared me to be in the right gear or going at the right speed to approach the hazard. I have to say my confidence grew and my complete faith in his judgement grew at the same time; meanwhile, Malissa just read her book and hardly ever looked up. We made slow steady progress with Nico's map reading and orienteering skills guiding me along rough little roads on which Tantetta and Nico had chosen for us to travel because they were so quiet. We travelled for four hours and then stopped near Chateauroux to let Hermes out to stretch her legs, have a drink, eat some grass, and Odin ran around delighted to be free from the confines of the horsebox cab.

We drank some homemade lemonade and ate chunks of fresh baguette and ham and then led Hermes back up the ramp, and we all piled into the cab again to continue our journey. We found the farmhouse called Moulin a Vent easily – it was two kilometres outside a village. Arriving at the farmhouse at 4.30 pm we were in good time to meet our hosts, let Hermes into a paddock and give Odin a decent walk. Odin nearly had a run in with the large rangy farm dog which came over to inspect him and for a moment I wondered if they would have a go at each other, which would have been embarrassing, but Odin wagged his tail, and they accepted each other. We had coq au vin for tea with a delicious tarte tatin for dessert, served with cream. Claribel and her husband Gregoire Albertine were delightful hosts and did everything to make us comfortable and welcome. They kept hens, geese, Gauloise cockerels for the pot, goats for their milk and cheese, plus bees for honey and a very productive vegetable garden. They had a walnut orchard to make walnut liqueur as, apparently, many years before, they had suffered from Phylloxera in the area, a pest which attacks grape vines by the roots, and any attempts to grow vines there now would be disastrous in the contaminated soil. A very busy and, obviously, a happy couple who were very pleased with the dry cured ham Tantetta had sent them and thrilled with the case of our best white wine. Their farmhouse was old, large, and rambling, with a steep roof almost to the floor on one side. It was comfortably furnished with quality furniture and oil lamps still in use. (As was usual in most farmhouses and houses in rural France then.) We chatted about their farm and the talk got round to the more than likely invasion by the Nazis. They were both worried but had no intention of leaving their farm or animals, and said everybody always needed food which they hoped to carry on providing. Their produce they sold in the surrounding area and at the local weekly village markets. It came up in the conversation that Monsieur Albertine had been in the Foreign Legion, which fascinated Malissa, and she became animated, discussing with him previous battles in various countries and tactics used by the Foreign Legion. It was a pleasant evening, which soon ended as they were early risers and we needed to be on our way at first light and we were all very tired by then. Madame Albertine showed us to our bedrooms, and Malissa and I were surprised to find we were to share a twin room. Neither of us commented, although I think we both thought it strange. We just got on with the situation without a word. Times were strange and about to get more so, though we were blissfully unaware of it at the time. Nico was taken to his room, and we were shown where the bathroom was. After cleaning our teeth and a quick flannel wash, we were all in bed – the house fell silent – except for Odin snuffling around trying to make his bed comfortable on the floor next to my bed.

It was soon morning, not even light, when our door was knocked on by Madame Albertine telling us it was time to get up and have something to eat. I rushed to the one and only cold, linoleum-floored bathroom and had a strip wash in barely warm water then rushed back to dress, passing Malissa in as much of a rush on her way to the bathroom. It wasn't that we needed to hurry to leave, it was just too chilly in the upstairs of the house to stand still! As soon as I went downstairs with Odin, the smell of freshly baked bread hit me and the kitchen was warm, lit by two oil lamps with the fire burning brightly and fuelling the oven which was set into the wall next to the fire. The kettle was simmering on a trivet over the fire and Madame Albertine filled the three mugs on the table with foaming hot chocolate topped up with fresh milk just fetched from the byre where the goats were being milked. The bread, fresh from the oven, was warm, and I dipped it into my hot chocolate and will never forget that delicious taste. Malissa preferred coffee in the morning and I wondered what she would say, but she sat at the large, scrubbed pine kitchen table and like me devoured her bread and drank her hot chocolate in silent appreciation. Finally, only minutes later, Nico arrived and slid into his seat, looking around the room approvingly, and he, also without a word, sipped his hot chocolate and dipped his fresh crusty bread into it, French style. Odin sat next to the fire, keeping an eye on Boss, the big, rangy, cattle dog also in front of the fire. I went outside to fetch Hermes from the paddock, tied her up and gave her a feed of damped chop with a small handful of oats. I quickly flicked a dandy brush over her coat to get rid of any mud and left her eating, then went to the barn to say 'au revoir' to Monsieur Albertine. He had just finished milking the goats and was putting them out to pasture for the day with their baby kids. His next job was to take the milk to the dairy, and I went to see the gorgeous young kids that were kept in a pen full of straw and hay. They were bleating and waiting to be fed. We walked back together, Monsieur Albertine carrying the heavy milk churns full of the morning's milk, and I followed him into the dairy next to the house. Inside there were rows of goats cheeses ready to mature or take to market. It was cold but everywhere was spotlessly clean and meticulously organised. We went to the house and Malissa and Nico were ready to leave. Madame Albertine gave me a large round goat's cheese, some fresh warn baguettes and some pain au chocolat, all wrapped up in oiled cotton and tied with string. I had brought my overnight bag downstairs and Malissa had kindly brought Odin's bed into the kitchen, and so we made our way outside. I loaded Hermes into the horsebox and gave her a full hay net to eat on our journey. Monsieur Albertine had kindly refilled all our water containers and as instructed by my Tantetta had fuelled up the lorry with fuel paid for by her.

We said our au revoirs and I was sad not to be able to spend more time getting to know this delightful couple; and then we were on our way again. This time my transmission through the gears was much smoother from the start and I accepted Nico's expertise with the map reading. Yet again we travelled for four hours before stopping for a break and we stopped on a side track which led up to an old, ruined castle on a hill. I parked up under some trees to provide shade for us and Hermes as the sun was getting hot. We climbed out stiffly and I opened the cloth containing the fresh baguettes provided for us by Madame Albertine for our lunch. Full of goats' cheese and mixed with herbs, they were delicious. We drank elderflower cordial made by Aurielle and munched last year's apples, which had been kept in the cool storeroom off our dairy at the Chateau. Malissa climbed the stony track up to the castle, watched by Nico; I followed with Hermes to stretch her legs and mine. Malissa, who had set off ahead, shouted to us, and tying Hermes to a post and joined by Nico, we scrambled up the steep rocky slope to see what she wanted. "Look" was all she said. We looked to where she was pointing and all I could see in the distance was a 'snaking line of black' on what looked like a road. Nico rushed down to the horsebox and reached into the cab, then ran back to us, carrying a small case. Opening the case, he pulled out a telescope. As always, I thought, very efficient. He fiddled around with it and froze before handing it to me. I could not understand what I was looking at. I thought Malissa had remarkable eyesight, until I realized that she already had a telescope too. I looked through and I could not believe or understand what I was seeing: it was a never-ending long line of vehicles and people slowly walking along the road. Some had cars, some had horses and carts piled high with belongings and some pushed wheelbarrows.

I handed the telescope back to Nico and asked, "What do you think it means?"

"It is the road going south which is a long way away and I think it is an exodus of people fleeing the German army. We need to keep going. Come on, we must get on with our journey." In silence we loaded up Hermes and with Odin we jumped in the cab and, suddenly, we felt fear in our hearts, well definitely in mine.

It was eleven-fifteen in the morning when we set off and we didn't stop again until just before three o'clock in the afternoon. I was feeling very stiff and tired. We came to a junction after a very long tree-less, exposed road and to the left was a rough track leading off towards a small wood and I needed to go to the lavatory. I decided the wood would do just fine so I started to turn the horsebox.

"No," said Nico, "we go turn right here."

"It's OK, I must go to the lavatory, and I need a drink and so does Hermes and Odin. I can soon turn round and get back onto the right road."

I unloaded long-suffering, gentle Hermes who was glad of the stop and began to crop grass. I had pulled off the road so that we were hidden from view but in a small clearing surrounded by trees. We all had a drink and then we heard some noises like gunfire. Malissa looked up at the sky, but the trees hid her view at first, then a few minutes later some aircraft flew low over us and off into the distance towards the road to the south.

"They didn't see us," said Malissa. "We should stay here for a short time to make sure they don't come back this way, they were German planes."

"I must go into the woods," I said, holding my little camping trowel and toilet paper as I scuttled into the undergrowth. A little later, as I filled in the hole, I turned, because I could hear a stream gurgling nearby. I saw a stone bridge a little further along the track, so for no reason I can think of other than natural curiosity and thinking we could fill our water carriers from the stream, I headed towards the bridge but came to an abrupt stop when I saw a car nearly on its side next to the stream. It was a very smart, big brown and custard-yellow coloured car, with lots of shiny chrome on its fenders and wing mirrors. I struggled through the undergrowth to see if anyone was in it as it half straddled the stream and had obviously come off the bridge. I could see the chauffeur in the front seat wearing a uniform with dried blood coming from his mouth and his eyes wide open and I was sure that he was dead. I was horrified and rushed back to fetch the others. I was learning to trust them as both seemed so worldly-wise. Nettled and prickled by thistles, I stumbled back to the clearing and almost speechless I beckoned to them to follow me, managing to whisper, "come quickly there is a crashed car", as we headed back to the stream. Fortunately, they had enough sense to follow me, and Nico, assessing the situation, went to see if the chauffeur had a pulse. He did not. Together we opened the back door, not an easy task as it lay at an angle. Nico wriggled in to see if the women on the back seat was alive. "No pulse," he said, as he backed out and stood up.

"What's that?" I whispered.

"What's what?" he said. "She's very dead."

"No, listen, I heard a whimper. There it is again," I said, and this time I climbed reluctantly in beside the dead lady and peering under her coat could see a furry little dog. It whimpered again. I put my hand in to try to get it out from the foot-well of the back seat and as I did so could feel a small, warm human hand. I recoiled quickly, and gasped.

"What is it?" asked Malissa.

"A child's hand and I think it's still warm. Wait a minute, I can reach the little dog." I carefully put my hand under the little dog and passed it to Malissa. It growled at us. I lifted the lady's coat from the hem thinking it was a heavy, expensive material and located a child's head covered in dark curls. I felt at the side of her neck and there was a pulse. "I need help please, she is alive." Just then the car creaked and shifted. I managed to put one hand under her arm and pulled, and as I eased the child out Nico reached into the car, grabbed her arm and together we lifted her out.

The little dog wriggled in Malissa's arms and whined towards the little girl. I got out of the car and Malissa passed the dog to me, took the child from Nico and we all headed back to the horsebox. We crowded round Malissa as she sat on the ramp and

instructed me to fetch a blanket which she wrapped round the
little girl. None of us could see any evident injuries or blood on
the child.

"It looks like the lady cushioned her on impact," said Malissa.
"Go back to the car and see what luggage there is, it might tell us
something about who she is or who they are. I will wrap her up
and keep her warm."

Nico and I went back to the car, and we managed to prise
open the box boot of the Armstrong Siddeley, because that's
what the car was. We discovered a large suitcase and a smaller
one. Opening the small one first it appeared to contain little
girls' clothes and then we struggled to open the big case, but
eventually we managed it, to find it contained ladies' clothes.
Digging deeper, we discovered a jewellery box and in a concealed
pocket inside the case with more pouches containing money and
jewellery. "Look for her handbag in the car," said Nico. "No wait,
I'll go, I'm slimmer."

'Cheeky,' and he slid into the car and found a leather handbag.
Carefully opening the glove compartment of the car, he found a
revolver and some more papers.

I was getting nervous about the time, the road ahead and
our journey, and suggested we went back. Then I had a thought.
"Wait," I said, "do you think the hem of her coat is heavy?"

Nico pulled out a pocketknife and slit open the hem of the
lady's coat hem – as he did so, diamonds fell out. We hurriedly
gathered them up, then made our way urgently back to the
horsebox. Malissa had lifted the child onto the front seat in the
cab and was watering Hermes when we got back.

We put the suitcases and handbag into the back of the
horsebox over in the Luton which was the part of the horsebox
that went over the cab, and I was backing out of the groom's

door when I heard a horse's hooves clip-clop sound. A strange sight came into the clearing and was as surprised to see us as we were them. A Normandy type of horse, a bay, was pulling a large bakers' cart. A young man dressed in oilskins and an old hat got down and walked over to see us.

"Bonsoir, avez-vous de l'eau s'il vous plait?" he asked.

Nico brought him a container full of water and gave it to him. Two children emerged from the back of the cart and a Brittany spaniel hunting dog with a very waggy tail jumped down. I thought I could hear hens in the back too.

"Bonjour, ou allez-vous tous?" I asked, very curious to find out who on earth they were and where they were heading.

"Nous allons en Espagne," said the young man, taking off his hat politely.

"Desole de demander. Je suis curieux." Then I asked Nico to fetch some cups for them and for no reason I spoke in English.

"Ah vous etes Anglais?" the young man asked and then spoke to us in good English. "These two are my brother and sister Claude and Simone, and my dog Tanner and my mare Trudi," he told us.

"I am Sid and my friends Nico and Malissa and my dog Odin and my mare Hermes," I introduced us to him.

The children had moved as near as they could to their brother and stared at us shyly, Odin went over to fuss them, and their dog was friendly and sniffed Odin.

"It's a long way to Spain and it is still a troubled country," said Nico. "What makes you want to go there?"

"I want to be un viticulteur," he said. "I am sorry, I have not introduced myself: I am Alex Bouchet," and he bowed to us.

"We are travelling north to St Malo to catch a boat to England," I told him.

"Why are you travelling to England?" he asked.

"My home is in Norfolk in England and my friends have business there," I replied.

"With your horse?" he said incredulously.

"Indeed, with Hermes. I travel with my horse as you do your horse," I informed him, smiling.

He turned to his horse and took her out of the shafts, but left her harness on. "She is old and very tired; we have been travelling for fourteen days now and we go slowly as I don't want to hurt her, and I am travelling on the back roads and avoiding villages when I can."

"Why?" asked Nico.

Alex explained how his Papa had joined the French army as a boulanger with his older brother to feed the French troops fighting the Nazis and that his wife, the young children's mother, had returned to Poland to nurse her sick mother in January this year and had not returned yet. The children were his half-brother and sister, his own mother was dead, but she had been a nurse and was English and had lived in Somerset before marrying and settling in France. Now his uncle's half-German wife was coming from Paris to run the bakery and she was sending the horse for slaughter and getting a van. He just couldn't work with her in the boulangerie, she was too bossy, so he has left and taken the horse and has been worried about the Force Publique trying to find him as he was a horse thief. The words all came out very quickly as if it was a kind of relief for him to tell us. "I have been the boulanger now in the shop whilst my Papa is away, but I cannot work with Hildegarde so I must follow my dream to run a vineyard and to learn all about wine and wine making. I must take my brother and sister with me as Hildegarde has a son who is so spoilt and cruel to his cousins."

Wow, now that was a fair story, I thought, and a young man after my own heart. Malissa told him we thought the Nazis had invaded or were about to invade France – we weren't sure which – and it would take too long to get to Spain, and they might not let him in.

"I have all our passports," he said earnestly.

"Look, let's have a drink," I said.

I offered Alex and the children ham and fresh bread, cheese, tomatoes, and apples with elderflower cordial to drink. Malissa went into the cab to check on our new passenger, so I followed to see how she was. The little girl was sitting up holding the little dog, staring straight ahead but saying nothing, no tears, nothing.

"I think she might have been concussed, or perhaps she is in shock," said Malissa. "She ought to see a doctor."

"Yes, I agree, but I don't know where we will find one. We need to be on our way. We were ahead of ourselves before our stop, but now we are going to be late arriving at our next overnight destination, and we need to be off very early tomorrow. I have an idea; I like this young man. I think he should head for the Chateau where he can learn about wines and help Marcell and Joseph. They need all the help they can get now we have left. I'm going to write two letters now: one for Marcell and Aurielle, and one for Monsieur and Madame Albertine who would put him up tonight I am sure and he could be at the Chateau de la Cascade in two days' time, saving him from these dangerous roads."

"Good idea," said Malissa. "Tell Nico, and he will give him directions."

I told Nico, who approved of my plan and laid out the map on the back of the cart while he discussed the best route with Alex. I also told Alex to feed his mare with some of our good hay as I set about writing my letters of introduction for him. Fortunately,

Alex could read a map as well as Nico and they discovered by using the map he had with him they could knock hours off the journey by using little known tracks travelling across the country.

It was now getting cold and looked like we were in for a storm, the clouds were thickening, and it was becoming very dark. I was feeling very sorry for Alex who didn't look old enough or big enough to be out on the road with his mare and family on the precarious journey he was taking. I urged him to leave and to arrive at the Albertines' farm as soon as possible. It was only just over an hour since we had met but I felt anxious for him and was urgently telling him to be on his way. At least his old mare Trudi had been fed and 'watered' and had enjoyed at least a short rest. I gave him a large piece of ham and some more bread for his journey, helped him put his lovely strong mare to the cart and wished him good luck. Saying au revoir to him and his shy young brother and sister, I said a prayer for a safe journey and no more German planes flying overhead.

After he left and anxious about time, we rushed around to load up Hermes and continue our journey north. Now we had two new passengers, both very tiny, very sweet and very quiet.

The road was devoid of traffic, and we made our way as quickly as we could. I concentrated on my driving, hoping the rain would hold off. We had about three hours of travel ahead of us and didn't need any more holdups. I had been hoping to arrive before dark and this was still my intention, but, yet again, we encountered a new problem. We had been driving for just over an hour when I saw a sad sight at the side of the road: a donkey on its side in a ditch, trapped by the cart it had been pulling. There was not a person in sight and there was no way I could drive by and not help the poor creature. Malissa agreed and Nico sighed but knew better than to argue with us. We jumped down (Odin delighted to enjoy another break) and using Nico's pen knife we freed the little fellow from the harness and pulled the trap from his back. He just lay there too frightened to move, so with Nico pushing and me pulling we got him to his feet very wobbly and as he walked forward, he was clearly lame with a cut on his thigh.

"Poor thing," said Nico. "But we must leave him and get going."

Undeterred by his comment, I pulled the ramp down without a word and with Malissa's help guided him toward the back of the horsebox. Well, there was a 'big no' from the little donkey; no way would he go up the ramp until Hermes nickered to him and with this encouragement, he went straight up the ramp and settled, travelling close by her side.

Now we were rushing. We fastened the ramp, piled back into the cab, and set off to our next overnight stop. Nico just shook his head and tutted, Malissa smiled at me, and I smiled back. The little girl remained silent.

Chapter 13

Meeting Jabbo

We arrived at the house near Chateau au Valettes where my father's friend's younger brother owned a vineyard, at five-thirty in the afternoon after over ten hours of travelling and I was tired at this stage. First thing I did was get Hermes out of the horsebox and as there was no one around to ask, I put her in a little paddock behind the stables which had a big oak tree in it. I checked for water and there was water in an old trough and fortunately it was clean. After that I helped the donkey into a stable and had a good look at his wound. Having found a tap I filled one of my buckets, thoroughly washed the wound, which didn't look too bad, and treated it with ointment I fortunately had with me in case of emergencies. The little donkey was as good as gold. I gave him some hay, clean water with some damp chop to eat, and decided it was for the best to leave him in the stable for the night to avoid any flies on his wound.

We carried our overnight bags to the kitchen door of the big house, and I was beginning to worry that no one was there.

Malissa carried the little girl in her arms and the child looked about but made no sound; something else to worry about. I pulled the bell chain and still no one came so we sat on the steps wondering what to do next when an old station wagon appeared and a dishevelled man of about forty-five got out and came over to us, his hand outstretched introducing himself as Howard Bathurst. Out of the back of the large estate car came two untidy, dirty young boys and a chocolate Labrador. "Sorry not to be here when you arrived, I hope that you have found everything you need, I asked my man to prepare a stable for you and Madame Sautaire has left us all a casserole, so we won't starve tonight, eh boys. Do come in, we are busy preparing to leave tomorrow, and it's all been very stressful."

We crowded into the big kitchen which fortunately did smell of food cooking and he ordered us to sit down at the untidy, debris-strewn table, plonked a large cooking pot in front of us and told us to eat immediately. He asked if the horsebox would be all right round behind the stables out of sight and I thought it would. He said Henrietta had insisted it was parked out of sight and I assured him that it was. I didn't know she had left those instructions; I wondered why, perhaps because of the extra fuel I was carrying; she had already warned me to keep it safe throughout the journey. He chatted to Nico who became quite animated, and I was interested to know what they were talking about, but try as I might I could not follow their conversation. I discovered later they were chatting about the merits of various firearms and their individual abilities and uses, just something else about which Nico was knowledgeable. Malissa and I tried to coax the little girl to eat some of the casserole, but she wouldn't, so we gave her soft bread and warm milk and she had a little of that. She was wearing a lovely emerald, green coat with a velvet collar and cuffs and a dress of bright ruby red velvet with smocking across the bodice. As we didn't yet know her name, I called her Ruby and Malissa agreed it was better than just calling her 'little girl'. The two boys were ten and twelve years old and they ate all their food but looked very tired and in need of a bath. The whole kitchen was in disarray, and I don't think any of us cared, we were all too tired.

"Well, I must get these boys into bed," Howard said, "or Genevieve my wife will be annoyed with me."

"Oh is she here?" I asked. "I thought she was in England?"

"Yup, that's where she is and we are joining her tomorrow," he said.

"I see, which port you are leaving from?" I was curious to know.

"Same as you, we are going on the same boat, Nico here has arranged it for us. The thing is, my car is full of our stuff and there isn't any room for the boys and as you have a big horsebox, I thought they could travel with you?" He beamed at me as if there couldn't possibly be any problem with that.

Theodore, the youngest boy, piped up, "And Lucy too."

Good heavens, I thought, there's another child and I must have looked surprised because Howard laughed and told us Lucy was the dog.

I fed Odin and found some food for Lucy about whom they seemed to have forgotten, then took some dog food upstairs for Ruby's little dog.

Then we turned our attention to Ruby (the little girl). Malissa and I took off her coat and dress and put on a nightie we had discovered in her suitcase. We put her into the big double bed that we had been given for the night and Malissa shrugged her shoulders and climbed in next to her to keep her warm. "No point in washing tonight?" she said, as she cuddled the little girl.

I prised the little dog from Ruby's grip and took it and Odin outside for a walk, I kept the little dog on a lead. Howard must have put the boys to bed as he was in the kitchen drinking wine and chatting to Nico. I decided I would go straight to bed and wished them bonne nuit and Nico got up, did the same and followed me upstairs. He had one of the boys' beds and the two boys were bunking in together in the other bed. I had to giggle as I found it funny to think of Nico who was so grown up in so many ways sharing with two young boys. He pulled a funny face, and we headed off to our beds. I let the little dog snuggle up with Ruby, and Odin jumped on a chair in the room to use as a bed. I just couldn't be bothered to make him get down. I slept like a log but was up very early, before anyone else, to check on the donkey and Hermes who seemed to be fine. Having fed them both, I let all the dogs into the garden for a run. I looked in Ruby's suitcase in the horsebox for a change of clothes for her and got out a different dress and cardigan and it was then I discovered an interesting small hairbrush which looked like it was made of something like rosewood inlaid with silver and some initials scrolled on the back. Interesting, I thought. I found her some underwear and went back to the house and started to hunt around for something for breakfast. Fortunately, a woman arrived and introduced herself as Madame Sautaire and she proceeded to clear the debris still on the table from last night's meal and prepare some hot chocolate and coffee. She had brought some fresh croissants and baguettes. I left her and went upstairs to get a cold strip wash and brush my hair before the others used the bathroom. I went to wake up Malissa and found little Ruby already awake and just sitting up in bed, clinging onto the bed clothes, staring and looking terrified. The little dog jumped into her arms, and she looked a little happier as she cuddled the dog. I picked her up and took her to the bathroom to wash her face and take her to the toilet, then as I dressed her and put on her shoes, she never said a word. I checked her for any injuries, but apart from bruises she seemed fine. I knew she needed to see a doctor, but it looked like it would have to wait until we reached England.

I left them eating breakfast and went to the horsebox, started it up and drove round to the kitchen door so we could load up again. I noticed Howard's Austin Shooting Brake crammed full of boxes and packing cases with barely room for him. I had no idea how many hectares of vines were grown here but it was odd there were no workers to be seen anywhere.

My aunt's estate was relatively small – we only had about ten hectares of vines, but they were part of the estate's income, not the whole. Uncle Edmund had been a wealthy man, the Chateau de la Cascade had belonged to his family for generations, even escaping the scourge of the French Revolution. The owners of the Chateau had cared for their tenants over the years, their family motto being, 'Acto non verba. Cura Semper,' 'Deeds not words. Always care'. Tantetta, in her own right, had her own considerable wealth, being the daughter of the Earl of Rimmington. The fact that this place seemed deserted added to my sense of urgency that we must hurry and get to the port. It was now the 7th May and the boat was waiting for us; the deadline given to us was May 8th.

I went to fetch Hermes and the little donkey, tying them both up to the side of the horsebox and brushed them quickly. Malissa brought Ruby down the stone steps and lifted her, still clutching the little dog, into the cab and then went back to fetch our overnight bags. It was decided that Theodore and George, the two boys, would have to sit on my trunk in the back of the horsebox near the groom's door and keep Lucy with them. Finally, we were loaded and ready to leave with Howard shouting that he would be following very soon.

We made good steady progress for the next four hours and then pulled over under some trees for shade and to hide from any aeroplanes and let Hermes and the little donkey out at about eleven-fifteen. I lifted Ruby down and then put her dog on a lead and she just stood where we had put her, watching us get a picnic out. We sat on the ramp and shared cheese and baguettes left over from this morning's breakfast and drank blackberry cordial with water. The road was very quiet, and we had noticed even the villages that we had driven through seemed deserted with all the shutters closed. Where was everybody? In less than an hour we loaded up again to resume our journey. We were all, unusually, very quiet.

It had been arranged by Howard that our next stop would be at a Chambre d'hote near La Guerche-de-Bretagne and it had a paddock for Hermes, which we could use for the night. Our journey remained quiet and the very few cars that were on the road seemed to be going in our direction and overtaking us. We didn't see any people working in the fields or walking in the villages. Nico's map reading skills brought us to the Chambre d'hote which was on a deserted crossroads a few kilometres outside the village. We pulled into the rough looking parking space at the rear of the place, and I went to let them know we had arrived. I knocked and finally hammered on the doors, but no one answered. It was empty – they must have forgotten all about our arrival. We found an outside toilet and an empty paddock at the back which sloped away from the building and gave us a wonderful view of the valley. I put Hermes and the donkey into the paddock and then we all sat on the ramp. Malissa opened our picnic food, and we feasted on salami sausages and the dry cured ham which was lasting very well. The cooked ham had long been finished. We had plenty of fruit cake, but only six apples left, and

I thought we should save those for the morning. We found an outside pump so were able to fill our containers with fresh water and give Hermes and the donkey a drink.

Nico suddenly announced, "Right, I think we should keep driving since our overnight stop is not available. There is a place on the map which looks ideal for us to rest and get a few hours' sleep, then we should only be two hours away from the port. With any luck we will be there for six in the morning." He stopped and turned to me. "If you can manage to drive another three hours, Sid."

I was shocked as I was looking forward to some rest – the jolting of the lorry and noise of the engine was beginning to make me feel ill. I held my hand up and walked to the fence round the paddock where Hermes and donkey were grazing and put my head on my hands on the fence. What should we do? I honestly didn't think I could carry on or was I just being a wimp? I stared down the valley and suddenly I longed for Norfolk and my home and everything I knew that I had left behind so long ago. It was four forty-five and still light – what should I do? I walked back to them all.

"Right, Nico, check the fuel and if we need any get it down off the roof and fill her up. Malissa, get Ruby into her nightie ready for bed, put her on the ledge behind us and make her as cosy as you can. I know there are some cushions up there and a blanket. George and Theodore, go and wash your faces in the water at the pump, get into the back of the box and find a horse blanket and make yourselves as comfortable as you can. You can take two cushions from the cab with you to sleep on and here, take some fruit cake in case you get hungry later. Here is a drink of milk for you both and here, Malissa, is some for Ruby." I went into the back of the box and rooted around for a bottle of good wine, opened it and sloshed some into a mug, hoping it would help to keep me awake. I poured some for Nico and Malissa and just a bit more for me. "Right, it isn't wine I need but coffee, but we don't have any hot water. Just in case we get lucky and find someone who will give us hot water, I've put coffee in the coffee pot ready! Poor Hermes and donkey travelling again so soon, and then they have the long sea journey ahead of them. Come on, please give me hand to put them in. I hope your idea for the next stop, Nico, is a good one."

I didn't think my sudden energy surge would last long, but I would give it my best shot; I turned the ignition, and we lumbered yet again off down the road. Suddenly I slowed to a halt. "Have we got Odin?" I cried.

"He is on the back ledge with Ruby and her little dog," said Malissa. "Lucy is in the back with the boys. I checked the water pump – there was one of our buckets left there so I collected that up and looked around to be sure we had left nothing behind."

Horrified I had forgotten Odin, I decided perhaps wine was not a good idea to keep me awake.

We trundled on with more cars passing us, all were laden with possessions. One and half hours later I knew I was beginning to fade; my neck and shoulders hurt. I asked Nico for some water, which he passed to me, and we carried on slowly for another hour in the dark until I just knew I couldn't drive any further. Suddenly, there was a pin prick of light, a small fire on our left ahead of us and I pulled over on a rough track near to it. I switched off the engine and rested my head on the steering wheel. The silence was bliss. Malissa climbed down and shone her touch over to where the fire was and walked towards it. I suddenly tensed as I realized Nico had a pistol in his hand. A black man came over to us with Malissa, and Malissa said, "He's alone and he has coffee. I can smell it; come on down."

Wearily and warily, we got down and followed them back to the fire, gratefully drinking the strong coffee we were offered. He told us he was travelling to the port in the hope of getting onto a ferry as he needed to leave France before the Nazis arrived since they did not like Jews, gypsies, or black people. He added that he had been with a circus for the last two years and had left them to escape from France. This, he thought, had made a big mistake because the circus was heading for Spain, and he should have gone with them. Nico appeared fascinated by this story and asked where he was from originally. He was Moroccan and so we agreed he should have travelled to Spain. However, it seems that there was something else involved in his decision to travel north.

"What did you do in the circus?" asked Nico.

He seemed reluctant to tell us and just then Hermes shifted in the box and blew through her nostrils. "You have a horse with you?" He seemed incredulous and then told us he had a horse with him too.

"Where?" Nico asked.

"I hid him from the road, he is tethered behind those trees." He took us in the dark to show us his beautiful grey Lipizzaner stallion.

Nico was enraptured. "He is magnificent, how far have you ridden him?"

"From Sarlat, I have been on the road for weeks," he told us and asked, "Where are you all going?"

"We're going to St Malo to catch a boat to England," I said.

"If you can get there in time I can get you on the boat," said Nico.

I was beginning to think Nico was a bit of a fantasist, always saying he could arrange passage on this boat, ship, whatever it was – it kept on getting bigger in my mind.

"I can't drive any further tonight and there is no room for you in the horsebox, but I could do with unloading my horse and donkey for a few hours and trying to get some sleep. Is there a field near here for my horse?"

"No, only a track leading up to I don't know where," he said.

"Thank you for the coffee; it was just what I needed. D'accord, I will just get her off and tie her to the side with a hay net." I unloaded Hermes and the donkey, tied them up to the side of the box and offered them some water, then I then gave them both some damp chop and Hermes a handful of oats.

"I am sorry I have no food for you. I have not eaten all day – do you have a little bread I could eat?" asked the man.

"Of course," said Malissa quietly and rummaged behind our seats for some salami and bread and gave it to him. He thanked us, gave a little bow and told us his name was Jabbo. He was obviously very hungry as he wolfed the food down and then without another word went back to his campfire to sleep on a bed roll. We put up the ramp and quietly climbed in through the groom's door over the sleeping boys and tried to make ourselves as comfortable as possible on the straw in the back. Nico decided to stay in the cab with Ruby (and his pistol) and we all went quiet as we tried to get comfortable and snatch some sleep.

Chapter 14

At The Docks

I don't remember going to sleep, I just remember being woken up in the dark by Nico. It was two o'clock in the morning and I didn't want to get up.

Malissa woke up and whispered to her brother, "What is the matter, why are we getting up now?"

"Come on," he said, "I've made some hot coffee and filled the flask to take with us. Jabbo has set off now to try to make it to the boat before she sails. I have given him and his dog some food and I hope you don't mind some chop and oats for his horse as well." He gave me some coffee.

"Not at all," I said, "thanks for the coffee. Fair exchange. What dog?"

"He has a small white dog which rides in a kind of saddle bag, it's a circus dog, it can ride on the horse's back, it's brilliant." Nico was clearly a circus fan – who would have thought it, this quiet studious intelligent young man, was bowled over with Jabbo, his horse and dog.

"How long have they been gone?" I asked.

Nico checked his watch. "They left one and a half hours ago. Do you need to give Hermes a walk?" he asked.

I agreed that I should and jumped up to untie my sleepy mare and walked carefully as it was still dark, and I didn't know what I might be walking on. I was back in less than ten minutes as it was scary in the dark, and I drank some more coffee. "It's not possible for Jabbo to make the journey as you know his horse is an old horse, the journey will be too much for him," I ventured.

It wouldn't be easy for any of us, but I suppose we could move the water buckets and feed up onto the roof and try to make way for him for a few miles to help him, but I can't expect us all to travel so uncomfortably for hours.

"Do you believe the horse is his?" asked Nico.

"I'd have thought maybe not, as you say, it is old, and circuses can't afford to keep animals they can't use in the show. Perhaps he has stolen it."

He shrugged and looked away. Oh well, no point in dwelling on it; Jabbo and the horse needed help now I thought. The boys and little girl were still sleeping so quietly, we loaded up the donkey and Hermes as quietly as is possible to load two equines, closed the heavy ramp and set off on our journey again.

It was awful driving in the dark on very black, unlit rough roads in rural France with not the most brilliant headlights on the horsebox, our journey was slow, and my eyesight was strained. All three of us were intent on watching the road ahead. Many of the rural roads in France were little more than rough tracks. All went well, if slowly, for an hour and then Malissa gave a small shriek telling me to watch out – and there half on the road half on the grass verge was a car. I swerved to miss it as gently as anyone can swerve a loaded horsebox and braked at the same time. It looked like it had been abandoned as the bonnet was up, I just kept going, hoping that I hadn't woken the children or upset the donkey and Hermes. It was a close call, and now I was even more alert and nervous, straining to watch the very dark road as we slowly continued our journey towards the port.

We passed more cars, some parked, some just pushed off the road and ditched, possibly we decided because they had run out of fuel. It was very scary just making sure I didn't collide with one.

"I have looked on the map and 'he' should be near the next village. I told him to stop there for a rest," said Nico casually.

So, he had guessed that I would try to help, and I smiled to myself. "OK, we will stop there and have a drink." After two hours I didn't think I could drive any further, but I knew I just had to so willed myself on with a sense of relief – surely one stop would not hurt, I thought.

It was very quiet in the village, no one stirred, and we parked in the middle of the square near a water trough. Even here I dare not let the donkey or Hermes out. We all stretched our legs, well the three of us did – the children were still asleep. We had a drink of water and some fruit cake, and our ears strained to hear a horse, but all remained quiet.

"We have to go, I'm sorry," I said. "We still have a way to go and there will most likely be a queue to the port."

As I turned and put my foot on the step to get into the horsebox we heard a faint clopping of a horse. Nico jumped down and ran a short way along the road. The white horse came into sight, and we were all pleased and relieved to see him. The horse was hot, sweaty, and obviously already tired., Jabbo jumped down and sounding despondent said, "Thank you for waiting for me, but you must go on, we will never make it; thank you for your help."

"We are going to give you a lift," Nico said.

"How?" said Jabbo.

We outlined our plan, and he jumped back on to his tired horse and followed us as I drove to the outskirts of the little village where we would not disturb the villagers. We lowered the ramp and Jabbo climbed up onto the roof and we passed him the horse food and buckets to put behind the wood screens put on by Marcell to hold the hay and fuel, leaving, hopefully just enough room in the horsebox for the horse. He took the horse up the ramp and he just fitted in. Jabbo said he would ride with the animals in the back, so we closed the ramp and slowly pulled off. I could tell immediately we were very heavily loaded. Not only would our journey be slower, but we would use more fuel now.

Finally at four-thirty in the morning I slowed to a stop and said I just had to go to for a wee and Malissa agreed so we jumped down and went right at the side of the road, with Odin too, in the dark and then we waited for Nico to pee as well behind the lorry. We all climbed back in, and Ruby stayed asleep, so we all had a drink of water. At this point we finally joined the main route to St Malo. On we went again, until Nico said he thought we were only three miles from the docks. After this we noticed there were more and more cars parked, waiting to get to the docks. I overtook them at the beginning, but it became more and more difficult to go round them and we ground to a halt at about five o'clock. Nico then said he was going to go ahead on foot and find out where exactly we needed to be as he thought there was a way for us to avoid the queue and get to where the boat was docked. This, however, made me anxious.

"No, Nico, we should stick together, please don't leave us here."

Malissa shrugged her shoulders and said, "He will be fine. He will run, he has won many cups for running and he is fit."

Was there no end to this young man's talents.

"Do you have a pistol, Sid?"

"No, of course not, why would I?"

"I do and it's loaded," said Malissa and she reached into my glove compartment and pulled out a gun. "It's a Webley MK VI revolver one of the most powerful top-break revolvers ever produced." She then passed me the revolver we had found in the glove compartment of the crashed car. "It's an Enfield No.2 revolver, you'll be fine with this. You can shoot, I take it?"

"Yes of course, I just don't like them. Is it loaded?" I asked.

"Of course, and make sure you are ready to use it if we need to," she added. "Nico is an expert on firearms. In this weird situation we both carry, you should too."

I was speechless – who are these people, I thought, why they are here, why are they so calm and capable?

I stared into the gloom and ahead at the long line of cars and could see a slither of pink-grey light in the sky: the dawn was coming. Ruby stirred but carried on sleeping, bless her, the poor mite, she was really no trouble. I slumped down in my driving seat as best as I could and putting a cushion next to the side window, I closed my eyes and fell asleep. I don't know for how long but woke to knocking. At first, I couldn't understand where it was coming from, then I realized the boys in the back were awake and wanted to come out. Malissa woke up too and lifted Ruby onto her knee.

"Can you get a drink for all of us please and I will let the boys out."

I opened the jockey door, and it was then the thought crossed my mind that we had never seen their father on the road; he had never caught us up. The boys squeezed in with Malissa and we all ate some of yesterday's bread and some fruit cake and drank some water. The tiny bit of milk we had left, I gave to Ruby.

"Oh, who are our new travelling companions in the back?" enquired Theodore calmly, as if a strange black man, a big white horse, and a little dog riding in the back was normal.

"Just some more crew I've picked up, just like you two," I joked.

I went to the ramp and let Jabbo, his horse and dog out, but still not daring to let mine out. Animals fed and watered, with fruit cake for Jabbo, I climbed back into the cab. We shared out the rest of the water and fruit cake then we fell silent as we waited and watched people emerge from their cars and scuttle off into the undergrowth at the side of the road return to their cars to stand around and stretch their legs.

All seemed calm so I suggested we got out to stretch our legs but stay next to the horsebox. I was very worried about Hermes and the donkey, but deemed it too dangerous to take the ramp down again at this moment in case Nico returned and we needed to move. I went through the groom's door to check on my wonderful patient mare and patted her and little Donk – I thought that's what I would call him. Feeling very guilty about their lengthy incarceration in the box, I climbed over to where the boys had slept and back to the groom's door in time to see Nico jogging back to us. Malissa, Ruby, Theodore, and George just stared at me as I climbed down onto the road.

"What," I asked, "what are you looking at?"

Then I realized what a state they were all in; George and Theodore had looked dirty and untidy when we first met them, but now, they looked even worse; they had straw sticking out of their clothes and hair and very dirty faces and hands and they had been eating with those, ugh. It was then I realized Malissa, whom I had only seen tidy, was dirty, scruffy and was now looking as bad as the boys, and she too had straw in her hair and her usually lovely long, black hair was literally in knots and her clothes were dishevelled. Looking at Nico, I realized poor neat, smart Nico with his wavy, black hair looked the same as Malissa, with his hair sticking straight up and full of straw. It was then I realized why they were looking at me and my hands flew to my hair, and I just knew it was a tangled mess and I could feel straw sticking out everywhere. I looked down at my jodhpurs now feeling glued to me as I had worn them for two days and slept in them and then my hand felt a large damp patch on my bottom. I looked at my dirty brown hand and smelt it – I had slept in horse poo. The look of horror on my face must have been the catalyst because at that moment they started laughing, which then started me off and I laughed until my tummy hurt.

Just then a jeep came speeding up to us with two soldiers holding Lee-Enfield rifles and I couldn't believe it was Tiff and Scotty, who arrived in time to see us falling about laughing. Tiff came over and then backed off and started laughing too. "Good journey, Sid, well done, you made it, but you don't half pong." He then noticed the crew travelling with me. "Good heavens, where have you all come from, Hamelin?"

Being dumb I had no idea what he was talking about, until Malissa said laughing, "The Pied Piper of Hamelin."

It was funny that I had been to school and been a lonely person apart from one friend, spent years in France mostly painting, walking my dog, and riding on my own, and now I had managed to collect all these people on this one journey.

"We need to move immediately – can I drive for you?" said Tiff.

"No, I understand this lorry and it understands me. I have driven it here and I can do the rest. Just show us where we need to go. Oh, and the guy with the horse is with us, so give him a chance to keep up."

"What, there are more?" He peered behind the box and jumped into the jeep, laughing.

"Stop, can you give these two boys a lift – they would love it and we would have more room in the lorry please?"

"Well, OK, we don't have far to go," said Scotty. "Come on, hop up."

We navigated a few cars and very soon we took a left turn down a small track leading towards the sea and finally through some big gates which were opened for us by soldiers, and we were on the dockside. Jabbo, his horse now rested, kept up, cantering behind us. Now I was very scared about what was going to happen next. We were told to leave the horsebox, unload the horses and dogs and then we watched as the horsebox was craned on board. A ramp was put in place which had railings on both sides, and we were told to lead the donkey on first, but I knew better – taking Hermes first who I knew would never look back and would give confidence to Donk and the Lipizzaner to follow onto the boat. Once aboard, there was another ramp down to the stalls in the hold. They were tied securely and then had slings put under them to help with the sway of the ship while at sea. They behaved well. Malissa brought Lucy, Odin and Ruby's little dog on board and we put them into cages near the horses. Ruby started to cry so I told her she would be with her little dog when we sailed. Jabbo refused to leave the horses and his dog, and said he would stay with them all the time. Nico was missing, I didn't know where, and I went up the ramp to the deck to look for him and found him talking to the captain. Well, I think he was the captain – he had braid on his jacket. They were looking at their watches and it appeared the captain wanted to leave. Just then the boys' father, Howard Bathurst, rolled up in his station wagon and the sailors leaping into action put chains on the car and the crane swung it into the hold. Howard Bathurst strode up the ramp looking just as untidy as his sons as he went over to shake the captain's hand and greet Nico. Then some people arrived and at first there appeared to be a discussion about them getting on board. Nico went down to read something they had brought with them, and he then waved them on. The captain shrugged his shoulders, ordered the ramp to be removed once they were on board – there were ten of them. I just couldn't understand – it looked as if Nico was in charge, so I went to ask him what was happening.

"We are getting underway," he simply said. "We must not miss the tide."

"Who are those people that just came, do you know them?"

"No, but your Aunt Henrietta has asked on behalf of Dr Bleumanthall that we give them safe passage to England. She sent a request by telegram for me to see, so they are here. I would not let the countess down, she is a very special lady and has shown us great kindness," he said.

"Nico, how can you be in charge, I don't understand?"

"Oh, it's my boat." And with that he turned leaving me open mouthed in wonder. It was then I was horrified to realise we had been so busy loading; I didn't know if Tiff and Scotty were on board. I could have cried, and I rushed after Nico to find out if they were sailing with us. Nico stopped, smiled, and calmly said, "Of course, they are," and with that he went after the captain.

I found a sort of lounge where people were standing around looking shell-shocked, obviously not sure what to do. They had very little luggage with them. A very attractive, tall blonde-haired girl clung to a big carpet bag, and I suddenly saw a little black nose peeping out. A very young girl had a French bulldog snuggled under her arm partially covered by a shawl. I smiled at them both and decided not to say anything to anyone. I went in search of Malissa and Ruby and found them watching the boat leave its moorings and slip out into from the harbour. It was now six-thirty in the morning and the weather was calm. We had made it so far, now, so fingers crossed for a smooth, safe crossing. Nico came and told us there was food and drinks for us and led us to a wood-panelled dining room where, on a table with a white cloth, was fresh bread, croissants, butter, jam, hot coffee, and hot chocolate. It all smelt delicious and then I saw Tiff and Scotty coming into the room. I was so relieved I nearly threw my arms round Tiff there, until I remembered I hardly knew him, I smelt of horse poo and was filthy! Malissa and I helped little Ruby to some food and hot chocolate which she drank, but she was still not smiling or talking. Theodore and George were with their father, and they were all tucking into the food, and I joined them as I was starving. More food was brought out and the ten people who had just arrived were brought into the room to have some food and drink. Nico was missing and I asked Malissa where he was.

"Oh he's gone to take food to Jabbo," she said.

Thank goodness he had, as I had temporarily forgotten Jabbo was looking after the horses, donkey, and dogs. How could I?

Feeling better, I went down to see Hermes and Odin to find Nico chatting to Jabbo and feeding the dogs at the same time. The dogs were separated in their kennels, and I hated to see them kept in cages, but knew they were better there than being lost overboard should they get loose. The horses were calm and so I left them all and went in search of Tiff. I found him outside the dining room watching the boat leaving the harbour, heading out to the open sea.

"Sorry I smell, but if you can stand it perhaps you can tell me why you are here and where you have been since you left the chateau?"

"We have had orders to escort embassy staff to the various French ports, so the Rolls-Royce came in handy," he told me.

"Have you left it in France?" I asked.

"No, it's here on the boat – it belongs to Nico's father, and he wants it in London now. I can't tell you anymore, sorry. I am very glad you made it here; some feat driving all that way and with so many passengers you did well. You must be very tired. I would love to hear how you met so many people on your trip, but perhaps you would like to get some sleep now, oh, and as for you smelling, I am a farmer's son so it's nothing new to me and I think I'm scruffy too." He was, but it suited him, and he smelt masculine not of horse poo. "I still think you look gorgeous. Come on, I will show you where you can get some sleep."

Glowing with his compliments, I followed him to a small room with comfortable chairs in it and I immediately realized just how tired I was. "Please will you find Malissa and tell her where I am and suggest she brings Ruby here. I will sit here with her while Malissa has a rest."

"Yes, Ma'am, I will go immediately while you stay here," and grinning, off he went. I don't remember Malissa or Ruby coming in, I must have fallen asleep as soon as he left the room.

I slept well until one-thirty and woke up to find Malissa asleep in the room, but no Ruby. I panicked and rubbing my eyes jumped up to look for her. I found her with Tiff, in his arms, looking at some pictures in a child's book in the captain's rest room. It appears she had woken up and Tiff who had also been sleeping brought her out for a drink. She had been playing with the young girl with the French bulldog. Apparently, the book belonged to her, and the young girl was now sleeping next to an elderly bearded man.

"Her grandfather asked if she was your daughter," Tiff said. "He thinks his granddaughter seems to know her."

"Where are they from?" I asked.

"Paris," he told me.

I then told Tiff how we had found the little girl, as I was quite sure she didn't understand English, and she sat on the floor turning the pages of the book. We had coffee and cake brought to us by a sailor and I told how we had found Jabbo and his horse and dog. I told him about our journey, how we had found the poor little donkey and how we ended up bringing the boys along with us and how kind the lovely Albertines had been, and I hoped they kept safe whatever happened to France. Tiff was a good listener and asked where we were travelling to, next. I told him about my home in Norfolk, about my brother and sister and that my brother was in the army and that Alastair, Portia's husband, was in the RAF. My parents were safe in Singapore, but I wished that they were at home. Tiff didn't know my father was a diplomat in Singapore as his orders to rescue Nico and Malissa had come from other government sources which he could not disclose to me.

I decided to go and see Hermes and Odin again and see how Jabbo was, and as I stood up Ruby raised her arms to me to be picked up. I was so happy. I picked her up, cuddled and kissed her; what a breakthrough! Malissa woke up, yawning, and said she would stay with Ruby and read the book to her whilst Tiff and I went down below. The horses didn't look happy, but they were quiet and Jabbo had a soothing voice, he was crooning to them, and they obviously trusted him. Odin and the other dogs were all ecstatic to see us and wriggling their bodies and wagging their tails. We fed them as it was four-thirty and we would be docking around six-thirty. We went back upstairs to the deck and were told a meal would be served at five o'clock in the dining room, so we made our way there and ended up chatting to the other passengers. Dr Bleumanthall had asked Tantetta if she could help them get a passage to England. The beautiful, tall, blonde-haired girl with the dog which fitted into her bag, told me her name was Miriam and she had done some modelling in Paris for the designers Marie-Louise Bruyere known as Madame Bruyere, Coco Chanel, and Madeleine Vionnet, under the French name of Veronique. She introduced me to her family, her young sister Anna-Sara, brother Noah, his wife Zelda and her parents Dr and Mrs Abelman. This interested and impressed me, and we chatted about her life and work, where she lived in the Marais with her parents. Her father was a doctor, a friend and associate of Dr Bleumanthall and her mother, sister, brother, and his wife were travelling to London with their housekeeper and her teenage daughter, Esther, and Mayo Monteux. Their friend and neighbour, the elderly man Jacob Goldbaum, had just lost his wife – they buried her three days ago; it was tragic, but it meant that he could now travel with them to England. The little girl Avigail was his granddaughter, her parents had gone to America to start a new business and had left their little daughter in the care of the husband's mother and father. Miriam had friends in St John's Wood, London and they were going to stay with them until they found a house they could rent. They were all Jewish and feared for their safety if they stayed in France. They were hoping to take the train to London, and I wished them all well and hoped the next leg of their journey would go smoothly for them. I told her my mother had a house in Primrose Hill and my father a house in Chelsea and suggested I ask if the Primrose Hill house was available for them to rent. We exchanged names and addresses and then our meal arrived, a simple vegetable stew rich in Moroccan spices served with chunks of crusty bread; it was all delicious. I then went to help Ruby eat.

Tiff and I stood together, close to the railings on deck as we approached land. Nico came to ask me if the horse would mind being craned off the boat in slings; I was horrified.

"No, don't you have the same ramp that was used before?" I asked.

"Yes, only the captain isn't sure where we will dock in the harbour and if the ramp can be set up. We ship cattle and horses between Albania and Italy and use the ramp, but in designated areas on the docks. I will tell him it is important we use the ramp; don't worry I will sort it out." He marched off up to the bridge and I trusted he would do his best.

We could now see Britain and I longed to be on 'terra firma' with the horsebox and all the animals. Tiff put his arm round me and said, "Look we won't have much time to talk when we disembark, I shall help you load up and then I must go to London immediately. Would it be alright with you, the next time I have leave, if I travel to Norfolk to see you? I want to, very much."

I looked into his eyes and nodded and then he kissed me. I felt a whoosh and heat, an incredible feeling swept all over me and I could hardly breathe, my head went back, and I opened my mouth to feel every sensation of him wash over me. He looked deep into my eyes, smiled, and said, "Is that your first kiss?"

I nodded, having temporarily lost all power of speech.

"I think you just had an orgasm," he joked.

I had to agree I had just had something.

He hugged me tight and whispered, "You're the one, do you know that?"

I just nodded again and felt like crying because we were about to part, but I was happy he felt the same way as me. I put my head on his shoulder and he kept his arms around me. We watched together as the boat manoeuvred into the harbour. For a time, all felt safe and nothing else mattered.

Chapter 15

Arrive In England

The morning weather remained dry and calm as we docked, and the stevedores had to unload the horsebox first with a crane which was just as worrying as when they had put it onto the boat ten and a half hours earlier. Next Howard's station wagon was unloaded followed by the army jeep, the Rolls-Royce, still dirty, and an army ambulance. Then it was time to unload the equines and I was scared for them. There was a lengthy discussion between a port official, Nico, and the captain. I think we won because next the wooden ramp, which was carried on the boat was winched and levered into place, but alarmingly we could see it didn't quite reach the jetty.

Nico waved and shouted, "Get Hermes and the others, they will have to jump the last bit from the ramp to the jetty; the tide is high, but we can't wait here for it to go down."

"You go and get them and tell Jabbo," said Tiff. "I'll wait with Scotty at the bottom of the ramp."

I ran down to where Jabbo was waiting with the horses and donkey and tried to explain the situation.

"The hay," he said. "Tell them to get a bale of hay from the horsebox roof and empty it where they have to jump off, it will give them a softer landing."

"Great idea." I charged back and up onto the deck to shout these instructions to Tiff who passed it on to Scotty and then I saw Scotty climb up the side of the lorry with mountaineering expertise (well, he was from Scotland). I ran back, Jabbo and I untied the horse and donkey, walked them up the steel ramp from the hold and onto the wooden ramp which now led off the boat. Malissa ran to get the little donkey and I half noticed Ruby being held by Miriam. Jabbo and the Lipizzaner went down the ramp and jumped the last three foot onto the jetty making it look easy. I followed with Hermes and never looked at her, just straight ahead. I was able to jump clear of the hay and Hermes had a soft landing. What a good horse she is, I thought, probably just glad to get off the awful rocking boat. Malissa appeared at the top of the ramp with donkey, momentarily hesitated and then walked boldly forward with the little fellow following until they reached the end of the ramp, whereupon he planted four hooves stubbornly and just wouldn't budge. Step forward the British army, and with Jabbo holding his halter rope, Tiff and Scotty physically lifted the donkey onto the jetty, at which point a huge cheer went up from watching passengers and the sailors. We were on British soil, and I was so relieved and grateful to Nico, Malissa, Jabbo, Tiff, Scotty and all the kind crew, I allowed myself a moment of euphoria but then started to worry about getting back to Norfolk.

Miriam brought Ruby to us, and Ruby reached for me and clung to my neck. It was lovely to think we were getting some reaction and trust from her at last.

Miriam said, "I will be in touch when we are settled, good luck with the rest of your journey, au revoir."

Jabbo and Scotty loaded up the horses and donkey whilst I said goodbye to Tiff. Meanwhile Howard came over to us with Theodore and George in tow and asked if I could take them with me as he still had no room for them. I was very cross, but the boys looked miserable so I just agreed they would be fine with us but wondered when they would be picked up.

"Are you driving all the way home now?" he asked.

"No, impossible, it is evening, nearly seven-thirty and it's a ten-hour journey so we are staying with a friend in Dartmoor tonight," I told him.

"I shall be staying in London tonight and will telephone Genevieve to meet you tomorrow. She's in Newmarket so you could meet up in Cambridge or take them to your place and we could pick them up in a couple of days," he suggested.

Not at all happy with that, arrangement, I replied, "No, one of you will meet me in in St Neots the day after tomorrow at five o'clock, and make sure you are there. Come on, boys, sorry, but you are still travelling in the back." I was determined not to have Howard Bathurst organise my life. I didn't look back at Howard Bathurst as I was beginning to think he was a waste of time. He certainly didn't have any time for his two young sons.

We loaded up Lucy the chocolate Labrador, Odin, Jabbo's little white dog, Zippy, and Ruby's tiny pooch, all three equines, Jabbo, Theodore, George, Malissa, Nico and me, and set off once again. Just before leaving I said goodbye to Tiff, who gave me an envelope with instructions to open it at some point on my journey home. Then he cupped my face in his hands, gently kissed me and without another word he and Scotty were on their way, heading off to London in the Rolls-Royce.

As I walked back to the horsebox there were big grins on the faces of everyone on board, even the boys in the back were wolf whistling me as they peered through the window in the back. The Rolls-Royce was fully loaded, heaven knows with what, stuff from the Embassy in Paris I suppose.

The roads around Plymouth were very busy with RL trucks, armoured personnel carriers and military personnel everywhere, but finally we left the chaos behind us and were on our way into the peace and quiet of Dartmoor. I stopped by a red telephone box to ring Merioneth to ask if we could all stay, and I was in luck as no one else was using the telephone or waiting to make a call. I had twenty pounds in British notes and coins for emergencies and I had plenty of pennies with me to make the call, so I put them in the coin slot and heard them drop into the machine then listened for the telephone ringing.

The telephone rang at the Rectory and was picked up by someone sounding very young. I pushed the A button and asked for Merioneth and whoever answered the telephone said hello then put it down and I could hear their feet running away. I thought I had been forgotten, holding this end of the receiver for what seemed ages, but eventually Merioneth came to take the call as I kept feeding pennies into the coin slot. I asked if seven of us and our animals could stay for one or two nights. Of course, she said, yes. I was visiting her after a gap of four years, and they would be thrilled to put us up. No questions asked; now that is what you call a true friend.

We made our slow journey through the narrow lanes to their big old Rectory and Merioneth and her brothers ran down the drive to meet us. Their Labrador was first to greet us. Merioneth's father, The Reverend Berwyn Alfred Jones, was out on Church business, but she assured me he wouldn't mind at all. We unloaded and I introduced her to everyone and the animals, which her brothers were delighted to have staying with them, and we put Hermes and the little donkey into a paddock and the Lipizzaner into a stable. Her brothers quickly bedded it down with straw for the horse. I felt a chill in the air and noticed a damp mist rolling in from the moors and I shivered, not used to such cold air. What a good job I had packed some jumpers. Our dogs all ran free and played with their dog, well Lucy, Zippy and Odin did, but Ruby still clung to her little dog. It was always difficult persuading her to let it go. The best time to feed the little dog and take it for a walk was always when she was asleep. We headed for the house, which was a vast, dark stone Victorian building surrounded by gardens, paddocks, and trees. There was a rookery at the end of one paddock and the young rooks were cawing and being very noisy. A fresh, damp, peaty smell was coming off the moors and a hint of sea air blowing this way. In the paddocks were sheep and a few goats mingling happily with hens, cockerels, ducks, and geese. Merry followed my gaze. "Come on, I know you have been travelling a long way and frankly you all 'pong'; however, Sid, you smell the worst, a mixture of BO, horse hair, horse poo, dogs, petrol and I can't decide what the rest is."

We couldn't stop laughing as we followed Merry along the long hall covered in grey flagstones, up the big staircase then along another landing to an austere but enormous bathroom with a huge clawfoot bath and toilet, the biggest highest cistern I had ever seen and a huge Victorian washbasin.

"All a bit big, isn't it?" said Merry ruefully. "I nearly lose the youngest boys in the bath but it was 'an offer' The Rev. couldn't refuse. You are lucky, we consider today quite warm, there is no heating in here and it's freezing in winter. You can't stand still on the linoleum floor, or you'd get frostbite in your toes. Now you're not supposed to fill the bath with more than four inches of water.

However, water is one thing we have plenty of here on Dartmoor and I built the fire up to heat the boiler as soon as I heard you were arriving, so we should have plenty of hot water by now. All of us lot will wait until the morning to wash so the water is all for you. Bring me your dirty clothes, as our help, Mrs Perkins, will be here for six in the morning and she will do all of yours first thing so they stand a good chance of drying before you leave, even if you go tomorrow. Towels are all ready for you, there on the stand. See you soon." Like a whirlwind Merry bustled away.

We ran the bath and put Ruby in first and discovered a few big bruises, but no cuts, only she must be sore and uncomfortable. We washed her hair, and she was a little angel all the time, lifting her arms to be picked up and have a warm hug in a big bath towel. Malissa took her to find some outgrown pyjamas belonging to the boys and left on the bed by Merry. I had the luxury of a flushing toilet and a hot bath of about eight inches; it felt decadent and was bliss. I reclined and went through the last few days, especially the last few hours and my kiss with Tiff, and I closed my eyes and nearly fell asleep. I let out the water and cleaned a very mucky-looking bath and refilled it for Malissa. I left her to enjoy her bath and took Ruby downstairs to help Merry. Ruby seemed quite pleased with her pyjamas and, with shoes and socks on and an overlarge jumper belonging to one of the boys, was taken outside to see the hens. Alone in the kitchen Merry made me my first good strong cup of proper English tea. I thanked her for having us stay and for the trousers and jumper I was wearing, which were hers. All the time we chatted, Merry was busy preparing the evening meal. I told her all about our journey from the very start and how we had picked up so many children and animals on the way. She then asked me about the man in my life which had apparently already been hinted about by the others. So, I went back to my first meeting with Tiff and our subsequent meeting on the boat, culminating in the kiss.

Then I asked her about her life since returning here from boarding school and I told her that she was doing a very good job, helping to bring up her brothers as they seemed, from first impressions, very well mannered. "Oh, thank you. They're not a bad lot at all, sometimes naughty, but overall, I am very proud of them, and it has given The Rev. time to run the Parish and establish a good rapport with everyone here in the local community."

"Sorry to interrupt, but why do you call him The Rev.?"

"Well as you know it's short for Reverend, and Gruffydd started calling him that as he thought it was his name. He heard so many visitors call him Reverend and just learning to talk he couldn't say the long word, so it became Rev., it caught on as a family joke and has stuck."

Malissa walked in to hear this story and said, "Well I like it. Does he mind if others call him Rev. now?"

"No, it's fine," laughed Merry. "As I was saying, I feel I should be doing something else with my life and I have been doing some nursing training part-time. Now we are at war I think I should be helping. Trouble is The Rev. is dead against me leaving the boys as Aled is only seven and Afan only nine years old and the others are too young to be left in charge. I know it's true, but I need a change, Sid. The Rev. thinks I will enjoy having the goats and making cheese because I am a keen gardener and grow all our vegetables. I look after the animals with Osian's help so perhaps I would, but it's time I contributed to the war effort and got out into the world to see what's going on, not just be here every day looking after my brothers, whom, although I adore, I just need a change. Osian is a brilliant person in the vegetable garden, proper green fingers and good with the animals."

We were all quiet, digesting this heartfelt outburst when The Rev. arrived home and we leapt about to finish preparing the table for tea. We were all introduced to him although I had met him once before at school and he took easily on board that they suddenly had seven guests plus animals to stay and didn't 'bat an eyelid'. He was a lovely man, a true, kind Christian gentleman as well as loving family man and I liked him very much. Merry called the boys in for tea and to wash their hands and they all trooped in and this time I was introduced to them all. Osian the eldest at nearly seventeen shook hands with Malissa and me, then Rhys, fifteen, shook hands with us, then Gruffydd, thirteen, Dylan, eleven, Afan, nine, and Aled, seven, all politely shook our hands. Little Ruby was introduced to The Rev., and she surprised us all by very shyly curtsying, but she remained silent and serious. Next to come in was Nico, so the introductions began again to everyone, and The Rev. asked about the man outside with the beautiful grey horse in the stable. Nico told him who he was, that he had refused to come in and insisted on staying with his horse. The Rev. jumped up. "Nonsense, he must break bread with us," and he rushed outside.

Osian pulled up a chair for Jabbo and sure enough The Rev. brought him into the big kitchen to join us all in prayer before we ate. Jabbo held his hands in front of him with his palms facing the ceiling during Grace and we all said Amen. The Rev. looked at Jabbo thoughtfully. "Ah, my friend, you are a Muslim, forgive me for not thinking before when you said you are originally from Morocco. You are very welcome to join us and share our food. We are delighted to welcome you all here." And without a break he changed the subject: "Osian are the hens, ducks and geese fastened up?"

"Yes, Rev., all in and checked."

"We can't afford to lose any to the fox now with the war getting worse and nearer and the rationing is bound to get stricter too."

"What do you mean, Rev., getting nearer?" asked a frightened looking Dylan.

"Sorry, son, you wouldn't know. Today Germany has invaded France, they have bypassed the Maginot Line and broken through any resistance in the Ardennes, sorry to be the bearer of such bad news. You have all got out just in time. You, Dylan, and all of us, will be fine here. Don't you worry and don't be frightened."

Silence, shock, horror. I couldn't breathe for a minute. I just held out my hands, I don't know why. Malissa took my left hand and Rhys my right hand until we all joined hands round the table in silence. The Rev. prayed: "Dear Lord, God bless all our soldiers fighting abroad, please give them strength and victory and give us strength and love to help each other through the dark days ahead. Amen."

"Amen," we all said in unison. At this stage, for no good reason, I suddenly realized that George and Theodore were still filthy and had not washed yet or changed their clothes. Oh, how the mind works at times of stress.

Nobody moved until Merry said, "I'm so very glad you have arrived safely here, home in Britain, especially as the news is so very bad, but please I have grown the food, and cooked the food, would you please now eat it."

There was a collective sigh of relief and we all tucked in as we were very hungry and us starving wasn't going to win a war tonight. We all enjoyed Merry's wonderful cooking and baking, thick vegetable broth with chunks of soft white bread, farm butter, and apple, rhubarb and ginger pie with custard followed by local cheddar cheese with celery and pickle, all homegrown and homemade.

Not sure about any rationing here! Merry was a brilliant cook. When the boys were told to go to bed, they each went upstairs as good as gold and George and Theodore trotted upstairs with them. I asked Osian to make sure they washed their faces before going to bed. Malissa insisted on taking Ruby up to bed so I could talk to The Rev., Merry and Nico. Jabbo had eaten well, but he had been very quiet and when asked if he was alright, said he was not used to sitting at a table with people and that we were all very kind, but if we didn't mind, he would go and check on Zoltan and take his little dog with him, then go to bed. He had absolutely refused to sleep in the house so Merry had insisted he sleep in the warm boiler room on a made-up bed next to the stables where there was an outside toilet and sink. I followed him outside to check on Hermes and the little donkey – they were both side by side, standing under a field maple tree, dozing. I went over to stroke them and check they didn't have temperatures as they were both quiet after their long sea journey. They seemed fine and Hermes knuckled to me when I went to her. I realized I could not put her through such an awful journey again and decided she should have her jute rug on overnight. I was just putting it on when Merry came into the field to meet them both and to check that the sheep and goats were all settled for the night.

"Come on, let's go in. I know you are shattered and need to get to bed," she said.

We went back to the kitchen, put any left-over food away, washed the dishes and then she made us both some warm milk.

"Leave everything now, Mrs Perkins will do it first thing in the morning. The Rev. is in his office on the telephone trying to find out what is happening in France so we may hear more in the morning. Right now, the telephone seems to take longer than ever to get through to anyone."

I gave her a hug and thanking her again for everything took my milk and wearily went to a comfy bed with soft, clean sheets.

After a good night's sleep, I woke up sleepy and comfortable and remembering the bad news of the night before became worried about Marcell, Aurielle, Joseph and all the people I knew in France. I thought about the Albertines and hoped they would somehow be alright. I wondered what it would mean for Britain, now, and felt the need to get back home to Norfolk. I decided I had better ring Grandora and let her know I was in England. Ruby had woken up and climbed into bed with Malissa, who was just waking up. We all washed, dressed, and went down to the kitchen. Of course, all the boys were up and helping in the kitchen. Theodore and George were outside with Osian letting out the poultry and collecting eggs. Merry was getting porridge from the bottom of the AGA cooker where it had been cooking, slowly, all night. We all sat down at the table and helped ourselves to toast, homemade jam or Osian's honey, and we passed the porridge round the table. Nico came in with Jabbo. Jabbo looked sheepish and Nico looked excited.

"I wonder if you would like to have a circus display this afternoon," said Jabbo.

"Hurrah, yes please," the boys shouted in unison. "First, I am going to take Zoltan out for a ride this morning to ease any stiffness in his joints," said Jabbo.

"I will come with you. Hermes could do with a walk before the long journey home." So, I jumped up and put on my only pair of reasonably clean jodhpurs and went for a ride.

The tracks up towards the moors were quiet and we followed a tumbling stream then turned for home as we both realized it was very chilly and we weren't used to the damp cold. Hermes was fine and so was Zoltan and we were soon back at the Rectory.

I went in for a cup of tea with Merry and Malissa, and The Rev. came into the kitchen to join us.

"It is not good news from France. The German army appears to be an invincible fighting machine and they are advancing further into France. I am very glad you are here and not stuck over there. Everything is going to change now and so many young men are going to have to fight. I find it heart-breaking. I am so worried for Osian, who is nearly seventeen, and if this war carries on, he could be called up to join one of the services. He is a pacifist. Look how they were treated in the Great War; ridiculed and imprisoned and treated in a diabolic way. Some were even put before a firing squad and shot."

"You don't think he could be made to fight, do you?" asked Merry, looking very worried. "Is he a pacifist?" I asked.

"Yes, and a vegetarian. He won't eat meat, which is why we have some sheep in the field now three years old. They came as lambs, and he will not hear of them being killed. He loves growing vegetables and fruit, is a wonderful beekeeper, and he loves studying wildlife which, of course, we have in abundance here on Dartmoor," added Merry. "I just know things are going to get worse and I am very worried for the boys and all of us."

"Well let's enjoy this afternoon. I hear we are going to have a circus display," said The Rev. kindly. "I understand Jabbo was with a travelling circus and was on his way to where? When you met him."

"I'm not sure where he was going, he seems to have been just running away. I think he was hopeful of getting to Britain and luckily met us, fate really," I answered.

"Indeed, and do you know if he has a passport? Was he checked when you arrived?" asked the Rev.

"No, there was no one there to check any of us, we docked at a
different place to the normal ferries. No passports or dogs were
checked on our arrival. There were other cargo ships there and
it looked as if the harbour officials were more interested in them
than us. Why do you ask?"

"Well, he needs a passport, or he could be interned in a camp
as a foreign national."

I was quiet, I had not thought of that. I must ask Nico what
he knew of the situation and why we were not checked when
we disembarked from the boat; neither were Tiff and Scotty
or Howard.

Merry put sandwiches on the table for lunch and then it was
soon time for our circus show so we all trooped outside and stood
by the paddock railings. I was surprised to see Nico lunging
Zoltan with a look of great concentration on his face, next Jabbo
ran out wearing a bright red satin shirt and white trousers. He
ran alongside Zoltan, vaulted on and was soon executing a series
of acrobatics whilst on the horse as Zoltan cantered beautifully
but slowly around Nico. He somersaulted off and his little dog
ran after the horse. In one fluid movement, Jabbo picked up the
little dog and put him on the back of the horse and the dog rode
around on his back. Then Jabbo jumped up onto Zoltan with a
large hoop and the dog jumped through the hoop repeatedly
whilst on Zoltan's back as he cantered round. Again, Jabbo
somersaulted off and bowed as the little dog jumped into his arms.
We all clapped as it was very good, then he took the lunge line
off Nico and Nico ran alongside the horse and vaulted on; again,
we all clapped, very impressed. Next Nico did a series of Cossack
moves riding Zoltan on one side, then hanging on to the saddle
pad at the other side, even doing it one-handed, then he jumped
off, landed on his feet and bowed and we all cheered and clapped.

It was wonderful and now we knew why he had been so quiet and hanging out with Jabbo this morning he had been practising. Quiet, confident, mature Nico grinned like a young boy, which he was, and was clearly besotted with the circus act. Then Ruby was allowed to sit on Zoltan and, taking it in turns, the three youngest boys. I rushed off to the lorry to get my box camera and took photographs of them sitting on Zoltan and photographs of all of us. The boys caught the little donkey and took Ruby for a ride, with all the dogs running madly around them and Malissa keeping an eye on them all.

I went to clean out the lorry ready for tomorrow and found that Jabbo had already cleaned out the back where the horses stood and put fresh straw down. I tidied around to make as much room as possible for George and Theodore as they would have to travel in the back again, poor lads. I went to the cab to tidy it, throwing out accumulated rubbish from the journey. We still had two cured hams – one for Grandora and a cured ham which we had been using. I took it into the kitchen for Merry and the family, plus a couple of bottles of our wine. She was very pleased and quickly put the ham into the meat keeper saying it was best if Osian didn't see it as he was trying to persuade them all to be vegetarian, but that The Rev. would love it and the bottles of wine.

"Merry, please visit us and bring the boys. We have plenty of room and surely The Rev. would look after the animals for a week. I know it's not ideal to consider right now, but who knows, maybe later this year and good luck with your nursing dreams. You are practical and capable of anything."

Changing the subject, I reminded her that I thought we should be on our way by nine the next morning as it would be such a long drive.

Merry then said, "I shall miss you Sid, it's been wonderful to see you again. Come on through into the back room and we can sit and chat while I do some sewing."

I followed her through to a room at the back of the house which had sewing in piles waiting for mending, and she sat at her sewing machine and showed me the incredible patchwork quilt she was making.

"You are so talented," I said.

"Yes, at cooking and sewing and gardening, which is not much good if you want to work or earn money," she sniffed.

"Merry, it's amazing you have skills so many people don't have, don't put yourself down. Is this the first quilt you have made?"

"No, I have made them for all of us here and I have two more wrapped up."

"You should try to sell them; they are wonderful," I declared.

We ate our tea and then the children played card games in the sitting room whilst we sat around the table and chatted. Jabbo left early again after saying he would leave in the morning, but he didn't know where to go. The Rev. suggested he stayed with them for a bit longer and said he thought it was for the best he kept a low profile just now as he didn't have a passport. Nico added that as Morocco was colonised by the French, he thought Jabbo was safe here from any Home Office officials as he was on our side, fighting the Nazis like the rest of France. I thought I should offer to take him with me and Grandora would have a plan. She always had good plans for solving problems. I was getting worried about my future when I reached home as I couldn't imagine a role for me there. Maybe I should be signing up for war service with one of the armed forces. It would help if I could read and wasn't such a dunce.

The nearer the time came to leave I looked forward to home and at the same time I was very worried about how we would all cope with the war. I asked if I could use the telephone and I rang George and Theodore's mother Genevieve and asked her to be in St Neots and meet me in the market square between four and five o'clock to pick up the boys. She couldn't miss me in a large, varnished wood horsebox. I thought Sunday would be a quiet day for her or Howard, but she started to ask could I take them all the way to my home, and she would pick them up on Monday. I said, somewhat crossly, "No," that it was time she had her young sons back with her. I rang Grandora and no one answered, so I would have to try later. I then told Nico that Jabbo had better ride back in the horsebox with us, even though it put a great strain on the weight of the lorry and the remaining fuel we had. Fortunately, he understood the problem even though he was pleased. He said he would think about what was best. I was sure many problems would lie ahead, but was too tired to think any more, I took Ruby to bed and once she was asleep, I too fell fast asleep.

Chapter 16

Leaving Dartmoor

Morning arrived damp and drizzly. I was no longer used to such chilly depressing weather, and I looked through the window to see the moors shrouded in a grey mist. I watched Osian busy opening the hen houses to let them out, followed by quacking ducks and hissy geese. The sheep and goats came to the fence where he was working, bleating at him, asking for their breakfast no doubt. I hoped Hermes would not have caught a chill as it was much cooler than the weather that she was used to in sunny France; I was glad I'd put a rug on her. Malissa stirred, Ruby woke up and I shivered as I trotted across the landing into the bathroom before anyone else wanted it. We were soon all having breakfast in the kitchen, and I thought what a lovely family they were and how much I was going to miss them, even though I had only just met them, apart from Merry. I was very sorry to be leaving and so pleased to have broken the long journey from the chateau and spent some time here with this honest, happy family. In the short time we had been here, George and Theodore had become firm friends with the younger boys and had played with them, done as they were told and behaved very well. It was obvious they too, were sad to be leaving their new friends and I saw them taking down the address of the Rectory although, unfortunately, they didn't have an address to give to Gruffydd and Dylan as they didn't know where they were going to live. George asked me if Gruffydd could write to me, and I could pass on their new address via my home in Norfolk and pleaded with me that if Gruffydd and Dylan ever came to stay – could they come too? Of course, I said, yes, because I couldn't see it happening for a very long time because of the wretched war. I am so often wrong.

It was time to move on. All of us climbed back in the horsebox for the last leg of our journey. We were getting very good at making ourselves as comfortable as possible in our separate small spaces. We all thanked everybody for our brief, but wonderful stay, and with a final farewell and a big hug for Merry, I turned the ignition key, the engine turned over, burst into life and we were on our way. As we drove slowly down the drive waving, we did the usual mental checklist aloud! Hermes on board, yup, little donkey, yup, Zoltan, yup, Lucy, yup, Odin, yup, Jabbo, yup, Theodore and George, yup, Ruby and pooch, yup, Malissa, Nico, yup and me driving yup.

"You forgot Zippy, Jabbo's little trick dog," said Malissa laughing, "and yes he is on board."

Still damp and cold with a moorland mizzle drifting in, we headed for the road and our destination, Norfolk. At that moment it seemed a long way off. I headed for Exeter; driving through the Devonshire countryside was delightful with frothy cow parsley lining the sides of the road with creamy white flowers and bright green, lacy leaves. The hawthorn blossom was out sweetly scenting the air, the drizzle stopped, and we had a few flashes of sunshine between the languid grey clouds. We travelled through

Buckfastleigh, Ashburton, Bickington, Chudley Knighton, and Chudleigh, all very pretty, quiet villages, but now there were sandbags placed in front of shops, houses, and churches. Military personnel were more visible in the villages and there were many more visible signs that we were at war than any I had seen in rural France. Road signs had been taken down or twisted around to fool any enemy army from following their real directions. There were the usual pony and traps on the roads, people cycling and still a mixture of horses, farm carts and the odd tractor working in the fields. Just not too many cars trundling around the country lanes. Perhaps that was just my imagination, I had been away for nearly four years, after all. As we drove nearer to Exeter there was a build-up of military vehicles, and I thought it for the best to push on to Taunton. I drove through a busy Taunton which seemed to be full of even more army personnel and massive army trucks and again thought it best to keep going. I agreed with Nico we should head for Glastonbury, Shepton Mallet and for Swindon. We stopped at lunch time in a quiet side road with a broad grass verge and let the two horses and the donkey out to graze and have some water. We all enjoyed the food prepared for us by Merry and we managed to sit on the sloping ramp for our picnic because the ground was very wet from the rain. We stayed for one hour for the horses and dogs to have a break from the confines of the horsebox. The boys wandered off and finding a little brook they threw sticks in for them to race and see whose stick had won. Malissa suggested we set off soon before we found anyone else who wanted to join us on our journey, and we all laughed at that.

We soon approached Oxford and I bypassed the centre and took a road going to Bicester and then across country to St Neots. I was going to need fuel very soon and I could see that was going to be tricky as none of us had any fuel coupons. We had one and a half jerry cans of petrol left and so decided to put one in before we arrived in St Neots. I was getting worried about getting home. I mentioned this to Nico and Malissa, saying we could end up getting poor Hermes to pull the horsebox home.

"Well surely that would be too much for her?" asked Malissa, looking worried.

"I'm joking," I replied.

"No need," Nico shouted happily, "I have just remembered Tiff gave me this envelope when he left. He said it might come in useful and I was to give it to you. Sorry I forgot about it until now."

"Hang on, he gave me one too; it's in the glove compartment; open them both please as I am driving."

He pulled out a wad of petrol coupons and food coupons from one envelope and clothes coupons and a wad of English notes in the other. We were amazed and I was so relieved to know I could now get all the way home. "Ah bless him, hopefully we can get some petrol in St Neots. I don't know how he got hold of them and I don't care; they will be jolly useful," I said.

Cheered up, I felt a new energy run through me and had a warm glow, thinking about Tiff and his kind gesture. We soon entered St Neots and as it was after five o'clock, I kept my fingers crossed that the boy's mother Genevieve would be waiting for us. Gosh, I bet she's glad she's here in England right now, I thought. Of course, there was no sign of her and my time to arrive home at about six-thirty was rapidly becoming a hopeless miscalculation. I parked, switched off the engine and waited nervously as I realized the last thing we needed was questioning about where we had arrived from. Not everyone would see us as innocent, having just arrived from France with two Albanians, a Moroccan, three equines, four dogs, a little girl whose name we didn't know and without any papers. Just didn't sound good. Between the back of the horsebox and the cab was a small hatch, so if a groom was travelling in the back with a horse, they could alert the driver to any problems. As an APR warden approached us, I warned George and Theodore to stay very quiet and to ask Jabbo to do the same. He came to the driver's door, and I opened the window.

"Good evening, sir," I said with a smile. "All quiet tonight I hope."

"Yes, Miss, and how long are you planning on parking here?" he asked.

"Oh, just about to leave, the engine was a bit hot, and I needed to wait while it cooled down, but it's all good and we will be off now."

"Just a moment, I need to check where you're from, where you are going and who you are," he said importantly.

"Oh, I have just been to fetch a stallion from Dartmoor for breeding and he's a bad traveller in a horsebox and I just want to get home as soon as possible. Not too far now, just into Norfolk and we should be home before dark if we set off now. I am The Honourable Cressida Welsby of Willup Hall."

"Right, M'Lady, so who have you got travelling with you?" he asked with his hand on my door keeping the window down.

"Oh, my groom and my spare driver and my daughter and my two dogs. We are so lucky to have people like you working all hours keeping us all safe," I told him beaming.

"Well, you best be off now and get home before dark. You don't want to be driving this truck with headlights dimmed on dark roads. Hope you know your way as there are no signposts, as I'm sure you already know. There's been more than enough traffic accidents because of the blackout and lack of lights, we don't want to show enemy aircraft where we are. I've got orders to keep these roads empty for essential vehicles only tonight, so be on your way now. There's a war on, you know." He patted the door and stood back to see us off. No way could I continue to wait for Genevieve. With that I was off and I kept going, but not before Nico broke the silence, mimicking the APR warden with "There's a war on you know," and we all burst out laughing.

Malissa said, "I can't believe you lied so convincingly to an official, Sid, that's so bad of you."

With that we all started laughing again.

"Well done you in the back for keeping quiet," I shouted to them. "Are you OK? Sorry your mother wasn't there."

"We're OK," said George. "Only Theo is upset our mother wasn't there."

"I'm sure he is, but there will be a perfectly good explanation, you wait and see, and the good news is you both get to come home with all of us and see where I live."

There was silence and then Theodore said very quietly in between a few audible sobs, "Thank you, I will like that."

We carried on in silence. At least the roads were better than those we had travelled in France over the last few days and again we saw very little traffic apart from around the few towns we travelled through. Everywhere, strangely, was very quiet. We hadn't known signposts had been removed so if the Germans landed, they would be confused about where to go, again thank goodness Nico was with me with his amazing map reading skills. At one point we all sang 'She'll be Coming Round the Mountain when she Comes', 'The Farmer's in his Den' and 'Ten Green Bottles' and then we were all just too tired. I headed for Chatteris, Wisbech and King's Lynn, by which time I was feeling ill. I ached between my shoulder blades, and I just wanted to fall asleep. I decided to go for broke and not stop again to let the horses out, but just get home – that was all I had on my mind. Hungry, thirsty and tired, I briefly did stop at a telephone box near Sleaford to

warn Grandora that we were nearly home and to be prepared for
a mini-invasion of seven people, three equines and four dogs, all
tired and ready for tea and bed.

I cannot describe how emotional I felt driving into the village
near my home and seeing it in the gathering darkness. Finally, I
turned into our long drive through an avenue of horse chestnut
trees and could just make out the Hall in the evening gloom. At
last, we came to a stop at the side of the house facing towards the
stables. Grandora came straight out to us, and dear Granger was
there to take care of the horses. Dear, kind, capable Granger, I
had known him all my life but until then he was blissfully unaware
of all the animals travelling with me. Then Mrs Revill came out in
her pinafore, and I was surprised to see her this late as she would
normally have gone home by now.

"Please," I said, "I would like you all to meet my dearest friends
and thank you for waiting for us." Then I sort of collapsed into
Grandora's arms and hugged her before helping Granger pull the
ramp down. I could just make out his surprised face when Jabbo
came out leading Zoltan down the ramp first.

Jabbo bowed and said, "Pleased to meet you, sir," and handed
the lead rope to a shocked Granger. Jabbo shot back up the ramp
for Hermes and handed her to me before going back for the little
donkey. Granger recovered from his initial surprise and quickly
told Jabbo to follow him, but not before he looked at Zoltan,
admired him and then he looked at Hermes and said, "Your Uncle
Edmund was a great horseman, he knew a good horse when he
saw one, she is a very nice stamp of a mare." He then patted the
donkey, sighed a bit and smiling shook his head as both he and
Jabbo headed off in the direction of the stables with the horses
and little donkey. Over his shoulder he said, "I be back for the
horsebox shortly and will unload your luggage for you."

All the dogs ran around the garden, glad to be out of the horsebox. We watched they didn't get lost as this was a new place for them all except Odin. After unloading the animals, we all trooped into the kitchen where the table was laid for our late tea. At this stage I was beginning to feel very ill as I fought down sickness which washed over me.

"Everybody, this is my wonderful grandmother know to us as Grandora or otherwise Lady Ellesdale, and the lady in the pinafore who has cooked this wonderful meal for us is Mrs Revill. Now I will introduce Malissa and little Ruby, Nico, Malissa's brother, George and Theodore Bathurst – and – the seventh one will be here shortly; he is called Jabbo. Lucy is the chocolate Labrador and belongs to George and Theodore. Zippy is Jabbo's dog and my Odin you already know. This little pooch belongs to Ruby. Ruby, as yet, doesn't speak, so we don't know the name of her little pooch; however, in time I hope she will be able to tell us. Please, everyone, sit down and eat and afterwards we will find you all your bedrooms." On the point of collapse, I sat down.

Mrs Revill, bless her, had made a simple chicken casserole with mashed potatoes and a lemon meringue to follow. Unfortunately, I just turned and said, "Sorry, I need the loo," just making it to the downstairs cloakroom where I was very sick.

Grandora, waiting in the hallway, simply said, "Bed for you," and thankful someone else was taking charge, I dragged myself upstairs and automatically went to my old bedroom which was ready for me with teddy still sitting there on the pillow. Somehow, I removed my clothes and put on a pair of flannelette pyjamas, ran along the corridor to the bathroom and was sick again. I held onto the spinning walls and made it back to my bedroom and lay on the bed. I felt cold, tired, ill, shivery, depressed, and numb with a terrible headache and my eyes felt full of grit. Grandora came upstairs with a hot water bottle and water and put the glass on the bedside table. I couldn't touch it – I would be sick again. Grandora sat with me, and I buried my head into the lavender smelling pillow and cried.

"You're exhausted, my darling, you must sleep and rest."

"Oh, I keep thinking of France; Aurielle, Marcell, and Joseph and how they are? What's happening there is awful. I want to help them. Did Tantetta get to Switzerland. Is she safe?"

"Yes, she is in Switzerland with Augusta, Bernadette, and Jean-Phillipe. He is yet to fly to New York, but they are safe. Now sleep is what you need. Odin is here next to you." With that she sat by my bed humming, and I didn't remember anymore that night. I was at home with my Grandora humming at the side of me as she used to do when I was little.

I don't know when I woke. But the house was silent and all I could hear were the birds singing outside. I just lay in bed half-asleep, half-awake, feeling numb, but not sick. I lay there, trying to work out where I was, then remembering and trying to think what I should do next. I looked around my bedroom and it was comforting to see my pink curtains and my pink flowered eiderdown on my bed. What on earth was going to happen with the others now, how come I had brought Malissa and Nico back here, why hadn't they gone to London or somewhere else? Why had they stayed with me? What was going to happen to Ruby and what was her real name? As I went to get up, my legs felt like wool but heavy at the same time, my arms felt weak, and I fell back onto the pillow. This is ridiculous. I have just driven from France. I must go to the toilet I thought. There was a light knock on the door and Grandora came in.

"You're awake, good, time for some tea," she said and brought me a tray with a cup of tea and a slice of toast. "Now sit up and eat this. Oh, you will find through the door into your dressing room your own bathroom, now. I thought you would like it when you came home, and I had it done before rationing and restrictions started. No need to come downstairs, everything and everyone is just fine."

"Where are they all?" I asked feebly, not sure at that moment if I cared.

"George and Theodore are with Hugh and Margaret at the kennels, and they have taken their dog Lucy with them. Did you know Lucy came from here? Henry Bathurst, Howard's brother, bought her when she was a puppy, as a present for the boys before they went to France. Malissa is still in bed like you and Nico has taken Ruby with Granger to the farm to see the calves. Jabbo is at the stables cleaning them out and Hermes and the little donkey are out in the orchard with the Lipizzaner Zoltan grazing in the paddock next to the stables. So, everything and everyone is sorted."

Then, I suddenly remembered: "The horsebox – it must be kept safe at all times, Tantetta insisted."

"I know, it will be emptied this morning and, it will be taken care of. Right now, it is locked up in the cruck barn."

"There is a cured ham in it for you," I remembered and told Grandora.

"Just what we need, thank you, that will help with the rationing. Now, you get some more sleep and rest."

With that she left me. I slept most of the day and stayed in my room, concerned at what was wrong with me, I felt so rotten. Malissa brought me a tray with a glass of milk, two boiled eggs and toast for my supper and to see how I was. Ruby came with her and climbed onto my bed and snuggled up to me. I was so pleased to see them, to find out they were in the next bedroom to me, and they too were sleeping a lot and felt so tired. They stayed, Malissa chatting to me, whilst I enjoyed my supper and then they trooped off to bed and I slept again all night.

The next morning was May13th, and I woke up feeling better, but depressed. Something was missing, I didn't know what. I stared at the ceiling and stared and stared. I didn't want to get up – how ridiculous: I usually loved getting up. Dragging myself out of bed, I went to use my lovely new bathroom, which was fabulous, I was very lucky. But I just didn't feel lucky, just empty. I looked onto the lawn and past the Tree of Lebanon down to the ha-ha, park and onto the sheep's field. It was a dull cloudy day, not sunny like France. France, my friends, oh God how are they? What's happening? I should have stayed and helped them. What do I do now, here in England? All these thoughts raced around my head, and feeling exhausted, again, I flopped back onto the bed and just stared up at the ceiling.

There was a gentle knock on the door and Grandora came in. "So how is my girl today? Better, I hope. You have slept for over thirty-six hours on and off. Are you coming down for breakfast and to see what you brought home in the horsebox?"

"OK," I said with no interest in seeing the contents of my trunk whatsoever.

We went downstairs to the kitchen; Malissa was there with Ruby who ran into my arms which felt lovely of course. I gave her a cuddle and a big kiss.

"Morning, Sid," said Malissa with a big smile. "Finally we are both up. I think I have slept as much as you and I feel so much better now. This house is lovely – will you show me around today? Ruby wants to ride the donkey again and Jabbo has said he will take her around the garden. Her little dog gets on with his dog Zippy very well. Ruby has let her pooch run around. Odin has been looking for you – he is outside playing with George and Theodore."

I nodded and smiled and sat down to toast and tea which was OK – just not croissant and hot chocolate, which I longed for. Oh God, I must get rid of this feeling. What's wrong with me? I'm home safely and should be pleased. Grandora was staring at me and asked if I had any thoughts about running through the jobs that needed doing or popping down to the farm to see what we were growing for the war effort. She asked if I would like to see who the ARP was in the village and the plans in place in case of an air attack. I felt sick.

"Of course, yes, that sounds err interesting. I'll show Malissa around and then we could walk to the farm and take Ruby on the donkey." I wanted to go back to my room and lie down. I didn't though, but gave Malissa and little Ruby a tour of the house and gardens, finding little had changed since I was living here, but then my parents were away and Grandora had been touring the world and now there was just me out of all the family to be responsible for everything. The thought filled me with dread. The Walled Garden was looking dilapidated and overgrown. That apart, everything looked pretty much the same. The thought came again, and with a jolt. Was I expected to run the estate? No, that's not possible; Grandora will do it, although she's never wanted to have anything to do with it, since Grandfather died. I'm sure I am far too young to take charge of estate business. Humphrey Clayton was the estate manager – shouldn't he be responsible for it? Surely my parents should be home now to sort everything out. I don't want to do it. With these angry thoughts racing through my head, we walked down to the farm to see Ted and Nora Staples, our farm manager and his wife. The trees were glittering with fresh green leaves as the sun finally came out and

it was lovely to see old friends. Ruby loved running around, seeing
the calves again and Donk was as good as gold. Ruby was happy
to go into the farmhouse for some homemade biscuits, but she
was still not talking at all. Ted took me on one side and asked me
if I knew about the new orders to increase food production and
what did I think about ploughing up some more of the parkland.
I was horrified. I had noticed some of the park had been put to
crops. I told him I would be discussing it with my grandmother
later and I would let him know. Seriously, I had no idea what to
do; nor did I care.

I didn't do much all day apart from learn why the horsebox
had been so heavy. Apparently, I had on board, secretly hidden,
many valuable works of art. Tantetta had taken as many as
possible to Switzerland for safekeeping and other paintings had
made the journey across the Atlantic to the New York Gallery, and
I had been the courier for many others now taken to our cellar,
which had been prepared to maintain the correct temperature for
their storage. On board I had a painting by Georges Braque who
was born in Argenteuil near Paris and a compatriot of Cezanne.
Another painting was an early work by Marcel Duchamp, a couple
by Henri Matisse, Joan Miro the Spanish painter, Piet Mondrian
the Dutch painter, sketches and some paintings by Pablo Picasso
and many others. It seems that these artists who had been in
Paris at some time during their careers had either met my great-
aunt or she had followed their careers and bought their paintings.
She had a keen eye and a knack of finding or following great
artists. There were other paintings by Uncle Edmund and some
of mine, but mostly they were outstanding works by great artists.
No wonder she always wanted the horsebox secure during our
journey. Marcell had worked on the inside of the lorry making
secret compartments which had made it so much heavier. I had

also brought some of the family silver with me, valuable porcelain, several crates of best vintage wine and some very fine brandy, along with some French cheeses and my Grandora's cured ham. I wondered that there had been any room at all for Hermes and all the rest of us.

I went up to my room to unpack my trunk and was delighted to discover Aurielle had packed separately my Swiss duvet and covers. How glorious for my bed, instead of the British sheets, blankets, and eiderdown. The small suitcase from the crashed car had also ended up in my room along with the expensive-looking handbag. I called Malissa and Nico to come and see what was inside, but Nico had apparently gone to Peterborough. I asked where Ruby was, and she was having her afternoon sleep. I opened the beautiful leather case in which I knew were some of Ruby's clothes. I took out her clothes and the child's hairbrush with initials in silver. Malissa thought the initials were RA. We rooted round in the case looking for more information about the little girl and discovered a small jewellery box with some sweet little bracelets and a few necklaces, the sort of thing a child might wear. They were gold coloured with sparkly stones and very pretty. I then checked the red satin lining but there was nothing. I sat back on my bed, disappointed. Malissa started knocking all around the case on the outside and the inside and I watched attentively.

"I think there is a false bottom in this case," she said calmly, as she gently pulled back the lining, and running her fingers along the bottom and edges of the case, cried, "Found it".

"Found what?" I said, impressed by her determination and knowledge that there could be more.

"I have found the catch, look, it's tiny." It took several minutes of Malissa's infinite patience to finally open the lock. Inside were several little black velvet pouches and we eagerly opened the first to find it contained beautiful glittering diamonds. Each pouch contained diamonds of different sizes and each diamond glittered as it fell onto the tray we had now put on the bed. Malissa rummaged around again and found one larger pouch. In this were pearls, all the same size, and they, too, were emptied onto the tray, alongside the diamonds. We were mesmerised and just stared at our find.

Malissa smiled, looked at me and said, "We are looking after an heiress."

"I think Grandora should see these and then they must be put away for safekeeping in a safe. I will go and fetch her," I said.

I ran downstairs and into the small sitting room which was her private retreat and found her reading some letters.

"Sorry to interrupt you, but you have to see what we have found before Ruby wakes up."

We hurried upstairs, well I did, Grandora was slower, and into my bedroom. We showed her the case, diamonds, and pearls. She sat on a chair, counted them and looking closely at them declared, "Little Ruby must be a millionairess."

It was then I remembered the big blue handbag and so we carefully opened it. It seemed awful to open someone else's bag, especially someone we had never known who was now dead. There were two opera tickets from some months ago, a lipstick, a pretty gold, jewel-encrusted powder compact, a matching gold jewel-encrusted little hairbrush and comb set, an exquisitely embroidered handkerchief, a purse containing francs and a wallet containing paper money. Which Malissa counted. She said it was high denomination money coming to £2,000. Finally, we opened a heavy leather jewellery roll to find it held quality gold and diamond necklaces, rings, earrings, and bracelets and lastly a baby's hairbrush in dark wood with the initials JA inlaid in wood. We were all silent and just stared in awe at the amount of wealth in front of us.

After some minutes of astonished silence, Grandora said briskly, "We must make an inventory of everything here, put it all back in the pouches and jewellery roll and it can all go in the safe. I suggest we do it now before little Ruby wakes up and sees anything which could upset her. Then I suggest we tell no one, except Nico; it remains a secret. The time will come when we find her father and family. In the meantime, we know she must want for nothing, and we will look after her. I think I will inform my solicitor of the child living here and ask his advice, without revealing all her wealth. If we don't find any of her relatives this is her legacy, and we must protect it for her."

We all agreed, when I suddenly remembered, jumped up and cried, "Wait there is more," and I ran to my cupboard to get out her beautiful emerald-green coat with the velvet collar and cuffs and we had already noticed how heavy the hem was.

Malissa was soon at work again; I think she should have been a sleuth. Bit by bit she carefully checked every inch of the coat, hem collar and pocket seams and we found even more diamonds. Thirty in all, much smaller than those in the pouches. She sat back and sighed, "What a lovely coat. She was obviously a much-loved child from a wealthy family. This coat is expensive and beautiful, even the buttons match the coat."

Grandora picked up the coat and looking intently at the buttons on the cuffs and down the front as well as on the little belt at the back, said, very quietly, "These are emeralds, in each button is an emerald held on by gold filigree."

We all laughed, almost in disbelief, and I suggested when she woke, we checked her red dress to see if there were rubies in the buttons on the dress. I was half-joking. Malissa ran to the next bedroom and came back with the pretty red velvet dress with the smocking on the bodice and Grandora confirmed she was sure they were all rubies on the buttons down the back of the dress. Grandora went to fetch a satin pyjama case in which to put the dress, we repacked all the diamonds, pearls, and jewellery and Grandora took them away to place in the safe.

"Leave the coat in your wardrobe for now and I will buy some buttons to replace those on the coat then we can put the emeralds in the safe too. Whoever put these precious stones here was planning to escape from the Nazis. It's a pity you didn't find any documents."

"We did, we found the passport of the chauffeur and I wrote down his name; he was Swiss, I kept all the details in my journal," Malissa told us.

"I didn't know that you wrote the details down," I said, thinking she was a smart girl.

"You were busy driving us all safely home, Sid, you had plenty of other problems to think about. I also have the make and registration of the car," she added.

Right on cue a sleepy head came tripping along the landing to see us. Fortunately, we had put everything away just before she came in with the little pooch at her heels. After lots of cuddles and giggles we all went downstairs to look for tea and cake. I felt slightly brighter. It had been an enlightening and interesting day.

Later, after tea, George and Theodore played snakes and ladders with Ruby until it was her bedtime when I took her to bed and showed her some of my old nursery books as I knew the stories from memory. She enjoyed the pictures I was not at all sure if she understood the story in English.

I went downstairs to sit with Grandora and enjoy with her a glass of wine. Malissa joined us and we played a game of cards with the boys until it was time for them to go to bed. We told them to help themselves to a glass of milk before going upstairs. After they had gone, we discussed the new appointment of Winston Churchill as Prime Minister and the speech he had delivered to the House of Commons that day, when he had said he could only offer, 'blood, toil, tears and sweat'. Grandora had met Winston Churchill years before at some function in London and said how pleasant his wife Clementine was, but that Churchill was not always popular. He had had some failures in the past, including the catastrophe of Gallipoli, but hopefully he would prove that he was now the right man to lead Britain to victory against Nazi Germany. It was soon time for bed; all the blackout curtains were checked at every window downstairs, and we all said goodnight to each other.

I still had no idea what I was going to do with my life here in wartime Britain. It still all seemed surreal to me. With these thought and worries trampling around in my head, I finally fell asleep.

Chapter 17

George and Theodore

Some days later when I woke up, thinking as usual about the fighting in France and the devastation being wreaked across Europe, I seemed to be unable to do anything of any use to help fight for the freedom of France and the safety of Britain. Depressed, I went down early, straight to the stables to see Hermes, tacked her up and went for an early ride to clear my head, with Odin running next to me. I went onto the Pedders Way, a lovely old track originally a Drovers Road for taking cattle to market and runs around the coast of north Norfolk and down towards Thetford. It was a day which could go either way, not cold, just not sunny. Odin ran as free here as he did in France, and after reaching a neighbouring village, I turned for home on more tracks belonging to a local landowner and finally onto our estate tracks and back home for breakfast. Mrs Revill was putting breakfast on the table for everyone except Grandora. Just like Tantetta, she breakfasted in bed, something to do with their upbringing and a life of servants I suppose. Nico was back from his trip to Peterborough and explained he had been asked to go there to meet up with some 'Home Office' people to verify his presence in England, his journey here and to discuss all he knew so far about the Nazis and what they were doing. They knew his parents' ships were being used to transport supplies to Britain. He was able to discuss the maps he had with him and pinpoint areas of interest to them. He never seemed to be treated by anyone like a boy, which was strange, although he was soon to be fifteen years old, he was so much more mature. He asked me if I was agreeable to him taking my mother's mare Polly out for a ride with Jabbo. Of course, I told him it was fine with me if Granger was happy for her to go out and assuming she was fit enough. I trusted Granger to only act with the mare's best interest in mind. Jabbo knocked on the door and came in for breakfast, accepting coffee and toast. They both left to find Granger who I had a suspicion was already at the stables with Polly tacked up and ready to go. It would be good for the mare to have some steady work and Nico was clearly a decent rider.

The post arrived and Malissa opened a letter asking her to go to Cambridge University for an interview. I knew she had sent a CV and was waiting to hear from them. With her mathematical mind and her skill as a strategist combined with her languages, she was bound to be called by the Government for inclusion in their gathering of people with extraordinary abilities to fight against the Nazis. She seemed pleased to receive the letter and said, "I was thinking of taking Ruby into King's Lynn. I think Pinocchio is showing at the cinema and I'd like to buy her some new clothes, especially trousers and wellingtons. Could you come too; would you fancy coming?"

"I would love to, and we still have plenty of coupons Tiff gave us. I will have to ask if I can take the car."

As I went upstairs to ask Grandora I allowed myself time to think about Tiff and wonder what he was doing right now. I prayed he was safe wherever he was. Grandora was delighted with the idea and offered to take us to King's Lynn. She needed to see the solicitor and suggested we go early, have a bite to eat in the Dukes Head Hotel before we went shopping and to the cinema. We asked George and Theodore to come with us and we had such a lovely time.

We found vests, pants, a couple of liberty bodice, some jodhpurs and a sturdy pair of leather boots, wellingtons, and warm socks for Ruby. They were for winter, and we were buying them before there were more shortages. We also bought her two cotton dresses, skirts, and blouses, white socks, sandals, a cardigan, two swimming costumes and some shorts for the summer months, looking ahead. I bought her paints, drawing paper, crayons, and a new jigsaw. For the two boys I bought footballs, playing cards, two jigsaws, two new pullovers, two pairs of long trousers and shorts. I bought them each a dog whistle as they were learning how to train dogs with Hugh. They were thrilled. We went to the cinema and enjoyed the film then met up with Grandora who was looking very pleased with herself, but said it was a surprise for later. All this time the little pooch came with us and was happily carried everywhere. Odin had reluctantly stayed at home with Lucy the Labrador, Trig and Spruce my father's gun dogs who had been very young when he left for his diplomatic duties abroad and were pleased to have lots of people staying in the house again with them. They had been kept in the kennels with Hugh Brownlow our gamekeeper and his wife Margaret whilst Grandora was travelling. Now back at the Hall, they loved everyone they met.

Back in time for tea for the boys and Ruby because tonight they were going to bed early, and we were going to have dinner with Grandora later in the breakfast room, like we used to when my parents lived here. The dining room was considered too big for fewer than six people, as the table could seat twenty people. It was the first time we had the chance to talk about our journey from France and listen to Nico and Malissa talk about their time in Poland. Malissa had been in the wrong place at the wrong time, for a chess tournament, and Nico, who had been studying in Ukraine, was sent with a chauffeur to fetch her home. Unfortunately, they were in Poland when the German army had invaded but had no idea how bad things were at that time for so many Polish people and sadly their chauffeur went missing. Their father, away at sea, had managed to contact my father through diplomatic channels. Our fathers knew each other, having met in London during trade talks between Greece, Albania and Britain, and had remained in touch and friends. Something to do with supplies to Britain which came on their father's ships. He had asked if my father could help his two children escape from Poland, which he did. Tiff and Scotty, who were already in Poland on some secret undercover works, were dispatched by my father to get them out of the country and into France. I discovered that their father had promised any help he could offer in return for Nico and Malissa to travel with me to Britain after he had disclosed the brilliance of his two children and their incredible abilities and high IQ. It was in this way I learnt just how big their father's fleet of ships was and how important they were as they transported merchandise all over the world, vital to the continuation of food and products reaching Britain's shores at this precarious time. So, hey presto, that's what got them passage into Britain. They had been marvellous to have with me and I readily admit that without them my journey home would have been almost impossible. Not only that, I had also become very attached to both and regarded them as my best friends, just like a brother and sister to me.

During dinner Malissa said she felt different with me now after our journey, she thought it had changed her. She had never felt so at home with anyone before, was relaxed and had learnt to see the funny side of life. Nico said he was pleased she now talked to people instead of being reclusive, always reading and avoiding conversation with anyone. They both said the journey had been life-changing; a journey of discovering they could face new situations, putting their past training by their parents and tutors to good use.

We discussed the diamonds and precious stones found in Ruby's coat and her mother's handbag – well, we presumed it was her mother's bag. Grandora said the craftsmanship of the buttons was superb and she was sure the diamonds were of the best brilliance and of a high carat and therefore very valuable. It was important we try to locate her father or any of her relatives and it was fortunate that, for future reference, Malissa had the car make and registration and Nico had all the map details of where we had stumbled across the accident.

The conversation turned to the future of Nico and Malissa. They were unsure about the exact whereabouts of their parents, although they thought that their mother was stranded in Greece. Their parents' wish was that they stayed in Britain and that Nico attended a nearby boarding school which had been arranged for him. Malissa had received a request to go to Cambridge University to discuss her education and her skills which appeared to be in demand, but she didn't know yet what her role might be. Then it was my turn to discuss my future role here in wartime Britain. I was very quiet because I was uncomfortable about having to admit that I didn't think I could contribute to the war effort. I could not imagine an artist being in great demand to fight a war. My French was now good, and I understood German and Spanish without being fluent in either language. Could I be a translator? Yet I still found reading and writing difficult and that was so embarrassing to admit. I could drive. Perhaps I should become an ambulance driver or maybe learn to fly a plane?

Grandora spoke up: "You are needed here now. We must increase food production on the estate to supply as much food as we can to support our troops and help reduce the need for food being brought in by the convoys. Every day they are facing terrible challenges on the seas from attacks by the German U-boats. I have already volunteered to take in some refugee children from London and they will need organizing whilst living here. More volunteers are needed to help with the Home Guard and the Women's Voluntary Service."

"Yes, I know, but I am young, Grandora, I need to be doing more than just fiddling around here. There are soldiers younger than me joining up to fight for our country."

Nico joined in, "Your time will come, Sid, be patient, get things organised here and when you have done your best to see that the estate is running to its full potential, you will find out where your skills will be needed next." He was so wise, I struggled to believe he was only just turning fifteen, next week.

We wondered what would happen to Jabbo. Would he be interned in a camp? – but Grandora pointed out he was from Morocco, which was a French colonial country, so, technically an ally. Anyway, we would have to wait and see as he was to be interviewed by some people from the 'Home Office'. Grandora told us she had put in a good word for him.

"Do you think it's time we provided better accommodation for him?" I asked.

"All in hand," Grandora told us. "Granger and Jabbo get on very well and Granger is pleased with the work Jabbo is doing and has been having him stay in his house, as you know. He has suggested that, with a few repairs, we could get the old Woodsman's cottage dry, warm, and comfortable for him, so I said I would ask you, Cressida, what you thought about the idea."

"Brilliant," I enthused. "I will go and look at it tomorrow and will see what materials they need to do the work. We must have got most of the stone, wood, and slate here on the estate."

On that positive note we cleared the table and headed off to bed. As we went, I mentioned it might be a good idea to try and get some more help in the house if we were expecting more children coming to stay and we all agreed with that, as none of us wanted to wash the dishes after the evening meal.

The following days became busy as we arranged for the Woodsman's cottage to be renovated for Jabbo and he worked tirelessly on his little house and continued working with Granger around the estate doing any jobs my Grandora needed doing. We were all nervous when some very important and grim looking 'Home Office' officials called to see him taking him into my father's office to interview. Much to our relief, they didn't take him away as it seems he had some sort of French status, heaven knows what. When we asked what they had asked him about it seems they wanted to know how much he knew about the geography of Morocco, where his family lived and how he had travelled to Spain before joining the circus and moving on to France. They 'quizzed' him about his political views, especially with regard to the current rulers in Morocco. Apparently, he had travelled with a young Jewish friend whom he had met at a riding school in Morocco where they shared a love of horses. Jabbo went to muck out and sweep up the yard in exchange for any rides, whereas Moshe went there to ride as his parents paid for him. His friend was sick of the hostility constantly directed at

Jewish people in Morocco and decided he would travel to Spain for a new life. The two of them had stowed away on a cargo ship at the end of June 1936 and managed to get to Motril in Spain. On arrival in Spain, they soon found the beginnings of the Civil War was much worse than they had expected, so they split up. His friend Moshe decided to travel to Portugal and Jabbo headed for France. During his journey he came across the circus, fell in love with their horses and was taken on to help with them. Needing to escape the Civil War, he travelled to France from Spain and found he was good at vaulting onto the circus horses and doing somersaults and acrobatics. He fell in love with Zoltan and worked with him, developing a special rapport with the horse and little dog Zippy, thus creating a new circus act with just the three of them.

His father was already dead when he left Morocco and his mother and two sisters had been taken in by his father's brother and wife and they had taken control of all his father's possessions. He couldn't get on with his uncle and had nothing in Morocco to call his own so decided to leave and start a new beginning in his life. His father had been a carpenter, so he had grown up watching his father work and was expected to help him in the workshop. It was the first time I had heard Jabbo speak for so long and tell us about himself. It was a fascinating story. The 'Home Office' men went away and left Jabbo to stay with us. He had to sign papers promising to stay here, so we thought that was the end of it.

I decided that if we were going to have some evacuee children from London, I had better organise their bedrooms and on inspection with Granger and Grandora it was decided to paint the nursery and put some new beds in. As everything was rationed, I was worried about finding everything we needed, but no need to worry, my mother was a hoarder and we had plenty of paint, all white, and rolls of material bought in sales and waiting to be used. Jabbo said he would repair the two broken beds and make two more for the bedroom. I went into the village to ask Agatha Hubbard, 'the lady who sews curtains', as directed by Mrs Revill, to measure up the windows and make some curtains and bedspreads. Fortunately, she agreed to come the next day and then I asked if she knew anyone who could help in the house and help with children. I was directed to an end cottage built of stone and pebbles with a pink camellia climbing by the front door – there I met a Mrs Burden who had a daughter just out of school and wanting a job. She was nearly fifteen with grey serious eyes, a kind face, was pleasant and neat, so after a chat with her, I hired her for £3.00 a week on one month's trial, promising to supply her with a bike and some dresses for work. The days flew by, and we were all kept busy. Rosie Burden came to work for us and was a slow and steady learner, patient, and a real trier. Most important of all, Ruby loved her as she played with her, took her for walks and was capable of leading Donk the little donkey with Ruby in the saddle. Malissa disappeared to Cambridge for an interview and was told she was to go to a place called Bletchley for a further interview the following week. Following her, Nico was offered a place at Oxford because of his high intelligence. He had passed the necessary exams earlier in the year in Europe, so no boarding school for him. Things seemed to be moving very quickly in a strange direction. I would miss them when they both left.

Jabbo proved to be an excellent joiner and made some interior shutters for the nursery which were painted white and better than curtains. Then, 'the lady who sewed curtains', Mrs Hubbard, made lovely yellow-flowered, quilted bedcovers for the four beds and some pillows and sheets out of sheets we already had stored upstairs which had holes in; she repaired them by putting them outside inside. Mend and make do was Britain's new slogan. We rubbed the floorboards down and painted them white – we did have an awful lot of white paint. Next, we put some lovely bright rugs, down on the floor which I had found when rummaging around in the old attic rooms. I decided to paint some pictures for the wall, so I asked Grandora which room I could call my own for painting. I did fancy my father's office because of the light flooding in and the view across the park. Plus, he was the one choosing to gallivant around the world which did rankle me at this moment in history – so why shouldn't I use his office? It was next to the games room with its vast mahogany billiard table made by Thurstons of London on a four-piece slate bed with six cushions and brass pocket plates. I know all that because I found the receipt for it when going through Father's drawers looking for any details regarding the Woodsman's cottage. It would be impossible to move the billiard table anywhere, it was so big and heavy, so I couldn't use that room though I had to admit it seemed sacrilege to use Father's office. I thought I could use my bedroom and went upstairs to see how I could re-arrange the furniture when I bumped into Grandora and told her what I was going to do.

"I was thinking about a room for you before you came home," she said, "I was thinking about you having my little sitting room."

I opened my mouth to start to speak.

"No, I have thought it through, hear me out. I have a lovely big bedroom upstairs and a slightly smaller bedroom next to me. I would like to change the rooms around and use the smaller room as my bedroom and the larger room as my sitting room. I even have a fireplace in there and a large linen cupboard in the hallway which I can open into the bedroom as part of a dressing room. I've worked it all out."

We both went into her bedroom and the next bedroom was nearly as large as hers; I could see how it could work for her. The view of the park down to the river was amazing from upstairs and it would be marvellous for her as a sitting room. That discussed, the decision was made.

Now to find out how the cottage was developing so that I could nab Jabbo and Granger for some more alterations in the house.

The little cottage was looking watertight and nearly ready for the installation of a new floor. The windows were in – well there were only four windows and two doors. Jabbo had repaired one door and made another for the front. I asked Granger what he had in mind for the floor, and he thought red and black quarry tiles down would be his choice, if any could be found. Anxious to help, I went back to my father's office and looked through his list of business-people, those we had dealt with over the years, and found just the right person to supply us with some tiles. It was a struggle to read them all, but I was pleased that I had managed on my own. Off I went in our station wagon to Snettisham, looking for a pottery that might make floor tiles. The first I found sent me off to another place, and two hours later I located a man on a sort of a farm with a junk-filled, very weed-ridden yard, scruffy poultry, free range lambs and lots of free-range children all running about! He told me he knew a man, who knew a man that could supply some tiles! And yes, he would. To my delight, and with a lot of 'haggling' over the price, he agreed to deliver the exact tiles we wanted, the very next day. So, with my fingers crossed, I returned home via the beach at Wells next to the Sea and, with Odin went for a bracing walk on the beach. Just what I needed. It felt good to be mindless for an hour and on my own, apart from Odin, of course. I was very proud of myself completing my first purchase for the estate and it was later that night I started to worry that I hadn't seen the tiles and what if they were the wrong sort.

After Ruby, George and Theodore had their tea, I played snakes ladders and dominoes with them before bed. Rosie had bathed Ruby. I took her to bed and managed to tell her stories from some of my children's old story books and snuggled her into her bed, kissed her and said goodnight, God bless. Then I made sure George and Theodore cleaned their teeth and talked to them about how their dog training was coming along. When I was sure they were all settled down for the night, I went to join Malissa, Nico and Grandora for dinner. It was very cosy in the breakfast room at night with the crewel embroidered thick curtains drawn. I told them about my purchase and Grandora was pleased that I had used my initiative and gone ahead on my own to find and buy the tiles. Grandora told us she had managed to speak to Genevieve, George, and Theodore's mother. Howard, their father, had not been seen by her, or anyone for that matter, since he left France to return home. She had returned home to buy a house in England for herself and the four boys, before Howard completely bankrupted them. The vineyard was hers, left to her by her French grandfather, but at first Howard didn't want to live there. Because of his gambling problems they had decided to make it their home with their four boys, to get away from gambling temptations in Britain. Howard, it transpired, was always in debt and she thought when living in France and working on the vineyard he would be too busy to gamble, and it would be a new beginning for them. But it hadn't worked out that way and he had lost half of their possessions through gambling. They never had any money, were always broke and unable to pay bills. With the war being a possibility, she had no idea what the eventual outcome would be. She had returned to England to buy a house with money she still had and to stop him gambling it all away. His brother, Henry, had put the new house in Newmarket in his and her name. She was going to meet me in St Neots when she received a telegram saying her eldest son William was going to join the RAF. He was not eighteen for two more weeks, so she had rushed off to find him and stop him from leaving his boarding school to join up, throwing away his chance of going to university. His fifteen-year-old brother Tom was at the same school and had sent the telegram to his mother, warning her. They did find William, just in time, and he agreed to return to Newmarket to reconsider his decision. After much persuasion he agreed to stay at school until the end of the summer term afterwards he would join the RAF and train as a pilot. She is very grateful we have kept the boys here and she is going to London next to try and find Howard and to file for a divorce. She asked us to keep the two boys here a bit longer whilst she tried to sort out her life. Grandora concluded that she had told her that the boys were no trouble and that they could stay here, but they ought to be going to the local school until the end of summer term and that she would enrol them there. I knew Howard Bathurst was dodgy: now I knew why. He had a gambling addiction.

With that I decided it was time to go to bed with a lot on my mind and secretly worrying I had bought the wrong tiles. I couldn't possibly admit to them I had bought the tiles without having seen them.

I was up and out by six o'clock in the morning and rushed down to the stables to wake up Hermes and go for a ride. However, I had not beaten Jabbo, who was already mucking out and sweeping up. I rode round our park on a chilly morning, through the woods and the trees which were covered in varying shades of soft greens and smelling fresh and sweet. Then crossing the little lane, I rode back in through the main, large wrought iron gates and on down to the stables. Having untacked Hermes, I washed her down and gave her breakfast which Jabbo had left ready for her. Arriving in the kitchen at the same time as Rosie, I went upstairs to wake Ruby for her breakfast and found her coming downstairs with Malissa. Just as I was having a cup of tea, a truck arrived with my tiles, so I sprinted down to check them first – fingers crossed. There was the cheerful man, Arthur Laxton, just as jolly as yesterday with a truck load of beautiful Pamments, a traditional, Norfolk, handmade tile made from local clay and sand. I was overjoyed because I thought that they looked lovely. I paid him cash, as agreed, and he asked me if they were alright.

"I'm delighted, they look perfect."

"Well, 'me Lady', if you're 'appy then I'm 'appy, I'm 'ere to please. Anything you require, ANYTHING, you ask me first." He tipped his bent shabby trilby to me and got on with unloading the tiles.

Fortunately, Jabbo, too, was very pleased with them, and when Granger arrived, he too thought they were 'fine'. Humphrey arrived to see how the work was progressing and 'chunted' a bit about the price I had agreed to pay. I asked Arthur Laxton, the smiling man with the truck, if he had anymore, and on learning that he could get plenty I bought a job lot and paid less for them all. He said he knew my father and grandfather well, having supplied the estate in the past and had always respected them for fair dealings and he was happy to do business with me, anytime. Given this information I next asked if he could get me a stove to heat the cottage, one with a hob and little oven, fired by wood or coal and could possibly heat the water, as well?

He said, "Blimey, you don't want much, do you." With that saying 'leave it to me' and tipping his hat, he left with a whistle as he drove off. I was sure the other tiles would come in very handy somewhere in the future. I loved their warm, sandy colours and was pleased as punch with my purchase. Gradually I could feel I was becoming more positive and decisive, and I went back to finish my breakfast a lot happier. Lord above, was I becoming grown up, how frightening.

It was now May 20, 1940, and Nico was to go to Oxford today. We didn't know how long he would be there. There was a telephone call for him which he took in my father's office, and he came back to the kitchen looking very grave and worried. Malissa and I asked him what was wrong.

"That was my captain on The Hestia asking for permission to volunteer my boat to go to Dunkirk in France to rescue the soldiers there who had been ordered to evacuate from France."

We had heard on the news that our army was in retreat and were around Dunkirk and that an order had been issued by Winston Churchill, our new Prime Minister, to the commander of the British Empire Force, Lord Gort, to evacuate as many troops as possible back to Britain. A call had gone out for as many navy vessels as possible to assist the Royal Navy, and for any private seaworthy vessels to join in the rescue of British troops.

"I told him he must go, and I wanted to go and help too, but he has flatly refused to allow me to go with them and it's my boat. I'm now worried my father will be cross I have allowed her and our crew to go into danger."

"No," said Malissa heatedly, "not at all; you have done the right thing. Go to Oxford today and come home after your interview and we can listen to the news together. In fact, I will go with you and keep you company – I want to see Oxford and see if I would be better there, than in Cambridge. Any chance of us borrowing a vehicle please, Sid?"

"Leave it with me, I'll sort it immediately. Just get ready both of you," I replied.

I pedalled frantically to Woodsman's Cottage and there was Granger getting the chimney ready for the stove, which I hadn't got yet.

"Please could we use your van today?" I asked.

"Help yourself," said Granger. "We are going to help Alford with breaking in a young hunter at the hunt kennels today after putting in this chimney and we could ride over with Zoltan in the trap, or could I take Hermes?"

"Hermes needs some exercise, take her, it will do her good and thanks for the van," I trilled.

I drove the van back, hoping Malissa could drive. How come she never offered on our journey home? Still, it was a big horsebox, the little van would be easier for her. Then I thought I hadn't been to the kennels since I returned home, and I used to ride over regularly with Grandfather and loved going out on hound exercise. I made a mental note to go as soon as possible and see Alford and his wife Martha.

They were both ready and waiting at the front door to the Hall. I gave the keys to Malissa and asked if she had any papers with her and petrol vouchers.

"I have my invitation to an interview at Cambridge and Nico has his to Oxford University. We have our passports with us and one voucher for petrol," she said.

"Please be back before dark, it's awful driving in the dark and without any signposts, there have been lots of accidents on the road since the blackout and you can only have your headlights on very dim. Oh, and it's left-hand side of the road remember?" They gave feeble smiles and drove off. Nico was so worried; we all were as the news was so scary.

I went back for a coffee hoping the weather stayed good for them and bumped into Grandora, so we took our coffees back to her lovely flowery sitting room. I told her all that had happened that morning and she told me she had been listening to the news on the wireless. It was very worrying. Then she added, laughing, it was even more worrying Malissa driving the two of them to Oxford.

"By the way do you have any plans to go up to London?" she enquired.

"Good heavens, no, why should I?" I replied, intrigued. "You know your mother inherited a house in Primrose Hill from her mother. Well, it's coming empty, and you mentioned meeting a family on the boat who needed a house to rent."

"Oh, Miriam, yes. She might be interested if they haven't found anywhere yet. I'll look for her number and call her. Thanks, Grandora."

Mrs Revill knocked on the door and came in. "There's a gentleman asking for you by the name of Arthur, Miss."

I jumped up. "The stove!" I said. "Scuse me," and I was off hurrying to see Arthur.

It was a first-class piece of kit, a stove with boiler, a small oven, and a large circle on the top for pots. Not cheap, but worth the money. I rode on the lorry running board clinging to the open window as we round to Woodsman's Cottage. No-one there and I remembered they were going to the kennels, but no matter, Arthur had a strong man with him, and they managed to unload it, just. I paid Arthur and rode my bike which I'd left at the stables, down to the farm to ask if anyone was available to help Granger and Jabbo lift it inside the cottage.

I rode slowly back enjoying the drive through the park and worrying about what to do next. I stopped by our huge walled

vegetable garden which was only in part-production – the rest
was overgrown – and I looked over the long greenhouse which
had many panes of glass missing; it all looked forlorn and a mess.
I was confident Arthur would be able to find me some more glass,
but who could I find to step up production in the garden. Osian! It
came to me in a blinding flash – and we can make loads of honey
and have some goats! With this sudden thought I pedalled back
to write a letter to Merry requesting he came to work for us as
we needed his expertise in bees, goats and vegetable growing.
I knew Merry could decipher my misspelt words and uneven
writing – she could at school. The day passed very quickly, and
I went to help feed the horses and hay them up; I didn't need to,
just wanted to.

Granger and Jabbo were both very pleased with the stove and
would try, with Dan's help, to install it the very next day. As Rosie
had looked after Ruby all day and was going home, I put Ruby to
bed, and then started pacing, worrying about Nico and Malissa
and when would they be home. I took my bike the half mile down
the drive to the road and sat on the wall next to the big wrought
iron gates. I studied the beautiful intricate gates and wondered if
we would be made to hand them over to be melted down for the
war effort. I must take a photograph of them, I thought.

It was just beginning to drop into darkness, the light was
fading, and the sun had gone to bed, when I saw a pin-prick of
lights coming round the bend towards me. It was them; they had
made it home. I ran into the road, waving my little torch and they
turned into the drive, grinning at me. I was so pleased they had
made it back in one piece. I cycled after them and we all went
into the kitchen for supper which had been left out for us by Mrs
Revill. Both had been accepted at Oxford University and were so
pleased they would be together but would have preferred to go

to Cambridge as it was nearer here and 'us'. So, an application was going to be made for Nico to go to Cambridge, instead. I was pleased for them but upset they would not be staying here all the time. I had become used to their help and having them around. I did so enjoy their company.

We listened to the news on the wireless which was awful; all about our soldiers being in retreat and I went to bed very worried about the future for us all, and again prayed Tiff and Scotty were not in France or part of the major retreat from Dunkirk.

Chapter 18

Ruby's Trip to London

After breakfast, I went to talk to Grandora about the amount of money being spent on Woodsman's Cottage as well as just money in general, wondering if we had enough. I thought it was time I understood our income and expenditure. Seriously, the figures shown to me didn't mean much – I understood we were solvent, but needed to be prudent and it was important that the estate generated money. However, in these difficult times it was understandable there would be extra expenditure. It was our duty to provide food for the country and do our best to help people who needed it during the war.

There had been very little done to improve the buildings and to expand the business since Grandfather had died; so much had changed and in many ways much had deteriorated. Grandora thought my father, her son George, now Lord Ellesdale, would have taken over the running of the estate, the village and all the tenant farms, but he hadn't; instead choosing the diplomatic life. Grandora admitted her travelling around the world had not helped with the running of the estate, but now I was here, she hoped things would start to improve. She hoped I approved of the new bathrooms into six of the bedrooms and the improved facilities downstairs. She was going ahead with the changes to her bedroom and was putting more bathrooms on the third floor.

"We'll be a hotel next," I joked.

There was silence from her.

"Oh, seriously is that your plan?" I asked, laughing.

"One should always have a plan," she said firmly. "If your father has no wish to return, Lysander and Portia continue to prefer Scotland and you go back to live in France, what will happen here?"

I was seriously shocked and speechless but, eventually continued, "Well I was going to suggest we improve the living conditions in the servants' quarters. The old cottages have never been lived in since the Great War, when everyone seemed to leave. I understand the last person there was our resident gardener or was it the laundry staff?" I asked, adding, "If we put bathrooms in downstairs leading off or over new kitchens at the back, they will always be available for staff, whatever your plans. I also understand we can apply for help on the farms from the Women's Land Army which was re-mobilized last year in June."

"Yes, it was started originally during the Great War in 1917 and disbanded in 1919. The women who are called up now are between twenty and thirty years old," Grandora responded, then added "Are you thinking we could use the cottages for them to stay in if we improve them?"

"Yes," I replied, "we could, and we desperately need someone who will come in to do all the extra washing we will have when the evacuees arrive. There are seven beds to change weekly, now, plus all our clothes and we don't yet know how many evacuees there will be. I would struggle to do it all on my own and Rosie has enough to do looking after Ruby, helping Mrs Revill with the meals, and keeping the kitchen clean."

"What about Mrs Burden, Rosie's mother?" asked Grandora. "Do you think she could do with the money?"

"I'm not sure as her boy is in France at the moment and Rosie is beside herself with worry about where exactly her brother is and if he is all right," I replied.

"Oh dear and I'm sure we will be hearing of more worried families and where their sons and daughters are before this awful war is finished," Grandora added sadly.

"On another subject, I hope you don't mind, I have taken the liberty of arranging for a Harley Street specialist to examine Ruby to ascertain whether her inability to speak is physical or mental," she added.

"No, Grandora, I think it is a very good idea. When is the appointment?"

"The day after tomorrow, May 23rd. If it is acceptable with you, I will confirm the appointment and book the train for you and an hotel," she replied.

"An hotel?" I queried.

"Well, I thought you would like to meet up with the girl Miriam you met on the boat and arrange to show her the house in Primrose Hill. The appointment for Ruby is in Harley Street and I have also spoken to a trusted associate who has suggested an honourable person who can be trusted to look at just one pouch of diamonds and two buttons to try to value them for insurance purposes. I think you need a full day there and you're travelling so that would be two nights. I think, too, you should ask Malissa to go with you to help with Ruby. I have checked with Jabbo and Granger, and they know what they are doing, so will be fitting the stove, repairing the chimney, and doing the horses. If you agree,

I will ask Arthur to call and see me regarding materials needed for my new sitting room and ask him to have a look at the cottages about their renovation."

Whew! What a plan – what a list – no flies on my grandmother, I thought.

The next day flew by as they all seemed to, and after an early evening meal, I decided to have a shower and get my clothes out for my trip and put them in my small, brown leather suitcase. I chose my brown Harris Tweed costume suit and a cloche hat, three blouses, one to go in, another one for the evenings and one to come home in, plus stockings and a few changes of underwear, comfortable court shoes and pyjamas. I knocked on Malissa's door to get Ruby's clothes ready and took her emerald-green coat with the velvet collar and cuffs (now minus the emerald buttons which had been replaced with very pretty green buttons). Ruby was asleep in her new bedroom just off Malissa's big bedroom. What had been a dressing room had been freshly decorated with a new little bed and I had painted a section of one wall with characters from J.M. Barrie's book Peter Pan. It had been written in 1904 and showed pretty fairies darting through the trees; and Ruby loved them.

"Do you have any shampoo?" Malissa asked, "I thought I would have a shower now as it's a very early start in the morning."

"I was just going to ask you the same thing, I'll go and ask Grandora now." I trotted down the landing to Grandora's bedroom, knocked and put my head round the door to ask for some shampoo. I was surprised and amused to see Nico, George, Theodore and Grandora all in night attire playing whist, sitting round Grandora's beautiful little card table. "Have you any shampoo in your bathroom please? I seem to have run out," I asked.

Up she popped, taking her cards with her – she always was canny – and came back to tell me she had a hoard of shampoo somewhere but couldn't remember where and she couldn't find any in her bathroom. However, she had been recommended to buy this shampoo in this box here as it was very good and very good for evacuees. So back I hurried to have my shower and fortunately I did have some lovely French rose scented soap which I used. Whilst in the shower I opened the box of shampoo soap to find it contained foul smelling black soap called Derbac. Shampoo for hair and the removal of nits. For goodness' sake, what next? Anyway, I used it, well I was wet, and my hair was wet, so I just hurried up and washed my hair; the smell was dreadful. I was soon out and, in my towel, and I trotted along the landing to give it to Malissa, which I had put back in the box. I saw her sniff at her door but said nothing and rushed back to my room to dry myself and blow my hair dry. Well, I didn't need to do that as it was now dry and tangled up from the soap; so there it was: ginger, thick, wiry, and now frizzier than ever. I plaited it before I went to sleep, thinking, surely it will be better in the morning.

Early morning came and my hair looked as if I was constantly standing in a force ten gale. I folded my hair into a kind of bun and pulled the cloche hat on my head, hoping that would hide it. I went down to make tea for us and porridge for Ruby. It was five-thirty in the morning and, dressed and ready to go, Malissa arrived in the kitchen with Ruby and their bags. I didn't know whether to laugh or not. Malissa had the most beautiful, long, thick, black wavy hair which right now resembled a flying witch. She had obviously had the same struggle with her hair as me and with the same result! She had rammed a stylish mauve beret over her hair, that is over the bits not sticking out. Nothing was said as we drank our tea and little Ruby ate her porridge.

Granger knocked on the door and came in. "Your taxi is waiting," he said, giving us a strange look. We followed him to the Rolls and as we set off to the Narborough and Pentney Station I could hear him sniffing and I caught Ruby with her hand to her nose just staring at us, looking puzzled. I caught Malissa's eye and we dissolved into fits of giggles; even Ruby giggled although I'm not one hundred per cent sure she knew why.

Granger said nothing until he opened the door for us at the station and handing our suitcases to the porter then said to us, "I hope you all have a good trip and enjoy London and be careful, but at least there won't be any nits on you two." He then turned and was at off at speed, chuckling as he went back to the car, and all we could do was laugh.

Once on the 08.54 a.m. train we made our way down the corridor looking for our compartment which we found had three occupants already. We took our seats, and I could see one bowler-hatted gentleman sniffing as we sat down. The lady stared ahead with a look of distaste, kept her bag on her knee, sat bolt upright and never spoke. The second bowler-hatted gentleman never looked up from his newspaper, but just kept sniffing the air, which was so funny. We chatted and played 'I spy with my little eye' with Ruby to keep her amused. So, the steady journey began to King's Lynn where we changed for the 9.30 a.m. for Liverpool Street station. A rattling stop-start journey finally got us to Liverpool Street, London at 12.43 p.m. to find it was extremely busy as usual, but with even more soldiers about. They had their kit bags with them and there were many tearful goodbyes taking place, it was so sad. We saw our first evacuee children at the train station all in a line with brown cards pinned to their coats. They looked worried and scared, poor things. After what seemed to be an age a taxi arrived, and it was our turn at last. The driver took us to

Harley Street for our appointment and we were in plenty of time because of our early start. The specialist, booked by Grandora, was called Mr Pomsward, and he was very kind and patient with Ruby. He tested her for deafness, but we knew she wasn't deaf, then looked in her mouth and eyes trying to discover why she wouldn't talk. We thought it all a bit strange. Ruby was as 'good as gold' and held my hand during the tests. Afterwards Malissa and Ruby waited in the reception area whilst Mr Pomsward told me he was convinced there was nothing physically wrong with Ruby. The accident was obviously a terrible trauma for the little girl, and she had simply 'locked her voice shut'. The day would come when she would talk again, she just needed more time; we should be patient. Well, that was a relief. I thanked him and left.

We caught another taxi to Primrose Hill, and we all walked through Primrose Hill Park to see the wonderful view of London spread before us and the incredible dome of St Paul's Cathedral glinting in the pale May sunshine. It was odd to see the ugly barrage balloons flying all over the city. They were there to try and stop enemy aircraft flying low over London. Ruby enjoyed running in the park and playing on the swings at the bottom of the hill. We walked into the village and found a little cafe with yellow gingham curtains and matching tablecloths, where I had arranged to meet Miriam. Rationing was in evidence here and there was little choice on the menu, so we had vegetable soup and egg sandwiches. Miriam arrived and joined us for a cup of tea as the coffee was now made with Camp coffee, a sort of liquid substitute made with chicory, which none of us could stand to drink. Miriam looked stunning. It wasn't just her Parisian clothes which were lovely and stylish, but how she walked and carried herself and her lovely genuine smile. She brought her little French Bulldog with her as she had walked from St John's Wood. As we chatted, Ruby was kept occupied playing with the little dog called Bing after Miriam's favourite crooner, Bing Crosby. We had insisted Ruby left her little dog at home as we thought it unfair to expect it to travel with us on the train and spend time in London. Miriam seemed a little strained and tired. She told us it was difficult living in somebody else's house, and she was trying to find work but so far without success. It was interesting to hear how the family had fared since we had last seen them in Plymouth. Her father had applied for a position in the hospital, but had not been employed, even though he was an ear, nose, and throat specialist. Her mother was not used to being unable to run the house and make the everyday decisions, and her brother and his wife were so unhappy they stayed out as much as possible. Her sister, Anna-Sara, was going to the local junior school and her English was improving. Their housekeeper Mrs Esther Monteux and her daughter Maya were staying in Camden in bed and breakfast accommodation until they could all be together again. Miriam asked what the specialist had said about Ruby, and when she heard she agreed that as there was nothing physically wrong, it was just a case of waiting for Ruby to speak.

I was very pleased to be able to tell her about my mother's house being available for rent and Miriam was thrilled, so we called at the solicitor's office who had the key to the property and walked along Erskine Road and round the corner onto King Henry's Road and there was the house, all four storeys. Ruby ran up and down stairs, exploring all the rooms and outside into the delightful little garden overlooking the village just down Erskine Road. Miriam was delighted that there was space for the whole family and a garden for the two dogs. We agreed a rent and went back to the solicitors to draw up the agreement. After that she was so excited and couldn't wait to tell her parents. I suggested she tried the French Embassy to see if they had any work for an interpreter who could also type; as apparently, she could. I invited her to visit us in Norfolk, as any time she wanted a break she would be very welcome. I asked how the old gentleman was who had travelled on the boat with his little granddaughter. Miriam told me Mr Abe Goldbaum was staying in a lovely flat overlooking the park in St John's Wood and had been paying their housekeeper Madam Monteux and her daughter Maya to cook, clean and help look after the little girl, Avigail. The money for the flat had been sent from America by his son who was living and working successfully in New York. This was the little girl who, interestingly, thought she had seen Ruby before at her school in Paris.

We then said our goodbyes and managed to get a taxi to Mayfair where Grandora had booked us into her favourite hotel, Claridge's, because she thought we would be safe there. It was a first time visit there for me and Ruby, but Malissa said she had stayed before with her parents, when visiting London. The foyer of the hotel was spectacular, and you just felt special the moment you walked in. We had a lovely suite of rooms with our own lounge and two bedrooms. It was beautiful, very luxurious, even glamorous in an art décor style. Grandora had arranged for the trusted jeweller to meet me the following day to see one pouch of the diamonds and just two buttons, one with a ruby and one with an emerald. He was to give us an estimate of their value. The first request I had to the concierge was to put our valuables into the hotel safe and secondly to ask for some shampoo and conditioner to be sent to our room. We still both smelt of Derbac – at least we were convinced that we did. Our suitcases were brought upstairs for us with a lovely shampoo and conditioner. I jumped into the shower to wash my hair followed by Malissa. We had both had enough of smelly, sticking-up frizzy hair. I put on a fresh pale green silk blouse with my tweed suit, and we went downstairs to explore the amazing public rooms of the hotel, ordering a fresh pot of tea and tiny, tasty sandwiches for Ruby in the lounge area. Malissa looked amazing in a pale grey fine wool suit with a pale pink cashmere short-sleeved jumper, and her long black hair, now smooth and shiny. We were soon out exploring Mayfair and we took Ruby into the garden square to play and count how many squirrels we could see. It was sad and frightening to see sandbags round all the shop doors and windows in case of bombs and flying glass. There was no colour or glamour in the dress of the people of London – they all seemed to be wearing sensible austere clothes in dark, drab shades of khaki, grey and olive green. It was a relief to get back to the safety of the hotel and we went upstairs to enjoy our beautiful suite and listen to the wireless. The news was constantly updating us on the latest situation in France and about the armada of boats big and small bravely being sailed to Dunkirk to rescue so many of the soldiers from the beaches. One boat was called Daffodil from the General Steam Navigation Company of London and we knew one ferry boat called The Hestia belonged to Nico and Malissa's family. We prayed the operation would be successful and the boat and crew stay safe. Although the news bulletins regularly updated us, it remained sketchy, and it was hard to grasp just what was happening. At the same time, we were enjoying our stay in a beautiful hotel.

At six-thirty we went downstairs to be ready for our table in the dining room for an early dinner with Ruby being allowed to have a late night. Here rationing was also in evidence, but there was more on the menu than we had expected, and we dined very well on Scottish salmon and new potatoes. Ruby managed a small portion of poached chicken and we all enjoyed raspberry ice cream for dessert. The dining room was amazingly busy with elegant ladies, lots of military uniformed personnel adorned with gold braid, and the conversation floating round the room in many different foreign languages. We were very excited to see the King of Yugoslavia entering the dining room as we were preparing to leave. We didn't know him, but we were told it was him by our waiter and that he was living in the hotel because of the war. We learnt that the Kings of Greece and Norway were also using Claridge's Hotel as their current home. Malissa hoped to see the King of Greece as, although her mother was from Albania, she was a 'Tripolite', a Greek Albanian and her father was Greek. Her father had a fleet of cargo ships and ferry boats running under the Greek flag delivering goods and people from around the Mediterranean and Adriatic seas. I was constantly learning more about Nico and Malissa and their amazing lives.

Then it was off to bed, in wonderful feather soft beds with the softest sheets, and room service brought us hot chocolate drinks upstairs. It was wonderful luxury far away from reality and the unfolding horror of Dunkirk.

Next morning, we enjoyed breakfast and Malissa had eggs benedict and Ruby I enjoyed freshly baked croissants and jam, boiled eggs with bread-and-butter soldiers. Then we went to Harrods and while Malissa took Ruby to the toy department, I explored the food hall and looked at the produce on offer. Here was plenty of food for those who had enough coupons and I checked out the honey and jams as an idea was beginning to form a small seed in my head. I joined the other two in the toy department, and it was exciting for Ruby, but toys were not a priority during a war and there were not that many on offer. I bought a new monopoly game which I thought looked fun, five new packs of cards, a newly designed snakes and ladders board, ludo and tiddly winks games and some very pretty marbles to keep us and our evacuees busy during the long winter evenings. Malissa bought a chess set and games compendium, a beautifully decorated box full of a variety of games. Ruby had her mind set on a particular doll and so when she wasn't looking, I bought it her for Christmas and she was very happy with a new Harrods' teddy bear to hug and take with her. Then, I don't know why, but I bought another teddy bear and a similar doll. We went into the book department and Malissa was in heaven browsing and choosing books to buy and I was fascinated by an art book about Wyndham Lewis and his choice of painting geometric abstraction and the history of the artist; so, I bought it. Next, I bought a variety of children's books for different ages for the library at home, including Peter Pan, The Secret Seven and Grimm's Fairy Tales. I loved the art section and bought myself a new little box of travel watercolours, some sable brushes and a small book of quality watercolour paper. I bought some divine books with marbled paper on the covers and plain sheets of paper inside to write in or draw on whatever you wanted to do. Downstairs we discovered a department of hair adornments and another of scarves, so I went as mad as allowed with rationing, and bought new scarves and hair slides for Christmas presents. I must admit we had a wonderful time choosing and buying without thinking about getting it home, but since it was to be packed and delivered to Norfolk by Harrods, we didn't have to worry, leaving everything to them. We went to the Harrods restaurant to eat, caught a taxi to Hyde Park and walked through the park to see the swans, ducks, and geese. I wondered if they would stay or fly somewhere else, should London be bombed, or God forbid would they be eaten, should rationing get worse.

At three-thirty in the afternoon, we were back in the hotel, and I waited in the reception area to meet the gentleman coming to value the diamonds and buttons belonging to Ruby, which I had placed in the hotel safe. As I waited for the jeweller to arrive, I noticed how many high-ranking uniform personnel were using this hotel for meetings. Malissa had taken Ruby upstairs for an early bath and to have her tea delivered to the bedroom as she had enjoyed a busy and exciting day and was very tired. The gentleman arrived and we were shown into a private room just off the foyer as had been instructed by my grandmother to the concierge. The gentleman was called Mr Jakabus Guilhem and after our introduction I showed him the pouch full of diamonds and the two buttons, one with an emerald and one with, we believed, a ruby.

"These are magnificent," he said, immediately. "The emerald is a lovely green saturation colour and very likely Russian. Most possibly it has been in another setting in a piece of jewellery before being separated to make a button," he added after studying them through his jeweller's loupe. He carefully replaced the loupe into its sleeve because if the magnifying glass was scratched it would be useless. He wrote their value onto a piece of paper and passed it to me. I was stunned! Little Ruby was indeed an heiress.

"May I ask how you came by these incredible jewels?"

I breathed deeply – should I tell him? "We found a child in a car accident; she was alive but the other two people in the car were dead. We brought her to Britain with us and are caring for her. Efforts are being made to trace her father, as we believe it was her mother who was dead in the car, although we are not sure. The jewellery was found in her belongings, and for the purpose of insuring the valuable jewels we have come to you on behalf of the little girl to ensure whatever happens she has a secure future.

It is for that purpose you have been recommended. We have been assured you will give us an honest valuation." I hoped I had said enough without saying too much.

"May I meet her?" he asked.

"Well, after a busy day she has gone to bed. Why would you want to meet a little girl who we believe to be only three or four years old and has not spoken one word since we found her? We call her Ruby, but we don't even have a correct name for her."

"I would like to put a face to this child and assist you in locating her relatives, nothing more," Mr Guilhem concluded.

I went to the door to summon a waiter; however, the concierge was waiting for a signal from me and came immediately so I instructed him to ask Malissa to bring little Ruby downstairs.

Waiting for Malissa and Ruby to appear, we spoke briefly about the demise of the British army fleeing from France and the many refugees in desperate need of sanctuary on our shores. When Malissa arrived, I introduced her to him, and he immediately recognised her name, Angelopoulos, from the Greek Albanian shipping family and was surprised that Malissa and her brother Nico had accompanied me on my journey from France. He spoke to Ruby and told her he was enchanted to meet her; he spoke to her in French. Ruby just smiled shyly at him and cuddled up to Malissa. He then spoke to her in a language I didn't recognise, and Ruby showed him her lovely sparkly bracelet. He spoke to her again and she lifted her necklace for him to see. Malissa and I were speechless.

He smiled at Ruby and spoke to us, again, in English. "Well, Ruby understands Hebrew, so I think we can be sure she is Jewish."

"What did you say to her?" I asked.

"I asked if I could see her beautiful bracelet and then I asked to see her necklace and as you saw she understood me. Oh, and her bracelet and necklace are real, and I am sure a closer inspection would confirm that they are both Cartier. Her father is either in the jewellery trade or her parents are extremely wealthy people. What kind of car..."

I put up my hand. "Not now, we have a rule not to discuss such things in front of her." I nodded towards Ruby. "It is not a great secret, but for her sake some things are best not spoken about."

He nodded and said, "I understand; if I can be of further help, please let me know." He stood up to leave and I walked to the door with him. "Do you think they were heading for Switzerland?" he asked.

"Very possibly Switzerland, as that was the direction, they were going in," I agreed. "Thank you for your help," I added.

"I will send a written estimate to your grandmother's solicitors, it's been a pleasure to make your acquaintance." He shook my hand. "You are very kind people taking care of Ruby. Could I ask if you would consider helping some more Jewish children and their families escaping from the Nazis' regime?" He included Malissa in this request with a nod of his head towards her.

"Of course we would; you may include us in any rescue plans you have. We have room at the Hall in Norfolk. If we can assist in any way let us know. My parents have a house in Chelsea should you need extra accommodation at some time," I added.

Malissa nodded in agreement, and he bowed and left.

As we were on our way back to our rooms a note was delivered to Malissa by a well-dressed young man, and she looked very surprised to receive it. "Sid, it's from the King of Greece. I must go immediately. He is waiting to see me in the lounge, please come with Ruby and stay just a distance away in case I need you."

She left for the lounge. I followed at a discreet distance and sat with Ruby leafing through a Tattler magazine while Ruby sat next to me studying her Rupert Bear book. I kept my eye discreetly on Malissa who was introduced to King George II of Greece, and I watched her curtsy and refusing a drink began to listen intently to what he was saying. She answered at length about something, and he just kept nodding. Finally, he stood up and Malissa did too. He then indicated to me to join them and nervously I went over with Ruby.

"You are both remarkable young women and it's that kind of spirit we need right now to help destroy the Nazis. I have heard about your journey through France and about this little child you are looking after. I thought Malissa would like to know that her father and mother are both safe on the island of Santorini and her father has his ships delivering essential supplies to our Allies as we speak. I also wanted to personally thank Malissa and her brother Nico for the use of their boat The Hestia during the evacuation of Dunkirk. She is back with some bullet holes, but safely in port. Sadly, two of her crew were killed as they were strafed by enemy aircraft, but I am proud a Greek boat was used during the evacuation and was proved to be invaluable. Don't hesitate to ask my staff here should you need any assistance regarding anything and good luck with your studies at university and the valuable work you will be doing for the war effort." He nodded to both of us and then turned to speak to his aide.

"How very thrilling to meet the King and hear that he was pleased. Nico will be thrilled you met him but saddened to have lost two of his crew," I added.

Not wishing to leave Ruby alone in the suite, we ordered our meal to be brought to us by room service and Ruby was tucked up in her bed and fast asleep when there was a knock on the door and our meal was ready and brought to us on a trolley table with everything we could possibly want. Such luxury. We listened to the wireless again and the news was dire. Eventually I put on the music of Benny Goodman, and we listened to Big Band and Swing to lift our mood. After another good night's sleep and first-class breakfast, we headed for the train station to catch the train to King's Lynn. The station was even more packed with people, and, it seemed, judging by their luggage, they were trying to leave London. We were early and while waiting for our train, we sat in the waiting room watching the people in the station. Some appeared completely lost and others just tired and frustrated. Some of the soldiers looked very worn-out, exhausted with lost, haunted looks in their eyes and we feared they might have been Dunkirk victims.

We both wondered about Nico's boat and just where she was now. She had been built to travel between the Greek islands and was able to dock in Albania, Italy, Portugal Spain or Greece. First and foremost a ferry, used to transport people, animals, food and spices around the Mediterranean, she was not suitable for an Atlantic crossing and could only just manage the Bay of Biscay in good weather. Nico liked to nurse her and was very proud of her.

We eventually got on the train and made an incredibly slow and jolting journey north to King's Lynn and then on to Narborough with lots of stops, starts and shunts onto sidings. The delays were caused as we constantly had to make way for trains carrying troops or machinery. Eventually we arrived in King's Lynn only to discover our train was running two hours late. Signs were everywhere which read 'Is Your Journey Really Necessary' and 'Careless Talk Costs Lives'. One which I took very much to heart read, 'Grow Your Own Vegetables'. I convinced myself it had been important to discover if Ruby had a physical disability stopping her from talking and to find out the value of the gemstones as well as to rent out my mother's Primrose Hill house to a grateful family, very much in need. It was good to have found a solution to Miriam's London home problem. So, yes, my journey had been necessary. However, I was not sure about our spending spree in Harrods. I was relieved we weren't carrying dozens of Harrods packages for people to see and that they would arrive by carrier later. Now I studied thoughtfully the 'Grow Your Own Vegetables' poster. Well, we did grow vegetables on the farm, but I had only recently been looking at our Walled Garden and it was enormous, and no way was it growing as productively as it could be. I knew of one young man who could help us! Osian. And we could keep bees for honey, goats for cheese and milk. I was determined to call Merry when we arrived home to ask if they had decided about Osian coming to work at the Hall. If Osian was occupied growing vegetables, he could be excused active service and as he was a pacifist and short-sighted it might just work out for the best for all of us and our country, but especially him. Since he was part of a large family he was used to children and with evacuees arriving shortly, to keep us busy, this environment might suit him well.

After hours of a very slow journey and many delays, we arrived at Narborough, and there was Granger, waiting for us; thank goodness. Feeling grimy after our long journey on the steam train billowing out clouds of smoke, it was bliss to sink into the leather seats of the Rolls-Royce. Thankfully, it was home in time for a late tea for Ruby and then bed for her as she was a very tired little girl.

We had a later dinner with Nico and Grandora, and told them all about our adventures of the last few days. Nico was pleased to hear about his boat, The Hestia, but sad to hear that two of her crewmen had lost their lives. We were able to tell him The Hestia was in Falmouth Harbour and the captain was considering mooring in Dartmouth.

We were shattered and as soon we had told them about all our trip we were ready for bed. It was then that Grandora dropped the bombshell about evacuee children being expected in two days' time. She explained I would have to go and 'choose' to which children I wanted to offer a home for the duration of the war.

I thought it would be easy, but we just didn't have enough bodies to help with all the washing and meals and then I remembered, whilst in London I had offered to have more children, who would be arriving from Europe, and probably didn't speak English.

I didn't tell Grandora about my offer to Mr Jakabus Guilhem, it would do for another day. Malissa caught my eye as we left the table and grinned at my cowardice.

Chapter 19

Operation Pied Piper, First Evacuees

So, the day arrived bright and clear that I was to pick up our evacuees. I had ridden Hermes the day after our London trip and was out again, very early, riding on a fine clear May morning. It was the day before June 1st, and it was wonderful to canter along the edge of the beautiful green park which was disappearing little by little under the plough to grow wheat to make more bread for the war effort. Next, I had breakfast and then a quick look at how the cottages were coming along with their new downstairs bathrooms and more up-to-date kitchens. I walked on, checking the new cesspit, but I could see the brick work coming along and it looked enormous. Perhaps that's where the term 'built like a brick s..t house' comes from, I mused.

Next, I changed into a blue tweed skirt, white cotton blouse and knitted fair isle blue gilet and prepared to drive to Narborough station. I was apprehensive, even worried about the new children and how we would get on with them and they with us. I arrived at the station half an hour before the train was due to arrive, parked up, noting there were a few people waiting to collect the children, and for the first time wondered how they would be allocated to each prospective 'foster' family. A lady sitting behind a desk outside the station ticked my name off from the list on her clipboard – here it said I was to be allocated two children. She was very prim and proper, and I discovered she was called Miss Pearson.

I waited in what I think was a sort of a queue and recognised some of the people already there from our village. Strangest of all the people in the queue was a man I knew because he had a very untidy ramshackle farm which belonged to our estate. I had earmarked a visit to him regarding the state of the property. He lived alone and reared pigs for meat and slaughtering them at his farm. Surely, he wasn't a suitable candidate to take on an evacuated child who I would have thought needed a family situation. The train arrived and we heard doors opened and slammed shut and then out onto the front of the station came a small line of children looking terrified as they anxiously stared at us. Another lady with a clipboard started calling out names and suddenly 'our' queue jumped forward and started claiming the children they wanted. Jonas Black jumped forward, which was surprising for such a rotund man, and grabbed the arm of the biggest boy there and started dragging him towards the car park.

"Mr Black, you have to register and sign for his ration coupons and your money and put your signature by his name," shouted the lady with the clipboard.

The money was just over ten shillings a week towards the expense of keeping an evacuee, and eight shillings for any other children staying in the same house. Mr Black turned back and loosened his grip on the boy who, like lightning, sprinted back to two smaller tearful children that he had been standing alongside.

"Oy, you come 'ere," shouted Mr Black.

Everyone waiting to sign for the children were now all staring at the scene being played out in front of them. I then realized that the two children the boy had gone back to were standing alone because no one had picked them. I went over to say I would take them as my heart went out to these two. The boy was about nine years old, and the little girl couldn't be more than five. She had what I knew to be referred to as mongolism, she was clinging to her young brother and reaching out for the older boy whom I now presumed to be an older brother. It was heart wrenching, and I could not stand and do nothing. I knew then I would take them all home with me.

"Mr Black," I said, coolly keeping my temper as much as I could. "Why would you want this boy? I hope you are not planning to make him work on your farm?"

Mr Black gaped at me open-mouthed, and his brain started to engage as he realized just who I was. Gripping his greasy battered hat in both hands, he replied, "No, no, just thought I was 'elping 'avin a lad to tek care of at me 'ome wif job bein' what it is like, you know. If you want 'im you tek 'im, me Lady, I can alus wait a few days fur next lot."

"Excellent then, I will," I said crisply, and turning back to the sobbing children and their brother who looked at me full of hostility, I said, "Come along then, let's get you signed for and home for some lunch." I walked over to Miss Pearson, the lady with the clipboard. "Might I suggest in future you check out who puts their name down to give a child a home, you know where the home is and in what condition. You should not let just anyone put their name down without all necessary checks having been completed beforehand."

"You were down only to take two children," she said reproachfully. "You haven't been allocated more money."

"It's clear to see they are siblings and should stay together. If you have any complaints take it up with my grandmother, the Dowager Lady Ellesdale, Chairwoman of the Board for the homing of evacuee children in this area."

With that I turned sharply and, ushering the three children out towards the station wagon steered them all onto the back seat, put their three tiny suitcases and gas masks into the back of the car, noting how small their cases were. I was yet to discover that the evacuee children were only allowed to take to their new homes a kit bag or case containing very little. So, this was going to be interesting, I thought, as I drove home. I hope they all get on with Ruby and it was going to be difficult as Rosie had been off for two days, adding yet more to my workload. Her brother had been rescued by a boat in the armada of ships which had been over to Dunkirk. He had been badly injured in his shoulder prior to the evacuation and had been taken to the beach because of his injuries without his unit, the 2nd Battalion Royal Norfolk Regiment, and now he was in a hospital in Plymouth. Mrs Burden and Rosie were going out of their minds with worry about how Frankie was and there was no way they could visit him. I had wondered if Merry was now nursing and if she would do me a favour and find out how he was – only possible if he was at the same hospital of course. A long shot, I know, but you never know if you don't try. I had been waiting to hear from her regarding Osian coming to run the market garden side of our farming enterprise and to get cracking with some bee colonies, and so I had telephoned to speak to her about what The Rev. had thought about my offer. So far it was good news, and I was expecting to hear from them any day as to when he might arrive. Since his arrival was imminent, it was important to get on with the refurbishment of the servants' old cottages. We needed more help and Humphrey Clayton had told me that several of our tenant farmers had applied for help from the land army girls and he thought that we should too. We certainly needed help on the Home Farm with farm duties.

I turned into our drive and parked by the front door.

"Come on then, how about some lunch?" I asked.

"Where are we?" asked the eldest boy as he stayed in the car.

"We're home," I said patiently. "Let's go in and have some lunch; I'm starving, and I bet you are too; then I will show you around." I opened the back door and they all stayed on the back seat looking worried. "Come on, I'll get your luggage." With that I opened the back of the station wagon. Still no movement from inside the car. I sat on the tailgate and breathed slowly. Time passed and I waited silently. "Can I help you?" I asked. "Is there a problem?"

"We were told we were going to a family home and staying together, not to an institution for Lottie."

"What institution?" I asked curiously.

"This one," the oldest boy said.

"It's not an institution, it's my home, it's a house. I am very sorry that's what you think; it's my parents' house."

"It can't be, it's too big," piped up the younger boy.

"Please, come on, I'll show you the gardens and the horses first, then you can make up your mind."

Just then Jabbo came round the corner leading little Donk with Ruby riding in her little jodhpurs and boots.

"There's a blackie 'ere," said the young boy. "Why's 'e 'ere and 'oo's that girl?"

"Come on all of you, please meet Jabbo and Ruby and little Donk," I said, deciding now was not the right time to correct his comments.

The young girl was excited and started saying donkey, donkey and her older brother got out of the car with her and let her stroke Donk's nose.

"This is Jabbo, he's from Morocco and he lives here. He has a beautiful white circus stallion called Zoltan and he will show you his trick riding one day. This is Ruby and she is from France, and she would probably like to play with your sister. Would your sister like to ride on Donk with Ruby?" I picked her up and put her onto the donkey's saddle pad behind Ruby, and Jabbo set off towards the stables with the two boys following behind him. The little girl was hanging onto Ruby and her older brother was holding onto her. Just then Odin came running from the house and wriggled and squirmed with delight to see me. Breathing a sigh of relief, I took the three little suitcases into the house and went to the kitchen for a cup of tea.

Grandora had opened the door but missed the three children and, taking one look at my strained face, said, "That bad? You need a decent coffee." She soon returned with her French coffee from her hidden store and we both savoured the peace and quiet and a real cup of coffee. I related to her the events at the train station, and she was as annoyed as I was at Jonas Black clearly trying to get hold of cheap labour for his farm. "I'll sort him out, don't you worry. Now what are the children like and what are their names?"

"Oh my, I never asked them their names and I never read their name tags – what a good start! They have gone off with Jabbo and Ruby to the stables. I ought to fetch them."

"Leave them to Jabbo, he has plenty of good sense. I thought you would like to know what Merry has found out for us about Rosie's brother, Frankie?"

I sat up. "Is he all right, can he come home, how is he, how did Merry find out?"

"Slow down and enjoy your coffee." Grandora then told me that Merry was doing more nursing practice in Plymouth and one of her fellow nurses in post-operative care had met Frankie. "He is recovering very slowly and nearly lost his arm – he still might lose it – but the doctors are hoping there might be some ability to use his hand slightly as time goes on. He won't be going back to fight again and so will be coming home eventually, after a time spent at a rehabilitation home, that is. Apparently, he has been having bad nightmares as have a few of the soldiers who have returned from France. Evacuation from Dunkirk sounds horrific.

"On a more urgent note, here, I sent Granger into the village to update Rosie and her mother of our 'arrivals' and to beg them to be here tomorrow as we need their help. So, Rosie is coming later this afternoon to meet the children and to give Ruby her tea and put them all to bed. Merry says her father is delighted that Osian will be coming here, and it will be a wonderful place for him to contribute to the war effort. Osian has been for a medical for the navy, but he is very short sighted and so he failed."

"Well, you have been busy! Have you seen George and Theodore today, have they gone to school?" I asked. "They will be surprised when they meet the new children, the older brother looks about twelve I think, the same age as George, so should be company for each other."

Grandora said the boys were at school and told me that Hugh Brownlow and his wife Margaret had enjoyed having the boys over with them training and walking the gun dogs. They now wondered if they could stay with them at their home, until their mother was able to have them back, especially as we are now having some evacuee children and will be pulled out with cooking and washing. "Hopefully I will be able to play whist with them from time to time and I was teaching them how to play Bridge. Jabbo said he will teach us how to play Ronda, a Moroccan card game, and the good news is Margaret will come three days a week to help with the extra work here, especially if we have some land army girls staying with us as well," she added.

I then dropped my bombshell about agreeing to re-home some Jewish children who are escaping from the Nazis and have nowhere to go. They could only come to Britain if they had a sponsor and somewhere to stay.

"You did the right thing; I am pleased you offered to have those poor children who need all the help they can get," said Grandora.

"Well, that's not quite all; when I spoke to Mr Guilhem on the telephone, I agreed he could use my parents' empty house in Chelsea for any new homeless Jewish arrivals; just for short periods and only the first two floors. I suggested he had a word with you to confirm."

"Right, I see, I will speak to him." With that she added, "Ah, at last, Rosie is here early so you had better get her briefed about the new children, I'll leave you to it then as I have more letters to write."

As Grandora left she put both our cups into the sink and gave them a little rinse. Rosie looked surprised as it was so unusual to see Grandora do any sort of housework. I just shrugged my shoulders to Rosie. Little did Rosie know but Grandora was secretly trying to get rid of the smell of the delicious real coffee we had just enjoyed. Best not to say anything; Grandora was so funny, I did love her.

I chatted to Rosie about her brother and my friend Merry whose brother Osian was coming to work here in the Walled Garden and hopefully keep some bees and make honey. She told me her father used to keep bees and Frankie always helped him when he was young, so if Osian needed any advice Frankie might be able to help. Very interesting, I thought. I told her about the new children and that I was very worried about how they would fit in with all of us when Jabbo brought all of them back. He came through the utility room and knocked on the kitchen door.

"Hello all of you, we need to introduce ourselves. I am Sid, this is my friend and helper Rosie, you've met Jabbo and Ruby, so can you now tell us your names?"

The younger brother said, "I'm Lennie and I am nine, this is my little sister Lottie, and she is five, and he's...."

"Shut up, Lennie," said the oldest boy and then with a frown on his face said, "I'm Larry."

"Good heavens, all Ls, so is Larry short for anything?"

"Laurence," he replied with hostility in his voice.

"I'm Leonard and she's Charlotte," said Lennie.

"What cracking good names your parents gave you," I said, still feeling on shaky ground with Larry. "So did you see Zoltan?"

"Yes, 'e's smashin' an' we stroked 'im," said Lennie.

Jabbo turned to leave. "No, Jabbo, do stay and have a cup of tea with us," I cried rather too loudly, but not wanting to be left alone with just Rosie and these children. "Please do stay."

He looked surprised but sat at the table. Ruby went to Lottie, took her hand and took her to the table to sit next to her and Rosie made tea for us with milk for the children and I put the cake, I had made earlier, proudly onto the table.

Larry stared at Ruby and said, "Ow cum she niver speaks?"

"She doesn't want to yet, but when she's ready she will," I told him and smiled at my gorgeous Ruby who happily beamed back at me then at Lottie, bless her. Rosie put a plate of egg sandwiches onto the table, and they tucked in. I told Jabbo about Osian and the work he would undertake and our hope that one of the cottages would be ready soon as that was where he would stay.

"Be a few more weeks yet," he replied, "I think the problem is the piping for the new bathrooms. Metal is hard to get hold of just now; it's needed for the war."

I nodded; it was getting noticeably worse trying to get hold of many products. Manufacture of everyday goods was halted, and every effort was being put in to producing bombs, guns, aeroplanes, and tanks; even material was all being directed to make uniforms. "Ok, I will see what I can find to help; meanwhile, Osian will have to stay here in the house somewhere."

Rosie, Ruby, and I took the children upstairs to show them their bedroom and the bathroom. They couldn't believe they didn't have to go outside to the lavatory. Larry remained hostile and I decided there wasn't much I could do except hope that he would eventually come round, when he realized we didn't mean harm to any of them. Odin followed everywhere we went, wagging his tail and enjoying the children's company as he loved playing catch the ball with the children. Well, he just loved playing with children. I found Grandora in the sitting room, knocked on the door and took the children in to meet her. Ruby ran to sit on her knee then jumped back up and shyly took Lottie over to meet Grandora. The two boys stood awkwardly by the door, not happy about going into the room. Grandora asked them to come in and solemnly shook hands with both and asked if their journey had been a good one. Lennie answered Grandora's questions, but Larry remained silent and withdrawn.

He looked around the pretty sitting room and then just stared at his feet.

Trying to sound cheerful, I said, "Right then, off we go, we could walk round the gardens. But, oh, look, here's George and Theodore back from school; they can show you where the tree swing is and where we go swimming when it's nice day, can't you, boys?" They opened their mouths to say something and then looked at my face and agreed they would show the two boys around. "Ruby, show Lottie your toys and your dolls; off you go." I sat on the nearest chair.

"Not going well then?" Grandora sensitively asked.

"The oldest is difficult, but it's only his first day or should I say couple of hours. I just don't know how it's going to pan out; and it was your suggestion we had them, not mine," I reminded her. Grandora then informed me, "I have bikes coming soon, they have been on order for several weeks. I'll hunt them up and would you mind getting in touch with Arthur, the man you bought the tiles from and ask him if he can locate any piping for us for the new bathrooms?" I slumped further down the chair feeling low and exhausted.

"Sit up dear, remember posture and the family motto 'Dum Spiro Spero'." I grimaced and translated it, "Oh, yes, 'While I Breathe I hope'. I'll try to remember that over the next few weeks." Grandora chuckled.

I went into the kitchen to prepare tea for the children, mashed the potatoes with a little butter and milk, heated the chicken soup which had been prepared earlier by Mrs Revill (today was her day off), and put the enormous apple pie into the oven to heat. Then, just in case they were very hungry, I cut thick slices of fresh wholemeal bread and buttered them. I added cheese from the dairy and homemade pickle. We were lucky to have our own dairy farm, a herd of Ayrshire milking cows and a herd of Lincolnshire Red suckler cows for meat. My grandfather had always kept a few Long Horn cattle and we still had a bull and six cows which had been preserved; well, allowed to wander wherever they wished; and they still did. So far, we had not suffered food shortages as they were in the towns and cities, although we were short of sugar, tea, and coffee. Flour was becoming difficult to buy, but there again we grew wheat for flour and oats for our horse feed. The windmill was still working at Bircham, and they bought our corn, so we always had a good supply of milled flour. An announcement had been made forbidding horses from getting corn – this should be used to feed people. We were lucky to have plenty of grazing and our own chaff and oats to feed to our horses. Pity some horses, who were now receiving few hard rations, were short of grazing land so, of necessity, were sent for slaughter.

Jabbo came back with the children at five o'clock followed by Odin, Lucy, Zippy and my father's two dogs, Trig, and Spruce. I left him in the kitchen with them all and went to the little family sitting room to fetch Rosie and the two little girls. Ruby's tiny pooch was there, as usual, watching them playing with dolls. No doubt at some point she had been dressed in a dolly's cardigan and neck scarf and lined up with the dollies for a tea party. The little dog put up with all the dressing up and playing with Ruby. She just had to be with Ruby; the pair were inseparable. Lottie and Ruby seemed to be very happy playing together and Lottie's disability did not seem to be any trouble to her; she was just a little bit slower, that was all. When they had washed their hands and were sitting down for tea, a 'hush' descended around the table which didn't normally happen. I had asked Jabbo to join us for tea and he told us the boys liked his home, the Woodsman's Cottage, and they had been looking at his woodwork as well as helping get the stables ready for Zoltan, Hermes, Donk, and Polly. Even George and Theodore seemed quiet tonight.

"Did Margaret speak to you about us staying with her and Hugh?" asked George.

"Yes, Grandora told me, is it something you would both like to do?"

"We enjoy being there very much and it's interesting helping train the dogs and walking round the estate and helping breed the pheasants and partridge and, yes we have both said we would love to stay there," said George.

"I hope you don't mind us going there, and she's a very good cook and I have learnt how to bake cakes now," added Theodore.

"Very well. It's fine with me. We'll still see you every day and don't forget to come over and play cards with Grandora," I said, laughing.

"Do you play cards?" Larry asked, looking interested. "What do you play?"

"Whist, canasta, and bridge and Jabbo is teaching us how to play Ronda, a Moroccan game of cards, do you play?" asked George.

"No, but I'd like to," Larry replied.

"Can we play here when we have eaten?" asked Lennie.

"When you have finished eating, I don't see why not. We don't usually play here, we have a games room, but tonight you can stay here until it's bedtime." I got up to clear the table and made up a tray of simple food for Grandora and myself, and left Rosie and Jabbo with them in the kitchen; they had agreed to stay and supervise the card games.

I ate with Grandora in her sitting room at her small round table and we said little as we both were tired and deep in our own thoughts, but comfortable with each other. I did tell her they were playing card games, with Jabbo and Rosie watching over them. I told her that George and Theodore were happy to stay with Margaret and Hugh, and that I thought it was a good idea. Grandora was more interested to hear that Jabbo could play cards and was going to teach the boys Ronda. I told her he didn't say he could play Bridge or whist. "However, he is from Morocco, and they play Tute and Ronda and I had forgotten that until just now."

"Oh, brilliant, I have someone else to play cards with and he can teach us all how to play Moroccan cards," she said beaming. She turned on the wireless and we listened to the six o'clock news which didn't tell us much about the evacuation of Dunkirk; only that it was ongoing. I picked up the tray, kissed her goodnight and left her listening to the musical broadcast coming from Alexandra Palace wireless station. All seemed to be going well in the kitchen and Rosie had taken the two little girls upstairs for a bath and to bed. I suggested the game was wound up and could be continued tomorrow. I thought Lottie would be comforted, knowing her brothers were in the bedroom with her. Lennie went up as good as gold, and George, Theodore and Larry put the game away and Jabbo said goodnight to us and left with his little dog. I let all our dogs out for their ablutions, waited for them to come back in, then locked the door and went upstairs with the three boys. Odin came with me, and Lucy went up with George and Theodore, which surprised Larry and Lennie.

"Our dog stays outside round' back all time," said Lennie.

"Does he?" I said. "And where does he sleep?"

"On chain in yard wiv 'is little kennel. Lottie loves 'im, wanted to bring 'im wiv us."

"So, your parents are both out working all day, so who walks the dog?"

"Nobody walks him," Larry said.

I was mortified for the lonely dog and worried for his safety if they were going to be bombed. "Where do you live?" I asked.

"East End, Docklands on account of our dad's a docker." Said Larry proudly. "Oh yes, essential work in peace and war." I agreed. There was little more to add right then, but I was determined to rescue their dog and bring it here; and wouldn't Lottie just love that.

Ruby was in her bed and Rosie was putting Lottie into her new bed. She had a dolly and a teddy with her, which Ruby had given to her. She was pleased to see her brothers, and Rosie and I left them to get themselves to bed. Well, we checked Lennie had everything he needed as he was only nine. Rosie had unpacked the evacuees' suitcases and was surprised to see how few clothes or personal items they had brought with them. We found a list of their requirements for evacuation in Lottie's suitcase and on it was written: change of clothes, house shoes, plimsolls, spare socks, stockings, toothbrush, soap, face cloth, handkerchiefs, warm coat, mac, packet of food for the day and a label with their surname and Christian name, plus their school and evacuation authority. Not much when they had no idea when they would go home or see their parents again. Rosie was staying for the night to help with all the children who would need help getting ready for school in the morning. Rosie asked if we should sing the song 'Goodnight, Children Everywhere' to them?

"Good heavens, what are the words?" I asked.

Rosie started singing the song composed for evacuated children and sung by Gaby Rogers and Harry Phillips.

Sleepy little eyes in sleepy little children
Sleepy time is drawing near
In a little while you'll be tucked up in bed
Here's a song for baby dear

Goodnight children everywhere
Your Mummy thinks of you tonight
Lay your head on your pillow
Don't be a kid or a weeping willow

Close your eyes and say a prayer
And surely you can find a kiss to spare
Though you are far away she's with you night and day
Goodnight children everywhere

Soon the moon will rise, and caress you with its beams,
While shadows softly creep.
With a happy smile you will be wrapped up in your dreams,
Baby will be fast asleep. Goodnight children everywhere.

"Oh, right. Very good, Rosie, not sure about Larry and Lennie needing to hear it. Perhaps Lottie might enjoy it, I'll leave it up to you." Smiling I then bid her goodnight, even though it was only eight o'clock. I was too tired to stay up, went for my shower and tuned in to listen to the Hi-gang with Bebe Daniels, Ben Lyon and Vic Oliver; they were so funny. Day one with the evacuees; over and out.

How do parents of large families manage children without servants? The effort to get everyone up, dressed and at the breakfast table was exhausting and it was only eight o'clock in the morning, and I had Rosie helping too. I had yet to drive them all to school. I could have asked Granger, but he was working on the cottages after doing the horses. He was our coachman/groom/chauffeur/handyman, and he was without doubt the most important person on the estate as far as I was concerned and had been part of my life for as long as I could remember.

Today was a day of assessment to discover which children should be in which class in their new village school, or should they be going to the senior school which was across the road. George was at the senior school and Theodore was at the village junior school. I expected Larry to be in senior school and Lennie to be in the juniors, and Lottie to be in the first-year infants. Ruby, we thought, was only three or four years old and too young to go to school, so we had never enquired if there was a class for her. We arrived at the school as other evacuee children were arriving with village children too. I went in with them all after seeing George across the road and into the senior school. Larry was deathly pale, serious, and sullen. He was taken off to see the headmaster with several older children to discover their level of education, before being placed in the appropriate classrooms. Lennie went into a different room, and I waited with Lottie who was clutching my hand and was very quiet. Lennie came out eventually and he sat with us, waiting to hear how his test had gone. Finally, he was told to go into a classroom, and he seemed very pleased as he had passed the appropriate test for his age group. Larry came out and sat opposite us, lolled in a chair with his legs stuck out and looked mutinous. I was called into the reception class with Lottie and a teacher sat with her and gave her building blocks and a jigsaw to do. Other children of the same age were starting to read and write. We were sent back to the waiting room and waited with Larry for what seemed a long time. I was then told to go alone into the headmaster's study and asked what I knew of Larry and his mardy disposition. I innocently asked him what he meant and told him I had picked the family up yesterday at the station and had been acquainted with them all for less than one day. What was I supposed to know about them? He then said he didn't think Larry was suitable for the senior school. What! I was so angry with the headmaster and with Larry. How can an opinion be formed in such a short time. He then suggested that Lottie could not attend school because of her disability, and they did not have the correct facilities for her. They suggested she be sent to an institution for people the same as her. I told him she played beautifully with Ruby, my ward, listened to story books and was trying to learn to read and would benefit from following other able children. The reception teacher was called and seemed embarrassed by the decision. I stood up to leave.

"I will leave you to reconsider your decision and I will bring Ruby in to show you how well she plays with Lottie."

"How old is Ruby?" he asked.

"She is four next week, it's her birthday," I replied, feeling a bit guilty about inventing Ruby's birthday for Lottie's sake. I was so mad though. "And you might like to reconsider Larry's attendance since I was prepared to host a garden party for the school at Willup Hall and organise some tours for the children round the farm to see all the farm animals with a day in the park to study painting and sketching."

The mood suddenly changed. "Oh, in that case, that would be marvellous. Then I will organise Larry to be in the last year of juniors for the rest of the term and look forward to seeing your ward, Ruby, tomorrow." The headmaster was flustered.

I marched out and saw Larry had been listening. "Right, I will take Lottie home now to play with Ruby, and you can go with the teacher here to your classroom. I will pick you all up at the end of the school day."

He said nothing but followed the young teacher to his classroom. So that's how things are done, I thought; I was learning fast.

Later in the day I picked them all up from school, then dropped them off by the kitchen door where Rosie was waiting with Ruby and Lottie with tea prepared for them. I went to the stables to ride gorgeous Hermes, my beautiful rock, because I needed time to think. It was a warm, pleasant, sunny day and a ride alone always made me able to think through my problems and then I would feel calmer. It was much harder work than I thought it would be, having the children. It was tough for them to be carted off to some stranger's house, go to a new school, meet new friends and, how must they feel leaving their parents and family behind, whatever the circumstances. I remembered how much I had hated boarding school.

The ride did me good. I felt so much better riding through the park with Odin running with us and it helped to clear my head of clutter and think through possible solutions. I chatted to Jabbo and Granger about how the cottages were coming along and assured him I had some metal piping arriving the next day. I talked about the Walled Garden and about Osian arriving to turn it into a productive market garden. Jabbo had some good ideas about what to grow and revealed he loved cooking and growing vegetables as they did in Morocco, but he liked to use herbs and spices. He wondered if we could try to grow a few spices in the long greenhouse when all the glass had been repaired and I told him I was sure Osian would be delighted to have some help. I walked through the Walled Garden and looked at the salad stuff growing for the household and thought how sad and weedy the rest of the garden looked and wondered what we would eventually find growing amongst the weeds. I walked into the rose garden and sat under a pergola walkway of softly scented, creamy pale pink roses and breathed in their perfume. Then I saw Larry sitting under the bower of roses watching me. I walked over and sat on a wall opposite him. "I am truly sorry you are mad and sad about being here." He said nothing. "Do you want to go home?"

"I did, but not now you were good with the headmaster. Thank you for sticking up for Lottie," he replied.

"Was it alright in the classroom, after I left?" I asked.

"Well, it's too easy. I've done the work before," he said.

"So why did you fail the exam?"

"I didn't," he said, "I just didn't want to talk to them or answer stupid questions."

"Oh, so why are you mad?" I asked.

"Because we were sent away from our home to come 'ere on the train and I can easily look after Lennie and Lottie 'miself', at home. I do, after school every day and I could get a job and earn some dosh to help mi Ma, then instead, I've come 'ere and I see 'ow much you 'ave and it aint fair. Why should you 'ave so much and we've so little. I've never seen an 'ouse as big as this and all the posh stuff you've got in it. We've got an outside lavy, a tin bath which we all use once a week and we never 'ave enough money for food an' rent. It don't seem fair."

"So do something about it," I said.

"Like what?" he asked. "It's all right you are sayin' that, but what can I do to change things?"

"Be political," I said. "Get educated, be as good as anyone, go to university, speak out, join the debating society, make changes, get into Government. Talk to Grandora – she was a suffragette and knows how to demand change, how to work for change, how getting people together can and does make a difference, stand up for yourself and your family and fellow workers. Do you like reading?" I asked.

"I love reading," he replied.

"Oh, what kind of books do you have at home?" I asked.

"We don't, we can't afford books; don't be daft. Sorry I shouldn't say that to you. I go to the library when I can." He kicked a loose stone with his toe.

"Well, we have a library here and you can read what you like. I'll take you there now. Just read them in the library, it's quiet in there but the books do have to stay in the library as they're my father's books."

"What do you read?" he asked, as we walked back to the house.

"I can't read," I replied. "I wish I could, but the words are jumbled up to me and when I try to read a page, I have forgotten what I've read at the top by the time I've got to the bottom."

"You can't read?" He was incredulous.

"No, I paint instead."

"Where are your paintings?" Larry asked.

"Stored away since I came back from France."

"You went to France?" he asked, surprised.

"Yes, I have been living there for nearly four years with Grandora's sister Henrietta, but now because of the war, Tantetta, which is what I call her, has gone to stay in Switzerland with her sister Augusta and I have come home to help Grandora run the estate."

"Where are your parents?" he asked.

"In Singapore, out of the way of the war here in Europe, but I just wish they would come home." I suddenly shivered as I thought about them; the sun disappeared behind a cloud and a chill wind blew off the sea.

I showed him the library and he was transfixed. "I've never seen nuffin like this in somebody's 'ouse before." Just then Grandora came in. "Oh, it's you, dear, I wondered who was in here."

I explained Larry's love of reading and told her, "I'd said he could read in the library, and I told him you were a suffragette."

She twigged, smiled, and was delighted. It seemed I had made a break-through with Larry and Grandora went over to chat to him about the books. I left them talking together to check on tea and what the others were doing. It was non-stop and I wished Malissa and Nico were here.

The weekend soon came, and it didn't bring Nico or Malissa, but it did bring Osian and I was delighted. That young, cool, uncomplicated, calm young man arrived and from day one brought a can-do-anything attitude to all of us. He was quite simply a Godsend.

I had received a letter from Merry telling me about her training and about the boys and The Rev. and just at the end she added that Osian would be arriving at the train station on June 1st eleven o'clock Saturday morning. The letter arrived at seven o'clock Saturday morning, so it was a mad dash to be ready and at the train station. The morning had started very early, with me riding Hermes at six o'clock. It was a short ride, we followed the river as far as the cows' pasture at the end of Home Farm where we crossed the river and came through the farmyard past the Gamekeeper's cottage, and the kennels and back up the other side of the river to the stables. What a joy my mare was. The sun had risen, and it promised to be a glorious warm June day with endless big blue Norfolk skies. I arrived back at the house where everyone was still sleeping to find Arthur had arrived with the pipes for the cottages. He apologised because some were copper, and some were lead. He thought the copper could be used in the houses and the lead for the connections to the toilets. As I was talking to him Larry came over to see what I was doing. I introduced him to Arthur and left them talking while I went into the house to get the cash to pay him, a mug of tea and a slab of toast dripping in butter and honey. I passed Larry a mug of tea and a slab of toast at the same time, and they seemed to be hitting it off. They seemed to understand each other and be getting on well and Arthur asked him if he would like to spend the day in the lorry with him and help collect a new stock of hens for me. I could see Larry was thrilled to be 'working' and Arthur winked at me, counted his money then they both jumped into the lorry and left. What a good if unexpected result.

I went into the kitchen to get myself a cup of tea before the others came downstairs. It was nice to have a quiet time to myself. I was reading the 'bumf' on the land army girls and when they would be arriving, when the postman brought the letters. After that Lottie and Ruby came downstairs in their nighties carrying teddies, dollies with the little pooch trailing after them. The two girls decided to help themselves to the porridge I'd put on the table and leaving trails of porridge across the table. I quickly took charge and finished filling their bowls for them. Next downstairs were George, Theodore, and Lennie, none of them dressed, and they proceeded to make just as much mess getting their porridge. They were so busy chatting I don't think they noticed me there. Lucy wandered over to Odin and Pooch and climbed on top of them in the dog bed, sighed and went to sleep. The little pooch fought her way on top of the two bigger dogs and then went back to sleep with a big yawn and a sigh. I considered how lucky we all were, here, with good food, we were safe and very comfortable. I made more toast on the AGA for all of them, buttered it and added the honey myself to try to lessen the mess they might make. Then it was time to make a tray up for Grandora, a lightly boiled egg which I took to her room. I took the post with me and gave her the letters addressed to her and opened my one letter – which is when I discovered Osian was on his way and arriving in two hours' time. Fortunately, Mrs

Revill had arrived, and Rosie was just coming down the drive as I ran out to drive to the station. I was glad I was on my own apart from Odin who always made sure he was with me, and I enjoyed a lovely drive over to Narborough station. It wasn't likely the train would be on time, so I stopped to buy some lavender plants from a stall at the side of the road and the car then smelt wonderful. I bought a mug of tea from the WVS and sat in the sunshine to watch comings and goings. All life's emotions were displayed in front of me, joy, elation, grief, sadness, beginnings, and endings. I felt at peace in that moment, closed my eyes and turned my face towards the warm sun. Then a shadow blocked the warmth of the sun, and I opened my eyes. Before I could focus on who was standing in front of me, I felt a light kiss on my lips, and I knew instantly who it was; it was Tiff. Before I could get up, he had wrapped his arms round me in a big hug and kissed me again properly on the lips. I was in heaven.

"Well, I wasn't sure how to find your home and I was going to hitch, but I didn't know you were telepathic and would be here waiting for me," he laughed.

I just stared at him, rendered speechless and enjoying being in his arms. "No, I'm here to pick someone up and I'm so pleased I am. Why are you here?"

"Just to find you before I travel to Ireland to visit my parents. I haven't seen them for a year."

Pathetically all I could stutter was, "But the war?"

"Not part of it at the moment," he said ruefully. "So, who are you waiting for?"

"A young man," I said.

"Competition?" he joked.

"No, no." I felt myself going red. Just then I spotted Osian looking up and down the road, searching for me. "He's there,

Osian." I shouted, "Over here." I jumped up and took Tiff over to meet Osian.

"Gosh, were you the girl being smothered by this soldier, no wonder I couldn't see you," Osian joked.

They shook hands and I led them to the station wagon. Osian was a small, wiry, young man wearing spectacles and was engulfed by Tiff's large six-foot two-inch frame. It was then I noticed Tiff limping and leaning on a walking stick. "What happened to you, how are you? Oh, I am so sorry, what can I do to help?" I wittered on.

Osian took Tiff's kit bag from him.

"Oh, thanks, don't worry, I'm on the mend but I need to sit in the back of the station wagon so as to put my leg up on the seat." We sorted him out and Osian loaded his bags and Tiff's and commented on the lovely lavender. He then surprised me and ran back to organise a large trunk which was being brought to us by porters.

On the journey home Osian and I chatted about what he was going to be doing at the Hall in the two-acre Walled Garden, and about the bees and goats which, so far, we hadn't bought. I learnt more about Merry and how all his brothers were. He told me The Rev. was now chaplain to the naval personnel which meant he needed to stay in Plymouth every weekend. Weekdays saw him busy with parishioners and being Minister to the Home Guard; he had much to do. Now, with Osian leaving home he would be looking after his own large vegetable garden at the Rectory, while Gryffydd would look after the goats and the bees.

"So, does Merry ever get home to look after the little ones?" I asked.

"So far, she has a long weekend every fortnight and we have a local lady called Mrs Jones who comes every day except Sundays to clean and cook from twelve o'clock until six o'clock. Her sister Mrs Perkins, you met her, still comes every Monday and Tuesday to do all the laundry, so we are doing quite well really. Merry is loving nursing and is convinced it's in her blood because our mother's sister Bettina became a nurse and went to France just after The Great War and her father was furious and wouldn't speak to her again even though she found and rescued her brother."

"How did she do that?" Tiff asked curiously.

"She knew he was injured, and rumours were spreading about a bad killer influenza called Spanish Flu spreading everywhere, especially in crowded places like hospitals, and so she travelled alone to France to find him and bring him back. She did all that on her own and then went back to France as she had fallen in love with a French man, a baker, and she married him. Our grandfather was furious with her and never forgave her for deserting her brother."

"I thought you said she found her brother in France and brought him back home to England?" Tiff questioned.

"Yes, she did, but her brother was so badly injured he was confined to a wheelchair and needed round the clock help and nursing care. My grandfather thought it was her duty to stay at home and care for him. Instead, they had to pay for all the nursing care he received. I think that she had a child, a boy and she sent a photograph and a letter to apologise and explain that she had instantly fallen in love with the French man, but Grandfather never forgave her not marrying the man he had chosen for her."

"What about her brother, didn't he stick up for her after all she had done for him?" I asked.

"Of course he did, and so did his mother and sisters, but their father was very strict, a Presbyterian minister, and didn't back down; she was forbidden to return or even write. He didn't like foreigners and blamed all of them for the war which caused his only son's injuries."

"You could say not a very good Church minister," commented Tiff wryly and asked, "So is your uncle still alive?"

"No, sadly he died five years after the war from his injuries which never healed properly. Uncle Alexander survived the Great War and the 'Spanish Influenza Pandemic', he even married, but the Great War did kill him in the end. His name should be on the war memorial in their village, but it isn't because he lived for a few years after. On top of all that my grandfather died a broken man from grief."

"Oh, Osian, that's so sad and you have a cousin in France, and nobody knows him. Has your Aunty Bettina been to England to see you all since her father died?" I asked.

"No, we know she died of tuberculosis when her son was six and my grandmother has tried to trace him, but his father won't answer any letters."

Tiff and I were both quiet, digesting this sad story of how families fall out and lose touch. We wondered how the young man would be coping with the invasion of France when he should have been with his family, here in Britain.

I turned into our drive and there were children playing everywhere. As we came to a halt they swarmed around the car. We helped Tiff out and I left the children to claim Osian who was in his element of course, being used to such a big family. He was soon in the garden kicking a football around with George, Theodore, and Lennie. I took Tiff into the kitchen to meet Rosie and Mrs Revill, and arranged for a pot of tea to be brought through to Grandora's sitting room and we went through the hall to find her. She was sitting sifting through papers in my father's office, and I surprised her with Tiff. We gravitated towards her comfortable sitting room, and I left her talking to Tiff and went in search of Osian to rescue him from the boys. Returning with Osian, I found Tiff and Grandora deep in conversation about the awful situation with the war in France. So many countries were now under Nazi rule and there didn't seem to be any stopping the onslaught of the Nazis' war machine rolling across Europe. Grandora asked him how he had been injured and he made light of it, skirting round what had happened. When she asked him about his unit, he skipped round that subject too, but it soon became apparent they both knew a certain very top Colonel in the army, Colonel Charles Haydon, and Lieutenant Colonel Charles Vaughan.

Eventually the conversation turned to Osian and his plans for the Walled Garden. We told him we had ten new beehives waiting to be started and that we were working on a new goat house and milking parlour for them. We had already organised for them a designated field and paddock with extra strong fencing in place. However, we still had to purchase the goats! The hens were arriving later that day and Jabbo was very keen to help look after them and get them settled in. I also told him that Jabbo was hoping Osian would let him help in the garden and the glass house and he was hoping to grow some spices. We chatted about the renovation of the servant's cottages and the Woodsman's Cottage where Jabbo now lived. I told Tiff about the evacuee children, and we were probably going to have some Jewish children joining us soon, escaping the tyranny of the Nazis. Tiff told us about his parents' home and farm in Northern Ireland, how many cows they milked, and how they had all hunted during the winter. His father was a noted breeder of Irish Draft horses. They also kept a few racehorses and did some point-to-point racing. Even I didn't know this and was fascinated to learn more about Tiff and his family. It was soon lunchtime, and we ate in the morning room, leaving the children to eat in the kitchen, supervised by Rosie. We then decided to let Tiff lie down and rest after his long journey and Grandora, Osian and I went into the Walled Garden to hear Osian's plans for the redevelopment. He was so enthusiastic and had brought a book with him of sketches he had drawn and had already made a list of the numerous plants and seed packets we needed to purchase. He said he needed to study the garden and dig around to discover the type of soil, what had been planted in the past, and what had survived. So, we left him in peace to plan how he was going to make it all work out.

I went back into the house to try to decide where Osian was going to sleep and now Tiff, and make up the beds. 'No rest for the wicked', came into my mind.

Chapter 20

Tiff injured

W hile I prepared the beds and then the meal, Tiff rested in the drawing room. Grandora went into King's Lynn, and I gave the children and Osian lunch, vegetable soup and sandwiches. I left Tiff sleeping – he was clearly exhausted and still in pain from his journey, so I went to check on the cottages again. I walked round the one that was nearly ready and could see all it needed was painting upstairs. I decided to wash everything downstairs and found there was enough hot water for me to thoroughly wash the floors, stairs, bathroom, and kitchen. We now needed some curtains and a rug for the sitting room, table and chairs in the kitchen-cum-dining room, and it would be ready for Osian to move in.

It was nearly teatime, and the house was quiet as all the children had gone to the kennels to Hugh and Margaret's to help take George and Theodore's clothes over to their house where they were going to stay. Rosie and the girls had gone with them. Lennie would miss the boys not living with us but would still see them every day. I went back to the kitchen to make a pot of tea for Grandora who was back, and take Osian and Tiff some of my cake. I went into the drawing room to see if Tiff was awake, and I thought although he was very hot, he was still sleeping; so, after opening a window to cool the room down, left him. I went outside to find Osian and told him about Tiff and then I went to find Grandora, and we both went back to the drawing room to find Osian very concerned about Tiff and suggested I call the doctor immediately. Grandora said he needed the ambulance too, so I called that as well. Dr Haigh arrived. The doctor gave him some medicine and looked at his knee injury which was weeping again and smelt. We were all relieved when the ambulance arrived and took him to King's Lynn hospital. I went with him and was shocked this had happened so quickly when he had seemed quite well. Grandora followed in the car with Granger to pick me up and she came into the hospital to find out how he was. Dr Haigh was there too, and he told us the hospital were quite sure his wound had gone septic, he had a fever, and it would be a case of waiting to see if he recovered sufficiently to have another operation. They asked if we were family and when we said no, they said his family should be informed. I was mortified he was so ill and couldn't understand why he had been allowed to leave the hospital he'd been in previously. I decided to stay with him all night and Granger took Grandora home. Thank goodness Rosie was there and Larry should have arrived back from his day out with Arthur to help with the children.

Tiff was seriously ill, and I was unable to leave his side, I was so worried. Dr Haigh came into the hospital on Sunday afternoon and said he had contacted a friend from his medical school days and if I could agree on behalf of Tiff or his family, they would try a new drug on him called penicillin. I now had his parents' telephone number and I spoke to them. They agreed the drug could be used. He responded immediately, thank goodness, enough to have an operation to try to remove the shrapnel still in his knee. A surgeon from London came to operate on him, he was the son of a good friend of Grandora, and the operation was successful. All Tiff had to do now was rest and then start therapy to help restore the movement to his knee. He was in hospital for two weeks and finally came home on the 22 June. He was anxious to hear the progress of the war but we had no good news to tell him. On June 10th Italy had declared war on France as they were part of the Axis alliance with Germany. Norway had surrendered to Germany after sixty-two days of fighting and Malta had been attacked by Italy. On June 14th German forces had entered Paris and we then had news that the Nazi occupying forces in France were slaughtering all cattle, pigs and chickens after France surrendered on June 15th to Germany. On the 22nd June Vichy France was established as a Nazi-run client state and the north and coast of France was under German control.

We were able to let him read the speech given in the House of Commons by Winston Churchill which was a stirring speech and at the same time very sad. It seemed that we in Britain were the only ones continuing to do battle with Nazi Germany. I think it strengthened all our resolve to fight on and defeat the monster that was Hitler. His speech was called 'This Was Their Finest Hour' and he had only been Prime Minister for one month at this time.

Tiff was angry to be lying in a bed at home and not fighting for his country – he needed to be with Scotty and getting on with his job. Then news came June 30th that the Channel Islands had been invaded by German forces and Tiff started trying to get up and walk. He was so angry with his inability to participate in the war and with himself for not being better. Jabbo was brilliant

with him and, using his carpentry skills, he transformed an old
hospital wheelchair, delivered by Arthur, into a chair Tiff could
propel himself about and keep his leg elevated. He no longer
had to wait and be pushed by someone. Tiff could get around the
downstairs of the house now and was soon wanting to get outside
into the Walled Garden and onto the brick paths. Granger and
Jabbo lifted him outside and took him to the garden where the
paths were being repaired with bricks and he could just manage
to get round the big garden, and this exercised his arm muscles.
He kept himself busy passing bricks to the men and I think they
made sure the bricks were placed so he could reach them. He
started to try to stand and walk with crutches without putting any
weight on his bad knee. Again, the crutches were made by Jabbo.
He then became sore under his armpits from the crutches and
kept having to stop and rest, so they were padded with sheep's
hair covered in cotton. Finally, he progressed to just a walking
stick and weight bearing on his knee and was told by the surgeon
to swim. As we only had the river, Jabbo, and Osian helped him
into the water and supported him to the deeper water where he
could gently use his leg, move it and start to swim. At this point
his wound was fully healed, of course, and the cold water seemed
to help him use all his muscles. He always had a bath with plenty
of hot water after being in the river and a long rest until lunch
every morning. He started to cycle and could soon cycle round
the village. He was very determined to recover fully as soon as
was possible.

When Tiff had first left hospital it happened to coincide with
Ruby's 'birthday', her fourth birthday so we were able to have a
joint celebration. It was her fourth birthday so it meant she could
continue to attend infant school with Lottie, mornings only. They
were allowed home every day at two o'clock, so it wasn't too long

a day for the young pair. I had made a birthday cake with our butter and eggs, and we had saved our sugar ration for the cake. I used last year's raspberry jam for the filling and Mrs Revill found some candles. The best bit of the party was the arrival of a small lorry and the unloading of a new red tricycle for Ruby and a blue tricycle for Lottie, and then bikes just kept being unloaded. One each for George and Theodore, second hand, but repaired, repainted, and looking smashing. Rosie had a bigger, newer bike than the little one I had given her, and I had a repaired 'new' bike, my mother's old bike repainted with new tyres. Grandora hadn't forgotten Larry and Lennie as when the boys arrived with us, she had asked the bike shop to do their best to find bikes suitable for them, which they did. All the children now had a bike and were over the moon. Soon they were all practising up and down the drive and down towards the stables. We all helped Ruby to learn to ride her bike and she picked it up very quickly. Lottie was a little slower, but within one week she was as good as Ruby, and they loved ringing their bells and taking their dollies and teddies for a ride in the baskets on the front, or in Ruby's case in her basket sitting amongst her dolls was the little Pooch.

As he grew stronger, Tiff joined us in our outing to the fish and chip shop on Friday night so that was George and Theodore, Larry and Lennie, Ruby and Lottie and Osian, Tiff and me all in the station wagon and usually singing very loudly all the way home. Fish and chips were not rationed as they were regarded as essential for people's diet and happiness. We had several trips to the cinema to see Rebecca and Gaslight on our own, and we took the boys with us to see The Thief of Bagdad. At other times we had happy trips with just the two of us, on one occasion driving down to the Norfolk Broads and taking a barge ride just for a day trip. It was lovely to do this trip now, because as the war progressed fuel rationing got worse until all private cars were banned from having any fuel at all. It was bliss for both of us to spend time alone and almost forget the war going on around us and not thinking about what lay ahead. He told me he was going to Ireland to visit his parents who had been very worried about him and asked me if I would like to go with him, but I couldn't. We were hay making for the cattle and horses' winter fodder and still completing the cottages and were expecting the imminent arrival of two land army girls. Merry was hoping to visit on her long weekend off from nursing and see how Osian was doing. We now had four goats in kid, and they kept finding new places to escape every day when we thought they were secure. The children loved running after them and catching them and returning them to their paddocks. So, we were expecting goat's milk and cheese, although I was beginning to have doubts about the wisdom of keeping goats. The Walled Garden now had all the brick paths repaired and it had lettuce, tomatoes, spring onions, cucumbers, radishes, broad beans, and peas growing, and we were able to take some to market in Swaffham. Osian was even growing sweet peas and hoping to have lots of chrysanthemums and dahlia flowers to cut for the house or take to market. Not essential but growing amongst the vegetables and salad they looked very cheerful and so were good for us in challenging times. Lots more produce was growing in the long glasshouse against the south-facing wall, which had now been skilfully repaired with glass by Jabbo and Osian. Some of the glass had been found in the garden, dangerously overgrown with weeds and some procured by Arthur Laxton. Jabbo had started to grow some spices with seeds he had from Morocco under the watchful eye of Osian. They were like a pair of kids in the garden, working hard, digging and lovingly restoring it all to its pre-Great War splendour. It wasn't work for the pair of them it was a labour of love. Tiff often joined them to sit in the sun and watch the plants grow. I am sure their banter in the garden encouraged the rigorous growth of the plants. It was always sheltered in the Walled Garden from any winds coming off the sea and the cordon of fruit trees were beginning to flourish again and produce flowers.

Tiff and I would regularly take Hermes out in the trap and enjoy driving around the estate on the tracks which joined all the estate farms up together, and the Norfolk countryside looked beautiful with the cow parsley just getting past its best and the wildflowers taking over in the hedgerows. Poppies were coming out, celandines, spearwort, red campions and white campions, bush vetch, ox-eye daisies and in the hedges wild honeysuckle and dog roses. The rooks had reared their young and the constant raucous, cawing of the baby rooks had been replaced by birdsong of every variety. We spotted hovering Kestrels and gliding Marsh Harriers and one day we saw a Merlin swoop down on its prey at the side of the track. We often took a simple picnic of Home Farm cheese and Mrs Revill's fresh bread, homemade chutney, and her delicious elderflower cordial. We discovered more about each other and found contentment in silence and just the sounds of the countryside and at other times we never stopped talking. He was the easiest person to spend time with. We kissed and held hands, but never took our intimacy any further in an unspoken agreement that the time was not right. We just took time to learn and understand each other.

We went to the Hunt kennels to see Alford Harrington, our huntsman, and to see the two new spring foals. They were both out of my father's hunters' mares and were by a local Cleveland Bay stallion with a royal pedigree. They were both beautiful, a filly and a colt. Alford told us no hounds had been bred that year due to the war and they had some hunt fixtures coming up at Christmas and New Year, but they would not be out as much as they usually would have been over winter. Their runners, who carried the scent, had been called up into the services. Tiff told Alford about the hunting in Ireland and invited Alford to visit when the war was over. They discussed hound lines and breeding, and horses, and Tiff told us he used to ride in Point to Points, but just got too heavy to make the weight. His father still had a licence and kept a few racehorses and point to pointers and always bred a few thoroughbreds and some useful hunters every year. They also bred a few Irish Draught horses keeping the line pure and not breeding them to thoroughbreds as so many people did. I told Alford that I would ride over early morning on Hermes, and he said I should go out on hound exercise with them come August as he thought they would be shorthanded. He was hoping George might help or Theodore, as they were keen on the gamekeeping side of the estate working with Hugh. He knew they could both ride and had ridden at pony club level, but it didn't mean they wanted to ride out with the 'hounds' early mornings before school. He was keen to know if I had heard from my parents, but I had no news. My father was now an aide to the Ambassador in Singapore, and I had given up hope of them coming home any time soon. Alford was very interested to hear about the evacuees we had staying with us. He told us he had joined the Home Guard with Humphrey Clayton and Granger and that Granger was talking about taking Jabbo to join. That was news to me. Tiff told him that Jabbo was a Moroccan, which was under French Colonial rule, and that it had been invaded by Nazi Germany and that it would be a good idea if Jabbo joined the Home Guard as well. Good old Tiff, that would shut up any dissenters at Jabbo joining. Just in case there were any, they really needed all the help they could muster to protect us.

We went home that day by way of Margaret and Hugh's house, the Gamekeeper's cottage, to see how they were and as it was four o'clock the boys were home from school. We could hear shots coming from the training field. Curious, we went over to the field first and Hugh had the clay pigeon trap out and was firing the clay targets for the boys to practise shooting, using under and over double-barrelled shotguns and a smaller lighter diameter barrel gun for Lennie. The four boys were taking turns to try and shoot the target. We wandered over and at first Hugh was worried I was cross with him and looked nervous until Tiff asked if we could join in. The competition was on: Tiff and I teamed up with Lennie and Larry, George and Theodore were against us. I am afraid we won which delighted Lennie and it wasn't my shooting which helped, it was just that Tiff couldn't miss a single clay, he was brilliant. Hugh and the boys were very impressed and so was I. It was good fun.

I had written to Mavis Evans to tell her we would have the children's dog here as Lottie missed him and would she like to bring him either to Norfolk and see the children, or meet me halfway at Stevenage with the dog. With all the travel restrictions I knew it would be difficult, but not impossible. I had not heard from her, but then it was a strange request, and I wasn't sure she would reply. Suddenly, however, out of the blue I did. She had a Friday and Saturday off work from the ammunitions factory and would love to see the children. She would be over the following Friday. Well, I had better get the next cottage ready quickly. Osian had moved into the first one we completed and loved living there. Tiff often went over in the evening and had a beer with him, although Grandora had discovered he could play Bridge and captured him at least twice a week to team up with her. It was some time before I knew that Jabbo played well, and it certainly wasn't just Bridge, and if the boys were included, they just loved to be in a conspiracy playing cards. Grandora said it helped with their counting. It had never helped my counting.

The Home Guard was organised in our area by Colonel Brian Orpington-Jones who was very 'old school' and very against Jabbo being part of their group. He came over to see Grandora and complain about any 'foreigners' being allowed to live at the Hall as "You don't know who you are dealing with, and you can't trust them". I think Grandora sent him off with a 'flea in his ear' and told him not to be so 'bloody nosy' and such an old fool. I didn't hear what she said, but apart from a very curt nod to me as he left, he stormed off in his car. When I heard about his complaint, I was angry, when I thought about all the entertaining done by my parents, he had always been first here with his snout in the trough.

$\mathcal{C}hapter\ 21$

The Garden Party

I had promised the headmaster a garden party and so plans had been made to hold one. It just so happened to be the same weekend that Mrs Evans was coming to stay. We had organised a sack race, egg and spoon race and a three-legged race, a wheelbarrow race, skittles, Quoits, hoopla and a prize for the best miniature garden (Osian's idea), guess the weight of the cake, and lots more, like splat the rat or others involving water, sponges and getting wet. Pin the moustache on Hitler was being prepared too. The school children had been making bunting at school and organising signs and the parents were contributing buns, jellies, and homemade biscuits; anything they could get the ingredients for. There was to be a best knitting competition for babies, socks, jumpers, and scarves. It was very exciting for some and exhausting for others like me. I invited Miriam to join us with the ulterior motive of cadging more help. Tiff was helping Osian and Jabbo prepare a plant stall where people brought donated plants they had too many of in their garden and sold them for school funds. Jabbo was planning a circus display as a grand finale and Nico was coming home to take part, with Lennie helping. Lennie had a good riding seat and was a natural horseman and sat a horse well. He had been taking Polly out and was really very good. It was a plan in the making, apparently. Hugo was going to give a gun dog display without any guns being involved. Just the dogs finding hidden dummies and finding 'pretend game' then standing completely still. Margaret was busy baking for us and promised to sell entrance tickets for six pence each. We now had some bees making honey so we would be able to sell some or give it away as a prize. It was to take place on the lawn at the back of the house next to Grandora's rose garden and we had been trying to make seats out of planks of wood we had found in the barn, but that was very much a work-in-progress. With increased vegetable production, slowly, we were beginning to take salads, vegetables and any surplus eggs and cream to the local markets and we were supplying the troops with beef, lamb, and venison. Soon we would have some turkeys as we were hatching off some eggs in our new incubators. Well, we wouldn't have too many of those, but enough to sell at Christmas and plenty of cockerels too. Just not my little Pekins, who were my pets. Arthur had brought me a trio of grey Pekins as a gift, and they were so tame and funny. Lottie and Ruby could often be found carrying the little fluffy hens around near their chicken coop.

The Friday before the garden party Mrs Evans arrived, I picked her up at the station. (I had sent her a return ticket.) I was surprised, she was lovely and so easy to get on with, which was silly of me as I should have known she would be as Larry, Lennie and Lottie were all lovely, happy children. She was very embarrassed about the invitation to stay with Arthur and his wife Violet, as they had taken a shine to Larry who worked there every Saturday. I didn't mind at all and was delighted that the dog

Spud had been bathed before coming on the train. She told me he had been very good and not cocked his leg up once on the train. That worried me. Did he usually cock his leg up anywhere? The children were thrilled to have their mother visit them and pleased to see Spud. Larry commented he could get some training with George and Theodore whilst he was staying here. He certainly was over excited whilst running around the garden and trying to mate the pooch, and the hens fascinated him. Thank goodness they were fastened up. He was a sort of cross with a Fox Terrier or a Bedlington or something similar with a wiry grey coat. He was put on a lead by the boys and pulled his way over to meet Hugh at Gamekeeper's Cottage. I think Hugh was in shock as Spud wanted to mate all the dogs there. It sounded like a trip to the vets was on the cards as soon as possible.

The day arrived, warm and sunny with little wispy cirrus clouds drifting across our enormous Norfolk sky. We were rushed off our feet getting tables ready with tablecloths and plates and games set up, the racetrack measured for the races, hessian sacks out ready to use, the list was endless. I insisted Tiff sat down and wrote out signs to keep his leg rested. Grandora popped out to check our progress, now and then, but apart from that kept a low profile until her moment came to declare the garden party open.

The people started to arrive at one o'clock and we were all kept busy manning the stalls. We also ran a knitting and crochet competition as nobody wanted to sell their work because they didn't know where they would get anymore wool in the future.

We had found some deckchairs stored away for cricket matches and we had placed these around the garden with the now cleaned planks of wood. These Jabbo and Osian had placed on straw bales and upturned small tree trunks with a few nails securing them. The bring and buy was not brilliant as we were all worried about rationing and wondered when we would need what was in our store cupboards, but some people had used it as a good way of getting rid of unwanted ornaments. Arthur came with his wife Violet and a horde of children – I counted six running around every stall and generally behaving themselves. All the school children came, which didn't count for many as it was a small village school. The teachers were helpful and blew up balloons for the children and helped put the food out and serve it. The races were run and won, one by Larry – he won the hundred-yard dash. Lennie won the wheelbarrow race using Theodore as the wheelbarrow and they both received a prize and were happy. It was a happy and successful day, and the culmination was to be the circus display by Jabbo, Nico with Zoltan, and Zippy. Off they went to prepare for the finale then suddenly an exuberant scruffy grey dog burst through from the entrance to the stables and galloped happily around everyone, jumping up, cocking his leg anywhere. He ran to the small fish-pond, threw himself in then continued running around, tongue out, jumping over people, sitting on picnic rugs, and shaking himself over everyone. Of course, it was Spud who was supposed to be locked up at the stables. All our dogs were fastened up as most of them would want to play with the games and run off with the skittles or hoopla hoops or balls. Spud carried on cocking his leg anywhere and by now he had a horde of giggling children trying to catch him. He headed straight for the pond again and then out the other side to start shaking himself everywhere. He was thoroughly enjoying himself and no one could catch him. Larry and Lennie were chasing him, and Lottie was calling him to her and in tears. Her mother went to comfort her and brought her to me nearly in tears herself.

"I'm so sorry, I will take him back with me; this is awful, he has ruined everything."

"No, he hasn't," I said, laughing. "It's funny and the children love him, he's certainly the best entertainment today." I smiled at Lottie. "Don't worry, darling, he's a lovely friendly dog, he can stay here with us, we like him."

Unfortunately, Spud spotted some food left on a table and with a flying leap he was on the table wolfing everything down and then he was on the run again, back to the pond, then another jump over a deckchair where the prim and proper lady with the clipboard from the station, Miss Pearson, was sitting drinking her elderflower cordial. He didn't quite clear her, knocked her backwards with her drink, which spilt all down her dress, and the deckchair collapsed. There was silence from everyone as they stared, not knowing what to do. Tiff used his 'I am In Command Voice' and shouted COME HERE to Spud, who was so surprised he went to Tiff, who caught him. Everyone then turned towards my very regal Grandora as if waiting for her command or reaction and she responded magnificently. She ordered someone to help Miss Pearson up off the floor, and suggested she be taken into the house. In a daze, many helpers rushed forward to help the poor lady out of the tangle of the deckchair. As she climbed the stone staircase following Miss Pearson to the drawing room, Grandora turned behind her and clearly stifling her mirth said, "Carry On," to everyone on the lawn. I started giggling, then Violet, Arthur, Tiff, George, Theodore, Lennie, and the headmaster started giggling and we all collapsed in laughter. Colonel Brian Orpington-Jones was overheard to mutter "Damn poor show", but was totally ignored as he'd come to the garden party, not paid, or made any contribution to the event; just enjoyed the free food. I was beginning to dislike him very much. Spud was taken back to his kennel and Hugh went with the boys to make sure he was secure this time.

"It was funny really, wasn't it?" said Mrs Evans. "Will that lady be alright?" She still looked worried.

"I can assure you my grandmother is a diplomat and will smooth everything over. In fact, the lady will almost be glad it happened to her by the time my Grandora has finished with her."

Half an hour later Miss Pearson did indeed come out in a different dress, one of my mother's I think, with a rosy glow on both her cheeks, clutching a sherry glass in both hands and giggling. Grandora was getting better and faster with her diplomatic relations, I thought. They both appeared at the top of the stone steps to the garden and a cheer went up. We all clapped, I'm just not quite sure who we were clapping.

There was a drum roll from Tiff on some weird bongo drums and Zoltan appeared from behind the gate to the stables with Jabbo, Nico and Lennie holding Zippy. They were all dressed in red satin Cossack-style shirts, white tights and white ballet-type pumps. Very fetching. There was a hush from the audience, which might have been because they were wearing white tights, and the trio went to a marked-out arena at the end of the garden. Everybody moved nearer to watch them. I think Jabbo was now well known locally as he often took Zoltan for long walks on a loose line, then he would jump on bareback and ride him home. He would stop and chat to anyone, and always let the children stroke Zoltan. Now he started to lunge the handsome white stallion into a steady rocking horse canter. Nico ran alongside the horse and then vaulted effortlessly onto his back. He sat up on Zoltan and then holding onto the surcingle he swooped to the ground, picked up a scarf held low by Lennie and Cossack-style crossed over sides and rode Zoltan with both his legs horizontal to the horse's body until finally he somersaulted off. Then he held the lunge line whilst Jabbo vaulted onto Zoltan, and Zippy the little white dog was passed to him. Zippy and Jabbo then jumped through hoops in unison. Jabbo somersaulted three times, and finally he held his hand out to Lennie who grabbing it, launched himself behind Jabbo. They jumped off, leaving Zippy still going round on the horse's back alone. Jabbo ran alongside and finally Zippy jumped into his arms. The crowd erupted with cheers, whistles, and clapping. It was spectacular and I was very impressed and proud of them. Lennie's mother was in tears again, this time with pride. "Wait 'till I tell their dad, he'll be so proud and pleased," she said and ran to hug Lennie.

Eventually it was home time, and everyone left saying what a brilliant day it had been. Rosie and her mother, Mrs Burden, took Lottie and Ruby inside and Mavis, Lottie's mother, went with them. The boys helped to put the deckchairs away and clear the tables. Lennie was tired and went in to go to bed and Larry asked if I minded if he went and stayed with his mother at Arthur and Violet's. So, when Mavis came downstairs, leaving a sleeping Lottie, they all left. Grandora said it was time for a glass of good wine and we opened a bottle of white from Tantetta's vineyard, one I had brought back with me in the horsebox. Then we opened another, as Hugh and Margaret stayed for a drink with Clarissa and Humphrey, Tiff, and me. Ted and Nora had already left for milking duties. Granger went and helped Jabbo with the horses, Osian went to his cottage after a drink of cider with us. I let all the dogs out and Tiff and I walked as far as the river with the dogs – the park was now mostly growing crops – and we took Spud with us on a lead.

It was a lovely, warm, peaceful evening. We watched the sunset in a burst of gold, orange, and many shades of red and then the darkening sky littered with thousands of stars. Tiff was quiet and I asked him what he was thinking about. He told me many men had been captured and taken prisoner at Dunkirk, many had been killed and the fighting had continued with the 51st Highland Regiment being left behind to fight with the French at St Valery on the coast. They had run out of ammunition and had been forced to surrender; those left alive had been taken prisoner. And he was standing here on this beautiful night with the girl whom he loved; and he felt guilty. He put his arms around me, and we kissed and stood like that, watching the stars in silence. Then he told me he had to leave and visit his parents in three days' time. He hoped that he was healed enough to resume active service. He had to be fully recovered as he didn't want to be a burden to any of his men when out in the field – they would have enough to think about without having to nurse him at the same time. The time he had spent here with me had made him quite sure of what he already knew: that he loved me, and he hated leaving, but he had to go and fight the German monster war machine now wanting to invade Britain. I dreaded him going as I realized just how much I loved him, and in this uncertain world I had no idea when, or if, I would ever see him again.

Of course, the next three days flew by – time always does when you don't want it to. Mavis Evans had returned home to London and the children were so sad to see her go. We decided to have a farewell meal before Tiff went too, and Jabbo wondered if I could get hold of one or two shoulders of lamb as he wanted to cook a Moroccan lamb dish for us. I managed a deal with the butcher which could be interpreted as black market racketeering, only I hope not. I was exchanging some cockerels which would be ready later in the year and some grazing for his sheep. Jabbo brought his recipe list which he had been checking with Osian. He had quite a few items, but many were impossible to find during the war. I went to find Grandora to see if she had any in her hidden emergency store; you never knew what strange things she kept in there. She always kept items that would store from Christmas hampers, and it was beginning to pay off during rationing. She did have some dates and flaked almonds, and wanted to keep some for the Christmas cakes; however, she loved spicy food, a taste developed on her travels, so was keen to share them with Jabbo for his Moroccan lamb dish. Jabbo always kept some spices with him and had some small packets which he had brought with him from France – turmeric and cinnamon and black pepper. We could not locate any ground ginger, but we found some tinned tomatoes in the pantry. Osian had started growing garlic which were very small just yet, but he donated two to the recipe and our onions were not ready and I wondered if I could barter two from Mrs Burden who had some tied up and dry from last year. Saffron stamens, very rare, were nowhere to be found. Osian had parsley and was growing coriander again in its early stages but could let Jabbo have a little to help with the flavours. The weirdest news was Osian had been to Ted's dairy experimenting with freezing cream with honey in place of sugar, and with some of our eggs' yolks.

The day arrived, Ted and Nora came bringing a metal container with the 'ice cream'. We had quite a gathering, including Margaret and Hugh with George and Theodore, Larry, Lennie, Lottie, Ruby, Rosie, Nico, Malissa, Grandora, Tiff, Osian and Jabbo. We all sat outside at six o'clock after another warm sunny day. There was a sea breeze beginning to blow in, but we were fine and sheltered in the Walled Garden. We had given Jabbo a big cooking dish from the scullery to cook the meal in and he had been cooking it on the fire which heated the glass house for hours. The smell of the sea on the breeze, the scents of the gardens, the lime trees in flower, it was all wonderful, and then the exotic smell of the Moroccan lamb, what a night to remember. It was so delicious even Ruby enjoyed the meal, although Lottie preferred the potatoes, cooked in the oven, more than the lamb. The rest of us found it the best lamb we had ever tasted. We drank cider or homemade apple juice made from last year's stored apples. The 'ice cream' was good, and very refreshing after the spicy meal. To be fair I think it was better than bought ice cream and everyone agreed. So, the night ended, and no one minded when Tiff and I left everyone to clear up and we made our way to the river before darkness descended, sat on our favourite tree trunk, and watched myriad stars appear. We walked back through the park to the enormous Cedar of Lebanon tree and here under the spreading branches with thousands of stars twinkling, Tiff stiffly got down on one knee.

"Darling Sid, when all this madness is over will you please marry me?" he asked shyly. "I don't have any right to ask you, when I am going away, and don't know when I will be back, but I would love to know we have a future together, when it's all over."

I flung my arms round him and laughing said, "Yes, get up, you'll damage your knee." What a perfect end to a perfect night.

The time came for Tiff to travel to Ireland. I took him to the station. He said he would come back when he received news of his next mission in one month's time if he was allowed. Sadly, we kissed goodbye like so many other men and women were doing now, and I stood on the platform with a heavy heart, waving him goodbye, until the train was out of sight.

Chapter 22

Horse Rescue

G etting the hay in was always a stressful time, making sure it wasn't too dry and dusty or too fresh and green to store in the barn. It was also a fun time probably because we were working as a team with the fresh sweet smell of meadow grass, and this seemed to make us all happy. Of course, it had to be made in good weather too, plenty of sun to dry the cut grass which added to the happiness we all felt after a long winter. Each day we prayed it wouldn't rain on any newly cut grass and spoil it. Luckily for us it stayed fine the first week and we made good hay, and the next week, after a weekend of light rain, we cracked on again and brought home a bumper crop of good hay for winter. Our new Land Army girls, Lucy Perkins and Sheila Beechcroft, tried hard to learn quickly but I know they suffered with lots of blisters on their hands. They were pleased with their new 'digs', one of the little cottages I had been renovating, as not many land girls had such luxury, and they knew it. They were fed three meals a day and then off they went to their own place to sleep, which pleased me not to have more people to worry about staying in the house. Lucy was small and slight, and at first, I didn't think she would manage the hard work, but I was wrong, again. She was great with the milking, and the cows liked her, and she had small hands to help if a ewe was in any difficulty lambing. Best of all she loved the horses and was always willing to help in her spare time. She had spent time working at a riding school, taking every opportunity for a 'free' ride. Sheila was taller and looked stronger, an efficient hard-working girl. Ted and Nora were pleased with their new helpers. Nico and Malissa had returned to Cambridge after coming home to help with some of the hay making and Malissa seemed to be always going to a place called Bletchley. But she never spoke about why she went there, and we didn't ask.

The news of the war in June continued to be depressing. On June the 22nd France had surrendered and on June 30th Nazi Germany invaded the Channel Islands. In France the German army took over the north of France. Vichy France was created in agreement with General Pétain as a Nazi client state mostly run by the French police on behalf of Germany. Our role was to carry on making sure we could supply all the food we could grow for our country and our troops. The news was depressing enough, the least we could do was try to provide as much food as possible and accommodation for people in need. I had a call at the end of June to ask if I was still willing to help two young Jewish children, so I discussed it again with Grandora and of course we both agreed we would help and sponsor them. I didn't hear from Mr Guilhem for a few weeks.

Given extra 'visitors', possibly on their way, I wondered if a former governess of ours would consider coming over to help with all the children. It was going to be too much for just Rosie and me. To that end I wrote to her with the suggestion that she might like to come and stay with us again if her family commitments

allowed. Margaret continued to come in three mornings a week
to help with the housework and cooking, and Rosie's mother, Joan
Burden, had been doing the laundry, but Frankie had come home
from hospital, and she felt that she had to stay at home to care for
him now. Rosie was very quiet about Frankie; she just said he often
had nightmares at night and woke up shouting and sweating. His
shoulder and arm were a mess, although there wasn't any more
that could be done for him in the hospital, and it was a case of
time. He was to try and to use his hand and arm a little more each
day. It looked as if he would not be fit to fight again, certainly not
anytime soon, in one way something of a relief.

A few weeks later I was out very early one morning riding
Hermes through the woods, when I heard what I thought was
sobbing. I stopped Hermes and looked in the direction of the
sound, nudging Hermes towards it. I slowly walked towards a big
fallen tree where a man stood with his back to me. The dead leaves
and pine needles muffled Hermes' hooves, I was nervous and not
sure I was doing the right thing, intruding on someone's grief.

I said, "Hello can I help you?"

A young man turned round, shocked that he had been seen.
"No," he said bluntly. "Go away. Please."

"Are you lost?" I asked, playing for time to see if I could show
him the way back to the village.

He said nothing in reply, he just slumped down with his chin
on his chest. I slid from Hermes and sat further along the log,
holding the reins and saying nothing.

Finally, he said, "You can go and leave me, I'm fine."

"Well, if, you're sure?" I looked at him and then I noticed a big
rope on the ground by his feet. "You know what, I don't know
your name and you don't know mine."

Silence again. Then he said, "Frankie, my name is Frankie."

So, it was Rosie's brother.

"I'm Sid."

He looked interested. "Our Rosie works at the Hall where you live."

"Yes, I could not manage without her, she is brilliant," I replied. "Would you walk back with me for a cup of decent coffee? I hear you know about bees and Osian is needing a bit of help, as two queens keep swarming and he's having trouble getting them back."

"Is he?" There was a spark of interest from him. "Rosie never said. She likes to tell us what's going on at your place. Oh, not nosy like, just chatting about the kids and what they get up to. Have you got real coffee?"

"Yes, don't tell anyone please." I got up. "Come on, it's breakfast time and I'm starving. If we're sharp, we can have a quiet drink before all the rest get up."

He stood and suddenly looked at the rope.

Quickly, I said, "Just look at that, someone has left a decent rope in the woods, we'll take it with us, shall we?" I picked it and threw it over the saddle and we both walked in silence through the deep woods to the path that led up back to the river and home.

We bumped into Jabbo, and I introduced them to each other, and they shook hands; Frankie used his left hand. I passed the rope to Jabbo and said, "Look what we found just lying on the ground in the woods."

Jabbo looked puzzled and Frankie looked embarrassed. I took Hermes to her stable and I came back out with her saddle and bridle and put them in the tack room. Jabbo kept him talking, showing him Zoltan and Donk and Polly. Jabbo looked at me quizzically, as I brightly asked him if he had a secret stash of good coffee, which I knew he did. He also knew I would normally never ask him for his good coffee in front of anyone, let alone a stranger, so he knew something was up. We were invited into his cosy warm cottage and were soon enjoying a fresh pot of rich coffee and tearing off chunks of fresh 'Moroccan' bread which we spread with honey. Frankie was starving and devoured the delicious simple meal in silence, staring into the fire which had been lit to heat the oven to cook the bread. I stood up to leave and Frankie started to get up.

"No, no, stay here with Jabbo and help feed the horses. Afterwards he is going into the Walled Garden to help Osian and you can give him some advice on how to stop the bees from swarming."

Jabbo stared at me and said nothing. He turned to Frankie. "Yes I need some help and it would be good to have some company." Jabbo never needed anyone for company if he had his horse and his dog, he was happy with his own company.

I left and quickly went to ask Grandora what I should do. Should I tell Rosie and her mother, or say nothing.

"We'll say nothing just yet but will keep an eye on him here. Do we have any work to keep him occupied?"

"Of course, there's always plenty of work, I'll go to Osian now, I might just catch him and tell him what I know. He's a good person, he will help, he always has some good ideas."

I ran and found Osian just about to leave his cottage. We went back into his kitchen, and I told him what had happened in the woods.

"Poor man, he's been through so much, he needs some peace and quiet and someone to talk to when he feels that he can. Leave it with me we will all try to help him." Osian was so calm and worldly wise for someone not yet eighteen. I thought he was amazing.

I had just gone back into the kitchen and started to prepare breakfast for the children when Rosie burst into the kitchen in tears saying they had lost Frankie, he had just disappeared, and he had not slept in his bed all night. I immediately told her he was safe, and I made her sit down and have a cup of sweet tea. I told her I had come across him walking in the woods and I had walked back with him. I told her he was fine and in the Walled Garden with Osian and Jabbo and I told her to go home immediately and tell her mother he was safe working in the garden here with us. Hopefully it would do him good.

Rosie left and I was organising the children when Mrs Revill and Margaret arrived with George and Theodore, so I took all the children to school in the station wagon. I wondered if I would ever have time to paint again – it certainly didn't seem possible when every day there was so much to do. When I returned home, I found Grandora in my father's office. We had coffee together and she told me I needed to fetch Spangles home. Apparently, the girls who had loaned him had gone to stay in Scotland for the duration of the hostilities. They had been too busy with exams at school to ride him and their paddocks had been dug up for food here in Norfolk, so they wanted to send him back. I was very pleased to know he was coming home as I had always loved Spangles. I went to tell Granger to organise a stable for him. I knew this would please him. An idea came into my mind to have a break away from everything just for one night. To do that I would take the horsebox and stay overnight at Grandora's horse racing trainer's yard which was near to where Spangles was. She used to have racehorses, but not anymore. I went into the Walled Garden and stopped and watched Granger, Jabbo, Osian and Frankie deep in conversation about some wood. Frankie looked animated and happy and was concentrating on Jabbo, who was describing something with his hands. I was pleased they seemed to be getting on well. Granger had been here all my life and had been a young groom here when I was born. He had never married, as far as I knew, and he was, I believe, an orphan. He was part of Willup Hall, just as much as I was, and he loved horses just as much as I did. He was fit for his age which I thought must be about fifty, and a lean, fit frame, grey hair, a kind, friendly, tanned, weathered, face, blue eyes which crinkled at the corners when he smiled, and he was always dressed in jodhpurs, leather leggings and riding boots. Jabbo was medium build, muscular and fit. He had fitted in here so well and loved horses as much as Granger and me. Frankie was in good hands with these two genuine, kind people. Frankie had brown, mousy hair, blue eyes, an open, honest face and a solid square frame. I went down to the steps into the garden to join them and tell Granger about Spangles.

"Champion, he's a proper good pony and was always best friend to Polly. I'll be right glad to have him back," said Granger.

"I thought I would take the horsebox now, and come home tomorrow," I said.

"The horsebox doesn't have any wheels as the bearings are being greased all round and serviced after your long trip home," Granger replied.

"Ah," was all I could think to say, as I was disappointed.

I was determined to go for Spangles and then I had a new idea. I decided to ride there on Hermes. I could use Pedders Way which would take me just about the whole way down to Thetford. I could stay overnight and ride back, leading Spangles the next day. I told the four men of my plan, and they were shocked! Shocked and speechless. Then I went up to the house to ask Grandora to ring her friends at the stud to ask them if they would put me up for one night and that I would be arriving the next day. Grandora was fine about it and said if I needed any help they would come and fetch me. I then packed my saddle bags and took them to the stables ready to leave early the following morning. Fortunately, Grandora soon came to tell me that her friends were looking forward to seeing me there the next day.

July was not turning out to be a good month and we were hardly halfway through it. Wick had been bombed, killing eight children and seven adults. Why Wick, nobody knew. The invasion of Denmark and Norway by Germany meant it was easier for their planes to get to Wick. The Luftwaffe had started bombing our shipping convoys off the southeast coast of Britain. Our Spitfire pilots were fighting the German air force in the air and our forces had shot down fourteen enemy aircraft and damaged twenty-three more. Bombing raids had started on the coast in the southeast of Britain. There was lots of talk about putting dogs and horses down because they ate too much food, needed to feed people, and cats were getting lots of flack about eating our food and should also be put down. There were rules about not feeding horses in summer and only feeding them what was necessary in winter. Even hens were to have their corn rations reduced and if they were not laying eggs, it had been suggested they be killed for eating. It was all this talk and the fact that the war was really coming to Britain now, that I felt it was important I went for Spangles. I just wanted him home. We were lucky we had some grazing land on the estate which was so hilly in parts it couldn't be ploughed up.

The next morning, I was up at five o'clock and in the stable yard waking up a sleepy Hermes. Granger was up to see me on my way.

"I'll do what I can to get the horsebox serviced and on the road in case you need me to fetch you," he said.

I was off, as the sun was rising, and dawn was breaking and fortunately it promised to be a beautiful day. This time I didn't take Odin with me, and I missed him running beside me, sniffing every hedgerow. However, I thought it was just too far and I didn't want him to have sore paws. Plus, I didn't know the people I was staying with and if they would mind having my dog stay too. The Pedders Way is a very quiet drovers track and mostly on soft ground where I could get on and canter. I walked, trotted, and cantered, trying to get there as soon as I could without tiring Hermes too much. I stopped for some coffee from my flask and a jam sandwich, and Hermes happily grazed. We travelled well and approached Swaffham at lunchtime and stopped again. I found a pub for lunch with a water trough and paddock for Hermes, so I took off her saddle and bridle and gave her one hour's rest and she grazed again. By teatime we were the other side of Little Cressingham and on my way towards Knettishall Heath. I turned off the Pedders Way and had to ask my way to the farm where we had been told Spangles was being looked after. Finally, I rode up a pot-holed farm track to a rickety old ram-shackled farmyard and I could see horses' heads looking over broken old stable doors. I tied Hermes up and looked over the doors into the stables to find they were filthy with horse droppings and no bedding, no water, and no food. I found Spangles in a stable with a smaller pony in the same dirty conditions. Spangles whickered to me. I was so pleased, he obviously remembered me. I was furious at their disgusting conditions and marched over to the equally dirty farmhouse and hammered on the door; but there was no one in. I was disgusted by how much junk and discarded broken items were lying around the yard and supposed garden, so I set about finding hay and buckets to water the horses. One bucket was all I could find so I watered each horse and found some dubious hay in a shed and gave it to them. I took Spangles out of the stable and fortunately I had Hermes' head collar with me, so I put that on him, and I left for the stud with him and Hermes.

It didn't take me long to find the stud where I was to stay for the night after asking directions in the next village. Granger had described the entrance to me accurately and a groom was waiting for me to take my horses, and care for them. Spangles was just ribs, no neck or covering of flesh on his rump and in a poor state. I was very angry and so relieved I had come to fetch him. The groom asked me how far I had come and seemed annoyed with me for expecting a horse in such poor condition to travel so far. I explained why I was there, and I told him about the horses in the stables at the dirty farm. He told me the man who lived on the farm bought horses and supplied them for the horse slaughterer. I was even more angry that Spangles was there; how dare the Marlowe family, to whom we had loaned Spangles, allow this to happen.

My hosts for the night, the Carlton-Jones, were very kind and I washed and changed into clean slacks and blouse from my saddle bags and joined them for dinner. They told me they had some good foals born this year and they would take me to see them. Their mares were put in foal before they knew we would be at war; however, they would not be breeding any more until after the war. They told me many racehorses were going for meat, as trainers and owners couldn't afford to keep them and there was so little food around for them as it was being kept back for the beef and dairy cattle. I told them about the farm I had been to, and the horses left there and the conditions they were kept in. Apparently, it was common knowledge that Terrance Mickle bought horses and sent them for meat, but they agreed it was unacceptable to keep them in dirty conditions without food or water. They agreed to go with me early in the morning, to see if anyone was there feeding those I had left there, in the dirty stables. We agreed there wasn't much we could do to stop them going for slaughter, but we could call the police if the horses were being starved.

Next morning, I was up early and, in the yard, to check on Hermes and Spangles. Spangles had a decent bed of straw now and some sweet meadow hay and clean water. Their groom was in the yard mucking out and turning some of the mares and foals into their well fenced paddocks. What a contrast of horse care in such a short distance. This stud was clean, tidy and well run.

After breakfast I went with Clary and Sylvia to find out about the horses, and we discovered that there was still no one there. Again, we watered them and gave them hay. So, we drove to the local police station and then went back to the dirty yard. We found an old horsebox parked in the yard now and a man wearing filthy, greasy clothes answered the farmhouse door when we knocked. He had delivered some horses for slaughter and come back for those in the yard and would be leaving later with them. He didn't even know Spangles had gone as he hadn't been to feed the horses. Not to worry, Spangles was legally my horse and should never have been there; why he was there was a mystery.

I panicked, I admit it was too much for me to accept, and I offered to buy the remaining five horses, immediately, and gave him a good price. I think Clary and Sylvia were taken aback by my offer as they looked a sad bunch of scrap horses, and they didn't want them in their yard in case they had disease. I wanted to take them away from this awful yard as soon as possible. We drove back to the stud and over coffee we discussed my next move. I was beginning to feel a bit foolish and hasty in buying them as I knew I couldn't buy or rescue every horse in Britain going for slaughter. Could we even keep them at home? Would we have enough grazing for them all? I decided to set off for home the next day with Spangles who needed another day of decent food, his feet trimming, and a set of shoes put on by the farrier. I would have to take my time getting home with him in such a poor condition. I called and spoke to Grandora after waiting an age to get a telephone line. After a few moments of silence, after I told her my news, she just calmly said she would talk to Granger, and he would drive down with the horsebox and pick them up. Bless her, she was one of the best.

The head groom for the stud came and told us of a wooded area with a small, fenced paddock attached, where we could put the horses until they were picked up, and so we went back to Terrance Mickle's yard with one of the lads and Sylvia and Clary's daughters Serena and Susannah to fetch the horses and walk them three miles to the paddock. When we reached their new paddock and turned them out, they all put their heads down to eat – there was no cantering around or squealing from any of them. We noticed a slight problem in that the young grey racehorse was entire and hopefully he wouldn't mate with the two mares.

I was given a tour of the stud in the afternoon and admired the foals and their two resident stallions. We chatted about the war and the new laws coming into force in Britain, seemingly daily. Then we discussed the Nazis. Now they had invaded Norway, Denmark, the Netherlands, Poland, the Channel Islands, France, and Belgium, and we knew they were turning their attention to an invasion of Britain. Clary was in his sixties and had married Sylvia, a much younger woman, some years after his first wife had died. He was too old for National Service but had joined the Home Guard as he had seen service during the Great War. Plus, he was a Major, so he oversaw the men in the Home Guard. He moaned that they were still practising marching with wooden guns and would be pleased when they received real guns so they could practise shooting with real bullets, and hopefully their uniforms would arrive soon. He was on various committees which all focussed on ensuring everyone left at home did their bit for the war effort. Whether this was gardening for food, knitting, or caring for families or evacuee children. We all had a part to play to keep the country running whilst the young and fit went into action. They had friends in Jersey whom they had not heard from in weeks and their children who were here in Britain at boarding school would now be staying with them at the stud, during the holidays. They were very worried about their friends in Jersey as it wasn't like them not to write.

I got up early next morning and Serena was already in the kitchen, which surprised me.

"Oh, I'm always an early riser and like to be on the yard to see if any foals have been born overnight," she said.

"Were there any born last night?" I asked.

"Follow me," she said and took me to the box nearest the house and there was a bay mare with a beautiful black filly foal just up on its feet for the first time. I was smitten.

"Oh my gosh, she is beautiful. Oh, you are so lucky to see these foals every day. Isn't she a bit late foaling now for a thoroughbred?" I asked.

"Yes, and the mare is a very small stamp for a racehorse. She did race, but she's only here because her dam belonged to my father's first wife and so he won't part with her. Who knows, she might have been a successful racehorse, it's all in her breeding, but she only ran in a couple of maidens and came second and third in each one."

We left the mare and foal alone to carry on bonding and I was about to tack up Hermes when Serena said, "I gave both of them a feed not quite an hour ago when I took over foal watch from the night staff."

"Thank you, I'll give them a bit longer to digest their breakfast and I will fill my flask if you don't mind. Then I must be on my way."

"I was wondering if I could ride with you this morning, I'd like to go part of the way up the Pedders?" Serena asked me.

"That would be good, I would love the company," I replied.

Within an hour we were on our way with Spangles on a lead rope from Hermes. Serena was mounted on her good-looking chestnut thoroughbred mare Whisper. We chatted about our families, and she told me her boyfriend Miles was in the RAF flying Spitfires and how much she worried about him. We reached Swaffham and called at the pub I had stopped at on my way down and rested and watered the horses. We only turned Spangles out in the paddock, tying up the other two. Serena then was going to return home from here and she said it had been a lovely ride and how much she had enjoyed it. I invited her to stay with us anytime she needed a change, and Susannah was welcome too of course.

So, I was on my own, the weather was still warm and sunny, and it was a relief to be under some trees and in the shade away from biting flies. The Pedders Way was quiet, and we only saw the occasional person out walking. It was a slower journey going back because I was aware Spangles was not as fit as Hermes and I didn't want to tire him, so we mostly walked all the way home. Three hours after leaving Serena I stopped, rested, and drank the rest of my coffee. It was clouding over as I neared home and drizzling as I left the Pedders Way to join the quiet lanes home. I rode into the stable yard just before six o'clock, tired out and wet through. Spangles knew where he was and had jogged and pulled my arm the last few miles. He whinnied and Polly answered – they were thrilled to meet up again and there was plenty of neck nibbling and squealing from Polly. Granger was shocked to see how thin and poor he looked and said it would take several months to feed him up and get him fit, but we would soon have him looking right again. He thought Lennie was good enough to start to ride him if I was agreeable. Of course, I was.

They were all ready to travel down in the morning for the other horses, although clearly he thought I was mad, and shouldn't have considered buying them; I had probably just bought a load of trouble. He thought it might be difficult to load them all into the horsebox and was taking some saddles with them just in case one of them needed riding home. I didn't fancy riding it all over again the very next day, but they were my problem, I had bought them and was responsible for getting them home safely. Granger told me I wasn't needed as he with Frankie, Osian and Jabbo were going to collect them; 'phew', I was pleased. He and Jabbo could ride them back, if necessary and Frankie would drive the horsebox with Osian and the other horses. I didn't ask how Frankie would steer, change gear and drive with mostly his left hand, but he was, little by little, using his right hand more. I realized it was a bit of a jolly for them and I couldn't blame them – they worked so hard they deserved a break. I told them of the pub where I had stopped and how amenable they had been with the horses; they served good food too. So, early next morning I waved goodbye, and they all seemed very cheerful; it was nice to see Frankie looking happy. Apparently, he had been staying with Granger, and although he still had nightmares he managed to go back to sleep afterwards and not wander off alone, into the woods. Rosie and his mother were sad he wasn't living with them, but content he was home, alive and doing what work he could do, keeping busy and occupied.

Much later that day the horsebox arrived home and I helped unload the very poor bay mare with three white socks, the little roan pony and the big heavy chestnut type; could be a Suffolk only it was hard to tell, he was in such poor condition. Granger was riding the hunter and Jabbo I was told had immediately been drawn to the two-year-old racehorse and was part riding and part walking him home; interesting. Grandora came to the stables to see the motley crew of dirty, tired horses and said very little, only that her husband would not have allowed such a common assortment of horses in his stables, years ago. She did add that she understood me feeling sorry for them and that in a few weeks' time with good food and care they would hopefully all look very different.

Next the children came to see them and of course Ruby loved the little roan pony and sat on his back. Lottie preferred Donk, which was a good job. The big, heavy horse, a bright chestnut Grandora agreed was very likely a full or part-bred Suffolk Punch with a lovely kind face and a gentle way about him. I hoped he could be of use on the farm and exonerate me for buying him. The bay mare was very thin, looked nervous and clearly tired. She looked like a hackney sort, about fifteen hands high. I put her in the stable where there was fresh water and some good hay.

We then went up to the house for tea. Four hours later Jabbo and Granger arrived, and we all went out to meet them. The dapple-grey hunter was 'ribby', but he had good paces and a good mouth, Granger told me, and he had gone well. The young 'firey' grey thoroughbred, had been awful to start with, holding his head in the air and trying to buck, rear and back up, but Jabbo had persisted with kindness, and he had travelled quietly, walking well in the end. Jabbo had not ridden him all the way because he was so young, but had walked with him and clearly liked him very much. They had called at the dirty farm of Terrance Mickle to see for themselves where the horses had been kept. They pretended they were looking for the place where I had said the horses were and had got lost. The police and some people were there checking the premises so hopefully he would be stopped from treating horses so cruelly in the future. They all agreed I had done the right thing buying them and told Grandora they would have done the same if they had been in my shoes. Granger was clearly pleased to have a yard full of horses to care for again, and he and Jabbo were soon busy rubbing them down, feeding and settling them all in their stables for the night. Of course, I was pleased to see them having the care they deserved; no horse or animal should be starved or kept in filthy conditions; best of all I had got Spangles back.

Chapter 23

Refugees Talia and Adele arrive

The summer holidays were about to start when I received a telephone call to say my two sponsored Jewish refugees were arriving the next day and would I meet them off the train. For safety the lady travelling with them must stay on the train with some other children who were being delivered to their new homes. It didn't rain; it poured. I told Grandora, who nodded and said it was fine with her. We now had so many people and animals staying with us, escaping from the horrors of the war, she doubted the Ministry of Defence would eject us from the house and requisition it for Government purposes. Ah, golden lining etc. I was honestly just glad I was doing something to help these poor children.

I spent the day with Margaret preparing a bedroom for them, which I had started a month earlier and never bothered to finish. It had been painted white, of course, and I had painted flowers and vines growing around the door and on both the bed heads which looked very pretty. We put up the blackout blinds and the new white curtains which had appliquéd flowers along the bottom thanks to Mrs Hubbard. One eiderdown was green and the other was pink, and both were covered in a flowered pattern, and they also had pink candlewick bedspreads. The oak floorboards were gleaming, and I found a flower-patterned pale green rug which was perfect. We polished the furniture again and put two comfy chairs each side of the window and two little tables next to them. I put some flowers in two white jugs, one on each table and stood back to check how it looked.

"It looks elegant, fresh and cosy," said Margaret. "Those flowers you've painted on the wall look beautiful, yet I think it needs a couple of paintings over there. Do you have any?"

"I'll think about it, we must have somewhere. It does look nice, doesn't it," I agreed.

I spent the day looking at all the paintings we had in the house and went into the little sitting room; there were two lovely watercolour paintings of flowers in vases. I can paint something to replace them, I thought and whipped them off the wall and took them upstairs into the bedroom. I added a Venetian mirror to one wall and put an antique camphor wood box on some drawers for their secret possessions. It looked perfect.

I went to the stables and found Granger and Jabbo had just lunged the dark dapple grey thoroughbred colt and were very pleased with how well he had gone. They were taking the hunter out for a gentle hack with Zoltan, so I joined them with Hermes, and we followed the river and forded it at Castle Acre and then crossed onto the Pedders Way and back home. There was more cloud than sun and a slight sea breeze, so no flies to bother us or the horses. I could see Granger had really taken to the big rangy hunter and he sat easy in the saddle on a long rein; I was pleased yet another decision I had taken was working out. I was very worried about the next two children to arrive and how they would cope with all of us.

Time came for me to go for them, and I asked Granger to chauffeur me there, for support. I thought it would be better if I rode in the back of the car with them, rather than have my back to them if I had been driving. We set off at six o'clock after the other children had eaten their tea. They were excited to meet the two new arrivals and I explained we might be late home, it depended on the time the train arrived at the station. They promised to be ready for bed when we got home. Larry was not always included with the others as he was always reading and studying in the library. He was turning out to be brilliant at school and he loved our library and said he might just as well make the most of it while he could.

It was a long wait at the station. So many trains were sidelined to make way for more important cargo; we just had to put up with it. The train was one-and-a-half hours late; we waited. The lady with them met me on the platform, checked who I was and giving me their papers said goodbye to the children and jumped back onto the train just as the whistle went. So, that's how I met the two little girls; eleven and thirteen-year-old sisters were both holding little suitcases and their gas masks in boxes round their necks, and one was clutching a large cloth bag. I will never forget their frightened, white, strained little faces. I just wanted to scoop them into my arms and promise them everything would be all right. Instead, I shook their hands, smiled, and showed them the way to our car. So far, I had spoken to them in English and had not received an answer. I tried French and that's what they understood because they were French. 'Naturellement!' They didn't speak any English and they were so shy and tired we could find out more about them from their papers tomorrow after they hopefully had had a good night's sleep. How awful for them to leave behind their parents and friends and not know when they would see them again. This awful war was horrible for everyone, but for children it was an abomination; their lives uprooted and torn apart when they should have been enjoying a safe and happy childhood. Quietly they followed me into the reception hall of the house, and we met Grandora waiting for us. I told her they spoke French and she greeted them in French.

"Bonjour mes cheries bienvenue."

They whispered, "Bonjour madame, mercie."

I then took them through to the kitchen to have some tea. We had prepared chicken soup with chunks of bread and egg custard tart which they ate slowly, furtively glancing at us like frightened mice, so I prepared hot milk for them and took them upstairs to bed. We both realized these were two shattered and traumatized children. I ran a warm bath for them over the four inches we were only supposed to allow for bathing and left them together to bathe and change into the night clothes I had bought for them. I then took them into Lottie and Ruby's bedroom to see the little girls asleep in their beds to try to reassure them they were safe here, like the sleeping girls. Then I took them to meet Lennie and Larry, who were awake in their bedroom both reading and pleased and interested to meet them. After that I settled them into their beds in their lovely new bedroom, each with a hot water bottle, covered each child, making sure they were cosy. I left a little night light burning in a deep dish, so they weren't plunged into instant frightening darkness. I noticed a man's black hat had been put onto a chair at the side of a bed and it appeared to be a special hat with a high crown so I just left it where it was; why would they have a man's hat with them I wondered. Suddenly the penny dropped; that's what the cloth bag contained. I would check the night light had gone out before I went to bed.

Feeling pretty shattered I went downstairs to hear the latest news on the wireless with Grandora. It was dismal as usual, although our Spitfire and Hurricane pilots seem to have given the Luftwaffe a run for their money and shot down more of them than they us. The attacks by German raiding airplanes against our RAF were relentless. Their fighting in the sky was referred to as 'dog fights' and I didn't know how they had the guts to fight up there in the sky, their sole aim to kill each other. We witnessed one fight take place and saw a plane plummet into the sea, leaving a plume of smoke from the burning wreckage and a parachute canopy floating into the water. I just hoped they were rescued whoever they were, German or British. They had started to bomb our cargo ships on July 10th in the Channel and apparently had sunk three of our ships. Poor people on board; how horrible. There had also been a bombing raid on dockyard installations in South Wales. We sat in contemplative silence after listening to the news and then with a sigh Grandora turned on the light entertainment channel and we listened to 'It's That Man Again' by Ted Kavanagh, the show starring Tony Handley, which was very funny and was always related to the current war news. We didn't mean to be uncaring about the news, we just needed to listen to some light relief to help us think about something less gloomy.

I went into the kitchen and made us a light supper and we both had an early night; I did remember to check the night light in the new girls' room, it had gone out and they were both asleep.

I was generally up early every morning and out riding and the next day after the arrival of the girls was no exception. I was surprised to see Lennie come into the kitchen for a drink as he was going to ride Spangles. We both went to the stables,

Jabbo and Granger had tacked up four horses and off we all went. Lennie was a surprisingly confident rider, a natural, and Spangles was beginning to look better for his new regime of light exercise and good food. It was a chilly start to the day and looked as if it would rain later, which was a shame as it was a Saturday and no school, but it might mean the children would need to be inside all day. We didn't go far as Spangles was not fit to be seen by anyone, but the ride out proved he was still the forward-going happy pony he always had been.

Back from our ride the rain started and lasted all day, so I was pleased we had at least kept dry when exercising. I soon found Lottie and Ruby giggling and introducing the new girls to their toys and dolls. I managed to get the little girls dressed, or at least dressing themselves and into the kitchen for breakfast. They were called Talia and Adele and it was obvious Ruby understood their French conversation. I wondered if Lottie would feel left out, but not a bit of it. Lottie was as busy as they were and just chattered away to them in English which they all seemed to ignore or understand. Talia and Adele were still quiet and reserved, and, although they played with Ruby and Lottie, they were kind of in the background. They met Rosie and Mrs Revill and Margaret who came over with George and Theodore. As it was Saturday Larry had gone to spend the day with Arthur and Violet and work at their place. Lennie was happy playing with George and Theodore. We read aloud to each other, played charades, card games, snakes and ladders, and I found a few children's books in French only; hopefully they would start to read in English as time went by. I was so pleased to have Rosie and Margaret to help me and Mrs Revill to prepare the food for the day. I wondered why I had not heard from my old governess Miss Thompson, since I had written to her over five weeks ago asking her for help. Grandora came in to spend some time with us and decided to try to teach all of them how to play bridge; she then got out the chess set, and that was it, bingo, we found out what the two French girls liked and were good at: chess – and they didn't need to speak English to beat us. I was just thinking Malissa would enjoy playing chess with them when in she walked, immediately squashed by Ruby rushing up to hug her.

We were all so pleased to see her and have her back home. Nico was with her but had gone straight off to see Osian and Jabbo. I went to tell Mrs Revill there were more for tea, but she already knew and was preparing food for everyone. As soon as it stopped raining, we just had time for a walk with the dogs before tea. We called in to the stables to see the horses and left Lennie there helping Granger, and to the kennels along by the river. Even the little pooch was getting stronger now as Ruby didn't carry him everywhere, and the tiny chihuahua nearly kept up with Spud, Odin, Lucy and my father's dogs Trig and Spruce.

We arrived back for tea and Mrs Revill had prepared a feast for us of sausages, jacket potatoes and apple pie with homemade custard. Larry was back and asked if they could learn how to play billiards. Grandora surprised me and said yes, but only under strict supervision. The green baize on the table must not under any circumstances be ripped as it was my father's pride and joy and very expensive to replace. Given guarded permission, we all trooped into the games room. Ruby and Lottie set up house in a corner with their teddies and dolls, and Talia and Adele sat on chairs and quietly watched as Grandora taught George, Theodore, Larry, and Lennie how to hold the cue and the fundamentals of the game. This involved using your cue ball to push the striker ball into your opponent's cue ball. Then I teamed up with Lennie and Theodore, and Malissa teamed up with George and Larry and we played a game. We were still playing when Nico walked in and gave pointers to George and Larry which meant they then beat us. It was all good fun and soon time for warm milk and bed.

When the house was finally quiet, and we had checked the blackout curtains were all closed, we went into the sitting room with Grandora to talk about the war, Cambridge, and what Nico and Malissa were doing. Of course, they could only tell us so much about their study life there. We were sorry to have missed Nico's birthday which had been a quiet meal with friends in Cambridge. Now a year older, he seemed to have grown even taller and thinner. He was still studying geography and survey maps and preparing them for 'something', just what seemed 'hush hush' and we didn't ask. Something to do with silk, whatever that meant. Malissa was using her mathematical knowledge for something else, but we weren't told what, and again, we didn't ask. They had both been to Oxford on several occasions and said there were more foreign people in Oxford than they had noticed before as so many refugees were coming to Britain to escape the war in Europe. Food was scarce and the cafes and restaurants seemed to be offering less every day. We were lucky here, having the farm and garden produce. And the Walled Garden under Osian's care was providing in abundance. Sugar was rationed, so the bees were a 'godsend', providing a substitute sugar. We discussed politics and Europe and where abouts in Greece their parents were now. We asked if their father's ships were still carrying cargo and were told a simple 'yes' and no more. Nico mentioned the attack and destruction of the French fleet was necessary to stop the Germans using it, but not good for Anglo-French relations. Likewise, he had heard that the Royal Navy had destroyed the French Fleet in Miers-ell-Kebir, Algeria, and the French had broken off diplomatic relations over it. The navy had been ordered to destroy the French ships to stop them falling into enemy hands. Sark had surrendered now to the German army and so the invasion of the Channel Islands was complete. Brighton beach was now closed, covered with mines, and barbed wire and defences. The Luftwaffe had attacked Scotland, Northern Ireland, and Wales. All shocking and depressing news.

We chatted about the children staying with us, what we were doing on the farm, how much we were producing and how we were working hard to increase our yields. Nico said the Government was asking for more aluminium and asking the population to hand over their cooking pots and pans to make more aeroplanes. Well, we had some aluminium pans, and we could send those. However, most of ours were made of copper and Mrs Revill wouldn't like to lose those. I said I was worried about the Government wanting our enormous wrought iron gates at the front of the drive, but if the steel was needed, they must go. I mentioned I had taken a photograph of them with my box camera and thought if we took them down, we could save the heraldic signs in the middle towards the tops of each gate and let the heavier bottom part go and we should get on with it before it was taken out of our hands by government officials, and they just took the lot. We didn't look very patriotic keeping the gates though, did we? We enjoyed a bottle of white wine before we went to bed, and it was wonderful to have Malissa and Nico back home.

After I had ridden on Sunday mornings, I had been taking the children to the village Church service, and even Ruby loved the singing, smiling and tapping her feet. I didn't think Talia and Adele would want to come as they were Jewish and probably understood it would go against their faith. Ruby had come with me before we knew she was Jewish and she was so young she just enjoyed the singing, not that we ever heard a sound from her. In the morning, after riding Hermes with Lennie riding Spangles, I asked Jabbo and Granger if the girls could come down for a ride on the horses or just help with the hens whilst I was at Church. I asked the girls if they minded going down to the stables and I could see they were reluctant to go alone, so I asked Lucy our Land Army girl if they would stay with them. Sheila was on morning milking duty and Lucy was having a day off, but she agreed to take them to the stables as she wanted to see the new horse they were going to hopefully use on the farm. I found some trousers for the girls and took them to the cottage to stay with Lucy, telling them why, in French. They understood and seemed happy to stay with her. I thought they would be fine at the stables when they realized Jabbo spoke French. We all cycled to Church; we must have looked like a cycling club only we were wearing our Sunday best clothes. The lane to the Church was hardly ever used by traffic and we were fine pedalling all over the road, even with Lottie and Ruby on their tricycles. There were eight of us and we left our bikes outside and made it on time to Church. Grandora was driven there by Granger, of course. We met Mrs Revill, Frankie, Rosie and Mrs Evans, as well as Hugo and Margaret with George and Theodore. After the service I don't know how, but Ruby fell on the gravel path and made her knee bleed. She was heartbroken and cried. Malissa held her as I wrapped a handkerchief round her leg and suddenly, we heard her saying 'Nu-nu Nu-nu je veux Nu-nu' in French. We were, at first, shocked, and taken-aback, but so excited and pleased to hear her talk; but who was Nu-nu – was it her little pooch? Malissa asked her, "Is Nu-nu the name of your little dog?"

"No je veux Nu-nu."

"So, what is the name of your little dog?" asked Malissa. "If it was my dog, I would call it Sweetie."

"No Zissa is name,' said a sobbing indignant little girl.

That is the day Ruby started to talk in a mixture of French and English. We asked her name, but the only answer was something that sounded like Ruby, or it might be Ruth, Rosa even Rosina, so we weren't sure if she had said the right word. I had a feeling I had got the first letter of her name right. So, one up to me.

We all pedalled home with Osian racing Larry and Lennie, and Hugh slowly overtaking us in his car, with George and Theodore hanging their heads out of the windows to cheer them on. When we arrived home, I was cheered up no end to see my Governess from years ago standing outside the house and smiling at all of us. Grandora was driven up to the house by Granger in our Rolls-Royce, the Sunday car, and was as delighted as I was to see Audrey Thompson back to take on some care of all our visiting children. Part of her delight was because she knew Audrey played Bridge.

"I am so sorry not to let you know when I was arriving, I have had a difficult time these last few months and as soon as I was able, I have jumped on a train to get here," said Audrey.

"You're here now and we are delighted to see you," Grandora said.

She took Audrey inside to her sitting room to tell her what had been happening here and why we had asked for her help. I joined them as soon as I could and took a pot of tea with me, keen to hear the reason for her delay. It seems her mother had become very ill and didn't recognise her anymore. She kept walking off into the road in her nightie. It had been a very difficult time for Audrey who had looked after her on her own, until she died a month ago. Audrey had dealt with the funeral and had inherited the house near Norwich, which she had decided to rent out for one year. This meant she could come and stay with us and work here.

"I hope I am still wanted?" she added.

"Of course you are, we have eight children staying here, well two are staying with Hugh and Margaret Brownlow, but spend plenty of time here and as it's the school holidays I was hoping for help with them. They need some structure during the holidays, and I don't mean school lessons – I have a plan to keep them occupied for two to three hours every morning and the rest of the day they can be free. They can learn to swim in the river, learn how to ride our horses, have some baking lessons, chess, play cricket, tennis, rounders, and camp out; there is lots for them all to do. I will be doing some things with you, and Rosie will be looking after the little children at the same time. I just need more time to run the estate and deal with any problems that occur, and I admit I would like some free time to paint again. I ride early every morning and Lennie often comes with me; he is such a good rider. I want the holidays to be a fun time for all of them. The boys have started to play billiards, but only with supervision and they go clay pigeon shooting with Hugh in the fields at the kennels, and Grandora has started her own junior Bridge club," I added laughing. "Oh, and I mustn't forget, they are learning how to play croquet with Grandora."

"Oh, is that all," she said laughing. "If that's all I'm sure I can help. It sounds like it will be fun."

I took her out to show her the cottage next to Osian which was to be hers and she was very happy with it. I left her to put her things away and suggested she came with me to re-acquaint herself with the surroundings and to meet everyone who was living or working here; she must meet the children, of course. As it was Sunday we tried to have as near to a Sunday roast as we could with very little meat but plenty of Yorkshire puddings and roast potatoes, vegetables, and lots of good gravy. It was my job to cook today, and I needed to get on with it. Malissa also helped as it was Rosie's and Mrs Revill's day off. I had managed to buy a small joint of beef and sausages with my ration books and just hoped I had enough for everyone and made a sausage pie to make it all go further. I hoped Talia and Adele didn't ask me if it was Kosher as I was quite sure it wasn't, but what could I do under the circumstances?

What a crowd round the table it was going to be, so I decided to split lunch into two sittings and feed the children first. Six children were fed round the big table in the kitchen and introduced to Miss Thompson, their new Governess.

"What's that then?" said Larry. "What does that mean?"

I explained that 'Governess' meant a private teacher and outlined my plan to him which he didn't seem to like; tough, I thought. I told him he was essential to the success of the plan, and I was relying on him to help with the farm, and the harvest. He could still go to Arthur's when they needed him. That seemed to please and settle him. They finished lunch with jam roly-poly and I then served Sunday lunch a second time – to Osian, Audrey, Malissa, Nico, Lucy. Grandora joined us at the table in the kitchen, which was unusual. It was a happy, relaxed meal and once I put it on the table everyone helped themselves, except Grandora who I took care to serve myself. I produced my 'plan for summer' to aid a smooth holiday with the children until autumn, when they would return to school. The activities were all my idea, but Grandora helped to put them down on paper and sort a detailed programme.

"I think it's going to be fun," said Audrey. "Where shall I start my lessons?" she asked.

"Do you remember the old school room we used in summer, but it was freezing cold in winter, it joins onto the old dairy? Well,

I have had it painted, there's a new floor and new fire with a back boiler to heat some radiators and keep it warm, plus some tables and chairs. I'll take you to see it this afternoon and then you can meet Jabbo and Granger."

"Granger is he still here?" she asked, blushing slightly.

"Well yes, he is still here. I forgot he must have been here when you were here before, well he is a vital cog in the working of the estate," I replied.

"What about Lord and Lady Ellesdale – are they here or still in London?" asked Audrey.

I sighed. "They are in still living in Singapore, my father is working with the Ambassador there and I keep hoping to hear that they are on their way home."

"Oh, sorry, I didn't know. You must miss them terribly," Audrey sympathised.

We cleared up after the meal and I went with Audrey to walk to the Walled Garden to show her how well Osian was doing.

"Marvellous, we can get the children to name all the salad and vegetable plants in French and English," she enthused.

The repaired hot-house was marvellous and growing in it was a grape vine and lemon tree, peaches, nectarines, and lots of seedlings ready to prick out. We walked on to the stables, and she met Jabbo and saw his neat cosy cottage. She was fascinated how we had met on my journey home from France. As we were about to walk back and look at the old school room, Granger appeared and of course they knew each other. I realized there was something unsaid between them as their usual manner changed. He was awkward and she was coy. How very strange, I thought, and intriguing.

Frankie still stayed with Granger during the week although he was spending more time working with Osian in the gardens. They

had many ambitious plans, and it was an exciting time for us and
very necessary to contribute to the country's larder to help with
food distribution. He always went home at the weekend to stay
with his mother and sister. He seemed happy and although only
able to use his arm in a limited capacity, it was slowly improving.
Over the weeks he had become a valuable member of the team,
showing a real talent with machinery and engines. I had decided
to pay for him to go on a mechanics course for tractors and farm
machinery and had arranged a place for him. I told him one
Monday morning when he came to work with Rosie. He was
thrilled and I just hoped it wasn't too much for him and triggered
a depression. I had picked a local tractor repair garage so I could
receive regular updates on his progress, not to spy on him, but
to keep an eye on how he was doing emotionally, and to be sure
he was coping. The children enjoyed being together during their
morning lessons with Audrey and the lessons were a great success.
They had instruction in preparing a camp-fire in the woods, with
Jabbo and Granger helping Audrey keep them all safe and not set
the woods on fire. They then cooked spare-ribs on the fire and
ate them with chunks of fresh bread and homemade biscuits for
afters which they had learnt how to bake the day before in the
kitchen. They learnt how to make the fire safely and how to put
it out correctly. They did camp out for one night in the orchard
in tents borrowed from the scouts in exchange for them being
allowed to camp in the orchard for their annual week of camping
during the summer holidays. A long hike was also part of their
lessons, along the Pedders Way to Castle Acre to see the Priory.
It was a great expedition and just organising them to go off on
their own with their equipment and food, was exhausting. They
had backpacks with sandwiches, water and even bandages and
a first aid kit; well, you never knew when that could be needed.

Osian gave them a lesson in first aid, how to put on a sling, how to deal with stings and splinters, and George was their elected first aider for the day. They had to plan everything themselves and discuss the day before what they needed to take and who should carry what. The boys loved the military style planning of it all. They had to plan the route from a map and get themselves there without any help from grown-ups. (We did take the precaution of having three grown-ups with them all the way, but they weren't allowed to interfere or help if they went the wrong way.) They didn't know that Granger would be waiting for them with the station wagon to bring them all home if they needed a lift or a helping hand. That was a surprise for later. Jabbo took Donk for the girls to ride if they got too tired and it was Audrey and Rosie who went to keep an eye on them all. I decided, as it was a hot day, and it was so quiet at home, I would have a nice swim on my own in the river pool. Grandora was busy writing about the history of her ancestors, a job she had decided needed doing, and it kept her busy. Osian had gone on his bike to a local nursery to discuss plants with their plantsman; I was alone at home which was unusual.

I walked down to the river without any dogs as they had all gone on the great expedition; even Odin had joined them. I realized I had left my costume and towel on the hall table. Just for madness and as it was a glorious August day, I stripped and jumped into the water naked. It felt decadent, free, liberating, crisp, cool; I loved it and swam, floated, and lazed in the clean flowing water. I didn't want to get out. Then a voice called out to me, and I saw it was Howard Bathurst, George and Theodore's father, and as I listened to him, I realized he was drunk and threatening me.

He shouted, "I have your clothes here and a camera to take your pictures for the newspapers when you get out of the water. You'll freeze if you stay in too long. Unless you are willing to tell me where my boys are that you have kidnapped, I will report you to the police for indecency. Of course, I can forget it all for five hundred pounds paid to me now, today. I can wait for your answer; however, can you stay in that cold water?" He laughed and sat down on the bank.

I was shocked at his rude audacity which I wasn't used to. How dare he? I stayed by the far bank planning what to do but couldn't think of any plan. If I went downstream it was shallow and no cover for me at all. If I went upstream, it was narrower, and you could touch the banks at each side for a short distance. I eventually started to feel very cold and started shivering. He had a whisky bottle with him and just sat drinking. I was frightened of him and what he could do in his drunken state. He was obviously desperate for money. I very much doubted he wanted to see the boys. I stayed where I was, getting colder and colder; my teeth were chattering, but I wondered might he fall asleep?

I was feeling desperate when a figure appeared behind him. The figure just stood and stared at us, trying to sum up the situation. I couldn't shout out; I was too frightened and frozen cold. What could he do? How could he help, would he help? Did he realize what was happening? Howard was at least six foot tall, and drunk could he be violent? Would Frankie with a ruined smashed shoulder and weak arm be able to defend himself against Howard if he had to? He was almost one handed.

"Have you decided yet to give me the money and I'll give you your clothes back?" shouted Howard, slurring his words.

Frankie moved so fast I couldn't believe I was seeing what was happening. He leapt forward and with his good arm, grasped

Howard round his neck and brought his right knee up into the back of Howard's shoulder blades. I thought he was killing him, and I think I screamed. As Howard's head was wrenched backwards Frankie fell on top of him and pushed him head first into the water and held him there shouting to me to get out. I was numb from cold, but somehow, I thrashed my way across the pool, dragged myself onto the bank and grabbed my clothes, stuttering, "Don't kill him, let him go."

I pulled my clothes to me and stumbled towards the house; I couldn't feel my feet. I then felt Frankie steering me towards the Walled Garden and into the greenhouse. It was red hot inside. He left me and ran up the steps into the house urgently calling, "My Lady, help."

Grandora came and helped me upstairs to my bedroom and stuck me in the shower, but I couldn't stand up. She helped me onto the bed and started rubbing me with a dry towel all over. Once in bed and covered, she left the room, but was soon back with two hot water bottles covered in towels and a warm drink of sweet tea. I felt ill, but not bothered somehow with what happened to me. I can't remember the doctor arriving, but he came immediately and removed the hot water bottles to the very bottom of the bed, gave me another warm drink of warm sweetened water and told Grandora to sit with me and keep giving me warm sweet drinks. I believe he stayed for one hour and said he would pop back after his surgery. I slept on and off in between being given warm drinks by Grandora. I didn't hear the children arrive back home after their long hike. I slept all night and felt woolly and weak in the morning and was ordered to stay in bed for the day. When I got up to go to the bathroom I nearly fell on the floor as my legs didn't work. The next day, however, I was nearly back to normal and began to wonder what happened to Frankie and Howard.

I heard later that after Frankie brought me back to the house, he found Osian cycling back, balancing plants in the bike basket and on the back of the bike. He kind of grabbed him off his bike to go to Howard. The bicycle tipped over to Osian's horror, but all credit to him, he left it and ran down to the river. Howard was unconscious, and Frankie was worried he had killed him – even though he was still mad with the man, he was now also scared. They dragged him away from the river and on finding the doctor who was about to leave as soon as he had finished with me, they took him to Howard and the doctor said he was in a drunken stupor and leave him to sleep it off. So, they put him in the feed shed, wrapped him in a blanket and kept an eye on him until Granger came back. Granger consulted with Grandora and when Howard was dry, he was transported in the back of Granger's van to the local hostelry and carried upstairs. The stay at the Inn was paid for by Grandora. A letter was left for him to open in the morning advising him to get in touch with our solicitors. It was several weeks before I found out why, but just after the event I didn't want to know anything about Howard Bathurst. When the 'incident' occurred, Frankie had been looking for me to show me his first certificate saying he had passed with a gold merit his first stage tractor mechanics course.

August was a very bad month for London and Londoners. It seemed that The Battle of Britain, as it was called, had been won by our young RAF pilots and we had triumphed over the German Messerschmitts, so now Hitler was going to start bombing us relentlessly into submission. I was so glad 'our children' were with us in Norfolk. The German bombers increased bombing strategic targets, particularly in London day and night. Barrage balloons flew all over London trying to force German bombers to higher altitudes. Coventry city centre was bombed and destroyed, killing an estimated five hundred people. The Auxiliary Fire Service was organised by the Government and was manned by civilians. Fortunately, over three million women and children had been evacuated to live in the country and an 'Air Raid Precautions' organization made sure everyone kept their blackout curtains closed and built air raid shelters in their gardens. Hundreds of people sheltered in the Underground stations during the bombing raids. In the very beginning this had been banned by the Government, but pressure was put on them to open the deep underground tunnels to accommodate people during the bombing raids. The people who were worst affected by the raids were from the East End of London and round the dockland areas. These were the people who had the least to start with and now they were being hit the hardest. Yet we knew many people were losing their lives to the bombing campaign and it was a frightening, horrible and exhausting experience to live through day and night. We had the newspaper delivered every day and Grandora read it first, then always left it in the library where I would find it and read the headlines. The rest of the news I listened to on the wireless set, although we knew much of it was censored so as not to upset the British public or inform the enemy how well they were doing. I hadn't realized Larry was reading the news when he was in the library reading the books. I saw him looking very glum one day and he told me he was getting scared for his mother and father in London's docklands which were frequently targeted.

"Look, it's not good news, I know, but remember your mother and father are working for the country and they let you come and stay here knowing you would be safe and it's one less thing for them to worry about, well three less things. Make sure you keep writing to them, and Lottie and Lennie. I'm sure they will always be glad to hear news from all of you." I put my arm round him and gave him a squeeze, trying to reassure him; however, even I was worried for their safety; they were in the thick of where the bombs were falling.

We had an air raid practice in our cellars, well, not the one where all the paintings were stored – that was strictly off limits. It was difficult getting us all in, so I ordered Anderson shelters for five farms and three for the estate. Granger, Jabbo, Frankie and Osian had help putting them up from Hugh Brownlow.

I called to see Alford and his wife Martha to check where they would go in case of an air raid, and he was quite grumpy about it saying they "didn't need no Andy Shelter thingy there". They had a perfectly good strong table to get under and a strong larder under the stairs. "Besides," he added, "I'd be out with the horses, keeping them settled and safe." So that was that. Martha was worse now and unable to help him with the horses or the hounds; her arthritis was crippling her. He obviously needed more regular help – he said he didn't – but as they were our hounds and my father's good hunters, I thought I had a right to insist he had help to ensure everything was running smoothly for when my father came home.

"Do you know when his Lordship will be home, my Lady?" Alford asked.

"Galling as it is for me to tell you, Alford, I don't know; I wish they were here now, very much."

I told Grandora when I saw her, and she said she would make a point of going over to see him and agreed I should organise more help for him. Later I suggested to Granger that he or Jabbo went over, but Granger had never really seen eye to eye with Alford and said, rather grumpily he would think about it. Before I left the yard, mellowing a little, he suggested Lennie rode over early morning before school and helped with hound exercise and any horses that needed riding out. Lennie agreed he would go over on Spangles and help walk the hounds and help with the feeding and exercise any horse that needed riding before going to school. It would have to do for now and I agreed to pay him three shillings a week; this pleased him very much.

When the scouts came over during the holidays to camp in our orchard, the boys were very impressed, and they all thought they might give scouting a go. During their stay we were invited to join them for a barbecue and fireside singalong but without the fire, as this would just be an open invitation to enemy aircraft. During this jolly night I came up with the mad idea we would have a football match against them. Their scout master was keen and so were the scouts. George and Theodore looked at me in horror but Larry and Lennie agreed it would be fun.

"I think you need eleven players," said George, clearly dismissing it as a mad idea. "You have just suggested we four boys play as a team or do you have anyone else in mind?" he asked dryly.

"Ok, let me think." I was stumped. "Oh, the girls can play, not all the scouts are over ten years of age, are they?" I asked the scout master.

"Not sure about girls playing," he said.

"Oh, go on let them," chorused half a dozen scouts, falling over laughing.

"I will find a team and we will play on the village football field," I said in my best determined 'can do anything' voice. At least I think it sounded like that.

"You can't, it's been ploughed up for spuds," said one of the scouts.

"Ok then, here on our lawn, this Friday and we will put on a tea for you all after the match."

"You're on," said the scout master and shook my hand.

I beamed at my lot who scowled back at me as we left and went back to the house. "Oh, come on, it can't be that bad, it will be fun, you have three days to practise." I was not popular that night.

It occurred to me to ask Osian if he would join the team and he said yes, and suggested Frankie and he agreed too. Things were looking up. Granger said he would coach them, and Audrey went along to the first practice session, with a whistle to referee. Adele and Talia were very doubtful and didn't want to tackle anyone. Rosie agreed to play, so things were improving. I thought we should have a bet on here with the scouts, so I suggested we did and was shouted down, Noooooo. OK, so no bet. Then I had a brainwave. We must ask Lucy and Sheila, so I did, and they said yes, they thought it would be fun. We had a team. The only problem was they really weren't very good. We did laugh a lot though, at practice; well, the boys didn't, to be fair, they were not pleased to be playing in a team made up with girls. The day arrived and Grandora insisted that a large Indian cane chair was carried down to the pitch, so she could watch.

"Put it behind our goal," she ordered.

No pressure there then, on Larry, our goalie. I explained to Grandora that if the ball got past Larry, it could hit her square in the face and that would not only hurt, it would be undignified. She agreed and ordered the chair to be carried back to the terrace and said she would watch the game through her binoculars. We didn't have any kit, but the scouts did and looked very smart and keen as they ran up and down the pitch, jumping up and down, warming up! Our lot, dressed in an assortment of shorts and jerseys, just stared at the opposition, and looked terrified. Well, we tried, and they all ran up and down, not doing a great deal. Larry made lots of good saves and the scouts scored a goal, so we were losing when Adele fell and hurt her ankle and had to retire, so we were one man/girl down. Then like a knight in shining armour Nico appeared in very respectable university sports attire and took Adele's place and scored the equalizer and the final whistle suddenly was blown, and it was over; thank goodness. I pulled Audrey to one side and told her I thought she blew final time a little early.

"Who cares, it's a draw, and I am out of breath from running, I couldn't go on any longer," was her excuse.

So, it was potted meat or boiled egg sandwiches for everyone and little pieces of sausage pie, squares of our farm cheese, cold slices of Queen of Tarts and Victoria sponge cake with homemade lemonade. It was a success. Best of all, Adele's ankle was better by bedtime; much to everyone's surprise!

There were only two weeks of the holidays left when I had a phone call from Merry to say she was coming for a holiday with the boys if it was still all right with me. Off course Osian was thrilled and worked out he could put them all up in his cottage, if Merry could stay in the house with me. They arrived and we had a wonderful week with their 'lessons' as usual in the mornings and the 'visiting boys' all joining in. Riding, swimming, cycling, playing rounders, camping out, hiking, they did it all. Merry and I managed some peace and quiet and were able to chat. I found out how busy she was in the hospital and travelling home regularly. No special man on the horizon yet because there was no time for one. I told her I corresponded with Tiff, but I hadn't seen him since he went to Ireland. He had hoped to return here before he was back on duty but had been recalled because of the worsening situation and I didn't know where he was; only that he was somewhere in Britain. Malissa came home to see her, and we enjoyed time with Grandora in the evening, listening to the news on the wireless and just chatting about the situation. Benito Mussolini, the Fascist leader of Italy, had sent Italian troops to Africa and had killed fifty civilians on a raid of Jerusalem. In East Africa, British Somaliland was invaded by Italian troops.

We seemed to be winning the war in the sky as the Luftwaffe were reported to have lost seventy-five aircraft compared to us losing thirty-five on August 15th. The Germans were now blockading British waters, had mined our seas, and were now attacking all approaching ships whether allied or neutral. Nico didn't want his boat to leave harbour as it was so dangerous, and he was worried for his men.

Grandora's junior Bridge school was a success and we decided to have a two-night tournament to find a winner. Of course, the Welsh boys were invited to play, and the two girls, Adele and Talia, were very good, but Larry was the winner; he had mastered Bridge during the summer holidays very well. It did his confidence a great boost to know he could play on an equal footing with anyone. Whilst they were staying with us a discussion was had regarding Adele, Talia and Ruby being Jewish and what it meant. I discovered all the children were interested and curious to know more about the Jewish faith, so I asked Adele to explain, with me translating if she didn't know an English equivalent for a word. It was during this lesson, held in the old school room, we decided to make Friday night a celebration of Shabbat. Adele was very pleased and started to tell us what we needed for the meal. Bread, fish, soup, meat or poultry, side dishes and a pudding. They would recite the kiddush blessing over the wine and a challah over the bread. We were to make matzo ball soup which are light dumplings made with matzo meal, eggs, water and oil or chicken fat. The dessert must be pareve. I was beginning to realize we needed an expert for this meal. I rang the solicitors in Primrose Hill and asked them to get in touch immediately with Miriam for me and ask her to ring me straight away. I hoped it didn't sound too dramatic. Miriam rang me from the solicitor's office that afternoon. She was worried at the urgent message.

"Miriam, I need you here this Friday, please come and help me to prepare Shabbat for sixteen people," I pleaded.

"I don't have enough coupons for so many people."

"Just catch the train and I will wait at the station for you," I told her, "and it's time we organised a telephone in the house there for you all."

I explained about the two Jewish girls now staying with us and she said she would come on Thursday to meet them and to help prepare the Shabbat. Result!

Chapter 24

Celebrating Shabbat

W hen I picked Miriam up at the station on Thursday, she had her young sister Anna -Sara with her and Avigail, the young girl we had met on the boat with her grandfather. "I am so sorry, I hope you don't mind me bringing them too, they can sleep with me. It's awful seeing London burning every night and so frightening to hear the planes coming over and the crump of the bombs falling. You just don't know whose house will be hit next. My mother thought it would do Anna-Sara good to be in the country for a few days and I offered to bring Avigail too."

"Of course, I understand, you poor things; how dreadful. I would not be able to sleep with worry," I replied.

I didn't have any idea of the horror and misery in London's Dockland area of the nightly bombing and the destruction taking place. The lack of facilities for people now homeless, dust everywhere, no bathrooms, no washing facilities, shared rancid toilets or the lack of safe bomb shelters. I could not imagine the horrors being endured and it seemed to be the poorest people of London who were suffering.

"The girls will love having others to play with, I'm sure. It looks as if you have brought some food with you?" I said.

"Just the dumplings for the chicken soup. My mother's dumplings are always very good, and she insisted I bring them."

"Well, I hope I have all the right ingredients for you to work miracles." I laughed.

Once home we introduced her to everyone as and when we bumped into them. Adele, Talia, Ruby, and Lottie all rushed to meet Anna-Sara and Avigail, and dragged them outside to play with their bikes and the two dolly prams we had found stored in the attic. We had bikes for Adele and Talia now, but not for the others – they would have to share for now. Perhaps we should order some more or ask Arthur to magic some up for us. Audrey came over to meet Miriam and they got on straight away. Miriam's little French Bull Dog Bing was not too keen on all our dogs at first, it was just too much for her to have them all sniffing her at the same time. We always had a wooden crate in the kitchen for any dog which might steal food, so we popped her in there with a comfy bed and she settled straight away.

Grandora had really been pleased with my idea to celebrate Shabbat and insisted we did it in our dining room. This was a splendid idea but a logistical headache. We didn't have lots of footmen and servants to wait on the table and carry the food from the kitchen anymore. However, she insisted, and it would be lovely and very grand for us all. I prepared the enormous table in the morning and was informed by Audrey that this morning's lesson for the children was how to lay a table and which cutlery to use with each course. Apparently, she had split the children into two groups, one lot to be guests and the other to serve them correctly, and then they swopped over. This was especially for Friday night Shabbat, but hopefully a lesson learnt for life. While I had been in King's Lynn I had popped to the cinema and bought tickets for the Saturday matinee for all of us to watch The Wizard of Ozz, and now I needed another two tickets for Anna-Sara and Avigail. These thoughts ran through my mind as I prepared the table, and Grandora came in to check that I was doing a good job.

Over tea Miriam chatted to Adele and Talia in French and it was clear Ruby understood the conversation as did Audrey and me. Adele and Talia were not trying to speak English very often because they had each other, so, no necessity. As Merry and her young brothers were with us it was an interesting noisy meal with French, English and Welsh all being spoken at the same time. Larry and Lennie were picking up words here and there and practising any word they liked to roll around their tongues. Miriam was very taken with the two new girls and at bedtime put them to bed and talked to them. I asked her to ask them about the big black hat they kept in their room. Miriam stayed with Audrey, and Anna-Sara and Avigail had a small room near to the girls. One by one we all went to bed.

Next morning, after I had ridden Hermes, I found Miriam up early in the kitchen already preparing the evening meal. Anna -Sara was still snuggled up in bed with Avigail, Talia and Adele reading books. Miriam told me that the girls had described their journey here and how traumatic it had been. Their father was a clock and watch repairer in a small town, and as the war approached, he listened to the news and knew they should leave France. They lived in the southwest of France near Bordeaux. Their grandmother lived with them, their mama's mother, and she became very ill and was hospitalised. Their mother would not leave her as the hospital had said she was dying and there was nothing more they could do for her. So, their mother insisted on staying in France with her until she died. Their father would not leave without his wife, and he wanted to repair all his clients' clocks and watches and return them. He was a conscientious man and didn't want to just close the shop with other people's property still there. He had applied for visas for all his family to the Portuguese Consul General in Bordeaux. This was Aristides de Sousa Mendes, and he gave them the visas they needed. His brother had already decided to go to Spain (travelling by train), as the Nazis were on the borders of France in the north and he agreed to take his two nieces with him and wait there for their girls' parents to join them. So, they left with their uncle, crossed the border into Spain, and made it to San Sebastian where they waited for the parents. On arrival in their small hotel, the girls' uncle had a heart attack and died whilst they alone were with him. They were left alone with his body in the small hotel foyer waiting for someone to help them. They kept his hat with them because he had hidden valuables in it, and this was just as well because his suitcase went missing soon after he died. The owner of the hotel was not very pleased to be stuck with two young Jewish girls and had been in touch with an organisation which helped Jewish people fleeing from the Nazis. The organisation had arranged for them to be taken to Portugal and wait for a suitable boat to bring them to England. This organisation was the Hebrew Immigrant Aid Society and the leader in Lisbon, Portugal was Moises Bensabet Amzalek. He was a known respected friend of Antonio de Oliveira Salazar who had founded Estado Nova, meaning New State. Salazar was now the leader of Portugal. They not only had to wait for a ship to bring them to Britain, but they had to obtain sponsorship from someone to pay and care for them in Britain. They have no idea where their parents are now or when they will see them again. I thought the 'poor things', meeting so many strangers and not knowing what will happen to them next.

I hoped they were beginning to feel safe here with us in Norfolk.

I hoped Larry would not become argumentative during Shabbat. It was noticeable how he was increasingly augmentative regarding politics, and especially passionate about the rights of the working population. He read extensively and his rhetoric was becoming exceptional for his age. I mentioned this to Grandora who was frequently his mentor and encouraged his ability to debate his point. Grandora took him aside and told him the art of good debate was the ability to listen and learn and not shout or lose one's temper: to have correct facts to hand and to use them to your advantage. It was important never to lose focus on the core of the conversation. Then she told him tonight was not a good night to become embroiled in a heated conversation with anyone who might listen to him as to the state of the war and its handling by our Government and Churchill. There was a time and place for everything, and although she was pleased he was honing his new skills as a speaker, there would be plenty of time at school and later hopefully at university, to practise. Lennie, on the other hand, was becoming a country loving person. Every day enjoying riding, clay pigeon shooting, exercising the blood hounds and farming, and certainly not school. His enjoyment of clay pigeon shooting was curtailed, of course, after the ARP Warden stopped the sessions, asking us not to 'waste' ammunition.

Preparations completed; we had our Shabbat dinner on that Friday night. Miriam blessed us, reciting the Kiddush. The Challah followed which blessed the plaited bread and wine before it was distributed. Candles were lit and blessed. Miriam had brought a small 'menorah' with her which she explained was a candlestick with seven branches which refer to human knowledge and representing the seven days it took to create the world, with the centre light representing the Sabbath. We ate gefilte fish, which was stuffed fish, chicken soup with the matzo balls her mother had made, cholent, a stew made with meat and kugel potato and noodle pudding, roasted vegetables. To finish the meal there was fruit, cheese and pareve, which for us translated as cake for dessert. We were told to greet each other saying Shabbat Shalom. Miriam explained that it said in the Bible that God made the earth in six days and on the seventh he rested which is why in Jewish tradition no work is done after sundown on Friday until sunset on Saturday. The food was served on our best porcelain, and we all dressed in our party clothes for the occasion; it was very interesting and hugely successful. Adele, Talia, Avigail and Anna-Sara loved it, and Ruby seemed to know automatically what to expect. This must have come from her distant memories with her parents, I suppose. I will never forget that Shabbat dinner in our home in August 1940 knowing we were safe, well fed and realizing so many others were less fortunate and suffering horribly.

It was a quiet and reflective time and Grandora said grace for us before the proceedings and afterwards she said prayers for everyone involved in fighting to rid the world of evil and bring freedom and peace back on earth. We had learnt so much that night about unity and togetherness and all helped to clear the table, only not the tinies; it was best porcelain and cutlery after all. We also excused Miriam, Talia and Adele from doing any work on that special occasion. It was a time of reflection, and it was moving and spiritual and it did us all good to learn about Shabbat.

Miriam stayed a fortnight with Anna-Sara and Avigail, which was fine and at least they were away from some of the awful bombing in London, referred to as the 'London Blitz'. Merry's brothers went back to the Rectory in Dartmoor just before the start of the autumn school term and I missed them all very much.

I wished that they could stay with us, but 'The Rev' needed that
at home to help him there. Rhys at the age of fifteen had been
tasked with the job of making sure they all got home in one
piece on the British wartime railways, a job he did very well with
military precision, bless him. Mrs Revill had packed a feast of
Spam and tomato sandwiches and homemade buns for their long
journey. Merry had left her brothers here with us while she went
back to work after her week off. They were such polite, good boys
and had done camping, football, cricket, rounders, long hikes,
picnics, and swimming all through their stay, and Audrey had
been wonderful at guiding them through all the fun stuff without
any arguments or accidents. The girls loved making things and
painting pretend boats made from sticks they found on their
walks, and then they all went down to the river to let them race
in the current and watch whose 'boat' had won. The boys joined
in this, and it became a favourite pastime all through the holidays.
We were lucky and enjoyed fine weather with some very hot sunny
days and we all became tanned by the sun; in my case this always
meant my freckles exploded all over my face and became even
more prominent, which I disliked intensely.

Osian's garden efforts were beginning to provide a healthy
and bountiful harvest of marrows, courgettes, tomatoes,
cucumbers, beans, peas, potatoes, carrots, onions and even
garlic. Mint for mint sauce and tea, lemon balm for tea, lovage
for soup and lemons in the greenhouse. He grew a plethora of
herbs which enhanced our wartime diet, although I confess, we
were luckier than many people, living as we did in the country
and having so much produce for our own use and the surplus to
sell. The list was endless. We were producing chutneys, baking,
bottling, and oven drying all the garden produce, utilizing
the vast array of stoneware storage jars and bottles from the

storeroom. The honey, produced by the bees, and managed by Osian, had Frankie and Lennie learning fast how to help him. Jabbo made more beehives for them to put in different places over the estate, so it was a successful joint venture. Shortly after arriving, Osian had asked for permission to study any plans previously made of the planting of the Walled vegetable plots, the gardens and parkland. He could often be found poring over the drawings made in the previous century of the plans, design, and planting of the grounds of Willup Hall. Now I discovered he was making a new journal, recording where everything was planted, measuring the trunks of trees, recording their names, their age and the exact position of their planting. He discovered we had an old Mulberry tree which we didn't know about. He was making a record of the fruiting trees and recorded each of their yields in the Autumn of 1940. It was an incredible challenge he had set himself, but he knew it was a record to be kept for now and for future generations. He was logging in his journal every plant and tree all over the estate and trying to know when they were about to bear fruits so he could beat the squirrels or jays. We were discovering we had more fruit and nut trees and bushes than we realised and now we were going to have a detailed log and map of where all were planted. He had made drawings and diagrams and as yet the records were in their infancy; yet already, it was possible to see how useful it was going to be. Self-taught and an amazing 'plants person', he deserved to learn more and to share his findings. I thought he should be going to university or writing in a gardening magazine, and I wondered how I could help him. Since arriving he had developed a healthy brown outdoor complexion from the sun and wind, and he was developing a more muscular body from all the digging, lifting and carrying he was doing. The same could be said of Frankie.

He too looked much fitter, healthier, and happier from working outside and from the healthy wholesome diet we all enjoyed.

The lovely chestnut, Suffolk Punch, now called Alfie, was a sweetie. With Frankie learning to ride they would go out regularly with Lennie, to Alford's hunt stables to help with the hounds. Lennie had taken to Spangles and was riding him every day he could; they were becoming a good team and improving all the time. Frankie mostly worked with his left hand and used his right to hold things still or to turn an ignition key, but not to hold weight; he could ride Alfie using his left hand. The lovely horse had such a good mouth and was turning out to be a gem, he could be used in harness or ridden. Lucy and Sheila adored him; he was so kind and gentle.

As summer turned to autumn Granger was taking the grey hunter gelding, which he now called The Brig, out with the hounds for some gentle exercise. He clearly adored the horse and had taken him over which was fine. Jabbo was working with the young thoroughbred colt I had brought back with me and saved from slaughter. Grandora was investigating the colt's breeding to see if he qualified to race. Hey ho, here we go; Grandora has a new bee in her bonnet. The little roan mare now called Tizzy had taken to Spangles and didn't like being left behind, only just tolerating staying with Donk the little donkey. The girls all liked riding, with someone leading them. Tizzy was inclined to just put her head down and snatch grass if a small child was in charge, which usually meant whoever was riding catapulted over her head. The only doubtful one was the hackney mare who had been so poor and nervous when she arrived. We were still just letting her build up her strength, and get to know us; so far, we didn't know what she could do or might do in the future; these were early days.

For most of us here at the Hall, our lives jogged along nicely, unlike those living in other parts of Britain. The Battle of Britain started in May and continued into September with an onslaught of Luftwaffe attacking London, trying to draw the RAF into submission. One thousand and five hundred aircraft took part in the many air battles which lasted often until dusk. The RAF were victorious in repelling the Luftwaffe. This was the climax of the Battle of Britain. So, the Luftwaffe started night-time bombing, trying to terrify Londoners into submission. London docks had three hundred and thirty-seven bombs dropped on it and four hundred and forty-eight civilians were killed in one afternoon and evening.

It was at this time in September that we received the news that Larry, Lennie and Lottie's father Ernie Evans had been killed. Their mother survived, even though she was at great risk, working in an ammunitions factory; the factory, luckily, wasn't hit by the bombing that night. Mavis came over to tell them and she stayed with Arthur and Violet; the children went to stay there with her. I was shocked by her appearance: she was thin, grubby, and grey-skinned, and, well not at all clean. Of course, it was easier to understand after she told me about the water pipes not working, destroyed by the bombing; no water to wash in or to wash clothes; even water to drink or cook with was in short supply and had to be delivered. The streets were full of bricks and rubble, the roads full of craters, rows of houses destroyed, and the electricity supply cut off. Homeless people everywhere wondering where to go, some pushing prams, holding a few possessions retrieved from their bombed homes, and dirty children trailing behind. No homes, beds, food, or a safe place to go. It was a sad time, and the everyday topic was the horrendous and continuous bombing of London. We couldn't believe that so many were being killed in London and other cities in Britain. London was burning yet the British stiff upper lip remained, and those brave people who were able to, carried on with the clearing up, extinguishing fires and nursing the sick and injured. I just knew we had to help as much as we could.

Sadly, it was just too dangerous for the children to go to their father's funeral but Grandora persuaded our Vicar to allow him to be buried in our Churchyard as the children were residents here now. The power of Grandora's word meant a great deal and he was buried in our village Church yard, and we all attended the funeral of the brave man who had worked right through the German bombardment in the London Docks, doing essential work. Their mother had compassionate leave from work and stayed in Norfolk, but the bombing had taken its toll and she was understandably reluctant to go back to the ammunitions factory and risk being killed, making her children orphans. At least staying in Norfolk, she managed to get some rest while she decided what to do next. For weeks the children were understandably quiet and depressed, but we kept them as occupied as we could whilst giving them time to grieve.

All the children returned to school in September, and we carried on getting in the harvest which was vital as so many merchant ships were being targeted and sunk by German U-boats and our food supplies were being destroyed. This required all of us working flat out using Alfie to pull the dray as we loaded it up with the sheaves of corn and Hermes chipped in pulling a hay cart. Lennie would jump on whilst Alfie was harnessed up to the dray, and ride him round the field as we picked up all the sheaves of corn. We owned a tractor which was used in turn on all six farms on the estate and the tractor pulled a binder which was employed cutting the corn; it was this that Frankie now drove for everyone. He was very good at sharpening the blades regularly and changing any pulleys or belts which constantly seemed to break. We stooped up the sheaves of corn to dry before the threshing machine came and we fed the bundles of grain and straw into the feeder of the threshing machine in the farmyard. The threshing machine was pulled by a steam roller and was owned by the Baines family. It went from farm to farm in our area of Norfolk throughout the harvest and was always in a hurry to get the job done and move on to other farms. The straw passed over the straw rack that removed the straw from the kernels then kernels passed over a cleaner that blew away the remaining straw and chaff. The cleaned kernels were dumped into sacks and taken to the granary and tipped up until we filled the storage barns. These jobs needed at least five to six men or women to keep production going. It needed all of us working on the farm at harvest time as many of our farm workers were away fighting. Alford, Granger, Jabbo, Frankie, Osian, our land army girls Lucy and Sheila, Ted, Hugh, Humphrey, and I all battled to get our harvest 'home'. We worked like the clappers to get the harvest in before we had any rain. Clarissa kept our spirits up with a constant supply of picnic food and beer or cider, which she brought to us in the fields. Fortunately, the sun shone, and the weather was kind, and we achieved a record harvest to support our contribution to the war effort. Every day after school the boys came to help us in the fields and Audrey looked after the girls whilst we worked from dawn until dusk. It was tiring work but satisfying and the banter was good between us all.

There were peas to harvest, carrots, turnips, swedes for animal feed and then we ran straight into the potato harvest and then came half term in October when the women and children came to help us collect the potatoes after the tractor, with the spinner attached to the back of it, lifted them. We also used our old horse drawn spinner, with Alfie and Hermes working together they proved to be invaluable all through harvest saving us valuable fuel which was rationed and in short supply. The team of helpers from the village would rush in to pick as many potatoes as they could into their wooden trugs which were then tipped up into a cart and taken back to the yard for cleaning, riddled and sorting before being bagged ready for transportation to market. Some were collected in hessian sacks and taken straight to the RAF bases in our area and as far afield as Lincolnshire or London. Everyone who worked was paid and they were also allowed to take potatoes home in their bags or metal buckets. Our boys and girls all got stuck in and worked all day; well, the girls didn't manage a whole day; usually by lunchtime, if not before, they were very tired and allowed home with Audrey. They all got very dirty and muddy and had a great time.

My birthday was in October, and I had a lovely day. We had just reached the end of the potato harvest and I was brought tea upstairs and woken by Grandora and four little girls. I had a lovely cake baked especially for the occasion by Mrs Revill and it was big enough to share with everyone at five o'clock with afternoon tea. This was all arranged by Audrey and the girls in the school room which was decorated by Osian and the girls with ivy, garlands of wild berries and autumn flowers like the orange Chinese lanterns and Michaelmas Daisies. I received gorgeous gifts which I knew I would always treasure. Audrey had organised a scrapbook of mementoes of the year. There were travel bag tags pinned to the pages and everybody had written a sweet message to me and a happy birthday greeting. The girls had made pretty little cross stitch patterned squares of material to tie into the book's pages with ribbon; it was delightful. Lucy and Sheila had surrounded a little table mirror with shells, collected, heaven knows where or how, as most of our beaches were out of bounds now. Jabbo had made a beautiful keepsake box made of cherry wood and smelling divinely of the sweet wood. Granger had made a plaque in wood for Hermes' stable door with her name on it. Frankie had plaited three pieces of polished leather to make an unusual key ring, and Rosie and her mother Joan had made a wreath of dried flowers. Audrey had sewn a hand-embroidered lavender bag and filled it with dried lavender. Osian had dried herbs and made a sweet-smelling potpourri to put into a dish to remind me of the smells of summer. It was all wonderful and had to be my best birthday ever.

In the evening Malissa and Nico made the journey home to join me for dinner with Grandora and Audrey. Grandora had bought me a small watercolour of army horses by Lucy Kemp-Welch whom I greatly admired; it was gorgeous. I loved it. As I was getting ready for my special birthday dinner the front doorbell was pulled. It appeared there was no one in the house available to open the door so I flew downstairs in my dressing gown. I didn't want to be late for a pre-dinner drink of champagne and was wondering who on earth could be here at this time. I was just thinking if it was Gilbert Long, our ARP Warden, grumbling about our black-out curtains; if so, I just might be impolite to him or shock him with an invite for a drink.

I opened the door and there was Tiff. I fell into his arms I was so happy. I turned round to hear and see all the children out of bed and giggling at me and Tiff, so were Audrey, Malissa and Grandora. They all knew he was coming and had kept it a secret. After they had said 'hello' we ushered the children all back to bed and went through to the drawing room for a toast with Dom Perignon champagne. I was just worrying about serving

dinner when in walked Rosie with some canapés of little flat
dough squares, slithers of cheese and herbs and halves of tiny
tomatoes. Apparently, Rosie and Mrs Evans had agreed to serve
dinner for us as my birthday treat and Osian had made the little
cocktail treats for us. Next Osian himself arrived for dinner and
was pleased to see Tiff again, then we all went through to the
dining room.

"It's beautiful,' I said, "this is the best day, and you are all so
kind and here is my best surprise." I slipped my arm through
Tiff's, and he kissed my cheek in front of everyone.

The table had a low arrangement of late-autumn garden
flowers and leaves turning gold, reds, and rich browns. Grandora
had lit three candles in the silver candelabra, and it all looked
very special. We enjoyed cubes of beef cooked in red wine, with
little shallots grown by Osian, and his garden peas decorated
with wisps of pea shoots and sweet little carrots just pulled from
the garden. I had made a tarte tatin the day before and it was
delicious served with dollops of fresh cream from the dairy. Nico
and Malissa had brought a bottle of Portuguese port and a box
of Harrods chocolates which we all appreciated after dinner. It
was the most divine evening and day and I had been spoilt rotten.
After the meal and Grandora had gone to bed, we put on the
gramophone and the six of us danced to the Glenn Miller band
and The Squadronaires, the main RAF dance orchestra. We
listened to Charlie Parker and Dizzy Gillespie and Thelonious
Monk and their new style of Bebop Jazz; we all tried the new
dances now in fashion. It was a happy dream of an evening.

When everyone had gone to bed accept for Tiff, we cuddled
on the sofa in the sitting room. Questions 'poured' out! "Where
are you stationed now? Is your knee completely better? How long
is your leave?" I asked.

"Whoa," said Tiff, "one question at a time. I have four days' leave, two of which are mostly travelling here and back. My knee is pretty good now, thank you. Not as good as before, but it's good. I can't discuss where I'm stationed, sorry, but that's how it is now. I just had to see you on your birthday and pulled all the strings I could to get here. Oh, and I forgot, your present, it's here." He casually rummaged in one pocket, then another, then another and, finally, from his top pocket he pulled out a tiny box.

"Oh, I do love you," I said and opened the box to see a gold horse on a gold necklace. It was exquisite and the beautiful horse's eye was a tiny diamond. I was speechless. Tiff put it on me, and we kissed. "I love it. I can't believe you have been able to get me such an amazing gift, but I love you most and you just coming here today is the best present ever; I will always remember today."

He asked if I was still going to marry him when the war ended. I flung my arms round him and told him yes of course. Later he went to bed, alone, and so did I. We just wanted to be together, but not now, not here and not yet. We were both elated and exhausted and he insisted we wait until the time was right for us to make love.

We enjoyed our two whole days together although the children, who were delighted to see him, claimed him for a game of cricket, and Nico and Malissa had questioned him about the progress of the war and how our fightback was progressing. He could only discuss what we already knew, but it was interesting to hear his point of view. He was very interested in how Osian's gardening project was developing and his log of the current garden and park contents.

Nico and Malissa sadly went back to Cambridge two days later; I was always sorry to see them go. When he saw the new dapple-grey hunter gelding that I had rescued, now called The Brig, Tiff loved him and we rode out together both mornings on him and Hermes, with the dogs following us. We drove the car, went for a pub lunch and a walk for some special time alone, and all along we knew he had to go back to be a soldier and fight, not knowing if this would be the last time we were together. I was so happy he had been to see me, and it was with great sadness I took him to the station and kissed him goodbye yet again. Strange though it seems, it was only now I told Grandora about his asking me to marry him when the war was over, and my acceptance. She told me he had asked if it was alright with her for him to ask me. In the absence of my father, she had told him it was fine, but soon my father would be home and he should then ask him. I told her he had proposed under the Cedar of Lebanon Tree, and she smiled.

"Oh, that reminds me, have you seen two paintings which used to hang in my sitting room?" Grandora queried. "They were gifts to me from your grandfather on our engagement. They are watercolours of flowers by Samuel John Peploe."

I confessed to her I had moved them, and feeling very guilty, said how sorry I was not to have told her. I intended to replace them with my own paintings but only one was completed.

She then amazed me by saying, "I might prefer to have yours when they are finished. Let me see them, so I can decide."

Phew, she was brilliant. I had forgotten all about the paintings.

I loved wearing the necklace. I touched it to remember Tiff, our last kiss and remembered his love for me. It wasn't right just now to be so in love, as daily the news seemed to bring more problems in the world. Since August 15th the Luftwaffe had constantly fought battles in the air, pitching their Messerschmitt 109 against our young pilots flying their Hawker Hurricanes and Spitfires. They outnumbered our planes four to one, but we had radar from a chain of radar masts stretching all over Britain, plus

30,000 people plane spotters looking out for any sign of enemy aircraft, so were fighting back. August 18th was the 'Hardest Day' when the Luftwaffe attacked Biggin Hill, trying to bomb our planes on the ground. Hitler failed to gain control over our fighter planes and by September 15th we had won the Battle of Britain in the skies, but we were now short of planes and pilots. After this they started bombing London again and there seemed to be no end in sight. On October 31st, 1940, the Italian submarine Scire attacked the British Naval Base in Gibraltar, but the bombs failed. London was still being bombed and people slept in underground stations and air raid shelters; but many civilians continued to be killed. Liverpool, also a target, suffered heavy attacks with two hundred bombing raids on the city.

Nico and Malissa were very worried about the possibility of the Italians attacking Greece which seemed to be a case of when, not if. Albania was already in the hands of the Italian Army, and they were turning their attention to Greece, now. No fireworks or bonfires would be permitted in Britain this year on November 5th, so it was a quiet day, but for tea we did mark the occasion with sausages inside jacket potatoes and carrot ears, so they really did look like little pigs in blankets, and afterwards homemade toffee, in the Hall.

Our thoughts then moved on to Christmas. Another Christmas and with rationing getting worse, how would we manage?

Chapter 25

Christmas Party and Boxing Day Hunt

N ovember flew by, the days grew shorter, and the fields were sprinkled with hoar frosts. We hardy souls still went out early mornings, blowing clouds of steam into the cold morning air just as the horses did. Hunting had started and we were often out riding with Alford and the hounds on morning exercise. Our fires were now lit every day in the Hall; with logs constantly being used. These were piled up outside the scullery door by Frankie, every day. We were very lucky to have a ready supply of logs from our own woods and we made sure those in need in our villages were also supplied.

November 12th saw a major air raid on Sheffield, followed by another on November 14th on Coventry City, which was hit with the most concentrated attack, lasting for eleven hours. The Luftwaffe had dropped on the City hundreds of tons of high explosive bombs along with thirty thousand incendiaries and fifty land mines. The great medieval church of St Michael, the

Cathedral, was destroyed along with the central library, market hall, the 16Th Century St James Palace, countless shops, and public buildings. Forty-three thousand homes were destroyed or damaged: fifteen acres of the Daimler factory were turned into a blazing inferno, and it was said that over five hundred people had been killed, but no one knew for sure if that was the right number; it was impossible to know. On November 24th Bristol was bombed and then on the 20th of November Liverpool had a major raid. November 22nd saw Manchester on the receiving end of massive bombing from the Luftwaffe and on November 28th Liverpool was again hit by German bombers, killing one hundred and sixty-six people. Poor Liverpool was constantly being bombed and the people were suffering badly; many made homeless, many losing loved ones, jobs, schools, and shops. It seemed a relentless campaign to destroy our cities, our citizens and our morale. The firemen of Britain were an amazing, resilient body of uniformed men who never gave up in the face of such tremendous adversity and were heroes to us all.

We all listened to the news on the wireless and read the papers following the reporting of these horrendous disasters. I felt I was not doing enough to help with the war effort. It made me despondent, and I discussed with Grandora what more I could do; should I sign up? I had heard about women being wanted to fly new planes from the factories to the airfield. Planes were in constant demand as countless ones had been lost, along with young men fighting the enemy.

"But you have a vital job here," she said. "You are always on the go running around from farm to farm sorting out problems. The children would have nowhere to go if you hadn't taken them in and given them a home. The villages depend upon you supplying food for their homes and the street markets and now people need fuel as well. I don't think that you have any idea how vital you really are in keeping the home fires burning. Because of you there is a knitting club meeting every week in our school room providing socks and jumpers, scarves, gloves, and blankets for refugees, and because of you it is heated and warm. You have made sure the school has food from our farm every week providing hot lunches for the children, and the elderly now have a rota of neighbours helping them through this desperate time, all because of you. You have even organised a transport system to take those in need of treatment, to hospital. Who would be doing all these things if you weren't here?"

"Somebody else would do these jobs now everything is up and running, I just feel worthless not being in uniform and doing a proper job. Granger, Jabbo and Hugh are members of the Home Guard, are in uniform and preparing to defend us to the last man, and Osian is learning how to drive an ambulance and taking his First Aid Certificate," I said, sighing.

It was left there, hanging in the air, an unfinished conversation.

Christmas came quickly as usual; one minute it's weeks away and then suddenly it's just days away. We had many crisp, frosty days with our early rides before Christmas, now dark in the mornings, and the pale sun came out slowly to try and warm the cold earth. The park seemed to have turned grey-green and dark brown overnight. Indeed, the earth seemed to have lost her rosy glow. I still was up and out of bed early every morning and rode out sometimes alone or with Jabbo, Granger, Frankie, or Lennie. They were all keen to be out with the horses no matter how cold it was. Osian was busy putting the garden to bed for the winter, planting new plants, bulbs and tending winter vegetables. The greenhouse was kept constantly warm and was still producing some exotic fruit, and lemons and oranges. Grandora spent more time researching the family tree in the library or playing bridge with her friends. Audrey made a new worthy partner for her at these events, which pleased her no end. Our junior Bridge club was still running once a week and as playing games outside became impossible in the dark for the children, they became skilled at snakes and ladders, dominoes, card games like snap and seven up. They were still allowed a game on the billiard table once a week, always with an adult in the room guarding the green baize of the table. They all became better readers and their writing improved. The girls loved painting and I helped them with their art in the heated school room.

Audrey spent hours each day helping the children make paper chains and Christmas decorations for the house and their school room, in the run up to Christmas. There was to be a nativity play held at the village school and conversations centred on who would be Mary and the Angels. It turned out Ruby and Lottie would be Angels, with six other children, and Mary was played by a village girl so none of our children could be disappointed at not being picked the lead. Talia and Adele were asked to play musical instruments for the choir and after some soul-searching discussions it was decided they would and were excited to be part of the production. Lennie was a Shepherd but didn't really want to be in the play as he thought he was too old. Larry and George were at the local grammar school now, so they were preparing for a musical recital as their Christmas contribution. We all went in the afternoon to see the village school nativity play and we were very proud of 'our' girls in their white sheets or white crepe paper outfits, their home-made white feather halos, wings, fashioned from wire and wrapped in silver tinsel. Lennie reluctantly wore a paisley shawl over a long old coat tied on with a big leather belt round his waist. He carried a wonderful shepherd's crook made for him by Jabbo and just the right size. I think they were all proud of themselves and we enjoyed seeing them doing so well and integrated into the small school.

It was at this time we discovered Talia was an amazing piano player when we found her tinkering on our grand piano. She was embarrassed to be 'caught' playing it in the sitting room. We were told by the girls that their mother loved music, played the piano, and had encouraged her daughters to play. Adele preferred the violin, so we went about finding a decent violin for her. Lydia Ann, my father's sister, found a good one for us. The girls had our permission to practise in the sitting room and they played beautifully, every day they were with us.

The musical recital was surprisingly good as some of the sixth form children were nearly eighteen and accomplished musicians. The theme throughout was Christmas through classical music, including Victor Hely-Hutchinson's Symphony of Carols. Larry was a stagehand; George played the flute and Theodore played the harmonica. He had been practising this for weeks everywhere he went, and I understand the gun dogs in the kennels seemed to like it and had nearly stopped howling whenever he played. Towards the end we all joined in singing more popular Christmas songs by Bing Crosby and poignant songs by Vera Lynn. The finale was the usual Christmas carols we all loved. It was very Christmassy and almost got us in the right mood for to celebrate; not easy knowing so much of the world was in turmoil.

I organised the tenants' Christmas dinner in the school-cum-knitting group room. We had always held one every year. I did my best to ensure we had the usual decent meal, and it was an opportunity to talk about farming without rushing off to feed livestock or do the milking.

Granger and Osian chose the huge Christmas tree for us, cut it down and brought it to the Hall. We put it up in our large reception hall and the four girls loved it and helped to decorate it with tinsel and with the Wesleyan Baubles we had collected over the years. It was strange, and to see the same decorations I had put on the tree when I was young, giving the girls as much pleasure as they had to me. It made me feel very sentimental and long for my parents to come home. Grandora wrote to them regularly and we received their letters through diplomatic sources in London. They were happy to stay in Singapore and keep away from the war waging in Europe, although it was now beginning to spread to parts of Africa. Grandora and I sent them a Harrods hamper and hoped they received it. In return my parents organised a fabulous Harrods hamper with toys and games for all of us at the Hall.

On the afternoon of Christmas Eve, we held a 'carol singing get together' for everyone we knew, which included the Rector and his family, Arthur and Violet with their enormous brood of children, everyone who worked on our estate and the tenant farmers was also invited; a family tradition going back many years. We were lucky to have plenty of wine in our cellars and our home brewed cider made from our own orchard apples meant we had plenty of alcohol for the adults. The children had diluted homemade blackcurrant juice, and everyone enjoyed homemade sausage rolls and sandwiches. We finished with everyone carol singing round the Christmas tree in the reception hall; it was a huge success and a lovely way to start Christmas. All our guests left in the dark at five o'clock and found their way to their homes, no easy task during the blackout when we were not allowed to show much light on our bikes or motor vehicles. Our local ARP Warden, Gilbert Long, was a keen detective type who checked every curtain every night, cycling around the village and neighbouring farms making sure no light was visible after dark. He was even known to have cycled over to us and gone around shining his torch shouting, 'PUT THAT LIGHT OUT' just in case we had a light on. Bless him!

Christmas morning arrived with noisy, excited children opening their presents; it was such fun listening to their happy squeals of surprise and delight. I had decided to use pillowcases for their gifts at the side of their beds and our old Christmas stockings, plus some recently homemade replica stockings which were filled with nuts and a little chocolate. Each one also had a torch and some tiny gift, like a packet of pencils or a notebook, or playing cards. The chocolate was very hard to get hold of, but we had slightly more success saving our sugar ration and making fudge for all the children. Even paper was in short supply. All the children received hand-knitted new gloves in their stockings made by the knitting club. Their pillowcases were not completely full as it was so hard to buy gifts for Christmas, but they all had new books and little wooden toys, or metal airplanes or cars, and the girls had shuttlecocks. They all had new bike bells and the boys had kites made by Jabbo and Osian. Mrs Hubbard in the village had been given some wonderful Indian material from Grandora, purchased on her travels, just right for the job of making kites. Lennie was delighted to receive a silver stock pin and white stock from Grandora and me to put on when he was whipper-in for Alford out trail hunting with the Willup Hounds. Grandora and I gave Larry a book of famous political speeches and gaffes, many very funny, which he was very pleased with. George and Theodore received gun bags from their Uncle Henry and cartridge belts from Grandora and me. Lottie and Ruby had prettily-dressed little hand-size dolls, and Jabbo made peg dolls for them with dolls houses made from old fruit boxes, sanded down and painted. Inside were tiny beds and chairs plus miniature paintings on the walls painted by me. I gave all the adults soap which was much appreciated and the ladies the pretty scarves I had bought in Harrods much earlier in the year. We gave bottled jars of produce and seeds (collected by Osian) with bottles of cider and homemade rhubarb wine to our tenant farmers.

Sadly because of the constant nightly bombing many people around the country spent Christmas Eve in air aid shelters. There had been fifty-seven consecutive nights of bombing during what was being referred to as the Blitz.

Fortunately, we had a lovely Christmas Day which fell on a Wednesday with Nico and Malissa coming home for the holidays. We all went to morning service at Church and then home for elderflower cordial for the children and sherry for us. Larry, Lennie, and Lottie's mother, Mavis Evans arrived to spend Christmas Day with us. She had left her job in the munitions factory in London after her husband Ernie had been killed and now had a job on an airbase in Norfolk; she was working in the kitchen and lived in digs near the base. Arthur and I were trying to find her suitable accommodation near us so the children could spend more time with her. On her visits and when not working, she stayed with Arthur and Violet, but we had agreed to have the children stay here for Christmas as they had been so excited preparing for it here. We had a joint of pork, plus a chicken, lots of home-grown vegetables and homemade bread sauce. We were very lucky growing all our own food; I knew many people who were really suffering with food being in short supply and rationed. After clearing away the debris from the meal, I left the children quietly playing with their toys. Grandora was asleep so I went to see Hermes and to prepare the horses for the Boxing Day Meet being held at the Hall. Plaiting up had been done already and I groomed Hermes, oiled her hooves, and then checked my tack, then I offered to clean any tack which still needed doing. I went back to the house and persuaded the children to walk the dogs with me before teatime and games; I thought some fresh air would do them all good. After plenty of grumbles and moaning we all enjoyed walking down to the river and back up through the park. The children were excited as, after tea, we were going to play Charades, pass the parcel and find the thimble. Tea was cold pork or chicken with salad and trifle. We had lots of fun, with Grandora joining in briefly and Nico and Malissa organising everything. Audrey stayed to help and after they'd all gone to bed said she was off back to her cottage to put her feet up and listen to Elgar on her gramophone. I preferred the Glenn Miller orchestra or George Gershwin. We adults had listened to George VI's Christmas broadcast, which was sad but uplifting, a time of reflection, yet again. He remembered those who were prisoners or wounded and bereaved. He was confident the service and sacrifice of the British people would win the war and a lasting peace. For us it was a good Christmas, and we knew we should count our blessings. We were so aware that, many, many people were suffering under the Nazi regime as well as from hardship caused by the ongoing war. It was a nightmare the magnitude of which we still had little knowledge – eventually we would find out just how vicious and violent it was, especially in Europe as well as here at home.

Morning soon came and there was more excitement as the Hunt was meeting on the lawn in front of the house. I was riding Hermes; Granger, the grey hunter, The Brig; Jabbo was on Zoltan; Frankie on the Suffolk Punch Alfie, aka Alfie Punch aka AP. Nico was riding my mother's sweet grey mare Polly and Lennie rode Spangles. Jabbo and Frankie were not riding but happy to be part of the field and hound control. Jabbo led Alford's second horse from the hunt stables, for when his first horse became tired. The field was very much reduced as so many were away either in the services or no longer had a horse to ride. As usual the 'Old Faithfuls' turned up, as always to support our Hunt and we had quite a few children on their ponies; some were home from boarding school and of course there was the pony club 'lot'. The Hunt Cup, served on the lawn by Malissa and Mavis, was a tiny tot of mulled red wine served with stuffing rolls. This was my invention of chopped sage from our garden, chopped onions we had grown, crumbled bread and eggs from our hens in a baked pastry case. I had also been inventive, trying an old recipe I had found in the kitchen pantry: chestnut stuffing rolls – we even had some hazelnuts to go with the chestnuts from a tree in the garden. Again, I mixed it all with chopped sage, breadcrumbs, butter, onions, and boiled eggs, wrapped the mix in pastry and served in slices. Served up as bites for everyone, warm from the oven, they were a great success. Grandora wandered around meeting up with old friends, villagers and generally enjoying the occasion. Audrey made sure our four young girls didn't get trampled on by any of the horses; they of course loved the excitement of seeing everyone, and petting the hounds, who were very friendly. Our dogs had to be fastened up for the duration of the Hunt.

It was a damp, cold day and rain threatened the whole time we were out with the hounds. I returned to the stables early with Jabbo, who at 2.30pm was now bringing home the first hunter Alford had ridden. We prepared the stables for when the others arrived back and Jabbo made a bran mash which he covered with a sack to keep it warm for all the horses for their night feed. He was so careful of old Zoltan and hosed his legs to wash off any mud then he sponged him over with warm water and dried him off. He rugged him up with a light jute rug and a hay thatch and popped him in his stable with its thick straw bed while he started on Alford's hunter, doing the same for him. I took care of Hermes, stabled her, and popped a light rug on her. Then I went to the paddocks to give feeds to the Hackney-type mare who was turned out with Donk and Tizzy the roan pony. With her thick winter coat and having gained weight, she was beginning to look well at last, and was noticeably less nervous. I then went to the tack room, put more wood on the boiler and started to clean my tack and Alford's hunter's tack. I put a kettle on the boiler and Jabbo joined me with some of his 'special Moroccan coffee'. He cleaned Zoltan's tack, and we drank the delicious coffee. It was bliss after our day out.

"Jabbo, is your name a Moroccan name or is it from somewhere else?" I asked.

"My name is Jabbour, and it is Moroccan, but I have always been referred to as Jabbo as my father was Jabbour as well. My full name is Jad-All-Jabbour." He told me this as we munched on homemade oat biscuits.

It was dropping dark when we heard the clip clopping on the metal road into the Hall and we scurried around to help clean and settle the horses with only the dim lights we were allowed. We even had the wooden sliding shutters closed at the stable windows, so as not to allow even a chink of light through. Lennie was splattered with mud and wet through from the rain which had finally decided to come down in spades. He was grinning and clearly very happy as he jumped off Spangles and started to clean the tired gelding with a sponge and warm water. I scraped the excess water from Spangles' coat and we both towel rubbed him down and rugged him up. Then we helped Nico with Polly and settled her in the stable. Frankie and Jabbo worked just the same on Alfie and put light indoor rugs on them with hay underneath, before leading them into their deep straw-bedded stables. They all had slightly warm water to drink and some hay to munch on whilst they dried. Granger had gone back with Alford to the Hunt kennels still on The Brig as he was going to help Alford feed round and settle the hunters into their stables.

"I'm going to help at the kennels and I'm taking Granger's van over to fetch him back. The Brig can stay there until tomorrow," said Frankie.

"Should I go too?" asked Lennie, jumping up.

"No, George and Theo are going with Hugh to give them a hand feeding round the hounds, it's getting to be hard for Alford with Martha being disabled with arthritis," he added.

"I think you had better have a warm cup of tea, take off your wet Hunt coat and put on your stable coat, then you can check on the horses here. We can take off their 'hay coats' when they are dry and then rug them all up with their night jute rugs," I told him as I put the kettle back on and made hot tea and dug out some more biscuits for them. I hung his maroon Hunt jacket on a hanger in the warm room so it could dry overnight. They were expensive to replace.

I thought we were lucky as we were still drinking real tea, but for how long for we didn't know. Our losses at sea were enormous and tragic. In December alone we lost forty-two British, Allied, and neutral ships in the Atlantic. Every month our losses at sea were catastrophic and our vital supplies were just not getting through. We had already decided our Hunt would only be going out once a month in future, because of the difficulties we were all facing. Dog racing continued to be run, but horse racing had been banned when France was invaded. Later in the year it had been reinstated but with many sanctions, minimising and restricting the amount of racing allowed.

We made our weary way back to the Hall from the stables to be met by our ecstatic dogs and a quiet, warm kitchen from which came the good smell of rich vegetable stew on the range. Our vegetable stew was always very good and tasty because of the vast array of herbs from the garden supplied by Osian, and it was just right after a day's hunting. Malissa came into the kitchen and brought a good red wine with her, which Nico and I enjoyed with our meal.

"You've got some apologies to make tomorrow," she said with a long face.

"Why, what have I done now?" I asked.

"Osian is not pleased with all the mess on the lawn made by the horses' hooves, you are in his bad books," she laughed.

"Oh yes, I suppose I am. I'll give him a hand tomorrow treading in the holes."

"Me too," said Lennie, smiling. "It was worth it though, what a great day. Thank you, I really enjoyed it, goodnight."

We all wished him goodnight; he was a good lad. It was lovely having Nico and Malissa home; they were such fun and so supportive. It was my time to support them, though, as they were worried about their parents. Greece had been invaded by Mussolini in October and since then there had been no news from them. It was presumed they were on one of their ships dodging U-boats and the war, but that could not last for ever, unless they managed to get to South America.

Chapter 26

Uri Berman escapes

Uri knelt scraping in the growing dark at the rotten floorboard. It was going from dark to completely black as night fell in the foul-smelling cattle wagon. He only had a pen knife with a saw and some other gadgets on his Swiss army knife – his grandfather's – the one item his father had insisted he had as a memento of the old man. He had it hidden in the hem of his jacket along with his identity papers, a photograph and a little paper money. The only other thing he clung to was a small pewter cup which had been his mother's and if there was a drink to be had he could use his little cup. There was no drink, no water, no food, no toilet; nothing on the train made up of cattle trucks, but the moans and crying of the suffering people. The girl he was next to in the corner of the wagon clung on to a boy with her and when she saw him scraping at the rotten wood, she stood square to protect him from other people; stood over him to give him chance to loosen the board. He had seen her pushed on to the truck clinging to the boy and dragging him with her;

she was bruised all over, wearing a dirty, blood-stained rag of a dress. She was small, thin and had pain in her huge dark eyes.

He was tired and his body was sore; he just felt it was his only chance to escape and he mustn't give in. His fingers were cut and bleeding from wooden splinters, but the smell of so many unwashed human bodies crammed together in the dark trucks spurred him on to escape. He thought and hoped that they were still in France. They had left Paris the night before, but the journey was slow and painful; the last sign he had seen was ages ago and it had been in French. Gradually he made the hole bigger and bigger, and he thought he just might squeeze through. He worked on it a little longer and then decided he could do it; he should go now; it was dark so hopefully the guards on the roof wouldn't see him. If they did a bullet was better than this. He gently knocked the girl's legs to try to tell her he was going to jump but it was too dark to see her and now he was on the floor it was too crowded for him to stand up. He was suffocating; he just had to chance it. The girl touched his head to let him know she understood and then he was gone.

He lay still on the dark track, terrified. He stank as all the urine and effluent from hundreds of people crammed into the cattle trucks relieved themselves where they stood. It seeped through the floors of the trucks, and he was covered in 'shit'. As the train rattled over him, he lay motionless, waiting for the guard on the roof to see him and shoot him. Silence came and the train packed with wailing, tortured people passed over him; he was left in peace. At first he dare not move but then realised that if he didn't, another train would likely come along the track. Bruised and hurting all over, he shuffled over the rails, scrambled down the loose pebbles and into some brambles. He struggled to free himself from the grasping thorns, finally coming to rest on gentler grass, exhausted. He thought he was in a field, but it was very dark, no light and no moon. Slowly, he made his way through the field and suddenly heard running water, maybe a river or a stream he thought. Making his way to the water, he used his precious cup to drink as much as he could. He washed his hair, face and hands but dare not wash his stinking jacket yet; if he did, he might die as the air was cold. However, whoever he met would smell him and might be reluctant to help him. Would anyone help him anyway? Everyone turned a blind eye to the treatment given to Jewish people by the Nazis. There was nobody to help any of them. He went back to the field and crawled through the grass, too scared to stand. He reached a wood and with his hands feeling his way and frequently stumbling, he went from tree trunk to tree trunk until he could feel he was facing another field. He felt for the hedge and crawled through and then he heard something breathing near him and he froze. Fear struck him rigid, and he could hardly breathe. Something got nearer to him and breathed on him as it munched on the grass. Relieved it was just a goat – he felt its face gently, stroked its neck and an idea came to him as he felt along its belly and underneath; and, yes, it was a nanny. He was a town boy, but he knew an udder when he felt one. He got out his cup and pulled at her teat as she walked away. He crawled after her and tried again and squeezed; she stood still and he put the teat inside his cup and squeezed again; he heard the milk hit the bottom of his little cup and so he kept on squeezing her teat, then he drank the warm milk and knew he must have more. He squeezed and drank more milk until he was exhausted. Crawling to a hedge at the side of the field, although it was dark, he found a small gap and soon he was in a field full of strange shapes. He approached one and found it was straw or hay stooped up waiting for collection. The milk was good, and he felt a bit better.

Crawling inside a stoop of hay for warmth, he fell asleep.

Dawn had just broken when he heard a voice calling which woke him; he wondered where he was, then quickly remembered that he didn't exactly know where he was. He moved slowly and saw a girl walking through the field calling for the goat. She caught the goat and walking back to the farmhouse she spotted him. He knew she had seen him, and he was about to move when she bent down to fiddle with a rope on the goat's collar.

"Do not move," she said, not looking in his direction. "Stay where you are and I will come back for you, don't move."

He stayed where he was, frightened, but with little choice. Could he trust her? After what seemed an age, she came back and told him to wait until she reached the farmhouse and then he should follow her, keeping low. He did as she told him, she opened a barn door and told him to go inside. An older man appeared and asked him where he was from.

"I am from the Netherlands, but I have been staying in Paris," Uri told him.

"Were you on a train?" asked the man.

"Yes, that's why I smell. I'm sorry."

"Take off your clothes and leave them on the floor. We must burn them. I have some more for you. If you have anything you wish to keep, take them out so we can clean them. I have a bath ready for you in the house." He gave him a towel and walked back to the house.

Uri took out his few precious belongings and followed him into a scullery where there was a small tin bath waiting for him. He got in and gratefully washed away the horrible stink of his journey. He climbed out, dried himself and put on the clean clothes left for him. They didn't fit very well, but they were clean, the old shoes were slightly too big, so the man gave him another pair of socks to wear on top of the others. So far, few words had been spoken and the girl had disappeared. He was taken into the kitchen and given a bowl of warm goat's milk and bread to dip into it. He was starving and ate quickly. The man told him to slow down, or he might be sick. He did as he was told.

"Are you Jewish?" he asked Uri.

"Yes," Uri replied, hesitantly.

"I thought so. Your hair needs cutting, it is too long. I will do it now. Sit here." He pointed to a chair, and he proceeded to cut Uri's hair, much shorter; so that he looked more like a French boy. "Do you know where you are?"

"No, I think I might be near to the middle of France."

"You are not far from Limoges, and you can rest here until it is safe to move you. Do you have papers?"

"They are here," said Uri.

The man read them and grunted. "You need more papers. You cannot use these or carry them with you; leave them here. I will take care of them. My daughter will be back very soon, and I will carry on working in the fields. Come, I will show you where you can wait." He took him to a field where there was a small goat shelter. He left him there and went to collect the sheafs in from the field and Uri went back to sleep.

Later that day the girl brought him into the house and gave him a bowl of vegetable broth with more bread and he saw a fire had been lit in the grate, no doubt for his disgusting smelly clothes, he thought. That night a man arrived at the farmhouse and Uri was told to follow him closely as they set off into the night. After about three hours they stopped to rest and drink water before continuing for another three hours When they stopped again the man produced some bread and cheese. No words were spoken. Eventually they met another man who had two bikes.

Again, Uri was instructed to closely follow on the bike. It was
very difficult riding in the dark not knowing where he was going.
He cycled with the new man, and they travelled on rough tracks
and roads until dawn was almost breaking and reached another
farm where they stopped and were given food and met a girl on a
bike The second man left him and cycled away, leaving him with
the girl. Together they travelled on for hours, through forests
where they often had to walk and could only cycle where there
were tracks or roads. Hours later she left him alone and went
back through the forest. He waited alone with the bike and was
scared, so stayed hidden in bushes. Hours later a man arrived on
a bike and just stopped where the girl had left him, spoke and
gave a password. Uri slowly came out of hiding and the man told
him to follow him, and they carried on cycling. Uri was tired,
scared, hungry and thirsty as they cycled on for most of the day
and next night. Finally, they turned into a long drive and rode
towards a large Chateau. The man was Marcel, and he took him
to the farmhouse at the back of the Chateau and put both the
bikes away. A young woman with a toddler by her side gave him
bread and soup and showed him a place where he could sleep,
which was hidden in a cupboard behind a bed. He slept until
teatime but stayed where he was, waiting for what would happen
next. He stayed in the tiny cupboard until he was told he could
come out. He was fed again and then the man told him to follow
him. They set off walking towards a lake, staying close to the
trees. It was evening and dropping dark. Crossing over a small
stone bridge which straddled a waterfall, they followed a shallow
river for some way until it went into a thick dark forest, then they
carried on walking for over three hours until finally they met a
young man who was waiting for them. The two men greeted each
other warmly, exchanged some words, then Marcel passed the

rucksack he had been carrying to the young man. He squeezed Uri's shoulder and shook his hand saying, "Bonne Chance." So, he left the young Jewish boy with the young dark-haired bearded man who now led Uri high into the forest hills where other resistance and refractors were hiding and living, waiting for a time to hit back at the tyrants occupying their beautiful country.

Chapter 27

Danielle and Tad Arrive

ew Year was a quiet affair. The weather was awful with
freezing days, snow always threatening to fall and when
it did, we had blizzard conditions. The youngest children
all went to bed after tea on New Year's Eve. Larry went to stay with
George and Theodore at Hugh and Margaret's as they were letting
the boys have a later dinner to celebrate the New Year, but they would
all be in bed well before midnight as they planned a long walk with
the gun dogs in the morning. Grandora, Audrey, Malissa and Nico,
Osian and I had dinner in the morning room. Malissa had prepared
some traditional Albanian food, Tave me Presh ska Mish meatless,
leek baked pie with rice and red peppers from our big glass house
in the Walled Garden, Kulac soda bread and Shendetlie honey and
nut cake. I had chosen a light white Riesling wine from the Alsace
region in France and Grandora had chosen a delicious champagne,
a Charles Lafitte to drink with our Shendetlie dessert and toast in
the New Year. Did we feel guilty about having our decadent war
meal? NO. It was all delicious and a happy evening with us being

together and alive, even if being a little subdued due to the events in December. In Egypt our British forces had launched an offensive to retake the Egyptian port of Sidi Barrani, which fortunately had been successful. However, the Calabria, a passenger and cargo steamer, had been torpedoed and sunk by a German submarine off Ireland with all three hundred and sixty innocent people on board losing their lives, which was just horrendous. Southampton had suffered three nights of heavy bombing at the beginning of the month and Sheffield had suffered four nights of heavy bombing the same as Southampton with heavy loss of lives and awful fires and destruction. Next to follow was Liverpool with three consecutive nights of bombing, which the papers called the Christmas blitz. At the end of December, Manchester was bombed and six hundred and fifty-four people were killed and over two thousand injured. It just didn't seem right to celebrate New Year with so much destruction going on, but we were lucky to be alive and it was important we carried on trying to help our country succeed here at home and defeat Hitler. So much of our supplies had been sunk on its way here in the convoys of ships. It was so important we had to keep trying to increase our food production. Granger and Jabbo had declined an invitation to join us, opting for a quiet meal together and for Granger no doubt some whisky and an early night. Jabbo was anxious about the events in north Africa and Egypt and his family and friends living there, as the news was far from good. We all went to bed before midnight, but it was a pleasant evening and one I shall always have as a treasured memory.

As January trudged along with its usual dreary, cold, often wet and stormy weather, I felt more compelled again to try to do more than just run our home operations. However, a telephone call from Mr Jakabus Guilhem, the jeweller I had met in Claridge's, put that plan on hold as he wanted me to take a young lady and

her young brother for a few months. They had only recently
arrived via Portugal and had endured a traumatic journey and
were in shock. He hoped my peaceful location would restore their
spirits. He considered our Hall to be a safe house. Safe from what
I wondered? I hesitated momentarily, as I didn't think we were
peaceful with the children playing and running around shouting
to each other and rarely, if occasional arguing. Anyway, of course,
I agreed to them coming and enjoying a normal life, so he said
a car would arrive with them the following morning. Yet again
it was all hands to the cleaning and decorating. Fortunately,
this job was well in hand upstairs in the stable yard. We were
busy converting two bedrooms, formerly used by grooms, into
a flat with a downstairs kitchen-cum-sitting room. Our addition
had been a small bathroom with a shower, and this was nearing
completion. I spent the morning working on the flat upstairs
whilst Jabbo and Granger were busy finishing the floor tiling
in the cosy living room. The Pamments were marvellous and
looked good everywhere. Margaret helped me to finish painting
the bedrooms and, in the afternoon, we hung the check curtains
and put up the blackout curtains. By six o'clock in the evening,
it was looking very good, the beds were in place and made up,
the fire was lit, and the back boiler was warming the downstairs,
feeding the two radiators upstairs in each bedroom. I helped
feed round the horses and we chatted to Osian and Frankie who
were fastening up the poultry for the night. They had a look at
the latest accommodation which was now finished and admired
all our handiwork. We were all intrigued to know who was
arriving next, and Margaret went home to give Hugh and the
boys their tea.

By eleven o'clock the next day the two had arrived by military
car, which was strange. A petite slim young lady slowly alighted

from the car followed by a boy of about eleven and I shook their hands and took them into the reception hall to meet Grandora. It was then I realized that she was not just slim, but skeletal, with protruding cheekbones and bony shoulder blades. Her clothes just hung on her; in fact, they didn't look like they were her clothes. She was extremely quiet and very protective towards the young boy who was also thin, but nowhere near as thin as her, and she kept her arm around his shoulders. She had a small, elfin shaped face with short curly, patchy, dark brown hair and enormous sad eyes. I left her talking to Grandora and took the driver and the other person travelling with them through to the kitchen and made tea for us all with some cake which had been made for their arrival. The man in the suit indicated he wished to speak to me alone, so I took him into the morning room and left the driver who was wearing army uniform in the kitchen.

"I would like you to be aware this young lady has suffered a dreadful journey here from Europe and needs rest and recuperation and it has been suggested that she would be safe and looked after here by you."

"I am not sure what you mean by safe, we are a large group here who are all family to us now and we all have a large degree of freedom on our estate. Are you suggesting she is watched and kept in like a prisoner, because if you are then this is the wrong place for her," I replied.

"I was informed this would be a safe place for her from stress and fear where she can learn to live happily again," he said, adding "she has helped us with information, and we don't want the wrong people knowing she is staying here."

"Oh well, I hope she will be fine here, we are tucked away in this 'neck of the woods', so to speak, so I have prepared a little house for her in the stable yard and there are always people there to give her help or advice or leave her alone," I added as I showed him into Grandora's sitting room and then went back to fetch some tea.

Leaving the chauffeur with Margaret and Mrs Revill, I went back to Grandora's sitting room and took a tray of tea. We sat having our tea and any questions I tried to ask were fended away by this quiet man, so gradually the conversation dried up. Grandora chatted about the weather, and I suggested I took the young girl, who had remained very quiet, to her little house with the boy so she could rest and later she could join us for lunch and the young boy could meet the others when they returned from school. The mysterious man in the suit left with his driver and I was glad. I thought he was a bit of a dark character. We were informed her name was Danielle Becker and the boy was Thaddeus, her brother; they were very quiet when I showed them their new home. Jabbo came round to say hello, as did Granger, and she said hello without any smile or warmth; the boy stood shyly behind her. I decided she needed some clothes, so I needed to have a word with Agatha Hubbard, Grandora and the knitting club about making some jumpers for them.

I went back to ask Grandora to write my letter to the training board for pilots in Docking airfield to apply for pilot training. That done, I put it onto the post tray for collection by any member of the household going into the village to post. Later, as lunchtime approached, I popped over to the stables to fetch our new arrivals for lunch. Danielle declined at first, but I insisted and reluctantly she walked over to the Hall with me. I introduced her to everyone there and had briefed them beforehand about her reluctance to engage; she seemed reticent and tired. We chatted as usual about the estate and what needed doing and just got on with eating. The boy Thaddeus did eat well, while Danielle was slow and ate very little. Afterwards I took her for a walk around our Walled Garden and introduced her to Osian and Frankie, but she soon became tired, so I showed her the way back to her little house in the stable yard and then I went with the dogs to the river. I had started sketching anything and anyone, and was now on my second sketch book. It was small and easy to carry with me wherever I went. I was pleased with some of my sketches and looked forward to showing Tantetta what I had been doing. I frequently sketched the river and the trees hiding its secrets and following its route like a row of gnarled guardians as it made its way sedately to the hidden meadow. The trees were now bare but had fascinating shapes and one day I hoped to paint them and their glorious greys, greens and khaki trunks and branches.

Some days later I had a letter giving me a date and time for my first flying lesson. I was so excited because, when I could fly, I would be able to join the WAAF and fly the new planes from the factories to the airfields all over Britain. I could be an ATA girl, a nickname for Air Transport Auxiliary service female personnel, a civilian service that was tasked with the delivery of aircraft from factories to squadrons of the RAF and Royal Navy. The day arrived and I drove over to the aerodrome with Grandora, who suddenly decided she would like to come with me. I had been trying to study a manual with Grandora's help on how to fly a Tiger Moth – a small training plane – which was what I would be using to start with. Because of my poor reading ability, I had roped in Grandora to help me with this task.

I was given a flying suit to wear and a leather helmet and goggles. The helmet kept my wild hair in check and the goggles hid my freckles. I liked it already. My flying instructor, Pete, was very serious, but jolly at the same time. We ran through all the instruments, and I was told to get in, and on this first flight he

would do the flying, just possibly giving me a short go at taking
the controls. I was so nervous, but I loved driving and just knew I
would love flying. The weather was perfect for my first ever flight
and there was the hint of an insipid winter sun in a pale blue
cloudless sky, when the propellers were turned, and the engine
fired into life. We taxied down from the hangar, turned onto the
runway and with full throttle we sped along the runway past the
control tower, and we were suddenly climbing into the sky. It was
marvellous and amazing. I listened to Pete and tried to memorize
everything he said as we circled and headed out to sea over the
Norfolk coastline, then turned back towards land and I allowed
myself a glimpse of the fields and villages below. It was then I
realized we were a very long way up. It looked interesting to see
everything in miniature, but suddenly I felt queasy. The plane
dipped her wings, we banked towards the earth, and I started
to retch so I closed my eyes to control myself and just wished we
would go land. I didn't take over the controls and I wasn't sick, but
I just knew I didn't want to fly. It was a fantastic experience, and it
was wonderful to feel free in the skies for a moment, but I knew,
sadly, it wasn't for me. Thank goodness I hadn't volunteered to
parachute into France. There again, to help the French Resistance
it was important that I could read and learn codes to be able
to use the radio. Unfortunately, with my dumb brain I was very
likely to struggle with all that stuff. I couldn't type or translate
as I couldn't read. We landed and I climbed out, relieved to be
on terra firma, thinking about our RAF boys flying every day
facing the enemy and how incredibly brave they were; they had
all my respect.

　　Meeting up with Grandora I thought I detected her trying
not to laugh.

　　"So what's funny?" I asked.

"You, you're green, it goes well with your red hair." Then she burst out laughing.

"It's not funny," I said crossly. "That was my future contribution to the war effort. Do I look that green?"

Pete came over and said, "Yes you do, very fetching. Sit down and I will organize a cup of sweet tea for you."

I sat down and as I was starting to feel better, just had to see the funny side of it too.

Pete continued, "You know there are lots of other jobs that need someone like you, and from what I hear you already have a full-time busy job getting food out to the Air Ministry and the rest of the country. If you agree, I know someone who would come over to your place and chat to you about a few additional ideas for you to help the war effort."

"Yes OK, that sounds like a good plan and thank you for your patience this morning. I don't think I will be flying just yet," I replied.

We all laughed and Grandora and I went for lunch at a pub on the way home, which I managed to eat. We enjoyed our freedom from the Hall and our special time together, as we always did.

January flew by, which was good really as it always seems to be the one month of the year that drags by, hindered by horrid, cold wintry weather and constant grey short days. February weather didn't improve much, but the snowdrops started to appear and always made me think spring was round the corner, though this wasn't quite true this year as we had lots of snow throughout the month. The bombing of Britain by Nazi Germany had continued all through January with Llandaff Cathedral in Cardiff, Wales sadly being severely damaged. Our troops were fighting in Eritrea, Sudan, and Tobruk in Libya. The United States President, Franklin Roosevelt, had made a speech on January 6th, during his US State of the Union address calling for freedom of speech and worship from want and fear. What a pity those values were treated with such contempt by the Nazis in every country they controlled.

We shovelled snow and struggled to feed the horses, all of whom came in from the fields during the harsh weather through January and February. This was as much to save the paddocks from being turned into mud when the thaw came as to protect the horses from the harsh weather. As all the water troughs in the fields froze, it was another good reason to keep them in their stables. Hens fluffed out their feathers and stopped laying eggs due to the short days and extreme cold. That is, all except the ones in the two large sheds, here we left some light on overnight. This was a new venture as we needed fresh eggs – the powdered eggs used at this time of rationing were awful. We were trying to fool the hens to think it was daylight so that they would keep on laying. They were all free to roam in the sheds and it was working. My little flock of Lavender Pekins were kept in during the wet days but were surprisingly resilient to most of the bad weather. They were so tame, the children loved them. The farms all struggled during the cold weather with turnips and swedes freezing and hard to lift from the ground and those that had been lifted freezing in heaps waiting to be sorted and delivered. Livestock stayed in the barns and ate the precious hay, straw and our cattle feed far too quickly. The dogs loved it though, and played and galloped in the snow with the children, chasing sledges and trying to catch snowballs.

The knitting group who used our school room rarely missed an afternoon of knitting and chatting, but the snow called a halt to their gatherings for a week. They all arrived the following week and were soon busy in the warm room knitting for Britain, which included the children, the elderly and all military personnel and refugees. So many people had lost everything because of the bombing and so many seeking refuge in our country, arrived with nothing. I had chatted to Danielle about her life prior to the hostilities and discovered that she was a fashion and design student in Paris, preferring to use fabrics for her art to the paint that I used. So, I introduced her to the knitting group, and she loved being there, designing new patterns for jumpers, cardigans, scarves, gloves and even skirts. This seemed to revitalize her and give her a new beginning and a reason to live. Four afternoons a week the ladies met up in the school room creating wonderful garments to be sent to the WVS for distribution. Danielle mentioned how much she would love a spinning wheel to be able to make the skeins of wool and dye it herself. I thought it was a brilliant idea. It was just one more item we needed and even these were in short supply. Danielle also confessed she loved reading and so I offered her the use of our library and told her no books were allowed to be removed from there so would she mind sitting in the library each evening to make sure everyone using it respected my wishes. She was very happy to do that. The library was my father's domain and many of the books were valuable; some were locked in cupboards, and I just wanted him to find it the same as when he left. I wrote to Portia asking if she could help us out with more wool from their sheep and to provide us with a spinning wheel. Of course, she wrote back saying she thought she could get us a spinning wheel, but the wool would be harder to find as it was winter and in demand. No one was shearing sheep yet, but she would ask local farmers for us. Thaddeus stayed at home, perfecting his English before going to school. He soon settled and found he enjoyed the boys' indoor games and cards and was a useful partner for them; his English improved every day. They soon started calling him Tad, so we all did the same and he seemed to like it.

I had a visit from some RAF person who introduced himself as Group Captain Richard Petersfield. He had been told I was keen to help the war effort in some way. I agreed I did, with some trepidation about his proposal – I just didn't want it to involve parachuting! I had thought it would involve driving, telegraphy, telephony, intercepting codes and ciphers or interpretation of aerial photographs, radar control, the list was endless. It didn't though; he wondered if I would consider having men and women staying at the Hall who needed rest and recuperation from flying duties but didn't need be hospitalised. The men and women would be suffering from 'Burn Out', a term given to those on the edge, after living in danger every single day flying and fighting in the skies or involved in other demanding and dangerous wartime duties. Well, I couldn't say no, and even when Grandora came in to meet him and discuss his proposal, my mind was already on where to accommodate them, how to bed and feed them.

"There will be a doctor visit to check their progress, but apart from that it will be straightforward, they will be dropped off here and picked up when they are considered fit for duties again. It's a wonderful place here with walks in the park and reading, peace and quiet; it's just what the doctor will order for them." He stood up to leave. "Well thank you, and lovely to meet you both." With that he was gone.

Grandora and I looked at each other and burst out laughing.

"Quiet," chortled Grandora.

"Peaceful." I giggled. "Best be off and climb the stairs to the third floor and check out the rooms there," I said. Kissing her on the cheek, I jumped up to start planning two bedrooms and a sitting room and check out the bathroom up there.

We were soon into March, and it was still bitterly cold, with biting winds coming in off the sea. However, there was no snow, just gloomy grey days, and we were all looking forward to spring. We had started out with two young pilots staying with us and then progressed to four: all polite, quiet young men. They were easy to get on with and patient with our children. We knew not to question them about why they were with us or about what their jobs were in the RAF and they kept mostly to themselves. I had managed to provide two cosy rooms with twin beds in each and electric bar heaters and the carpets were colourful. I had turned a larger bedroom into a comfortable sitting room with a heater and four utility armchairs with steam bent wooden arms which I 'cheered up' with colourful cushions: thanks to Grandora's Indian travels and Mrs Hubbard's sewing skills. They came downstairs for their meals, and we gave them the use of the dining table in the morning room next to the kitchen. Danielle and Tad came in every night to share a cooked evening meal with us, and she seemed to be able to smile more, but remained reticent to join our conversations. The doctor who called to check on their progress, called Professor Dendy Hillingdon, was a retired hospital consultant and an old friend of Grandora; she perked up considerably when he called, and he seemed to call often. He was a keen bridge and chess player and I'm quite sure Grandora wore lipstick on his visiting days.

Miriam wrote asking me if she could come and stay with us and bring her mother and sister-in-law, and of course Anna-Sara and Avigail, as the bombing was causing them stress and they needed to get away from the visible presence of the war all over London. On March the 8th Buckingham Palace had been bombed causing our Queen Elizabeth to comment that she felt more at one with the people of London who were being bombed every day. Poor Portsmouth had suffered terrible casualties on March 10th because of heavy bombing by the Luftwaffe, whose bombing was relentless everywhere. So far, we were lucky to have avoided any bombing in our area. Of course, I said yes to Miriam and doubled up Adele and Talia with Anna-Sara and Avigail for the time they would stay with us and put her mother and sister-in-law in a spare room. Miriam could stay with Audrey, which was Audrey's suggestion. I seemed to spend my life juggling people, beds, and meals. I asked Granger to pick them up for me as I was going to Arthur's to pick up some wooden chairs which folded up that he had managed to buy for me. With more and more guests we were running out of chairs for everyone. He had also managed to get me a kitchen larder cabinet for Danielle's downstairs kitchen, and I hoped they would all fit into the station wagon. Miriam and her family were arriving on March 19th for at least three or four weeks. I loved them all but wondered if I could cope with so many people staying here. I arrived home to find tea had been served by Margaret and Rosie, and all was quiet in the Hall. I put mine on a tray and crept into Grandora's sitting room to spend some precious time with her, alone. I must have fallen asleep in my chair because I awoke to hear the wireless reports of extensive and heavy bombing taking place in London right now. Reports came in of Plymouth and Bristol being under heavy attack. Well thank goodness Miriam and her family are coming here, I said to Grandora, who agreed. It was so awful to think of the poor people having their homes destroyed, burned by incendiary bombs. I went to bed depressed.

The following Friday we held Shabbat again in our dining room, inviting everyone to join us. Danielle was impressed with our effort to provide enough of the right food, and that we celebrated it. She worked in the kitchen with Miriam and her sister-in-law Zelda and Miriam's mother, Sarah. They were helped, as well, by Adele, Talia, Ruby, and Lottie; preparation completed all before sundown. We invited our visiting RAF guys and Audrey, Sheila and Lucy. Osian came too and it was a serious, meaningful, and happy night.

April arrived and we had golden daffodils lining our driveway to the Hall and they danced in the wind in the park and gardens. Such a glorious reminder surely of better times to come. Miriam was still with us when Easter came on the 13th of April, and we enjoyed a low-key celebration without any chocolate Easter eggs. We painted real eggs and had fun judging whose was the best. Nico and Malissa came home for Easter Sunday and Monday and so twenty of us attended Church on Easter Day and we enjoyed a lovely sunshine walk home but still very cold with continuing biting winds. I found Miriam and Danielle with Talia, Adele, Zelda, Anna-Sara, and Sarah in the kitchen preparing a turkey dinner for us all which was a wonderful treat. The RAF guys staying joined us in the dining room and I noticed Danielle seemed uneasy with them and avoided any conversation. Miriam, however, immediately found a rapport with Danielle and looked happier than I had ever seen her when chatting with her. There seemed to be no doubt Miriam had a skill when talking to people. She was a good listener. Clearly that's where her talent lay in helping troubled people to unburden themselves. Nico and Malissa spoke about their dismay at the invasion of Greece and the withdrawal of British troops to Crete. I told them my parents had written saying they were hoping to be home very soon as there was tension in the area from Japan. They planned to be home in time for Christmas.

I had managed to buy Danielle and Tad new clothes after they arrived. They had landed at the Hall with only the clothes they were wearing and one change. On June 1st clothes were rationed and I was relieved I had enough money and coupons to buy extra clothes for all the children ready for the changes in the seasons and weather.

A pie was introduced called the Woolton Pie named after the Minister for food, the 1st Lord Woolton. It was meatless, a pastry dish of vegetables and we had been making it at the Hall well before it was given a name. We had been making it using real pastry not potato pastry as we still had access to butter and flour, being farmers. Although we had to answer to the newly set up Agricultural Executive Committee, whose job it was to make sure all farms were producing as much food as they could, we were easily ahead of them. All the estate farms had been regularly visited by me and I had insisted they improved their growing capacity. We nearly ran into trouble with the authorities as I had kept half the park as grassland for our sheep and cattle, but we were supplying the RAF with plenty of meat so we were allowed to keep our grass. The cattle grazed it in summer anyway. We had a sort of hidden field of pasture the other side of the river that was easy to miss if you didn't know where it was, so we cut it for hay and then grazed horses there, afterwards. We grew barley, oats, and wheat, and although some was milled locally, most of our cereal went to the Government. On five of the farms the tenant farmers milked cows and produced an outstanding amount of milk, cream, butter, and cheese; of this I was very proud. The bee population had been increased by Osian and Frankie, and we now produced plenty of honey and the surplus we were able to sell. The market garden had been increased now to four acres, two of which were outside the Walled Garden. The goats had not been a brilliant plan although on a small scale we produced some milk and Osian was working on increasing this to make cheese, but I had my doubts; at least he was a trier. Much as I liked them, they were a nuisance and Granger was constantly moaning about them getting out into the wrong fields eating anything they found, real opportunists! Osian would go totally mad if they found their way into the Walled Garden. The hens were a great success and three of our tenant farmers were copying the idea of lights on in some hen houses at night to increase egg production. We had to use petrol driven generators so it was hard to juggle the end result i.e. extra eggs with the use of valuable rationed fuel. Our turkeys were, so far, a small flock of one hundred and fifty outdoor reared Norfolk Blacks and we were working to increase the population. They grazed in the field all day but had to come in every night to avoid predators like the foxes.

Osian had decided he needed to learn how to drive, and Granger had been giving him lessons in his van. As a result, his next ambition was to drive an ambulance and to take a First Aid course. Granger let him take his van into King's Lynn to the Hospital for the first aid course. He hadn't taken a driving test as these had been suspended in 1939 because of the war, so we were all concerned about him driving in the dark as he could not use full headlights because of the blackout. I took the decision that he should have someone with him as he was inexperienced and with the conditions so challenging. In view of my concern, Granger went a couple of times and then the day came it was my turn. I decided I would listen in to the First Aid course. I found it interesting and fascinating, and decided I would volunteer as an emergency ambulance driver. As usual I had to learn the theory and as my reading skills were so poor, Audrey and Osian went through everything with me and I managed to pass. Osian joined the ambulance service, and he was driving 24 hours on and 24 hours off, which he assured me left him enough time to work in the garden with Frankie's help. I asked Larry to help us when he had time. He was reluctant so I pointed out that if he had ambitions for a political career in the future, he would need experience working with people and the land – this opportunity would give him that experience. That did it, he finally got stuck into gardening for food, not for flowers. I think he became quite proud of what he grew as time went by and he saw the produce sold in the local markets and ate the results of his labour.

Progress as well for Danielle; she started spending time in the Walled Garden pricking out seedlings and helping Osian potting up plants. She said it gave her great contentment and peace.

I was soon on call three nights a week driving the ambulance, arriving home at 6.45am and going straight to the stables to ride Hermes. I was so happy, at last I felt I was doing something worthwhile. Grandora, however, was not so pleased; she said very little, but I think she was annoyed, convinced I was doing enough at home with all our visitors and supplying food for Britain. Best of all, I finally got to wear a uniform at last.

Chapter 28

Stan Hardy

After another uncomfortable night in the stable, daylight arrived and the Hardy family went outside to a smell of acrid burning and smoke in the atmosphere, and they looked towards Hull city to see much of it was still on fire. The night had been awful, and they had been kept awake with the noise of the bombs dropping constantly throughout the night. Well, Roscoe had slept all night, but he was the only one. They had to take the children to school first, that is if there was still a school for them to go to.

School was still standing so they dropped off the children, then Stan and Lacey went home to check what remained. Their street was cordoned off and blocked by police, the fire service, and ambulances. There was nothing left; flattened by the bombing; the houses were in ruins and smoking. Work was still taking place to extinguish the fires and carry out the dead, look for the injured or anyone who might be buried, but still alive. Thank God they had slept at the stable on the outskirts of Hull. Stan and Lacey were allowed through the roadblock to look for any possessions not destroyed, while Lucky their black horse was tied to a lamp-pole at the end of the street, waiting for them. Their tiny tan and white dog they also left with Lucky tied on to the cart. Trip was a ratting dog and very useful at the stable. There was very little to be rescued from the debris of what had been their family home. All Lacey's plants and herbs which filled the yard behind the house were burnt and ruined. Lacey was very quiet and reminded herself that the main thing was her family; all were alive. She cried inwardly for the loss of her precious plants, but far more for her neighbours, injured, missing or dead. A choking dust and a foul acrid, stifling smell filled the air.

Stan was told to go to the council offices in Hull with all the other now homeless people to be re-housed. Stan went to work and left Lacey standing in the queue as she had been told to do – she waited hours only to be told that they had been allocated spaces at a Church Hall on the north outskirts of Hull with 'no animals allowed'. She was advised to come back the next day for their new ration books for food and clothes. Stan had found similar miserable conditions at the docks with people clearing debris and others trying to make their way to work and unload fishing trawlers. He met Lacey and they picked up the children from school and went back to the stable for the night. They bought fish and chips for tea and some milk for the morning. There was no field with the stable, just a yard, and not much food or bedding left for Lucky, and with no work today, so no pay, it was going to be difficult to feed the children or the animals.

The next day they repeated their experience of the previous day and went to the council offices with no more luck than before. A council worker who had children at the same school as Reuben and Star and knew Lacey, met them and felt very sorry for the family. Lacey was a little weird with her flowery skirts and a long plait down her back and lots of bangles, but she was genuinely kind and thoughtful. She was very good with her own children and other people's and always had herbal remedies ready for most coughs or sore throats and these she would give away to anyone. They left in despair.

Suddenly they heard a council worker running after them and calling. She'd run after Stan to tell him the council had been offered accommodation in North Norfolk for any family who had lost their home. So far no one had accepted the offer as it meant travelling away from Hull, family, friends, and work. He asked if they would they be interested in travelling to Norfolk to take up the offer. Stan jumped at the chance to get away from the bombing and said they would be glad to accept the offer. He was given the address and travel expenses, new ration cards and was told that the family in Norfolk would expect the Hardy family in a few days' time. Stan told her about Lucky, and she said she would check if they could take him. They waited two hours and were given tea and scones by the Women's Auxiliary Voluntary Service from their mobile cafe unit at the end of the street. Finally, the council worker found them with the news that their horse would be welcome too.

That night was their last night sleeping in the stable listening to more bombing of the docks and wondering if one would find them and kill them all. First light saw all of them on the road out of Hull heading towards South Cave. Kind, patient Lucky pulled their cart with the four children, the stable cat tied to the cart and with Trip sitting on Star's knee. Luna was next to her mother and Reuben and Roscoe walked at the side. Their three hens had been put into a crate for the journey so hopefully they would have a supply of eggs until they reached Norfolk. They were to be a gift for the family who were offering them a home. The first night they slept in a field underneath the cart on top of a tarpaulin with bedding and eiderdowns they had used at the stable. Stan lit a campfire in the morning and then boiled a kettle of water from a stream and made tea and boiled three eggs which they gave to the children for their breakfast. Soon they were back on the road heading towards Walkeringham, making their way around the Humber River. A kind farmer gave them the use of an old barn the next night and they bought some potatoes to boil for their tea and a bit of bacon with their ration books for breakfast. Travelling the next day, they stopped at a bakery and bought sausages, bread and scones. They felt rich and lucky to have so much food. Stan and Lacey told the children they were on holiday until they reached their new home and then they would all have to be on their best behaviour. Lacey promised them if they weren't happy, they would leave and find somewhere else to go.

They eventually arrived after many long days travelling on the road at the village where their host lived and they met a lady riding a beautiful dark chestnut mare. It turned out she was the very lady they were looking for. She was their rescuer, their host, and she took them to an enormous Hall which was her home, and Stan and Lacey were very nervous. They were all very tired and dirty, having not changed their clothes for over a week or washed themselves apart from their hands and faces in cold water. They followed her to the stables and rested Lucky who was tired, and then they were given their first decent cooked breakfast in a long time and were even given jam and honey.

They all loved the horses and dogs at the Hall and Lacey admired the Walled Garden and could name all the herbs growing there. Stan was anxious to settle the children into where they were going to stay and was relieved to be told they were having their own cottage to live in, so he was eager to be off and get there straight away. He was thrilled and over the moon to finally arrive at a lovely cottage with stables, fields, places for their animals and lovely beds and furniture, all ready for them to move into. They had never had a bathroom in a house before, just the outside lavvy and a tin bath to bathe in; it was all too much for them to take in. There was a meal in the oven just waiting for them and food in the little scullery to tide them over for the next week. They were overawed by such friendship and generosity and so tired they hardly said anything to the wonderful people. The whole family was in shock at such a lovely place to be told it was to be theirs to stay in. Stan vowed he would do what he could to repay the kindness shown and find any work to keep them all together safe and snug in this paradise.

Chapter 29

The Hardy Family Arrive

May soon became June and the nightly bombing of Britain had only slightly lessened and 'The Blitz' as it had become known from September to May had failed to stop Britain's ability to continue in the war. It had though, caused massive destruction and killed forty-three thousand British civilians and wounded some one hundred and thirty-nine thousand. Hitler had decided to invade the Soviet Union and the Luftwaffe could not wage war in two places at the same time, which gave Britain a respite from the wave after wave of heavy bombing. The biggest raid on London had been on May 10th when one thousand three hundred and sixty-four people were killed and one thousand six hundred and sixteen, badly wounded. How horrendous. We continued to be a place of 'rest and recuperation' for airmen needing time away from the war or in recovery from injuries, and we were always saddened to see them go as they had an uncertain future. We didn't just have British RAF men here, there were Free French, Polish, Canadian,

American, New Zealanders, Czechoslovakians, Belgians, South
Africans, Southern Rhodesians and Australians. There were
even some men from Newfoundland, Northern Rhodesia, South
Africa, Barbados and Jamaica all here to fly for Britain and fight
against Hitler. The summer holidays arrived, and Ruby had
another birthday celebration and Miriam, Zelda, her sister-in-
law, Anna-Sara, Avigail and Miriam's mother Sarah all came to
enjoy a country holiday and share Ruby's party. This time Maya
Monteux came, and she was a great help enjoying life here away
from the bombing. Audrey ran the after-school activities and the
most popular summer sport that year was cricket. I had been
persuaded by Arthur to buy a table tennis table he had found
loitering somewhere and that was a great hit. We put it under
cover in the cart shed. We all played, and I loved it. We had
managed to measure out a temporary tennis court at the back
of the house behind the Walled Garden and that also became
an instant hit, although without any high fencing the balls
went everywhere, and a few willing fielders were necessary to
keep fetching the errant balls, or the game took forever. Our
visiting airmen happily joined in with the children's games and
one American enjoyed the rounders and then tried to teach the
children how to play American Baseball. The scouts came again
to camp in the summer holidays and there were lots of laughs
around the campfire which could only be lit in the daytime due
to the blackout and was put out by Granger strictly before dusk.
Looking back, we were either incredibly lucky or we were just
good hosts; I'm not sure which, but our guests were all polite,
well-mannered, and good fun. I worked three nights a week
driving the ambulance and rolled into bed about 6.30 - 7 am after
my nights on duty. Most mornings when I came off-duty, I would
ride Hermes. I just needed to clear my head and relax after a busy

night and if it was a lovely morning, going to bed, however tired, just didn't appeal to me. I really hoped I was making a difference and freeing up more important staff to sleep or do better things. My work was mostly ferrying locals with illness, heart attack, broken bones, and pregnant ladies to hospital; a vital job that needed doing regardless of the war. Occasionally I took injured RAF personnel and once I took a German prisoner of war to hospital – he was working on a farm and had 'speared' his foot with a manure fork. He was surprised that I had a smattering of German, curtesy of my professor in France and my private tutoring lessons.

Back at the Hall the funniest game was invented by the four girls. They decided to build a cross country course for the dogs. I think they had been watching Jabbo and Granger training the racehorse I rescued. Now three years old, he was maturing nicely and showing great promise although a shame he had missed racing as a two-year-old, due to horse racing being banned because of the war. Broken to saddle by the two men, he was now learning how to race from the farm to the stable paddock a good mile and a half. An edge of grass around the park meant he could canter round once a week and get into a good sprint on the run up the hill. He was even doing some hurdles although he was bred to be raced on the flat, we were hedging our bets as to what he would eventually do when racing resumed.

So, the girls were now training the dogs. They carried chairs, buckets, sacks and even a ladder onto the large garden near the Cedar of Lebanon and started training the dogs to climb along the rungs of the ladder balanced on two chairs and crawl through a sack and out the end they had cut open. They made small jumps with branches and mop handles balanced on buckets and even trained them to run up a ramp they had found somewhere, and when the dog was at the top they had to turn round, sit down and then run back down the ramp. The next trick was to catch a ball thrown for them and return it to a bucket. The tiny pooch was surprisingly good for Ruby and tried very hard running around the course often missing out loads of obstacles. Spud loved it and learnt the course quickly, barking ecstatically all the way round. Spruce and Trig, my father's dogs, were agile and loved the attention, so tried hard to please. Odin was just a natural and loved playing with children, but the star was of course Zippy, Jabbo's little white dog. He flew round the course and was so quick he could not be beaten. Jabbo had to show him first though, as he didn't like leaving Jabbo, unlike Odin who would chase a ball for anyone who would throw it for him. The rest of the time he never left my side. Lucy the chocolate Labrador now spent most of her time in Margaret's kitchen since George and Theodore stayed with them and refused to do any of it when the boys tried to train her. She just lay down to have her tummy tickled. Still there were six dogs being trained so they could have as many competitions as they wished. It was very amusing to watch, and it was soon a favourite pastime for the RAF guys staying with us and Grandora; I think they took penny bets, but they wouldn't admit to it. Those who came to stay and could play bridge were seconded onto her team if they were any good. One American staying with us spent his time teaching the boys and Grandora how to play poker. I think Jabbo was even good at that, though, and won some money from him. Only pennies were allowed to be used, so I was told.

Grandora had made a lengthy search into the grey colt's breeding and had successfully traced it back from his sire Mr Jinks to Tetratema, son of The Tetrarch. All these were speed machines over short distances, so we were doubtful about our young colt being able to prove himself racing as a two or three-year-old. Some racing had been resumed, but you needed the fuel to get to the racecourses and that was a problem. So, it had been decided by Jabbo and Granger to train him to jump to increase his stamina so he might be able to hurdle in the future. At least they were enjoying training him, and we all enjoyed watching. It gave us all hope for a brighter future plus the horse enjoyed a good life being cosseted and looked after.

Britain had now signed an Anglo-Soviet Agreement forming an alliance against Nazi Germany in July 1941 following what Hitler called Operation Barbarossa – the invasion of Soviet Russia. Again, we thought this was good news as we in Britain had stood alone against Hitler and we needed allies to help us defeat the tyrant. Our Prime Minister Winston Churchill gave a speech which we listened to on the wireless in Grandora's sitting room. He spoke of how we faced the 'storm alone after France fell to German invasion' and how the Royal Air Force had 'beaten the Hun raiders out of daylight air raids and warded off the Nazi invasion of Britain'. Thirdly he spoke about the United States lease and lend bill enactment signed by President Franklin Roosevelt devoting 2,000,000,000 pounds sterling to help us defend our liberties and their own. He then went on to say the fourth turning point is now upon us, telling us that at four that morning Hitler had invaded Russia with no warning. He said, 'Hitler was a monster of wickedness, insatiable in his lust for blood and plunder.' He went on to call Hitler a 'bloodthirsty guttersnipe launching his mechanised armies upon new fields of slaughter, pillage and devastation'. He then declared that 'we are resolved to destroy Hitler and every vestige of the Nazi regime'. We agreed.

The Government announced a War Weapons Week for all communities throughout Britain to get together raising funds towards the cost of building weapons for the war. Meanwhile, the children and adults all contributed to the war effort in our area by trying to raise money towards buying a Spitfire. We organised a concert which was held in the park behind the Hall, and we had music from George and Larry's school orchestra. Dancing from the local village young dance troop which included jive and cha cha to music of the big band sound of Glenn Miller and his orchestra. This was followed, of course, by our dogs doing their assault course for the four little girls with Lennie and Tad helping; very entertaining and funny. Jabbo gave another excellent acrobatic display with the ever-beautiful Zoltan, Lennie, and Nico, and of course Zippy. The local Thespian Society put on a short section of Shakespeare's 'A Midsummer Night's Dream', which was also entertaining and quite funny although I'm not sure it was supposed to be funny in the way it was. We raised lots of money towards our area target of £70,000 and most importantly had a wonderful night.

Larry wrote a short poem which he read out after much cajoling from us all.

Where have all our horses gone
Lost in battles on the Somme
Where have all our horses gone
Dead, forgotten in French fields
British horses from Wolds and Weald

Touch our horses' velvet nose
See kind eyes now closed
Heaving flanks caked with mud
Their kind hearts that would
Break and give their all

And fight with courage
By your side to hear you chide
Come on my beauty on again
Fight with me ignore the pain
Where have all our horses gone
Lost in battle everyone

No more war we promised them
No more war and yet again
Here we are losing kith and ken
Friends, family young and old
To fight an evil foe

Where have all our horses gone
In our hour of need
This time our horses plough and pull
To feed us through this war
And give their soul once more

To hear our gentle chide
Come on my beauty on again
Please keep beside my side
We'll weed and scatter seed
Thank God for horses
Here as always in our hour of need.

Larry read this beautifully as dusk was just beginning to signal home time. There was first silence, then tears and then he brought people to their feet clapping. All our players came back to stand before the cheering crowd and Zoltan came on last to take a bow with Jabbo standing to one side as Zoltan bent his knee and touched the ground with his nose.

Our gates had now gone to help the war effort and railings around the park had also gone. We had taken off the heraldic signs off the gates and delivered them ourselves in pieces to hide the removal of our beautiful old signs. The rails, hidden deep in hedges and undergrowth, remained where they were, and I was glad we had a big wall around most of the park which nobody wanted.

I went with Miriam, Audrey, Sheila, and Lucy to the village dance to raise more money. Danielle would not entertain leaving her little house to come dancing and so reluctantly we left her babysitting for us at the Hall with Tad sleeping in Larry and Lennie's bedroom. Miriam was staying with us and said she would stay at home with Danielle and Grandora, but we insisted that she came dancing with us. There were plenty of RAF men there a long way from home, so we danced with them all to a band from Swaffham who played the popular songs of Vera Lynn and Ann Skelton. Of course, our favourite Glenn Miller sound got us all up on the dance floor and we boogied until 10 pm. It was great fun and for those few hours I hope all thoughts of the war were banished for these brave young men. Driving back was the usual eye straining nightmare, with this time lots of giggles as we were all happy and had enjoyed a very happy night, free of worries.

The City of Hull had been ferociously targeted by Luftwaffe bomb attacks all of 1941, resulting in many people being killed or made homeless and children orphaned. This was not reported on the wireless or in the papers, I found out during a visit by Group Captain Richard Petersfield whilst he was visiting some airmen staying with us. I made him a cup of tea and we chatted outside in the rose garden on a sunny morning; it was peaceful and quiet. He told me where he was from, and about his wife and children. He was in the RAF at the start of the war; this had been his ambition and what he had always wanted to do. He went on to say he was saddened and shocked at the use of planes to bomb innocent people, he had hoped to fly planes for the good of mankind not to destroy cities. He told me he had moved his family from Cottingham (a village just outside Hull), as the bombing of the city was some of the worst in Britain and many people were now homeless. They were now renting a house outside Swaffham. How interesting that due to news reporting restrictions not much had been written about Hull's devastating bomb damage. I asked Grandora to write on my behalf to the town council, offering refuge for a family or orphaned children; even though Grandora thought we were already full of people, she reluctantly agreed we should help. It was August when I heard that they had one family willing to leave Hull for their safety. Their house had been completely destroyed on 18th July and it was because the family had taken their horse to their stable that night, they had missed the bombing on east Hull and the Victoria Docks. The horse was used to pull a flat wagon which took the fish boxes from the docks to the market and to take the market waste out of the city. His tiny paddock, no bigger than a back yard, had a stable and the family had been sleeping there most nights. I immediately agreed to take them and their horse, as normal committing myself to the animals as well as the humans. I knew how I felt about my animals and would have hated leaving them behind. I then started wondering where I would house a family of six. Luck was on my side: I asked Grandora to tell me just how much property the estate owned in, and around the surrounding area. I left her going through my father's papers and calling our solicitor to check things out, as I left for my night job driving the ambulance.

I arrived home on what promised to be a warm, sunny day and as I drove down the drive, I spotted deer in the park, quietly grazing, enjoying the morning peace just like me. I went to the stables and changed into my spare jodhpurs which I kept there and hopping into my boots I ran into Jabbo leading Hermes in for me to ride. Zoltan was already tacked up and so without grooming Hermes I tacked up and we rode down towards the river and into the woods. It was bliss cantering up the grass track that led to the farm and seeing Lucy and Sheila turning the cows out that had been milked that morning. The day promised to stay sunny, and I loved this early time of a new day, full of promise. We turned for home and I left Granger to untack Hermes and turn her back into the field for me and I headed to the house for breakfast and bed. I said hello to all the children who were dressed and ready for school and having their breakfast prepared by Mrs Revill. I went through to Grandora with my cocoa and toast, and she was dressed and reading some papers.

"It looks like good news for your family and bad news for a tenant of ours," she told me. "We have a smallholding near Ashwicken and the old lady living there can no longer manage the place. We must help her relocate and the cottage will then be available for the family from Hull. I didn't know about this cottage but have been informed by our solicitors of a few more in area that I didn't know about. The rent from them is paid monthly and has been used to support the Hunt kennels and Alford's wages," she added.

Funny, I never thought about the money to support the Hunt being separate to the Hall. "Thank you so much, that sounds great. Will you let the people in Hull know please? I am off to bed for some sleep. I will be up at one o'clock, so will see you for a late lunch."

When we got back to the council about re-locating the family,
we were then given the additional news that two children, now
orphaned, would be coming down too if I had accommodation
for them. It had taken ages to get through on the telephone, but
finally I managed and that's how I heard this extra news. Wow, we
were going to be busy, as if we weren't already. Poor children, how
awful for them. I was pleased to offer them a safe home; it was the
least we could do. I waited for the secretary to tell me when they
would arrive and the next day, I went with Humphrey to visit Mrs
Robinson, the elderly lady on the smallholding at Ashwicken to
talk about her move and, at the same time, assess what needed to
be done at the cottage. Mrs Robinson was very elderly and bent
with arthritis; I found it hard to believe Humphrey had allowed
her to stay there for so long. The place looked run down but had
great potential. She was pleased to see us and fussed over our
visit, preparing a cup of tea for us and some home-made plain
biscuits. Her old dog shuffled over for a fuss, and we had to shoo
cats off the hairy chairs before we could sit down. Outside were
two nanny goats and a couple of their kids wandering loose in
the yard. She cried about moving and told us she didn't want to
leave, but knew it was all too much for her. The fields were getting
overgrown with weeds, but she hated leaving her geese and hens,
the cats and goats and could Jed her dog go with her? She had
lived there for thirty-five years with her husband who had died
three years ago. It was so kind of Mr Clayton to help her and let
her stay knowing she could not keep it as smart as it used to be.
I quickly glanced at Humphrey who looked embarrassed, and I
assured Mrs Robinson he had done the right thing, but now I had
a family in need who had lost their home in a bombing raid. I also
told her the animals would all be looked after and the goats could
live with our herd at the Hall, the geese could live in the orchard

and swim in the river and hopefully the new family would like the cats and, yes, of course her dog could go with. All we had to do now was find a safe place for her to live in and then redecorate the cottage. Result! We drove home!

Grandora had more news. She had agreed to buy a seaside house in Hunstanton which was near a park and a shop and not far from the shops in Hunstanton; she thought it would prove a good investment for the future. My Grandora was a fast worker. "Who knew if any more of our loyal tenants would want to retire and it would be a handy place for them," she said. Then we heard that our family would be arriving next weekend which was just six days away. The orphaned children would be arriving the following week after we had been checked out. Oh, that was a new one. Now we were going to be checked out! I drove myself back to Ashwicken to see Mrs Robinson to tell her I had found a place for her in Hunstanton, and she could move immediately, so I was shocked when she told me she would only consider moving after she had seen the new place. I told her I would take her, so she put on her coat and off we went to view the house. She declared it was far too big for her to clean, so I suggested she had the downstairs rooms. This she agreed was the best idea, so I took her back and now I had the headache of planning and making the house into two flats. This mission seemed to take for ever, well it took all morning, and I was anxious to get back and plan how I would complete the task. I called at Arthur's farm to ask for help, but he was out working somewhere so I had a cup of tea with Violet and outlined my plans to her; she wrote them down and I left her to explain to Arthur for me. The house in Hunstanton had a downstairs toilet so I decided she could move in as soon as convenient and use the bathroom upstairs until we had added facilities downstairs for her.

Jabbo and Granger rose to the challenge and Osian and
Frankie went along to look at the land to see what was growing,
apart from weeds. Over the next few days, a plan of action was
put into place with military precision and Audrey, Danielle
and Rosie came to help with the redecorating and cleaning.
They were long days for us all and poor Mrs Revill did all the
cooking for everyone until Margaret knew we had an emergency
job on, and she worked extra days to help us. Osian and I still
had to go to work driving the ambulance, I was on the night
shift and Osian drove during the day. We had just two airmen,
both Australian bomber crew, staying with us at the moment
and when they heard our dilemma, they volunteered to help
us immediately. I thought Mrs Robinson was going to be a
problem as she nearly decided not to leave, but with so many of
us there and Jabbo and Granger taking her bed down, she had
no choice and I drove her over to her new flat. Mrs Hubbard
was there putting up blackout curtains with Mrs Burden and
hanging some decent curtains of a thick material we found in
the attic at the Hall. By the end of the day the bed was up and
made, the kitchen was ready to use, and the fire was lit. We even
put her a cooked stew into the gas cooker and a 'Mrs Revill's
cake' in the pantry plus some of our jars of preserves and a vase
of flowers on her table. We then left and I took Mrs Hubbard
and Mrs Burden back to the village. Frankie came with us to
start doing the horses' night stables. I went to work, which was
a bit stupid as I was so tired, but a cup of tea and a slice of apple
cake set me up for the night shift. Thank goodness it was not
too busy a night, ferrying people to the hospital. I was too tired
to go to Ashwicken the next day and slept until two-thirty in
the afternoon. I just had to leave everyone else to do their job
at the small holding.

The following morning, I went over with Frankie to see how things were progressing and to listen to Frankie's report on the land. Arthur was there with two men finishing building the downstairs bathroom extension onto the scullery, and Jabbo and Granger were fitting in the pipes and doing the plumbing. The cottage was now painted with fresh white paint, and the scullery and bathroom were nearly ready for plastering. The old oven range in the kitchen would still be used for cooking, and the water box next to the fire, which was part of the range, heated water which now had pipes fitted from it leading to the bathroom and scullery. I hoped they worked when we tried them, but I was confident 'the team' would have done a good job. I walked over to the fields with Frankie and listened to what Osian had decided we ought to do with the land. It was too late in the year to start growing potatoes or carrots, cauliflower, cabbages – well, just about everything. Hopefully, we could seed down a few acres for hay for next year and cultivate the rest to stand fallow, ready for early planting in the New Year. So much had been left to grow wild and had gone to seed, and the ditches were overgrown and choked with weeds. We wandered around the yard, exploring amongst the weeds to see what treasure trove of old farm implements there were hidden and rotting; very little it turned out; we found a broken hay rake and an old roller. The sheds were falling down and filthy with age and old rotting animal dung. So, we all set to clean out a brick built stable attached to an old hay store with no hay in it. After that, we went to work on the shed the hens were using as a night roost, which was filthy and deep in hen dirt. We cleaned the dirt encrusted water and feed bowls. Not sure where the goats went at night, but goats liked to be warm and dry so perhaps they had been living in the empty hay barn. We stopped just after six o'clock at night; all of us were tired and had our jobs to do when we got home. The next day Granger would mend the broken fence round the paddock so the horse could be turned out and take a load of chopped wood for the fire. I had no idea what time to expect the family and had been informed by Hull council relocation department that they had left Hull and were travelling to us by horse and cart. Interesting.

The next morning, I rode Hermes early as usual. It had been raining in the night and was a dull, cloudy, moody start to the day but great to be out on my own with just Odin and Hermes. As I skirted the village a strange sight was coming down the little hill to the Green and it looked like gypsies were arriving in the village. A man walked at the side of the horse, holding the reins, and a boy walked on the other side. The flat cart was loaded with chairs, a luggage trunk, pots and pans and plant pots. A woman with three children and a dog sat on a box seat at the front. A cat was sitting with them, tethered to the cart. The horse was black with four white socks, lots of feathers and a long black mane, and as he got nearer to me, I could see he had a white face with a moustache and a tail nearly on the floor. As they reached me, they stopped, and Hermes reached her nose to the horse, and I gave her a long rein. The horse nickered softly, and they nosed each other and blew down their nostrils in greeting. The man was roughly dressed in a long thick overcoat, wearing big boots, a flat cap, and a blue neckerchief round his neck, he had blue eyes, a tanned face, black hair and looking me in the eye he asked me politely if I knew the way to Willup Hall. So, here were my new refugees! Good heavens, they had travelled a long way with their horse from the east riding of Yorkshire through Lincolnshire and into Norfolk.

"Are you Mr and Mrs Hardy, the family from Hull?" I asked. "I have been expecting you to arrive today and you are early. I am very pleased to meet you. I am Cressida and you can follow me to the Hall."

He jumped on to the flat cart and dangled his legs over the side as he drove the horse and cart behind me along the lane to the Hall.

I went straight to the stables, jumped down and took Hermes to her stable, then I went to meet Mr Hardy's family and show them where to put their horse.

"Do you want to put him in the paddock to graze or pop him into a stable while we have some breakfast?" I asked him.

"Are you The Honourable Cressida Welsby?" Mr Hardy asked.

"Yes, I am, and I'm amazed by your journey, you must be tired, all of you."

"I'll turn him out if that's alright," he said. He took the harness off with his son's help and they put the harness on the cart.

Meanwhile, his wife remained very quiet, and the three younger children stood very near to her, looking shy. I shook hands with him, and he introduced me to his wife and children. The oldest boy was Reuben, he was twelve, and the next was Luna, ten, then eight-year-old Roscoe and the littlest was six-year-old Star, and his wife was called Lacey. She had serious calm grey eyes and was slim, medium height with long black hair plaited down her back.

"Come on," I said, "let's go and get some breakfast and I will tell you about your new place."

"New place – what do you mean?" he asked surprised. "I thought we were staying here." He looked about, baffled, and faltered. "We don't want to cause any bother, we just don't have a home anymore and we just want to be somewhere safe."

"Of course, and hopefully, you will be safe, well at least safer than Hull." I added, "Please follow me, the horse will be fine in there. Close that gate. I'm starving, so let's go." He put the docile horse into the paddock and his horse was down cropping grass, instantly. We made our way to the kitchen and found Mrs Revill ready for us with cocoa and a pot of tea with porridge, sausages, and eggs. They sat down clearly uncomfortable to be in the kitchen. But one by one the children came in to eat and soon the table was full of people, food, dogs, and noisy chatter. The children left for school with Audrey driving them there and I finally had time to talk to the new family about the smallholding I had waiting for them. Of course, he wanted to leave immediately, but I persuaded them to stay and let their horse have a rest and I took them into the Walled Garden to show them all the work that Osian had been doing. Lacey was very taken with all the herbs growing there and knew the names of each one and its use. Mr Hardy was interested in the number of vegetables growing in the beds and the cordon fruit trees growing against the walls. Of course, the interior of the long glass house was the main point of interest and fascination, and the peaches, lemons, oranges, bananas, and nectarines growing in there and the vine growing against the south facing wall, but nearest to the fires keeping the glass-house heated in winter.

I took them to the stables and introduced them to all the horses Tizzy, Donk, Hermes, The Brig, Spangles, Polly, the shy hackney mare, the young grey racehorse now called Timefortea, 'Timmy' and Zoltan. Alfie was out in the fields working on the farm. They thought Zoltan was very beautiful and of course he was the best-looking horse there. Well, to me Hermes was the best-looking mare in the yard. They loved the goats and Lacey said she had always wanted to keep goats; an idea immediately came into my mind. They just seemed anxious to get to where they were to be staying so I suggested that I take them in the car, and they could come back for their horse and all their stuff later. No, they insisted they took their horse, Lucky, with them, and they wanted to set off as soon as possible. I knew their new home was still being worked on, so I was playing for time. Anyway, they were keen to leave so that's what they did: three hours later they were on the road, but not before I had shown Lacey the schoolhouse and introduced her to Danielle and all the ladies busy knitting. She held Danielle's hand and looked intently into her eyes and said she had felt great pain inside Danielle and that she was still in pain, and she could feel it through her hand. Danielle was clearly surprised that a stranger could read her thoughts and see through her to the pain she felt. Gosh did we have a mind reader or a fortune teller staying with us now. Time would tell.

Chapter 30

We Meet Susan and Roger

F our hours later they pulled into the driveway to the smallholding, and they were shocked to see so many people working very hard to get everything ready for them. I had driven there ahead after giving them good instructions. There would always be work at the smallholding, but at least it was now tidy and clean and ready for the family. Granger showed him where to put his horse in a clean stable as Lucky was a bit sweaty, and gave him a bucket of warmed water for him. Trip their dog stayed by their flat cart on guard. The oldest boy Reuben rubbed Lucky down and I showed him where the hay and straw were kept and where the horse food was. We then stood back and let the family explore the house on their own. It was now painted, white of course, with a new pamment tiled floor in the kitchen, a new bathroom off the scullery and newly rubbed down wood floors in the sitting room. It had bright green flowered curtains and furniture from the second-hand shop in King's Lynn. Upstairs the three bedrooms were clean and painted, had a double bed in one room and four singles in the other two made up and ready and with more new curtains made by Mrs Hubbard and blackout blinds to all the windows put up by Mrs Burden. Jabbo had mended three broken windows and put a new tap in the kitchen. Audrey and Margaret had cleaned the house and Granger and Frankie had swept the yard. Mrs Revill had sent a venison stew down for them and some fresh bread, oats in a sack, tea, camp coffee, butter, cheese, homemade jars of jam, honey, chutneys, and belly pork to cook later. Osian had brought a sack of potatoes, a bunch of carrots and a basket full of fresh green vegetables, salad, and tomatoes. Osian and Frankie showed Stan and his son Reuben the paddock and goats, geese, and hens, and then we walked to see the twenty-four acres of land surrounding the property. Nothing had been done in the short time we had to get things ready, but Osian explained his plans to grow some hay, potatoes to sell and a lattice work of different vegetables growing in square patches in the fields so Stan could sell them at his gate entrance or in the markets. This was if he wanted to as we knew he hadn't grown things before. Lacey came over to us with Star, Roscoe and Luna, and said she was hoping to grow herbs and flowers to sell. They were all excited to meet the goats, geese, and hens. I was so relieved she had hopes and plans to grow produce and so was Osian. Hopefully, just maybe it would work out for them, after all.

We decided there was nothing more we could do for now, but leave them to explore and settle in. Just one question was on my mind.

"Before I go would you tell me where you were when the bomb flattened your house and most of the street where you lived?"

Stan recounted their story: "We lived near the docks, but Lucky and our dog Trip stay just outside Hull where I have a rented stable with a very small yard. We had been staying in the stable every night for weeks, just going home for a wash and to cook. That night I said we should stay at home and sleep in proper beds for a real rest, but Lacey said no, and insisted we all went back to the stable; so, we took Lucky back that night after work. We had been sleeping in the straw for weeks. Little by little we had taken a few home comforts like pillows, blankets, and a trunk with some clothes in. Every morning the children went to school and were laughed at because they smelt of horse and horse manure, yet we are alive because we stayed there. Me and Lacey found out our house had gone after we took the kids to school, and we weren't allowed down our street. Didn't matter as there was nothing left to go back for; they were just taking our neighbours' dead bodies out and their gorgeous little girl. I saw her blonde curls from under the blanket covering her. When I told the council we had nowhere to live they offered us a school to sleep in with many other families, but it's been easier to be on our own in the stable. The school they offered us was a long way from Lucky's stable to the north of the city. I went back to the council to ask for some coupons to buy food and bedding as we had left our ration books in the house – lost them all. It was then a lady there said she knew of a place to stay here in Norfolk with my family and our horse, so I jumped at the chance, and we have been travelling for just over a month. Thank you for everything you have done, all of you, hopefully, I will get to know you all in time."

We were all humbled by his story and how awful this terrible war was for so many people. We said our goodbyes and left them in peace.

I was so proud and pleased of how the Willup Hall team had pulled together to help those less fortunate than ourselves. I drove home with Audrey, Margaret and Agatha Hubbard and Joan Burden, dropping them off in the village. I left Jabbo and Granger to do the horses and went in to see if Grandora was back from visiting her sister-in-law, Lydia Anne; I wanted to tell her all about my day. She was home and we enjoyed a glass of wine and chatted about everyone staying with us and about the new orphans arriving next week. We now had two South African RAF guys staying with us, and both liked long walks and spent time reading and resting so we didn't see much of them. The Australians had already returned to their duties, bless them. I had seen them before they left and thanked them for all their help.

I had a room ready for the children and so was calm about their arrival, just concerned about their 'minds', poor things; losing their parents in a bombing raid was dreadful. I was soon on my way to bed with nothing to eat, I was just too tired for tea; it had been such a long day.

The orphans arrived the following week and I picked them up from the station and there they were looking scared and tearful. Bless them. I hugged them and carried their little suitcases, and they carried their gas masks; a little girl of ten and her brother seven, Susan and Roger Brownson. We were soon home in time for tea and the children were introduced to everyone else. The poor pair had to put up with such a noisy lot round the table it must have been quite a shock. We took them to see the horses after tea and all the dogs went with us; and they seemed frightened of the dogs. Apparently, they didn't have any animals at home as their mother was allergic to them, Roger told us. There was an awkward silence then Susan burst into tears.

Ruby went and put her hand into her hand and turning to me said, "I'll take her home now and show her my dollies. Come on, Lottie, let's go."

It was so sweet of her – she was the loveliest child. I helped in the yard and then went in to get ready for my night-time ambulance job. Rosie had taken the new children to their room, and I found her unpacking their few possessions onto the bed. Their gas masks hung on the bedroom door just as all our gas masks did in the house. We were all attached to the awful things and couldn't go anywhere without them, carried by straps on our shoulders.

I had painted their room, white – what else? They had one blue eiderdown and one pink one with regulation government type cream blankets, flannelette sheets and now on each bed a beautiful, knitted patchwork cover of rainbow colours. These had been knitted by Danielle and her team of knitters – Danielle in the nicest way possible had taken over as leader and teacher of the knitting group. Her designs and use of colours were worthy of any fashion show. She had enthusiastically rushed through these covers which were being made for refugees, but the knitters agreed no one could need them more than our two new orphans. Both children had been staying at a friend's house overnight as their parents were out working on night shift when the factory where they worked was badly bombed and both their parents had been killed. It was hard for us to comprehend the mindless killing and destruction caused by this war; how much worse (and unfair) it all was for the children. Now with a cheerful rug on the dark wood floor their new bedroom looked lovely; I did so hope they would be happy here, with us. I had painted some a scene from the Walt Disney film Snow White and the Seven Dwarfs on the wall, along with birds, butterflies, and flowers.

I hoped in time they would settle down to school and home life here if we gave them lots of love and patience. Audrey was brilliant as usual, helping with their schoolwork and getting them to mix and play with the rest of our refugees. The RAF personnel staying with us at this time numbered three new men who were kind and helpful and enjoyed playing board and card games with the children. Roger continued to be frightened of dogs but seemed a little better with Ruby's little pooch, which still followed her everywhere, except to school. Susan became a fantastic table tennis player and as time went on could beat all of us.

Christmas was coming again, and I wondered how we could buy presents for so many children, but I needn't have worried, Grandora and her sisters-in-law Lydia Anne and Rose Mary were already gathering presents for everyone and told me not to worry as they had it all in hand. I trusted them – well, I had to trust them, as rationing was making everything more difficult all the time, although a black market had sprung up across the country dealing in every commodity needed. Again, we remained lucky, having our own farm, here on the estate, plus access to the other five farms, and a healthy market garden with hens supplying eggs, chicken for the 'pot' and the occasional deer from the Park. It was the growing population of stags which needed containing. Plus, we always had too many rabbits making dangerous rabbit holes the horses could break their legs in. So, with Hugh being a good shot we often had rabbit pie or stuffed roast rabbit to add to our range of food. At least our extended family ate well.

I frequently sent little notes and sketches to Marcell and Aurielle in France, but I am not sure how many reached them. In nearly two years I had only received two letters, each telling me how well they were and that Alex and his two sisters, his brother and nephew were well. Who on earth was his second sister and a nephew? I was quite sure he only had one sister when I met him and one brother; it was impossible for anyone else to have been on the cart with them? I just know that they were all having a rough time with many food shortages as the German occupiers took all the food, fuel, wine, and coal to Germany along with fine art, paintings, leather, perfume, and strangely, axe handles. The Germans had stolen many farm animals, corn, potatoes, and farm machinery –these they sent back to Germany. I knew this from reports in our papers, but not from their letters, which were censored. The people of France were starving and indeed struggling just to keep alive and survive during the occupation; my heart literally ached for them all.

As November arrived, I was excited and nervous about the return of my parents and how my father would react to so many people now staying at the Hall; my new building plans; and, well, everything I had done here since I arrived home. The news was sketchy; but the situation created by the Japanese in the countries near Singapore, where they were, was troubling and serious. Singapore was impregnable, with guns guarding the sea around the Island; there were hundreds of our troops stationed there.

I could not understand the delay in my parents coming home. They should let other people look after the running of the Embassy now and get home for Christmas. All was ready for them in their bedrooms and their sitting room near Grandora's two rooms and mine. I would not let anyone use their rooms; they were always left ready for their return.

November became December and the worst news came on the wireless on December 7th: Japan attacked Pearl Harbor and the Hawaiian Islands causing utter devastation and killing a reported 2,400 people and wounding over 1,178 people. This attack came without warning because the Japanese Ambassador did not inform the President that the attack was imminent. There was a time difference due to the distances involved and the message was delayed. On December 8th Singapore was attacked and on the same day the Japanese invaded Hong Kong and the Philippines. By December 11th Germany and Italy with Japan had declared war on the United States of America. This meant America had now joined with us in the fight to destroy Hitler, we no longer stood alone.

Christmas came quickly yet again, and Miriam and Anna-Sara came to stay with us. She always stayed in Audrey's cosy cottage now and was a great help with all the children's needs. It was becoming increasingly obvious that she was an extraordinary listener, easy to talk to and someone to whom you could unburden your troubles. She would always spend time with our visiting airmen, and they would tell her about their fears and anxieties. She never shared these conversations with any of us. She had spent long hours with Danielle and Tad, and I knew Danielle always seemed more positive after their chats. Now she would sit and draw with the two new orphans and spent time with them, letting them tell her their secret thoughts and worries. It was obvious that she should become a sort of counsellor and take a course at college or university. I started to discuss this idea with her and my wonderful Grandora, and we came up with a promising course available to her at Cambridge University, so we sorted it all out and she was enrolled to start after Christmas in the New Year.

We had the best Christmas possible for the children, with carol singing on Christmas Eve, the Christmas party for everyone in our large reception hall around the beautiful Christmas tree, which Granger and Jabbo had found, cut down and brought in for us. Rose Mary, Lydia Anne and Grandora chose some wonderful gifts from Harrods, and everyone contributed with a selection of inspiring homemade creations which suited us all. I had purchased plenty of scarves on my trip to London the

previous year and there were plenty left to give out to everyone
again this year. I don't think anyone minded getting a pretty
scarf again. Christmas dinner was a mad affair with two of our
airmen staying with us for Christmas Day as they lived so far
away, from their homes in Poland and Canada. We managed to
feed everyone, and it was all a great success. We sent our food
parcels to the village in plenty of time and made sure there
were enough vegetables, turkeys, and capons for everyone. The
festivities went on after all the children had gone to bed after
they had played charades with us and enjoyed playing with their
new board games. As usual The Hunt met on the front lawn
on Boxing Day to the delight of everyone and we worked hard
in the kitchen to make tasty bites for our visitors to go with
the punch we had made. It was much more sensible making a
punch with plenty of blackberry juice and then add some of
the strong stuff. Our new refugees, the Hardy family, were not
forgotten and were well taken care of, supplied with food for
their Christmas table and invited to join us for the Christmas
Eve Carol Service. It was during this event we discovered that
the youngest Hardy children Luna and Roscoe knew Susan and
Roger from their school and arrangements were made for them
to visit the Hardys during the holidays. Another surprise was
that Lydia Anne had decided to look after three children from
Jersey. The mother of the family they had been staying with in
Kent had suddenly died and it was for the best that they were
relocated again, poor things. Aunt Lydia Anne was so impressed
with how we were coping and helping refugees, she had decided
to help and do the same. Of course, I told her, they were all
welcome during the holidays. It was all becoming completely
mad, but how could three more make any difference to the gang
we had now? After the hectic Christmas, New Year's Eve was

comparatively quiet. 1942 – a New Year – but given the war news, none of us felt like celebrating.

On 15 February Singapore fell to the Japanese easily as our guns faced out to sea and the Japanese attacked from the hills behind, getting through difficult terrain, which our top Military had declared impossible for anyone to traverse. One hundred and thirty-six thousand British, Canadian, Australian, Indian and Malay soldier surrendered to the Japanese. It was a disaster and what of my parents? When would we hear from them? I had never felt so low in spirits before. Where was Tiff? I had not heard from him in weeks.

I sat with Grandora and Audrey in the sitting room when our Prime Minister Winston Churchill broadcast on the wireless the news of the defeat of Singapore. He said, 'I speak to you all under a shadow of a heavy and far-reaching military defeat; it is a British and Imperial defeat. Singapore has fallen.... this therefore, is one of moments when the British race and nation can show their quality and their genius. This, is one of those moments when we can draw from the heart of misfortune the vital impulses of victory. We must remember we are no longer alone.' We sat in stunned silence and misery.

"Dear God, give Bertie and your mother strength to survive," whispered Grandora. I cried for them; tears of mixed emotions, of sadness, fear and anger that they were there at all and not here safe here with us.

The only news of my parents came weeks later telling us briefly that they were alive, but held prisoner in different places. I was so sad to hear this and remained annoyed that they were there when they should have been at home. I know this was bad of me, I just couldn't help how I felt that could not get them out of my mind. We wrote to them through the wonderful Red Cross. Now our knitters, who had been knitting for the refugees in Britain, started knitting for the Red Cross as well. More ladies joined our group, and we were able to increase our output of much needed jumpers, cardigans, hats, socks, gloves, and blankets. We were always needing more wool, often in short supply.

One morning in March whilst on my early morning hack with Hermes and Odin, I stopped to sketch the valley before me and the rising mist over the frosty landscape. It was very cold, and I tethered Hermes to the tree next to me. I did my sketch then lightly watercolour washed it and put away my paints and the little water bottle into the bag which usually carried my gas mask. It was to make it look like I was carrying my gas mask which I wasn't; a big sin. Honestly, who would find out in the middle of nowhere in Norfolk? I was frozen to the tree trunk I had been sitting on, and with a very numb bum I went to untie Hermes and, catching my foot in a root, somehow twisted backwards, with all my weight on my right wrist. Ouch! It hurt, I felt dizzy, and a wave of sickness washed over me. I sat down and, nursing my wrist, I put my head down towards my knees. I'm not sure how long I was there but can't think it was too long as it was so cold, I started shaking. Somehow, I had to get home so, with one hand I untied my quiet patient mare and limped down the bridleway onto the little lane leading towards my home. I felt sick again and stopped briefly and then carried on hobbling. I was sure I could get on Hermes if I found a handy big stone to stand on. I carried on to the crossroads to the old stone way-marker where a slightly bigger lane carried traffic back to Willup Home farm.

Then I heard a cycle bell ringing and Albert our postman came pedalling furiously into view. He slowed down. "Morning, me Lady, anything wrong?"

"Hello Albert, are you heading to the Hall?" I asked, feeling faint again.

"Oh, you look white," he said.

"I feel very white," I joked. "Could you cycle to our stables and tell Granger or Jabbo to come and fetch me and Hermes please, Albert?"

"Of course, M'Lady, I'll go now." Off he pedalled furiously.

Granger and Jabbo were soon with me in the van; Jabbo rode Hermes home and Granger took me home.

"Did you fall off?" he asked incredulously.

I understood his surprise – Normandy Cobs rarely ditch people, ever. "No, I was on the ground, and I twisted and fell onto a fallen tree trunk. I had just been sketching," I answered wryly.

"Hospital for you, Sid," he said. "I'll be back with the car for you pronto."

I limped into the kitchen and Mrs Revill went to fetch Grandora. Grandora was hardly awake and although I told her to stay at home, she insisted on dressing immediately and going to hospital with me – but only after she had drunk a cup of her best coffee to revive herself. She told the Canadian airman who was off for an early morning walk to look sharp and make sure all the children were up and down for their breakfast when Rosie or Audrey arrived, and that he was in charge of organising them until we got home.

He saluted her, "Yes ma'am," with a smile and then said, "It was a smell of delicious real coffee that got me up, or was I dreaming, Ma'am?"

She sighed and went back into her room and came back with enough for a cup of coffee for him. He grinned at me, and we went outside to find Granger waiting for us with the station wagon.

It was definitely a break, and I was potted up and put into a sling, but at least I had only twisted my ankle. I was mad that it had happened, mainly because I wouldn't be able to ride or paint for a while. I went back to meet all the children and give them the lecture on behaving themselves and doing as they were told and went to Grandora's sitting room to put my feet up and fall asleep on the painkillers I had been given. Of course, my arm swelled up and gave me grief and pain over the next week, and I was well and truly depressed. I struggled to do my hair, pull on my trousers, socks, or my bra, and I couldn't cook, ride or sketch and plenty of other things too. Thank goodness we still bought fish and chips once a week – they were never rationed and were brilliant on Mrs Revill's evening off and more so now with me in a pot.

More bad news – Grandora received a letter from Portia saying Alastair was missing and as her baby was due in two weeks and she was devastated about Alastair, PLEASE could we visit. "That's it, my dear, we are going, and you are coming with me. I need help and so do you, we will go to Scotland and help Portia with her new baby. We can't be told it's an unnecessary journey; it's a vital journey." The Government was always asking people 'Is your journey really necessary?' as they needed transport and fuel for important Military people, and we were always being told to save fuel. "I'll ask Rosie to pack for you right now and I'll tell Granger to get some fuel for the car."

Off she went in a flurry. I didn't argue – I quite fancied a change as I was sitting doing nothing, anyway.

Over the next two days we fluctuated between whether it would be better to drive up or take a very slow train; either way it was not going to be a luxury journey. The train would give way to all troop trains and those hauling products for the war. The car would use more fuel than we could carry with us, and we could not guarantee being able to buy enough on the way, to complete our journey. After much discussion it was decided Granger would take us by car to Narborough and Pentney station and help get us, and our luggage, onto the train.

Tickets for first class were booked and we were to leave in three days' time and be away for at least four weeks. I was upset to be leaving Hermes and all my family for so long, but at least Odin would be with me. Then Malissa decided to come too, and I was delighted. She had been working so hard since May 9th last year, bouncing between Bletchley Park and Cambridge. Something to do with a U-110 being captured and some machine I think; I didn't ask; best not to these days. She needed a break as she was clearly very tired. Lottie's mother was going to be staying with Violet and Arthur for a short holiday and was planning on taking Lottie to stay with her, so we decided to take Ruby and her Pooch with us too. I was pleased to have my special people with me on the trip and to spend time with them.

Chapter 31

Portia in Scotland

I asked Miriam if she would come and stay at the Hall and take on the responsibility of looking after all the children and she jumped at the chance even if it delayed her course, which so far was going well for her. Grandora suggested her sister-in-law Lydia Anne came too, but I squashed that notion straight away. Lydia Anne could be far too bossy and would try to order everyone about and do exactly what she wanted. Now was not the time for her to arrive with three more evacuee children from Jersey. No, they would all cope without us for a few weeks Portia needed us more and I needed more wool for the knitters and another spinning wheel. We were soon packed as apart from plenty of warm clothes I didn't envisage us dancing the Highland fling or attending dances. I was wrong: I soon found the ceilidh was keeping spirits up in Scotland, so, it was a good job Grandora insisted I pack some evening attire just in case! I just hoped we didn't get trapped in any snow drifts when on the cold train or travelling around Scotland. The departure day arrived, and I hobbled downstairs and was very glad of help from everyone to get me, Odin, and my luggage into the car with everyone else. All the children waved us off as we left them with Miriam and Audrey busy organising games to play or do their homework in the school room before they had their tea. It had been decided we would take the sleeper Scotsman to Perth, leaving Narborough and Pentney station at 16.56 for King's Lynn, where we would change for Peterborough, arriving at 19.45 and departing at 21.53 for Edinburgh Waverley and finally arriving into Perth at 08.34. It was important to book 14 days in advance and we were just a tad shy of this, but Grandora's charm and the luck for us of another family's cancellation bought us three and a half tickets. The roads were quiet as we made our way, with Granger driving us in the station wagon, to Narborough and Pentney railway station. The main traffic we saw were some RAF lorries full of military personnel, no doubt for all the airports dotted around our Norfolk coast. We were soon on the train with our two dogs in our first-class sleeper compartment all to ourselves. Books were brought out and Malissa or I read to Ruby, and we played I-spy and snap. It was just what I had expected: a long, dreary, cold journey. The high spot was making our way to the dining car at mealtimes and these little episodes broke up the travelling. Not that we were treated to a cooked meal – it was just soup and biscuits and some weak tea which was at least warm. We had milk with us for Ruby, which was heated up for us in the dining car and we enjoyed the egg and cheese sandwiches Mrs Revill had prepared packed with slabs of fruit cake. The fruit cake was minus most fruit as it was impossible to buy or get hold of dried fruit unless you dried the fruit yourself – which is what we tried to do at harvest time. Ruby was put into a bunk bed hopefully to sleep for the whole journey, and Grandora broke out the hip flask and gave us a tot of whisky to help us sleep. Which fortunately it did until early morning and I awoke and just rested, warm and comfortable in my little lower bunk bed, listening to the steady shuttle and rattle rhythm of the train on the tracks.

On reaching Perth we took a taxi to the Salutation Hotel overlooking the River Tay for breakfast and to await Portia's transport to take us to her farmhouse. This turned out to be her housekeeper's husband Mr McGregor in Alastair's Humber Snipe, which was a bit of a squeeze with all our luggage. I didn't know what to expect to find when we arrived at the farm of Portia and Alastair... well, I expected a farmhouse. No, wrong again, it was a large white mansion between Killiecrankie and Pitlochry. Set back a mile off the road with trees lining the long drive, it climbed slightly up the hillside and there were sheep grazing everywhere, little white dots all over the landscape and what a beautiful landscape. The house was set in an arboretum of trees and gardens and the views were amazing, just breath-taking. There was me with a vision of a crofter's cottage and Portia struggling to feed baby lambs and striding out with her crook across the mountains in search of missing sheep. No, it was not quite like that at all. I should have known: it was stylish Portia who lived here after all. The cottages at each side of the gates to the drive housed the housekeeper/cook, Mrs McGregor, and her husband in one, and the shepherd Wullie Bruce in the other. Portia's little boy Hamish, now nearly two years old, had a nanny to look after him. So why were we needed so desperately, I wondered, and I am sure Malissa and Grandora wondered too. Oh, who cared, it was a fabulous place and I realized I was enjoying the break already. Portia was big and was due in 10 days and was clearly scared now Alastair wasn't there and had gone missing. He had been reported as crashed over France and unaccounted for. She was clearly deeply traumatised as to what had happened to Alastair and the thought of him never seeing their unborn child or not returning home. I was glad we were there to keep her company and try and support her. So, we chatted the rest of the day and Ruby played with Hamish and obviously relished having 'a baby of her own' to organise with a watchful eye on her from the nanny Betsy. The house was stylishly decorated in a modern 40s style with a Scottish flavour. I took the Pooch and Odin all around the garden, which was mostly designed to look like a small park. It was soon time for Ruby to go to bed and then we had a small dinner party and Portia got to know Malissa and heard about our adventures travelling home from France. We then told her about all the people we had staying with us at the Hall at the moment, and the changes I had made to the cottages, old schoolroom, and stables. It was all very cosy and relaxing and a long way from our busy lives at the Hall and even further away from the horrors of war affecting so many people. Hopefully it took Portia's mind off her troubles, even if for only a short time. Grandora told her it was important she stayed calm for the sake of the new baby who needed her to be relaxed and focused on the poor wee mite's imminent arrival. It was a big house and a little draughty in the hallways and upstairs, but with the fires blazing downstairs and several hot water bottles and some bed socks and a cardigan over my flannelette pyjamas, I slept reasonably well apart from the nuisance of my pot. I actually fancied an old-fashioned nightcap for my head, one that fastened with ribbons under my chin. I tried my woollen beret, but it kept coming off in bed.

The next day Malissa, Ruby and I went for a walk to see Portia's Highland ponies grazing behind the house. She had two grey mares both in foal, two unbroken young geldings and her handsome dun riding mare. I couldn't walk far as my twisted

ankle soon became swollen if I stood for too long, so we soon
returned to the warmth of the house. Portia was knitting in the
sitting room by the fire when we got back, and Malissa took Ruby
to play with Hamish and then she said she was going to do some
work in the library. I asked Portia if I could sketch her and she
agreed, so I did a series of quick very loose sketches which was not
easy with a pot on, but I thought they looked good. They showed
Portia big with child and concentrating on her knitting. Another
I did of her looking pensively out through the window, and finally
when she was tired, I did one of her sleeping with her feet up.
She was such a beautiful person in every way, and I captured her
beauty in pregnancy and her serene radiant face. I knew I had to
paint her when my arm was fully recovered. Feeling tired myself
and with my arm now hurting, I nodded off by the fire.

Over lunch we discussed the plight of my parents and the
stupid war, and we all wondered when on earth it would end.
I also asked where she planned to have the baby as I would be
useless to help with one arm.

"Oh, at home here, of course, it has all been arranged and my
midwife only has six miles to travel here, and the doctor is just in
Pitlochry so I will be fine. I just want Alastair to be here, close by."

Thinking about all the travelling and the possibility of bad
weather, I thought we had better have a plan. However, none of
us knew what plan we should have ready for the event in the
worst-case scenario of us being on our own here when the baby
decided to arrive. After lunch, Grandora and Portia went for a
nap, Malissa went back to working in the library and Ruby had
a snooze in the nursery. I decided to ask Mr McGregor to drive
me to see the Soldiers Leap, a place where a Redcoat soldier is
reputed to have leapt eighteen feet across the River Garry when
fleeing the Jacobites and to the southern end of the Pass of

Killiecrankie where a footbridge crosses the River Garry. Then, feeling sore and tired, I was taken back to the Mansion for a cup of tea. I did telephone home to ask if everything was alright and I spoke to Miriam who asked how Portia was. I told her about Alastair crashing in France and being unaccounted for and she asked me where in France he was believed to have come down and could we find out. Strange question, but I told her I would ask Portia to enquire, although they might not tell her as I was sure it must be classified information. Why she wanted to know or what she thought she could do, I had no idea. We spent the following week much the same, resting, sleeping, sightseeing, and learning about the Grampian Mountains, but mostly waiting.

By the third week I was able to walk much better due to all the resting, I think. It was bitterly, bitingly cold, and as usual after lunch Grandora went to lie down as did Portia and Ruby; Malissa went to the library to work. I was restless and thought a walk would do me good as I hated doing nothing during the day. I wrapped up warmly and put some warm trousers on and snow boots, gloves, hat, scarf – all very difficult with only one arm working and a sling – then I set off up the hill behind the house. I walked slowly, but I managed pretty well and passed the Highland ponies hiding from the wind in a shelter belt of trees and bushes. I reached a wilder moorland part of the farm and in the wind, which seemed to be getting worse, I spotted a sheep on its back, and I knew I had to rescue it somehow even though I could only use one arm. I knew sheep died if left on their backs. So, I struck out off the path and made my way downhill to where the poor sheep was lying still and unable to move. Not sure what to do next, I went to the side of the sheep where I could grasp its legs and with one good hand and my shoulder, I sort of pulled it over and it jumped up, knocking me backwards into a very muddy bog. I now struggled to get out, floundering on my knees, conscious that I must not get my pot wet and sort of holding my arm out of the way. With a huge effort I managed to grovel my way onto my feet and stagger back up to the path and make my way home. Suddenly it started snowing so badly I could hardly see my feet never mind the path, so with my head bent into the wind and my clothes covered in smelly bog mud and snow I fought my way down past the ponies and towards the house. I honestly thought I might have had it and died of exposure on the hillside. I tumbled into the reception hall and knew I had to have a wee quickly, but it was difficult getting my mud-caked boots and snow covered coat off. As I danced from foot to foot that's when I realized I was not alone. I had a shocked, open-mouthed audience also in the hall.

Ruby said, "It's Aunty Cwessy not a snow man," then she started giggling.

I slowly realized as I danced across the hall, dragging my coat off, which was stuck because of my pot, that a man was smiling and staring at me: it was Tiff.

"Someone help me quick please," I said to anyone, and it was Tiff who leapt into action first and bundled me towards the cloakroom door, pulling off my scarf and gloves and then he started helping me wriggle my bog-caked trousers down. "Oh, I'm fine, I can manage now," I said breathlessly.

"Will I ever find you clean?" he said, laughing.

Malissa sprang into action and pushed me through the cloakroom door, closing it in Tiff's laughing face. She helped me take off my dirty outer clothes and boots, all the time laughing at me, and when I had been to the lavatory, she suggested I had a bath and washed my hair. We went into the hall to find Tiff, Portia and Grandora waiting for me, suppressing their giggles, or not. I suggested I would need a stiff drink when I came downstairs after I had washed and changed.

"A stiff drink at four-thirty in the afternoon is the slippery slope, Cressida it's far too early," Grandora said, hiding her amusement.

"Don't talk to me about slippery slopes just now, Grandora," I said, and I limped upstairs to make myself presentable with their laughter ringing in my ears.

I went downstairs clean with glowing cheeks and straight into the waiting arms of Tiff and then I headed for the fire and my stiff drink, a decent Malt. Well, when in Scotland and all that.

"I am so pleased to see you again. How did you know where I was?" I asked.

"Well, I called at Willup Hall to see you and was told you were staying here, so I decided to travel here to find you."

"What, you came all the way to Scotland just to find me?" I asked incredulously.

"Well not quite, there's a training camp up here and that's where I'm going in a few days' time."

"Near here?" I asked, sounding like an echo.

"No, up towards the Highlands and don't ask me anymore," he chided.

"Oh, who cares where, you're here now and that's all that matters," I said.

The others came in for pre-dinner drinks and we all chatted about the snow and my escape from the bog, which could have been worse apparently as there are bogs around here which are not at all easy to get out of. We were treated to cream of parsnip soup and a Homity Pie for dinner with roast potatoes and carrots, followed by apple crumble. We had not made Homity pie at home but as it used potatoes, leeks, apples, garlic, egg, cheese, thyme and pastry, I thought I would try it when we went home. Of course, the conversation turned to Alastair and how we could find out what was happening about trying to trace him. Then the telephone rang, and it was for me. Miriam had Danielle with her and told me that Danielle had been able to get in touch with 'Some People' about evaders and their whereabouts in France. Anyway, they had information concerning Alastair, but would prefer to wait a few more days before confirming what they knew, but they could confirm that he had survived the crash. I walked back to the dining room and went straight to Portia and, smiling, I hugged her and told her what I had been told verbatim. She hugged me back so relieved and seemed to relax just a little. Tiff was interested as he had met Danielle for the first time when he called at the Hall, and he commented to us how quiet and withdrawn she was with him. I told him about the odd circumstances around her arrival at the Hall, but I didn't know what had happened to her in France.

The next day Tiff and I drove to Blair Castle and walked round Blair Atholl and visited the Queen's View on Loch Tummel. The snow had stopped overnight, and Tiff was driving a military vehicle which was cold, but robust and it managed the roads well. We both sat on sheepskins, and I had a thick tartan rug lined in fur wrapped round my knees and feet. We soon headed back though, arriving home well before dark and any further freezing weather. That night Portia had arranged a bit of a ceilidh for us and a few of her hardy neighbours braved the cold to visit us. Two carloads arrived and arrangements were made for them to stay overnight with us. The musicians from the village played until eight o'clock, which was by no means late, but with the weather, the dark roads, and the blackout they were soon on their way to their homes a couple of miles down the road. We enjoyed a pleasant night, meeting new people and enjoying Portia's hospitality. She clearly had some good friends where she lived, and the Scottish hospitality as always was warm and welcoming. The next day passed in a leisurely way after everyone left early in the morning, and Tiff and I enjoyed precious time spent together walking a little and, well, just chatting. That evening the weather worsened and the snow turned into a blizzard with fierce westerly winds blowing. The ponies were brought into their stables and Tiff helped the shepherd Wullie Bruce and Mr McGregor fetch the sheep into the home pastures with the collie sheepdogs doing most of the work. We had an early dinner and played cards with Grandora; well, I watched as they played Bridge, my least favourite card came. Then Malissa played the piano, and I was roped in to play chess with Tiff and I beat him. So now I loved playing chess with Tiff, but then it was my turn to play Portia and that didn't go well for me, but I knew she couldn't beat Malissa. Well, I jumped up to pour out a drink and as Portia sat opposite Malissa to play a game of chess, she pulled a face and winced. Every head in the room noticed and swivelled in the direction of poor Portia.

Grandora said, "Right, Portia, no chess for you, sit on the sofa and put your feet up."

Tiff helped her to the sofa, and she winced again. I went to make some warm milk for her to sip and we all wondered what to do if this was the baby coming during a great storm. The telephone rang and I went to answer it and found it was somebody in London asking for Lady Portia Sinclair, wife of Alastair Sinclair.

"I am afraid she is indisposed at the moment as we think her labour has started," I told him. "I am her sister Cressida – can I give her a message?"

"Tell her that her husband is in Gibraltar and will be..." The line went dead.

I ran back to the sitting room in time to see Tiff picking Portia up to take her upstairs to her bedroom.

"Call the doctor and the midwife," Grandora ordered.

"The line has just gone dead during the telephone call, but I will try to get through," I said.

Malissa and Grandora followed Tiff upstairs and I watched them go then I ran back into the freezing cold hall to try the telephone. It was no good: the lines were definitely down in the storm.

I took the hot milk upstairs and bumped into the nanny Betsy on her way to find out what the commotion was.

"Portia has gone into labour, so I've made her some warm milk."

"Have you called the doctor?" she asked. "Or the midwife?"

"The telephone lines are down because of the storm," I replied.

"Right, go downstairs and boil plenty of water and collect some clean towels from the laundry room and bring them upstairs. I will go and see how far on she is."

"Do you know what you are doing?" I asked in surprise.

"Well, I am the eldest in a family of seven girls and one boy, and I have helped my mother at the birth of the last four babies, so yes, I know what I am doing as long as it is straight forward; if it's not then we need the doctor." She hurried off down the landing to Portia's bedroom and knocked on the door and then went in.

I went downstairs to do what I had been told to do with my one free arm; fortunately, Tiff came down into the kitchen to help me. We went back upstairs to Portia's room where it was warm, and a fire was lit in the hearth, and she was lying on the bed with just Malissa and Grandora sitting by her bed.

"Where's Betsy?" I asked in alarm.

"She has gone to her room to change out of her night clothes and put on a clean uniform," said Malissa.

Grandora held Portia's hand and Portia looked wide eyed and frightened.

"I just want Alastair," she cried.

"He might be here soon," I said, soothing her hair.

"What do you mean?" Portia asked tearfully and they all looked at me.

"The telephone call was from somebody in London to tell you Alastair was in Gibraltar waiting for an available plane to bring him home." Anyway, I hoped that was the end of the message that I had missed.

"Why didn't you say?" she gasped and broke off with a groan of pain.

"I came to tell you, but you were already on your way here with Tiff. Well, look, I'm telling you now and isn't it the best news. Now just concentrate on seeing your baby soon."

"Where's the doctor?" she moaned.

"I'll go back and try the telephone again." I hurried downstairs glad to have something to do.

Tiff went upstairs with the towels and water, and I followed him to open the door and Betsy was just going into Portia's bedroom with her sleeves rolled up. I tried the telephone again for the midwife and the doctor, but it was no good: I couldn't get through. Tiff and I sat on the stairs ready to help. Then I paced the landing as it was warmer to keep moving, Tiff paced too, but was much calmer than I, then Malissa asked for more towels and hot water. I went back into the room and held my poor sister's hand while Grandora sat at the other side of her bed. Malissa was helping Betsy and seemed very calm and proficient and looked as if she knew what she was doing.

Then Betsy said, "I can see the head, stop pushing, Portia, wait. Now I want you to push as hard as you can."

Portia gave a great scream-cum-groan and out popped the baby. Betsy wrapped her quickly in a towel and rubbed her gently and the baby cried. "You have a daughter, it's a little girl." She popped the baby onto Portia's chest so Portia could see the baby. The baby had lots of downy dark hair and looked very contented. As Grandora and I crooned over the baby Betsy and Malissa waited for the afterbirth. Tiff knocked at the door with more water and towels. Malissa went to take them off him and left him outside on the landing. We seemed to wait for ages and Betsy massaged Portia's tummy and looked worried. She went to the door to speak to Tiff and came back and told me he wanted a word with me.

He was very serious and said, "I am going to try and get the doctor. I am going down the drive to tell the McGregors we need help, so keep the lights on and stay here and keep the fires going." With that he was gone.

I went to the inside coal house and shovelled coal into the coal buckets with one hand and took one upstairs and then took one into the reception hall for the big fire and another into the sitting room. I made tea for everyone and took it upstairs. Betsy said Portia could not have any tea yet as we were still waiting for the afterbirth.

Betsy and Malissa cleaned the baby and popped her into a cot and attended to Portia – basically, waiting for the afterbirth. She looked very worried then finally the afterbirth came away and we could see how relieved Betsy was. Tiff had driven here in a Willys MB jeep and hopefully had a decent chance of driving through the snow to fetch the doctor or the midwife back to the house. Mrs McGregor arrived with cheeks red from the cold wind and came upstairs to ask if there was anything that she could do. I was glad I now had someone who could help and direct me where to find whatever we needed in the house, and she promptly made some fresh tea for us all and was delighted to hear it was a baby girl. Tiff finally arrived with the frozen doctor and midwife and Betsy said all was well now as the afterbirth had come away. We went downstairs and left him with Betsy and the midwife going through the procedure of the birth and checking all was well.

The doctor eventually came downstairs for a tot of whisky, a cup of coffee, a warm by the fire and pronounced all was very well and that mother and child were both sleeping. Betsy followed him into the room. He complimented her on her midwifery skills and suggested she considered taking a nursing course and completing her midwifery exams. How did she know to worry about the afterbirth?

"It happened to my mother with her fifth baby, and we thought she would bleed to death, but the midwife somehow stopped the bleeding and then the afterbirth came away," Betsy told us.

Just then two little children appeared and hand in hand they slowly came downstairs in their dressing gowns. Ruby guided Hamish to Betsy and then she came to sit on my knee and asked where was breakfast and who was the gentleman with the big bag. So, I told her that Hamish had a new baby sister and the man with the bag was the doctor.

"Can we see the baby please?" asked Ruby excitedly. Betsy speedily took charge and said they may peep quietly in to see the baby then it was back to bed until six o'clock in the morning, and off she swept, gently shooing two little children in front of her.

"Well, if Tiff doesn't mind, I will doze by the fire for a few hours before heading home. Clara will stay upstairs with Lady Sinclair and keep a check on them until I can return later today, weather permitting," Dr Green announced.

Tiff agreed he would quite like to have a rest himself and with that we all went to our rooms for some much-needed sleep. Mrs McGregor was soon knocking on my door with a cup of morning tea; it was nearly nine in the morning and so I got up and went downstairs for my breakfast. The windows in the bathroom had lacy patterns of frost on the inside it was so cold outside. Malissa was at the breakfast table and Betsy had taken the children to the nursery for some more sleep as they hadn't settled very well all night. Dr Green was just finishing his breakfast when Tiff came in to say he would take Mrs McGregor back to her home for some rest. I went with him to the kitchen to thank Mrs McGregor for all her help and I noticed her lovely hand knitted cardigan and asked her who had knitted it.

"Why, I have, of course; can you knit?"

"Well, no, but I am going to try and knit something," I replied, feeling awkward as I didn't fancy knitting – I would rather paint, but I didn't want to hurt her feelings. I asked if she knew where I could buy a spinning wheel and told her about our knitters at home. Apparently, they had a group of knitters here and they were busy knitting for the War effort and the Scottish soldiers and although wool was hard to get hold of, she told me I had come to the right place.

"I have?" I said, puzzled.

"Your sister, ask her," she said, smiling.

Tiff tucked into Scottish porridge oats and toast with homemade jam on his return and told Dr Green he would take him back when he was ready to go.

"So, whose is the little girl called Ruby, I hope you don't mind me asking?" Dr Green asked.

I hesitated and looked at Malissa and then I decided to tell him the whole story with lots of help and information from

Malissa. We told him about finding her in the crashed car with her little dog and with whom we presumed to be her mother, dead in the back seat. We told him about choosing Ruby as a name for her because of her lovely ruby-red velvet dress. At first, we didn't mention her jewels. We told him that in the beginning she didn't talk at all, but now she chatted all the time. We added that we didn't know her real age but had guessed it so she could go to school. Malissa was able to tell him the make and registration of the car she was travelling in. Again, I hesitated, but then I told him about a few precious diamonds discovered and that her jewellery appeared to be real, possibly made by Cartier. I mentioned our trip to London and our meeting with Mr Jakabus Guilhem who had spoken to Ruby in Hebrew, and she had understood him. Then I was quiet as I had recalled all the details about my Ruby, and I knew deep down I didn't want to be without her, I didn't want her to find her relatives.

"You both love her very much," Dr Green said.

I looked at Malissa and knew she felt just the same as I did about Ruby. Ruby and Hamish came into the room with Betsy at that moment. They had brought a pull-along toy for Hamish and they both played with it by the fire.

"Ruby, can I have a word with you please?" asked the doctor.

Ruby shyly came over and waited to hear what the doctor would say.

"Would you like to come and play with my little girl, Ruby; is your name Ruby?"

She looked at Malissa then me and shyly whispered to the doctor, "It's Roza, but I like Ruby too."

I was very surprised, as was Malissa. We realized we had not asked her if she knew her real name, had just called her Ruby when she didn't talk. Her little dog was with her.

"What is the name of your little dog, Roza?" asked the doctor, smiling.

"Her name Pooch now, but I call her Zissa," said Ruby, seriously, adding, "What you call your little girl?"

"Her name is Elizabeth, and she would love to see you."

Ruby put her head on one side and asked, "Can Hamish come too?"

"Yes, he can, I have a little boy called James and he would love to play with Hamish."

"When can I come?" Ruby asked.

"Tomorrow, you can come and stay all day, would you like that?"

"Yes, please, goody we will come tomorrow." She clapped her hands and ran back to play with Hamish.

Dr Green told us he would make extensive enquiries with some colleagues of his who were making records of people taken to concentration camps and trying to track down missing relatives in Europe, a difficult and painstaking job which would most likely take years or very likely never be completed.

"Thank you," I said with some sadness that I might lose my charge one day.

We went upstairs to see the gorgeous new baby and Portia was very happy, but soon tired and we left her with Clara the midwife. The morning flew by, and Tiff didn't come straight back and we all had a quiet morning after a long night. The big surprise was Lysander turning up with his wife Fiona to see us all and in time to welcome the new baby into the family. It was lovely to see him after so long. He was very much grown up now and I could hardly recognise him as my older brother in his smart army uniform, he even looked taller. He was pleased to meet Malissa and hear about our journey from France and all the people now living at the Hall. He was very interested to hear that Malissa worked at a place called Bletchley Park, but when I asked him what went on there, he said he had no idea – yet it was clear that he did. I didn't pursue my question – there was a war on and sometimes you just knew when to shut up. Sadly, Lysander and Fiona hadn't brought their baby son with them as the weather was unpredictable and it seemed wisest to leave him with his nanny at home. Tiff arrived back and I was surprised to discover that Lysander and Tiff knew each other, and it seemed they knew each other quite well. Grandora was delighted to see us all together again and just wished my parents were with us and here to welcome the new baby. We discussed my parents' situation, yet none of us could discover their whereabouts at the present time. It was very worrying for all of us. Malissa beat Lysander at chess that night and I enjoyed learning all about Fiona who was a nurse, and about her family and her future plans with Lysander. Basically, I was wondering, as was Grandora, if they were eventually planning on living in Norfolk at the Hall. It sounded as if Lysander wanted to stay in Scotland as he was married now, which would disappoint Grandora and my parents, but I was beginning to think it wouldn't disappoint me at all.

The next morning there was another surprise when Tiff, who had disappeared early in the morning, returned at lunchtime with Alastair. We were in tears at his appearance – he had lost weight and seemed very demoralised, pale, and exhausted, yet he was clearly thrilled to be home and went straight upstairs to see Portia and the new baby. Hamish was at the doctor's house playing with Ruby, James, and Elizabeth, while Betsy was having time to herself to recover from her busy night. I was so happy to be with my family and I realized I didn't want to go home and leave any of them. Tiff told me Grandora had asked him to organise a delay of one more week with our train tickets before we went back to the Hall, and he had managed to get new tickets for us to leave in ten days. The bad news was that he had to travel back to his unit in four days and we were both sad to be parting yet again. We valued all our days spent together, knowing other families and couples were facing the same situation as we were.

Alastair was so grateful to Betsy for stepping in and taking charge of the situation with the birth of the baby. Portia was surprised that Betsy knew what to do and declared her a miracle nanny. "I never asked her if she could help me with the birth and both she and Malissa were so calm and capable, you were all wonderful," she concluded.

I asked her about buying some wool from them.

"Don't tell me you have started knitting?" Portia laughed and added, "please don't knit me anything, you'll never keep count of your stitches." Which I admit was very true although I had never thought about counting stitches before. "Well, you know we shear our sheep here and we have plenty of wool as you have had some already, so no problem at shearing time. We have been creating a consortium of sheep farmers to store wool to supply the forces for material. I can find out what we have stored here at the moment and let you know later. Not sure about a spinning wheel though, I will ask around for you."

I told her all about Danielle and her marvellous patterns and how she was creating new designs and how talented she was and French.

"Oh, now that sounds interesting. I would love to see what she designs and maybe we can do some work together," said Portia, adding they could provide good quality wool for her designs.

As the time came for us all to leave Portia, Hamish, Alastair, and Rhona Isadora Sinclair, the new baby, I felt enormous sadness. Tiff had gone and it had been such a sad goodbye on my behalf

– he was now part of my family and they all kept leaving me, or me them. Lysander had left with Fiona just after Tiff, and I was beginning to feel empty. Alastair was a bit down and reserved and Portia said he was not himself, just not communicating with her as he used to. I had a brainwave that if she wanted some extra help for some weeks maybe she should consider having Miriam to stay with her – she would be great with the baby and could listen to Alastair if he would talk to her as she had great counselling abilities. Portia thought it was an excellent idea and wrote a letter for Miriam, inviting her to stay there, for a wage of course. So, with lots of tears and hugs and sad goodbyes, Grandora, Malissa, Ruby and I headed back on the train to Norfolk.

Chapter 32

Rory's first visit

We were all tired on our return journey probably because of the stress of leaving our dear relations and the continuing uncertainty of the war. Travelling on the overnight sleeper again seemed a long and cold journey, so then finding Granger waiting for us at the station was a great relief. Once back at the Hall we were treated to some scones and tea, while Ruby ran off to play with her toys and check that all her dolls were safe and just where she had left them. We had a run down on what had been happening here at the Hall and who was staying with us from the RAF by Miriam and Audrey.

Granger knocked on the door and came in. "All your bags are in and the box full of wool is in the schoolroom. Ahem, I must tell you Jabbo has gone."

"Gone, how do you mean gone?" asked Grandora in shock.

"Well, he saw Tiff and they had a long discussion and then Tiff went up to Scotland to see you and then a black Humber, the sort used by the military, picked Jabbo up and he has gone to help the army. He agreed to go, he wanted to go. He was very worried about Zoltan and Zippy, but I promised him they would be fine and waiting for his return."

I was gutted to hear this. Jabbo was safe here; why didn't Tiff mention anything about this to me. "Are Zippy and Zoltan all right?" I asked.

"Well, Zippy is comfortable staying with Danielle and Tad. Zoltan is very quiet, moping for Jabbo and not eating very well, I am worried about him."

"How long has Jabbo been gone?" asked Grandora.

"Nearly two weeks now," replied Granger.

"Do you know how long he has gone for?" Grandora asked.

"No, my Lady," said Granger.

There was silence as we all digested the fact that Jabbo had gone to war; Jabbo, who we had all come to rely on, always helpful, always kind, always just there when he was needed. I wanted to cry, and I wanted to rage at Tiff for allowing it to happen, but I knew there was nothing I could do. I was so proud of Jabbo for wanting to go and be counted and for wanting to make a difference. Anything Jabbo felt he could do to be effective in defeating our enemies was important, very brave and understandable.

I was glad my pot had been taken off in Scotland by Dr Green and although my wrist and arm were still swollen and weak, I was exercising my hand and fingers and hopefully should soon be able to help Granger with the horses. I was glad we didn't have any goats anymore – we had given them to the Hardy family as Lacey was keen to have a goat herd and make goat's milk and cheese. I had sent her everything we had bought for the venture here at the Hall; they were one less problem for us just now. Now I was home I had started helping with the poultry enterprise which Jabbo had helped with up until now.

We knew Jabbo was always busy, but now it was obvious just how valuable he had become to all of us and the work of the Hall. I know Granger missed him; we all did.

I had only been home for three days when I had a telephone call from Granger at four-thirty in the morning. The hackney mare Scarlett, named after Vivien Leigh in Gone With The Wind, had been a problem since I had brought her home from the yard of Jonas Black. She was nervous of people, and it had taken months for her to gain our trust and to put any weight on and begin to look healthy. She had been turned out with Zoltan as he had constantly jumped the fence into her paddock. We had never witnessed him mount her, but obviously we knew he probably had. Over the last few months, she had been wintered out in the paddock with a barn to shelter in and the company of Donk and Tizzy and ad-lib hay. Then she seemed to be getting too fat and Granger said he thought she might be in foal, so the vet was consulted, and he had agreed she was in foal, and now it seems was her time to foal. I was up out of bed and down at the stables immediately, it was freezing cold and there was a late frost carpeting the ground. We had a large foaling box and Granger had brought her in and was just quietly keeping an eye on her without interfering. Granger could deal with the foaling but wondered if I should ring Alford who had dealt with more mares foaling than he had.

"I'll go up to the house and give him a ring," I volunteered.

So, I ran over to the house and bumped into another early riser whom I had only met once since my return, an RAF flyer called Rory from Canada.

"You're up early," we said to each other simultaneously and we both laughed.

"We have a mare foaling and I have just come up to telephone for Alford the huntsman at the hound kennels to come over and help us keep an eye on her," I said.

"Can I help?" he asked, making coffee for both of us.

I sipped my coffee and was surprised it was decent.

He saw my face and said, "A secret stash from my mom in Calgary."

"Lucky you," I said approvingly.

Rory then asked, "Look, can I help? I'll go down with you, we let our mares foal as naturally as possible back home, but sometimes they need a little help and if I can help, I would love to give you a hand."

"Oh thanks, do you mind if we take Granger a cup of coffee too."

"No probs," he replied and so, carrying our precious coffee, we tootled over to see Granger.

The mare was restless and trying to get comfortable and we watched her for half an hour. She was often not easy to manage due to her lack of trust with people. The best person with her had been Jabbo and she had slowly been developing a good relationship with him. Rory quietly went in to her, and she tensed up until he crooned to her, and we could see her visibly relax, put her nose down to him as he slowly ran his hands over her and along her tummy. Then he lifted her tail to check what progress was being made. He patted her and came out of the foaling box and saying, "She's doing OK, right now, we would be best just waiting, and we can assist her if necessary."

So, we sat on some straw bales outside the foaling box waiting and then Granger said, "I'll go and feed round the horses and be back shortly."

We sat quietly not wanting to disturb the mare from her exertions. It was now five-thirty in the morning and finally I went to see Hermes and give Granger a hand.

Granger and I went back almost on tiptoe just in time to see Rory taking the birth sack off the foal and the mare was letting him deal with her precious new-born. He patted the mare and slowly came out of the box. The mare started to lick the foal and bond with him whilst she was cleaning him up. We watched the magic moment of new life and the mother's instinctive love.

"It's a colt," said Rory, "and he's got some long legs and a proper white star on his forehead. He'll need a name," he added.

"Rory's Star," I said, "that's his name. Thank you so much for helping us. Now I'll go and cook us some breakfast. I think we've all deserved it. See you both in half an hour," and off I toddled to tell Grandora the good news. Not the children though, until later, when the mare could let them see her quietly and when the foal was on its feet and suckling.

Rory came into the kitchen; his legs were so long, and he was so tall he filled the kitchen. He had oh, such blue eyes, straw coloured wavy hair with a lock falling over his eyes and a warm mischievous grin. "So, do you know the stallion? Is the foal well bred?" he asked.

I told him we thought it had to be Zoltan the Lipizzaner stallion. Then I told him about my trip to fetch Spangles and about ending up buying five more horses at the same time, as they were destined for slaughter, one of which was Scarlett the nervous mare.

"You did well then, I wouldn't let it happen to the horses on our ranch, but plenty of folks do. I rode to school every day on my pony and he's still at home and being ridden by my niece to go to school on now."

We chatted amicably about horses and not once about the war while I cooked some bacon and eggs.

Granger came in, followed by Miriam and Audrey. It was one of the most pleasant early mornings of my life, feeling safe, warm, and comfortable with my fellow travellers on this earth. Lennie came in and Granger told him about the foal, and we allowed him to run down at full pelt to see him as long as he was quiet when there. He came back elated – he had been in the stable and touched the foal along his back, down his legs, on his face, imprinting a human hand upon the new foal and the mare had let him and he loved the little colt. I told him Rory had been there when the foal was born, and I had called the foal Rory's Star.

"Rory's Star, I like that," he said. He had his breakfast and jumped up saying, "Right, I'm off to start mucking out."

Granger stood up as Lennie left and commented, "That's a decent lad, he's really good with the horses and helpful in the yard. I'll go down and give him a hand." Rory said he would take a breakfast bacon and egg sandwich upstairs to the New Zealander, Jim, we had staying with us.

"Would you mind one more down there later today?" he asked Granger as he was leaving.

"Not at all, you're always welcome in the stable yard, there's always plenty to do," said Granger.

I handed Rory the bacon and egg sandwich and Miriam and Audrey left and then I was left alone in the kitchen, and I contemplated having half an hour in bed. Mrs Revill arrived, followed by Rosie, and then Larry came in with Susan and Roger, and moments later followed by tousled haired, yawning Ruby and Lottie, both clutching dolls and followed by Zissa, the ever-faithful Pooch. I helped with breakfast for everyone as Mrs Revill took charge of the cooking and I went to call Adele and Talia who were dressed, bright and breezy and already on their way into the kitchen. I prepared a tray for Grandora and took her hot water, a boiled egg and toast up to her bedroom. I forgot about having half an hour extra in bed.

Grandora was pleased to hear about the new foal, and I relayed to her all the events of the busy morning. I shared a wonderful cup of real coffee from her stash and listened to the morning news on the wireless. I had grown to love the chatter of the children and the hectic lifestyle we now lived with them, but it was bliss to escape to Grandora's haven of peace and quiet and to have some time to relax. It had been decided to leave her sitting room downstairs for the present time and that the bedroom next door to hers would be my art room for the time being. I think she had realized that I was the best option to be next door to her than any more children having the room. I had left this wing of the house alone and refused to contemplate anyone using my parents' rooms. I had only just started to move all my art stuff in when I had broken my arm and we had rushed up to Scotland. So now I went next door and started to organise my art room for the first time in several weeks. I knew I wanted to sketch the new foal and I wanted to sketch Rory lounging, relaxed, and laughing down at the stables, a place where he was clearly happy to be. I wondered why he was staying with us, but I knew not to ask – there would be a good reason and no doubt a sad one. Hopefully here they had time out of the war to recover and rest from the stress and turmoil of the battle which they called burnout. I had quite a collection of sketches now and I longed to show them to Tantetta. I thought that the loose sketches I did of Portia in Scotland were brilliant and just needed framing; the very fact they were just a few simple pencil strokes made the subject, ie pregnant Portia, more poignant as she was waiting for Alastair and for the arrival of her baby.

Miriam came upstairs to find me and let me know she was leaving the next day for Scotland and to thank me for the continuing support I gave her and the jobs I found for her. She was now pretty much the official counsellor at the Hall for the RAF guys who came to stay here with the blessing of Captain Petersfield and the RAF and Professor Dendy Hillingdon.

"You are the reason you have these jobs, Miriam, you have the personality that encourages people to open up to you and you are such a good listener. Somehow you are able to let people find their own way through their problems, you are there to guide them and gently enable them to face their demons and find a way forward. I believe you have a God-given gift and you are using it now at a time when so many people need mental help as well as physical help. Fate guided you here and I am so glad to have met you." We hugged and went downstairs together to help with lunch for the children.

Larry came into the kitchen, looking worried.

"Anything on your mind, Larry?" I asked.

"I had permission from Grandora to speak to Malissa and she has suggested that I go to Cambridge University with her to discuss with a tutor the possibility of going to do a degree there," he told me.

"That's a lovely idea," I said, "so why do you look so worried?"

"I think it will be too posh for me," he said.

"Nonsense, it will do Cambridge good to have you studying there. Travel down and have a look round, stay with Nico and Malissa, and then decide if you would like to go and which course would suit you."

"All right, I will, but how do I get there? I have some money saved from every Saturday when I work with Arthur," he said, looking more cheerful.

"I will arrange the journey and any money you need; you deserve it, you are working so hard."

"Oh, by the way, Larry added, I spent some time in the library reading a little about the findings of a Rudolph Berlin, a German ophthalmologist, a Professor in Stuttgart. He has studied people unable to read and has called this 'dyslexia'. It might be interesting to find out more," he added.

I was stunned and very interested – my problem had a name. Perhaps I wasn't just dumb after all. "Thank you, Larry – if you learn anymore I would be grateful. Back to practicalities: in fact, could you do me a favour and take all the dogs for a walk after lunch and any children who want to go with you, please."

Miriam chipped in, "I will come too if I may, I need some fresh air; it looks like the fog is lifting and the sun will come out."

Then everyone seemed to pile into the kitchen at the same time and we served lunch as if we were a cafeteria. After lunch I told them all about the new foal and I walked to the stables with them to let them all have a peek at the beautiful new-born foal on his long wobbly legs.

The children all made good progress at school and after Larry's trip to Cambridge he was working even harder to get into university. He was now fifteen and growing into a polite young man, although his passion for social reform never dwindled. Lennie was not a star at school, just a steady trier, and he had expressed a desire to stay at Willup Hall with the horses forever. Adele and Talia were now both accomplished young musicians and their schoolwork was outstanding. They practised endlessly on the piano in the big sitting room which had been cold and without a fire in the beginning, but when we realized the extent of their dedication, we had made sure a fire was lit every day during the cold months for them. Ruby was seven and still at the junior school with her best friend Lottie. Any work Lottie found difficult, Ruby helped her with and was a patient understanding little teacher. She had Lottie's back whatever the situation at school or at home. To me Ruby grew prettier in looks every day and she had the sweetest temperament and I loved her dearly. Susan and Roger had settled in very well and they enjoyed going to see the Hardy children during the holidays to help on the farm and to play with Star, Luna, Reuben and Roscoe. Lacey had become keen on the goats and their new kids which had been left behind on the smallholding and so after a discussion with Osian she was thrilled to have our goats to increase her herd. She was now producing goat's milk. There was a collective sigh of relief from Granger and Osian that the goats had at last gone as we had all been forever catching them from their 'walkabouts' and mending broken fences.

We saw Malissa and Nico every month when they would spend a long weekend with us and join in with whatever the children were doing according to the weather. Chess or Backgammon if cold, Bridge with Grandora and Audrey of course, card games, snakes and ladders and in the good weather, riding, cricket, football, rounders and table tennis just about any time as the table was now indoors next to the school room. They all went on long walks called expeditions, complete with sandwiches and flasks, and they would take every dog we had on the place. Sometimes I would plan to pick up the youngest in the trap with Hermes at an arranged place and then I would drive back with them in the trap. I had resumed my ambulance duties but doing two nights a week and one day. Osian was still working four nights a week and still in the Home Guard and on night duty as an incendiary fighter one night a week. He looked very tired as he still tried to work just as hard in the garden during the day. I was struggling to help him in the garden and learn as much as I could, but I didn't have Ossian's green fingers – sometimes I think a plant just looked at me and

died. Frankie was now back in the army, training new recruits
in mechanics as he had passed his mechanics exams with flying
colours. He was not likely to go back into active combat as he still
had difficulty using his arm and hand, but was needed to help
maintain all the vehicles at the army depot whilst training others.
We missed him dreadfully and I wondered how long it would all
go on, this living with constant uncertainty of who we would
lose to the war next. Rationing continued to blight our lives: in
March electricity, coal and gas were rationed and our clothing
rationing was decreased, although as always our farm and Osian's
gardening activities produced plenty of food for the war effort
and us – we ensured the villages didn't go hungry either.

I regularly oversaw the estate more as Humphrey, a kind and
patient man now in his seventies, was slowing down. He followed
the old way and didn't understand the need to modernise and
increase production. My grandfather always wanted to be ahead
of the game and was always trying new methods and machinery,
and I wanted to emulate him. I saw our Vicar Bramwell Stevens
every few weeks for tea to hear his view on how the people in the
village were coping and who might need some extra help of food
and fuel. Odin loved to meet up with his sister Poppy as she was
always with Bramwell. I heard just as much and more from Rosie
or Mrs Revill, however, and I continued the tradition of caring
for the villagers' needs started by Grandora many years before.
I visited all our farms now with Humphrey or without him, and
had at last become more confident when dealing with everyone
and any problems which arose, as they always did.

Jabbo came home. He just strolled up the drive with his kit
bag and went straight to the stables to see Zoltan and it was then
he found him in a paddock turned out with the hackney mare,
now Zolly's girlfriend Scarlett. Also there of course was little

Rory's Star enjoying having a mummy and daddy to annoy. It was the only way we found we could get Zoltan to eat and stop moping: allowing him to stay with his girlfriend. Since he had been turned out with Scarlett he had changed and almost settled down. Then Jabbo came home, and he was so happy to see his old friend nuzzling him and wanting his ears rubbing. We left them spending time alone together and Scarlett was pleased to see Jabbo, the one person she had always got on with. Jabbo was thrilled with the foal and later Lennie was quick to show Jabbo how well he was doing training the little fellow to the halter and to be led up and down the paddock.

I didn't hear from Tiff, and I didn't ask Jabbo where he had been. He either would tell me in his own time or not. The summer holidays arrived, and all the children got on as usual, running around the estate on bikes or on horses and ponies or just lazing under trees on hot days reading. Swimming continued in the river and a couple of visiting Australian RAF men strung up a swing from a tree over the river where it was shallow and so we heard lots of screams and laughing coming from there on hot days as they swung over the water and got a dunking when they fell off. Audrey organised lesson mornings, which could one day be following the countries where the war was taking place, or craft mornings and there was crochet and knitting for all with Danielle holding the class. Jabbo came into the classroom to give a demonstration on whittling for the older children and how to make little wooden boats to race under the bridge, which was a very popular pastime. I could see a change in the children now, though Theodore and George still came and joined in with Larry, Lennie, and Tad, but they were growing up and away from the games the little girls played. Roger still followed his sister Susan everywhere and they played with Ruby, Lottie, Adele, Talia and

Anna-Sara and Avigail, who always spent the summers with us away from London. Reuben and Star came over for games of football, cricket and camping out with everyone. The scouts still joined us for their summer camp and games of rounders, cricket, and the now annual football match.

Everyone took part in the planning for the annual Garden Party. This was a highlight of the summer calendar, and we always invited our local soldiers and RAF folks to join in with the villagers. Of course, Jabbo gave a vaulting demonstration with Zoltan and Zippy, and the girls had a dog's obstacle course competition with outsiders allowed to compete with their dogs too. All the usual competitions took place, and we had music from our two young ladies, Adele on the violin and Talia on an old accordion which she had been practising on, accompanied by Tad on a flute, George on guitar and Jabbo on some Moroccan drums. Osian's plant and honey stall did very well as usual and Mrs Revill's jam stall sold out. We made carrot scones, and cold sausage and egg pie, and wartime almond biscuits to serve on our stall. The games were Pin the moustache on Hitler and Slat the Rat, Skittles, guess the weight of the cake, the sack race, flower arranging competition and the best embroidered tea cloth; it was a busy day for all of us. Oh, and the best poem judged by Grandora. Won by Larry in his age category and by Talia in her age category.

Talia wrote:

I love Norfolk
Where Marsh Harriers hover high

I love Norfolk
Where sand and sea meet the sky

I love Norfolk
Where valleys flow before your eyes

I love Norfolk
Muddy pigs enjoy open sties

I love Norfolk
Where crystal rivers birth mayflies

I love Norfolk
Where prowling foxes call and cry

I love Norfolk
Fields of bright pheasants in a nye

I love Norfolk
Green and fertile as ships pass by

I love Norfolk
Now you know some reasons why.

I was so proud of them. Again, I hoped in our little corner of Britain we gave happiness to so many people if only for a day. Lottie and Ruby won their age group poetry competition with a poem about snakes:

Super slimy sand snakes
Swimming south for supper
Such sea weedy stormy seas
So swimming south for supper
Sea urchin sausages

Sounding sweet and smelly
Said super slimy sand snakes
Sleeping snoring on seabed.

A bit yucky, but Malissa and I were very proud of the effort they had made.

A Padre stationed at the same army camp as Frankie came with him and brought some soldiers to the Garden party to enjoy a day away from their base. The Padre opened the Garden Party with prayers and then Grandora officially welcomed everyone and declared the Fete open. Rory came with several RAF guys and eight American flyers from their base, and all the villagers turned up and the men in uniform caused quite a stir with the ladies and young girls. On hearing Miriam was due back from Scotland to help at the garden party, Rory jumped into the enormous troop carrier and drove to the station to pick her up. Miriam was shocked and very amused to be picked up with her little suitcase in such a huge military vehicle. Rory was clearly very taken with her, and it was obviously mutual. They both soon got stuck in at the party and helped with the games. The local dance group danced to the music of Glenn Miller, with the girls in bobby socks and dancing shoes, with ribbons in their hair, and the young boys with Brylcreemed slicked back hair. We finished the Garden Party with a singalong to several Vera Lynn songs – I'll Be With You in Apple Blossom Time and of course We'll Meet Again, followed by God Save The King. It was a great success.

The rest of the summer we held friendly cricket matches on the village field or here at home on our pitch in the park, now officially Willup Hall cricket ground, and sometimes we travelled to local away matches. Those not too far away as fuel was becoming harder to buy. These matches now often included any military personnel staying with us, plus Jabbo, George, Theo, Osian, Reuben, Tad, Lennie and Larry, and with Granger often officiating as umpire. The girls went to watch with Audrey and myself, but I think meeting other girls to play with and the picnic was what appealed to them more than the actual game. Our boys always hoped that any visiting Australians, Indians or New Zealanders were going to be on our side as they were usually such good cricketers It always depended on who was available as many were away fighting or couldn't get leave from their bases.

Colonel Brian Orpington-Jones had been round again complaining about us turning the Hall into a dangerous bed of foreigners and spies and that my father would put an end to it when he returned. He was disgusted with the RAF pilots and crew staying with us and said they were a disgrace to the Military, they were cowards and in the Great War he would have had them shot. He continued to complain about Jabbo not being the 'right sort' to have in the Home Guard. Grandora decided enough was enough and he was not welcome at the Hall anymore. We had allowed the Home Guard to use the woods and estate to practise on and the village hall for their meetings, and if the Colonel continued spreading his malicious views, we would have to rescind these privileges.

We knew we were lucky in this part of Britain as we heard so many awful stories of destruction and death going on all around us. We didn't need a horrible stupid gossip like Colonel Orpington-Jones spreading hurtful lies. We had all been jumpier about the bombers flying over us and on more than one occasion we had all run down to the cellars and spent the night there trying to sleep on the camp beds which was a nightmare and ended up with us staying awake most of the night. It was on those rare occasions I was glad I was driving the ambulance on the night shift.

One night when I was not on duty, June 12, 1942, we heard loud explosions and crumps in the distance on the evening of that awful night. We headed for the cellars. We found out later that a 500lb bomb had been dropped and smashed through the roof of The Eagle Hotel in King's Lynn, destroying it completely. It destroyed the fish shop next door and 42 people were killed and thirteen were injured. The nearby cattle market was damaged and the council dump, plus St Faiths Church, Greenland Fishery, and the Victory Pub. It was thought a single German aircraft flying home after a bombing raid had decided to get rid of any bombs still in its hold and ditched them over King's Lynn. I was disappointed not to have been on duty that night to help in any way, and also relieved I had missed the carnage.

The children went back to school in September after helping us with the harvest. Reuben came and stayed with us during harvest and Lennie took time off school with George and Theo. All children were expected to work when they could and help the war effort. Harvesting of all food was considered important and essential work. Larry was working hard at school to pass his exams and much of his spare time was spent helping Grandora with her research into our family's ancestry, but he enjoyed helping in the Walled Garden. As a result, he was excused from the corn harvest as growing produce such as salad and vegetables on a big scale, as we did, was also classed as war work. October came and on the 5th we celebrated Eid, the Muslim ceremony following Ramadan, with Jabbo doing the cooking again outside in his replica tagine. I managed to swop two big capons for a front of lamb with the butcher again and we sat outside in the Walled Garden and the meal was delicious. Whenever Rory had any leave he would spend his time with us, well particularly Miriam, helping with the harvest, horses, apple picking when we made cider and gathering apples for winter storage. He was very handy with the lug pole, being so tall. He soon had the apples falling.

November arrived and we all walked to the village church to see the scouts and brownies marching from the school behind the village brass band. This year was different as we also had a contingent of soldiers and RAF men marching to the church, which gave even greater solemnity to the occasion, and we all squeezed into our beautiful little church. Afterwards we gathered around the memorial to the local soldiers who fell in the Great War and laid our wreaths, then part of the beautiful poem by Laurence Binyon was read.

They shall not grow old, as we that are left grow old
Age shall not weary them, nor the years condemn,
At the going down of the sun and in the morning
We will remember them.

This always moved me and more so than ever as the names of two local lads killed at the Battle of Dunkirk were read out.

News filtered in that another offensive was underway in North Africa and I listened enthusiastically as I was beginning to wonder if that's where Tiff and Jabbo had been. It would make sense regarding Jabbo going over there when he was from Morocco and Tiff knew him and his background. I began to switch the wireless on throughout the day hoping to hear good news from there. Finally after helping Granger with the horses I returned for lunch to hear the news I had been waiting for. Operation Torch in November 1942 has been a success.

The bombing continued in all our cities and ports and casualties remained high and people were made homeless. I had a telephone call from a contact asking me if I could find room for an Asian family of Sikhs, a mother, two boys and her mother-in-law. Their home had been destroyed in Birmingham and they had no other family to help them. Of course, I said yes, and they duly arrived with next to no possessions at all. We had to house them in the schoolroom for a week whilst work was completed on an old groom's quarters, similar to Danielle's only slightly bigger. We had already started developing the upstairs rooms in the loft with a downstairs sitting room and kitchen; now we added the bathroom. Thank goodness Jabbo was back here working with Granger. Arthur came to the rescue with a decent second-hand pot sink and units for the kitchen and piping for the plumbing. I don't know how he did it, but he always did, bless him, and I wasn't going to ask him how because these people from Birmingham needed a home and that was the priority. Mrs Hubbard was given some material from our attic's store for curtains and bedding. The knitters diverted their attention from knitting for the army to knitting for our latest refugees, cardigans, jumpers, and bed covers. They came with nothing as everything had been lost in their bombed house. We moved Mrs Singh and her family into her new quarters exactly one week after she had arrived, and they were delighted. They were neighbours to Danielle and Tad, who immediately got on well with the two boys Ashneer and Virinder. Mrs Singh's husband was Dr Gurdas Singh, who had joined up with the British army medical corps and he was believed to be in Burma. Bargitta, the mother of Dr Singh, was soon knitting and helping serve tea at the Knitters Club gatherings and her daughter-in-law Panaya was soon cooking light bites and spicy vegetables like karri with lemon juice, red peppers, turmeric and flour for the knitters to try. She had to be inventive as many of the ingredients were not available because of the war and restrictions.

Christmas arrived and we found the rationing even more tedious and difficult. No wrapping paper this year as paper continued to be in short supply so we had to be inventive. Osian had woven baskets during the summer when the willow trees' branches were green. These grew by the river and in early summer the stems were pliable. There was a basket for every child to have a few presents put in, plus they still had their Xmas stockings from previous years. Of course, Susan and Roger were also included this time with new stockings being made by Mrs Hubbard with some of Grandora's exotic material from her travels. We had to be inventive with the presents, and the soap I had given to friends in the past was now almost impossible to buy – all we were allowed was 4 ounces of household soap and 2 ounces of toilet soap per month. Sweets were still rationed to 12 ounces a month and now alcohol was difficult to buy. Shortages of everything were getting worse and worse. We had cockerels and some turkeys, which were all destined for the canteens of the RAF in Norfolk; feeding our fighting men was of major importance though. Our beef regularly went to the government, but we had never been successful with the goats as we had planned. Osian was our poultry farmer now and he was doing a marvellous job. He assured me we would have some cockerels and least a few turkeys for our village and ourselves. That was for all of us to share. We had a large amount of people to feed and plenty of vegetables for our table and for the villagers. Hugh told me he would have some rabbits ready for Christmas for us and for the Salvation Army and the Red Cross to cook for Christmas dinners for those in need. He had culled a stag for us, and it was hanging in the game house ready for us to use. Hopefully, there would be some pheasants for the Christmas holidays too. Instructions had gone out to our farms to make sure they had something for us to give to charities which prepared food for the community and the elderly at Christmas and our village. Cheese was produced at two of our farms and we also had plenty of eggs from our hens, all because of Osian's good husbandry. We had plenty of wood for our fires and we shared what we could in the village, and we made sure the Hardys had enough to keep their fires going.

The knitters had been knitting soft teddies, rabbits and ragdolls as presents for all the children in the area and for the Red Cross and Salvation Army. Baby cot blankets were being knitted and socks, gloves, scarves and hats. They catered for everyone. There were teams of knitters working in shifts in our schoolroom during the weeks up to Christmas. Mrs Revill had been saving the sugar ration allowed for all of us to be able to make a Christmas cake and truffles using cake crumbled up and mixed with honey and a little milk hardened in the freezer and then rolled in a little melted chocolate, mixed with condensed milk, and melted butter. I managed to get some chocolate from Rory who was given it from some American flyers. Grandora bought a selection of sweets, rhubarb and custard boiled sweets, gummi bears, jelly babies, candy canes sherbet and liquorice, Fox's mints, boy blue whirls and Cadburys Caramello; she was brilliant, sweets for all the children – we just had to divide them up and make paper cones. We made the cones from newspapers, filled them with sweets and tied at the top with any ribbon we could find. We had nuts from our own trees for their Christmas stockings and little wooden boats crafted by Granger, each one with the children's names on.

We had managed to protect our children staying here with us from having to contribute to the war effort by working as so many children had to do. Children were expected to salvage scrap glass or paper and grow vegetables, so our girls and boys had to learn how to knit. Knitting comforts for the troops was a great way for them to contribute to the war effort. Many children in Britain between the ages of fourteen and seventeen were in full-time employment. They worked in aircraft production, shipbuilding, and vehicle manufacture, or in shops. They were needed to work because so many men were away fighting. From sixteen to eighteen they had to register for some form of National Service, even if they had full-time jobs. Boys would get their call-up papers for the armed forces when they became eighteen and girls had to join the Women's Auxiliary services or other essential war work. Ours had been too young for work and had been protected by us so far, yet as they grew older, we knew they would be expected to do more to contribute to our country. Luckily, they really did have jobs on our farm producing food and they really did do some hard work, particularly at harvest time.

We held our customary Christmas Eve carol service in our large reception hall round the Christmas tree in the early afternoon Although we were two hours ahead on Daylight Saving Time as we remained throughout the war, we thought it was prudent to finish early for everyone to get home before blackout if possible. This year the hall was jam packed with servicemen and friends and family. We served a punch concoction made with fruit cordial produced by us from our fruit and our own elderflower wine; it was definitely an alcoholic punch, and we were all merry. The children had their own non-alcoholic fruit punch. One of our estate farms had been making beer with potatoes which was interesting, but not to my taste. However, it was enjoyed by some of the men at the parties. We sang carols to Talia and Adele playing on the piano and violin, with Tad on his flute; and passed around, with great difficulty in the crush, trays of homemade plain biscuits with tiny slithers of cheese from our dairy and homemade mushroom and Spam pâté. It was a fun evening, and we all appreciated the merriment of the occasion and the camaraderie. As the children were being either got ready for bed or taking themselves to bed, a knock on the door stopped them all in their tracks. It was Tiff and Scotty. I was thrilled, and I think I laughed and cried at the same time. The children mobbed him and had to be chased to bed by Tiff, all laughing – they were so happy to see him. We were expecting Malissa and Nico to arrive on Christmas Day and having Tiff and Scotty here was a bonus. We had invited Rory plus one to join us for Christmas dinner, so as usual we were a full house which was lovely even though a bit tiring. Scotty dropped a bit of a bombshell that evening, hoping I didn't mind him staying with us as he was meeting Merry here on Boxing Day. I didn't mind at all. I knew Merry and the boys were coming to see Osian and stay with us for the rest of the Christmas holidays, I just had no idea that Merry and Scotty were seeing each other. How exciting and interesting.

Christmas Day raced by with the best food we could serve, and it was imaginative and good to eat and a happy time for all of us. The children were pleased with their new pencils, crayons and fountain pens, and all the rest of their homemade presents. Grandora had managed to buy each one a diary containing plain paper so they could write whatever they wanted whenever they wanted. We played hunt the thimble and then charades with them. Tiff bought me a Scottish Faire Isle patterned scarves, beret, gloves and jumper in shades of autumn browns and ochre golden yellows. Is this a hint of where he was stationed? His unit must still be in Scotland as I had thought when I was staying there. He never discussed his work as it was all very hush-hush. He had brought hand knitted gloves for us all which we all thought was very funny as we already had lots of hand knitted gloves and scarves and hats from our knitting team. At least they were different patterns and colours. I gave him a fountain pen and a hand knitted jumper designed by Danielle, so it was very special. We laughed at our choice of presents. He stayed until New Year's morning and had to head back as it seemed something big was happening. I just overheard him talking to Scotty. I did find out he had been to Greece, Africa and Italy since I last saw him. We didn't talk about the war – it was the Christmas holidays, after all. He met and liked Rory, well who wouldn't; and Rory's plus one was Miriam. How curious everything was getting. We had some interesting billiard games with the boys taking part against the men and everyone having a go at table tennis and some wonderful cold and frosty walks with all the dogs. Dendy was another regular visitor – as a retired hospital consultant his wartime job was to report on the men's recovery progress and of course he always took time to see Grandora. It was a happy time in spite of all the difficulties. We also managed to give food parcels to all the villagers and attend church. We had quiet candlelit suppers with Grandora, playing bridge or chess afterwards and found out how everyone was fairing in their everyday lives. Of course, they all got roped in to play chess with Malissa or Nico, and Malissa was always the winner. I was so pleased to have Merry stay with us and catch up on what we had been doing since 1940 when I had stayed with her at the Vicarage on Dartmoor. Plus, I wanted to hear about all the news about her and Scotty, where they had met and when they had fallen for each other. George and Theodore were pleased to spend time with the Welsh contingent and their friendship with the boys grew stronger.

The Boxing Day Meet was a quiet affair this time as so few people were able to attend. It was a token Meet really as we only had four young teenage boys willing to be the quarry and run about

five miles with the hounds in hot pursuit and followed by just ten
mounted riders. Everyone else seemed to be on duty or serving
away from home. The war divided many families across the globe.

I gathered we were bombing in Europe much more now as we
heard the rumble of the enormous bomber planes taking off from
the runways near us. We had witnessed some of the dogfights
which took place in the skies, which thrilled the boys and horrified
me. Now it was the turn of the DH Mosquito, Lancasters, the
Boeing B-17 Flying Fortress, and the Boeing B-29 Superfortress
and all the rest of the bombers. We heard their engines growling
as they left in the night; it was frightening, and we all prayed
for their safe return. Sometimes in the early morning hours as
dawn was about to break, we heard them returning and I was
glad I didn't have the job of counting them in and waiting for
the stragglers. These brave young men were the same men who
came to us suffering from mental exhaustion or recovering from
injuries which they no longer needed to stay in hospital for their
recovery, but they were not yet fit enough for active duty. Burnout
was the stress they faced after doing so many flying missions that
they knew their chances of surviving diminished each time they
went on another mission. They witnessed the death of so many of
their comrades fighting in the skies. I hope the time they spent
with us was an oasis of calm, peace, fun and a time away from the
horror of what they were doing, which was so necessary if we were
to stand any chance of winning the war. Rory from Canada and
all the others who spent time with us could play sports together
or with our children, read in the library or sleep as much as they
wanted, and there was always someone to talk to about anything
other than the war and planes.

We had a very quiet dinner on New Year's Eve when all the
children had gone to bed with Tiff, Scotty, Merry, Grandora,

Miriam, Osian, Nico, Malissa, Audrey, and Danielle. Rory was held up at base and couldn't make it. I think we were all deep in our own thoughts about would we meet again here next year and how much longer could we go on with the war. So as 1943 arrived we were having more battle successes now, but it was far from over.

The year passed by in whirl of work and worry. No news was good news and we concentrated on caring for the children and the farm. The Battle for Stalingrad ended with a surrender by the German 6th army which was their first defeat, and we were all pleased. An interesting story emerged about the Calcutta Light Horse. They had managed to attack a German merchant ship, called Ehrenefeis, sheltering in Mormugoa Harbour a neutral Portuguese protectorate, in the Indian territory of Goa. The ship had been transmitting Allied positions to U-boats. Although the ship's Captain had declared it was having repairs done. They were brave men to conduct the attack when they had so few weapons. They had used rowing boats and limpet mines, so ending radio transmissions. We continued to lose far too many ships in convoys in the Atlantic trying to bring supplies to Britain.

It was reported in the papers of the success of the Dam Busters' raid called 'Operation Chastise'. Our brave pilots had flown their bombers low over the German dams in the Ruhr Valley, bombing the Mohn and Eder Dams, crippling the heart of Ruhr industries. The man who had made this possible invented the 'bouncing bomb' – he was called Barnes Wallis and he became a hero. Sadly, of 617 Squadron 145 Bomber Crew who left Scampton Grass aerodrome in Lancaster Bombers, only 80 returned from the mission back to Lincolnshire. They were all brave young men, most just in their early twenties.

We continued to enjoy films which came to our cinema and a favourite of mine was Humphrey Bogart in High Sierra plus

The Maltese Falcon and Casablanca. The children loved Charlie
Chaplin in The Gold Rush and all Walt Disney's cartoons like
Mickey Mouse and The Silly Symphonies and of course Snow White
and the Seven Dwarfs, Fantasia, and Pinocchio. Meanwhile, the
boys raved about Donald Bradman, the Australian cricket player,
the most perfect high-scoring batsman they said. Or they just loved
to discuss and try the techniques of Dennis Compton, the new
English star batsman. Cricket continued to be played during the
war as it was deemed a great morale booster. Our children all loved
the game and if there was a game being played in the locality they
would cycle there to watch, or to hopefully be allowed to play if the
team was short of players, which they frequently were. I listened to
Bing Crosby on the wireless, and Miriam and I gave performances,
singing his songs to anyone who would listen. Seriously, we were
not very good, but it was fun even when everyone shouted, 'Oh no
not again.' I loved his film Going My Way and the successful song
White Christmas. Marlene Dietrich singing Falling in Love Again
was a favourite for Grandora. She loved the ballet and before the
war had frequently been to Sadler's Wells and had seen Margot
Fonteyn in Swan Lake, Giselle and The Sleeping Beauty, and she
was hoping to be able to follow her career again if the horrid
war ever ended. Audrey, Miriam, Lucy, Sheila, Rosie, Grandora,
Danielle and I all went to see Gone With The Wind, and we were
all smitten and loved the fabulous film; well, I should say we loved
Clark Gable. So, it was horrible to hear on June 1st that Leslie
Howard, who also starred in the film, was on a scheduled passenger
plane flight 777 DC-3 BOAC flying over the Bay of Biscay when it
was shot down by eight German Junkers JO88s with the loss of all
seventeen people on board. Why eight Junkers? It was rumoured
the Nazis thought Churchill was on board. We heard such sad news
daily and never got used to it.

Chapter 33

Alex Bouchet, Brutal Attack

Alex worked his way down the row of vines, pruning and tying up; meanwhile, Marcell worked opposite him; they worked in companionable silence. Aurielle and Nadine were working up at the farm cleaning out the hut where their few chickens lived and then weeding their precious vegetable patch. Simone and Claude where at school and Jacques was following Aurielle and playing with a kitten. It hadn't been easy for any of them since the occupation had begun. The lack of food was difficult because as soon as they grew any, first the Milice, the French police, then Nazi Germans, came and took it. It was against the law to keep any food secretly or even wine. Their wine now was taken from them every year – all the wine they grew and bottled was claimed by the German government. French people were now forbidden to drink wine. At least they managed to have some bread now that Alex was the village baker. Every morning he brought back supplies for the soldiers living in the Chateau and some for them. He was allowed to hunt with the Gruppenfuhrer for wild boar, deer, pheasant and partridge. Well, he was allowed to find out the location of the prey and take the Gruppenfuhrer there astride his very own mare Trudi. He more or less lined up the shot for the Gruppenfuhrer, then Alex organised carting the carcass back to the Chateau, butchering it, cooking it, making sausages from it and having any scraps that were left over for the family. When he could he made some pork sausages at the bakery and made sure there were some little sausages for the village children. Aurielle cooked for the soldiers in the Chateau everyday using produce from the farm which was intended for themselves. The rest of the time they all kept themselves to themselves and kept busy, always working and finding jobs to keep out of the soldiers' way. They did not antagonise the soldiers on instructions from Marcell, who needed to keep a low profile so he could continue to liaise with the Resistance without causing suspicion.

Alex would take acorns and waste vegetables – not that there were many of those – deep into the woods and put on the trails which he knew the wild boar used to encourage them into clearings where they could get a good shot at them. He understood they were nervous of humans and kept hidden in the forest and they were difficult to track and find. By regularly going into the woods and leaving food, he began to build a picture of their favourite haunts and their most likely locations. After the fall of France, Alex and Joseph regularly made trips deep into the forest for boar or deer hunting to supplement their food ration. After June 22, 1942, when Pierre Laval encouraged French workers to volunteer to work in Germany to secure the release of French prisoners of war, Joseph started to make plans to go into hiding deep in the forests and hills of the region. He was determined to escape the Service du travail obligatoire which was forced labour in Germany. Finally, when Fritze Sauckel, called the 'slave master of Europe', was charged with obtaining labour from across Europe, he used intimidation and threats to create the workforce needed in Germany as more and more German men were conscripted into the German army. Joseph went into hiding, like so many other young men and women. After Joseph had gone into hiding for good, Alex would go with Marcell to find provisions they needed in the forests. Marcell needed a reason to go into the forest to operate his wireless. It was Marcell who had insisted Alex had new papers forged saying he was married to Nadine and that the baby was his. This was to protect Nadine from being made to work for the Government. It also protected the baby and with Alex having poor eyesight and being a farmworker, he hoped to keep them on the Chateau estate. He did succeed in this objective, and they had no orders to go and work elsewhere.

The Gruppenfuhrer did not like them disappearing at all and demanded an explanation for their reason for going into the forests surrounding the Chateau. So, Marcell explained they hunted for wild mushrooms and truffle as well as wild boar, deer and pheasant, and that is what Aurielle had cooked for him, and that Alex made sausages from the boar meat. The Gruppenfuhrer insisted he rode Trudi and that he was taken into the forest to see where they went. He took one soldier with him who had orders to shoot them if they were lying. That was the first time the Gruppenfuhrer shot and killed a boar in France. Apparently, he had land and a house in the Black Forest to hunt there. After that he insisted on going every Sunday with Alex, who was now allowed into the forest to find the trails or the boar and put food out for them. One day Marcell heard from a distraught villager that the baker had been marched into the village square, stood against a wall and shot for refusing to give all the food in the bakery to the soldiers. He had insisted it was to be sold to the villagers.

The Gruppenfuhrer was not pleased when he discovered there was now no one to bake bread for the chateau. That is, until Alex volunteered to bake in the bakery every morning. It was agreed by the baker's widow he could use the bakery from four o'clock in the morning and then go home to work in the vineyard and she would take charge of selling what he had made. This worked well for both of them. Alex had more flour to use and could supply the soldiers in the Chateau with good bread and pastries, plus the village, Nadine, Marcell, and the children. Another bonus was the widow of the dead baker was able to earn some money to keep for herself.

It had been bad enough when the Vichy Government was in charge, acting on behalf of the Nazi regime. They were as cruel if not much worse than the Nazi Germans against their fellow French compatriots. The laws inflicted on the people living within the borders of the Vichy government were Fascist and draconian, and the French police were rigorous in enforcing them. Now since 1942 they had fifteen German soldiers billeted at the Chateau and they ate a great deal of food, all stolen from the local people. Marcell insisted they did their necessary jobs and kept their heads down and didn't do anything to antagonize the soldiers. If there was the smallest amount of food that they grew that they could sell, he now took over the job of taking it to market in the nearest local small town. Here he had a contact with a forger who made the necessary documents with the photographs of people the resistance group were trying to move on or hide. Marcell had contact with Joseph and the small but growing band of men living rough in the forests who were escaping from being forced to work in Germany. Sometimes they needed papers for their contacts and to help them move around France, and they had various drop off zones deep in the forest behind the Chateau, exchanging photos and new forged documents. Marcell was always careful to appear compliant with the German soldiers staying at the Chateau so he could carry out his clandestine duties without suspicion. It helped to say they were tracking deer and wild boar for the table and so far this had been believed and it was true. When Alex was pretty sure of some tracks repeatedly being used by the wild animals the Gruppenfuhrer would accompany him mounted on Trudi with his right-hand man walking with them. This German soldier was a Unteroffizier, well over six feet tall and a huge muscular man who seemed to be his most trusted man. His name was Horst, and he was kind to Claude, Simone, and Jacques when he saw them.

The weeks turned into months and the months into years and eventually the Gruppenfuhrer had to return to German to see his family. He told Alex he would be back in two weeks and to keep feeding the wild boar and tracking them until he returned for some more hunting. He left thirteen soldiers behind to carry on with their administrative work and some soldiers to implement any orders. As it was very rural so far they had not been kept very busy. Within three days of his departure, a black military vehicle appeared at the Chateau and out stepped a tall man dressed all in black leather; he was a Sturmbannfuhrer working for the SS and dealing with enforcing the strict code of racial isolation of the Jews, seizing their assets, and deporting them to concentration camps. It filled the family in the farm with great fear and misgivings. They carried on with their work as usual, quietly and discreetly. Aurielle carried on doing the cooking and Louise carried on doing the washing and ironing and Marie came weekly to clean. As two weeks came to an end and before the Gruppenfuhrer returned, Alex went into the forest with a knapsack of food for the wild boar so he could have an idea of the best place to find them to hunt. He had no idea he was being followed by the Sturmbannfuhrer and some soldiers. Alex stopped in a clearing to look for any evidence of boar activity and putting his knapsack on the floor he reached in and withdrew a water flask. "STOP what you are doing." It was the Sturmbannfuhrer, surrounded by armed soldiers with their guns trained on Alex. "What are you doing here?"

Alex was about to say hello when he recognised who it was, but the guns aimed at him froze him in his tracks. "I am bringing food for the boar and tracking where they are." He faltered because it sounded stupid as these soldiers had not been served any roast boar or venison by Aurielle.

"I don't believe you, give me your bag. Stand back," he screamed as Alex bent down to pick up his bag.

"It's just old waste vegetable roots," Alex added.

"You don't bring food into a forest unless it is for somebody," the Sturmbannfuhrer snarled. He indicated to a soldier to bring the bag to him and to empty its contents onto the forest floor.

"It is just for the wild boar," said Alex trembling.

"You liar, tell me why you have come so far, are you meeting someone here?"

"No, not at all," Alex began.

Next a soldier who had moved behind him slammed a rifle butt into his ribs, breaking first his humerus and then five ribs. Alex bent over with surprise and a pain seared though his whole body. Next as he collapsed on his knees a boot met his femur, he heard the crack, and he sank to the earth floor in a new world of unbelievable pain. Another boot met his jawbone and the side of his head. His glasses flew to the ground and a boot ground them into shards of glass and mangled wire. Alex tried to speak but found he could hardly breathe with the blood in his mouth; he tried to move and just as a new wave of agony engulfed him he heard a voice he knew: "Hor auf damit" – stop it. Alex lapsed into unconsciousness. The Gruppenfuhrer had returned, and Marcell had rushed to him saying he believed Alex had been followed into the forest by the Sturmbannfuhrer as young Claude had seen them follow him. He had ordered that Trudi be saddled up and he had cantered her into the forest, taking the path he had taken before with Alex. His Unteroffizier followed on, running and nearly keeping up. Just when he thought he had gone the wrong way he heard a scream and went in the direction it came from. He saw Alex on the floor and shouted to the idiot man in black to stop. "Do you realize he is here on my orders? He is tracking wild boar to feed us all and he is the village baker – now we have neither meat nor bread." He wanted to say you fool but knew better than to say that in front of the soldiers. The SS had many ways of getting back at you if displeased. He briefly wondered if people like him had ever had a mother and been nursed and at what point in their lives had they become sub-human serial killers. "I believed he was meeting with Resistance workers, and it is my duty and yours to keep track of everyone's movements. I will leave him to you; he was dishonest in my view and deserves all he got." With that the Sturmbannfuhrer marched away with the soldiers. The Gruppenfuhrer told Horst to stay with Alex and he would tell Marcell to fetch the mule with the cart for him. The Sturmbannfuhrer had wreaked many troubles onto the tiny town in his two weeks stay at the area and he moved on the next day to chase any 'undesirables' hiding in the next area he terrorized.

Alex was unconscious for most of the week. The local doctor was called, and he insisted Alex went to hospital and organised for an ambulance to fetch him. Alex made a very slow recovery. He was unrecognizable for three weeks and unable to leave hospital for six long pain filled weeks. Finally, he was brought home and remained bedridden for weeks until Marcell managed to make a rudimentary wheelchair by cobbling a chair to some old pulley wheels and welding pipes on to it to make handles. He also took Alex out in the little farm cart with Flavie pulling it and took him to see how the grapes were growing. Alex started to walk in time using homemade crutches made by himself as he waited for his bones to heal. He even carved new clogs for them all. Shoes were impossible to buy or find, and many people in the towns now wore clogs as they all did on the countryside. He had pain relief from the doctor, but like many things now unavailable medicine was hard to come by. The Gruppenfuhrer managed to get hold of some pills for Alex and they helped him sleep at night. Nadine and Aurielle were now pulled out with work and looking after the children. Marcell did go looking for boar, but without the success Alex had achieved; at least he was able to liaison with the Resistance. The Gruppenfuhrer riding Trudi went with Horst and managed to shoot two stags which fed the soldiers, but not the family in the farm. Nadine cooked for the soldiers in the Chateau and Aurielle became the baker in the village, and so life jogged along with many trips and falls on the way. When they started the vendange with help from the village, Alex was able to sit on the cart and drive Flavie up and down the rows of vines, collecting the panniers of grapes tipped in by the pickers and take them to the hopper where they were taken out for him. At least he was doing something and that made him feel better and helped with his long recovery, even if all the wine was stolen and shipped to Germany. Marcell had brought him some second-hand reading glasses from a trip to the market so at last he could see quite well again.

The days came when they knew the Allies were back on French soil fighting to free France and Marcell would go into the forest as much as he could with Alex in the cart looking for boar tracks while Marcell would use the wireless and listen for news. They knew the Resistance were now fighting and making a difference, and they had new weapons, food, boots, and money parachuted in by the Allies. Then the day came when the Gruppenfuhrer went to Alex who was sitting in the sun making clogs.

"We are leaving now. I advise you to disappear from here for a few days, there will be other fighting soldiers coming this way and I doubt they will be soft with anyone they find. Go now, that is my advice. Good luck." He clicked his heels and turned and went to the front of the Chateau and in a cloud of dust all the soldiers sped away in their vehicles.

Alex had no idea they were going – there hadn't been any indication to any of them of their imminent departure. He sat alone in the sun and silence. He then hauled himself to his feet and blew on his little used whistle given to him to summon for help since his attack. Claude was the first to ask him what he needed and on hearing the news he rushed off to fetch the others.

"Right, plan A, we are going to the caves for a few days; we have prepared for this, now get Trudi harnessed up in her cart and Flavie in his," said Marcell, anxious to be away from their home.

With the goats now four of them and the hens loaded up, they started their journey of three miles to the hidden valley where there were caves only locals knew about. Marcell had cycled to the few houses at the crossroads to advise the occupants to join them and told them where he would meet them. He then made his way to his radio wireless and sent a message to the local Maquis warning them and a message to the villagers to vacate the village if they could and to be on their guard against possible reprisals. The little group spent the next few nights hiding out without any fires and little food until they had the all-clear from the Maquis

who now had some SOE, Special Operations Executive, with them.
These had been parachuted in to conduct espionage, sabotage,
and reconnaissance to aid the local resistance movement against
the Axis powers. They returned to the Chateau and finally a man
called Tiff called to see them with a Moroccan called Jabbo. They
had come to give them the heart-breaking news that Joseph had
been shot and killed.

Chapter 34

The Archer Children Arrive

New Year's Day arrived on a blustery, cold morning and we all sat around the breakfast table in the kitchen chatting. No one wanted to move or break the spell of our few days of happiness and being together safe here in Norfolk. The world and war seemed far away for those precious few days we spent together. I had at last received news of my mother who was a prisoner in a camp in Singapore, but no news about the whereabouts of my father. My mother had been allowed to write a very short letter telling us, briefly, she was well and not to worry about her. It was so brief it was odd and when I told Tiff he said it would have been censored by the guards and just be pleased for now that at last we knew she was alive. We sent a parcel of knitted shawls, knickers, playing cards, paper and pencils, which seems odd, but it was Grandora's suggestion. I just prayed she was allowed to receive it and would let us know.

We continued to see Rory and he became one of our family. Miriam was still working on her counselling course and spent more time working with the guys who came to stay with us as part of her course project. She always stayed with Audrey, and they had become firm friends so Rory would often spend his time staying in the cottage when he came over on his motorbike. He had bought it once he realized he could visit us whenever he had some leave. Sometimes he brought other 'flyers' with him for the weekend and we loved meeting all these brave young men from many different countries. Talia and Adele mixed easily with everyone; however, their bond as sisters was very strong and they were rarely seen apart. They loved their music and long walks with the dogs. They could often be found in Danielle's and Tad's cottage at the stables, or they spent time with Miriam, Anna-Sara and Avigail when they were staying with us in Audrey's cottage. Susan and Roger were invited by Margaret down to Gamekeepers Cottage on many occasions to join them for tea or to join in with whatever they were doing. Theo and George were now doing more homework and like all children over twelve in Britain, had jobs to do on Saturdays and after school. I suppose Margaret just liked having the children with her now and I know we were all aware of the trauma Susan and Roger had been through and were still battling with the shock of losing their parents so suddenly, in the bombing. They were constantly frightened of the planes flying over us and any loud bangs, and Roger didn't want to be away from his sister, Susan. When the Avro Lancaster bombers flew over there was no mistaking their four Merlin engines growling in the sky, and it was a menacing sound even though we knew they were our bombers. We had become pretty good at recognising the sights and sounds of aircraft and were able to identify them, the German planes or ours. Roger had also been frightened of dogs and Margaret had decided that if he saw them enough and helped with their care, he would get used to them, and it was working.

We heard that the siege of Leningrad had at last been lifted on January 27th, 1944, when the Moscow to Leningrad rail line re-opened after two years and seven months of the German army's forced containment. It would take time for the dreadful news to be reported to us, of the full extent of the siege and the thousands that had either frozen or starved to death in Leningrad during those two years. By March news filtered through that the Allies were bombing Cassino in Italy in a new offensive to take control of the country. It was there a contingent of Polish soldiers fought a bitter battle with thousands losing their lives.

Here at home, we had endured a biting cold January and February and it was a constant struggle to keep the Hall warm and the fires lit with our logs. Coal was used for industry and to fuel the production of bombs and machinery, so coal for domestic use was rationed and our supply limited; a better supply would have kept the fires going longer. As it was, we were forever feeding logs onto the fires which burnt away so quickly. The hallways in Willup Hall were draughty and freezing and so we all rushed from room to room, from fireplace to fireplace. The knitting group were kept busy taking old jumpers to pieces which had been outgrown, and re-knitting new jumpers using all the old wool. We kept the old school room fire and boiler constantly lit so that was always a warm, welcoming place. March arrived with the same horrible cold weather, with icy ponds, hard frosts and more snow.

We sent the children out with Granger and Donk, pulling his little cart to collect kindling and firewood from around the estate on Saturday mornings. Fortunately, the children loved doing this and never thought of it as work. They would all scamper around the woods, racing each other to pick the most wood, screaming with joy and laughter.

I also heard that the French Resistance Movement had been formed. I knew the Free French were trying to fight against the Nazis in France with what few weapons and little organisation they had. Now they were going to be an officially recognised body of people helped by the Allies to damage the Nazis' occupation as much as possible with weapons and radios being parachuted in secretly. So now the Resistance were to be equipped to organise and instigate more sabotage attacks. They were not going to be alone any longer. I prayed for the safety of my friends, and I wished I was over there helping them.

Best news of all was the heavy U-boat losses suffered by the Germans as a result of new Allied anti-submarine tactics and although thirty-four Allied ships were tragically sunk, forty-three German U-boats were sunk by the Allies. The Battle of the Atlantic was almost over, and the German U-boats were in retreat from the Atlantic. Was this the 'beginning of the end' – we could only hope.

All of us did our daily jobs and kept working to provide food for our country and in my case somewhere to stay for yet more children – another young family of four siblings who were evacuated from London for the second time. Their father was a dentist and their mother a nurse, and their work meant they were unable to be always available for the children. Their father held his practice in some rooms in their house and worked throughout all the bombing, but preferred the children to be somewhere safer. The children had first been evacuated in 1940, but they had not been happy where they were, so had returned to Clerkenwell at the end of 1940, with their parents arranging for a live-in housekeeper. Unfortunately, the housekeeper had died in a bombing raid when visiting her own mother in London, and so now it was decided they should be evacuated again. They were understandably very nervous when they arrived. To be fair to them, they settled very well and very quickly. Both parents came to visit them after four weeks and they didn't fret or cry when their parents returned to Clerkenwell. Gerald, Helen, Linda, and Christopher Archer mixed well with everyone and did their homework without having to be told. They loved all the dogs but were terrified of the horses and the cattle on the farm. Jabbo and Granger arranged for them to learn to ride on Donk and Tizzy, and the two youngest took to riding under the watchful eye of the two men. Gerald was adamant it wasn't for him and bravely Helen was led round the paddock on Spangles, at the walk, once only, but never again.

Gerald soon palled up with the boys for cricket, table tennis and bike rides. In fact, cricket was the passion for all the children, but particularly the boys, and they were thrilled to discover that Ashneer and Virinder were brilliant cricketers. Cricket had always been a favourite sport here at the Hall and now more so than ever; the boys were always discussing who were the best bowlers or batsmen. Hedley Verity, the Yorkshire cricketer, was always a top favourite, although Larry declared Bill Edrich the better player and so the friendly banter continued as they tried to emulate their chosen bowler or batsman. Another favourite topic for discussion was the merits of a Supermarine Spitfire over a Hawker Hurricane and which were the bombers they would choose to fly; always Lancs, 'Avro Lancasters' or sometimes the Boeing B-17 Flying Fortress. Rory told them the true story about a young trainee pilot called Everard Bacon taking a Spitfire for a spin without permission and upon landing flipped the plane over. He emerged from the upturned plane unscathed but was last heard of on his way to a new posting in the Shetland Islands, not as a pilot. They loved to hear these stories. If the girls joined in these discussions – and they often did – they loved to mention the wonderful women's cricket team England fielded before the war, naming Marjorie Pollard as an outstanding player and thoroughly modern woman and supporter of women's field sports. She wrote a book Cricket for Women and Girls in 1934 which the girls loved to read. They would then cite the women now helping to fight the war in the Women's Auxiliary Air Force who were telephonists, ambulance drivers, radar direction find operators, fabric workers in balloon command, orderlies, ammunition workers, planes and tank builders, riveters, and cooks as trail blazers for the ability of women to be as good if not better than the men. Best of all, they would mention the women who designed aircraft like Beatrice Shilling, a talented engineer. She studied the problem that occurred when planes dived to avoid enemy fire and there was a great risk of the engine flooding with fuel and cutting out the engine. This was happening to the Rolls-Royce Merlin engines in the Hawker Hurricane and the Supermarine Spitfire fighters. Shilling designed a solution: a brass disc with a hole in it which could be fitted without having to remove the engines, saving valuable time. She rode her motorbike from airfield to airfield, helping to install them herself. It was wonderful for the girls to have these female heroines. It was a known fact that Hazel Hill had helped her father, Captain Fred Hill. Both mathematicians, they worked out how to fit eight guns on to Spitfires and Hurricanes instead of just the four they had in the beginning. They worked out how to concentrate the trajectory of the bullets into a single flightpath, aiming at their target instead of them firing directly forward. So, life at the Hall was one of struggle and hardship combined with camaraderie and good spirits.

I still rode Hermes early in the mornings and when Rory was staying with us, he would join me on The Brig. They were lovely quiet times in my busy world, and we would talk about his life in Canada and the way they farmed there. He spoke about the wide, open spaces, the mountains and the wild animals that could be found there. He clearly loved his county and spoke of the lakes and rivers, the colours in the forests in the fall and the Indian Reservation and their customs. I was fascinated to hear first-hand all about the enormous, spacious country called Canada. I gave him permission to take Hermes out in the trap with Miriam as he had a real affinity with horses, and I knew Hermes would be treated well, with kindness and care. Ruby and Lottie would rush out to go with them if it was Saturday and they were well wrapped up with hot water bottles on their knees under fur rugs in the trap. He was so patient with the girls, and they adored him. Lennie admired him and would jump at the chance to ride out on Polly or Spangles with him. They both spent time training the colt foal Rory's Star to walk off a halter and started to long rein and lunge the foal's mother, the Hackney mare, Scarlett. Rory was so easy going with a casual manner, he had time for everyone with a slow smile which would spread to his clear blue eyes and his blond hair would flop over his forehead. With his long legs and blue jeans, he looked just like a movie star straight out of a Western cowboy film. Miriam told him about her trip to Scotland and he decided he would love to go there. So as the weather turned warmer at Easter, he rode his motorbike to Scotland with Miriam riding pillion to visit my sister Portia. We thought they were slightly mad, but that's what the war did; it made us all a bit mad and determined to live every minute of our lives while we were here. He found he loved Scotland and the wide, open spaces, the mountains, hills, and lochs reminded him of his home back in Canada. When they returned to the Hall it was obvious, they were even more in love than ever.

We attended church at Easter as we always did and had
an Easter lunch all together and a long walk with the dogs
afterwards. We held the Easter Egg Competition in the morning
before church and it was lots of fun, as usual, with some hilarious
weird painted duck, geese, and hen eggs, which were cooked and
used afterwards. No wastage was ever allowed. The children had
been busy in the school room on the Saturday under the guidance
of Danielle and Audrey, and even I had painted a blown goose egg
just for fun, not for the competition. We had four men staying
with us: this time two Americans, a Welshman and an Australian.
Two had been flying bomber planes and two were Spitfire pilots.
We knew the Avro Lancasters carried a crew of seven men: the
pilot, navigator, bomb aimer, flight engineer, wireless operator,
and mid and rear gunners. The B-17 carried a crew of nine men.
Again, we never asked why they were staying with us and again
they were at liberty to sleep, eat, walk or join in with us to play
billiards or table tennis, or to be captured by Grandora for a
game of Bridge, Backgammon, or chess. They smoked upstairs
in their rooms or outside, but nowhere else in the Hall. They
often walked to the village pub and some of us would join them
from time to time. It would generally be a jolly night, sometimes
with music and dancing: the pub would become a fog of smoke,
though, which I didn't like; it seemed that so many people had
taken up smoking during the war. We had a very busy household
with certain rules, but peaceful and relaxed at the same time.

We had a visit by some army 'bods' one day and they asked
me to direct them to the farm and the field we had the other side
of the river; they wanted to check out the access to it. I pointed
out where it was, took them to the farm and showed them the
track leading over the bridge to the field with an alternative route
through a wooded area. It was our summer grazing pasture field

for the horse, or milk cows and was a hidden field. It was accessible from the road the other side of the river by heading toward Home farm, then turning down a track and to the field. They spent some time tramping around the park and the other farms and then just left, abruptly without any explanation for their visit. Within a few days we were informed we were not allowed to use the field anymore as it was earmarked for Ministry business and they showed me a map they had drawn up of some other land belonging to our estate which was now out of bounds, at least for the time being. The telephone rang all morning from our tenant farmers irate about losing grazing land or crops and I tried to explain there was nothing we could do about it. I also had to explain it was 'hush hush', we were not to talk about it to anyone, especially in the village and would be in big trouble if we did so. We soon had noisy nights as machinery was taken to the fields over many days and it was then hidden by camouflage netting. It was intriguing and we had to keep quiet about the army lorries, motorbikes and tanks arriving and being stored. It was very exciting and mysterious. I kept my fingers crossed that the weather stayed dry to avoid the land being churned up by the heavy machinery. We heard more bombers taking off every night now and heading over to Europe with their deadly loads. Sad to say we were glad that someone 'over there' was getting hammered by bombs instead of it always being us and our cities. It was time the tide was turned.

May arrived and one day Tiff turned up out of the blue as usual, driving his army jeep. I was walking back for breakfast from my early ride and was so relieved to see him again. He was in army fatigues and wearing a leather flying jacket and his Captain's hat and he had an overnight shadow on his chin. He looked tired, but still gorgeous and I ran into his strong arms and breathed in his wonderful masculine smell. We went into the kitchen, and no one was up yet so I boiled the kettle and was about to take the mugs up to Grandora and ask her for some of her diminishing supply of real coffee when Tiff produced a packet from his saddle bag of real coffee. I buttered some slabs of bread, covered them in honey, and we quietly went upstairs to my bedroom. He showered and dressed again, and we sat on my old club chairs, sipping the coffee and ate the slabs of honey-smeared bread. I waited for him to talk to me; just happy to see him alive and well, even though clearly, he was exhausted.

"I am on my way up to Scotland," he said. "Just got back from Italy. I have some bad news. Howard Bathurst is dead."

The last time I had seen Howard, he had threatened me, as I froze stark-naked in the cold river, unable to get out of the water because of him. I was sorry he was dead, but not as sorry as I should be. I was silent. "How do you know?" I asked.

"Because I was with him. He has been part of my team now since he left here the day he trapped you in the river. I admit I was angry with him and not prepared to work with him. After he was taken to the pub by Frank, Osian, and Granger to sleep off a hangover, your grandmother made plans for him. She contacted his brother Henry and between them they agreed to pay off whatever his debts were for the sake of his sons. They didn't deserve to live with the shame of his gambling debts. The next day your grandmother went to the pub and met him before he left. He was told his debts would be paid and that he had to sign up immediately; the unit he was joining was in Scotland and his transport had been arranged. He had no choice unless he wanted to face the people he owed money to, for his gambling debts. Your grandmother is a good friend of the colonel in charge of my division, and so it was swiftly arranged. He had an escort to the station and on the train to us and my team. It was already known that he was a crack shot and had been the best marksman in his boarding school shooting competitions and against other schools. He was a rugby first, a brilliant prop and still reasonably fit. He had been a good cross-country runner once upon a time. The gambling was a sickness ruining his life and that was why Genevieve had taken the opportunity to live in France when she inherited the vineyard from her grandfather. I understand she hoped that living in rural France would take away the opportunity or desire to gamble anymore. Life was very hectic with their four boys and the vineyard to run, but Genevieve soon found it was always left to her to do all the work and childcare as he found excuses to go off to gamble every day in town. When he arrived in Scotland, I wanted to break his neck when I heard what he'd done to you, but every man is needed right now so instead I gave him constant drills, runs, fitness tests and every difficulty I could put his way. He actually excelled at everything I gave him to do. Hats off to him, he fitted in with the men, obeyed orders and worked hard. He has been on many missions with us, and he became a well-respected member of our team. He always had your back, no matter how bad the situation; he would always put himself forward and volunteered to tackle any obstacle or task. He was a crack sniper, and he gained the admiration of all of us, and died whilst rescuing a wounded member of our team. I am here to tell his sons how proud they should be of him and how proud my men and I have been to serve with him. He is going to be sadly missed," he finished.

I listened in silence and felt sad. Poor boys, they were going to be devastated. I knew I had to review my feeling about Howard, poor man.

"The boys are at school at the moment, Margaret has taken them, and she was going to the doctors afterwards for some medicine for Martha. Rest here, have a sleep and I'll go and tell Grandora the news and wait for Margaret to come back. I can call Hugh to come over. I think he should be here when you tell them. They really like Hugh and respect him," I added.

Tiff agreed and told me, "Their mother is on her way over with their two older brothers, she is hoping to be here by the time they get back from school. I will have a sleep though, just until lunchtime."

I kissed him, left him to rest and went to find Grandora with my emotions in turmoil.

I found Grandora sitting up in bed, sifting through some paperwork. I immediately thought of Tantetta sitting up in bed in the mornings, checking the art auction catalogues whilst having her morning coffee. Bless them, they certainly knew how to live. I sat on her bed and told her about Tiff's news. She stared out of the window across the park and was thoughtful.

"I feel as if I am responsible for his death," she said finally. "I sent him away; I suggested he joined the army, made himself useful and his sons proud of him: I feel terrible."

I didn't see that coming. I was very surprised by her reaction. I hugged her and told her, "It's definitely not your fault at all. He had turned his life around and that was because of your intervention. He has acted bravely and made an enormous contribution to the war effort, which has been far better than gambling and taking his family into ruin. His death has nothing to do with you; it is the result of a mad man wanting to rule the world and populate it with a pure Aryan race."

"Bless you, you're right; I am getting old and fed-up with this dreadful war. Would you fetch me some coffee and I will get ready to see Genevieve when she arrives; she must be in a state."

I gave her another hug, because I loved her so much, and just then she sounded too vulnerable. I went downstairs to prepare breakfast for her and found Mrs Revill and Rosie cleaning the kitchen. We were constantly trying to keep on top of the cleaning at the Hall. The army of servants that 'lived in' before the Great War had kept the Hall running smoothly for the previous generations of my family who lived here, but those servants were now long gone.

The Great War had changed the way many people thought about working for 'upper class folk' and they had found other more lucrative and rewarding ways of earning a living. I told them that Tiff would be here for lunch and that Genevieve, and her two older sons, were arriving later. I had no idea about their overnight plans, but we should be prepared for them all staying. I told them why they were arriving and everything Tiff had told me about Howard's bravery in battle. They were both quiet and Mrs Revill then was her usual self; wiping away a tear, she started to check the store cupboard and busy herself with meal preparations for the next two days. Rosie said she would take the tray up to Grandora and then make a start on cleaning the children's bedrooms. I went down to the stables to relay the events of the morning to Jabbo and Granger. Osian was home and talking to them in the warm tack room. He looked tired; he was working too much, driving the ambulance every day and most nights, as well as trying to cope with all the gardening. We all tried to help, but none of us were as good as him at growing plants. They were shocked by my news and felt just the same as me; that any previous actions and mistakes made by Howard were now exonerated. We all felt our main concern was how the boys would react. Larry would never stop missing his father, dead because of the bombing, but never talked about him. Lennie and Lottie must be upset, we knew that, but they didn't cry anymore, and they had accepted his death. Larry seemed even more determined to right the wrongs of mankind towards the working classes, filled with anger over his father's untimely death. Now, sadly, it was time for George and Theo to hear about their father's death.

We looked out for Margaret arriving back and Granger went to prepare Hugh and suggested he came to the Hall as soon as he could. We did all we could to help Genevieve and the oldest boys, William, now a man of twenty-one and in the RAF, and Tom nineteen, at university, training in medicine and working at the hospital. Genevieve clearly was very upset about Howard and proud of the father of her four children; she asked if they could stay with us overnight. Of course, I said yes. When George and Theo came home from school, we gave them some privacy in our sitting room alone together. They asked for Margaret and Hugh to join them after their mother had told them the awful news, then Tiff went in to tell them about their father and how brave he had been.

Tiff left them alone and came to join me; we walked to the stables for some time to ourselves. He stopped and put his arms around me, and I breathed in his man-smell which I loved. He cupped my face in his hands. "I have to leave early in the morning; something big is about to happen and we are all preparing for it. I can't say anymore. I love you so much, just remember that. I am determined to get back here and marry you if you will still have me," he joked.

I stared into his eyes alarmed at how earnest he was – clearly something very dangerous was going to happen. I kissed him passionately. Returning his fierce passion, I was suddenly scared to lose this incredible man and I didn't want him to leave. We stood still, not speaking, just treasuring the moment in each other's arms.

As we continued our walk down to see the horses, Rory roared up the drive on his Harley-Davidson WLA motorbike and stopped by us, smiling. He dismounted, saluted Tiff, and shook his hand. He was just slightly taller than Tiff, but his long legs and lean frame somehow made him appear much taller. "Glad to get this opportunity to see you guys," he said, "I came over to see y'all as we might be just a touch busy, and leave has been cancelled for the time bein."

Tiff smiled dryly and replied, "Yes, same here. I'm off first light, I have orders to be back at our base camp."

Rory went on, "I'm goin't' see Rory's Star. I've just seen Miriam and she's comin' down shortly; I believe she's up at the Hall with George, Theo and their brothers and mama as they've learnt of their pa bin killed in action. I'm truly sorry to hear about his death, I understand he was a top guy."

"Yes, he was with me at the time over in Italy. He was incredibly brave and will be sadly missed in our group," said Tiff.

"I'm truly sorry; we're losing too many good men and women. It's time we put a stop to this 'damn' war once and for all," said Rory grimly. "I'm just goin' find Lennie and I think he'll be with the horses as usual." He saluted Tiff, shook his hand, and kissed my cheek. "Thanks for everything, you've made life over here a real pleasure for me and other lonely, homesick guys. Look after my Miriam for me, won't you?" He kicked the bike into life, gunned the engine and with a roar carried on down to the stables.

We followed slowly, deep in our thoughts and arm in arm. I went to see Hermes, and Tiff went on to talk to Jabbo about something or other; I had no idea what.

Later, over our evening meal, we were all strangely quiet; there was a definite difference in how we usually chatted and laughed with each other. Grandora asked me to go to the larder and get out another bottle of good white wine from Tantetta's Chateau in France. We had already enjoyed a decent red Malbec from my father's cellar, but I went for the wine which was right at the back in the larder. I brought a port as well and our cheese made on the farm. I decided we all needed to lighten our mood and remember tonight as a night of joking and light-hearted banter. It worked and Larry came and joined us as he was now nearly seventeen. Lennie came downstairs in his dressing gown, sidled into the room and we allowed him to sit in on our conversation after the meal. Margaret and Hugh had insisted on William, Tom and Genevieve staying with them at the Gamekeepers Lodge with the boys so they could stay in their own beds after their news, and they could stay up and talk as long as they liked. Hugh and Margaret went to stay with Humphrey and Clarissa. Rory joined us for the evening meal with Miriam and Audrey. He was clearly madly in love with Miriam and she with him. Our own supply of food was limited due to rationing and the loss of so many merchant ships trying to bring supplies to Britain, but we did better than most, we just had to be creative with what we had and could produce on the farm. Much of our produce was requisitioned by the government and Osian who had been busy working all hours driving the ambulances, when not working in the Walled Garden, was now being sent to Plymouth to drive ambulances there and had suggested his brother Rhys, now nearly nineteen, came to help this year in the garden. Rhys had been working on a farm in Devon but was good with bees and poultry. The Rev. was pleased to know Rhys was going to stay with us and be working in the vegetable garden looking after the poultry and helping Ted on the farm. We were desperate for more help, and I had been contacted by Maisie Morton, our maid from nearly eight years ago, asking if there was any work for her.

I was delighted and had replied by the next post, asking for her to come immediately.

I suggested Tiff came to my room that night, but bless him although he did, he insisted on sleeping on my sofa. I was beginning to worry there was something unappealing about me. We just sat and talked way into the night, and he assured me he was determined to come back and marry me first before we made love. He was shattered and so was I, but we never knew when we would see each other again or if we would ever see each other again. I had to remind myself about all the wives, sweethearts, siblings, and children going through the same agonies we were going through, and I admit it seemed inappropriate to make love on the day Tiff had brought us the sad news about Howard Bathurst. When I woke Tiff had gone; he said he was going early, but I was sad I had missed saying goodbye, although our parting would have been even more painful. The awful thing was he had told me he had asked Jabbo to go back with him as he had a job coming up and he needed Jabbo to translate for him. I didn't get the chance to say goodbye to either of them.

Jabbo left me a letter which Grandora read to me. Apparently, he had married a girl when he was in Morocco, who was a nurse. Well, he kept that secret. Her mother was Moroccan, and her father was a French soldier, both had died when she was very young, and she had been sent to a convent in France. She trained as a nurse. She had gone to Morocco to work in a hospital there at the start of the war to escape a possible invasion of France by Nazi Germany, never thinking war would go to Morocco. She was hoping to return to France, but the war had made it impossible so now she would like to work in Britain and if we didn't mind could she live in Jabbo's Woodsman's cottage until he returned. She was now in Gibraltar waiting for a hospital boat to arrive and hopefully it would need her to do nursing work for her passage to Britain. Strangely, she had omitted an address so we couldn't reply, but I sent a letter to Merry and Osian who would be spending any leave he had at the Old Rectory with his family to listen out for any possible news of her on a hospital ship arriving in Plymouth. I presumed there would not be many Moroccan nurses serving on hospital ships.

Genevieve stayed for five days to comfort the boys. They had not spent much time together in five years and it was good for them to be a family again. William soon had to return to his RAF base as his leave had been cancelled, so they said their goodbyes again. Life returned again to what was as normal as it could be, and I got back to the job of running the estate, the Hall and looking after the children. Maisie returned and I was worried she didn't seem to like the new way things were run now or how many children and RAF personnel we had staying with us. I think living at the Hall before had been more orderly and refined. Her jobs had been defined by rank and she was expected to help my mother, or Portia and me. Now I expected her to do any job that needed doing, from cleaning the house, lighting the fires, and changing the beds, looking after the children, helping in the kitchen. Unless she could change, it was not going to work. I discussed this with Grandora as there was no way she could devote her time to just looking after Grandora or doing light cleaning jobs. I left her for a few days before I asked her to see me, so we could talk about the difficulties she had with all the changes, and the slightly chaotic atmosphere. When my parents left Singapore she had taken up a new position in Windsor, looking after an elderly couple who had since died of old age. Maisie, in her fifties, was not really that old, but was struggling to change her ways, which I understood. I told her about the children living here and how their lives had changed because of the war. It wasn't what they wanted, but I was doing my best in trying to help them reorganise their shattered lives and find safety, security, and happiness with us. I suggested she carried on for a month and then decide about her future and what she wanted to do.

Rhys arrived with his brother Gruffydd, which was brilliant as they both knew us and understood the way we worked. Osian was now in Plymouth driving ambulances there, as they expected to be busier than usual in the future. I still worked driving ambulances for two nights a week, plus now I was expected to be available on a third night if there were extra emergencies. Meanwhile, Rhys and Gruffydd did get on with working in the garden and they soon had everything planted and growing ready for the summer, just like Osian would have liked. They were very anxious to please and not disappoint him. Gruffydd was very good with the bees and poultry. Granger liked both boys from the many times they had stayed in the past, so I had no worries with their competence and ability to do Osian's and some of Frankie's work. We missed Frankie and Osian very much, but the two boys just gelled with us at the Hall and helped to make everything run smoothly.

Funnily enough, over the next few days I had managed to do some sketches of all the children and most of the people living here as I had, at last, started painting again. I managed to ride too; as the weather grew warmer and the days longer, most days I went out early in the morning. Then Grandora received a telephone call from Clary Carlton-Jones at Clearmore Stud near Thetford. He told her that Serena's fiancé, Miles, had been killed when his Spitfire went down over the Channel and now Serena had ridden off on her horse. They had been searching for her but hadn't seen her for over five hours and would we keep an eye out for her should she head our way. Granger tacked up The Brig, rode down the Pedders Way, successfully found her and brought her back to the Hall. She seemed fine, just not speaking as if she was in a trance, but otherwise not hurt physically. Grandora telephoned her parents and told them she could stay with us for the night and then we would get her home. Miriam was studying for her exams in Audrey's cottage when I knocked on the door and told her what had happened, so she came straight over with me to see Serena. Serena was sitting in Grandora's sitting room, staring out towards the big Cedar of Lebanon tree and not talking. Miriam suggested a hot bath and bed for her. I suggested my bedroom immediately as the sheets had just been changed and I could keep an eye on her. We soon had her bathed, warm, and ready for bed. I gave her a whisky to drink, putting the glass into her hand. She drank it all down, so I gave her another. Miriam raised her eyebrows but said nothing. Serena sipped her third drink and colour flooded back into her cheeks. I had lit the fire in my bedroom because some of the nights were still chilly even though we were getting to the middle of May. Serena sat still, just staring at the fire and saying nothing. Miriam whispered to me that she was in deep shock, and we may need to call the doctor. I went downstairs and brought back four mugs of warm milk. I took one next door to Grandora and told her what was happening or not actually happening to Serena and then went into my bedroom and gave Serena hot milk, and Miriam and I sipped ours. We put Serena into my bed with never a sound; she just went to sleep. I made up my couch for Miriam and, leaving her with Serena, went into Grandora's room. She was now asleep, so I quietly climbed into her big double bed and after mentally mulling over the sad events of the day, I went to sleep.

Morning came again, thank goodness, and I went to the kitchen to stoke up the fire and riddle the AGA. The AGA and I did not like each other, our relationship was fraught with problems – quite simply, it would not 'go' for me, it just went out. Now Granger and Jabbo were its 'Masters' and broke no argument with it; they tackled it with gusto, riddled it, fed it and made it behave. Well, I had a go, and fingers crossed it would respond and we'd have warm kitchen and hobs to make toast when everybody came downstairs. Thank goodness we still had a swizzle trivet over the open fire and an old oven range. I put the kettle on the trivet and swung it over the fire after filling it with fresh water and it soon boiled. I took mint tea upstairs. Miriam was awake, but still lying on the sofa wrapped in blankets and clearly warm and comfortable. I gave her the herbal tea and kicked a log on the fire, then sat in an armchair by the now, almost dead fire, looking for a spark. Amazingly the log 'sparked' and came to life, so I added coals, then snuggled into my warm, long, red Scottish plaid dressing gown.

"Serena hasn't stirred all night," said Miriam. "But I am worried about her, she is in shock or denial, and as she isn't talking, I can't see when she will snap out of this stage of her grief. I want her to talk about Miles and the happy times they had together. I just want her to talk. As I said last night, we might need to call the doctor; in fact, I think we should."

"OK, I'll go and telephone him to let him know to add us to his list of visits for today," I replied, and went downstairs into the chilly hall to telephone for Dr Haigh. I then telephoned Clary Carlton-Jones to let him know how she was. He told me they were struggling to get enough fuel for the journey to fetch her. We weren't that far away, but fuel for private cars wasn't allowed anymore and so I told him if necessary we would bring her down in the trap and Lennie would ride her mare back at the same time. I told him what Miriam had said about Serena being in deep shock and that I had called the doctor.

I was down to the stables visiting Hermes and checking on Serena's chestnut mare Whisper when out of a stable popped Lennie, a bucket of water in one hand and a dandy brush in the other. He looked so happy doing what he loved most – just like Granger they both loved being around the horses more than anything else. I loved Hermes and I stroked her velvet nose and breathed into her neck, smelling her horsy smell. She had lost her winter coat and was beginning to gleam with a healthy shiny coat of burnished copper. Her coat was the same colour as my hair, only mine didn't gleam with smooth waves, it crinkled and frizzled and reached for the sky.

"How is Serena this morning?" Granger asked.

"No different to yesterday so far. We gave her a few stiff whiskies last night, and she has slept, but I have asked for the doctor to call and see her," I replied adding, "I think I'll just take the dogs for a walk, I need some fresh air."

Odin was already with me, so were Trig and Spruce, Spud joined us running in circles and Jabbo's little dog Zippy came with us, running ahead, in excitement. I had forgotten Zissa the little pooch who was with Ruby anyway. I took them to the river and down to look at all the vehicles hidden in the field and was surprised to see some of them had gone. It was all quiet and the field was a mess. I hurried back to make sure Rosie had arrived and that Mrs Revill and Margaret were getting the children ready for school. I wondered if Maisie was helping them and starting to fit in and not think she was here to be a ladies' maid. They were all organised in the kitchen and asked, of course, about Serena.

"It's a miracle she rode her horse here in the state she was in," volunteered Margaret.

"I know, I thought about that, she was just in some sort of a trance doing ordinary things, but not knowing what she was doing."

"I put some toast into the round wire toast holder and put it onto the hob."

"Was the AGA on when you arrived?" I inquired airily, hopeful I had done a good job.

"No, it was going cold, Granger has been to sort it out," Rosie replied.

I said nothing, but I wanted to kick the damn thing.

Serena slept on and off most of the day until Dr Haigh arrived and left some sleeping pills for her. She was sleeping so much I couldn't see why he had left sleeping pills! He said sleep was a great healer, which I thought was true. Later that night as I was preparing to sleep on the couch in Grandora's room after spending time with Miriam in my room watching over Serena, the big doorbell rang at the front door. Worried, I ran downstairs, unlocked the door to find Susannah, Serena's sister, on the doorstep with her suitcase. Could life get any stranger?

"I got a lift with some army guys heading this way. My boyfriend fixed it for me when he knew where Serena had ended up after hearing about Miles. I hope you don't mind, I just want to be with her."

"Come in, of course, completely understandable; I'll take you straight up to the bedroom. I hope you don't mind, Miriam is staying with her and sleeping on my couch. You can share the bed with Serena though. I am bunking with Grandora on her couch in her room."

I took her upstairs and then went downstairs to get her a drink of warm milk. Larry was on his way downstairs and asked me if he could do anything to help. I explained what was happening and who had just arrived, but said I would be grateful if he just kept an eye on all the children over the next few days and made sure they behaved and did their homework. I made him some milk and gave him some of Mrs Revill's homemade biscuits and he went back to bed. He had turned out to be a really good lad, Grandora had a soft spot for him. I took a sandwich and some biscuits upstairs for Susannah and found her cradling a whisky, so I joined her and Miriam and we sat by the fire in my room, chatting, and watched poor Serena sleeping.

In the morning I woke up in Grandora's room after a surprisingly good night's sleep on her sofa: must be the whisky and warm milk. I went straight down to the stables; it was just five-thirty, but Granger was there working already with the kettle on for a mug of tea. I helped him in the yard until Lennie arrived and then went back to get breakfast ready. Mrs Revill arrived, followed by Rosie, and I took porridge and toast upstairs for Grandora, Miriam, Susannah, and Serena. Serena stayed asleep and Miriam went back to the cottage for a change of clothes. I took Grandora her breakfast while Susannah used my bathroom.

Lennie, meanwhile, was mucking out Serena's chestnut mare when Serena appeared at the stable door in her pyjamas.

"Oh hello, have you come to see your mare?" asked Lennie cheerfully.

Serena didn't answer, just went into the stable and put a halter on Whisper.

"Are you going riding?" asked Lennie doubtfully, looking at her pyjamas. Then he remembered her fiancé, Miles, had been killed. "I am so sorry to hear that your Miles has been killed, he was a brave man and I liked him a lot," he said sympathetically. "I remember what a good cricketer he was. We won our last match because of him, he scored record runs, he was a great bloke."

According to Lennie, Serena sort of gurgled and sank into the corner of Whisper's stable onto the straw and was quiet. As Lennie went to help her up, she started to wail loudly, and sob, and a very frightened Lennie ran for help. Miriam on her way back to the Hall was the first person he met and together they ran to Serena, whereby Miriam crouched beside her and held her as she sobbed and sobbed. Susannah, on realizing Serena had left the bedroom, had run down to the stables, guessing that's where she would be and arrived just before me. I had seen Miriam and Lennie running to the stables from Grandora's bedroom window. We waited as Susannah knelt next to her grieving sister and rocked her as she wept. Finally, we all helped her into the warm tack room and sat with her until her sobs subsided and she grew quiet. She looked about her and at all of us.

"Thank you," she whispered as she closed her eyes and leant on Susannah. "Why am I here?"

Miriam gently explained to her why she was with us in our tack room at the Hall. A while later Grandora appeared at the door and suggested a nice hot bath for Serena and so we all went up to the house for some tea and breakfast. Coming downstairs was one of our resident RAF guys and I was shocked when I realized that I knew him as he was a former school friend of Lysander's. I thought I knew the racing green MG roadster parked by the Hall. It was Thady, his sister, who had been an awful bully to me at my boarding school. Brennan Shillington had even stayed with us one Easter and I'd liked him. He had a younger brother Hywell who was a really cheeky, funny young boy, always teasing his older brother and climbing trees. Clearly, they adorned each other.

"I hope you don't mind me intruding, but I noticed you helping a young lady in her night attire on her way back from the stables. Is there anything I can do to help?"

"I know you, don't I, you're Brennan, Lysander's friend. I didn't know you were staying here. Of course, that must be your MG Roadster outside. It's just like your mother's car. No, thank you, you can't do anything, she's had a shock, her fiancé has been killed flying his Spitfire, she's with her sister now and when she's ready and rested we'll be taking her home. Thanks anyway and good to see you. Maybe I will see you later." I smiled and went upstairs. I wondered why he was staying with us. Best not to ask though.

Serena and Susannah stayed for a few more days and during that time Serena grew stronger and started to eat a little, but there was no cure for her broken heart. She needed her family and friends, love, and care and time for the healing process to begin. And she was needed back at work in the operations room at the airport where she had been working during the war. Finally, the day came for them to leave. I harnessed up Hermes and Lennie tacked up Whisper, and we set off with Susannah and Serena to meet her parents halfway. They met us driving a strong Cleveland Bay gelding to a wagonette and we unharnessed the horses and let them rest as we all had a break at a local inn, then Susannah climbed on Whisper to ride the rest of the way to their home on the 'Stud Farm'. Serena rode in her parents' wagonette, warmly wrapped up in a fur blanket and with her mother Sylvia's arm around her. Lennie climbed into the trap with me, and I let him drive Hermes back to the Hall. He was having lessons with Granger on the art of carriage driving, coachman style and he was a natural. I was impressed and proud of him.

It was a long day, but fortunately the weather stayed dry and reasonably warm even without much sun, but best of all Serena had started her long road to recovery. Miles would stay in her heart her whole life, but she was beginning to come to terms with life without him by her side. So many people throughout the world were learning to live without their loved ones due to this stupid war.

Chapter 35

Flying Bombs in London

G radually over the next few nights all the army vehicles stored in our fields disappeared as magically as they had arrived; there one day, gone the next, or so it seemed. I can't explain, there was something almost electrical in the atmosphere, and a tension in the military personnel we kept meeting. As Tiff had told me, something big was about to happen. I suspected something was taking place somewhere, but I had no idea what. Soon, however, I was to find out. Until then we were busy at home with our hens and the new baby chicks that had been hatching, and the young turkeys we had brought in. I helped move the beehives to a new location; an old pasture field full of wildflowers just coming into bloom. Lucy and Sheila were busy feeding the young stock and milking every day, and the sheep had been lambing since early April. There were more lambs still due, but some of the ewes and their lambs needed moving into a new sheltered pasture and we were about to start the hay season. I was helping to bottle feed any cade lambs, a job I loved, with help from Ruby and Lottie. I had always fed the dogs, and there were six to feed morning and night so none of us were ever still. I just bounced from one job to the next. Grandora manned the telephone and kept rotas for us all, a new idea of hers with which we all struggled. Granger was busy running the stable yard, keeping the boilers going, getting fuel to the fires and mending fences, sorting any problems in the Hall which needed repairs, fetching feed for the horses. Arranging for them to go to the farrier and keeping Hermes and our Suffolk Punch Alfie ready for any work for which they were needed. His list was endless and on top of all these jobs he was in the Home Guard with Hugh and Humphrey and there were practice sessions three nights a week to attend. They still used our park and woods to practise their army drills, without the obnoxious Colonel Orpington-Jones who had retired due to ill health. His poor wife had been to apologise for his behaviour which she explained was getting worse. Dr Haigh had prescribed complete rest for him as his outbursts were becoming increasingly erratic and his mind forgetful. Meanwhile, the drill and imaginary 'invasions' held in the park by the Home Guard were sometimes very funny to watch. Fingers crossed we would never need them, but the men were all deadly serious and at least they tried to be 'ever ready', and we were very grateful that they were there for us.

We had just two young aviators staying with us at this time; they were both polite, but very quiet and clearly in need of peace and rest. Grandora told me that she had been told they were both evaders from France where their bomber had crashed. Rosie was brilliant with the children as always, and Larry was helping with their homework and any extra reading practice they needed. He made sure they were ready on time for school every morning. I missed Osian, Jabbo and Frankie so much. Gruffydd and Rhys were brilliant and doing their best to do everything Osian would want them to do. They worked so hard in the garden and with all our poultry and the bees. I could not fault their work ethic and they were always very good with the children. Of course, they knew George and Theo well from the first time they met, way back in 1940, at the start of the war when we had just arrived in Britain. They had spent most of their holidays with us at the Hall and they knew Ruby, Lottie, Larry and Lennie from the very beginning of them arriving. Now they hardly had any spare time to play football or join the others for a board game or table tennis. When they weren't working, they went to Osian's cottage to sleep, and they had to do their own housework. That said, they always found time for a game of cricket. They managed to have their breaks in the cosy tack room with Granger, and Lennie and Tad often joined them with Larry for chats and discussions about the war. Favourite conversations centred around which was the best fighter plane, a Spitfire 'Spiffy' or a Hawker Hurricane or the Messerschmitt Bf 109, and why. If they could collar an RAF guy staying with us, they would rope him into the discussion. I always thought how lucky we were with all our children who rarely argued and generally helped each other. I had taken them to see Ali Baba and the Forty Thieves before we became busy with our harvests, and they had loved it. Now Audrey, Danielle, Miriam and I went to see Double Indemnity, the psychological thriller film starring Fred MacMurray and Barbara Stanwyck, which we enjoyed, although as I often say I prefer to watch a comedy.

It was early one morning, when I was making myself some toast as I prepared breakfast for the children, that Maisie came in and asked me if she could have a word with me later in the morning. Of course, I told her to see me in my father's office when the children had gone to school. Later that morning Maisie came and knocked on the door and came into the office. I was not doing a very good job of filing some invoices, hoping that Malissa would do my paperwork, when she came home.

"Sit down, Maisie, how can I help you?" I asked.

"It's about what you said the other day to me, my Lady. Well, I have been thinking about my role here and I would like to stay here. I came here before your mother had her children, to be a Lady's maid for her. I was very sad when they left for Singapore as I loved my life here, looking after your mother and Lady Isadora. As you know I have recently been working in Windsor looking after an elderly couple, where it was very quiet, but they have now both died. I wrote to you asking if there would be any chance of a job back here for me. When you replied, yes, I was so pleased, but when I arrived, I couldn't believe how busy the Hall is now with so many children and those poor brave men staying here too. I must confess it wasn't what I was expecting, and at first, I didn't like it. I am one of a family of six children from a small farm near Boston, Lincolnshire, so I was brought up in a busy, noisy house. I suppose I had just forgotten what it's like. I have been watching the children here and they are good children; heaven knows where they would be right now if it wasn't for you. What you are doing here is amazing and I want to help and be part of this wonderful family. I can read well and help with their reading; I can cook and clean and I've seen the knitting club and all those blankets and jumpers being knitted for those poor souls who've lost everything. We're always being told to make do and mend and I can do that; I make rugs from unwanted scraps of material I can, peg rugs – some people call them clip rugs – and I'm very good at it, I can teach anyone if they want to learn. Most of all, I want to be here when your mother gets back. I can't imagine it's very nice in a prison camp in all that hot weather. She'll need me when she gets back, and she knows me, and I can help her, and her Ladyship will be needing assistance as she gets older. I just got a bit above myself when I came back, things being so different here now, but I know I want to help if I can please. So, I want to stay very much and be part of the team you have here."

I smiled, "I am pleased, Maisie, there is so much to do sometimes I wonder how we get everything done and I miss those now away on war duty. You are needed and very welcome."

After this, Maisie started to pull her weight in the household duties and turn her hand to any job which needed doing and she remained cheerful too. We were very lucky to have her back with us and I was sure my mother would be pleased to see her when she finally arrived home. Whenever that might be.

It was at this busy time I was asked to take Gerald home to Clerkenwell to his father's dentist surgery to have his brace replaced with a new one. I said he could see a local dentist instead, but his mother protested, saying he was receiving treatment from his father and they both felt it should continue with him. I wasn't thrilled about making a needless journey escorting Gerald to his father's surgery then back home. His mother pleaded saying she wanted to see him so much and he would be seen immediately, and she would be at home to feed us. Then added Gerald had told them about the good food they had to eat, and could I possibly take some eggs and butter down at the same time and of course they would pay me. It was the first time I had been asked to provide what would be 'black market' goods if I sold them. Of course, I could only take them as a gift for them. I agreed to take him, and I would let them know the day and week I could arrange time off from my jobs and ambulance driving.

June arrived with windy days and scudding clouds racing across our vast Norfolk skies and the sun playing hide and seek with the clouds. I managed to ride Hermes in the early mornings again, which was my special time often alone with my own thoughts. The hay was nearly ready to harvest, and Granger and I were watching daily now for the right time to cut it and lead it home, hoping for a window of good fine weather. Our horses were still being rationed in their paddocks as we didn't want any of them going lame with laminitis from eating too much rich sweet spring grass and Tizzy and Donk were kept in a very small paddock as they only had to look at good grass and get fat. Then we heard on June 6th about Operation Overlord and the D-Day landings in France, finally we were on the offensive on land in Europe, it had started at last. The weather over the last few days had been stormy and I prayed that the troops weren't seasick in the Channel and the boats had sailed to France safely. We heard through the wireless that the Allies, specifically the United States fifth army, had liberated Rome on June 4th, two days before our push to liberate France. The Allies had landed in Anzio and bombed Monte Cassino the Medieval Monastery there, sadly destroying it. We had an Allied victory in North Africa which had enabled the invasion of Italy to begin. Everything now seemed to point to the end of the war becoming a reality. The Soviet offensive was gathering pace in Eastern Europe, and they were on their way to Germany. Now more than ever before, we were glued to the wireless, listening for any news of our achievements in France. I was so scared for Marcell and Aurielle – how were they coping with the bombing and fighting?

On June 7th Grandora read to me some sections of our King's speech to me. He said: 'Four years ago our Nation and Empire stood alone against an overwhelming enemy, with our backs to the wall.' He mentioned the 'Spirit of the people, resolution, dedicated, burned like a bright flame lit surely from those Unseen Fires which nothing can quench. Now once more a supreme test has to be faced. After nearly five years of toil and suffering we must renew that crusading impulse on which we entered the war and met its darkest hour'. He mentioned the Queen joined him in sending this message to us. 'She felt that many women will be glad in this way to keep vigil with their menfolk as they man the ships, storm the beaches, and fill the skies.' He added that the predications of an ancient Psalm may be fulfilled. 'The Lord will give strength unto his people: the Lord will give his people the blessings of peace.' It was a stirring speech from His Royal Highness George VI.

Tiff and Jabbo, where were they? It made sense now why Jabbo had gone with his ability to translate for Tiff if they were in France. I was sure that was were they were. Over the following days and weeks, we heard that 6,500 vessels had landed 130,000 troops on the beaches of Normandy and 12,000 aircraft had ensured air superiority for the Allies. Nico came home and let me know he had been able to help Tiff with maps and terrain of a certain area in France, but he could not confirm why they required this information, and he would not say any more on the subject. He looked tired and he slept for the best part of the first day he was at home. I believe his knowledge of map reading and of minimizing maps and putting them onto silk had been very useful to the military all throughout the war. We heard that our troops had landed, but judging by a report from Osian now ambulance driving in the Plymouth area, he was busy ferrying soldiers to the hospital from the port. These were the lucky ones brought back by the ships taking troops out to the beaches. We also learnt that the landings were taking place in Normandy on the beaches there. They had called the beaches Utah, Omaha, Juno, Sword and Gold. We heard the planes flying overhead now night and day and our two airmen were quiet as they were not part of this momentous operation. They too remained glued to the wireless, waiting for orders to return to their squadrons.

The older children took a great interest in the events taking place and were constantly listening for news of how the invasion was going. Fortunately, our young children continued with playing and their schoolwork and didn't show any interest in what was happening in the world. When not at school, Audrey and Danielle kept them occupied with nature walks and hobbies, and Rosie as always was brilliant with Ruby and Lottie. Susan and Roger spent all their spare time with Margaret and Hugh and helping George and Theo walking the gun dogs. Margaret had become the best surrogate mother to these four children, and she had become devoted to them all, as had Hugh. They had been childless for so many years and now Margaret had found her raison d'être. George was now taking his exams and preparing for university and studying. We knew he could be called up any day now and he was wanting to join the same unit that his father had been in when he was killed. Hugh told me that he was an excellent shot, just like his father. He ran every day and tried to keep fit and was looking forward to seeing Tiff again to question him about the commando unit. Theo was different and loved taking photographs of the natural world around us, walking and being close to nature. He was learning how to develop his own films, and had a sound knowledge of wild animals and their habitat and foraging habits.

For the rest of us, life continued as usual, cleaning, cooking, washing and for me running around making sure everything ran as smoothly as possible and checking that repairs were mended and that we had enough food to keep supplying the country. We had a quota to keep to and fortunately we usually exceeded it. Gruffydd and Rhys worked their socks off to provide us from the

Walled Garden and now they were planting the newly ploughed area just outside the Walled Garden. Granger had nothing but praise for these two. Any problems they had they had learnt to contact Stan and Lacey, who had become proficient at growing vegetables, salads, and herbs. Their letters zinged backwards and forwards and when Stan came over for market day they would call and see the boys and bring whatever they had requested. Reuben got on with them very well and was going to stay with them during our hay harvest and later in summer our corn harvest. They swopped seeds, bulbs, and new ideas with them. Best of all, as Stan and Lacey had adopted our goats, it was a relief not to have Granger moaning about what the goats had been doing or eating and where they had got out and broken the fencing yet again.

We listened to the wireless telling us about the British landing on beaches named Gold and Sword and that they had come under heavy fire, but that they had established a toehold in Nazi-occupied France. It was momentous news and scary at the same time. The Americans and Canadians had huge forces landing on other beaches at the same time. Now we had some hope for the future and dread for our loved-ones fighting for our freedom. I had a decision to make at home: the weather was too poor to make hay and I decided to leave it growing in the fields as I didn't want to risk it being cut and then due to severe weather being too wet to gather in and then left to rot on the ground. So should I take Gerald to London to have his brace re-fitted? I decided that Gerald would have to wait – I refused to miss a few good days should we get some to cut the hay. Then we had a good spell of weather, and we rushed out to get our valuable hay crop in. Again, all our farms helped each other, and we shared our tractor, trailers and tools, horses, and our helpers. Hermes and AP, our

Suffolk Punch now called Alfie Punch, were brilliant again and worked all day in the fields with Lennie and Granger in charge of them. I had so far refused to have any German prisoners of war working on the farms. This was because of the trauma Danielle had suffered at the hands of her Nazis captors. I was not sure what had happened, but I thought it had to be torture and possibly rape and I couldn't risk upsetting her. I was quite sure that Miriam knew, but she was very discreet, and I would never ask her what the truth was. One of our farms, Castle Hill, had an Italian POW working for them and I admit he was cheerful, helpful, and hard working. With Rhys, Gruffydd, Granger, Lennie, Reuben, Lucy and Sheila and now the Italian POW Enzo, we made a great team and went from farm to farm making hay. The good weather held for the first week then the heavens opened, and we had some days of constant rain; luckily, we had cut several hay pastures and led the hay in. They had baled the hay with our recently acquired New Holland baler and taken the bales to the barn, so we were able to leave the rest of our grass crop standing in the field until the next run of good weather.

As we had several days of continuous rain, I took the opportunity to take Gerald to Clerkenwell on the train. We managed to obtain enough petrol for Granger's van, and I drove to Narborough with Gerald to catch the train. I was hoping to do this journey in one day. I took a basket of produce for Gerald's parents, butter, bread, flour, and a ham hock. They were thrilled and his mother kissed me and hugged me and took me into their parlour. They had a large house in a row of similar red brick houses. Theirs was a corner house with a large corner bay window surrounded by a neat brick wall. The dental practice was through a side door in the house and further down the side passage led to a large garden where their Anderson shelter was and a pretty summer house and a small orchard. There was a drive and garage for their car at the back of the orchard. It was a lovely garden, and they were obviously keen gardeners with an amazing vegetable plot. I had a coffee with Mrs Archer, the camp variety, and I asked her about her job, which turned out to be nursing at the local Maternity Hospital. She told me that despite the war they had been kept very busy with new babies arriving.

"Heaven knows how much busier we will be when our young men come home," she laughed.

I hadn't thought about that. They had a lovely light sitting room pleasantly and comfortably furnished, velvet curtains and flowered covers on the chairs. We had a good lunch of homemade vegetable soup followed by fresh salad with spam and a Bakewell tart in their dining room, and they were a very interesting couple to listen to. They had loved travelling Europe before the war for walking holidays and knew the area of France where I had been living so we had lots to talk about. Gerald was soon sorted out with a new brace for his teeth by Mr Archer after lunch, as Mrs Archer showed me the garden. Gerald was pleased to be back home and beetled up to his bedroom to search for a book he needed before we left and a favourite toy for Linda.

We were to leave in the afternoon to get the train back when there was a terrifying explosion, and we could see billowing smoke away into the distance and we all were shocked and frightened. We went into the road and found other people looking towards London city to see what had just happened. The air raid siren had not been heard.

"Should we go into the shelter?" Mrs Archer nervously asked her husband.

"No, I think these two had better hurry up to the tube station to catch a train for King's Cross and I will attend to my next patient. If the siren sounds we will go to the shelter then. It's very strange I didn't hear a plane, just a buzzing sound."

We said our goodbyes and Mr Archer went back to work and Mrs Archer walked with us towards the station. Suddenly we heard another strange buzzing noise, similar to an aircraft engine.

Gerald pointed. "Look, there in the sky, it's a strange long thing, buzzing."

We followed his gaze and heading towards London was a big cigar-shaped thing. We were transfixed as were several other people on the street. We all saw it stop, then an eerie silence and it fell from the sky and then we heard an almighty explosion and smoke billowed up, then the sirens sounded. We all ran into the underground station with other people doing just the same thing. It was horrible panic and pandemonium as we jostled each other. I grabbed Gerald and pulled him to the wall; his mother saw us and followed.

"Mrs Archer, we must go now to get our train – will you be alright?" I asked.

"Yes, you go, we are used to bombing although I don't know what that was. I will run back; it won't take me long. I would prefer you just to get back to Norfolk and my other children. We are ever so grateful you are able to keep them safe for us. They are very happy with you. Thank you." She hugged Gerald and kissed him and left us and was swept back into the daylight with a crowd of people.

We arrived at King's Cross and going upstairs to the arrivals platform we were swept up in another panic as people rushed into the building and down the stairs to the underground. We then heard another much louder explosion nearer to us. It was horrible. We crouched onto the ground as I didn't know what to do; other people did the same thing. Our train was waiting on the platform, so we dusted ourselves off and ran and jumped on the train. I don't know why I thought we would be safer on the train, but at the time it seemed the best place to be. Sitting in shocked silence, we waited as other people boarded the train and everyone was shell-shocked. Within twenty minutes we were pulling out of the station; all I wanted to do was get away from London. Oh my God, how awful for all the soldiers in France, they were living through the hell of bombs and gunfire constantly. I was shaken and terrified from hearing three weird bombs as they came down and exploded. As our train journey began we heard someone muttering about a flying bomb and Gerald and I discussed could it be possible that was what we had seen and heard?

Finally, we reached the station at Narborough after what had turned out to be a long and alarming day. I drove home in the van we had left parked all day and arrived home late, although it was still light as we were still on two hours ahead of normal summertime hours as we had been since the war started. The Hall was quiet, and it seemed that everyone had gone to bed so we went into the kitchen to find something to eat as we were by now both hungry. A note had been left by Mrs Revill telling us there was some soup for us and sandwiches. I went to the pantry and retrieved our supper which was vegetable soup and spam sandwiches. We both laughed at the same time when we realized what our supper was.

"So, we've had a memorable day of new teeth braces followed by veggie soup, spam and flying bombs in-between, then more veggie soup and spam," said Gerald dryly and we both giggled. He took out of his mouth his new brace and put them into a clean hanky whilst he ate and pulled a face. "Can't say it's comfortable," he admitted.

I made us hot milk and he thanked me for taking him to his parents and then, taking his milk, he went off to bed. I took mine upstairs and gently knocked on Grandora's bedroom door. She was awake and reading. I told her about our day and the explosions, and she said they were flying bombs and that they had been reported on the news on the wireless. They were a new deadly threat to our country sent from Hitler in retaliation for the Allies landing in France. Since we left London there had been more bombing in London, causing a large amount of death and destruction. How awful, how much more could London take? How much more could we all take? Norwich had been badly bombed in April 1942, killing 229 people and injuring 1000. It was called the Baedeker raid as it was thought the targets were chosen by the Nazis from a tourist guidebook. London had lived through the Blitz and now we were being attacked by flying bombs. I was so grateful to be back home in the countryside and just hoped these new bombs didn't get this far.

We celebrated Ruby's eighth birthday – we think it was eighth, we were guessing – with a party in the rose garden with sandwiches, a cake with candles and buns, jelly and blancmange. She invited her classroom friends, which was the whole classroom – thank goodness it was a small church school. We made silly hats for all the children to wear, well those who would, from newspaper, and played musical chairs with Theo playing his recorder, pin the moustache on Hitler whilst blindfolded, splat the rat, the farmer's in his den, pass the parcel, and hide and seek. Finally, we went into the park to the Cedar of Lebanon and split into two teams and played Ralico, which was hysterically funny and exhausting, which was the general idea for all the children to get them as tired as possible. The weather was wonderful, and the sun shone for us, and it was a great success. We would repeat this throughout the year for all the other children's birthdays with varying games depending on their age at the time. The boys always wanted cricket parties with cricket teas, which was very civilized, and everyone took part. The boys with winter birthdays were treated to bow and arrow lessons with Hugh in the fields behind the kennels and they were trained how to use, clean and shoot a riffle which they loved. At the end of June, we were told that Cherbourg had finally been liberated.

July followed much the same pattern as previous Julys with lots of work outside on the farm and in the Walled Garden. We followed the news on the wireless and the newspapers and it sounded as if the Allies had their work cut out pushing the Nazis out of France. Many problems bogged down their process of driving through France with their armies and tanks. Narrow roads and high thick hedges held them up and the fighting sounded ferocious, and many villages and towns were destroyed, and more sadly, civilians and soldiers killed. It was reported that many countries were involved in the invasion, the Greek, Dutch, Czechoslovakian, Belgium, Free French Forces, Australians, Canadians, The Norwegian Navy, The United States, The New Zealand Airforce, and Polish forces units. It was wonderful to know that at last we in Britain had many friends now coming to our aid to rid the world of the Nazi menace. Osian remained in the Plymouth area ferrying wounded soldiers from ports to hospital. Frankie was now down in the south of England making sure army vehicles were in working order before being taken over to France. Mrs Hubbard was now more occupied than ever working for the Women's Voluntary Service, and Grandora helped out too on a number of occasions, dispensing tea and scones to service men. She enjoyed Dendy visiting our RAF men and spending time with her afterwards, either discussing the war's progress, playing chess,

bridge or walking together. Mrs Revill made large numbers of
scones every week for the WVS.

I remained envious of the many women who ferried the new
planes from the factories to the airfields. They often had to fly
many different types of planes without having used them before.
I loved listening to the pilots staying with us, arguing which was
the best plane, the Spitfire, or the Hurricane, of which there were
1,700 of the latter against just four hundred Spitfires. I just felt
useless, and I always felt I wasn't helping enough with the War
effort. The V1 flying bombs continued to batter London, falling
hourly on the city, creating a reign of suspense, panic, and terror;
they were nicknamed doodlebugs or buzz bombs. During all this
terrible time I managed to take the older children to the cinema
to see Going My Way starring Bing Crosby and Barry Fitzgerald.
On another occasion we went to see Roy Rodgers with Dale Evans
in Cowboys and the Señorita, which became a firm favourite
Western film for all the children. They spent days afterwards
running around pretending to be Cowboys and Indians and
saddled up Tizzy and Donk to ride them around the paddock as
they pretended to shoot each other.

It's strange what is accidental and innocently mentioned. I
was asked by an RAF man staying with us if I had a boyfriend
and of course I replied yes, he was in the army. When asked
what branch of the army I struggled to answer, saying finally I
thought it was logistics and he was always training somewhere
in Scotland. I was careful what I said; there seemed to be spies
everywhere according to the Government. Later in the week the
children were talking about Jabbo and the circus tricks he could
do with his horse and the same airman listened to them and said
he thought he had seen Tiff and Jabbo at Templeford some weeks
before. I reported this to Grandora who telephoned Squadron

Leader Richard Petersfield, who came over and questioned the RAF guy. It was all innocent and above board, but we were all reprimanded for tittle tattle.

It was on August 15th we heard that Operation Dragoon was ongoing in the South of France in Provence and that Allied forces had landed there to take Marseille and Toulon. Meanwhile, a battle to liberate Paris took place from August 19th until the German Garrison surrendered on August 25th, 1944. So finally, after nearly five years, Paris was liberated. Operation Dragoon took 4 weeks to succeed in liberating the ports in the south of France whilst inflicting heavy causalities on the German forces. I kept my fingers crossed that Marcell, Aurielle, Joseph, and Alex, the young man we had met on the road, were safe at the Chateau, and I kept asking Grandora if she had heard from Tantetta in Switzerland. I had heard from Rebekkah in New York and from Phillipe, but little news had arrived from France for years now. It was very worrying, and I prayed they were all safe. More to the point, where were Tiff and Jabbo now?

We started the harvest as Britain urgently needed food and we kept on providing it. The baler was a brilliant tool, and the farmer John Bagshaw on Castle Farm soon was an expert at operating it for all of us. As we used a binder machine pulled by a tractor to cut the corn and then the steam driven threshing machine came to each farm to thresh the wheat, it was all hands to get the harvest in. This meant Rhys, Gruffydd, George, Theo, Larry, Lennie, Gerald and Virinder and Ashneer all helping Sheila and Lucy. Hugh and Ted worked together with Granger and me. Help came from all our farms, and we moved from field to field on each farm, praying the weather would hold fine whilst we worked to bring in a bumper harvest. Margaret and Clarissa provided all of us with food in the fields and we worked from dawn until dusk.

Hermes and AP worked hard carting in the corn, and Polly, my mother's grey mare, did her fair share of carting the sheaves of corn into the barn. John never stopped baling the straw and was getting exhausted and so Granger stepped in and learnt how to drive the tractor and baler slowly round the fields baling under John's watchful eye. He was very proud of his tractor driving prowess, but we all missed Frankie and his mechanical skills being at home to help us. I made a mental note to discuss purchasing a combine harvester with Frankie for use on the farms in the future.

Reuben and Stan came over to help and slept under the stars for a week, which was their choice, and they made our boys jealous, and they insisted they joined them sleeping in a tent in the paddock for a night. So off they went and put up two tents and they stayed out all night near to Stan and Reuben and thought it was wonderful. We cut oats, barley and wheat, and our barns were soon full. The young children had plenty of fun making jumps out of the bales of straw, jumping over them with all the dogs and playing hide and seek round them. On the last day of harvest just before dusk I sat on a bale, drinking cider from a bottle, and watched these conker brown, wild children running around screaming, laughing, and chasing each other. I felt contented and for a time I felt I had been useful – I had saved these children from bombed out cities and fates not worth contemplating and here they were cheerful, healthy, and hopefully these happy times would live in their memories for ever. We celebrated the finish of the harvest with a barbecue courtesy of Hugh, held in the orchard with venison, and chunks of bread. We were lucky our estate did provide for us; oh, and that Hugh was a good shot.

It was soon October and time for the fruit and nut harvest. We always had plenty of cob nuts, hazelnuts, and walnuts; as I say, we were blessed. London now had V2 rockets being fired from somewhere in deepest France. It was proving difficult to find the correct location from where the rockets were being launched. Barrage balloons had helped, but the damage to London by the flying bombs was horrendous. Over an 80-day period more than 6,000 people were killed by these flying rockets and 17,000 people were injured, and a million buildings were wrecked. The fear of hearing those doodlebugs as they were flying overhead was real and terrifying, as I had personally experienced. The nerves of people living in London must be in tatters.

We all worked hard to collect our apples and pears to make cider and lay apples down for the winter months ahead. The children loved running around the trees picking up any apples and running to the cart to put them in. Again, everyone came together to help, and our cider press worked hard to make apple juice, apple or pear cider for us and the other farms. On October 31, 1944, during Halloween a rare full moon occurred, which we thought was a good omen for the harvest being another bumper one. I'm not sure that the moon had a lot to do with it, but it turned out to be a good harvest. Next, Rhys and Gruffydd started to harvest their two acres of produce of shallots, onions, garlic, carrots, parsnips, turnips, swedes, beetroot, marrows, and runner beans. They had successfully grown strawberries, gooseberries, raspberries, redcurrants, blackcurrants, spring onions, broad beans, garden peas, and in the glasshouse tomatoes, courgettes, cucumbers, lemons, and peaches. Plus, we had been supplied with honey all year and they had many jars of honey stored for the winter months ahead. We now scoured the hedges for blackberries, rosehips, damsons, crab apples and sloes. More wine was soon fermented in our demijohns made from the produce of our hedgerows. I had invested in more clay storage jars for preserving and bottling and had managed to get hold of some more Kilner jars with the help of Arthur Laxton. So now it was over to the team in our kitchen to begin making chutneys, preserves, jams, lemon curds, pickled eggs and onions, jellies, and sloe gin. The team consisted of Mrs Revill, Audrey, Danielle, Margaret and me with help or hindrance from Lottie and Ruby. This year we had the added help of Helen Archer, who at fourteen was particularly good as she had always helped her mother with her garden produce. Grandora's contribution was to supply the gin; I did not ask from where it came. Mrs Revill had been saving sugar from our sugar rations for this occasion. I was convinced we should set up a shop selling our produce and I had plans in my head for a name to put on the jars. I had discussed the idea with Grandora, and she was just as enthusiastic about the new venture as I was.

November came, and as some blackout restrictions had been lifted in September, we were able to use the lights in the stables as the nights grew darker much earlier again. Plus, no ARP warden yelling at us to 'PUT THOSE LIGHTS OUT'. I dreaded the dark nights and short, chilly winter days making outdoor jobs difficult in the dark. The fighting in Europe dragged on and we continued to hear nothing of my parents. Grandora kept ringing up important people she knew to try to find any news of them, without any luck. President Franklin D. Roosevelt was re-elected as President for an unprecedented fourth term. A successful Allies operation continually located and destroyed the locations of the V1 rockets which had been fired on London, but now Joseph Goebbels had announced the V-2 rocket campaign had begun and Winston Churchill announced that the explosions of the last few weeks had been these new weapons. Malissa came home at last and told us that the Allies had recognized the government of the Albanian partisan leader Enver Hoxha, who she hoped would prove to be a good leader, but she was full of doubt. We also heard the good news that all German troops had now left Greece. Malissa slept for a day after her arrival and then told me she was staying at the Hall for two weeks' holiday as she was over-tired and not able to concentrate on her work. I was just delighted to have her at home. We celebrated the destruction of the German battleship Tirpitz in Operation Catechism by RAF bomber command; in celebration the lights of Fleet Street, Piccadilly and the Strand were turned on after five years of blackout. Were we finally winning this dreadful war? Well, we lived in hope that we were.

On November 11th Armistice Day, we all walked to the Church Remembrance Day parade which was mainly made up of the Home Guard. There were uniforms from all the Services, but not as many as usual as most were away fighting the war. The youngest children ran on ahead home as we older ones walked home. I was deep in thought, thinking about Tiff, Merry, Osian, Jabbo, Scotty and Rory. I could go on and on naming all the other young men who had stayed with us over the last years. Portia's husband Alastair was now involved in training new recruits in the RAF and Lysander was stationed somewhere in France. Towards the end of the month a V-2 rocket fell on Chancery Lane and High Holborn, killing 6 people and injuring 292. Then another one landed across the street from Woolworths department store in New Cross South London, killing 168 people. It was sad and depressing news. Then we heard that another V-2 flying bomb had killed 157 people in Antwerp. It was truly sickening. Sometimes I didn't want to hear any news at all, just pretend none of it was real and not happening.

December brought little joy to us in comfortable Norfolk, and I mean the joy of hearing from our loved ones. I received a request to house two children from London whose father had been killed in a V-2 bombing; their mother was a nurse and needed to keep on working. The parents were from the West Indies and the children were seven and three years old. Of course, I said yes, and this time they were delivered to the Hall one day, in time for children's teatime, so Amani and Linford Bailey joined our war family. Amani was only three years and gorgeous, and her brother was seven and quiet and serious. They were dropped off by a lady who had to hurry off to catch the train back to London and she thrust a folder with their details into my hands and was gone. The poor bewildered children just stared at me with big brown eyes, looking very frightened. I smiled at them.

"Come on, you two, let's go into the kitchen and meet the children staying here, and don't be worried because we have been looking forward to you coming to stay with us. Oh, my name is Sid, and I can see from this letter that you are Linford and Amani, I am pleased to meet you."

I took them into the kitchen and told them to sit on the chairs waiting for them. There was immediate silence in the kitchen as all eyes turned to look at them.

Gerald got up and walked over to them and said, "Hello, I'm Gerald and I'll introduce you to my brother and sisters. You won't remember them straight away, but you will soon get to know us all."

How kind of him, I thought.

Rosie asked them if they were hungry, but they remained silent. She gave them plates of toad in the hole, saying, "If you like this there's more for you and would you like some gravy?"

Still silence from the little ones.

"I think it would be for the best if you got on with your tea and I will help Amani to eat hers," I said to them all, and I sat next to her and cut up the sausage and Yorkshire pudding. There was apple pie and custard for afters and milk to drink.

Ruby finished hers and came over followed by Lottie and asked me, "Can we show her our toys? Can we play with her?"

"Yes, of course, if she will go with you," I said.

Ruby gave Amani a teddy bear to hold and Amani held both their hands as they toddled off to see their dolls.

"Do you play cricket?" asked Roger who was seven and Christopher looked on waiting for a reply.

Linford nodded. "I play in the park with my daddy. I mean I did."

Tears filled his eyes and Linda went over to him and gave him a hug. "Come on, Linford, you can play snakes and ladders with me." She took his hand and led him into the playroom.

We have lovely children staying with us, I thought and sighed. "Poor things, they must be exhausted, I'll start taking hot water bottles upstairs to put into the beds."

Larry and Gerald helped me to ferry up six hot water bottles then went back for six more. I had put the two new children together in a room next to Linda and Helen, as I was sure they would keep an eye on them for me. Their room was warm and cosy and had a new brightly coloured peg rug on the floor made by Maisie and bright yellow patchwork patterned curtains with patchwork covers on the beds made by Merry. I had pushed one bed up to the wall so hopefully little Amani wouldn't fall. It was soon bedtime for them, and I took them upstairs and helped them get ready. Linda and Helen came in and took over from me and began to read a book of nursery rhymes to them. These traumatised children settled in over the next few weeks with the help and kindness of all our war children.

Linford soon became best friends with Roger and Christopher, and they all played well together with Ashneer and Virinder, usually playing cricket. Little Amani latched onto Ruby and Lottie, and spent time helping them to dress and undress their dolls. Amani couldn't go to school – she was too young – and Rosie was busy helping in the house, so we took her into the old school room where Bargitta and Panaya were happy to keep an eye on her whilst working with the knitting group. We soon made up an afternoon bed for her to sleep in whilst staying with all the ladies in the group and they all made a fuss of her. Maisie turned out to be brilliant and took over looking after little Amani when she wasn't working, and between her and Audrey, she began to learn nursery rhymes and even read some words.

That year we made the usual effort to celebrate Christmas and it was a mend and make do Christmas regarding presents. Audrey and Maisie helped the children to make gifts for each other and to make more Christmas decorations for the Hall. Gruffydd and Rhys helped Granger to choose a tree to bring into the house and this was the first year it was only about seven feet tall; still not bad, but not as tall as the trees we usually had in the big hall. It was going to be the first Christmas without Jabbo staying with us since I had arrived home from France, and I missed his help and cheerfulness. Gerald's parents were joining us over Christmas, and they had booked a room in the pub in the village; Larry, Lennie, and Lottie's mother was busy working at RAF Scampton in the kitchen there and was unable to visit us until New Year's Eve. The week before Christmas Rhys received his call-up papers as he was eighteen years old, nearly nineteen and he was willing to go, but was worried about leaving Gruffydd on his own with so much work needing to be done on the garden. Grandora was on his case in a flash and registered him as an essential worker, a land army man. So, a Ministry man called to see us, and we were able to show him just how much Rhys was needed to grow food and how much he had achieved whilst he had been working here. I was seriously concerned how we would manage without him. We now had three hundred egg laying hens, two hundred cockerels, three hundred turkeys, all looked after by the two boys, and they cared for the bees. When he saw our food store and checked the inventory of our farm produce the Ministry man was impressed and agreed he needed to stay with us. He suggested at first that we employ a German prisoner of war, but when I explained one of our refugees had been very badly treated by the Gestapo, he understood my reasons for refusing. He was able to see how productive we were, and he left empty-handed and happy; well not literally empty-handed as he left with eggs, butter, farm cheese, cider and honey; and we were able to keep Rhys.

We had twenty-five for Christmas lunch sitting at the table and it was a very jolly affair with homemade hats and homemade crackers without any bangs. It's difficult making pretend crackers with just newspaper. We managed one turkey and one large capon, two stuffed rabbits with homemade stuffing, roast potatoes, carrots, roast parsnips, cauliflower, and mashed swede. We even had homemade Christmas pudding with fruit in it, not a lot, but we poured a little of Grandora's brandy over it and set it alight and it looked impressive. We had yet again managed to make presents for the children and Grandora had bought pencils, crayons and notebooks for each child and little jigsaws for them all. Bless her, she had managed to buy kaleidoscopes for them and whipping tops, chalks and skipping ropes. The Knitting club had made little dresses and jumpers for the girls' dollies, plus jumpers for each child with hats, scarves, and gloves. I had drawn all of them illustrations of their favourite cartoon characters and turned them into Christmas cards. Maisie had knitted characters from Peter Rabbit for the girls. For the rest I had made sketches of our glorious countryside and turned them into Christmas card keepsakes. Malissa was most impressed. Well, she said she was. Mr and Mrs Archer loved seeing their children and spending time with us all at Christmas. They were a lovely family. In fact, Malissa and I cleared up with Audrey and Maisie while Nico and the Archers went for a walk in the park after lunch with all of the children and the dogs. Susan and Roger were invited for Christmas lunch with Margaret, Hugh, George and Theo. Meanwhile, Rhys and Gruffydd had travelled home to see their family in Dartmoor, not an easy journey, in view of all the restrictions, but they hadn't seen any of them for ages. Merry was in Scotland staying with Scotty's parents, helping Scotty recover from serious injuries. I hadn't been told how or where he had been injured, Merry had just told me she wouldn't be home for Christmas, and could I organise the boys going back to Dartmoor to see their father and brothers.

As usual it was a quiet New Year's Eve, with the adults sharing a meal together after the youngest children had gone to bed. Miriam and Rory joined us as Rory had leave. Larry and Gerald were allowed to stay up late for the celebration as they were now young adults. They disappeared after the meal with Nico and Rory for a game of billiards and we sat around the table for ages discussing the war and what was happening in Europe. It was the first time Rory hinted at the murder of Jewish people by Hitler and about the horror of the concentration camps. He only hinted, but we were all shocked and worried – what if it was true, what did it all mean? What about my parents and their treatment in Japanese prisoner of war camps? We were all quiet when it was twelve o'clock and we toasted in the New Year of 1945 with a prayer for all the people in Europe and the Far East, fighting evil doctrine.

Chapter 36

War in Europe Ends

January had only just begun when one morning after helping at the stables I returned for breakfast and Rosie arrived to say Mrs Revill had influenza. First of all, we prepared breakfast for the hungry horde, and it was ready for them as they came downstairs for school. Granger rode with them on his bicycle as they all had bicycles now to ride along our quiet lanes to school. Even Ruby and Lottie and now Linford and Roger cycled the three miles to school, winter, and summer. If it was necessary because of bad weather, we took the horses and two traps. Fuel shortages were hitting everyone and there wasn't any petrol allowed for privately owned cars. It had been too icy for me to ride Hermes, which was just as well because now I had to plan our meals for the week. However, I had been to the stables to help muck out the horses, so before I started cooking, I just had to remember to take off my jumper first, as I was generally covered in horse hairs, and it wasn't a good idea to serve hairy food! I soon organised wartime cauliflower with bacon and spam for tea, and cheese and potato dumplings for Talia and Adele, with Danish apple pudding for us all. I then went straight round to visit Mrs Revill who lived alone, but she insisted I left in case I caught influenza as well. Mrs Hubbard said she would look after her, so I left and went home. Despite the precautions, by the end of the week we had Gerald, Linda, and Larry with influenza and for some reason Helen had tonsillitis at the same time. What a nightmare running up and down stairs with soothing drinks for them all, plus medicine brought by Dr Haigh; it seemed to last for ever and we isolated them to minimize the others catching it, in particular, Grandora.

My meals were reasonably well received – well they had no choice – and I prepared carrot scones, and teatime sandwiches of gooseberry jam, rhubarb jam and marmite, which was a love it or hate it sandwich. I made rabbit stew for tea the next day, as I personally didn't fancy pigeon pie, so that was never going to be on the menu. Most days I made vegetable soup, as I could throw everything into it from the kitchen garden. We had ration books for all of us, including the children, it was just that having a farm meant we had access to more food and a greater variety. We regularly were able to exceed our food quota to the Government. We couldn't abuse the privilege we had with so much food available from the farm; that just wouldn't be right. I'm just saying we did very well, and I should add Mrs Revill did very well for us all; she was an excellent cook. I took her some chicken broth, blackcurrant juice and rose-hip syrup, hoping it would help her to recover quickly. I raided the larder and discovered her recipe for Lord Wootton pie and the rolled out mashed potato looked just like pastry. It was a great success on the top of the vegetable pie and tasted good. Mrs Revill had also, by now, been making a drink, every autumn, from acorns – she just boiled them for fifteen minutes until dark brown, then peeled them. After this the acorns were split, dried, crushed and briefly grilled to make a nutritious drink. Unfortunately, it was just another drink that I didn't like much, it was a definite 'ugh' for me. In fact, very few of us liked it. I discovered jars of the stuff as I beetled through the larder.

Rhys supplied all the vegetables for my pie, and I found dried lovage to add, hanging up in the larder. Short of spring onions, I used shallots instead. Another good standby was Colcannon, cooked cabbage and potatoes fried together, and I decided to make that one day with sausages. Poor Mrs Revill, it was several weeks before she could get rid of an awful cough following the influenza and I was very glad of Margaret's help with the cooking during that time. We needed more help in the Hall. I wondered who I could employ to help Mrs Revill more in the kitchen. The housework took a back seat yet again.

We heard that the Battle of the Bulge in the Ardennes had finally been a success for the Allies, and they had broken through to the Siegfried Line after the collapse of the German troops. It sounded as if it had been a long and difficult battle and the American army had suffered significant losses. 'The Screaming Eagles' of 101 company held out in the Siege of Bastogne under extraordinary and harrowing circumstances until the American P-47 Thunderbolts went to their rescue with reinforcements and supplies via airdrop, it was reported in the papers. It had taken from 16th December until January 25th for the Battle of the Bulge to reach a successful conclusion, with great loss of life. We heard most of this from an American airman staying with us. He had been injured when landing his crippled plane back in Britain at Great Massingham. The landing gear on his bomber had been smashed up. His crew of eight men were thankfully all OK.

It was shortly after hearing about this that we heard about a new bombing campaign in Germany. We always heard the heavy rumble of the bomber aircraft as they took off for their targets in Europe and we were so used to them we hardly noticed. It was a frightening sound though. However, on February 13th there seemed to be more throaty rumbles than usual throughout the day and night. It was early evening, and I was walking up from the stables towards Audrey's cottage when Squadron Leader Richard Petersfield was driven down the drive. The car stopped alongside, and a sombre Squadron Leader got out and came over to me. I saw his face and held my breath.

"My dear, can we go in and find your grandmother?" he asked, gently steering me towards the house.

"What is it, why are you here?" I asked, as we walked towards the door.

Grandora was in the reception hall and walked over, smiling at first, then she stopped. "What is it, Richard?"

"I came in person as I believe you have been good friends to Rory Kaiholm, and I regret to inform you that he has crashed on his way back from a bombing raid and I am afraid he didn't survive."

The world stood still. I walked in a daze towards the door.

"Cressida, stop, wait."

I was through the door, I didn't know where to run. I just had to run away, only I could not run, my legs were like lead. I didn't see, I didn't look anywhere, I could only see Rory grinning, blond hair flopping onto his face, playing with the children, playing cricket, riding, at the stables talking to Granger, Jabbo and Lennie. Rory with his sleeves rolled up, strong brown arms hoisting sheaves of corn onto the cart. Rory roaring up the drive on his motorbike, Rory laughing and dancing with Miriam, love in his bright blue eyes. Miriam, Lennie, Oh God, Ruby, and Lottie, Oh God.

I reached The Tree, I put one hand onto the tree, Rory's favourite tree, The Cedar of Lebanon, where he sat with Grandora in the shade and watched the cricket, the horses grazing, the children playing. I heard a muffled howl, a sort of animal moan – I didn't recognise it or know where it came from; I couldn't get my breath. I heaved for air, moaned and then I sobbed and sobbed. My chest hurt, my head hurt, and I leant onto the tree and felt its rough bark on the palms of my hand. This was Rory's tree and then I saw him easing the birth sack off Rory's Star as the mare gave birth. Oh, poor Rory, how could so much love of life be gone, snuffed out in this hateful war.

"I HATE IT!" I screamed.

I felt a hand on my shoulder, but I continued to sob for the brightest life, the blue eyes, blond hair, for his kindness, his gentleness. I looked up and saw Miriam next to me, her face stricken with tears coursing down her cheeks; she put her hand into mine. Danielle was next to her with Tad, Grandora, and Audrey. Then one by one they all came to The Tree. Mrs Revill, Rosie with Amani and Linford, Mrs Singh, Ashneer and Virinder, Gerald, Helen, Christopher, and Linda. Granger and Larry appeared with Lennie between them, Larry had his arm round a sobbing Lennie. George, Margaret, Susan and Roger, Theo and Hugh, Lucy and Sheila arrived. Word had spread fast of the saddest of news, about the man we had all grown to care for and respect. Ruby ran to me, and Lottie sobbing followed her, and they wrapped their arms around my waist and I hugged them tight with tears running down my face. In the shadows was Squadron Leader Richard Petersfield, silent, with his head bowed, next to him were the two pilots staying with us. Somehow in silence we all held hands round

Rory's favourite tree; all of us crying. He had touched every one of us with his bright aura of love, friendship, and kindness. No words were spoken, none were needed. We stood in silence and companionship; all of us remembering our friend.

Squadron Leader Petersfield then said the words: "O God by whose mercy the faithful departed find rest, look kindly on your departed veterans who gave their lives in the service of their country. Grant that through the passion, death, and resurrection of your Son they may share in the joy of your heavenly kingdom and rejoice in you with your saints forever. Amen."

There was silence; then Granger suddenly quoted with passion the last verse of the poem by Lieutenant Colonel John McCrae, 'In Flanders fields':

Take up our quarrel with the foe:
To you from failing hands we throw
The torch; be yours to hold on high.
If ye break faith with us who die
We shall not sleep, though poppies grow
In Flanders fields.

Slowly in silence we made our way back to the Hall until Ruby pointed at the sky and said, "Look, a shooting star; Rory said, Night Night."

We all saw it and somehow, maybe, she was right. Perhaps he was saying Night Night. I hugged poor distraught Miriam, and she was led back to the cottage by Danielle and Audrey. With tears still streaming, I hugged Lennie who was inconsolable. Larry took him back to Granger's cottage. Spud, Lennie's dog, followed them with his tail trailing. When we got back to the house, Rosie, Gerald and Helen took charge of the children and put them all to bed; they were all subdued. I went to my bedroom and Grandora soon came in with two glasses of whisky. We sat in silence on my sofa, and I curled up next to her with my head on her shoulder and fresh tears fell. Eventually I looked at Grandora and she was crying too.

"He was a star," she said. "I was very fond of him." She sighed. "You must get into bed now. Just take off your jodhpurs and boots, I will stay with you tonight." She held me like a child as I cried, then my door was quietly opened, and two little girls crept into my bed and snuggled next to me and Grandora. Finally, blessed sleep came for all of us.

Every time I heard the unmistakable sound of the Avro Lancaster bomber's four Rolls-Royce Merlin engines flying overhead, I looked up for a moment, thinking of Rory. I never stopped looking, hoping... Sometime shortly after that awful day, Grandora called Lennie and me into the study. She proceeded to tell Lennie of a conversation she had had with Rory some weeks before he died. Apparently, he wanted to buy Rory's Star and at that time Grandora had discussed it with me and we both had agreed to give him the colt. Now unknown to me he had written a will bequeathing Rory's Star to Lennie along with his motorbike, flying jacket, boots, and camera, plus enough money for Lennie's education and enough to keep, train and equip Rory's Star with any tack he needed. When Lennie heard this, he was overcome with sadness and burst into tears.

"He thought of you like the son he didn't have, but if he ever had a son he hoped he would be like you," said Grandora gently. "He knows you adore the colt, and he trusts you will always take care of him. He has helped you with his training and knows you will carry on with fear-free training and give the young colt time to understand you and to grow and mature."

"I don't deserve it; I just want him back. I want to talk to him again and hear about his home in Canada, I want to see him, I miss him so much," Lennie jerkily said between sobs.

I started to cry. "I miss him too, I miss his smile, his laid-back way, his jokes and his long legs stuck out always in the way, and his gorgeous cowboy boots."

Lennie slowly smiled suddenly. "They were always stuck out, weren't they; he was so funny, and so good to be around. He made everything seem OK."

I put my arm round him and hugged him.

"Go and tell Granger and Larry. They will want to know why I asked to see you. It's wonderful he has left you enough money for your future. You have a nest egg, Lennie, he wanted you to have a good future and freedom to choose it," added Grandora.

Lennie looked shocked and muttered, "Thank you," as he rushed out.

I sat down in silence, relief, and shock. "That's a lovely thing he did." I sighed. "He was a lovely soul with the biggest heart of gold, but what about Miriam?"

"I have a letter for her and a parcel, but I don't know what's in it. I knew about what he left Lennie if he didn't make it, as Lennie is underage, but I am not privy to his private gift to Miriam," said Grandora. "I will give it to her this evening."

We had an enormous problem keeping the children in clothes that fitted them as they grew, and material was almost impossible to find, as were shoes. They were rationed in America too: all manufacturing was for military fabric and footwear for the services. We all had ration books, and coupons with which to buy clothes. Eleven coupons were needed to buy a dress, two were needed for stockings, five for ladies' shoes. It was difficult deciding what you needed most as there were not enough coupons for everything. School uniforms had to be worn and they had to be correct, so children swopped them as they outgrew them, and they were passed around and used by many children. Gaberdines were a nightmare to find for all the children. These were made of wool or cotton and were supposed to be a raincoat although not all worked very well in heavy rain. They were a smooth fabric, usually lined in a check or tartan and were worn belted. They were standard school uniform for all the children. Outgrown cardigans and jumpers were either passed on or unravelled and then re-knitted into new jumpers made to fit and then passed on to other children. The WVS helped by taking clothes from people who no longer needed them and giving them to someone who did. The make-do-and-mend campaign was launched to encourage people to make their clothes and make them last for as long as possible. Mrs Hubbard was a genius seamstress who helped us alter clothes to fit different children and to be worn for different occasions. I looked in my old school trunk and discovered my school uniform and Portia's tunics, girdles, our blazers and blouses. The brilliant Mrs Hubbard soon altered them to fit Lottie, Ruby, and Susan. It was a good job we could buy some material with our coupons and give it to Mrs Hubbard to make some clothes for the children. Not only did Grandora have a supply of materials she had bought and stored over the years, but so did my mother. The problem was my mother's material collection was mostly silks and velvets or brocades and my grandmother's were rolls of exotic Indian sari material and African brightly coloured tribal cottons which she had collected on her travels. We put most of them to good use though. We sent to Harrods for shoes for the children and managed to keep them in one pair of sandals each, every summer with one decent pair of school shoes for the winter. They wore wellington boots all through the winters, even in summer with shorts, well pretty much all the time. Meanwhile I too wore wellington boots and jodhpurs or trousers every day to the despair of Grandora. She was a very modern forward-thinking grandmother, but even she got fed-up with my constant horsey clothing attire. In the summer I confess to wearing long shorts and sandals with a short-sleeved shirt – I was too busy to worry about what I looked like.

We had always allowed the pony club access to the estate during the summer months for their riding practice and summer camp, but this had petered out during the last few war years. I now had a request from Davinia Hardcastle-Cord for permission to start using the field during the Easter and summer holidays, the same one they had used before. They were going to start the pony club activities again for the local children. The field in question was now growing potatoes so I said I would find an alternative and be in touch with her later in the week. There was always something to deal with, but I was keen to help the pony club. Lysander, Portia and I had all been members in the past and it had been great fun. I decided to consult with Ted over the right field, but I thought what was left of the park might be the best place. We now had a permanent cricket field and Granger and Jabbo had been planning to build a small stand. I thought a pavilion would be a good idea although perhaps it would be a step too far. As the weather improved the children, girls and boys were always out practicing their cricket skills every day after school and at weekends, weather permitting. Larry had discovered that my grandfather and my father had been keen collectors of the hard-backed Wisden and we had always taken the monthly cricket magazine as well. He regularly poured over these tomes with Gerald, discussing the best cricketers of the past and of their present favourites. The Yorkshire cricket writer Jim Kilburn called Yorkshire County 'one of the best-rounded teams of all time, with men of true genius in Headley Verity and Len Hutton'. I think they also wanted to emulate Denis Compton and they would try hard to capture the prowess of the great cricketers in British cricket, many of these now in uniform and fighting for us.

We earmarked a part of the park nearest to Ted's farm for the pony club and Lennie, Ruby and Lottie wanted to join with Donk, Tizzy and Spangles, so, I paid their subscription; they were very excited about their first pony club meeting in April. As usual in the run-up to Easter we started the tradition of making Easter eggs after school in the school room. Larry, Lennie and Gerald, George and Theo declined to paint any this year; well, they were grown up young men now. Helen, Linda, Christopher, Susan, Roger, Linford and Talia, Adele, Tad, Ruby, and Lottie all painted eggs and collected sticks for a 'boat' race to be held on the little bridge over the river after Easter Sunday lunch, helped by Audrey.

Easter Sunday arrived and we all walked to Church for the Easter Service, as did practically all the villagers. We had two 'flyers' and an RAF guy staying with us, and they walked with us, giving the youngest children piggy backs if they became too tired. I realised that the RAF guy was an old school friend of Lysander called Brennan Shillington, back to stay with us again. He had been to stay with us one summer and it was his sister Thady who had been one of my tormentors when I had been at boarding school. He was great with the children, and I had found an old pushchair for Amani, which Brennan proudly pushed. At one time this had been a very smart pushchair, which I suppose, I had also been pushed in, a long time ago. He was soon zooming around the group with Amani giggling in her pushchair. The four youngest children wore brightly coloured dresses made from cotton sari material and Linford had a bright shirt made from

some fabulous material from Africa. All of us wore our coats as it
was a chilly April 1st, and a strong wind blew from the direction
of the coast. Once back at home the small children had potato
piglets for lunch which they loved and were easy to make; just
jacket potatoes with sausages pushed in the middle with carrot
ears on top and carrot legs. We all had sausage roll, steamed
pudding, and cheese and red lentil savoury, followed by bread-
and-butter pudding. Later, after changing from our Sunday best
clothes to our knock about ones, we walked down to the river
to race the sticks under the bridge and then went for a walk in
the woods with the dogs. Back home, it was indoor board games
before beetroot, marmite or jam sandwiches for tea and carrot
scones and homemade biscuits before bed.

The next day I bumped into Brennan, and we chatted about
the horses and what Lysander was doing now. I knew not to ask
why he was staying with us, but I was very curious. I asked how
Thady was.

"Oh, she's doing OK. She finished 'uni' studying Botany and
was working at Kew Gardens cataloguing seeds from all over
the world: now she's working for the Government making sure
farmers are reaching their potential food quotas, assessing their
food producing ability and advising as to how it can be improved.
She's based somewhere in Kent."

Thank goodness she wasn't working in Norfolk, I thought.
"How is your younger brother Hywell? He was such a lively chap,
up for anything I thought he was great fun." I stopped when I
noticed his ashen face and his eyes fill with tears. "Brennan, what
is it? Oh no, I am sorry, I shouldn't ask." I was so mad with myself
for asking.

"No, don't worry, I just can't accept it yet. He joined the RAF to
train as a mechanic first and a flyer after; he thought it would be

useful to understand how a plane worked. He loved fiddling with engines. He was working on a Hurricane, going for a quick turn around when the airfield was attacked. He wasn't yet nineteen." He paused then went on, "I see young men every day coming to me for advice or help before their missions, and they don't return; you know so many don't return. I see their earnest faces at communion and then they're gone. And now my little brother Hyewell. It's too much."

"Are you a padre?" I asked surprised.

"Yes, but I haven't worn my collar here, I can't really face it at the moment. I'm a C of E padre in the RAF stationed in Norfolk, I don't have my own Church. I was a curate in London before I joined up. That's why I'm here shirking my duties, hiding from the truth I'm not as brave as those young men and I don't think I have done enough to help the war effort." He tapped a cigarette on a silver case, put it in his mouth and with shaking hands he tapped the lighter and lit it.

I was in earnest when I told him, "No you're not shirking, don't think like that. You did support those young men when they needed it, and no one can blame you for taking time out after hearing about the death of Hyewell."

I sat next to him in silence as he drew deeply on his cigarette – "thanks for listening," he said, "you're doing a great job here. I'm leaving today off to my unit. Oh, I've seen Serena, she works on the same base. She said to say hi to you." He left later that day to join his squadron.

It was towards the end of April the Pony Club held their first rally since 1939 and our three excited young riders took part for the very first time. Fortunately, we had one of those rare April days of sun lighting up the park and a crisp breeze keeping the clouds on their toes and sending them scudding across the sky.

There were hints of new, bright green growth creeping along the boughs of the trees and along the hedgerows showing new life and new hope springing up everywhere. I had caught a glimpse that week of a new fawn in the woods running with its doe, such a wondrous sight which always delighted me.

All the children were given the opportunity to ride but not all of them wanted to take it up as a hobby. Donk was safe and sweet with Lottie on board and trundled around the laid-out riding school area as good as gold. Tizzy went well for Ruby who had become quite bossy when riding her which was exactly what naughty Tizzy needed, a firm rider. Spangles was an old timer at the pony club and knew what was expected of him and so Lennie did very well. They had all helped Granger to groom, clean prepare the ponies and clean the tack for the occasion and I was very proud of them all. We were the biggest group of people there on the side of the arena as all of us had gone to support our three intrepid riders.

Ruby and Lennie jumped cavaletti poles and Lottie took Donk over a series of poles on the ground. Donkeys don't usually like jumping unless tempted with food. They all had a lot of fun playing mounted games after the serious business of learning how to be better jockeys. Lennie won the bending race because Spangles was always brilliant at pony club and Ruby won the sack race with Tizzy, and Lottie came second in the apple bobbing contest. Davinia had a booming voice like a Sergeant Major and kept control of all the exuberant children and their errant ponies. They came home very happy and had made lots of new friends.

Happily, Frankie arrived home on leave one weekend at the beginning of May and we were relieved and thrilled to have him home. Of course, he had to go back, but he had a whole week to spend at home and we were eager for news of what had been happening. He told us he had been in France servicing army vehicles However, his injured arm and shoulder meant he was kept behind in Dunkirk with the mechanics working for him. He had been promoted to Sergeant, so we were all very proud of him. He was puzzled not to hear any news about his missing regiment the 2nd Battalion Norfolk Regiment. It was mystifying many people how so many soldiers had simply disappeared during the fighting at the time of the retreat from Dunkirk. This must have been just after Frankie had been taken to a field hospital. Were they made prisoners, if so, where were they? Meanwhile Mrs Burden and Rosie were made up when he arrived back; it had been so long since they had seen him at home.

I was in the stable yard helping untack the ponies, washing them off and making sure the happy, but very tired children looked after their ponies before going for tea, when Jabbo casually walked round the corner of the yard and just stood grinning at us. We all rushed over to him, and Lottie and Ruby swamped him with hugs. Lennie shook his hand and I just stood and smiled; I was so relieved and pleased to see him. He was in army fatigues and looked worn out, dirty and unshaven. Who cares, he had made it back home and that's all that mattered. As soon as was decent I asked where Tiff was. He just grinned and pointing, announced, "Behind you." I whirled around and flung myself into his arms with Ruby and Lottie now clinging onto his trousers. We couldn't stop laughing. With the horses munching a feed we went up to the house leaving Jabbo shaking Granger's hand and Lennie grinning like a Cheshire cat. Grandora came into the hall to see Tiff and we went into her sitting room with Lottie and Ruby who were so excited to be with him and rushing to show Grandora their rosettes. I suggested they went to show their dollies their rosettes and they thought that was a good idea and left us alone. We both wanted to know where he had been, but it was classified so we didn't ask again. We did learn they had hitched a ride home on a plane from somewhere in the Netherlands and come straight to see us. He asked if he could shower before having dinner, and I remembered I was in charge of the children's tea and our dinner so jumped up and rushed into the kitchen. It was a noisy tea and I juggled getting our evening meal ready at the same time. I had made a mince pie which had plenty of vegetables in it to make it go further and served it with roast potatoes with rhubarb pie and custard for dessert. There was just the three of us in Grandora's sitting room which was lovely, we shared a bottle of Sancerre from Tantetta's vineyard, and I served a little of our farm's cheddar cheese with some oat biscuits. It was very decadent for war food with rationing, but what the heck my hero had come home. Jabbo stayed to eat with Granger and Lennie as he wanted to be near Zoltan and Zippy and have an early night. As before, when Tiff had stayed, he was exhausted and slept in my room on the sofa. We didn't talk for long, but we chatted about Rory, and he hugged me tight as I cried again. He said he was going to be here in the morning for breakfast, but had to leave late morning, for London, for a debriefing. I just hoped and prayed he didn't go back to fight or get into the path of a V-2 doodlebug. He did hint that the Allies were closing in on Berlin and that the war was definitely going our way at last. I was tired out having prepared breakfast, made sandwiches for a picnic lunch for everyone and run around at the pony club meeting pushing Amani in a pushchair and having nightmares she might get trampled by a horse as she toddled round. How do couples have more than one child as it's so exhausting and surely they are too tired for any more rumpy pumpy.

I still rode my gorgeous mare every morning and after a
peaceful start to the now warming, sparkling green, spring days
I just seemed to rush around arranging everything and still
checking we had met our expected Government food quotas.

Tradespeople were hard to come by and were often needed
on the Estate but so many had enlisted in the forces, the file was
endless and then I had to see children's teachers, tenants, or
our customers. Thank goodness Granger kept tabs on when the
horses and ponies needed to visit the farrier for new shoes. It was
everyday something needed fixing or fetching or taking, and I
loved it. I did find time to sketch and water colour, but I never had
the time to do any oil painting.

May 5th arrived, and it was rumoured the war was nearly
at an end; amazing and wonderful. On the 30th April it was
reported that Hitler had committed suicide with Eva Braun whom
he had married forty hours before their suicide. More reports
kept seeping through the cracks of atrocities committed by the
Nazis against the Jews, Gypsies, black people, disabled people,
communists, homosexuals' political prisoners and prisoners of
war. At first many people found them to be incredulous stories
and wondered how they could be true. There were some horrific
stories coming from the whole of the Continent and it seemed
to be of starving people everywhere with many displaced trying
to find their way home.

We had endured an awful time with shortages and suffered
so many deaths from the bombing. So many of our young men,
soldiers, seamen and airmen had been killed in action and many
civilians lost their lives from Nazi attack, but it was the people in
Europe who had suffered the most.

May 7th came, and it was announced at 7.30 pm that war had
ended, and that May 8th was to be a brief holiday for everyone

to celebrate. The Church bells rang out throughout Britain signalling war was over. Our dear 'Winnie' added we could not lose sight of the fact that we were still fighting a war against Japan. At 3 p.m. on Tuesday May 8th, 1945, Winston Churchill announced on the wireless to all of us that Nazi Germany had surrendered to the Allied Forces calling it Victory in Europe Day. At that time, we were in our village celebrating with everyone, the end of the war in Europe. We had trestle tables out in the street from the village hall, full of food, for everyone. Margaret, Mrs Revill, and I had baked buns, scones and cakes and prepared sandwiches for everyone. We had kept red, white, and blue bunting stored in the village hall since the end of the Great War and this had hastily been erected on the road around the village green. Talia, Adele, and Theo brought their instruments, and the few players of village brass band were there too. They played every merry song we knew like Roll Out The Barrell, and we did the jitter bug and boogied. Finally, we did the conga all around the village square. Fires were lit in a metal barrel and as dark descended, someone, I don't know who, gave us a brief firework display. Our crew wandered home afterwards a bedraggled crocodile of happy, tired children and adults, up the dark lane home, all shining our torches and singing Vera Lynn songs. After six years of fighting, peace was at last to be restored. We had listened to the Prime Minister, Winston Churchill calling for a brief celebration and offering his gratitude to the Allies. He then reminded us that Britain was still at war with Japan a point all too real for me, my family and all the relatives of the thousands of prisoners held captive by the Japanese. The Allied forces were still fighting in the Pacific. On May 8th the Channel Islands were told the war had ended and they were liberated on May 10th. Then and as the days passed awful stories of the cruelty of Nazis came to light.

Tiff came back to Norfolk for a much-needed break and told me he was ready for a holiday and could I manage a week in Scotland with him. Even though Germany had surrendered he needed to go back to his base in the Highlands of Scotland. I was delighted and more than ready to travel away with him. First though I had a telephone call from Mr Archer saying they were looking forward to having their four children home and could I arrange their journey on the first available train to London. As Gerald was now seventeen he was more than capable of shepherding his siblings on the train. Mr. Archer thanked me for protecting and caring for them and asked if they could all come over to see me when petrol was available again. I told him I would like that very much. Over the next two days we seemed to just rush around getting train tickets, gathering their possessions which were all over the Hall, as they bicycled everywhere saying goodbye to all their new friends. We had already organised a cricket match to be held at the weekend and the boys were hoping Gerald would be able to play as he was a decent bowler. They were playing the scouts group even though some of our evacuees had joined the scouts they still played for Willup Cricket Club Junior Team.

After a successful win for Willup Hall, scoring 365 all out to us and 360 all out for our visitors, Gerald, Helen, Christopher, and Linda Archer departed for London. The very next day I had a visit from two official looking people, a man and a woman complete with briefcases. I asked them in and took them into the study, curious as what it was all about, and why they had not made an appointment to visit me.

"We believe you have two orphans living here as evacuees which at the cease of hostilities are no longer evacuees. We have come to collect them and take them to the orphanage," said the dour-faced lady official wearing a dark grey suit.

I was stunned and rendered speechless and very angry.

"We are here to collect Susan and Roger Brownson and would be pleased if you would bring them here to us so we can leave with them as soon as possible," she insisted.

Grandora walked into the office and in controlled anger I explained to her why this lady and gentleman were here. "I will need to speak to your superiors first before you remove any children from our care, so I would like you to leave your names, which office and department you are from, and leave my house immediately," Grandora told them sternly.

The man started to say something when there was a knock on the door and Tiff walked in. He took in the atmosphere, my strained face, as well as Grandora's grim and determined looks, and, turning to the couple without extending his hand, said smoothly, "Is there a problem?"

"Yes we have come to collect two children Susan and Roger Brownson to take to the orphanage. Now war has ceased they are no longer officially evacuees, and these ladies are refusing to let us take them: and who are you?" added the man.

"Major Tifford, and I agree with Lady Ellesdale, there won't be any children leaving here until all your papers are checked and we talk to your seniors to establish your authority; so, until then we wish you good day." With that he opened the door and showed them out.

The couple hesitated but Tiff had such an air of authority and determination they left without a word.

"Could they do that?" I asked, shocked by their appearance, and demands. "Take Susan and Roger away to an orphanage?"

"How awful, they will be devastated, and Margaret will be heartbroken now George is joining the army and Theo is going to university, she loves having them all staying with them," I added.

Grandora was studying the papers they had left. "I will phone my friend and we will sort this out. Where are the children right now?"

"They went to Hugh and Margaret's for tea and to walk the dogs?" I told her.

"Then we will all go over to see them immediately; ask Granger to bring the car round will you please. I will telephone to let them know we are on our way."

As it was just over half a mile, I didn't see the point in taking the car or fetching Granger, but Grandora had her mind set on sorting the job out immediately with no detours and definitely no quibbling.

Whilst the children were playing outside we quickly explained to Hugh and Margaret what we had just been told. They were both horrified, of course. Margaret looked at Hugh and a silent message passed between them; Hugh spoke first. "We have been discussing their future and we would like it to be with us; we know we are too old to have our own children and we have loved having George and Theodore staying with us, so we would like to adopt Susan and Roger. We have grown to love them very much. Do you think the authorities will approve of us?"

Tiff spoke up, "They will if I have anything to do with it. You are marvellous with the children."

"Very good and you are quite sure this is what you want to do?" asked Grandora.

"Yes," they said, in unison, holding hands.

"Right, we will set the wheels in motion with the relevant authorities immediately. Now, how about a nice cup of tea?" Grandora suggested.

"Oh yes, and what's that I heard about you being a Major?" I asked smiling.

Tiff took a mock bow. "At your service," he declared.

We all congratulated him; I was so thrilled and knew just how much he deserved it.

Days later Miriam who had been to see her family in Primrose Hill, London returned looking pale, drawn and was very quiet, as she had been since the awful news of Rory dying in action. I went round to Audrey's cottage to see her whilst Audrey was helping Granger tidy the tack room. I found her in tears, so I made some mint tea and sat with her waiting for her tears to stop. She had lost Rory and I knew it was impossible to move on; he was such an unforgettable presence in our lives and always would be.

"I am pregnant," she finally told me quietly. "And I am pleased, just so sad I can't share my news with Rory. My parents aren't too bad about it, but not thrilled, because he wasn't Jewish. They are pleased for me, but worried about me coping on my own."

"I am thrilled for you, and you will never be on your own you've got all of us to support you," I said, hugging her. My head was spinning with the implications of her news, but we would solve any problems, I just knew it.

"We were married you know in Gretna Green when we went to Scotland. We didn't tell anyone as we both wanted to tell our parents first and have a proper wedding celebration when the war was over. I have the marriage certificate to prove it. I just loved him so much; he was my world, and I am glad I have a part of him growing inside me," she added.

I was so happy for her and then I asked, "Rory left you a letter and a small parcel did he...?" The question hung in the air.

"Yes, he did." Her fingers touched a pendant of a gold tree; a Cedar of Lebanon hanging on a beautiful gold chain. "A reminder of where we had our first kiss and where he asked me to marry him," she said.

I admired it. "It's beautiful."

"He also left me his inheritance. I have no idea what it is, though, I have to contact a solicitor. I don't want his money I just want him back."

Fresh tears fell and I held her hand saying nothing. I felt a pain in my chest for her and Rory and at the same time I almost felt guilty about Tiff's safe return. We sat together in silent shared grief until Audrey and Danielle arrived. They both knew already, and Audrey put the kettle on again and the three of us stayed with Miriam offering our support and consoling her in every way we could.

Next morning after I had ridden and got wet through in unexpected torrential rain, I went into the cosy tack room, which always smelt of leather polish, for a drink, to dry, and chat with Lennie and Jabbo as I noticed they were both there. I turned the conversation round to Jabbo and Tiff's recent trip to wherever?

"Oh yes, I can tell you now, we went to France to help with the Marquis," Jabbo announced, "I know Tiff can tell you more about it so I think it would be best if he told you." He added, "He is an amazing man to be with I have great respect for him."

I needed to ask Tiff, then, where they had been, and I wondered why he hadn't told me anything before now. I left them and went back to my bedroom to pack for my trip to Scotland thinking I would ask him on our journey. I was desperate to know if he had visited the Chateau de la Cascade or contacted my friends there.

Odin came with us as he always did and at the last minute I decided to take Ruby and Lottie with us for a holiday and the little pooch of course. Rosie and Mrs Burden were having a week off to spend with Frankie now he was back, and that meant The Hall was short-staffed. To fill the gap, Audrey moved in, and with

Maisie's help they would look after Linford and Amani and the others. Susan and Roger would go and stay with Margaret and Hugh full time. Lennie and Larry were capable of looking after themselves apart from cooking meals and Talia and Adele were always reading, revising, or practicing playing their instruments and were never any trouble – so, for them as well it was just meals and washing. There were no airmen in residence and Grandora had gone to stay with her sister Lydia Anne. Gruffydd and Rhys were easily catered for, just an evening meal, so with everyone taken care of, we decided it was a perfect time to go away.

We took the sleeper train, and our journey followed the same route I had taken when we had visited Portia when she had been about to have her baby Rhona Isadora. We stayed at the Salutation Hotel on the River Tay again, and finally reached Portia and Alastair's house. I couldn't believe how much Hamish and Isadora had grown; they were now five and three years old. Ruby was soon playing and taking Lottie everywhere, showing her the school room, nursery, and playroom. The new nanny was in charge of Hamish and Rhona Isadora, so we were able chat for ages catching up on the last three years. Betsy had gone to do a midwifery course. Portia looked wonderful, glamorous as she always did, and we talked about the new venture with Danielle, designing and creating fashionable garments from Scottish wool. Now the war was nearly over we could make a start and plan for the future, especially the exciting business venture. Of course, after dinner Alastair and Portia played cards with us; they won and then we played chess, and they won again. Poor Tiff was not going to do very well with me as his partner when it came to cards or chess games.

Portia took me aside and asked if Tiff and I had 'done it' yet. Embarrassed I said, "No, we were waiting to be married first."

"You silly billy," she laughed. "I didn't know whether to give you a double bed or two single bedrooms."

I giggled and said, "Go on then we'll have a double."

That night when Tiff knew we were sharing, he stopped in the doorway. He looked at me intently, his eyes burning with love and desire. I went to kiss him slowly.

"I want my parents to be here for the wedding if that is possible," I said in a low voice, my arms around his neck. "But I don't want to wait any longer, I mean that is to wait for you."

He scooped me up into his arms and carried me to the bed. Slowly with my help he undressed me and not so slowly he wrestled out of his uniform and then just lay next to me stroking my skin, legs, shoulders, breasts then slowly, gently his fingers stroked me, and I gasped as he went further and then he lay on top of me, and I was scared and excited and in ecstasy. We moved together and I felt as if I was exploding. I shuddered over and over again. I kissed him and lifted my body up to him, over and over and pressed myself into him. Eventually we stopped and as the moonlight sought us out though the windows I touched his body all over with my hands, exploring every part of him. I snuggled nearer to him, and we needed each other again and this time we came together in a frenzy of lust and love. Then we slept in each other's arms until dawn peeped in. I moved towards him and climbed over him in silence, begging him to wake up which he did. This time he guided me onto him, and we rocked in rhythm, all the time staring into the depths of each other's souls, his magnetic eyes drew me in to kiss his lips and ignore his scratchy chin. We slept again and then started another passionate embrace and coupled again, hungry and starved for so long of this new beginning. We had a lot of waiting time to make up for. It was nearly breakfast time and we showered together – he pinned me against the cold tiles and I and pulled him towards me and I came the minute he entered me, and I moaned long and low as he kissed my nipples and moved down kissing me. I came again and whimpered for him to be inside me again and we rocked rhythmically together..

We had dressed by the time there was a knock on the door and Ruby came in to ask us when we were going down for breakfast – she added, "Aunty Portia wants to know."

I bet she did. I was glowing when we went into the morning room, and I felt my cheeks burning from so much kissing. Portia looked hard at us as we walked in, then grinned at us both and smoothly said, "It looks like you're both ready for a cooked breakfast, unless you're too tired."

I flushed and glared at her, Tiff smiled and buttered his toast replying, "You're right, I could eat a horse."

Alastair glanced up from his newspaper and reaching for the toast added, "My word, Sid, you are positively glowing this morning." Smiling at us all, he bit into his toast and lovingly glanced at Portia. I wondered if everyone knew or just guessed.

After breakfast Tiff rode around the enormous sheep farm with Alastair on two of the Highland ponies and Portia and I sat outside in the sun with our scarves, gloves, coats, and boots on, each clutching a coffee. It was never very warm in Scotland in May.

"So, was it good?" she asked.

"More than good, I want more right now." I closed my eyes and thought about his touch. I shuddered in ecstasy.

"Wow that good, so when's the wedding?" she teased.

I became serious. "When we hear some news about our parents, and we get them home where they should be."

Portia sighed, "The minute you hear anything I am coming down, I am so excited to show them their grandchildren. I hear things have been difficult for them and indeed for all prisoners held in captivity by the Japanese. I don't know what to believe. Have you heard about the concentration camps in Europe that disgusting man Hitler, created. He's been murdering people ever since war began and even before. Starving, torturing and murdering Jews. Eliminating millions of people because they weren't Aryan. Bless you, Sid, for sponsoring the Jewish children you have been looking after and for looking after all the evacuees. You have been amazing; driving ambulances and running the estate all through the war. Grandora is so proud of you and all the food you have supplied towards the war effort and the changes you have made to the estate. She says the estate is viable now as an ongoing business and the Hall should survive for many years to come."

"She said all that. Goodness me I am shocked," I replied. "Oh, that reminds me. Dr Green wants to see you; we are all invited for lunch tomorrow. I think he has news concerning Ruby's father; I think they know who he is," Portia went on.

I went quiet, it was the news I had been dreading.

"You really love her, don't you?" Portia said gently.

I nodded my head, too emotional to answer.

"But you know you must do the right thing for the child. Anyway, unfortunately there are thousands of displaced children around Europe and Ruby could be the wrong child for this man; it could be him clutching at straws of hope."

The next day, after I admit, another night of unbridled gorgeous passion where any thought of finding Ruby's father went right out of my selfish head we went to Dr and Mrs Green's for lunch. Ruby was thrilled to meet Elizabeth and James again and they all disappeared into the playroom to be cared for by their nanny. After lunch we left the three men to talk about the dreary business of the continuing war against the Japanese in the Pacific. We chatted about my new business venture which included Portia and Danielle. Victoria Green had some very good ideas to contribute towards its success. Notably the sale of quality Scottish cloth in the shop, as well as Scottish wool, traditionally-made knitted jumpers including the exciting new designs by Danielle. I couldn't wait to get back home and discuss these ideas with Danielle; I thought they were brilliant. Dr Green joined us in their garden room and the conversation which I had dreaded, came round to Ruby.

"I have contacts in London, and they are working hard trying to reunite Jewish children with their missing parents or relatives," he began. "It's a complex and difficult job, I have written to Mr Jakabus Guilhem the gentleman you spoke about, and we have come across an application from a certain man living in Switzerland, who just might be the father of Ruby. He says, however, there was a baby boy travelling to Switzerland with their mother. Do know anything about a baby being in the car at the same time, has Ruby ever mentioned a baby brother?"

"There was no baby in the car just the chauffeur and a lady who we presumed to be the mother and she was dead on the back seat," I stated. I thought about the beautiful, engraved hairbrush in my drawer at home. I had used the brush on Ruby's hair on our journey and somehow it had ended up in my travel bag. I decided it must be Ruby's brush – it had the initials JA engraved in silver on the back. "Can you find out the baby's name – the brush I have was in the lady's handbag?" I asked Dr Green. I always presumed it was Ruby's hairbrush, but it could have been for a baby instead. Of course, I didn't know her name then and I thought it must be something beginning with J. But she seemed to say her name was Roza but we stuck to Ruby because of her ruby red dress the one she was wearing when I found her. "There was definitely no baby in the car or baby clothes," I remembered triumphantly hoping that this was not Ruby's father after all.

"Well, if you can remember anything at all let me know, will you?"

"Yes of course," I acknowledged and smiled at him.

"The gentleman will be in Britain about Christmas time, and he would like to visit you to see Ruby and see if he thinks she is his daughter and if she remembers him," he announced.

Bombshell, reality time; I could not pretend to myself I could keep her as my own forever. I sighed, "Yes of course we will be pleased for him to visit us."

"You love her, don't you?" said Dr Green gently.

"Yes, as if she was my own; she feels like my own child, and I dread the emptiness if she leaves," I added.

"I understand, just imagine the emptiness her father has felt these last six years," he said.

Portia put her hand on mine but said nothing.

The next day we left to travel to Lysander and Fiona's home and Tiff to his unit. I was looking forward to meeting their new edition to the family Flora Henrietta Welsby and their son Sanders Broderick George Welsby. I had almost forgotten what my father's Scottish estate looked like, as my mother didn't like visiting it. My father usually travelled up alone for some fishing or deer stalking and my mother would make the journey especially for Burns night or when they had lots of friends staying for the shooting or fishing. It was just too cold and big as I remembered, an old and rather ugly castle. I couldn't understand why Lysander chose to live here instead of the Hall in Norfolk. It was going to be his inheritance after all. I was surprised when we went inside to find it was much more attractive than I had remembered, so I presumed Fiona had been busy redecorating. Whereas Portia had decorated her home in an art décor style with a very Scottish twist, Fiona had embraced all Scottish tartan, antlers, and baronial armoury on the walls. She had used strong colours effectively and it looked warm and inviting, thank goodness. I think Ruby and Lottie were scared when we first approached the castle set in a landscape of hills and trees stretching for miles into the distance.

They got on very well with Flora and Sanders just as I knew they would I was always proud of how kind and friendly Ruby always was and Lottie was just a very happy little soul all the time. It was very interesting to see Lysander's photographic collection of sea life and the rocks, beaches, and islands. His photographic collection of bird life was amazing he was clearly an expert photographer and ornithologist. Over our evening meal he told us he was passionate about making films of the life in and around the seas of Britain.

I interrupted, "Surely you are going to run the estate in Norfolk when you leave the army?"

"No, never, I could not live with my father and work with him, I run the estate here – well, Fiona does, bless her. But it's much more low-key and laid back and it gives me time to work on my wildlife projects. No, I love it here. When I leave the army, my life will be focused on my family and staying here in Scotland. Sorry, that's my plan; I hope it doesn't drop you in it. I hear you've done a damn good job of running the estate and turning it round and making it profitable, but I suppose you want to go back to France." He looked at me, they all did.

"I did love my life there, and I love Tantetta and being able to spend time painting; the light there is amazing, and I am fascinated with the production of wine. But I have loved seeing our estate in Norfolk improving year on year, the expansion of the agricultural and horticultural side. I have plans to turn the courtyard stables into a farm shop with additional shops for local crafts, knitted designer Scottish wool products, Scottish tweed clothes and an art gallery," I declared to an open-mouthed, silent audience.

"Wow that's awesome," said Portia.

"Bravo," declared Fiona.

I had so many plans to keep the integrity of the estate for many years to come as it grew and made more money. I had been delighted to share the beauty of the area we lived in with people who would probably not have had the opportunity to enjoy it in the past.

"A young man called Larry has opened my eyes to how fortunate we had been in our upbringing and that so many never have the same chance in life." Now I hoped to have the chance to improve the lives of less fortunate children although of course I knew when my father came home, he would have his own ideas. Or would he? I looked at Tiff. "Of course I plan to be part of Tiff's life and what he plans to do."

He smiled and said, "You already know I love your ideas and your passion. We have yet to make all our future plans; one step at a time, though. I'm still in the army and I think we should wait and see the war in the Pacific come to an end. I might be sent there yet; I just don't know."

Oh God, that was a bombshell. Next morning, Tiff and Lysander left for the Highlands and a place called Achnacarry Castle some army special forces training centre.

One addition to my brother's home was a fabulous indoor swimming pool. It was not the biggest, but it was warm and fun for us all to swim there every day. Before he left for the Highlands, I was so curious well just nosy to know how much it had cost and how did he manage to pay for it. Well, if you can't ask your own brother, it's a bit sad.

"Good lord, I didn't pay for it. Fiona's father thought it would be wonderful for his grandchildren and Fiona's sister Elsbeth who spends a lot of time with us. She has the same genetic problem, like Lottie, and, like Lottie is a gem of a girl and so wonderful with the children. We love having her here and swimming is something she does best; hence he paid for the pool. Remember, he is a wealthy man, through steel manufacture."

"Oh, of course, I forgot, how kind of him," I mused, ideas rattling around my head. "Is he a bit of a philanthropist?" I asked.

Lysander laughed. "My little sister's brain is whirring, I can hear it. He is a philanthropist, so if you have a good idea and need help, write it down and make a proper plan to put to him. Fiona will help you. So long as it is a good plan," he added and then said, "I believe it is now referred to as Down's Syndrome that is the genetic problem Lottie and Elsbeth have. It takes the name from John Langdon Down who published a work on the condition in 1866. Remember that name in the future."

I hugged him, I loved my brother so much. After a very pleasant three full days with Fiona and Portia who had brought her children to join us, Elsbeth, Fiona's sister arrived. She was fourteen years old and just wonderful company and brilliant with the children. She took to Lottie and Ruby straight away and was soon giving them swimming lessons. Elsbeth, in the water, was like a mermaid and enthusiastically encouraged all the children into the water with her.

Tiff and Lysander came back, and Alastair came over too, so it was a proper family reunion, but, we were very aware, minus our parents. Finally, and sadly, we started on our long journey home with invitations to return, and our invitations to them, to visit us in Norfolk. Tiff had to return to London, and I had a hay harvest to get in.

Chapter 37

Alex Bouchet, Reunion

Alex cycled back from early morning baking at the bakery; it was six o'clock in the morning and the incline up the little hill pulled on his leg which had been broken in several places. He had bread for the morning in his baker's basket. He had left Odette Vaubolon, the baker's widow, about to open to sell the bread Alex had made. It was extremely popular.

Alex arrived back at the Chateau, and he never ceased to love the entrance and view from the gates – today was no different as, bathed in warm sunlight, the Chateau glowed the palest pink. Inside it was being cleaned and furniture restored ready for the Countess who was shortly to return home. The fighting was still going on as the Allies pushed into Germany, but since Paris had been liberated on August 25th, 1944, and the Allies had pushed up though France, the German forces were being pushed out of France. This had been helped by the large-scale uprising by the French Resistance and it was here where Joseph had lost his life. They were hoping for the Countess to arrive soon; it had been six long years since she had lived in her beautiful home. Preparations were well underway for the imminent grape harvest, the vendange; life and work on the estate never stopped. They were always busy. Joseph's friend, a quiet young man called Uri, was staying with them to help on the estate and with the harvest. Alex liked him, but Uri was deep, and he had admitted to Alex he didn't know in which direction to go next in life. They had advised him to stay with them until he had made up his mind and so he did. Uri said it was nice to be part of a family, to feel safe, to live the life his friend Joseph had lived and to see the kind of life he had led before the war. Joseph had talked about the Chateau, his work, and friends and how happy he had always been there.

They worked hard to bring in the harvest and start the wine making process and they were helped by some of the young men and women who had fought alongside Joseph and Uri who were adjusting to 'ordinary' lives again. As the harvest neared to a close, the Countess arrived home with her sister Augusta and her sister's girlfriend Bernadette, with whom she had been living in Switzerland. The Chateau was looking clean and fresh; Aurielle and Louise had worked hard to get rid of any trace of the Nazi occupation. The next job was to remove the panels which had been placed over the precious wall covering and the hand paintings done by Cressida in the dining room. It was going to be a messy job taking them down. They all followed the progress of the war now in the Ardennes and they heard that the fighting was fierce.

It was a quiet Christmas, and they all took great comfort from being together and safe. Rationing was still in place; no Christmas gifts were available or needed. New Year came quietly in, and they continued repairing the Chateau and Estate from five years of neglect; not from Marcell, but from lack of funds and staff to repair everything. Spring arrived and Alex continued to make bread every day and his leg and arm grew stronger. Claude was now sixteen years old, soon to be seventeen and was a dark-haired strong boy who just loved working with his 'Uncle' Marcell who treated him like a grandson. Simone was a beautiful young teenager and still a great help to Nadine caring for five-year-old Jacques and cooking in the farmhouse. Life settled into a new steady routine much like the one that had existed there for centuries.

It was during the second week of September, as Alex was walking up through a row of vines with Tanner patiently following him (they both walked slowly now), that Claude, Simone, and Jacques came running towards him squealing and shouting, "Viens, Papa viens vite vite, Papa, regardez qui est la."

They grabbed his hands and tried to drag him to make him move faster, all the time their eyes were shining, and they were laughing. Alex looking ahead, through the row of vines, could see two figures. As they drew near, he was sure one was Uncle Albert with an old bent man. He tried to speed up even though his leg was hard to move, and he stretched out his arms to hug his uncle.

"Comment etes-vous le bienvenu. What are you doing here? I am so glad to see you, I have missed you. You look so well, not a day older."

His uncle smiled, hugged, and kissed him, and then holding out his arm, he turned him towards the old man who had come with him. Alex turned to say, 'hello nice to meet you' and held out his hand then stopped, scrutinizing the face before him, and he gasped in shock. "Papa!" He hugged him and looked into his eyes again. "Papa." Then he cried and cried as he hugged his frail father. He cried for his father, he cried for Gregoire, he cried for the victims of the Nazi reprisals, he cried for Joseph, he cried for Laurent Vaulbolon, the village baker shot dead, but mostly he cried for himself, he cried as he hadn't cried, not once, throughout the ordeal of his attack, pain, and suffering. He sobbed like a child as he hung on to his lost father and he hugged Claude, Simone, Jacques, and Albert. They let him sob and cry and they held him close, and his father wept with relief and sorrow for the time they had lost, the time stolen from them of being together and growing older together. They walked up to the farmhouse to the big table under the veranda where Aurielle, Nadine and Marcell waited for them with tears in their eyes. Henrietta, Bernadette, and Augusta were there too, standing with Uri, smiling and crying to see them reunited. All the time little Jacques clung to them, although not sure about what was happening. There was food on the table and wine from the walled-up cellar hidden all these last few years, and now opened ready to toast the reunion of the family.

Alex learnt that his stepmother had not survived the war, dying in forced labour. His father had been a prisoner of war since the fall of France, he too had been used in forced labour but was used in the kitchen to produce meals with next to no food for the hundreds of sick workers. He had a best friend working in the kitchens with him and it was their bond of friendship and loyalty which had kept them going. In the end, before they were liberated by the Allied armies, he had developed ulcers on his leg and under his foot and could hardly walk. His friend Andre was always there for him, had helped him all the time and when the camp was liberated, they held on to each other as they walked out and found help at a hospital. It was here that they were accidentality split up and Bernard was put on a train back to France. He had not seen Andre since, and then he was devastated to learn he had died in his sleep in the same hospital. The man who had kept him alive had died and he had not been by his side. They had promised each other they would see their families if only one of them made it back home and he hoped to meet Andre's wife and make sure she was alright. He wanted to tell her that her husband had been his hero. His brother Pierre was now home, and his wife Hildegard had finally made a decent job of running the two brothers' bakery. In the beginning she had antagonised the villagers baking German products, and her overweight son had been teased and tormented at school. Uncle Albert had put paid to her plans to prosecute Alex for stealing the horse that belonged to the business; he had bought her a little van. He had told her to make sure the villagers came first and bake for them what they wanted, she should not take notice of the German soldiers or try to please them if she wanted a business after the war. Fortunately, she heeded his advice.

Uncle Albert told Alex he had rented out his house and given up the funeral business and now he planned to retire from that life and become a cabinet maker of fine furniture. He would make exactly what he wanted to make for the joy of finally making beautiful things made of wood and to please himself. Henrietta asked where he planned to do this and where was he going to live? Uncle Albert told her he wanted to live near his family, so that he could see them every day he had left on this earth.

"Right then, firstly we will restore the cottage by the paddock, and you can live there and have a workshop next door to it," Tantetta told him.

Alex chimed in, "You, Papa, if you wish, can be a baker in the village so I can stop working there and concentrate on the vineyard here and work with Marcell every day."

His Papa was overcome with the kindness of everyone, something he had seen so little of for the last six years. So, it was agreed Uncle Albert and Bernard would stay with their family and, with joy for the homecoming reunion, there were glasses raised and toasts all round.

Chapter 38

Parents Come Home

S pring that year had been particularly lovely with hedgerows frothy with white and pink hawthorn, blackthorn blossom and the lanes and byways wearing lace trims of delicate white cow parsley, the smell everywhere had been a heady perfume of springtime in the country. I was up early morning every day to drink in the beauty of the sunrise and to hear the new lambs bleating for their mothers and the glorious early morning joy of spring birdsong.

We brought home a good crop of hay again with help from the boys Jabbo and Lucy, Sheila and Enzo, the Italian prisoner of war. The air became sweet with the smell of newly cut and drying hay. It was a great team effort because as we were out in the fields the others held the fort at home. Granger and Jabbo brought the horses every day harnessed up to the farm carts and the two tractors we now had worked constantly cutting and bailing the hay.

As soon as our hay was harvested, I turned my attention to getting my parents' bedrooms spring cleaned and decorated ready for their return. Maisie and I went upstairs to decide what needed doing first, and agreed they needed painting.

"I think a blue would be lovely," she said.

"Yes, but we don't have any blue paint, only white; my mother made sure we had loads of white paint."

"No, there's lots of coloured paint. I remember your mother buying it," Maisie replied.

"Where?" I asked, intrigued.

She led me to a cupboard full of small pots of paint. "Here it is," she said, opening the doors with a flourish, "the coloured paint pots."

"Oh, I've seen these, but they are too small, Maisie, we need much bigger pots than these."

Maisie stared at me curiously. "These are the colours you add to the big pots of white paint, and you mix them."

I stared at her in horror. I'd thought we only had white paint, all the bedrooms we have used had been painted white. Oh, if only I could read. Then I started laughing and so did Maisie. I rocked with laughter: I hadn't laughed so much since Spud had knocked the prim Miss Pearson lady off her deckchair and spilt her drink all over her at the first garden party we held. The same garden party when Spud cocked his leg everywhere, jumped into the fishpond and shook himself over everyone. I even snorted, I laughed so much. Grandora found us helpless with laughter and in between our giggles we told her why we were laughing. She sighed, raised her eyebrows, looked up, shook her head, then laughed, not as hysterically as us, finally adding: "You are a funny one, Cressida". Maisie then told us she knew where the new wallpaper was for my mother's bedroom which she had chosen before she left. She took us to another cupboard in between my parents' rooms and there was the most beautiful Arts and

Crafts wallpaper in gold, with twisted branches of wisteria and pink chrysanthemum flowers and butterflies. So, it was decided Grandora would look for the telephone number of the decorator my parents had used, and hopefully he would come and decorate their rooms. The expensive and exquisite wallpaper needed an expert to hang it, definitely not us.

Meanwhile, I concentrated for the first time in years on my artwork. I had made countless sketches of everyone I had met over the last six years. Many of all the children, the military personnel who had stayed with us. I had also made sketches and watercolours of the countryside around the estate. I studied all of these carefully to decide which I wanted to transfer onto canvas in oils. I had sketched the Hurricanes and B-17s and Lancaster bombers flying over the Norfolk countryside. I came across one sketch which made me stop, and immense sadness washed over me, and tears rolled down my cheeks. I walked towards the window and looked out at the park and towards The Tree, the special Cedar of Lebanon, and I just knew then that that would be my first painting. I worked as hard as I used to work in France, and I was enthused with a passion to paint constantly. I had to attend to estate duties, but now, after I had ridden, I would check what Rhys and Gruffydd planned to do and then talk to Granger and Jabbo about what needed to be done; then I would go to the kitchen for my breakfast, check what everyone there planned to do that day, and see the children before school. After that, straight away, I would go to my art room and spend the rest of the morning working. All this urgent plan surged through my head and took over my thoughts and actions.

Lottie was still with us as her mother had a new man in her life who was in the RAF working as a mechanic. They had met when Mrs Evans started working in the kitchen on the aerodrome base

Willup Hall

since deciding to leave East London after her husband was killed by a bomb. They planned to buy an inn and run it together and Mrs Evans had asked me if her children could stay with us until she was settled somewhere. Larry was studying, preparing for university, and he used our library, and it would be such a shame to change his school just now, before his exams. Lennie never wanted to leave us, which delighted me, he was so sympathetic with all our animals, a brilliant horseman, keen to work, learn and above all easy to get on with. I just hoped he would go to agricultural college first before he decided about his future. Lottie was such a sweetie and a lovely friend for Ruby, I dreaded them being separated. George had joined the army now and was doing his basic training while Theodore was going to finish this year at school before spending some of the summer with his mother getting to know each other again. Theo was keen on photography, ever since I had bought him a little Leica camara years ago, and he preferred wildlife and the natural world and wanted to make a career from photography of his favourite subjects. He was hoping to attend College in Newmarket to study photography. Susan and Roger had moved in with Margaret and Hugh, who had applied to adopt the two children it was going through, and they were all happy. Talia and Adele were just a pleasure to have around, always helpful, kind and dedicated to being good at their schoolwork and music. They practised for hours on their musical instruments. They were both applying for scholarships to go to music college, and I hoped they would pass because they so deserved to go. Of course, they were waiting to hear from their parents and wanted to make sure that when they finally did, their parents would be proud of them. My fingers were crossed but we did get some good news about their parents – mostly that they were still alive. Audrey still checked the children's schoolwork and organised

Saturday mornings for the young ones. Danielle was in charge of the knitting club, which was carrying on, and at the same time busy working on exciting designs for her new venture here at the Hall. Panaya had seen one of Merry's beautiful patchwork quilts and was enthused to begin working on one of her own in bright, glowing, spicy colours. Merry had written to her and they were corresponding over designs. I hoped I'd see Merry soon, as it was ages since we'd met up. Virinder and Ashneer were studious boys and were determined to go to university and make their parents proud. They were passionate about cricket and during the weekends and light nights, practised batting and bowling. Tad was a studious boy and had a gift with languages which he picked up easily, but he was wanting to become a doctor and hoping to get into university to study medicine. Panaya had heard from Dr Singh who was still working with the army in Burma at the military hospital there and she and his mother were sick with worry and lit candles and prayed for his safe return. We all longed for the end of the war with Japan. I was desperate to receive news of my parents' whereabouts and now I wanted it to hurry up and end as I didn't want Tiff to go and fight in the Pacific. I wanted him home and for us to get married and start a new life together.

Then one day at the beginning of July I heard from Jakabus Guilhem, the jeweller I had met in Claridge's, and who had asked me to sponsor Talia and Adele and other Jewish people needing refuge in Britain. I received a letter from him telling me the good news that he thought the organisation he was involved with had received news from Portugal that they believed they had traced the parents of Talia and Adele. Could I confirm their surname was Treves, plus their ages and the address in France where they used to live – and please to get back to him as soon as I could. It was important to get it right and save any pain and anxiety as soon as possible. I went with Audrey to find their details in the office and by return post I sent them back the information without telling the girls and getting their hopes up – not wanting to disappoint them if it didn't work out. Within the next week I had received confirmation that they were now sure their parents were alive, were well, and found in Portugal, and were hoping to be allowed into Britain to find their children. Grandora used the telephone and her enormous influence, and we were soon informed that the parents were on their way to Britain and on to Norfolk. We decided not to tell the girls yet, just to make absolutely sure their parents were the right ones before they arrived at the Hall.

Two weeks after receiving the first letter I drove to the station to pick up Monsieur and Madame Treves. I recognised them straight away. They were a worried-looking worn-out couple, wearing old shabby clothes, and looked in need of some good food. They were clearly bewildered refugees and had no idea where they were. I could now see the girls looked just like their mother. I approached them and they shook my hand apprehensively, so I drove to the next village tearoom and ordered tea and sandwiches. I wanted to tell them about their wonderful girls and how it had been a privilege to care for them for the last five years. I told them about their lives with us and how beautifully they played the piano and the violin. They told me how upset the girls had been when they had left their musical instruments behind in France. I added that they had no idea their parents were arriving today as I hadn't wanted them upset if they had not been the right parents, but I could see now that they were: with that I telephoned Grandora to tell her we were on our way and headed for the Hall.

We arrived to the beautiful sound of music in our reception hall. I took Monsieur and Madame Treves quietly inside so that they could see and hear their beautiful daughters playing on their musical instruments. Their faces were a joy I will never forget. Tears ran down their cheeks as, clutching each other, they stood in rapture at their two grown-up girls. Talia became aware first and slowly stopped playing and then Adele followed her gaze and all four rushed into each other's arms; Grandora and I left them alone. Of course, they stayed with us whilst they ate slept, talked, walked, and learnt about what had been happening in their respective lives for the last five years. It was clear now where Talia and Adele had inherited their good manners and ability to dedicate themselves to work whatever task that might be. Their parents were a delight, bless them; they had travelled for so long, their relief to be back with their daughters was palpable. They clearly doted on their girls, and I was again reminded why we had sheltered these children from the misery of war.

They were all special, each one in their own way and deserved love and care during those harrowing years. I assured Monsieur and Madame Treves the privilege of getting to know Talia and Adele had been all ours. Monsieur Treves was clearly very worried about getting back to work to support his family and he was concerned that their home and shop in France would no longer be standing. We did our best to contact the maire of their town and they wrote letters to the relevant authorities. We arranged for them to travel to London with the girls for their entrance exam to The Royal Academy of Music. They were then worried they couldn't afford for the girls to stay in London if they were offered places there, so for two weeks we discussed their best options and two weeks became four weeks and then longer, but we didn't mind at all.

During this time, we had another new arrival, and it was a surprise to welcome Jabbo's wife. This was the woman he had married after knowing her for only a few days, primarily to aid her entry into Britain and to rescue her from loneliness, her solitary lifestyle and of course, mostly the war. I think it had more to do with the fact that she was beautiful with a sweet personality and as she was half-French and half-Moroccan, she had a graceful, elegant way of walking. She was a nurse and had been nursing in Gibraltar whilst waiting for the opportunity to catch a ride to Britain. As there was a war on, her nursing skills were in demand, and she ended up working at the naval hospital on the Rock. I was pleased she was here and was surprised how she could be married to Jabbo in such a quick Muslim ceremony, when they didn't know each other. More surprisingly, it was agreed she would stay in Danielle's cottage with her for the time being.

All this news was put aside when we heard on the wireless and read in the papers on August 6th, 1945, that the first atomic bomb had been dropped by the United States of America onto the Japanese city of Hiroshima. The bomb was nicknamed Little Boy. President Harry S. Truman announced the news from the cruiser USS Augusta in the mid-Atlantic. Apparently, the device was 2,000 times more powerful than the largest bomb used to date. The bomb was dropped by an American B-29 Superfortress known as Enola Gay at 08.15 local time. I had no real idea at the time of the severity that such a bomb would have on a city or the people in its path. President Truman went on to say, 'If they do not accept our terms for peace they may expect a rain of ruin from the air the like of which has never been seen on this earth. Behind this air attack will follow by sea and land forces in such number and power as they have not yet been seen, and with the fighting skill of which they are already aware.'

We were shocked by this news and of course elated to think the end of the war was now in sight. Then we heard no more until it was announced on August 9th, 1945, that another bomb had been dropped on Nagasaki, nicknamed 'Fatman; again, we were shocked and saddened that it had come to such a drastic conclusion. Finally, Japan surrendered and signed the Instrument of Surrender on board the USS Missouri in Tokyo Bay. Yet again I prayed my parents could come home now.

We heard at the end of September, via the Red Cross, that they were both alive, so I decided to hold back my birthday celebrations in October until they returned, whatever the date. We were informed my mother was arriving in Southampton docks on 17th October so I telephoned Portia who said she would be arriving in Norfolk on October 12th and then would travel down to Southampton with me to greet our mother. We would catch a train to London from Southampton with my mother where Granger would meet us and drive us home in the Rolls. I doubt we would be able to buy any more petrol for the journey, but hopefully our ration would allow us enough for the return journey. We rarely used our petrol ration as we used our horses or bikes to get about, so we had some petrol at home for emergencies and fetching·my mother home after nine years away was one of them. We had not yet heard about my father's whereabouts. So, the time came, Portia and I were waiting on the docks for the ship Almanzora on October 17th. We were both strangely nervous of how my mother would be, and very pleased to know she was finally coming home. Of course, neither of us recognised her for a few moments as she walked down the gangplank. Always elegant and slim, our mother was now skinny and dowdy. Just not the radiant hostess she had always been before being incarcerated in a prisoner of war camp by the Japanese. She still had an upright, very regal posture though, and that's what I recognised as she stood on the quayside looking bewildered. Hopefully the fun-loving mother playing with us at home when we were growing up would return in time. We both fell upon her, crying and hugging; she seemed relieved to see us and hugged us, but she remained very quiet, almost reticent. She waved to another lady who obviously had been travelling with her and we picked up her very small suitcase which was clearly her only belongings and bustled her to the taxi which would take us to the station. We all fell quiet taking a cue from her and Portia and I exchanged glances of concern, but we had both been warned that her years of captivity would not have been easy and to just get her home to rest. I secretly hoped that she never wanted to go away again. We arrived at Paddington station and found the very welcome sight of Granger waiting for us. I think Mother was more pleased to see Granger than us.

"Oh, Granger, it's you, how wonderful," she said, sinking gently into the leather back seat.

"My Lady, it's a pleasure to have you back," he replied, tucking a rug gently round her knees. He stepped back onto the pavement, "Does she know we have a few people staying with us at the Hall?" he asked me.

"No, she is so quiet, Granger, not herself at all, we've hardly spoken. At least her bedroom looks gorgeous now and it's very private for her. I don't want to burden her with any news of home just now," I replied.

Portia called to us from the backseat, "Let's make tracks and be off, shall we."

We exchanged looks, I jumped in the front seat, and we started our journey for home.

Mother fell asleep and Portia asked Granger, "Have you seen my little ones, Granger, are they behaving themselves?"

"Yes, my Lady, they are indeed, and your little Master Hamish has been having a go at sending old Lucy off to fetch a training dummy. Lucy is a very old lady now and is very patient with Hamish," he added.

"Can't beat my father's breed of Labrador, can you, but which one is Lucy?" Portia queried.

I explained to her about Theodore and George Bathurst being the two young boys I had brought back from France with their chocolate Labrador, Lucy, who had been bred on our estate by Hugh Brownlow. It had been decided to keep her with Margaret and Hugh as she was too old to be taken somewhere else to live. We chatted about dogs past and present and about the possibility of puppies, as she would like one. My mother slept all the way home. Grandora was waiting for us and being intuitive got the picture immediately as we ushered my mother straight upstairs to her bedroom. She seemed overwhelmed by everything.

"My beautiful chinoiserie wallpaper panels, you've put them on," she exclaimed, delighted. Her hand-painted panels of wallpaper with wisteria and exotic chrysanthemums in pink, climbing branches covered in amazing foliage with butterflies on a gold background was called Empress and looked amazing in panels behind her bed. She was silent when she saw her new bathroom and we ran a bath for her. We all agreed, as we always did, to give the water to the person who needed our allowance the most. We would just have to have the quickest showers possible. It had been recommended that people only bathed once a week in four inches of water so at least a quick shower was better than a bath. The children had flannel washes all week and showers at the weekends. We were all used to water conservation though; hopefully it would end soon. Maisie brought a tray of peppermint tea upstairs for us with some tiny cress sandwiches and shortbread biscuits.

"Morton, oh my dear, you're here," my mother exclaimed, obviously very pleased to see her, and gratefully accepted a porcelain cup of tea. Tears rolled down her cheeks and I knelt beside her and put my head on her knee. Portia sat next to her and held her hand.

"We'll go now, Mother; you just rest after your long journey, and we will see you later," Portia suggested.

"I love you, Mother, I'm so glad you're home."

We left her with Grandora and Maisie.

"Gosh, I'm glad Maisie is here," said Portia, "they always did get on well."

We went downstairs to find Hamish and Rhona Isadora with their new nanny, Alison. I explained to Portia how Maisie had returned to us and that she had very nearly left straight away when she discovered we had so many people staying with us.

"Well, I'm jolly glad she didn't," said Portia. "Besides, the people you have here are lovely; you have been lucky getting such polite children."

I laughed and agreed. Hopefully Malissa would be here soon to meet up with Portia again. She had said she was coming home for a week.

We soon realized that Mother had clearly had a traumatic time as a prisoner of war, and it had made her withdrawn. Miriam said she would spend some time with her, and we agreed that would be marvellous, but first Mother needed some time to adjust to her new circumstances. She had endured a long journey and now she needed to lead a quiet life here, rest and recover.

I celebrated my birthday quietly with my mother in her room and then had a very noisy party in the morning room with the children. Malissa came home for my birthday and after our evening meal we played billiards. Then Benny Goodman and

Glenn Miller and swing music on the gramophone and we boogied and jitterbugged in the morning room (the room furthest away from my mother's bedroom), Larry, Malissa, Audrey, Danielle, Tad, Osian, Rhys, Gruffydd, Lennie, Portia, and me. It was a fun night and I realized how lucky I was to have such good friends. We finished the night singing Vera Lynn songs again, especially 'We'll Meet Again', always a tearjerker.

We received the news that our father was on his way home and would be arriving in Liverpool on November 15th, so my brother said he would meet him there and bring him home to us. Fiona was going to travel down on her own with her sister Elsbeth and her two children, Sanders and Flora Henrietta. My mother was very quiet when we told her Father was on his way home, so I asked why she was worried, and she told me she was concerned about his health and how much being a prisoner would have changed him. Yes, so was I, my father had always frightened me a little bit; the only time I had been happy with him was when we stayed in France for the Vendange. There he had been tanned and relaxed and a fun-father to be with. I was very worried about what he would say to me about the changes I had made at the Hall over the last six years. I was quite sure he would be angry about so many people staying at The Hall and those who were still here. Neither of my parents had any idea I had let their Chelsea home be used by refugees. Not sure which was my biggest worry.

Mother continued to improve slowly, and she now knew about all the people who had been staying at The Hall throughout the war. She never talked about her time as a prisoner of war, and I never asked her. I still hadn't told her that I had agreed to the use of the first two floors of their London townhouse in Chelsea by an organisation helping to resettle Jewish refugees. I had been asked for help by Mr Jakabus Guilhem and I had given his association the use of the house as a safe place for children and families in transit. My parents' good furniture had been moved upstairs to the two floors above the basement and the ground floor. Remarkably, the house had survived the bombing, thank goodness.

My father arrived home in a private ambulance organised by Lysander. Once he knew my father was ill he decided the train journey was too much for him. Margaret, Maisie, Audrey, and Granger were waiting with my mother, Portia and I to greet him. However, it was soon clear he was very ill and not able to talk to anyone. He arrived on a dull, chilly November day and we managed to get him and the wheelchair upstairs to his warm bedroom where a fire was burning brightly in the hearth. Jabbo had carried my father, and Lysander carried the wheelchair. I had asked Jabbo straight away if his wife Halette could help with my father and be his private nurse. She was pleased to help and to have some work and agreed straight away. We called Dr Haigh so he could help my father get the right treatment. He was so pale and thin, it was pitiful; his legs were weedy sticks, and he was very weak. His bedroom adjoined my mother's, and she sat with him all day when he arrived. They were two very damaged people, physically and mentally. I was so glad Portia and Lysander were here with me to look after them. They had decided to stay over Christmas with my parents and celebrate the first Christmas in ten years since we had all been together.

We left my father to the care of my mother, Halette and Maisie. Mrs Revill was soon making light and nutritious meals for him, and Dr Haigh came every day to check on him. I called each morning to see him after I had seen the children for breakfast in the kitchen. I still rode each morning and preferred to be helping in the stables, but I had to see so many people every day for the estate and farms to run smoothly. I went to paint in my room each day and I had pushed my bed to one side so I could make room for my work, my sketches, paints, work in progress and my new desk. Monsieur and Madame Treves had decided to return to France to discover what was left of their home and shop, taking the girls with them, but would return after Christmas for the girls to go to college in London. I had written to Fiona's father about him sponsoring the girls through college and Fiona spoke to him saying what brilliant musicians they were but how desperately they needed support. She told him how their parents had followed them to Spain and how they had crossed the Pyrenees, just like Danielle and Tad and countless others, to escape Nazism in France. They had been imprisoned in Spain because they were Jewish, and they were to be returned to France. They had no one to turn to or to help them. Eventually, they had been released after some intervention from the same Jewish organisation working tirelessly to assist Jews to escape – the same organisation that had helped Adele and Talia. As they had no money, they had walked through Spain to Portugal, travelling along the Camino Way, the old pilgrim's route to Santiago de Compostela, and once there they had looked for the girls and Monsieur Treves's brother. They had no idea he had died in Spain just as he and the girls had arrived. Finally, they were put in touch with the Jewish relief organisation, the HIAS-HICEM, which had been transferred from Paris to Lisbon on the authorization of Antonio de Oliveira Salazar. They were now informed that their two daughters had taken the same journey through Spain to Portugal with the help of the Jewish Relief Organisation, had found a sponsor and were now in Britain. They had had to wait for their visas before they could leave Portugal and they needed a sponsor to agree to fund them in Britain. During all this time no one could be sure where their daughters were. They had worked in Portugal to try and fund their journey to Britain to find their daughters, but with no money it had been tough for them for years, finding work and accommodation. Finally, before they left, Jakabus Guilhem had been contacted and had agreed to help them travel to Britain using our sponsorship. On their arrival they had stayed at my parents' house in Chelsea and further investigation had revealed that their daughters were staying with me. Now they planned to start again in France and help to rebuild the country they considered to be their home. Fiona's father, Lionel MacCloud, agreed to sponsor the girls through the Music Academy, and Grandora said she was sure my parents would help them and let them stay in their house in Chelsea. Before they left, my mother and father heard the girls play their instruments, the violin and the piano, and agreed they were wonderful, gifted musicians and deserved help with their course.

Gruffydd and Rhys had remained working with us and I was excited about showing my parents the Walled Garden and what had been achieved during their absence, but I was also dreading hearing my father's displeasure about the changes.

I spent more time working in my room painting when I was not working outside and attending to estate duties. Osian arrived home at last and we were all so pleased to have him back. Tiff came home for Christmas, and I was able to introduce him to my parents. They were told I would be bringing him upstairs to see them and they both dressed in readiness; my mother sat by the window and my father sat in his wheelchair, looking slightly better. He was not quite as yellow as he had been when he first arrived home. On a small round table Maisie brought a tray with tea, and then left. Tiff was introduced and we all sat making small talk about the weather and the farm. My parents had been briefed by the War Office not to discuss their experiences as prisoners in Singapore, so as not to upset the relatives of those prisoners who had died. They asked Tiff about his role during the war in the army and he was reticent about discussing all his exploits. When I mentioned he had spent time with Howard Bathurst before he had been killed in action during the war, whilst fighting alongside Tiff, my father became interested, and asked if it was one of Biffy Bathurst's sons – the same Biffy he used to shoot grouse with, before the war. After that he became very interested in Tiff and his new commando group and finally Mother and I left them chatting.

Tiff found me later. "Your father is a very interesting gentleman, he has met some amazing people and we are playing chess later today." He added, "But he is very tired and resting now."

Oh well, that was interesting and now he just had to be sure he didn't beat my father at chess.

Over the next few days my parents met many of my friends living at The Hall. My mother adored Ruby, Lottie and Amani and was soon spending time with them when they weren't at school or having lessons with Audrey. Larry was introduced to them by Grandora who had schooled him not to launch into his favourite rant about the working man versus the upper classes. Instead, they all played cards and Larry was a hit when they realized he was an intelligent, well-read young man about to go to university. When Father met young Lennie I could read the hesitation to connect with Lennie in his stable clothes and covered with bits of hay and straw. They slowly became respectfully aware of each other's knowledge of horses, a love of the hunt and watching the blood hounds track their quarry, usually a local cross-country running enthusiast. Lennie spoke with enthusiasm about the young grey racehorse in his care and the training he was receiving with Granger and Jabbo. My father was thrilled to consider getting 'his' racehorse into training and onto the racecourse. He was becoming more animated every day, although it never lasted for long as he was soon overwhelmingly tired and needed to rest or sleep. Jabbo was never far away to push him in the wheelchair and my father became increasingly reliant upon Jabbo being around to help him. He always asked for Jabbo or Halette, and I even began to breathe a sigh of relief that he was getting on with everyone living at Willup Hall and not mad about the people I had invited to stay with us during these war years. Squadron Leader Richard Petersfield came to see us one day, and of course he met my parents. I understand they had a lengthy chat, which my parents found very interesting.

December arrived and Tiff had to go back to his unit, but he wanted to ask my parents for my hand in marriage before he left. Since war had ended, I had worn the ring he had given to me on my right hand. Tiff had questioned this, but I had said until my parents came home, and he asked them if we could get married, I didn't want to tell people we were engaged. All the time he stayed with us he slept in his own room, and it was killing us since our lovemaking in Scotland. Of course, I had crept along the corridor to his room, and he had crept to my room like naughty sneaks, which we both hated. It was the 'being back in our own rooms' before dawn that was the horrid bit, it was so cold in my bed I just got dressed and went riding, even earlier than usual.

Then one morning, drinking a mint tea in Grandora's bedroom as she sat up in bed with her morning coffee, she said, "When is Tiff going to ask George for your hand in marriage? You seem to get up earlier and earlier I sometimes wonder if you have ever been to bed to sleep." She frowned, but her eyes twinkled.

Embarrassed, I muttered I would tell him to get on with it and fled to find Tiff. He was talking to Hugh in the kitchen and Hugh was pleased to see me; he had come to ask me which puppy he should save for Portia as he had a bitch expecting a litter of black Labrador puppies and already had a litter of working springer spaniels.

"I think Portia and Alastair are both hoping to have a puppy from our breeding lines, but I'm not sure which one they would want. I'll tell her to come over and see you. Will tomorrow be all right?"

"Yes, my Lady, I'll be off then, and it would be grand if his Lordship would like to visit us to see them anytime."

"Lovely, I will tell him," I replied.

Tiff said he was going down to the kennels so he would go with Hugh. Hugh went outside to his bike, and I pulled Tiff to one side.

"Please hurry up and ask my father today. I'll set it up for tonight before an evening meal."

He kissed me, conferring, "I never thought I would be so nervous, it's a worse prospect than scaling cliffs under fire." He laughed and left on his bike and pedalled furiously to catch up with Hugh.

That night he went upstairs to take my parents the small sherry they were allowed each evening before their meal. Mother, apparently warned by Grandora, left the two men alone. Half an hour later, Tiff leapt the stairs two at a time straight into my arms and twirled me around.

"It's a yes, darling, it's a yes, he can't wait to get rid of you," he teased. "We are all to go upstairs for a glass of champagne."

Lysander came into the hall. "Congratulations to you both, I am delighted for you. I'll fetch the champagne and bring it with me."

Malissa and Portia joined us after listening to bedtime stories told to Sanders and Rhona Isadora by Ruby and Lottie who did the reading whilst the children and Portia listened. Ruby loved to be centre stage in the nicest possible way; she wasn't bossy, she just had a way of taking charge of a situation. Maybe she would have a future in politics or perhaps a professor or head of a big business. Whatever she did she would be in charge, I was sure of that. Just before we went upstairs to join the others Tiff pulled me into the drawing room.

"You can put your ring on the left hand now," he said.

"Oh yes, of course, perhaps you should give it to me in front of them and I can pretend I've never seen it before," I suggested, as I handed it to him.

"Ok, come on then, I'll give you the ring in front of everyone."

We went upstairs and they all congratulated us again and then Tiff produced a gorgeous, expensive-looking little box and gave it to me. I opened it, planning to be delighted and surprised for my parents, but I *was* surprised to the delight of everyone because inside was the most incredible ring – it was a large, magnificent emerald surrounded by diamonds; I was amazed and thrilled. I still wanted my original ring though, because it was the sort of ring I could wear every day whatever I was doing, even riding, or mucking out; greedy me. Anyway, I was very surprised and couldn't believe he could afford it, but it was so sweet of him, and he looked so pleased. It fitted and I couldn't stop admiring it. Once on my finger it didn't look too big really. Everybody admired it and Grandora told Tiff it was lovely, and he had done very well to choose it as it was just the right colour for me; which it was.

Some days later after Tiff had gone away, yet again, I was talking to Malissa and asking how Nico was. It was then she told me he had gone away after May on The Hestia. She was sailing back to start work in the Adriatic Sea and he needed a long break away from the stress of map reading and translating for the Military and doing his master's degree. I asked why she hadn't joined him.

"I was worried that Ruby's father might now be found, and I want to spend time with her and you." She added, "I love it here, I think of here being my home now, I hope you don't mind me saying that. I love my parents, but they have worked so much in the business, always travelling, I have hardly seen them. Here has been a constant base for me and I love coming back to you all, knowing you will be here for me."

"Of course I don't mind, I want you to stay here for ever and Ruby too, I don't want her real father to be found, I can't imagine not having her here," I added.

"Me too, I know what you mean, but if her father is looking for her, he must love her and be upset not to have her living with him. We have to accept she might one day go away," she said sadly. Then she told me, "Nico is coming back in February and is looking forward to bringing you and Grandora some decent coffee and some saffron for Jabbo." That was really good news.

Unbelievably I received a letter from Jakabus Guilhem the very next day letting me know the man who was looking for his daughter had contacted him. He had been put in touch with his organization since certain research had discovered a possible match to Ruby. I understood this had been aided by information given by Dr Green in Scotland. He thought it was more than possible that he was the father of little Ruby. He had been searching for his daughter called Roza Aaronson and his name is Zac Aaronson. Roza would be ten years old now and his son would be six years old, his name is Jacques Aaronson. In his letter he said he thought he was the wrong man and not the

father of Ruby as there was no baby with them in the car. That
was, until it was mentioned the type and colour of car she had
been travelling in with her mother and their chauffeur. The car
matched the type and colour of the car Malissa Angelopoulis
had told Dr Green about which had been found crashed in the
forest. Malissa had given these details to Dr Green in Scotland.
He then mentioned his daughter had a little dog which went
everywhere with her, a chihuahua called Zissa. He added, this
made me decide we had the right man, and he was the father of
Ruby. I have given him your telephone number as you may wish
to speak to him first before allowing Ruby to see him or vice
versa. I hope I have done the right thing – it is very difficult and
upsetting trying to trace so many Jewish relatives now missing
in Europe. He concluded: I have been in touch with a Dr Green
who contacted our organization regarding this little girl, and it is
becoming evident that we think we have found her father, which
is a miracle. So that was that: it sounds like I was going to lose
Ruby, my beautiful little treasure. Thank goodness I was Aunty
Cwessy to her, and Malissa Aunty Lissa. Still, it was strange news
about her having a baby brother. I showed the letter to Malissa
and Grandora, and discussed it with my mother. They told me I
must contact him straight away and I must allow him to see Ruby
without telling her who he was. Perhaps she would recognize
him. Who knows how much a child would remember after all
these years.

Tiff returned to help us with the preparations for Christmas
and I told him my news about Ruby. He was very sad and
sympathetic towards me, but like everyone else he sensibly said
that if it was her father then we must let her go. He then asked
me if it would it be all right with me if we were married in April
and I was so pleased, what a perfect month. No hay ready to get

in, or corn harvest. Oh, my goodness I was turning into a farmer, not a painter.

Then later that same day he brought me a whisky and one for himself and said he needed to talk to me. That was ominous and I was subdued as he started to tell me about his time in France. We sat alone in my bedroom, and he told me how he had gone with Jabbo to France to help the Maquis fight the Nazis and create diversions during the time of the Normandy landings. They had parachuted into the hills not far from my Tantetta's Chateau de la Cascade. He had a good idea of the area where he would land and the terrain, thanks to Nico showing him on the maps. What he didn't know was that one of the main men in that division of the Free French was Joseph Denisot.

"My Joseph, how wonderful, how is he, is he back at the Chateau now?" I was so excited.

"Stop, Sid, listen to me, slow down. I'm sorry, I don't have good news, but you have to listen to me. I did help them set up sabotage for the Nazis, we did take them ammunition, weapons, dynamite, clothes, boots, food, and money. We lived with them in the woods, always on the move from the Nazis. They have lived like that since 1941 and they were a tough bunch of men and women. I took Jabbo to translate for me although it was difficult keeping him hidden as there were very few black men left in that area of France or anywhere else. One day we went to dynamite a railway bridge and it was successful, but we came under attack from a lorry load of German soldiers and Joseph was hit. He died in the arms of his best friend, a young man called Uri. We carried him to a nearby farm and gave him a quick burial, but now it is time to move his body to the village and to bury him properly. Fortunately, at least Joseph knew the Allies had landed and that Paris had been liberated. Your aunt is going to return to the Chateau soon and she has ordered a memorial stone to be erected there with all the names of the Maquis who fought and died during the war who were from that area. Uri will be there, and I thought you would like to meet him. I have seen Marcell and Aurielle and they are well and have survived all the hardships they have had to endure. The young man you met on the road taking his brother and sisters to Spain is there and has been working there throughout the war. He was beaten by Nazi thugs and now limps badly, but he has become a competent vintner and winemaker; also, he has been running the village bakery. His brother and his sisters and his sister's little boy are all very happy, living on the estate and I thought you would be interested to know that Flavie is still alive and the young man's mare Trudi is still there. I'm sorry I have not told you this before, but for security reasons I haven't been allowed to talk about my time in the army. I'm so sorry to have to tell you about Joseph; he was a remarkable, brave young man."

I sat in numb silence as he held both my hands and gave me this information. He handed me my whisky and I stared through the window thinking of our fun, carefree and happy times together, Joseph and I growing up in the lovely French countryside. How innocent we were of bad people and the evil which exists in the world. I remembered his passion to fight for France, his determination to make a difference. He certainly did that. I didn't sob or wail; I cried silent tears for our youth and innocence until Tiff put his arms round me and rocked me gently. There was no end to the suffering caused by the evil mind of one man and of how it had permeated down from him into the Nazi ideology, destroying and ruining lives, communities, and countries. I thought, in the name of Joseph Denisot, and all lives lost in this tragic war, we must never let it happen again and we must never forget.

Frankie arrived home on the 20th December, which was wonderful as he had been discharged from the army. He left with the rank of Sergeant which was really great. We were all very proud of him and his contribution to the war effort. Hopefully he would help out here whilst I was away in France – we needed the extra help. Sheila had now returned to her parents in Northampton, but Lucy had stayed in the cottage waiting for Frank to come home. They had become secretly engaged before he went away and that's why she had stayed to help us. Surprisingly I discovered he had asked her to marry him under The Tree of Lebanon in the park, how strange; it seemed to draw us all to be romantic. He told me that Lucy didn't ever want to go back to her home as she had been beaten by her father and was glad she joined the Land Army and got as far away from him as she could. He discussed his plans with me for opening a repairs garage for farm machinery and lorries. He had seen an empty garage on the outskirts of the village which belonged to our estate, so obviously I was delighted for him and gave him the go-ahead to get it ready for work and to let people know where he was going to be based and what he planned to do. No rent for a year; that is what I agreed. Local people needed help and an incentive to stay local and there was very little money anywhere.

Barbara Bailey wrote asking if she could spend her Christmas break with Amani and Linford here at the Hall. She was still bunking down in a friend's flat in London and it was not suitable for her to have the children to stay with her there. She was working lots of shifts to try and earn enough money to make a home for them. Unfortunately, it was a vicious circle as the more money she earnt the less time she had to look after Amani and Linford. Hopefully, if she moved to Norfolk to work in the King's Lynn Hospital, as she hoped, life would improve, and she would have more time for her children. Of course, I agreed it would be lovely for her to join her children here, only one thing – could she please bring some warm trousers to wear and some wellingtons. She seemed surprised but laughed and said she would do her best.

Rosie approached me one day and asked if she could have a word with me in private.

"Of course," I said, "how can I help you?"

"I was wondering, now so many of the children who have been staying here are going away, will you still need me here to help?" she asked shyly.

"Of course, I need you, you have been marvellous helping everybody all the time. You help Mrs Revill. You are invaluable, you have become a very good cook. I have new plans for all of us to increase the income of the estate and I want you to be part of the team. Did you want to leave?" I asked, hoping she'd say no.

"Oh no, I love it here, but I was worried I might lose my job with us being quieter just now," she said.

"Not at all, I couldn't manage without you," I assured her. Funny, I thought, is that what some of them think now the war has ended. I found Audrey and asked her if she planned to stay now the war was over and told her I wanted her to stay and help me with my new plans.

"I was going to ask you if there was a job for me here, only I want to stay because Granger has asked me to marry him, and I have said yes," she told me, smiling.

I flung my arms round her, "I am delighted, what fabulous news, so that's three of us getting married, Frankie and Lucy, Tiff, and I, and you two. You are perfect for each other, I am so pleased Grandora keeps her best Bridge partner," I teased. I then had to ask the question. "Where did he ask you to marry him, Audrey, if you don't mind me asking?"

"We were walking in the park with Zipper and Spud, and we had just walked up to The Cedar of Lebanon Tree, and we looked up at the stars and that's when he asked me. It was so romantic; I said yes immediately. I don't want to waste any more of my life living alone."

I hugged her, I was so pleased for the two of them. Well fancy that, had the tree got mystic powers, I wondered. Next day Danielle asked if she could stay as she had no plans to go anywhere and wanted Tad to finish his education anyway, plus she was hoping to carry on weaving, knitting, and designing for the new shop attached to The Hall, that I was planning. She also added that she loved working in the Walled Garden and seeing the results of her work. Was there anything in Grandora's suggestion that Danielle and Osian were really in love with each other, even though they didn't know it; and then she added that she would have to return to France at Easter to discuss with estate agents what to do with her house in Paris. She had no idea what condition it was in now the war had ended. I asked her what she thought she should do with it, and she thought she would keep it as apartments, as she needed the income to live on. She might keep the top apartment as a place to stay in Paris for holidays if her design ideas became popular and it would be handy should she need to go to Paris for any fashion shows. Wow, how wonderful, she was thinking big; I liked that.

We all worked hard to decorate The Hall for Christmas. Christmas Eve afternoon was always special with a carol party in the big reception hall. Presents were still difficult as rationing was still in place and so we continued to make our gifts and tried to be as inventive as possible with new surprises, as always. I did small sketches of The Hall and gardens from different angles and plenty of small sketches of cricket matches on our cricket field.

Jabbo made me natural wood frames for all these pictures, and I was very pleased with how they turned out and hoped they would be a permanent reminder for everyone, especially the children, of their happy life here.

Then the bombshell came. It was expected. I just hoped it wouldn't happen, but it did. Monsieur Aaronson rang and asked for me. We chatted in French, and I invited him to come for Christmas on the understanding that if Ruby was not his daughter, he would leave immediately he knew the truth. We all got stuck in, preparing accommodation for Monsieur Aaronson and all our Christmas visitors. We were able to include the rooms upstairs used by the recuperating RAF men during the war. Mavis Evans and Gilbert Newbert were arriving and staying with Arthur and Violet Laxton and family. Larry and Lennie were staying here with us until Christmas Day and then going over to Arthur's for Christmas dinner with their mother and Gilbert, her new man. They would be back for the Boxing Day Meet here at The Hall. My parents were thrilled it was still going ahead. Malissa was here all the time, as, just like me, she dreaded Ruby leaving and wanted to check out her father, if indeed he was? If we didn't like him, we had agreed we would fight him in the courts for her to stay with us. I think we both hoped we didn't like him. Granger and Jabbo were going to celebrate at Granger's house as they had every Christmas throughout the war, only this time joined by Audrey and Halette. Not that Jabbo and Halette celebrated Christmas, but it was a holiday meal and a get-together-with-their-friends day. Lucy was going to Mrs Burden's with Frank, and his sister Rosie would join them as soon as she had helped in the morning with the children and our Christmas dinner. Portia's nanny, Alison, and Fiona's nanny, Lisa, would look after their respective children and Malissa would take care of Ruby. Lottie was going with her brothers to stay with her mother at Arthur's house after opening her presents here. Osian had decided to stay with us over Christmas and so his brothers Rhys and Gruffudd went home to spend Christmas with their father and their brothers. Merry and Scotty were staying in Scotland in Linlithgow near Edinburgh with Scotty's parents. Scotty had lost his left leg below the knee during the war, which was why Merry had decided to live with him in Scotland. They had met at the Vicarage when Tiff had called with gifts sent by me. Scotty had been travelling with him. They had fallen in love immediately. I was beginning to think we were too quiet at The Hall as everyone was leaving us.

On December 22nd a tall, bearded man in army uniform and wearing a turban was dropped off by taxi at the door to The Hall. Of course, I guessed who it was and ran down the steps to greet him with my hand outstretched. "Safely home; Dr Singh, I presume. Lovely to meet the father of two fine cricketers Ashneer and Virinder. Oh, I am Sid. Follow me and I will show you where they are. I don't think they know you are arriving?" I added.

I strode ahead and down to the stables and to the neat cottage where his wife Panaya and his mother Bargitta lived. I stood back in wonder as he knocked on the door. It opened and Panaya stood there speechless, wiping the flour from her hands. She flung herself into his arms screaming, "Bargitta, come quickly, look."

Bargitta rushed to find out what the noise was about, and Gurdas Singh bent down and touched his mother's feet and then hugged her.

Panaya looked at me, her eyes beseeching me. "Where are the boys?"

"Cricket," I predicted, "I think they are practising their batting for the next cricket match, I'll fetch them."

"No," said Dr Singh, "I will go, just show me where."

I set off with him following and Panaya behind him and Bargitta now in a warm coat and boots and carrying a coat for Panaya behind her. I went to the back of the stone hay shed where, protected on three sides from the wind by stone walls, the boys always practised bowling or batting. I heard the boys shrieking "catch it, Vinny" and "well bowled, Ash". I hoped their father didn't mind their name's being abbreviated. I gathered their mother and grandma, whom the boys called Bibi, preferred the boys' full names to be used. When they realised their father was home, Ash ran first, followed by Vinny, tossing his cricket bat to the floor. They had not seen their father for six years. It was a very emotional reunion to witness, and I was honoured to see all their joy and emotion.

We had the usual crowded Christmas Eve party round the Christmas tree; Jabbo carried my father down, and Tiff his wheelchair. Alastair and Tiff mingled and helped hand out drinks for everyone. Mrs Revill, Rosie, Malissa, and I passed out the little canapés. Mushroom pate and little sausages, spam with homemade red onion chutney on homemade oat biscuits, and our own strong special cheddar on miniature homemade scones. The doorbell never stopped ringing and it became a case of whoever was nearest opening the door. Nobody knew who they were letting in as tenants and villagers joined us, plus there were still plenty of military personnel in uniform visiting relatives in the area. Some RAF guys came as they couldn't get home, so they too, were invited. The estate farmers were there and all our friends and helpers, Humphrey and Clarissa Clayton, Ted and Nora Staples, Hugh and Margaret Brownlow with Susan and Roger. Alford and Martha had been picked up by Ted and were to be taken back by Granger. Everyone wanted to see my parents now they were safely back home.

As I smiled, laughed, and chatted I offered a canapé to the man next to me and he said, "Merci beaucoup," without thinking, he then added, "I should say thank you." I nearly dropped the tray. The good-looking man before me had dark brown eyes. a shock of black curly hair and was about 5'11. He was physically strong and fit looking, not thin, not fat and I just knew who he was. Without a word I took his arm and directed him to the quiet of the drawing room to check he was who I thought he was. Completely unknown to me, it was where Malissa had gone and was now playing cards, on the floor, with Ruby, Lottie, Amani, and Linford. They all looked up and Malissa stiffened and looked from him to me. I knew she knew immediately; it was in her eyes. We both looked at Ruby, engrossed in finding matching pairs of cards. He followed our eyes, and he knelt on the floor to watch the game. Ruby looked at him, briefly, and then helped Amani find two matching cards. Then she looked at him again.

"Hello, you can stroke my dog if you like," she said to him and handed Zissa to him.

He nestled the little dog against his cheek and, never taking his eyes off Ruby, he said, "I love little Zissa, she always looks after you."

Ruby got up and went to take her dog back. "How do you know her name is Zissa?" There was silence. All the children went quiet and watched Ruby and the new man. "Are you my papa?" Ruby asked.

"Oui, ma cherie, je suis ton papa," he replied with tears in his eyes.

"Papa tu t'es absente despuis longtemps, maintenant tu es la tu peux jouer aussi said Ruby and then added, "Je m'appelle Ruby." She sat next to him and then started to show Amani how to find more matching cards, completely unconcerned about her father being there. Malissa and I held our breaths at this exchange. Clearly, he was her father, and we couldn't believe how matter of fact Ruby had been.

Later that night she took her papa's hand and led him upstairs to her bedroom and read a fairy story to him and Lottie. She was a remarkable little girl. I was concerned she had not mentioned a baby or her mother, not once.

Later Malissa came into my bedroom with Tiff, and we sat on chairs by the fire drinking nightcaps of good single malt whisky which Alastair had kindly brought with him. We were all shattered. Halette had helped my father into his bed after he had been carried upstairs by Jabbo. He liked Jabbo very much and Jabbo was teaching him how to play the Moroccan card game called Ronda. Maisie had settled my mother to bed as both my parents were exhausted after seeing so many people at the Christmas Carol Event. Everyone had been pleased to see them. Now all we had to do was make sure Christmas dinner on rations went well. Tiff asked us how the meeting had played out between Ruby and her father. Tiff had shown Monsieur Zac Aaronson to his bedroom and now we were just the three of us, alone.

"You're both sad, I understand, but it's the best for her, you know, and I am sure she will always visit you both in the future. After all, you saved her life."

Malissa and I agreed, but it was going to be difficult to say goodbye to our little girl. Malissa went to bed, and Tiff and I slept together after making sweet, slow, ever so quiet love.

Christmas morning was our usual procession to church, only Granger brought Grandora and my parents in the Rolls. Ruby's father came too and watched Ruby and Lottie enjoying singing all the Christmas carols very loudly. I approved of his approach with Ruby; stayed quietly in the background, giving her time to get to know him at her own pace. I was not sure what he thought about us always taking her to our Christian village church, but I didn't care; she loved going with us. Most of all she was alive and had been kept safe throughout the war years. It was a tradition and now part of her upbringing here at The Hall. It was a bright and very blustery, cold day and we all hurried back home and to the fires which were burning brightly.

After everyone had opened their Christmas presents, Larry, Lennie and Lottie were picked up by Arthur and taken back to join their mother for Christmas dinner. I dived into the kitchen to start finishing off Christmas dinner which had been prepped by Mrs Revill and Rosie the day before. Rosie had been in this morning to make sure the meat was cooking. Rosie had gone to church with us and then home to be with her family. Alastair had brought us a whole salmon and a lamb. I'd never seen so much food for years. Of course, we had always had lots of our own home-grown vegetables and fruit, but a large amount of meat was a rarity, unless it had been venison which we had always shared around the estate and village. We had sent some of the lamb to Granger and Audrey for their Christmas dinner with Jabbo and Halette, and also to Hugh and Margaret, Alford, Martha, Humphrey and Clarissa. I believed good fortune should be shared. Nora and Ted assured me they already had some lamb, having butchered a hogget, a two-year-old lamb, and shared it with the rest of the farmers on our estate. As always, baskets of provisions had been sent to the elderly who lived locally and food from the estate we shared with all the community. The potatoes were ready to start roasting with the parsnips, leeks in cheese sauce, cauliflower, carrots, and green beans, we had an ample supply and along with the stuffing had been prepared by Mrs Revill. So, I got cracking with Malissa in the kitchen. The salmon was beautifully cooked, and we sliced it to serve as a starter with a lemon and dill sauce. We soon were able to join the others for pre-dinner drinks. Audrey and Danielle had decorated the table with some new artistic ideas supplied by Danielle, and it looked amazing with the white damask tablecloth, silver cutlery, crystal glasses, homemade beeswax candles and winter twigs entwined with handmade tiny white wool pompoms. Miriam and Danielle were joining us with Osian, Tad, and Anna-Sara and now, also, with Monsieur Aaronson. Oh, why did I ever imagine it could be quiet here when we were cooking for twenty-five people? I was loving having The Hall dining room full of chatter and laughter and everyone enjoying Christmas here, just as it used to be in the days of my grandparents; I remember all the fun and gaiety when my brother Sandy, Portia and I were allowed to join everyone for Christmas dinner and then we were shooed away to entertain ourselves, which we always did.

This Christmas was just the same, only we didn't have staff; just me, Malissa, Miriam, and Danielle helping to serve the food. I loved that Christmas Day with the war over, and all of us at last, together.

Chapter 39

The Revelation

I finished painting for the day and washed my brushes and hands and went into the kitchen to make a pot of tea for Gandora and myself. I popped two homemade plain biscuits onto a plate and put an embroidered tea cloth on the tray, then the lovely porcelain tea pot and milk jug, no need for a sugar bowl. The Hall was quiet, we were alone, and we were slowly getting used to having more time just to ourselves. As I went in to Grandora's sitting room I realised that she was asleep, so I tiptoed in and put the tray down onto the table and sat back in a comfortable armchair, lay back and closed my eyes. Then I realised that the wireless was on, and I started to listen to it without intending to. I heard about the discovery of a place called Bergen-Belsen by our soldiers on April 8th and I listened with growing horror about the dying, starving and dead people they found there. They had liberated another camp called Neuengamme near Hamburg and discovered more corpses and living dead people covered in lice and suffering from typhus.

The broadcaster went on to report of camps found by the Russians and the Americans designed to exterminate undesirable people the Nazis felt were unfit to live. Many of the people were Jews, but there were also disabled, black, gypsies, political prisoners, and homosexuals. I stood up and couldn't breathe. I choked, I tried to speak – I couldn't. I stumbled past Grandora and into the hall, trying to get away. I tried to scream, I was choking, choking. Then I think I wailed, and it went black. I came-to with Grandora next to me, and I kept repeating 'I did nothing, I did nothing, I did nothing I did nothing'. I looked up to see Danielle with stricken face staring at me. "I did nothing, I did nothing," I ranted. "I should have done more, I should have fought, I should have been there."

Danielle stayed by my side and kneeling next to me, she stroked and held my hand. "You did everything, everything, you rescued so many people, you opened your heart to all of us, you rescued us, you saved us, you did everything you could."

They dragged me to my feet and led me back to the sitting room and made me sip some tea and I just stared through the window, feeling sick, revulsed, ill. I did nothing was all I kept thinking. I was cosy at the Hall here in Norfolk, I did nothing as the ghastly war had ravaged the world and wrecked people's lives. I moaned aloud and I started to weep uncontrollably. I rocked, and I wept for all the lost people and their agony as they had no one to protect or comfort them.

I don't know for how long I wept and shuddered: dusk came, and exhausted I stared through the window at the gathering gloom. Grandora and Danielle stayed with me and Grandora gave me a hot whisky toddy, a mixed drink of liquor, water with honey, spices, and herbs. I stayed the night on her sofa in her bedroom. Just before I slept, I remembered my Ruby, 'RUBY where are you?' I wanted to hug her, to touch her, to keep her close to me for ever. Then I don't remember anything.

Chapter 40

Miriam's Baby

Boxing Day was a big, hectic success. I rode Hermes and Tiff rode The Brig. At the Meet, as usual, Osian was pulling his hair out at the horses' hooves churning up the front lawn and rushing round 'shooing' horse riders off the grass and onto the gravel forecourt. It was agreed that we would hunt for one hour, then go to Hunt stables and hand The Brig over to Granger to hunt for the rest of the day. Lennie was going to whipper-in and ride a young homebred bright bay hunter from the hunt stables, Granger was briefly in charge of Ruby on Tizzy and Lottie on Donk, during the Meet. The other two whippers-in brought their own horses, and the field master was the redoubtable Davinia Hardcastle-Cord, the Commissioner for the Pony Club; the one with the voice of a sergeant major riding a strong bay gelding with a hogged mane. It was all very confusing, but the person to have us all gasping was my mother who appeared at the meet on her mare, Polly. Surely she wasn't strong enough yet? Well, why not, she looked calm and happy and very smart in her old Hunt coat even if it was too big for her now. She

told me she was only going to join us for the Meet then hack over to
Alford's hunt stables. She had arranged for Lucy to bring Polly back
to our stables. Alastair would pick her up there and take her back
to rest as she admitted she would probably be very tired and stiff.
Frankie appeared at the Meet on A.P. who looked amazing with his
chestnut coat gleaming, a smart trace clip and his mane and tail in
plaits, all the work of Lucy. Lysander had been put on a marvellous
rock of a grey hunter, bred by my father for himself and used by
Alford whilst my father had been away. To top all that off, Jabbo
appeared on Timefortea, our racehorse, now six years old, which my
father hoped would go hurdling. My father was plotting this with
Granger and Jabbo. Again, I was thrilled to see my family on Boxing
Day at our Hunt Meet. My father was watching from his wheelchair
and clearly loved it all.

The route had been planned by Alford and Hugh and it
allowed us to pass near the hunt stables within one hour of
leaving The Hall. The runner, a fit young student arrived, was
given the scent and we allowed him to get a good start. It all
went very well, which was unbelievable, given the changes we
made during the course of the day. Tiff handed The Brig over to
Granger at the hunt stables to carry on hunting and we brought
Polly and Hermes home. Back home at the stables we rubbed
Polly and Hermes down then gave them water with the chill taken
off and nets of hay, then left them in their stables with jute rugs
on. They both had a blanket clip and we had walked back so
they weren't sweated up. They would get a bran mash later when
the others were back. Tiff and I left the rest of the stable duties
to Jabbo, Granger and Lennie. Larry and Lottie had gone back
to Arthur's farm to be with their mother, Mavis, and to get to
know Gilbert, her husband to be. We went back to the Hall to
see how my mother and father were and to prepare a meal for

everyone when they returned. Tiff was a dab-hand at cooking which impressed me no end. Yea, more time for me to ride in the future; well, I could dream.

Lysander, Portia, and their families stayed for two more happy family days of meals together, lots of walks and getting to know each other and catching up on the last nine years of being apart. Six years of war and three and a half years of me being in France and my parents being in Singapore. They wanted to be back in Scotland for Hogmanay and plans were made for them to return in April for my wedding. My parents would then go back to Scotland with them. Much as I loved them all, I was tired and glad they were leaving. I prepared a simple buffet for New Year's Eve, in the big dining room, and invited all my friends, tenants and everyone I had met during the war, who lived near enough to visit, to come for an early evening celebration. We played swing dance music on the gramophone and danced in the great reception hall and then sang popular songs including Roll Out The Barrel, We'll Meet Again and finally Auld Lang Syne. It finished at nine-thirty as my parents still went to bed early and so did the children. When we had cleared most of the dishes away we sat in the drawing room with the fire burning brightly whilst Halette made sure my father was settled for the night. Maisie helped my mother retire and we opened some bottles of good white wine and chatted amongst ourselves about our plans and hopes for 1946. Grandora and Larry stayed to raise a toast of good health to us all for the New Year with champagne and we toasted those who never made it to the end of the war and would never return to their homes again.

We heard that on January 3rd, William Joyce, nicknamed 'Lord Haw Haw' by his British listeners, was hanged for treason. I don't think anyone was sad about his demise. This dreadful man had preached to Britain that we were doomed, and for years had said we should surrender to Hitler. It was also reported that the Reichskleinodien treasures of the Holy Roman Empire, taken from Austria at the time of the Anschluss, were returned to Vienna. At last, artefacts and treasures stolen by the Nazi regime were being found and returned to their rightful owners. Malissa didn't think they would be returning to Albania to live after hearing that the Communist leader Enver Hoxha was proclaimed the nation's Prime Minister of the new People's Republic of Albania. She said her parents would be living permanently in Greece from now on and she thought she would like to live in Britain. She now spent much of her time with Ruby as we didn't know when Ruby's father would decide to leave and go back to Switzerland; we both dreaded losing her. Tiff thought Malissa and Zac, Ruby's father, spent lots of time together and perhaps they were falling in love. I thought that was rubbish as she was Greek Orthodox and he was Jewish, so I didn't think falling in love was on the cards; they just both cared about Ruby as I did; well, we all did.

Before I could think more about my impending wedding, we had the imminent birth of Miriam's baby to think about. She had sailed through her pregnancy looking serene and radiant and we had all looked after her, making sure she didn't do too much and had lots of rest. Her sister-in-law Zelda had been living with her and Audrey for the last month, and her mother was coming to stay as her due date loomed nearer. Zelda and Noah now had a little boy of their own, a lively two-year-old and James could be a real handful.

I think every one of us was excited for Miriam and thrilled the new baby was going to be born here in Norfolk, a place Rory knew and had grown to love. Miriam had written to Rory's parents to tell them that she and Rory had been married in Scotland and to tell them that she was expecting Rory's baby. They had written back telling her how thrilled they were and that they were making plans to travel to England to meet her.

The days flew by with wedding arrangements and estate duties, horses to look after, children to care for; and we all watched over Miriam. Every week our worst job in my mind and the one I tried to avoid was the laundry. The bedding and the children's clothes were a never-ending chore. We all did muck in and help with every job which needed doing, but I much preferred outside work. Audrey came and helped Rosie and Maisie every day and Joan Burden came two days a week to wade through the massive amount of laundry we had. I needed extra with Miriam being less available – she had always helped with the everyday work of running the Hall, but now we forbade her to do any work at all apart from preparing the vegetables for the meals. Help came from Lucy who had been discharged from the army but wasn't needed on the farm. She, like me, preferred outside work, especially with the horses, but had agreed to help in the house and stay on in the cottage whilst waiting for Frankie to be discharged from the army. It was possible, too, that shortly, her sister Hazel would be happy to join us at The Hall and she had done a cooking course at college.

I seemed to be running backwards and forwards between the cottages, The Hall, and my parents' rooms each day. Thank goodness I managed to ride every morning and get into my art room at some point every day. Miriam's mother was arriving later in the morning with Anna-Sara and Avigail, and I was rushing up from the stables when I bumped into Audrey who asked me to fetch Halette and telephone for Dr Haigh, as Miriam was about to have her baby. I was like a 'headless chicken' in panic, ran into

The Hall and up the stairs two at a time to tell Halette who was
with my father. Then I told my mother and Grandora, and asked
her to telephone for Dr Haigh to come straight away. I then ran
'helter skelter' to the stables to tell Danielle and Granger. By the
time I arrived back at the cottage Miriam had delivered her baby
with Zelda and Halette in attendance, apparently as 'easy peasy'
as you please. A little boy; how wonderful; we were all so thrilled.
His name – Rory Junior Johannes Kaiholm.

I was so excited to be marrying Tiff and looking forward to
having lots of sex with him without creeping around in the night
to meet up illicitly. My mother began to make a guest list and
she started putting people down I hardly knew. I told her all
the people who had become my friends during the war were the
people I wanted to see at my wedding, not people I hardly knew.
So momentarily she faltered, then agreed it was not a social event,
but a time for me to rejoice and be happy with my true friends. I
then told her I didn't have any idea what I should wear as wedding
dresses were so expensive, practically unobtainable and material
was still hard to find. Later that day Maisie came to ask me to go
upstairs to see my mother because they had decided between
them that my mother's wedding dress might just fit me. It was
beautiful white, embroidered silk, with lace sleeves to the wrist,
a high neck and pearls sewn all down the bodice in rows to the
waist. If I didn't wear very high heeled shoes the length would be
ok as well. I was taller than my mother, but any changes could be
made by Mrs Hubbard. Then my mother surprised me by showing
me a sash of fine wool made of her family tartan to be worn on
my shoulder and tied at my right hip in a bow with a gold Celtic
brooch, pinned to hold it in place. My mother's father was Cedric
Cockburn, the novelist who had lived on his family's ancient
crumbling Scottish estate on the Scottish Borders, and it was their

tartan. My mother had been very lonely living with her mother Georgina and her father on the remote estate, and meeting my father had changed her life. With my father she had always been surrounded by family, friends, and a hectic social life. I tried the dress on and was thrilled by how well it looked and how well it had been looked after, in storage. So, I had my dress. Danielle then surprised me with a gift of a magnificent hand-knitted fine white wool cape with a high ruffle neck and trimmed with fur which went to my waist and fastened all the way down with pearl buttons. I was so touched that she had designed and made such an exquisite cape for my wedding day. Grandora brought me a veil of Leavers lace, a gift from her and Tantetta. They'd both worn it on their wedding days. Whilst I was discussing with my mother how to keep it on my head Grandora brought me her diamond tiara with an emerald set in the centre which she had worn for her own wedding. I truly knew I was going to feel like a princess. I almost felt beautiful. The Leavers lace was exquisite, had been made in Nottingham and created by John Levers it was very special. Ruby, Lottie, Anna-Sara, Susan, Abigail and Amani were to be my bridesmaids and we decided to have their dresses made from silk Grandora had brought back from India before the war. We chose a pale pink and gold silk brocade with borders of bright turquoise, greens, aquamarine blues which was unusual and gorgeous. It was so exciting after all this time, since our first meeting at the Chateau in France, we were to be married; and I was so in love with him.

Miriam's father arrived to see the baby and said he should be circumcised, but Miriam did not agree. It was a happy and tense time, but he accepted it was not going to happen and that the baby was half-Canadian. He was impressed that little Rory would one day inherit a ranch in Canada, all being well. He clearly loved the baby and was proud of Miriam and he did say there was no point in being sad about the baby not being all Jewish as that made him nearly as bad as the Nazis who had persecuted people for being different to themselves throughout the war. He stayed for five days and spent some time chatting to my father and playing chess with him.

I then received a letter from Tantetta in Switzerland saying she was arranging an exhibition of my work to be held in April in London and afterwards in Paris and she hoped very much I would attend both openings. She added that Grandora had informed her of how hard I was working on my paintings and that she was sure they were outstanding and that I had more than enough ready for an exhibition. The sneaky pair arranging an exhibition, my first, behind my back, how thrilling and nerve racking! I worked even harder to finish a few I thought needed more work to make them acceptable.

I had sent a wedding invitation to Aurielle and Marcell, and I questioned them as to the arrival of Alex in May 1940 and did he have more than one sister staying with him as well as Claude his brother at that time. Of course, a wedding invitation was sent to Alex and his family too. I soon received a reply accepting my invitation and the news that they were expecting Tantetta to travel to the wedding with Auntygusta and her friend Bernadette as they were arriving to attend first the re-internment of Joseph. There was also to be the laying of a Memorial stone to commemorate Joseph Pierre Denisot and others killed in action. with the Maquis, the French Freedom fighters who had operated in that area during the war. I knew I had to be there in March, and I knew Tiff would want to be too. She then went on to say Alex had arrived in May with Claude, Simone, and his older sister Nadine, who had a tiny young baby with her. During the war

Alex had been badly beaten by the Boche and nearly killed, but he had recovered after many months of illness. He walked with a permanent limp, but he had become the good viticulturist he had wanted to be. He had many talents including using a bow and arrow, which had kept them well supplied with venison and wild boar that had supplemented their meagre diet during severe rationing. He had also become the village baker after Laurent Vaulbolon, the village baker, had been executed by the Nazis for protesting about them taking all the bread he had baked, leaving nothing for the villagers. He had been taken to the little village square and shot in front of the villagers as an example to them all not to keep any food for themselves. It had filled everyone with fear as had been intended. She concluded that they were hoping to see us at the funeral for Joseph and then added she was sending us a recent photograph of them all standing in the courtyard in front of the farmhouse at the end of the war. It took me ages to try to read it and to stumble over the words, but I think I got the gist of it correctly. I looked into the envelope and pulled out a photograph of my good friends smiling for the camera in the sunshine. There was Marcell with his arm around Aurielle's shoulder, and Alex with his brother Claude, now a young man and Simone a pretty young girl next to Alex and there was also a young woman with long dark brown hair with her hands resting on the shoulders of a young boy. He had bouncy black curly hair, a bonny smile and looked to be about six years old. There was a stooped, thin old man and another good-looking upright man with a white beard and a mane of white hair standing next to him. I turned the photograph over and Aurielle had written their names Marcell, herself, Claude, Alex, Simone, Nadine, Jacques, Alex's father Bernard and his Great Uncle Albert. I looked at them again and again and I could almost feel the sunshine and smell the lavender in the garden. I ran my fingers over their faces and then I looked at the little boy again; he looked so familiar. How stupid of me, so did Alex, but why should he look familiar? Apart from the fact I had met him of course, silly me. I popped it back into the envelope and then realized there was another photograph inside, a smaller photograph. It was of two tanned men with stubble beards, old farm clothes, leather belts, army boots and both carried guns in the crook of their arms, one a Lee Enfield, the other an older gun I could not recognise. They were not smiling, but they were relaxed, happy and one had his elbow resting on the other's shoulder as their dark eyes stared intently into the camera. I suddenly realized I was looking at Joseph and he was staring straight into my eyes. I breathed deeply as I stared at my dear friend, Joseph. When was this taken, did he die soon afterwards, was this his friend who held him as he died? I would ask Tiff when he came home from London – he would know who he was. I gently ran my fingertips over the face of Joseph and felt immense love and sadness for him.

I decided to find Grandora and show her, but first I went into the kitchen to make us a pot of tea. Osian came in carrying a box of vegetables from the garden. I made him tea and thanked him, and we chatted about Merry, now nursing at a hospital in Scotland so as to be near Scotty who, since his injury and discharge from the army, was working in one of his father's pharmacy shops. He was a qualified pharmacist, but I didn't think it would be his job in the long term. I showed the photographs to Osian and told him we would be travelling to France in March for the re-internment of Joseph. I was thinking of Joseph sitting on the wall swinging his legs and teasing me for my poor French when I first arrived, and then trying to teach me the local patois, then I realised that Osian was telling me something about the garden. I looked up at Osian to focus on what he was telling me and stared at his fine boned face, his clear honest blue eyes, and his light brown hair and I realized I could be looking at Alex; except Alex had dark brown hair. They were both small boned and wiry, fit, and strong, and barely five foot eight. A thought came into my mind: "Osian, what do you know about your cousin in France, the one you don't know; I mean his mother was the older sister of your Auntie Vera and your mother, you know the one who went to live in France, called Bettina?"

Osian looked at me surprised. "Very little, Merry knows more than me. I could ask Aunty Vera if you like. Why, what makes you ask?"

"Look at the young man in this photograph, he told us his mother was an English nurse who went to France to marry a baker she had fallen in love with, and I think he has the same bone structure and eyes as you."

"Yes, perhaps he does and there's me thinking the young boy in the photograph looks just like Ruby," Osian replied casually. I took the photograph from him and realized I was looking at Ruby's double.

"Don't mention this to anyone. We can't get Ruby's father rushing over there unless we have a better idea it could be Ruby's missing baby brother. Get in touch with Merry please – come over and use our telephone tonight. I would love to speak to her anyway," I implored Osian.

I rushed off to find Grandora and bumped into Zac, Malissa, and Ruby. They were spending a lot of time together. They told me they had just been riding. Riding, Malissa?

"No, not Malissa, me and Daddy," said Ruby proudly. "I have been riding Spangles and Daddy has been having a lesson with Granger on Polly."

"Oh, that is exciting, darling, and was Spangles good for you?"

"Of course, I can ride him now, I am nearly ten and I love him, Lottie is going to ride Tizzy when she comes home."

"Well, I would like to come and see you next time you ride Spangles. Now off you go and get a drink of milk. I need to speak to Malissa, there's a good girl." I smiled at Zac, excused us, and pulled Malissa upstairs with me to find Grandora.

"What's the matter?" Malissa asked.

"I have something to show you, come and have a look."

I knocked on Grandora's room and found her resting in her armchair by the window, the newspaper as usual had slipped off her knee. "Grandora, look at this, well, both of you."

I gave the letter to Grandora to read. Aurielle had written it in French, but Grandora's French was excellent, and I wanted to be sure I had read it correctly as it had been a struggle for me. She read it and passed it to Malissa who read it slowly. They both looked at me waiting for me to reveal why they had been summoned to read the letter. I passed the photograph of my friends in France, smiling on a sunny day by the farmhouse, first to Grandora and then to Malissa. I never spoke but waited for their reaction – if there was one – if not I must be wrong and so was Osian.

Malissa gasped as she slowly looked at the photograph and then looked at me. "How can this be? I don't understand," she said slowly.

We asked Grandora what she thought, and she agreed it was a remarkable likeness of the two children then she hesitated and said, "I thought you were asking me if I thought the young man looked like Osian?"

Malissa looked carefully again. "Oh yes I suppose he does now I think about it."

I chimed in, "It never occurred to me that there was a resemblance, well why would it.? We met him in the woods for such a brief time and I hadn't met Osian at that time, but now I know Osian he does bear a remarkable likeness to Alex. Osian thought the young boy in the photograph looked like Ruby," I added and asked, "Should we show Zac?"

Grandora spoke first: "I will telephone my sister and speak to her. I hope the telephones are working over there. I will send a letter to her. Can you both help me to do it now, we need to know where Nadine is from and where Alex found her."

I suggested, "She was definitely not with him when we saw him, but by the time he arrived at the Chateau she was with him." I interjected: "We are going to France for the memorial ceremony for Joseph next week. I think Zac, you and Ruby had better go with us to meet this little boy. Perhaps Nadine was the nanny and she escaped from the crashed car and ran away."

"Well, we just don't know, we will write and try to ring Henrietta tomorrow and explain what we need to know," Grandora suggested.

Next, I showed them the photograph of Joseph and his friend.

"What brave young men, it's clearly been hell over there. Thank God for people like them, willing to fight for what they know is right. I will come to the ceremony with you and see my sisters and the Chateau," Grandora concluded.

So that was that; Grandora was coming too.

Meanwhile, my father was very excited about the prospect of racing Timefortea. The racehorse who had never raced was now hopefully going to be a hurdler or a point to pointer. My father asked me if he could have a chat with me and arranged a meeting for the next day in his office. What had I done wrong, I wondered? So, feeling like a nervous child, I was at the office on time. He was in his wheelchair and as we sat opposite each other I waited for the reprimand or whatever.

"Cressida, I am so proud of everything you have done here whilst we have been... away. I know you have run this estate, kept the harvest dinner going with our farmers and made sure everyone in the area has fuel for their fires and food. You have been a godsend for the young RAF men who have stayed here with burnout or injuries; it's been a safe haven for them. I know all about Miriam and her counselling, encouraged by you. You have provided a home for children and families in dire need of help. Isadora tells me we have made an enormous contribution to the war effort and all our food production has increased at the same time. The farms are running smoothly, and you have introduced new ideas and machinery. I want you to know, I am amazed and delighted to know my daughter has made such an enormous contribution to the war effort on behalf of the Willup Hall Estate. Your kindness to so many people in desperate need of help shows how kind-hearted you are, but then, I know you always have been. I love you so much and thank you for keeping everything going here; you are so much better than I could ever be at running the estate."

I breathed out – whew – what a surprise.

"That brings me to the next question. I was wondering with your obvious organizational skills, if you could arrange for us to have a training gallop for our racehorse, and with your permission, can we afford it and do you think we can do it? Oh, and I have bought a dark grey mare arriving from Clary's yard, to train with Timefortea. I believe you saw it the day it was born. The time you went for Spangles and came back with a small herd of horses," he added, smiling.

This long speech clearly was an effort for him, and he was now tired. Thrilled about the new mare arriving and in shock for a moment, I just stared and then I clapped my hands together, yes I clapped, don't know why, just so relieved I wasn't in trouble.

"Of course, it's wonderful and a brilliant idea, you must arrange it with Jabbo and Granger, oh, and Frankie and Osian. They will be brilliant at working out how to do it. I'll tell them to come and see you and at the same time would you look at the plans they have for a cricket pavilion on the West Road so we can have more cricket matches without any stray balls coming the way of The Hall windows, which has frequently happened over the last few years. Oh yes I'm sure we can afford it." I jumped up and put my arms round him and kissed him.

"Oh, and that reminds me," he continued. "What's happened to our gates?"

"Ah yes, the gates. I'll explain later, don't worry, they're flying around somewhere." I laughed. "I'll go now and find Granger." I skipped, yes skipped out and I think I was humming.

The next day there was a conference held in the dining room to discuss the proposed gallop for training our one and only racehorse. Soon to be two now, apparently. I wasn't going to fuss about it being a wasteful exercise as it was good to see my father energised and enthusiastic again. I'm sure we would exercise all the horses on the new track eventually. Tiff arrived home and I showed him the letter and told him all about my thoughts of who the little boy might be. He had met them all when fighting over there and helping to organise the Maquis. He clearly remembered the boy and agreed, now he thought about the child, he did look a lot like Ruby. He remembers the young girl he had presumed was the baby's mother having very long dark hair and green eyes and when he thought about it, he thought she might have had an Irish accent, but she was speaking French most of the time. He said he never thought about it and didn't pay much attention to the child at the time. He met them at the time of Joseph's death, and he had many other problems on his mind. At that particular time peace had not been declared in France and he (and the Maquis and Jabbo) were constantly having to hide from the German troops as they were heading back to Germany and causing maximum damage to people and places as they left. It was understandable that there were more pressing problems to deal with than wonder about a child, it must have been a chaotic and scary time.

We booked train tickets to France for us to travel in five days, and we decided to ask Zac if he would like to join us with Ruby and of course Malissa. He had to be told why, as he wouldn't understand the reason for the invitation to the memorial service of someone he didn't know. So, I showed him the photograph. It was a black and white photograph, but he was overjoyed and hopeful when he saw the little boy named Jacques. He finally put the photograph on the table and started to plan the trip to the Chateau with us and of course Malissa and Ruby.

Suddenly we all went quiet, when Ruby picked up the photograph and staring hard said, "Is this my Nunu, it is, it's Nunu, where is she?"

Well, that did it; so, she thought she recognised the woman in the photograph called Nadine. We couldn't go fast enough and Grandora declared she was ready for her break, already packed and looking forward to seeing her sisters again after so many years.

Chapter 41

Back To France

Tiff and I soon found ourselves rattling along very rough lanes in a 2 CV van driven by Alex. Meanwhile, Zac, Ruby, Malissa and Grandora were being sedately driven in Tantetta's Rolls-Royce by Marcell. I was now very excited to see my second home again. All along the roads were signs of the fighting which had taken place and we passed burnt out and ditched military hardware. They certainly had faced a horrible time here. The people we did see looked poor, badly dressed and worm out. Pretty much like us in Britain, only I must admit they did look worse. Turning through the gates and into the drive to the Chateau again took my breath away and I could have cried with joy to be back and relief that it was still standing. Aurielle ran out to meet us and we hugged each other for a long-time, crying tears of happiness and tears of regret that so much of our lives had been wasted because of a stupid war and because of a stupid, evil, mad man. I introduced her to Zac, Ruby, and Malissa; she knew Tiff and of course was overjoyed to see Grandora. Alex's old dog Tanner got up stiffly and came over to see who we were, and I stroked his old head and big floppy spaniel ears.

"Please will you be careful with Nadine; she knows why Monsieur Aaronson is here and she is scared to lose Jacques as he is like her own son now," explained Aurielle.

Tantetta came out of the Chateau with Auntygusta, and I hurled myself at Tantetta like a small child.

Grandora smiled and scolded me: "Cressida, let her breathe, don't knock her over."

We were all emotional to be together again and with my arm looped through Auntygusta's, we all went into the kitchen for a drink. I met Bernadette, or as she preferred to be called Bernie, Auntygusta's friend who lived with her. I liked her; she was a down to earth, no-nonsense woman.

I could see Zac was anxious to meet little Jacques. Ruby, who had not been told why we were there other than for a holiday, was just happy to be with us. We had all travelled light as we were here for the memorial service then we were all returning home for my wedding on Saturday, April 20th. After a much-needed cool glass of grape juice, we were told Nadine was waiting to see us with Jacques. We all went outside to meet her, Claude, Simone, and the little boy Jacques. Ruby was busy stroking Thor, Tantetta's dog, at first, then she followed us, curious to see who we were meeting. It was difficult – but we all knew to be casual, and we just chatted until Ruby said to Nadine, "Are you Nunu? You look like Nunu; do you remember me?"

Nadine burst into tears and hugged her. "Of course I remember you, my little one, where is Zissa?"

"She is at home with Odin and Aunty Romilly is looking after them for us. Is this your little boy? Can I play with him?" And without waiting for an answer, she took the little boy's hand and together they went into the paddock to throw a ball for Thor. They were so alike, side by side with their mops of bouncy dark curls and their merry, dark brown eyes.

Nadine suddenly started talking quickly: "I am so sorry I left her in the car. I thought she was dead, I think I was knocked out at first, I can't remember the accident and when I came round there was an awful silence and all I could think of was to get out of the car with the baby still in my arms. I could see Madame and the chauffeur were dead. I just had my travel bag and the baby's bag. I just started walking, not really knowing where I was heading, I just wanted to get away from the awful scene. Then it started to rain, and the road was so long and empty and the rain came down harder and harder and I was frightened that the baby might die of cold." Nadine stopped and started to cry. "I have wanted to tell you all for a very long time, but it's been so difficult here and it was best not to tell anyone." Nadine went on with her story. "Then this horse and old cart came along the road, and I was frightened, but there was nowhere to hide. A young man climbed down to ask me if I needed help, but I was frightened of him, and I could hardly understand what he was saying. My French was not very good then. He showed me under the tarpaulin, sheltering from the rain, were two children so I climbed in and went with him; I was so tired and we went to a farmhouse. I was cold and bruised all over and my head hurt. The man and his wife were lovely people and Alex went to dry Trudi, his horse, in the barn and Claribel the lady helped me and the children get out of our wet clothes and sit by the fire to get us warm. Then the baby cried, and she waited for me to feed him, but of course I couldn't, I just had an empty bottle. Madame Albertine, Claribel, prepared some warm goat's milk for the baby and I think she guessed he wasn't mine. I was so scared of any soldiers coming and finding out I was Irish or that the baby was Jewish and taking him from me that I said he was mine, but I couldn't feed him. I told them my name was Nadine instead of my Irish name Nula. Marcell quickly managed to have false documents made for me and the baby Jacques. I am sorry, but I never thought we would find Monsieur Aaronson–" she turned to Zac– "or you find us. After all, I never met you as you had travelled to Switzerland before I arrived in Paris to assist Madame Aaronson with her children. I think of Jacques as my own son now and I love him very much and he thinks I am his Mama." As this sudden outburst ended she started to cry again, and Alex put his arm around her to comfort her.

Zac said, "I don't blame you for doing what you did, you were very young and had only just arrived from Ireland to be his nanny. You've saved his life and I owe you an enormous debt; I can never repay you for what you have done. You have loved him and cared for him, and I thank you from the bottom of my heart. Look at Ruby here, she was saved that day by strangers who at first thought she was dead too. I can't believe the kindness of strangers to my little children; my poor wife was certainly looking over them when she died and guided you all into their lives. Thank you so much. My debt can never be repaid, but I am not here to drag my son away from you, he needs lots of time and patience to learn to accept me as his father and Ruby as his sister. I hope that you are coming to Britain to stay with us. Cressida says you can visit us there so we can slowly learn to be a family again."

Nula looked doubtful, but Alex said yes, they would love to come to stay with us. Tiff immediately said they must come to our wedding and travel to Britain with Aurielle and Marcell. Grandora asked who would look after the Chateau. Alex assured them his father Bernard, Uncle Albert with Marie Christine and

Louise would be pleased to; so that was settled: they would come to stay with us in Norfolk.

The Memorial Service was so very sad, as was the internment, but beautiful. The weather was sunny and warm, in marked contrast to the chilly breezes we still had in Norfolk. We followed Joseph's coffin draped in the Tricolour, the French flag. It was carried from Louisa's house to the little cemetery in our tiny village by six men, all wearing army boots, suit jackets, leather belts and black berets The road was lined with mourners and there were people following us as we walked behind Louisa, her daughter Cecile and her two grandchildren. Many strangers came to pay their respects as the six soldiers took the coffin into the Church for the service and the same soldiers carried Joseph into the graveyard after the service. The Priest paid great respect to Joseph and his fellow Resistance fighters and their sacrifice and service to France. The graveyard was overflowing with silent people as his coffin was taken to the waiting grave and lowered in by his compatriots. Then, after the priest had said the Our Father, Hail Mary and Glory Be as his coffin was laid to rest, six more men wearing black berets and in suits with Ml Carbines and bandoliers across their chests appeared and stood to attention and fired a volley of three shots and singing started: La Marseillaise Allons enfants de la Patrie, Le jour de gloire est arrivé, Contre nous de la tyrannie, L'étendez-vous dans nos campagnes, Mugir ces féroces soldats ? Ils viennent jusque dans vos bras, Egorger vos fils, vos campagnes. Aux armes citoyennes, Formez vos bataillons, Marchons, Qu'un sang impur, Abreuve nos sillons.

Tears silently ran down my face as we all sang and I remembered Joseph with his love of life, his humour and the fiery passion in his eyes and deciding to join the army to fight for his country, France. Then I saw him leading Flavie between the rows of vines during harvest time, pinching grapes and later tasting my culinary disasters in the kitchen and teasing me and laughing at my poor cooking. I was so sad and heartbroken never to see my good friend again. Then The Last Post was played by a bugler and slowly we all left the cemetery.

We made our way to the Chateau with everyone who was there, as they were all invited to join us. We were going to unveil the marble stone erected and paid for by Tantetta on the quiet road junction leading to the Chateau in a shady spot near a big Chestnut tree.

Talking to the mourners I discovered that Tiff was well known and respected from his time here by the men who had carried the coffin and those who had fired the shots over the grave. I was introduced to the best friend of Joseph, a man called Uri Berman, the man who had fought with Joseph for four years. He was the man who had cradled Joseph as he died from his wounds and who had carried him to a farm, insisting he be buried on the farm in secret because he had promised him he would make sure he went home one day. Marcell had sent Uri to Joseph for his protection after Uri had escaped from a cattle train taking him and the other occupants to a concentration camp. I realized then that he was the other man in the black and white photograph with Joseph. He had a strong, interesting face and I took more photographs with my box camera. I had been taking a few photographs discreetly before the funeral, and continued after the memorial service. Apparently, Marcell, Aurielle, Alex and Marie had been despised by the villagers during the war for appearing to get on with the Germans staying in our Chateau. What nobody knew was that Marcell was in constant contact with the Maquis and needed good cover to use his radio hidden in the furthest reaches of the estate. They had decided to look as if they were getting on with the Milice and the Germans, when they arrived, as a good way to discreetly rescue people who were running away from being sent for obligatory forced labour in Germany. They also found safe passage for airmen who had survived crash landings from their aircraft and now needed to return to Britain. They were part of an escape network operating throughout the war in France, assisting those people in urgent need to escape the Nazis. For these reasons they had kept their heads down and kept working on the estate, providing food and wine for the Nazis whilst all the time working with the Maquis and sending radio messages back to Britain. They could never let anyone know what they were doing for fear of exposure and then torture and reprisals. They all had risked death and were willing to give their lives for the freedom of France. I was in awe of what they had been through. Tiff and Jabbo had been parachuted into France by a Handley Page Halifax, the aircraft favoured for this mission, from RAF Harrington. This airfield had been chosen for Carpetbagger Operations to deliver agents and supplies into occupied Europe to support local resistance fighters as it was near to the supply depots of Cheddington and Holme. It was also near to Tempsford, the SOE base. The Americans flew B-24 Liberator aircraft on the same missions, giving vital support to the 23 Halifax doing the same job. They had formed part of a team called the Jedburghs, nicknamed 'Jeds' after their training in the Highlands of Scotland and then at Milton Hall near Peterborough. Jabbo had trained as a radio operator and Tiff was the only Major in their team. Their job was to liaise, advise, and supply arms and ammunition and money. Usually, a Jedburgh team would also comprise an American from the Office of Strategic Service, OSS, a Frenchman from the Bureau Centrale Renseignements et d'Action, and a British agent from Special Operation Executive, SOE. They all wore their uniforms in France so that if caught they could not be treated as spies. Their job had been to fulfil their motto: Surprise, Kill, Ambush. Tiff thought that the name Jedburghs was possibly chosen because of the town Jedburgh's history of raiders, known as the Border Reivers. I stood in awe of these incredible people and the full horror of what they had been expected to do and what they had achieved. We stood here in peace today because of their heroism and their willingness to lay down their lives for justice and for their families and for future generations.

We gathered around the white marble headstone bearing the name of Joseph Pierre Denisot and his fellow fallen compatriots. People shook hands and then melted away, leaving our little party to return to the Chateau, to sit and reflect upon all that had taken place that day. Uri came back with us as he had been invited to stay for the summer and join in the vendange, giving him time to reflect on plans for the next part of his life.

1945 had been a poor grape harvest and they were hoping this year would be a good one as they all needed some hope. Uri was a tanned, well-muscled, fit young man, very quiet, withdrawn and seemed to be on guard most of the time. I wondered if he would ever be able to relax after the strange existence he had lived for so long. I knew I had to paint him – he had a chiselled bone structure, and he was clearly a silent observer of life and people. Fascinated by the story of Ruby and Jacques, he spent some time talking to Zac, alone. They looked as if they were making plans for something then Tiff and Marcell joined them. I suppose they all had plenty to discuss. I felt so inadequate. My contribution in Britain during the war was nothing compared to the stories of horror which kept coming out on the news or just hinted at by my good friends here in France. I asked about the Albertines and was horrified to learn that shortly after we had visited them on our journey home in 1940, Gregoire had been attacked and killed by the Collaborationist police. He had remonstrated with them for taking their goats. Claribel had spent the war on her farm living with her brother's young wife Clemence and her three children. Her brother Robert de Rouille had been knifed by the French resistance in town one day whilst visiting his mistress and their Chateau had eventually been taken over by German soldiers. The eldest boy Florent de Rouille, now sixteen, had been sent to Marcell and then on to Joseph to avoid him being picked up by the Nazis. He was here and I knew I must meet him. Aurielle took me over to meet Claribel again as she, too, was here with her family. I was overjoyed to meet her again and so sorry Gregoire was no longer alive. However, a man I didn't know was with her. He was Spanish and his name was Mattias Otero, and it was because he had met Alex during his long journey that he had arrived at Moulin a Vent. How strange they had met because of the journey Alex made to the Chateau. He had decided to follow Alex and catch up with him and leave his life as a hermit behind, but had instead ended up helping Claribel and her family throughout the war.

I had never met her niece in-law Clemence and her twin girls Estelle and Celeste, so was fascinated by their escape from their Chateau before the Milice were about to turn into their drive. Apparently, Florent loved to visit Claribel and Gregoire on their farm. His mama and papa didn't have a good marriage as his father was always in town visiting his mistress and drinking in bars. Florent and Gregoire had devised a quick route from the Chateau to the farm which could be used by Florent. Florent had made his mama and little sisters practise the route through a secret tunnel and over a narrow shallow channel in the river. Anything of real value, not already sold by Monsieur de Rouille, had been hidden away and the children's little pony always grazed close to the escape route. When the Milice arrived at the farm searching for food, Florent had just returned with Claribel from the pastures a long way away from the farm, having visited the milking nannies and kids. Claribel and Florent hid in a hedge and saw Gregoire rushing out to protest to the Milice grabbing their poultry and carrying some of the bleating baby kids from the barn. They saw Gregoire attacked, and Claribel, protecting Florent, was helpless to do anything; it all happened so quickly. As they drove away she rushed to Gregoire to help him, but he died from numerous vicious blows to his stomach, ribs, and the fall backwards onto his head. It was some days later Matias turned up at the farm asking for water and telling Claribel he was trying to find a young man called Alex travelling with his brother and sister. This chance meeting resulted in Matias staying and helping on the farm with them all throughout the war. When the Nazis occupied Vichy France in 1942 an attachment of soldiers took over the occupation of the Chateau. Clemence was adamant she never wanted to live in the Chateau again and she hoped to sell it, but planned to add the estate lands to the farm as she said it was Claribel's land anyway.

Chapter 42

The Wedding

Time soon came for us to return home for my wedding. As I slept for some of the journey on Tiff's broad shoulder, I marvelled at how brave he was, how strong and dependable and how lucky I was to have the love of this good man. Little Jacques slept on Nadine's lap when tired, but watched Ruby and gravitated to be next to her when he was awake. We arrived home after the long journey very tired, and after settling the children for the night we enjoyed an evening meal prepared for us by Mrs Revill. Rosie had been in charge of Linford and Amani and they were in bed when we arrived home. The good news was that their mother had found a flat in King's Lynn and a nursery and school for her children. Rosie told us and said she had agreed to travel three days a week to help her care for the children and put the children to bed when Barbara was working at the hospital on nights. I was very worried about the hours she planned to work and knew I would miss her if she left us permanently. We would all miss Rosie here at the Hall. Mrs Revill wasn't getting any younger so I suppose I would have to find a new cook soon. I wanted to open a tea shop and a farm shop selling our farm produce. I had so many plans to improve our income and the lives of everyone working here and living in the village. Lucy wanted to start a riding school and had asked for my help, and I thought it was a great idea and as Jacob Black was retiring from pig farming I thought it could be the ideal place for Frankie's agricultural repair business and for Lucy's to start a riding school, especially as I planned to have some holiday cottages ready to rent. It would tie in very nicely. I was going to have an art gallery in part of our stable yard and open up the Walled Garden for people to walk around and see our produce growing. My mind was racing with plans for the future. We were all very tired after our long journey and I didn't care what anyone thought. Tiff and I went to my bedroom, I climbed into my bed with him and cuddled into his arms.

The next weeks were a whirlwind of activity. My feet didn't touch the ground. If I wasn't painting in my studio getting ready for the exhibition and my best critic Tantetta arriving, I was checking out the food for the guests, the accommodation for everyone and the decorations and flowers for the church. My father wanted beef served at the wedding breakfast and Lysander was bringing four whole salmon from Scotland. Osian supplied six cockerels from our flock of poultry. I had arranged for the villagers to have a party at the village hall on my wedding day and we were supplying the food for them. It was a very special all-round celebration; war had ended, and it was my wedding. Rationing hadn't finished, but we were going to try our best to treat everyone on my special day. Dr Singh and his family had now moved into the house he had bought in King's Lynn near to the hospital where he worked. As a result, we could use the cottage for some of the guests. We had booked the bedrooms at the pub and prepared the bedrooms in The Hall. Work had progressed on the old dairy rooms at Ted and Nora's farm ready to use for two holiday cottages, and we were going to use those for some of Tiff's family. I was getting married at eleven o'clock in the morning so we could have the wedding breakfast at one o'clock, and it gave many people time to go home before it was dark.

My father had insisted on giving me away and walking down the aisle with me. Lysander was to be by his side and Jabbo discreetly hovering nearby with the wheelchair just in case. My little bridesmaids looked so sweet in their Indian sari material dresses and Mrs Hubbard had soon made pageboy outfits for Linford and Jacques. Heaven knows how much my beautiful veil cost. It matched the Leaver's lace of the long sleeves of the wedding dress, and I felt like a princess. I had chosen my bouquet to be made of anemones, hyacinths, narcissi and tulips. These had been supplied by Stan and Lacey from their smallholding and from our glass house at The Hall grown by Osian. With everyone who had become my friends during the war watching, I went to church with my father in our Rolls-Royce, with Granger driving. As I arrived Wullie's son Garnet Lawrie, Alastair's shepherd's son resplendent in his regimental kilt, was playing The Skye Boat song and as I went down the church nave he played on his bagpipes the Wedding March by Mendelssohn. There was Tiff looking amazing in his Major's uniform, smiling at me, his warm eyes reaching into my soul. As I stood beside him I knew I had come home, I had found my other half, my sanctuary, my greatest love. It was the happiest day of my life to be married to Tiff and to be surrounded by the friends and family I had come to love. I was truly blessed.

I came out of church to the cheers and well wishes of the entire village and all our evacuee children and family and friends. Waiting to take me to the Hall for our wedding breakfast were A.P. and Hermes in shining patent collars and harness and pulling the family square bottom Landau from our coach house. They had all been so busy whilst I was away getting this surprise ready for us. Lennie as coachman with Lucy the groom were waiting to take us back. I was so excited to see the horses and the sun came out and shone for us all the way home. The wedding breakfast was a great occasion for us all, especially now my parents were home after their dreadful ordeal in Singapore. I saw Talia and Adele's father looking so happy and he told me that Zac had decided to spend more time in Britain, opening a shop in London selling Swiss watches. He needed a man in London to sell and repair them and he had asked him to be that man. He and his wife were thrilled at the opportunity to earn more money and to be near to Talia and Adele whilst they studied in London. The two girls played for us on the piano and violin as we greeted our guests into the big hall. Monsieur and Madame Treves had been told that Lionel MacCloud was going to sponsor them through Music college, and they were so grateful for their girls to have this opportunity. I told him the girls' dedication to their music was worthy of the award. Tiff's family were a delight, and I was so pleased to meet them for the first time. My father was soon deep in conservation with Tiff's father Mr Tifford, about horse racing, hunting, and shooting, and making plans to visit Ireland in the future. Our cake was a super three-tier affair with iced horseshoes round the bottom of the cake and a bride and groom on top; the groom was wearing an army uniform.

We had no immediate plans for a honeymoon, as next I had to attend my London exhibition. Following that we were going to Scotland for a month then whipping over to Paris for the opening of my exhibition. So, we spent the night at The Hall in my bedroom which was just so cosy after our busy day and we sat with a night cap of malt whisky before amazing slow sex and satisfaction in knowing we belonged to each other for ever.

Chapter 43

Uri Berman in London

U ri walked out of the airport and into the waiting car. The door was held open for him by his chauffeur who saluted him. His two male companions also joined him in the car, and they were driven through London to Carlos Square and the car pulled up outside the Connaught Hotel. Expensive, classy, and discreet, but Uri knew the Nazi criminals he was hunting liked just such a hotel – he wasn't going to find them hiding under rocks in some desert. He would find them though; he was determined to locate and punish the monsters who had perpetrated unimaginable heinous crimes against humanity. The full horror of the concentration camps, the gas chambers and the death marches were only just being revealed to the dismay and revulsion of the world.

He had lived, trained, and fought alongside a man called Joseph. It was Joseph who had taken him into the hills of France after his first meeting in the woods on the estate of Chateau de la Cascade. It was Joseph who had worked on the estate for the

Countess de Gaillarde and had fled to the remote hills and forests of the area when the Milice had started to round up young French men for transportation to Germany for forced labour. His group of the Maquis hid out in the hills waiting and hoping for help to come in the shape of weapons and more men with plans of how they could carry out acts of sabotage against the Milice, the Vichy government, and later against the Nazis. They had each other's back for four and half years, and Uri thought of Joseph as his brother, he had held him in his arms when he took his last breath drowning in blood which poured from his ears, nose, and mouth. Joseph was shot as the Allies fought their way back into France on the beaches at Dunkirk and up through France in Operation Dragoon in August 1944, landing on the beaches east of Marseille and Toulon. The combined forces slowly made their way through France fighting the German army and some of the retreating Nazis were killing people they met on their way, in retaliation, as, increasingly defeated, they ran back to Germany.

The Maquis had booby-trapped the road and as the German army truck passed by, it struck the mine and slewed to a halt; the soldiers left alive had poured out, shooting into the surrounding area. One of these bullets hit Joseph and he died in the hills overlooking the road, as the rest of his team fired their M1918 Browning Automatic rifles back at the soldiers. Their guns and weapons had been parachuted into the hills and woods, collected, and hidden until they had a leader to co-ordinate their fighting and a radio operator to assist them find their targets, and communicate with British intelligence. This was the (SOE) Special Operations Executive founded in Britain with orders from Churchill who organised money, weapons, food, boots, and radios to be sent to the Free French Resistance fighters. The French Resistance were significant in helping the Allies advance through France following the invasion on June 6th, 1944. They supplied the Allies with information about the German defences and the whereabouts of the German Wehrmacht. The resistance sabotaged the French electrical grid, transport facilities, railway lines and telecommunication networks. When Joseph died, Uri went mad with hatred and anger, he became a cold-blooded killer, intent on finding and killing every Nazi Collaborator and Gestapo he could track down, including the soldier who fired the shot that killed Joseph – this soldier he followed and despatched slowly, with more shots than necessary. They carried Joseph's body to a nearby farm and buried him, and then the rest of their team regrouped to carry on the battle to rid France of the Nazis.

After the war Uri had gone to the Chateau de la Cascade which Joseph had told him so much about; here he worked in the vineyard whilst he decided what to do next, and met up with Tiff and Jabbo, two of the men sent out to France to re-arm, organise and help the Maquis. He was restless and needed to keep fighting. Because of his bravery whilst fighting as part of the French Resistance, he was awarded medals by the French government. When the Resistance was disbanded, all he wanted to do was track down Nazis criminals and kill them. Then the chance came to go to Palestine and join the Haganah Jewish Army. His main ambition was to travel round the world hunting for and bringing to justice the Nazi monsters. His aim was to find the devils who had perpetrated monstrous acts of appalling cruelty and inhumanity; this became his sole goal in life. To his mind, not many he hunted deserved a court hearing – if he had his way – and he often did, when he found them, they would have 'unfortunate accidents' before reaching any court. Joining the Haganah and fighting for the protection and rights of all Jews was a step in the right direction for him.

He was in London on secret business for the Haganah at the same time as Tad and Danielle, and the same time that Cressida had her art exhibition in London. Once again fate or coincidence intervened on his behalf.

Chapter 44

Tad and Danielle Reunion

Tad made his way across Carlos Square and headed for the
Connaught Hotel. It was now 1946. He was about to start
medical school at university and was doing some training at
the hospital in Norwich. He had travelled to London with his sister
Danielle and her fiancé Osian. Danielle had fallen in love with Osian
when she started to help him in the Walled Garden, finding peace
in the process of growing food and flowers. Since then, the three
of them had enjoyed visiting museums, art galleries and theatres
together. Osian had been an enormous help and support to Tad
while making his choice of university.

They were looking forward to Cressida's art exhibition – their
reason for visiting London.

The Honourable Cressida Welsby had been the sponsor for
Danielle and Tad when they came to Britain after escaping from
France during the war. They had lived in a little house in part of
the stable yard at Willup Hall in Norfolk and been very happy
there. They had met many other refugees given shelter at the

Hall, by Cressida, during the dark years of the war. They had felt secure there, learnt to live again and remember that not everyone was evil and out to harm them. They learnt to relax and laugh with the other residents, adults and children, and enjoyed helping others with different mental or physical issues caused by the conflict. His sister had been given a chance to develop her design skills with textiles, knitting and weaving in a workshop of knitters in the old school room at the Hall. The workshop had been the idea of Cressida to encourage the ladies of the village to knit much needed blankets and jumpers, gloves and scarves for people who had lost everything due to the bombing and the war. They shared skills and taught each other how to read the patterns, and of course they had each other for support, company, and a chat. Cressida managed to get wool from her sister's farm in Scotland and had bought a spinning wheel which Danielle had soon mastered and in no time was spinning wool for the knitters, creating new patterns, designs and ideas. It gave her hope and a new interest in living, something which had disappeared after their traumatic escape from France. She had spent four weeks in hospital when they arrived in Britain and during that time Tad had visited her regularly and watched the doctors and nurses fighting for her life and that's what had made him decide he wanted to be a doctor and help people.

After her discharge from hospital, they had stayed in a small hotel by the sea on the south coast until she was able to travel to London; some people wanted to ask her about her role in the Paris resistance network. She was part of a group helping people escape from Paris, particularly airmen who had been downed over France by enemy fire and needed a route to get back to Britain and avoid capture, interrogation and being sent to prison of war camps. The people had been to see her in the hospital as they needed to hear about the organisation in Paris and the routes taken by the helpers of these downed airmen called evaders. Danielle told them that her basement flat in the large house she owned was still available for the hiding and use of the Resistance, as it was possible it had not been compromised before her capture at a station in Paris. Her ground floor apartment had a back door leading into her tree-filled private garden and a door in the wall led onto a quiet street. It was always important to get radio operators up and running in Paris, which was a dangerous and difficult job, and the SOE always needed safe houses made available to them. It was when they had all the information Danielle could give them that they were told a home had been found for them in Norfolk and the two of them had been taken there and met Cressida. It was here that Tad's badly damaged sister began the long process of healing from the torture and constant rapes by the Gestapo after her capture and detention in Paris. The result had been infection and subsequently a long time in hospital upon reaching Britain. How she had managed the journey after their escape from the cattle truck he could not comprehend. The pain she endured on the climb through the Pyrenees was unimaginable and yet she had kept going and kept him going too. The fact that their parents had been keen mountaineers and loved skiing had helped them both as they had been on many trips to the mountains of France and Switzerland until their parents' death in a mountaineering accident in Austria. This had left Danielle and Tad orphaned in Paris and their inheritance was their parents' large house, plus a substantial amount of money. Danielle was at art and textile college, and he was still at school, but there was enough money for them to stay in the house with the rents from the three other apartments and the two of them lived in the ground floor apartment. They

had used it as a safe house for evaders until Danielle had been
caught and questioned by the Gestapo for being under suspicion
of helping fugitives.

   He had been taken from school by the Gestapo and taken to a
station where lots of Jewish people were being held and there by a
miracle he had seen his sister brought in a truck with some other
bewildered, dirty women waiting to be loaded onto the train. He
had fought his way towards her and being of a slight built he
had gone unnoticed, and he used their signal, a whistle, taught
to them by their parents when they had been mountaineering,
to attract her attention. Miraculously she heard his whistle in
the noise and rushed towards him, but a soldier barred her way
with a rifle. Danielle had turned away and then whistled back
to let him know she had heard him. Then a commotion behind
him made the soldier turn, and in that minute, Danielle ducked
down, hid in the crowd and bent nearly double, fought her way
towards where she had seen Thadeus; the name he was called at
home. The Jewish people had been herded to the station in the
night and early hours of the morning and were being pushed
onto cattle trucks. There were people already in the trucks and
the smell was horrible. Little children were crying with hunger,
and old men and women had to be helped up into the trucks.
He and his sister had managed to get on together and found
themselves next to a teenage boy who seemed to be travelling
alone. They were pushed against him and could hardly breathe
for the crush; there were far too many people in the wagon. It
was filthy with faeces and urine on the floor, and they could only
stand up; to sit down meant suffocation. When the cattle doors
of the truck where slammed shut, the boy had shown them he
had a pen knife with many blades. It was larger than most pocket-
knives. He showed them because he told Danielle he thought that

a plank in the corner on the floor felt rotten and he was going to hack at it and see if he could make a hole in the floor. The train jolted off slowly and pulled away from Paris; everything they knew was left behind. Their future was uncertain. Danielle told him to take his glasses off and put them into his pocket to keep them safe from the crush. The teenage boy scraped away at the floor of the wagon, and at first it seemed an impossible task. He asked Danielle to shield him from the others in the wagon and then she bent down to try and see if he had made any headway. There appeared to be the beginning of a small opening. Danielle had shielded the teenage boy from the crush of people and, turning her back on them, she had put her arms round her brother and stood over the boy as he continued to cut and scrape through the floorboard. She had taken a turn herself when the boy was clearly exhausted. As the hole became bigger he would not let her touch the knife in case she dropped it through the hole, onto the tracks. As night came, the train slowed, just trundling along as if waiting for signals; they didn't know what. The boy decided the hole was big enough to slip through and he had signalled to us he was going; with that he was gone. There was so much crying and wailing on the train it was hard to hear, but they listened hard to hear any shots from the guards, but there were none.

Danielle told Tad they were going to go next. He was terrified and for a moment he would have preferred to stay on the train. He could not possibly squeeze through the small opening in the floor from a moving train, he thought. She promised to follow and said to lie very still when he hit the tracks until the train had gone. Scared to death, he sat on the floor, dangled his legs through the hole and thinking he would die, he too slid through the hole. Pushed himself through, falling hard on the track between the rails. He lay still in the filth on the rough ground as he let the long train pass over him. He was physically sick from fear and lay in his vomit, not moving. As the wailing from the poor inmates on the train became more distant, he continued to keep still until silence fell around him, but he could not move as he was gripped by terror. Finally, he started to crawl down the tracks hoping to find Danielle. He made a low whistle again but there was no response. He crawled on his belly and kept whistling until he thought he heard a moan. It seemed to take ages and then he reached a body and found it was Danielle, not moving. He wanted to scream; he shook her gently and whispered Danielle and then she moaned again, and he knew they had to get off the tracks, so he started to pull her. She came to and clutching each other they fell down a rough stony embankment into a hedge and just lay together for a few minutes. It was Danielle who said they must move away as far away as they could. They struggled through some fields and a wood, found a stream and drank lots of water and washed their hair. Danielle took off her dress and washed her body all over, so he did the same. There was no modesty between them, they were too tired and hurting to be bothered. They hated putting back on their filthy wet clothes. Danielle then took the time to look at the stars and decide which direction they should go in, and in between the clouds were bursts of moonlit sky. She found Altair in the east-southeast and Tarazed nearby. Venus burned brightly and then she saw Saturn rising in the east. She wanted to head towards the Pyrenees and get to Spain then Portugal, but she knew they needed help; but who could they find or trust to help them. Camping out with their parents had taught her how to read the stars and so they started walking to the west, following the stars.

When morning came the sun rose in the east and was warm and there was no road, so they lay down to sleep, wishing they had not washed their clothes in the stream. There was no food and not a house or dwelling in sight, so they carefully walked on until they found a house but wondered whether they dare ask for help. So many French citizens gave people up to the Nazis for reward, especially if the strangers were Jewish like them. By now the faeces on their clothes had dried and become crusty and they knew they had to find cleaner clothes even if they had to steal them. Finally, they saw a slim ribbon of a dirt road and they followed it carefully, staying in the fields, and then they saw a girl on a bike, and she stopped to tie up her hair and Danielle crawled near to her and asked urgently in French for help and to know where they were. She didn't look at them just stared away down the road as if she hadn't heard Danielle, then staring ahead she told Danielle to go to a copse of trees on the left and wait until it was dark, and she would come back for them. They were scared but decided to trust her as they were desperate.

She came back when it was dark and told them to follow her, at a discreet distance into a village and then she let them into her house, gave them food and hot water to wash, and burning their filthy rags found them cleaner clothes. Nothing fitted Tad. She gave them bread and lettuce washed down with fresh water – it tasted like heaven. She was a saviour; they were so lucky to have put their trust in her. After that they had to stay for many days in her attic, not moving during the day, just resting, reading and always keeping very quiet and out of sight. She fed them at night, and they waited for some new ID papers and travel documents to arrive. Danielle's beautiful long black hair had been pulled out in clumps at the back of her head by the Gestapo and it was decided to cut it all off and she would wear a wig of grey hair and pretend to be an old lady. Tad didn't have any idea about the tremendous pain she was in, and it was her determination to get them to safety which kept her going. She still had many bruises on her face and body, but they were fading to yellow, and she was given make up to cover them.

The girl told them she was called Marie, but they never knew anything else about her; it was always best not to know too much in case they were caught and tortured. Finally, they were taken to the station in Toulouse to catch a train to Foix. There were active resistance workers in the State Run Railway Company and Marie had a boyfriend working there. He told her which trains would be best for them to catch and the quietest railway stations and how to leave the stations from side doors. From Foix they were driven south by a woman who was part of the network of underground French Resistance. They did not ask her anything, nor did they tell her anything; it was a quiet journey. After several hours they reached a small town called Arignac and then were left hiding in a remote cottage until a man dressed like a sheep herder arrived later that night to guide them through the mountains. They were joined by two evaders, downed RAF pilots, from Britain, and it took them seven days to cross the mountains into Spain. They had new papers and Danielle was dressed like an old woman in black with a wig of grey hair under a headscarf and she leant on a walking stick. The papers said Tad was her grandson. The Passeur was annoyed Danielle was an old woman; he said she would never make it across the mountains and survive the cold. How she did while still in such pain, no one knows, but the mountaineering they had done with their parents helped them to keep up, stay on the track and cope with the exhaustion and the freezing cold and powerful mountain streams, and rivers they had to cross. Tad was certainly surprised by her ability to keep going and prove the Passeur wrong. They had two nights in Andorra before pushing on to Spain with the evaders, and without the Passeur who had now left them.

Their father was born in Switzerland and was a university professor of geology in Paris who loved skiing and mountaineering. Fortunately, so did their mother, which is how they had met on the ski slopes of France. They inherited a large rambling house in Paris from grandparents and changed it into four apartments. They wanted to spend more time travelling during the university holidays with no worries about running a huge house. The rents came in handy too. They travelled everywhere with them when not attending school. Danielle was at university in Paris on an arts and textiles course when she heard their parents had both been killed in an avalanche in the Austrian Alps. Tad stayed on at his private school as he was studious, clever, and enjoyed his schoolwork and the rents and inheritance kept them comfortably well off. Their apartment was downstairs with a garden, which was how Danielle had hidden people on the run from the Nazis; few people could see the side door entrance behind a high wall.

Danielle refused to get on any train when they reached Spain as she knew they could be arrested and sent back to France, so they took a bus journey to a small town and then another to the next town and they kept making small bus journeys until they reached the coast and made their way to Bilbao; there they found a place to stay, eat and rest. Danielle had sent a disguised message to an organisation that helped Jewish people cross to Spain and they finally made their way to their address in San Sebastian where they were expecting them, and with their help made it to Portugal. They had parted from the two evaders who were travelling on to Gibraltar, from there they hoped to be flown home to Britain. It was one of these men, George Blake, who had kindly given them just enough money to help them on their route. They had so many good-hearted people to thank for their kindness.

They waited in Lisbon while a sponsor was found in Britain and Danielle spent some time in hospital. MI9 heard about Danielle and the resistance organisation she was part of in Paris and wanted to interview her to learn more about the help the resistance needed to carry on their work in the city. So, after several interviews in Lisbon, it was decided she was to be trusted and flown to Britain to be interviewed again when they arrived. Unfortunately, she became seriously ill upon their arrival, and was rushed to hospital with a severe infection and it was thought that she would die. Tad was taken in by a family who lived near the hospital, but spent all his time, during the day, by her side. She needed emergency surgery and was in hospital for four weeks. During this time, he watched the doctors and nurses looking after her and decided that he would train to be a doctor. It didn't seem possible, but she became even thinner, reserved and withdrawn; at times, he thought, even from him. Finally, they were taken to London where she was questioned about her involvement in the resistance, their time travelling through France over the Pyrenees and to Portugal.

They were then introduced to a man called Jakabus Guilhem and he told them he had arranged for them to stay in Norfolk – they would be taken there, by car, straight away. It was the best thing that could have happened to them, and Danielle started the process of healing mentally, and physically and even learnt to trust and laugh again. Tad went to a good school and passed his exams for university. He enjoyed his childhood in Norfolk with lots of kind, helpful people, fresh air, outdoor games, and chess which he loved; and he became quite good at cards. He also discovered cricket, rounders, and football. He loved table tennis and helping water the plants in the Walled Garden and having long discussions about life, politics, war and the world with Larry, Osian, Frankie and Jabbo. Jabbo told him so much about Morocco that he promised he would go one day. Added to this Danielle started to join him in the garden and was included in their talks and discussions. She soon started helping in the garden which she began to enjoy, particularly with Osian.

Now the war had ended, and they were here in London, shopping and going to see Cressida's exhibition. Tad walked through the swing doors of the Connaught Hotel where he had arranged to meet up and have lunch with Osian and Danielle. As he walked through the swing doors his glasses perched on his head dropped onto the floor and as he stooped to pick them up his briefcase flew open. He rushed to stop his revision papers flying all over the foyer and went headlong into a man crossing the floor. As he picked himself up he apologised profusely to the big, strong, tough-looking man in dark glasses. He had two equally tough-looking men with him, and they were all wearing black clothes. These men helped him retrieve the papers whilst the man he had bowled into, stood back, and watched. They all had short army-type haircuts and dark glasses and were a bit menacing. Tad was very embarrassed and nervously said, "if my glasses had been in my pocket, it wouldn't have happened; my sister was always telling me to put my glasses in my pocket to keep them safe and not to push them on top of my head". As he spoke, the three men turned away to leave, but then the man he had run into stopped, turned, and stared at him, saying nothing; then he ordered: "Come, I will buy you a drink, we will go into the bar." It was so 'matter of fact', like an order, he dare not refuse. He put his arm behind him and steered him towards the bar.

"I don't drink,'" Tad mumbled.

"You must drink something," he laughed. "Have a shandy." He ordered a beer and lemonade and drinks for himself and the other two men who remained quiet.

"Well, I am meeting my sister and her fiancé, and I don't want to miss them," Tad stuttered nervously.

"When are you meeting them, what time?" he asked crisply.

"In an hour, here in the reception area for lunch. I was going to have a coffee and read through my papers," Tad replied.

"What papers?" he asked.

"My medical papers for my interview."

"What, are you a doctor?" he asked.

"Not yet, well I am working, for experience, at a hospital at the moment; before I go to university."

"Which hospital?"

"I am working for Dr Singh in Norfolk," Tad said, thinking he asked a lot of questions, and it felt more like an interrogation.

"Why are you in London?" he asked.

Gosh he was inquisitive and plain nosy. "We are going to see an art exhibition of work done by our sponsor."

"Sponsor! Why did you have a sponsor – and for what?" he asked, staring intently.

Well, he was still wearing his dark sunglasses: odd. Tad wanted to leave this blunt, rude man, but felt compelled to answer him. He took a deep breath. "My sister and I came here in 1941 and we needed a sponsor to come to Britain and this lady sponsored us and we lived at her place during the war. Now if you will excuse me, I need to go and find my sister."

"Your sister is married?" he asked.

"No, engaged. I told you she is to be married."

"Ah, she is; well, that is good."

"She was ill when we arrived and had to go to hospital for an operation."

"Where did you come from?" he asked me quietly, leaning forward and studying me.

Tad thought he was rude to ask so many personal questions, but he carried on answering him. "We came from France. We used to live in Paris."

"Are you Jewish?" he asked. Tad was now getting nervous, and it must have shown. The man leaned back on his chair and casually said, "I am Jewish, and I come from the Netherlands. First, I travelled to Paris from Amsterdam to escape the Nazis."

"Where were you during the war?" Tad asked, intrigued.

"I was in the hills in France with the Free French. I became a Maquisard."

There was silence.

"I was helped by a man called Marcell who works at the Chateau de la Cascade. How did you leave France?" he asked.

Chateau de la Cascade, why did Tad recognise that name? "We were loaded on a train in Paris with other Jews. As we travelled a young man dug a hole in the floor of the wagon, where it was rotten and he got out first and then we jumped out through the hole, onto the tracks. A girl helped us and kept us in her house until we had new papers then we travelled over the Pyrenees to Spain and then got to Portugal, then here," Tad said simply and quickly.

"With your sister?" he barked.

"Yes," Tad said sharply. He was getting exasperated by these impertinent questions. What had it got to do with him, he didn't like the memory.

"What train were you on, and where was it going?"

Tad put his hands to his ears to block out the sound. "How should I know, a cattle wagon; my sister was part of a Resistance group in Paris, she was captured and tortured before being taken to the railway station for deportation. It was fate we met there; we both got into the same wagon on a cattle train." He was remembering the wailing, moaning, and crying, the stench of bodies pushed together, he could feel the despair. He closed his eyes, and leant on the table with his elbows and pushed his fists into his eyes. He now knew what had happened to the poor people on the trains.

"How did he make a hole in the floor?" He persisted with his questions.

"He used a gadget like a Swiss knife, only bigger," Tad said, almost shouting, and looked at him angrily. This stranger was asking him questions he didn't like when he was trying not to think about the time on the train or the other people there, ever. So why did he feel compelled to answer him?

"Was it like this?" He casually felt in his pocket and placed a large Swiss army knife onto the table between them.

Tad stared and couldn't speak. He stared at the knife and then looked at him as he removed his dark glasses. Now without his glasses Tad stared into the face and the serious dark brown eyes of the teenage boy on the train and his hands moved across the table and gripped his hands and tears ran freely down his face. They hugged each other over the table and then Tad saw Danielle standing in the doorway with Osian, a questioning look on her face and she was just staring at them. They both turned to her and held out their arms and she knew instantly; she ran to them and fell into their embrace, crying.

Chapter 45

The Art Exhibition

I stared at my reflection in the lady's room mirror; I had to admit to myself I was glowing. Perhaps it was the result of being kissed so much and my cheeks were suffering from being rubbed by stubble. I checked my lipstick and tried to smooth my wavy, frizzy, chestnut hair. I had tied it back and put on an emerald-green velvet band and I was pleased; it looked pretty. Well, it matched my emerald-green velvet dress, and my hand went to my throat to touch my pearls. I loved them, they were stunning. I wasn't even bothered about my freckles anymore. The pearls were a gift to me on my wedding day from Zac, Ruby, and Jacques, so I felt as if they were always with me now, wherever I went. I went back into the gallery and felt another thrill to see my sketches and paintings hanging on the walls with appropriate lighting. Tiff came over to me, put his arm around me and we stood just staring in wonder at the art show which was all my work.

"Is there enough drink for everyone?" I asked anxiously. "Food, drinks, chairs everything."

"Yes, and yes, stop worrying, you look beautiful, I am the luckiest man alive. I have a beautiful wife who just happens to be outrageously sexy too; oh, and a talented artist," he added, waving his arm towards the paintings.

"When will they arrive?" I asked nervously.

"Possibly in the next five minutes, just time for me to kiss you again," he declared, grinning.

A waitress walked by and smiled as we kissed. We had spent the night together in Claridge's, courtesy of Grandora, her treat. We'd never left our room.

I wandered round the gallery looking at my paintings again. I stopped at my oil painting of Martha Harrington on her beautiful bright bay hunter mare, Pegs. I had found an old photograph in my father's office of Martha when she was whipping-in, and one of Alford on his bay hunter, Legacy; they were placed side by side. I hoped they loved them. I moved on to see the sketches of all the children who had stayed with us and then on to my sketch of Uri and Joseph taken from the photograph of them during their days with the Maquis in France, during the war. Next to it was a painting of Joseph, which I had painted only a few weeks before I returned to Britain. He was relaxed and smiling, holding Odin on his knees, sitting on a wooden bench with the vineyard behind him. I felt tears spring to my eyes just looking at my good friend, Joseph; happy days. Then I had painted a portrait of Uri, from a photograph taken by me at the Memorial Service to Joseph. I had captured his eyes full of sadness and a passion. The paintings were side by side, just as they had lived through the war, side by side. I slowly carried on round the Gallery, reliving the memories invoked by the images before me and of the time when I had painted the picture, met the person or seen the landscape. I came to the charcoal sketch of Tiff and Scotty reclining against the bonnet of the Rolls-Royce outside the Chateau just after they had arrived with Malissa and Nico. So long ago, yet it seemed only yesterday I was that carefree girl who did the sketch. I had wondered what these soldiers had actually done throughout the war. They had kept their secret. Only now I knew that they were Special Operations Forces, SOF, and finally SOE for Tiff, trained to conduct 'Special Operations – specifically designated, organized, selected, trained and equipped forces using unconventional techniques and modes of employment', obviously driving a Rolls-Royce was included. They were called Commandos and trained in Achnacarry in the Scottish Highlands. They had formed the Special Airborne Service SAS and they included Special Air Corp, Special Boat Service, and the Parachute Regiment. The Greeks had fled to Egypt after the invasion by the Nazis and there they had formed a unit called Sacred Bond which had worked closely with SAS under Lieutenant Colonel Stirling in the Western Desert and the Aegean. No wonder I had hardly ever seen Tiff during the war.

The trip to London had taken lots of planning; but my father had made it to my wedding, walked me down the aisle and finally made it to my exhibition. I was so pleased.

The doors opened and Tantetta swept in with Dendy and Grandora, closely followed by Auntygusta with her long-time special friend Bernadette. The three sisters looking regal and amazingly fit and well, still turned heads, even at their age. I kissed them all and they went off to study my works. Their opinions meant everything to me. Lysander and Fiona arrived with Portia and Alastair. I quickly went over to greet them with a kiss. Miriam and her mother Sarah, sister-in-law Zelda, brother Noah, their little son James and younger sister Anna-Sara were next with her father in a wheelchair taking it steady after his

heart attack. Miriam held the door open for Rory's parents who
were both manoeuvring the pram through the door containing
baby Rory, their beautiful baby grandson. They had flown to
England as soon as they heard they had a new grandson called
Rory Junior R.J. I hoped Miriam loved my painting of her half
turning towards me with her halo of golden hair and a sad half-
smile. I had painted it after the news had come through that Rory
had been killed in a bombing raid over Germany; news I still
could not come to terms with. I hoped they all loved the several
paintings and sketches of Rory, happy at the stables, with our
horses, and all of us at The Hall. My mother arrived with my
father, also in a wheelchair, pushed by Jabbo. Granger held the
door for them all.

"I hope the car is alright; I have parked right in front?"
said Granger, as he waited for Audrey and Halette to come
through the door.

"It all looks amazing, darling, so smart; oh, I am so proud of
you," said my mother, as she kissed me.

I hugged her. "There's champagne waiting for you all over
there." I directed them to the waitress standing with a tray
of drinks.

"Paintings first, Romilly please," insisted my father.

They drifted off round the gallery. The doors remained closed,
but as I turned away they burst open again as The Rev., Merry,
Scotty, Rhys, Gruffydd (now taller than Osian and twenty years
old), Dylan, Afan and the youngest Aled now twelve all arrived.
Osian remained the smallest brother even now at twenty-two, and
just then he walked in holding Danielle's hand, with Tad following
them. I was thrilled they had gone to so much trouble to come to
support me and went over to greet them.

I walked over to Tiff, had a drink of water, and wondered if any of the others would get here for my art exhibition premiere. I had invited so many dear friends to view before the public were allowed in. I watched Tiff's parents walking over to us and he handed them some champagne. I hugged them both. I instantly loved them when they came over for the wedding which is when I had met them for the first time; they were the kindest couple you could wish for. I had my back to the door and Tiff nudged me to turn round and there coming through the doors were more of my friends and war family. Lucy with Frankie, and Mrs Joan Burden with Rosie. They were quickly followed by Mrs Revill and Agatha Hubbard, Susan and Roger with their new official parents Hugh and Margaret Brownlow, and they arrived with George, Theodore and Genevieve Bathurst. Ted and Nora Staples had come with Alford and his wife Martha Harrington who was leaning heavily on sticks, but she was here. Humphrey and Clarissa Clayton came next and then Talia and Adele arrived with their parents Monsieur and Madame Treves, looking just so happy to be here. Then I went to the door to wait for 'my people' and at last he was here: Nico looking so tall, suave, handsome, and well dressed. He had decided for the time being to remain living with us at the Hall now he was back from his trip on The Hestia.

Nico kissed me on the cheek asking, "So, is everyone here, Sid?"

"Yes well, almost. Are Larry and Lennie and Lottie coming? I hope they are," I said, looking for them.

"Larry and Lottie are just coming now with Mavis and Gilbert, minus Lennie," Nico told me.

"Where's Lennie?" I asked.

"He has stayed at home to look after the horses and dogs with Sheila Beechcroft and her new fiancé Thomas Marshall from Tall Trees Farm and he's sent you this card." Mavis arrived and handed

me a card from Lennie apologising for missing my big day and
wishing me 'Good Luck'.

"That's lovely, but how come Sheila is back at The Hall, I
thought she had gone back home?"

"Well, she and Tom have become sweet on each other. They've
been writing to each other since she went home. Now she's come
back to help Tom with the milking, Lennie with feeding all the
dogs and horses so that Ted and Nora could come and join you
today. I think she will be staying longer though, as they are now
officially engaged; he proposed to her yesterday."

"Under The Tree," added Larry grinning.

"What, our Cedar of Lebanon?" I quipped, laughing. "That's
so kind of them to look after everything at home."

I was thrilled Larry had made it to London with his mother,
Gilbert, and Lottie. Then the biggest shock came when all the
Hardys arrived looking a little out of place in London. Lacey was
ethereal as usual with long dark hair, in a single plait, serious
grey eyes, a slender figure dressed in brown leather ankle boots
and an ankle length velvet moss green skirt with a waist hugging
matching jacket with a peplum. She only needed a wreath of hops
or woodland flowers round her neck, and you could believe she
was part of a woodland scene and just stepped out from inside a
tree into our world to see how we lived. She refused to eat animals
and her diet of their home-grown fresh vegetables, salads and
fruit gave her a healthy smooth skin, shiny hair, and a slim figure.
She was a great gardener and grew an amazing variety of herbs;
now she kept bees too and was now making candles as well as
honey. She was successfully making soap from the milk produced
from the goat herd they had built up on the smallholding, as well
as milk and cheese. Stanley had turned out to be a great worker
on the smallholding, a rough diamond as well as a loving, proud

father. I had grown to respect Lacey's quiet ability to get on with life and whatever came her way. The whole family had become a great asset to our community.

I had been disappointed to learn that Jean-Philippe could not attend my exhibition but was hoping to be in Paris to see us there.

The Singh family arrived smiling; as always so friendly and kind. Their boys were amazing cricketers and we had won all our games of cricket for the last two years because of their skill and passion. They had been very popular with everyone plus Mrs Singh's cooking was amazing. I went over to chat to them, and the time passed; it looked like no one else was coming, then Barbara arrived with Linford and Amani and bustled over to say hello before touring the gallery.

Where were the others – it was so important to me that they came? Finally, they arrived, and I flew across the room to welcome them. Ruby came in first with her father Zac, and Malissa behind her, then Aurielle, Marcell and then Simone and Claude, followed by Alex and Nula with little Jacques holding her hand; they had been picked up from the train station. I covered them in hugs and kisses and invited them to see the paintings and to have a drink.

Tiff came over to say hello and he put his arm round me and whispered, "Happy now?" And kissed me on the top of my head.

Over his shoulder I noticed three tough, army-type men come into the room. I didn't think they were invited, still they looked like security men. I turned back to talk to Aurielle and Marcell. Alex went with Nula to join his cousins, Merry and her brothers to talk to them all. Ruby took her brother Jacques to play with Lottie. Zac and Malissa stood with us.

"They are settling well," I said to Zac.

"Yes, thank you for letting me stay with you until they know me better, I can't thank you enough; words don't seem adequate to express my gratitude for caring for them and keeping them safe. Our good Lord was looking out for all of you that day," he said smiling.

"Thank you for these beautiful pearls, I love them, but not as much as I love my Ruby, I am dreading you leaving with her," I told him.

"Well now, I thought you might like to know I have bought a property not far from you in Great Massingham and I plan to live there and just travel to London or Switzerland for business."

I nearly shrieked with joy. "Oh, who will take care of them when you go away for business?" I asked.

"Well, I very much hope my new wife," he said, his eyes twinkling.

Malissa just held out her hand to show me her amazing diamond engagement ring.

"Wow!" I was thrilled. "Are your parents pleased?" I asked Malissa.

"Yes, and they are coming here today to meet Zac, the children and everyone. I checked with your parents who agreed and have invited them back to Norfolk with us all."

We hugged and I was thrilled for them.

Next a young man was brought over to meet us by Jakabus Guilhem. He introduced him to us as Connor Fitzpatrick. So, this was Nula's brother who had been searching for her since the outbreak of war when she had taken a job in Paris. Tiff took him over to where Nula was chatting to Merry. I watched as they hugged each other. Jakabus told us the young man had been in touch with him as he searched for the family Nula was working for in Paris. I love to see these ends tied up.

Time flew by and I was repeatedly congratulated on my work; mostly I think they loved seeing my sketches and paintings of themselves during the war years. Food was still rationed, but we had made sure there was plenty for everyone as they were all returning on the train after the showing. All except Miriam, as her family were still living in Primrose Hill, and Mr and Mrs Kaiholm were going to meet them. The Singh family were going back to their new home near the King's Lynn hospital where Dr Singh now worked after he returned home at the end of the war. They had decided they didn't want to return to Birmingham, and the boys and their mother and grandma had grown to love Norfolk where the boys were doing so well at school. I was pleased to see Susannah and Marcus, with Brennan and Serena with Clary and Sylvia all looking happy again. The Reverend Brennan Shillingstone as he was known now was going to be taking on a benefice outside of Norwich. He was now married to Serena so they would not be too far from her parents' stud farm. I understood it was a large old rectory with stables and a big field for Whisper.

Before everyone left, Tantetta tapped a glass and asked for quiet. She then spoke about my paintings, my work as an artist here and in France, and surprised me by talking about what I had done in Britain after returning home. She said she was proud of all my achievements, mentioning my ambulance work and the knitting group I had set up, the RAF men who had rest and recuperation with us, and the kindness I had shown to so many people, especially evacuees and refugees in need of help and that my contribution to the war effort had been amazing. Everyone burst out clapping and cheering and they all came over to thank me again before they had to leave for home.

I was overwhelmed by their gratitude; I still felt I had done so little to help during the war. It was nearly time for us to go to the station to catch the overnight sleeper to Scotland to continue our honeymoon on Lysander's estate. My brother, sister and their families were going to stay with our parents in Norfolk and with the three great-aunts Isadora, Henrietta, and Augusta, plus Bernie; they would spend precious time together and do some catching up. Tiff went for my coat, and he held it for me as we both said goodbye again to Miriam who had come back in for her handbag which she had left on a chair. Tiff turned to thank and tip the waitresses. I watched as Miriam dropped her glove as she rushed off to catch up with her family outside. As she picked it up, something caught her eye, and mine, at the same time. It was a tall, muscular young man with the short-cropped hair, standing alone looking at the paintings. He was just studying the painting of Joseph. At that moment he became aware of movement behind him, and he turned, and I watched as they saw each other and their eyes locked. I then recognised him from our meeting in France at Joseph's funeral. The world stood still. I held my breath.

Miriam uttered, "Uri? I am Miriam."

She held out her hand, never taking her eyes off him. Their hands clasped and they both jumped as an electric shock passed between them. Tiff stood next to me and took my hand; we smiled at each other. Their stars are aligned. The world starts to live again. It breathes and sighs new life and fresh beginnings. Our new world dawns.

Bibliography

BOOKS

Spitfire Pilot by David Crook
SBS Silent Warriors by Saul David
Escape from Paris by Stephan Harding
A Woman of no Importance by Sonia Purnell
Sleep in Peace Tonight by James MacManus
Midnight in Berlin by James MacManus
Parachute Doctor: Memories of Captain David Tibbs MC RAMC
    Edited by Neil Barber
The Dressmakers Gift by Fiona Valpy
The Final Innings by Christopher Sandford
The Story of Twenty Five Years 1910 1935 by Jubilee Book
The Perfect Home by Handy Woman
Marks and Spencers Makers of the 21st century
When Hitler stole Pink Rabbit by Judith Kerr
A Small Person Far Away by Judith Kerr
Bombs on Aunty Dainty by Judith Kerr
The Ripening Sun by Patricia Atkinson

The Guernsey Literary potato Peel Pie Society by Mary Ann Shaffer
& Annie Barrows
The Girl from Bletchley Park by Kathleen McGurl
War Dog by Damien Lewis
The Beekeepers Promise by Fiona Valpy
The Little Paris Bookshop by Nina George

The Times June 7ᵗʰ 1944 by permission of his Majesty the King
The Kings Message

Hermes, Greek Herald messenger of the Gods / God of road /
commerce / invention

Norfolk airstrips in WW2
Sedgeford decoy, Snetterton Heath USA, Thetford decoy,
Tibenham USAAF, Attlebridge 120 8 Af USA, Barton Bindish
RAF, Downham Market RAF, East Wretham USA 133 8 AF,
Great Massingham RAF bomber station, Marnham RAF,
North Creak RAF.

Wikipedia
The Gleiwitz incident. A false attack staged by Nazi Germany
which was an excuse for them to invade Poland saying Polish
soldiers had attacked Germany first.

www.wikipedia.org
Maginot line was impervious to most forms of attack, built and
controlled by the French. A series of concrete fortifications,
obstacles and weapon installations built in 1930. Germany
struck France May 10 1940 bypassing the secure Maginot Line
and slipping into Ardennes through thick forests. Failure of

leadership military and political meant the French army was poorly led and ill equipped with inferior arms. Ending the 'Phoney War' an eight month period at the start of WW2 during which there was limited land operation on the Western Front.

www.wikipedia.org

Kristallnacht or The Night of the Broken Glass also the November pogrom against Jews carried out by SA paramilitary forces and civilians throughout Nazi Germany 9-10 November 1938. German authorities watched and did nothing to stop the murders and destruction. The name Night of the Broken Glass refers to the glass littering the streets after shops and homes belonging to Jewish people who were attacked.

National Day of prayers on 29 May 1940 ordered by King George VI to pray for the safe evacuation of Dunkirk, code name (Operation Dynamo) which began May 26 and continued for 8 days. 338,221 Allied soldiers of the The British Expeditionary were brought back plus 140,000 French, Polish, Belgium saved. 700 little ships took part Medway Queen paddle steamer made 7 trips saving 7000 lives. One boat The Royal Daffodil was holed, but made it back she was a Mersey Ferry.

www.history.com

World War 1 caused the Great Depression in France and Germany. Hitler promised the German people a return to economic success and wealth.

www.wikipedia.org

Frederick William Hill "Gunner Hill" best known for his pre-war calculations that high speed fighters Supermarine Spitfire and Hawker Hurricane would need to be armed with eight machine guns in order for them to be potent weapons. Hazel Bertha Hill was thirteen years old when she helped her Father calculate how many guns and the trajectory of fire the new Spitfires and Hurricanes would need to bring down enemy aircraft

www.iwm.org.uk

Rationed foods----- jam, meat, cheese, lard, butter, eggs, milk, tinned tomatoes, dried fruit, cereal biscuits, peas, tea, coffee, fish, onions. People were encouraged to grow vegetables in their own gardens allotments and many parks were used for this. The scheme became known as 'Dig For Victory'

www.bbcnews.com

Churchill's speech. Never in the field of human conflict has so much been owed by so many to so few. Referring to the fighter pilots of the RAF

www.iwm.org.uk

Land army girls or known as the Women's Land Army made a significant contribution to boosting Britains food production during WW2 Many male farm workers joined the forces and the Women's Land Army provided a new much needed rural workforce. They worked in all conditions and weathers and could be directed to anywhere in the country

During the Battle of Britain German aircraft accidentally bombed St Giles Church in Cripplegate London accidentally dictating the future shape of the Battle on Britain. Churchill ordered the bombing of Berlin in retaliation August 30. London Blitz was in retaliation for the bombing of Berlin.

www.jewishfoodsociety.org
Jewish Sabbath dinner

www.thespruceeats.com
Food eaten on Jewish Sabbath Dinner

www.wikipedia.org
Grape Phylloxera is an insect pest of commercial grapevines. Originally native to North America. In the late 1800 French vines almost lost forever *–www.winemag.com*

www.wikipedia.org
Le Paradis massacre was a crime committed by members of German 3rd Company1st Battalion 2nd SS Division Totenkopf Riffle Regiment. They machine gunning of 97 soldiers May 27 1940 during the Battle of France. Soldiers of Royal Norfolk Regiment became separated from their unit. They surrendered after running out of ammunition and were murdered by machine gun on a farm in the village of Le Paradis. Two survived private William "Bill" O'Callaghan and Private Albert "Bert" Pooley who later testified against the commander Haupststurmfuhrer Fritz Knochlein who was later executed in 1949 for his part in the massacre

The SS open Dachau concentration camp in 1933 outside Munich
www.theholocaustexplained.org

www.maybourne.com
   Claridges history – London – Maybourne Hotel Group
      Kings of Greece Yugoslavia and Norway and the Queen of
   the Netherlands stay at Claridges on Brook Street and Davies
   Street Mayfair London during the war as did the Presidents
   of Poland and Czechoslovakia.

www.dulux.com
   Eau de Nil
      Water of the Nile light green hue, more saturation than
   celadon, less grey than sage, tan under tones, cool bluish cast

www.londonhouserugs.co.uk
Aubusson rug Emerged in mid-seventeenth century France in the
town of Aubusson.

www.wikipedia.org
   Battle of France 10 May-25 June
      the Battle of France known as the Fall of France and
   low countries. In 6 weeks May 10 Germany defeated Allied
   forces and conquered France, Belgium, Luxemburg and
   the Netherlands. Italy entered the war June 10 1940 and
   tried to invade France. Germany invaded Vichy France 10
   November 1942

www.foragedfoods.co.uk Acorn coffee

Lippizaner a breed of horse

Downs syndrome first identified in 1862 by John Langdon Haydon
   Down a British physician and later named after him.

Ronda popular card game in Morocco

www.britannia.co.uk
The Blitz A German bombing campaign against the United Kingdom in 7 September 1940 and 11 May 1941 during the second World War was an intense bombing campaign undertaken by Nazi Germany For eight months the Luftwaffe dropped bombs on London and other strategic cities across Britain. Bombing never stopped for 57 consecutive nights September – November in London

Hebrew Immigration Aid Society Moises Bensabet Amzelek leader of Lisbon Jewish community friend of Antonio de Oliveira Salazar in 1933 founded Estabo Nova – New State Portuguese. Leader

Professor Francisco Paula Leite Pinto saved Jews. Aristides de Sousa Mendes the Portuguese consul in Bordeaux issued substantial numbers of transit visas at his own initiative.

www.warfarehistorynetwork.com
Calcutta Light Horse December 1942 retired or part time soldiers in Goa attacked the German merchant ship Ehrenfels interned in Goa harbour for repairs. They attached, to the Ehrenfels limpet mines, so ending the German radio transmissions to Germany informing the Germans of the positions of Allied ships.

www.wikipedia.org
There were held captive two million French soldiers POWs, many used as forced labour in Germany, in agriculture or industry. Service du travail obligatory was a forced enlistment and deportation of hundreds of thousands of French workers

to Nazis Germany to work as forced labour for the German war effort. The German government promised for every three French workers sent it would release one French prisoner of war. Forced labour hostages ensured Vichy France would reduce military forces and pay tribute of gold, food and supplies to Germany. French police rounded up Jews without French citizenship or undesirables, communist and political refugees.

Marshal Philippe Petain Nazi collaborationist was in charge of the puppet government in Vichy France

HAL Id: hal-01740521 https//hal.science/hal-01740521 Maude Williams
To Protect, Defend and Inform:

The evacuation of the German-French border region during the Second World War

There was an evacuation of one million persons along the Franco-German border area. These evacuations were aimed at giving free space for military intervention on the border zone between the Maginot-Line and the border between the Siegfried-Line. Alsatians and Lorrainers were evacuated to assembly points from where they were travelled by train to various towns in southwestern France September 1939.

www.wikipedia.org
Home Guard set up in 1940 as Britains last line of defence against German invasion Members of this 'Dads Army' were usually above or below conscription age On May 1940 Secretary of State for War Sir Anthony Eden broadcast calling for men to enrol in a new force the Local Defence Volunteers later called the Home Guard

www.wikipedia.org – Channel islands evacuated around 25.000 children and people ten days before German troops landed there June 1940s

www.wikipedia.org
Special Operations Executive. Secret British warfare organisation formed by Hugh Dalton SOE suggested by Lieutenant Colonel Dudley Clark proposed by Sir John Dill Chief of Imperial Staff. Churchill wanted a Commandos unit of specially trained troops of hunter class who could develop a reign of terror down the enemy coast. 2000 men volunteered by 1940 and became the Special Services branch. It was involved in fighting and creating formations devoted to special operations behind enemy lines, airborne operations, counter insurgency, terrorism, covert ops, direct action, hostage rescue, high value targets/man hunt, intelligence operations, mobility operations and unconventional warfare. Trained in Achnacarry Scottish Highlands established by Colonel Charles Hayden under Lieutenant Colonel Charles Vaughan The commando depot responsible for training complete units. Includes Parachute regiment Special Air Corp and Special Boat Services

www.wikipedia.org
Special Air Service. Formed during Western Desert campaign of the second world war. Early operations North Africa, the Greek islands and the invasion of Italy went on to conduct operations in France, Italy, the Low Countries and Germany. The first modern special forces unit was SAS formed July 1941 by Lieutenant David Stirling (Scots Guards) motto Who Dares Wins He became Lieutenent-Colonell Sir Archibald David Stirling DSO OBE.

www.collinsdictionary.com-- Nye definition a flock of pheasants

www.wikipedia.org
British pet massacre At the beginning of WW2 a government pamphlet led to a massive cull of British pets As many as 750,000 British pets were put down in just one week.

www.wisden.com Cricket Almanack

75 years ago the earth experienced a great magnetic storm. It arrived at a poignant moment in history when radio and electrical technology was emerging and the world was embroiled in World War 2. On September 10 1941 there was an ethereal blitz. Auroras were seen in Europe 18-19 September.

www.airforcetimes.com
Downed aviators were called evaders (evading capture) as they tried to get back to Britain

www.collinsdictionary.com
Airgraph little letters. Photographed letters reduced to miniature and sent by airmail.
People made Christmas presents with cotton bobbins, anything which was rubbish peg rugs called clip rugs, beer made from potatoes, flagons made of pottery soap flasks, board games, Monopoly, Cleudo, Snakes and ladders, toy home made guns, yo-yos made of wood and string, knitted soft toys, felted toys, carved wooden jungle animals or farmyard animals, homemade crackers.

www.nationalarchives.gov.uk
WVS. Created in June 1938. To prepare women for civil
defence work. They recruited women for Air Raid Precaution
work. They ran field kitchens and rest centres for bombed
out homeless people; provided canteens at railway stations
for military personnel and escorted children being evacuated.
Women's Voluntary Service helped handing out second hand
clothes, knitted blankets and knitted jumpers and ran car
pools during petrol rationing.

Fruit picking lug pole used to collect individual apples off trees
at harvest t

Hull Blitz 1941. What happened between 1939 and 1945 Hull
suffered 82 air raids with an estimated 1,200 killed. At the
time reporting restrictions meant that a bare minimum of
news reached the public and Hull was just referred to as 'A
North East town.'

Mandatory work program for Germany started in 1942 were
French people were rounded up and sent to Germany.
Refractaires was the name given to French people evading
this forced slave labour in Germany.

www.wikipedia.org
North Atlantic air ferry route in World War 11
    Transatlantic flights left Prestwick in Scotland and would
leap frog via Greenland and Newfoundland then on to
Washington.

www.wikipedia.org

December 7 Japanese attack Pearl harbourer and the Hawaiian islands 2400 people killed 1178 wounded. The warning for the attack was delayed from Japan due to the time difference.

December 11 Germany side with Japan and declare war on the United States

www.winstonchurchill.org

The speech by Churchill 'We shall fight on the beaches; we shall fight on the landing grounds; we shall fight in the fields; in the streets; fight in the hills; we shall never surrender' was delivered in the House of Commons, but never broadcast it was reported in the papers

www.wikipedia.org

Operation Overlord June 6 1944 6,500 vessels landed 130,000 troops on Normandy beaches codenamed Utah, Omaha, Gold, Juno and Sword. 12,000 aircraft ensured air superiority for Allies. Allied progress slowed down after landings because of narrow lanes and thick hedges of the French countryside which impeded tanks progress Cherbourg liberated end of June. Paris 2

www.wikipedia.org

1945 Auschwitz concentration camp was liberated by Soviet troops. The sickening obscenity of the Holocaust revealed for the 1st time as more camps are liberated.

Harry Truman sanctioned the use of the atomic bomb against Japan and August 6th 1945 an American bomber plane called Enola Gay left Tinian island carrying an Atomic bomb nicknamed Little Boy which was dropped on Hiroshima at 8.15 am resulting in approximately 80,000 deaths. Thousands died later from radiation sickness. August 8 1945 a bomber was en-route to Nagasaki with a bomb nicknamed Fat Man another Atomic bomb which killed 25,000 and 25,000 more were injured. Japan surrenders on August 14 1945.

War lasted 6 years 50 million dead, 20 million people were militarised, 6 million Jews, 4 million Polish people, and 15 million soldiers all killed.

www.wikipedia.org

The Jedburgh's

Clandestine operation WW2 to drop three men teams of soldiers of British Special Operations Executive (SOE) the US Office of Strategic Services (OSS) the Free French Bureau Centrale de Renseignements et d'Action and the Dutch and Belgium armies in exile were dropped by parachute into occupied France the Netherlands and Belgium, usually by Handley Page Halifax aircraft, only 23 in use for this job for dropping agents and stores. To assist Allied forces with sabotage, and guerilla warfare. Nickname The Jeds. Usually consisted of a commander, an executive officer, non-commissioned and a radio officer. 300 selected and trained in the Highlands of Scotland paramilitary training base. Then further training at Milton Hall, Peterborough. Personnel weapons were an M1 carbine, colt automatic pistol and Type B marti radio Jed set B2.

The name was apt as the town of Jedburgh in the Scottish borders was notorious in the late Middle Ages for activities of the raiders known as the Border Reivers. Nicknamed The

Jeds in WW2 they were sent to Ambush, Sabotage, Assassinate and Demolish. Motto Surprise, Kill, Vanish. 'The Jeds' all volunteers were known by codenames. 300 'Jeds' selected in the Scottish Highlands for paramilitary training then sent on to Milton hall Peterborough London S.O.E. headquarters. Personal weapons MI carbine, colt automatic pistol, type b Marti radio Jed set B2. They carried pieces of silk with 500 phrases for radio signals, money belts with 100,000 francs £500 plus 500 US dollars. 93 teams in France, Lieutenants, Captains, Majors and Radio Sergeants Between June to September 1944 they wore uniforms. Their job to liaison, advice and show expertise and leadership to the French Resistance. A Memorial to them is in Peterborough Cathedral.

Lord Woolton Pie

A pastry dish of vegetables widely served in Britain during WW2 during rationing. Created at the Savoy hotel by Maitre Chef de Cuisine Francis Latry. Named after 1st Earl Lord Woolton who popularised the recipe after he became Minister of food.

www.bbc.co.uk

May 1940 Spitfire funds started. Funds were set up by councils, businesses, voluntary organisations and individuals. Funds raised about £13 million

www.wikipedia.org

The Squadronaires

A Royal Air Force Band started and performed in Britain during and after WW11

Official title of The Royal Air Force Dance Orchestra.

Kilner jars, preserving jars

www.history.com
Poet John McCrae WW1 wrote;
In Flanders Fields May 3 1915

In Flanders fields the poppies blow
Between the crosses row on row
That mark our place, and in the sky
The Larks still bravely singing, fly
Scarce heard amid the guns below.

We are the dead. Short days ago
We lived, felt dawn, saw sunset glow,
Loved and were loved and now we lie
In Flanders fields

Take up our quarrel with the foe
To you from failing hands we throw
The torch; be yours to hold on high
If ye break faith with us who die
We shall not sleep, though poppies grow
In Flanders fields.

Key Names of Willup Hall

- The Honourable Cressida Makenna Welsby, aka Sid.
- Odin her red /white spaniel x Labrador.

- Thor, Tantetta's dog, spaniel x Labrador blue roan colour
- Tantetta, The Comtesse de Gaillarde, Henrietta, daughter of The Earl of Riningborough.
- Lady Augusta Whitely, daughter of the Earl of Riningborough, lives in Switzerland.
- Bernadette Bartley, aka Bernie, live in friend to Augusta.
- The Dowager Lady Isadora Ellesdale, Grandora, their sister.

- Lord George Albert Ellesdale, husband of Romilly, aka Bertie.
- Romilly Lady Ellesdale, his wife, aka Rom
- Mary Rose and Lydia Ann Winteringham, sisters of George Albert Ellesdale

- Lysander Welsby, aka Sandy, brother of Cressida seven years older has dog called Puck.
- Fiona, wife to Lysander and nurse, daughter of Lionel MacCloud
- Flora Henrietta Welsby, baby daughter
- Sanders Broderick George Welsby, son
- Elsbeth MacCloud, Fiona's sister, has Down's Syndrome.
- Lionel MacCloud, father, Steel magnate and philanthropist

- Lady Portia Sinclair nee Welsby, sister of Cressida, five years older.
- Alastair Sinclair, husband of Portia, sheep farmer and Spitfire flyer in RAF
- Rhona Isadora, new baby daughter
- Hamish George Sinclair, son

- Working gun dogs at Willup Hall
- Black Labrador Venture Scout – mated
- Working Cocker spaniel Woodland Wanderer
- to produce Thor, Odin and Puck and Poppy

- Alford Harrington, Huntsman to the Willup Hall Bloodhounds a drag hunt, his horse Legacy
- Martha Harrington, has arthritis, her favourite mare Peg

- Humphrey Clayton, estate manager.
- Clarissa Clayton, his wife.

- Hugh Brownlow, gamekeeper at Willup Hall.
- Margaret Brownlow, wife of Hugh, no children of their own, loves children.
- Maisie Morton, ladies' maid to Romilly and the Dowager Lady Ellesdale
- Mrs Revill, Willip Hall cook.

- Twinkle, Sid'sfirst pony
- Spangles, Sid's second pony
- Hermes, Sid's Normandy cob mare chestnut, flaxen mane and tail
- The Brig, rescued dapple grey hunter

- Scarlet, rescued nervous hackney bright bay mare
- Rory's Star, her foal
- Timefortea rescued TB grey colt two years old
- Tizzy rescued strawberry roan 12. 2 mare
- Alfie rescued Suffolk Punch aka A.P. Alfie Punch
- Donk, rescued little French donkey
- Polly, Romilly's grey mare

- Granger Stokes, coachman/groom/chauffeur/handyman.

- Mrs Agatha Hubbard, Seamstress.
- Joan Burden, helps at the Hall.
- Rose Burden, daughter 14 years old, helps at the Hall with the children
- Frankie Burden, soldier...badly injured in France, mechanic and helps in the garden.

- Jonas Black, pig breeder, tries to have an evacuee child to use as cheap labour.
- Terrance Mickle, horse dealer, horse slaughter man.

- Merioneth Jones, school friend from Wales, daughter of The Rev.
- The Reverend Berwyn Alfred Jones aka The Rev, Eleanor his wife deceased.
- Osian nearly 17, Rhys 15, Gruffydd 13, Dylan 11, Afan 9, Aled 7.

- Audrey Thomson, former Governess at Willup Hall, good with children.

- Jabbo is Jad All Jabour, Moroccan owns Lippizaner circus horse Zoltan little dog Zippy.
- Halette his new French/ Moroccan wife. A nurse.

- LAND ARMY girls Lucy Perkins and Sheila Beechcroft

- Clearmore Stud people near Thetford
- Clarence Carlton-Jones aka Clary and Sylvia his wife, daughters Susannah and Serena
- Miles Crossland RAF pilot, Serena's fiance, Mark Favill, farmer, Susannah's fiance.
- Brennan Shillingstone, RAF Padre.
- Thady Shillingstone, his sister, a tormentor at school to Sid
- Hywell Shillingstone his younger brother
- Whisper, Serena's chestnut Thoroughbred mare

- Dr Haigh, local GP at Willup Hall

- Talia and Adele Treves sponsored by Cressida, refugees
- Monsieur and Madam Treves, their parents

- Ruby, little girl found in a car crash in France
- Pooch Zissa, her little chihuahua, whose name means sweet one

- Trig, black Labrador and Spruce, tan Cocker Spaniel

- Miriam Abelman, French model met Sid on the boat to Britain.
- Bing, her little French bulldog
- Mrs Sarah Abelman, Mother

- Dr Abelman, Father
- Anna-Sara Abelman, much younger sister.
- Noah Abelman, brother to Miriam.
- Zelda Abelman, wife of Noah, all refugees.
- Esther and Maya Monteux, mother and daughter, housekeeper to the Abelmans.
- Jacob Goldbaum, their neighbour in Paris.
- Avigail Goldbaum, Granddaughter, refugees

- Evacuees from London's East End Docklands
- Lennard Evans /Lennie, 9 years old loves horses and country life.
- Laurence Evans,/ Larry, 14 years old loves reading, politics and the right of the working man.
- Charlotte Evans/ Lottie, 5 years old, Ruby's friend, has Down's Syndrome.
- Mavis Evans, Mother works in ammunitions factory until husband Ernie is killed in the bombing.
- Spud their dog.

- Miss Pearson, lady with clipboard, prim and proper.

- Arthur Laxton, 'can get you anything' dealer. Wife Violet, 6 children

- Group Captain Richard Petersfield, organisers respite and recuperation at the Hall for RAF.
- Professor Dendy Hillingdon, retired consultant now working for the MOD, Ministry of Defence.

- Susan and Roger Brownson, orphans from Hull, parents killed in bombing.

- Gerald, Helen, Christopher and Linda Archer, from Clerkenwell, evacuees.

- Stan Hardy, from Hull
- Lacey Hardy, his wife, herbalist, spiritual, vegetarian.
- Reuben Hardy, eldest son, 15 years old, Star Hardy, daughter, 13 years old, Luna Hardy, youngest daughter, 6 years old, Roscoe Hardy, little brother 8 years old
- Their black Traditional gypsy cob Lucky
- Jack Russell called Trip

- Rory Kaiholm, Canadian, Lancaster bomber pilot.

- Doctor Bleumanthall, Tantetta's doctor
- Rebekkah Bleumanthall, daughter and friend to Cressida.
- Esther Bleumanthall, wife

- Jean-Philipe Delacroix, art dealer, business partner to Tantetta.
- Marie Christine, maid at Chateau.
- Elise, daughter of Marie Christine.
- Joseph Pierre Denisot, estate worker turned Marquisard during the war
- Cecile Denisot, sister of Joseph lives in Lyon with two children.
- Louise Denisot, mother to Joseph and Cecile, did laundry and ironing at the Chateau.
- Marcell Allard, Chateau estate manager and wine maker.

- Aurielle Allard, his wife, housekeeper at the Chateau.
- Monsieur Dalier, private French tutor.
- Uri Bermen, Young Dutch teenager escapes from a train.

- Dara Connel Tifford, aka Tiff, British Special Forces.
- Fergus Scott Mckinley, aka Scott, Special Forces.
- Howard Bathurst, Gambler joins Special Forces.
- Theodore Bathurst, his son lives with Hugh and Margaret Brownlow during the war
- George Bathurst, son lives with Hugh and Margaret Brownlow during the war
- Genevieve Bathurst, their mother, estranged wife of Howard
- Henry Bathurst, brother of Howard, uncle to the boys
- William Bathurst, 18
- Tom Bathurst, 15
- Lucy, the boys' chocolate Labrador.

- Malissa Angelopoulis, 18 Greek Albanian.
- Nico Angelopoulis, 15/16 Greek Albanian.
- The Hestia, his ferry boat.

- Alex Bouchet, 16 years old, baker wants to be an expert wine maker
- Simone Bouchet, half-sister
- Claude Bouchet , half-brother
- Mother Bettina Bouchet, sister to Eleanor Jones
- Trudi, Alex's Normandy cob mare, Tanner his Brittany spaniel dog.
- Pierre Bouchet, brother of Bernard, uncle to Alex, French POW.

- Hildegarde Bouchet, Pierre's German wife
- Gaston Bouchet, Hildegarde and Pierre's son
- Uncle Albert Bouchet, great-uncle to Alex, his grandfather's brother, undertaker.

- Claribel Aubertine, distant cousin to Comte de la Cascade.
- Gregoire Aubertine, ex Foreign Legion, her husband.
- Boss, rangy cattle farm dog of Claribel and Gregoire Albertine
- Clemence de Rouille, niece-in-law to Claribel.
- Robert de Rouille her husband and father of
- Florent de Rouille, son, 12 years old, Estelle and Celeste de Rouille twins 6 years old

- Matias Otero, Tall, Spanish school teacher turned Nationalist fighter.

- Danielle Becker, escapes train with her brother same train as Uri.
- Thaddeus Becker, aka Tad, her young brother

- Nadine, Irish nanny cares for a baby is found on the road by Alex.
- Baby, Jacques

- Zachariah Aaronson, aka Zac, watch dealer in Switzerland

- Evacuees from Bombing in Birmingham
- Doctor Gurdas Singh, in British army in Burma. Doctor to the troops

- Panaya Singh, wife; name means A girl will honour and applaud her family
- Bargitta Singh, mother to Gurdas; name means strong and powerful woman
- Ashneer Singh, son, eight years old; name means sacred water
- Virinder Singh, son, eleven years old; name means king of warriors

- Mr and Mrs McGregor, handyman/chauffeur and housekeeper for Alastair and Portia Sinclair.
- Betsy, Nanny turned temporary midwife for Portia.
- Clara Hutton, midwife.
- Wullie Laurie, shepherd, Garnet Laurie his soldier son, plays the bagpipes.

- Doctor Green, in Scotland.
- Margaret Green, his wife.
- Elizabeth Green, daughter 5 years old, son James Green 3 years old.

- Vicar Bramwell Stevens, his dog Poppy sister of Odin, Thor and Puck.

- Colonel Brian Orpington-Jones, in charge of Local Home Guard.

- Linford Bailey, seven years old.
- Amina Bailey, three years old.
- Barbara Bailey, nurse, their mother from the West Indies.

- Laurent Vaulbolon, village Baker near Chateau de la Cascade shot by Nazi soldiers.
- Odette Vaulbolon is wife.

- Davinia Hardcastle-Cord, District Commissioner for the pony club.

- Thomas Marshall, son of farmer on
Tall Trees Farm
Willup Hall estate farms
Tall Trees farm
Castle farm
Willup Hall farm
Home Farm
Green Leys Farm